PRAISE FOR

ALISON WEIR

Jane Seymour

"Highly recommended for fans of the period . . . As with the earlier novels in the Six Tudor Queens series . . . Weir focuses tightly on the sole perspective of her protagonist, thereby finding enough relatively fresh territory to keep even die-hard Tudor buffs interested. A fascinating afterword sheds light on Weir's departures from the confirmed historical record and on the additional research she did for this novel, including an investigation of how exactly Jane died."
—*Library Journal* (starred review)

"Best-selling Weir's impressive novel shows why Jane deserves renewed attention. Without any dull moments, Weir illustrates Jane's unlikely journey from country knight's daughter to queen of England. . . . This third volume in Weir's exceptional Six Tudor Queens series offers new angles on its earlier subjects. . . . From the richly appointed decor to the religious tenor of the time, the historical ambience is first-rate. With her standout novel in the crowded Tudor-fiction field, Weir keeps the tension high, breathing new life into a familiar tale and making us wish for a different ending."
—*Booklist* (starred review)

"Jane Seymour the shy mouse type? Think again! This superb book, the result of deep and meticulous new research, brings her to astonishing life—she is vibrant and determined, and she sets the king's court on fire. The fascinating secrets of the

Seymour family are deftly explored, the world of the Court painted anew—and Jane's romance with the king is an absolute revelation. Wonderfully written with sympathy and grace, this gripping book gives us the real third wife and shows her struggle to stay true to herself and survive in the toughest of worlds. A magnificent novel."

—Kate Williams, author of *Becoming Queen Victoria*

"In this gripping and utterly compelling novel, Henry VIII's third and—allegedly—best-loved wife is brought vividly to life. Forget 'plain' Jane Seymour: here is a woman to be reckoned with—strong-willed, brave, and tenacious. Her story is set against the rich and complex backdrop of Henry VIII's court at its most turbulent. Not to be missed."

—Tracy Borman, author of *The Private Lives of the Tudors*

Anne Boleyn

"This Anne is clever and clear-sighted. . . . Those sympathetic to Boleyn tend to stumble at her documented spite towards Katherine of Aragon and Mary Tudor, but Weir roots this bad behaviour in understandable insecurity, as the King's ardour for her wanes and the longed-for son does not arrive. This tale of Anne's ascent and demise cannot escape comparisons with Hilary Mantel's Wolf Hall series, which deals with the same events. Weir's version is . . . detailed, immaculately researched and convincing. She is particularly interesting on Anne's probable exposure to early feminist writings."

—*The Times*

"*Anne Boleyn, A King's Obsession* is beautifully written, exquisitely detailed, and gives readers a more down-to-earth picture of the often maligned Anne. . . . Don't miss this series."

—*Romance Reviews Today*

"[Weir] explores Anne's influences and motivations, creating a multifaceted portrait of an ambitious woman who reluctantly accedes to Henry's courtship and later acts out of desperation to protect herself and her daughter, Elizabeth. Even readers who know Anne's story well should gain insights from this revealing novel." —*Booklist*

"This is a well-written and fast-paced novel that should appeal to fans of Tudor-era fiction looking for a fresh look at one of the period's most popular protagonists." —*Library Journal*

"A marvelous book—Anne comes alive and leaps from the page, fascinating, enthralling, full-blooded—you can't help but fall in love with her. A brilliant evocation of the period—and a knife-edge moment in British history. Wonderful."
—Kate Williams, author of *Becoming Queen Victoria*

"Simply exquisite. Anne Boleyn is a tricky character and hard to like sometimes, but Weir has really brought her to life in such a compelling way. This is Anne Boleyn as you have never seen her before. I could not put it down."
—Tracy Borman, author of *Thomas Cromwell* and *The Private Lives of the Tudors*

"Anne Boleyn has always been one of the most hotly debated figures in history. Villain or victim? Schemer, sorceress, or saint who died for the new religion? Alison Weir's wonderfully detailed novel offers a spellbinding solution to the mystery of Anne's true nature. Carrying all the conviction of Weir's lifelong historical research, it both paints a wholly human portrait of Anne and places her in the broad European context that makes sense of her story. At once an enthralling read and a real contribution to our sense of the sixteenth century."
—Sarah Gristwood, author of *Game of Queens*

"As with all her books Weir makes history come alive as no one else. Her novels are biographical but with that comes that extra magic ingredient of a vividly imagined fictional framework that takes the reader there, then. I enjoyed it enormously. I finished it late last night and genuinely couldn't put it down. I'm still reeling from the horror of that final paragraph, which kept me awake for the rest of the night. Brilliant!" —Barbara Erskine, author of *Lady of Hay*

"The moment I opened Alison Weir's new novel I was transported back into the sixteenth century. Although a novel, Weir's outstanding and sound historical research shines through, shedding new light on England's most controversial queen. Weir provides page after page of utterly compelling detail, keeping the reader hooked from start to finish. This book is not only a world apart from any other novel on Anne Boleyn, it is also an exquisite work of literary art. I enjoyed it so much, I can't praise it highly enough!"
—Nicola Tallis, author of *Crown of Blood*

"Alison Weir is the doyen of Tudor fiction and nonfiction, in my book. She has that unique talent to transport her readers into the lives and loves of the people she writes about from the first line. *Anne Boleyn, A King's Obsession* takes us from the eleven-year-old Anne, worrying about her sallow skin and unwomanly figure, to the woman kings lusted after, and the woman who changed England—and thereby Europe and North America—forever. Anne shines through as the woman any king couldn't possibly resist! With Weir's light touch, it is fiction that reads as fact, and leaves us breathless, hoping. Then, of course, we recognize that we are not reading pure fiction after all, but a finely woven tapestry of fictional biography that stays with us long after we close the book at the final line. It is simply a masterpiece."
—Susan Ronald, author of *The Pirate Queen* and *Heretic Queen*

Katherine of Aragon

"Opulent . . . Weir is uniformly excellent at conveying the chaotic emotional give and take of the relationship [between Henry and Katherine]. . . . Katherine carried herself with a nobility she clearly intended to speak well to posterity. Alison Weir's novel captures that nobility better than any biography ever has."
—*Christian Science Monitor*

"As always, Weir demonstrates a keen eye for crafting dramatic scenes of beautiful, accurate detail, instilling in the reader a vivid sense of being there. . . . If this greatly impressive inaugural installment is any indication, Tudor lovers have much to look forward to." —*Booklist* (starred review)

"The novel provides a fascinating glimpse into the personal life of Queen Katherine behind the intricate and vicious political intrigues of the Tudor court. . . . Meticulous research, combined with Alison Weir's empathy for her subject, makes this an illuminating and engaging portrait of 'the true queen.'" —*Historical Novels Review*

"Vividly detailed . . . Weir brings considerable expertise to her fictional retelling of the life of Katherine of Aragon. . . . [The author] portrays her sympathetically as both credulous and steely." —*Kirkus Reviews*

"[Weir's] fresh approach to Henry's first wife [is] a wonderful place to start for those unfamiliar with Katherine's story. Weir's portrayal is far from that of a weak, victimized woman, but one of a courageous, strong, devoted queen fighting for her life and rights. An easy, quick read to begin the series." —*RT Book Reviews*

"Yet again, Alison Weir has managed to intertwine profound historical knowledge with huge emotional intelligence, to compose a work that throws light on an endlessly fascinating figure. But her real gift in all of this is making it feel so fresh and alive."   —Charles Spencer, author of *Killers of the King*

The Marriage Game

"Entrancing . . . [Alison] Weir manages to weave actual history and the imagined kind together seamlessly."
—*Huntington News*

"Weir's credible characters and blend of the personal and political will sweep up readers of this engrossing behind-the-scenes psychological portrait of Elizabeth."
—*Publishers Weekly*

"Based on historical events, letters and conjecture, Weir['s book] paints a fascinating picture of Elizabeth's years as queen. . . . There is enough drama here for a PBS series."
—*RT Book Reviews*

"Weir's impeccable reputation as both a historian and a master storyteller guarantees a huge audience for another intriguing Tudor-themed tale."   —*Booklist*

A Dangerous Inheritance

"A page-turner . . . too juicy to put down . . . Alison's Weir's strong suit as a fiction writer is making her novels living history."
—*The Courier-Journal*

"A juicy mix of romance, drama and Tudor history . . . pure bliss for today's royal watchers."   —*Ladies' Home Journal*

Captive Queen

"Engaging and dramatic . . . [Weir] laudably sticks to historic facts while simultaneously using her imaginative gifts."
—*The Star-Ledger*

"The history itself is inherently dramatic, augmented here by Weir's usual lush detail, which stimulates." —*Booklist*

The Lady Elizabeth

"A compelling, even irresistible, read."
—*Booklist* (starred review)

"Intrigue and maneuverings. Scandal. Schemers and innocents put to death. [This] history of Tudor England is an engrossing story. . . . Weir marries conjecture with what is known about the life of Elizabeth I from childhood to coronation, and it makes for ripping good reading."
—Milwaukee *Journal Sentinel*

"History buffs will enjoy this entertaining look into the rarely explored early life of one of England's most fascinating characters." —*Publishers Weekly*

"A gripping fictional portrait." —*Salon*

Innocent Traitor

"Engrossing . . . suspenseful . . . enormously entertaining."
—*The Washington Post Book World*

"Splendid . . . In giving narrative voice to her subjects, Alison Weir brings us into emotional contact with them in a way that an unadorned historical account does not."
—*The Boston Sunday Globe*

"[Weir] makes a familiar story vibrant and fresh."

—*The Atlanta Journal-Constitution*

"Completely absorbing . . . a brilliantly vivid and psychologically astute book."

—*Booklist* (starred review)

"Poignant and harrowing . . . a gripping finale."

—*The Seattle Times*

BY ALISON WEIR

FICTION

SIX TUDOR QUEENS:
Katharine Parr, The Sixth Wife
Katheryn Howard, The Scandalous Queen
Anna of Kleve, The Princess in the Portrait
Jane Seymour, The Haunted Queen
Anne Boleyn, A King's Obsession
Katherine of Aragon, The True Queen

The Marriage Game
A Dangerous Inheritance
Captive Queen
The Lady Elizabeth
Innocent Traitor

NONFICTION

ENGLAND'S MEDIEVAL QUEENS:
Queens of the Crusades
Queens of the Conquest

The Lost Tudor Princess: The Life of Lady Margaret Douglas
Elizabeth of York: A Tudor Queen and Her World
Mary Boleyn: The Mistress of Kings
The Lady in the Tower: The Fall of Anne Boleyn
The Mistress of the Monarchy: The Life of Katherine Swynford,
Duchess of Lancaster
Queen Isabella: Treachery, Adultery, and Murder in Medieval England
Mary Queen of Scots and the Murder of Lord Darnley
Henry VIII: The King and His Court
Eleanor of Aquitaine: A Life
The Life of Elizabeth I
The Children of Henry VIII
The Wars of the Roses
The Princes in the Tower
The Six Wives of Henry VIII

Jane Seymour

THE HAUNTED QUEEN

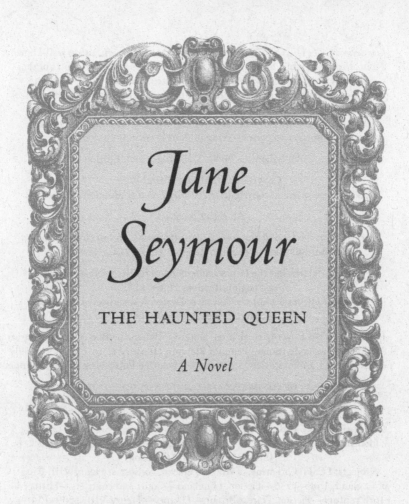

Jane Seymour

THE HAUNTED QUEEN

A Novel

Alison Weir

BALLANTINE BOOKS

NEW YORK

2019 Ballantine Books Trade Paperback Edition

Copyright © 2018 by Alison Weir
Reading group guide copyright © 2019 by Penguin Random House LLC

Published in the United States by Ballantine Books, an imprint of Random House, a division of Penguin Random House LLC, New York.

BALLANTINE and the HOUSE colophon are registered trademarks of Penguin Random House LLC.
RANDOM HOUSE READER'S CIRCLE & Design is a registered trademark of Penguin Random House LLC.

Published in hardcover in the United States by Ballantine Books, an imprint of Random House, a division of Penguin Random House LLC, in 2018. Originally published by Headline Review, a division of Headline Publishing Group, London.

LIBRARY OF CONGRESS CATALOGING-IN-PUBLICATION DATA
Names: Weir, Alison, author.
Title: Jane Seymour, the haunted queen : a novel / Alison Weir.
Description: New York : Ballantine Books, 2018. | Series: Six Tudor Queens ; 3
Identifiers: LCCN 2018005077 | ISBN 9781101966563 (trade paperback) | ISBN 9781101966556 (ebook)
Subjects: LCSH: Catharine, of Aragon, Queen, consort of Henry VIII, King of England, 1485–1536—Fiction. | England—Court and courtiers—History—16th century—Fiction. | Great Britain—History—Henry VIII, 1509–1547—Fiction. | Great Britain—History—Tudors, 1485–1603—Fiction. | BISAC: FICTION / Historical. | FICTION / Biographical. | FICTION / Sagas. | GSAFD: Historical fiction.
Classification: LCC PR6123.E36 J36 2018 | DDC 823/.92—dc23
LC record available at https://lccn.loc.gov/2018005077

Printed in the United States of America on acid-free paper

randomhousebooks.com
randomhousereaderscircle.com

Book design by Christopher M. Zucker

This book is dedicated to
my three amazing editors
(in alphabetical order)
Mari Evans
Susanna Porter and
Flora Rees

1518

THE ROYAL HOUSE OF TUDOR

HENRY VII
King of England
1457–1509

m.

ELIZABETH
of York
1466–1503

ARTHUR
Prince of Wales
1486–1502

MARGARET
1489–

HENRY VIII
King of England
1491–

ELIZABETH
1492–1495

MARY
1496–

m1.

m2.

m.

m1.

m2.

JAMES IV
King of Scots
1473–1513

ARCHIBALD
DOUGLAS
Earl of Angus
1489–

KATHERINE
of Aragon
1485–

LOUIS XII
King of France
1462–1515

CHARLES
BRANDON
Duke of Suffolk
1484–

JAMES V
King of Scots
1512–

MARGARET
DOUGLAS
1515–

MARY
1516–
+
5 OTHERS
died young

THE SEYMOUR FAMILY

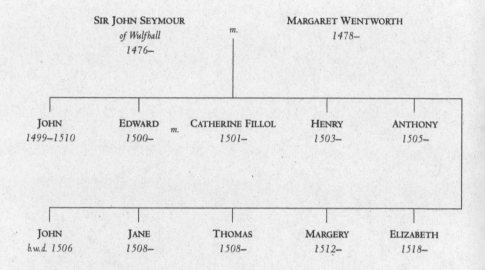

SIR JOHN SEYMOUR				
of Wulfhall		MARGARET WENTWORTH		
1476–	*m.*	*1478–*		

| JOHN | EDWARD | CATHERINE FILLOL | HENRY | ANTHONY |
| *1499–1510* | *1500–* *m.* | *1501–* | *1503–* | *1505–* |

| JOHN | JANE | THOMAS | MARGERY | ELIZABETH |
| *b.w.d. 1506* | *1508–* | *1508–* | *1512–* | *1518–* |

She is as gentle a lady as ever I knew, and as fair a queen as any in Christendom. I do assure you, my lord, the King hath come out of hell into heaven for the gentleness in this, and the cursedness and the unhappiness in the other. When you write to the King again, tell him that you do rejoice that he is so well matched with so gracious a woman as she is.

—LETTER FROM SIR JOHN RUSSELL
TO LORD LISLE, 1536

For jewelled crowns and gaudy sceptres
Are but harbingers of tragedy and death . . .

—FROM A POEM BY THE AUTHOR

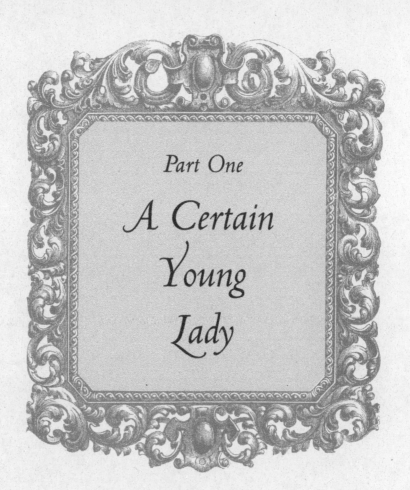

Part One

A Certain

Young

Lady

Chapter 1

1518

"A health to the bride!" Sir John Seymour smiled and raised his goblet as the company echoed his toast.

Jane sipped her wine, watching as her new sister-in-law blushed prettily. Edward seemed besotted with his new wife. At seventeen, Catherine was a very comely girl, a year younger than he. Jane had been surprised at how practiced she was at the art of coquetry, and how warmly the men were looking at her. Even Father seemed to be under her spell. Catherine's father, Sir William Fillol, was leaning back in his chair replete, looking well pleased with the match—as he should be, for Edward, being Father's heir, had good prospects and the determination to do well. Even at the age of ten, Jane knew that for an ambitious young man, marriage to the well-bred co-heiress of a wealthy landowner would be a great advantage.

Sir William had been boasting of how the Fillols could trace their ancestry back to one of the companions of the Conqueror.

"And we Seymours too!" Father had countered smugly, sure of his own exalted place in the world.

All in all, it was a most satisfactory union, and worthy of this great feast. The long tables in the Broad Chamber of Wulfhall were laden with extravagant dishes, all prepared under the watchful eye of Lady Seymour herself. Meat and fowl of every kind graced the board, the centerpiece being a magnificent roasted peacock re-dressed in all its glorious plumage. Sir John had provided the best wine from Bordeaux, and everyone was attired in the new finery they had worn for the wedding.

Sir William normally resided less than fifty miles away from Wulfhall, at Woodlands, near Wimborne, but he had opened up Fillol's Hall for the wedding, and Jane's whole family—her mother and father, and all their seven children—had traveled to Essex to be present. Father was so delighted with his new daughter-in-law that he had insisted that Sir William and Lady Dorothy accompany Catherine when Edward brought her back to Wulfhall to continue their celebrations. That had sent Mother into a flurry of preparation, and everyone agreed that she had risen to the occasion splendidly.

It was dusk now, and candles were being lit on the mantelpiece and windowsills, their flickering, dancing flames reflected in the diamond-paned glass in the stone windows. As Jane observed Edward and Catherine conversing together and stealing the odd kiss, it came to her that in a little over eighteen months she herself would be of an age to be wed. Fortunately, there was no sign that Father had any plans as yet.

For Jane had no desire to be married. She wanted to be a nun. Everyone teased her for it, not taking her seriously. Let them. Soon they would find out that she was as determined as her brother Edward when it came to getting what she wanted in life. She could not imagine her hearty, jovial father objecting, nor her adored mother. They knew of the dream she had had of herself wearing a nun's veil, kneeling before Our Lady. It had visited her a year before, on the night after her parents had taken them all to visit the shrine of St. Melor at Amesbury Priory. She had been overawed by the great church with its soaring octagonal steeple, and had prayed devoutly at the altar of the murdered boy-prince, kneeling beside her siblings with her hands pressed together, as she had been taught from infancy.

Since then, she had been certain that her future lay within those twelve holy acres. She could see herself singing the offices in the choir with the sisters, gathering apples in the orchard or fishing in the ponds, dedicated to God and manual labor for all her life. Next year she would be old enough to enter Amesbury as a novice.

For now, she was content to be with her family, laughing at the jests at table, enjoying the good fare spread out before her and sparring with her brother Thomas, less than a year her junior, who was at this moment throwing sugar plums at the newlyweds. Mother frowned.

"Catherine, you must forgive my youngest son," she said. "He never knows when to desist. Tom, stop that."

"Such high spirits will take the lad far," Sir William observed indulgently. His wife sniffed.

"He's a menace," Edward said, not smiling. Jane heard her mother sigh. Edward had no time for his youngest brother, and always treated him as a nuisance. And Thomas was adept at riling him, utterly resolved never to be outshone by Edward. It was an unequal struggle, for Edward was the heir and Thomas's senior by eight years. He would always have first bite of the apple. When Jane was six, he had been sent to France as a page of honor in the train of the King's sister, the Princess Mary, when she married King Louis, and the following year he had gone up to university at both Oxford and Cambridge, and thence to court, making himself useful to King Henry and his chief minister, Cardinal Wolsey, whom many asserted was the true ruler of the realm.

It was hot in the Broad Chamber. Despite it being high summer, Mother had insisted on having the fire in the hearth kindled, in case anyone felt a chill. Jane pulled off the floral chaplet she was wearing, for the blooms were wilting, and smoothed down her long tresses. They were the color of pale straw, rippling like fine silk over her shoulders. Edward, Thomas, Anthony and the baby Elizabeth were dark-haired, having inherited Father's coloring, but Jane, Harry and Margery took after Mother.

For a moment Jane felt sad that her beautiful hair would be cut off when she took the veil. It was her only claim to loveliness. Her cheekbones were too rounded, her nose too big, her chin too pointed, her mouth too small, her skin too whitish. Looking around the room at her brothers and her pretty little sister Margery, it came to her, without envy or rancor, that they were all more attractive, more jolly—more vital.

In bearing children, Mother had done her duty as efficiently as she accomplished all her other domestic responsibilities. Before Jane had come along, she had borne five sons, although the eldest, John, whom Jane could barely remember, had died when he was eleven, and another John had died just after birth. Harry and Anthony were cut from different cloth to their brothers: Harry was easygoing and had no ambitions beyond the Wulfhall estate, while Anthony was studious; he would be following Edward to university soon, and there was talk of his pursuing a career in the Church. Jane felt encouraged by that. If her parents could lay up treasure in Heaven by giving a son to God, how much more store they would have in giving a daughter too.

Six-year-old Margery had been allowed to sit up for the feast, but tiny Elizabeth, having been brought in by her nurse to be admired by the guests, was now sound asleep upstairs in what was called the Babies' Chamber.

It was a teeming household, and a happy one. As Jane looked about her at the large room filled with her merry, feasting family, a sense of well-being and contentment stole over her. Whatever the future brought, she was proud to be a Seymour of Wulfhall.

When Jane was little, she had thought that there must be wolves somewhere at Wulfhall. She had peered around corners and opened closets and cupboards in trepidation, lest one leap out at her. She had lain awake at night fretting about what she would do if she ever encountered one of the beasts. But hearing her screams one day when Thomas had sprung out from the dry larder shouting, "I'm a wolf!" Father, having clouted him for it, had reassured her that the name Wulfhall had nothing to do with wolves.

"It was once called Ulf's Hall, after the Saxon thane who built it hundreds of years ago," he explained, taking her on his knee. "Over the years the name has changed a little. Better now, sweeting?" And he had kissed her and set her down to go back to her toys, reassured.

Jane was aware that Wulfhall had been rebuilt and altered several times over the centuries. The present house was about three hundred years old, and it embraced two courtyards—the Little Court, which housed the domestic offices, and the Great Court, where she and her family lived. The lower walls were of ancient mellow stone supporting an upper story of solid timbers framing white plasterwork. You entered through the porch and came into a large hall. At the far end a door led to the smaller Broad Chamber, which the family preferred to the hall, since it was easier to heat. On sunny days, the windowpanes in the Broad Chamber and the chapel glinted with a thousand lights, and the vivid colors of the armorial glass blazed like jewels. At one corner of the Great Court stood a high tower, a relic of an older house.

Sir John was wealthy, owning extensive lands in the county of Wiltshire, enabling him to build a fashionable long gallery where his family could take exercise on a wet day. Their portraits, limned by itinerant painters who had visited the house looking for work, stared down from its lime-washed walls. Among them was an imaginary likeness of the founder of the Seymours' fortunes, a Norman knight called William de St. Maur.

Oh, no, thought Jane. Father is going to bore everyone with the family history.

"He arrived with the Conqueror at the time of the Norman invasion of 1066," Sir John was boasting proudly. "Seymours have served the Crown loyally ever since. We have been farmers and landowners; we have held public offices, and held them well. Some have sat for the shire in Parliament." He refilled his goblet, warming to his theme; his children had all heard it before, many times. "I was knighted at eighteen, after fighting the Cornish rebels alongside my father. As you know, it was upon the coronation that I was appointed a Knight of the Body to King Henry."

Sir William nodded. "It's hard to believe that was ten years ago. All that talk of conquering France, all come to naught."

Father had fought for the King in a French campaign (and probably exaggerated his exploits, Mother had said more than once behind his back, smiling affectionately).

"In time, in time," he said now, clearly more interested in impressing his guest with the family's achievements. "You see that horn on the wall?" He pointed to the great silver-bound ivory hunting horn resting on iron brackets above the fireplace. "I have the honor to bear that as hereditary ranger of Savernake Forest. Look at that line of trees yonder, through the window." He pointed to the dense woodland on the crest of a gentle hill. "That's the ancient forest, which stretches all the way west as far as Marlborough, and to Bedwyn Magna, which is our nearest parish."

Jane anticipated that Father would soon be enlarging on how capable an administrator he had proved since his fighting days were ended, and the diplomatic missions abroad he had undertaken on King Henry's behalf. Not for nothing was he sheriff of Wiltshire, Dorset and Somerset; not for nothing was he Justice of the Peace for Wiltshire.

But no. "I am content to farm these days," he said. "You have to be at the forefront of change. I have twelve hundred and seventy acres here at Wulfhall alone, and I've converted them all into pasture for sheep."

Sir William raised his bushy brows. "And you've had no trouble? Other gentlemen of my acquaintance who have enclosed their land for sheep have met with violent opposition. Even Sir Thomas More, whom I met at court, says that sheep are eating men. And it's true. For in growing rich on raising the finest and costliest wool, you noble gentlemen, yes, even men of God, leave no ground for tillage. It has put many a poor man out of work."

"There has been some grumbling among my tenants," Father admitted. "But I have made sure that none were left in want, and found them other work to do when they might have faced destitution. Thus, I pride myself, I have retained their love." Young as she was, Jane knew from her dealings with the people on the estate that Father was well thought of, and Edward said his success at managing his estates was even spoken of at court.

It was growing late, and the balmy late-summer night had covered the land. The men were growing noisier in their cups, and Mother was shooing her younger children off to bed. Catherine was yawning and her father suggested it was time for her to retire. Edward leapt up to accompany her.

Jane rose too and excused herself. It was still hot in the hall, and she was relieved to escape outside for some fresh air.

What she loved best about Wulfhall were the three gardens that immediately surrounded it. She wandered into My Old Lady's Garden, which faced the house and was named for her Grandmother Seymour, who had been born Elizabeth Darrell and died soon after Jane was born. She had had a passion for growing things, and the garden she had created was gloriously colorful with roses, gillyflowers and pansies in season, as well as pretty shrubs and bushes tamed into the shapes of chess pieces. To the east lay My Young Lady's Garden, which had always been Mother's domain. The herb beds she had planted after her marriage were still flourishing, useful for cooking, making medicines and unguents, and sweetening the rushes that carpeted the floors. To the west, there was the Great Paled Garden with its painted picket fence and the wilderness of wildflowers where Jane and her siblings still indulged in their childish romps.

As she sat on a bench, enjoying the night air, she thought how fortunate she was to have the most wonderful mother in the world. Lady Seymour was the heart of the household. For all Sir John's masculine authority, Wulfhall revolved around her. Most mornings found Jane and Margery in the kitchens or the still room, where Mother gave them instruction in running a great establishment.

"It will serve you well against the time when it pleases God to send you husbands," she had told them. Seeing Jane about to open her mouth, she had added, with a twinkle, "Nuns need to be good housekeepers too!"

Bustling about, she would be checking that the meats were being timely turned on the spits, and that the bread was risen for baking. For all her gentle birth—and she was descended from kings—Mother was not above attending to such duties or even carrying them out herself. She took her responsibility as mistress of a knightly household seriously. Her table was legendary in these parts, her reputation sterling. Woe betide any cook or kitchen wench—or any daughter, for that matter—whose work fell short of her expectations.

Not that the servants disliked or feared her. She was a humane lady, and kindly, but she would be respected and obeyed. Rarely did she have to raise her voice to anyone, or resort to the beatings so often meted out by others in authority. Even the unruly Thomas did her bidding without question. All her children adored her, and her servants blessed her for a godly and bountiful mistress. Few left her service through choice.

Mother strove unfailingly to instill in all her charges the moral virtues of chastity, honesty, humility and docility. Her girls were raised to be loyal and obedient to their parents and—when the time came—to their husbands, and to conduct themselves soberly as became Christian gentlewomen. Above all, she taught her children to love God, to respect their betters and to honor the King and the Lord Pope in Rome.

Often, as she stood at the large scrubbed table in the kitchen, or distilled perfumes and physick in the still room, Mother would reminisce, for she too believed that her children should be steeped in their family's history. They could all recite that she had been born a Wentworth of Suffolk, and that she was descended from Edward III, the mighty House of Neville and Sir Henry "Hotspur" Percy, hero of the long-ago Battle of Shrewsbury. As a young girl she had been a celebrated beauty. Even now, at forty-one, she was smoothly plump as a partridge with a clear, rosy complexion and fair hair.

"When I was seventeen," she liked to tell Jane and Margery, "I was maid to the Duchess of Norfolk in Yorkshire, and in Maytime they staged a pageant at Sheriff Hutton Castle, where a goodly laureate's garland of silk, gold and pearls was presented to a young poet, Master Skelton, in honor of his talent. He wrote me a poem." Her eyes would grow distant, as if she were seeing that long-ago summer and recalling how it had felt to be a young girl on the brink of life. "It was entitled 'To Mistress Margery Wentworth.' He called me a pretty primrose." Jane thought it a description that was still apt. There was a copy of the poem, written in some spiky hand, among the family papers. It had been taken out for display on several occasions.

As Mother's hands worked deftly at cutting pastry roses, she liked to reminisce on her courtship. "Two years after Master Skelton wrote that poem, I met your father. He had just been knighted, and he asked for my hand. Oh, he was a handsome swain, and I was smitten. He was accounted one of the new men, who were much favored by the old King; men who were making their way by loyalty, hard work and diligence, rather than by nobility of birth. Your Grandfather Wentworth perceived those qualities in him, and saw rightly that he would make me a good husband. For your father, of course, it was a highly advantageous match, much in the family tradition, for by marrying well, your Seymour ancestors increased their lands and wealth, and their standing in the world. But our marriage was the greatest of them all. And to be happy in it is the crowning blessing." Mother would dimple and blush a little, for all her mature years. That her parents were happy anyone could see, but Jane had observed other married people together, and knew that not all got on so well. Marriage seemed to be as big a gamble as the games of chance they played on winter evenings.

The morning after the feast, nearly everyone slept late, many nursing sore heads. Jane arose from the bed she shared with Margery, hoping to snatch some time alone in the chapel before Mother emerged and summoned her to help in the kitchens.

The chapel was beyond the Broad Chamber. Beneath its traceried windows of stone and the stained glass depicting the Annunciation stood an altar adorned with an embroidered silk frontal, a jeweled crucifix and an old and much revered plaster statue of the Virgin and Child. Jane thought that the face of Mary was the most beautiful thing she had ever seen, so calm, demure and serene, as she herself must always try to be in emulation of the Holy Mother.

The air was redolent with the scent of the flowers Mother had arranged in honor of the newlyweds. Kneeling at a prayer desk before the altar was Father James, the family priest, who had tutored Jane and her brothers from their infancy. How well she remembered the horn book that had hung around her neck and the hard labor of learning her letters, her numbers and her catechism. When she grumbled, she had been told that she was lucky indeed to have forward-thinking parents who believed that little girls would benefit from learning their letters. She had far preferred the needlework her mother taught her. The embroidered caps and bodices she made as gifts were the pride of many of her friends. The altar frontal was also her work, and she trusted that her skill would be put to good use at Amesbury. In her mind, her future was settled.

Father James crossed himself and rose to greet her, extending his hands in welcome.

"Jane, my daughter!"

He was a dear man, much beloved by his small flock, and to Jane a friend in whom she could confide.

"Father," she said, "I came to pray, but now that I find you here, I would seek your help."

"Sit down, my child," Father James said, indicating Sir John's leather-studded chair. "How can I help you?"

Mother was in the Broad Chamber, seeing to it that the servants restored it to normal after the feast.

"May I speak with you?" Jane asked.

"What's the matter?" Mother asked, frowning at one of the maids. "Nell, please wipe that table properly!"

"Can we be private? Please, Mother."

"Very well." Lady Seymour beckoned to the steward. "See that the room is left tidy," she commanded, then led Jane to her closet, the little room that was her personal domain, where all her papers and records were stored. From here, she ruled the household.

"Now," she said, sitting down at the table. "What is troubling you, Jane?"

Jane took the stool that stood ready for anyone wanting a quiet word with the mistress. "Mother, I really mean this. I want to be a nun at Amesbury."

Lady Seymour gave her a long look. "I know. But Jane, you are yet to see your eleventh birthday, and this is not a decision to be taken lightly. When you are older, some young man might ask for your hand, and all thoughts of being a nun might fly out of the window. I know, I have seen it happen—and too late, in one instance. The girl, a cousin of mine, met the youth when he came with her family to see her take her final vows. He was betrothed to her sister, but when she saw him after the ceremony, she was utterly smitten. It was the ruin of her. I would not have that happen to you."

Jane felt tears of frustration welling. "But I know I have a vocation. I've just told Father James, and he did not try to put me off. He told me to talk to you, with his blessing. Mother, you know how I long to go to the good sisters and live in the peace of that beautiful priory. I do not want to marry."

"Dear child, there is often no peace to be had in a convent, and inner peace is obtained only at very great cost. It is a hard life, not an escape. You must understand this."

Jane sighed. "Why does everyone try to make it difficult for me?" Mother smiled. "If you truly have a vocation, God will wait for you. But you need to understand many things before you take that step, not least what you will be giving up. Child, do not look at me like that. All I ask is that you stay in the world and learn more of it before you decide to forsake it. If you still feel the same when you are eighteen, then I will speak to your father."

"Eighteen?" Jane echoed. "That's eight years away."

"Jane, listen." Mother's voice was tender. "You will change in many ways over the coming years. At eighteen, you will be a different person, and much more mature. Bide-your time in patience. Good things are worth waiting for."

"But—"

"That's my final word at this time. And don't go running to Father. He and I are of one mind on this matter."

Chapter 2

1526

Jane held fast to her conviction that she had a vocation. After her eighteenth birthday, seeing her so resolved, her parents finally gave her their blessing, and letters were exchanged with Florence Bonnewe, the Prioress of Amesbury. At length, the Prioress invited Sir John to bring his daughter to the convent.

As the family gathered in the Great Court to say farewell, Jane knew a moment's hesitation. Of course she had understood that taking the veil meant leaving her family behind and renouncing the world; she had asked herself again and again if she could make that sacrifice, and felt certain that she could, if God asked it of her. But now, with all her loved ones crowding around, and Mother and her sisters openly weeping, she found herself doubting her resolve.

They needed her, an insidious voice whispered in her head. Edward and Catherine were clearly not happy, although it was hard to fathom why. What had gone wrong between them? They had seemed so joyous in the first months of their marriage. Catherine was lovely, with her honey-colored curls and dimpled smile, but that smile had been seen all too rarely after Edward had seemed to lose interest. It only appeared for their young son, John—the image of the grandfather in whose honor he had been named—who had been born a year after the wedding. He was seven now, the same age as his youngest aunt, Dorothy, whom Sir John always said should have been called The Little Surprise, for he and Lady Seymour had thought their family to have been complete with Elizabeth.

Her mother needed her especially. As Jane had grown into womanhood, Lady Seymour had come to rely on her more and more. And Mother seemed not quite her usual self these days. Something was preoccupying her. Even Father seemed concerned about her. Jane feared she might be concealing some worrying ailment. But when she pressed her, Mother always insisted she was perfectly well.

Catherine was crying now, her arms around a squirming John. She wept all too easily these days. Father put a comforting arm around her shoulders. It was touching, the affection he had for his daughter-in-law.

Jane embraced Edward, knowing that his stiff face masked the sorrow he was feeling at her going. Thomas was subdued as he bent to kiss her. Harry, blinking away tears, gave her a warm hug, and Anthony a blessing. How she would miss them all. She clung to her sisters, and then Mother clasped her tightly to her bosom.

"May God go with you, my darling child," she wept. "I will come to see you very soon."

The Prioress was a big-boned, formidable woman. Seated serenely in her parlor, her cheeks rosy under her snowy wimple, she made the very sensible suggestion that Jane live with the community for a few weeks, to test her vocation.

"We will not discuss a dowry until you have decided to stay with us, but a contribution toward your keep would be most welcome, since our order is vowed to poverty."

A glance around the Prioress's parlor with its Turkey rug, carved oak furniture and silverware rather belied that statement, but Sir

John promptly handed over a heavy purse. Then he squeezed Jane's hand, gave her his blessing and left.

Under the Prioress's strict rule, she quickly came to realize how much freedom she had enjoyed at home, and how indulgent her parents were. Coming from a noisy household, full of bustle, she found the silence of the nunnery hard to bear. The food was plain, and nowhere near the quality and abundance of Mother's; the mattress in her cell was thin and lumpy, and the black habit she was given to wear was scratchy against her skin. But she had known not to expect worldly comforts in the religious life. She had known that she would have to get up in the night to attend the holy offices, although she had not anticipated how draining the constant interruptions to her sleep would be. She had known that chastity would be required of her, but she had not realized that she would never again be allowed to touch another human, unless there was urgent need. She had expected to mortify the flesh, but she was freezing cold most of the time, apart from the one hour a day that the nuns were allowed to spend in the warming chamber, the only room with a fire.

She persevered. The glorious singing of the choir nuns sent her spirits soaring heavenward. She prayed for hours in the chapel, communing with God and striving to find the inner silence that enabled her to hear His voice. She reverently adored the statues of the saints and came to feel that, like Mary in the chapel at home, they were her friends. She grew fond of the sisters, with whom she became acquainted during their daily period of recreation. She was pleased when they praised her embroidery.

But at the end of her probationary time at Amesbury, she went home. The peace she had expected to find there had proved elusive. Always, it seemed, there was some worldly desire against which she must strive. She felt she did not have the stamina for it.

And there had been another thing, a disturbing thing. If the nuns were vowed to poverty, why was it that Prioress Florence wore a habit of good silk and was served choice fare in her own comfortable parlor? And why was she permitted a lap dog, a nasty, yappy little brute that showed its fangs whenever anyone dared approach it, yet suffered its mistress to take it on her knee and fondle it?

"I do not know if I have a vocation," Jane confessed on that last morning. What she had really wanted to say was that Amesbury was not as she had envisaged it.

"This life needs commitment," the Prioress said. "I had rather have a nun who knew she had a calling than one who doubted. Go home and think again, with my blessing."

So Jane had come home, in something of a turmoil. The further she traveled along the sixteen miles to Wulfhall, the more certain she became that Amesbury was not for her. There were things about it that she would miss, of course, but others she was relieved to leave firmly behind her.

Her family were all jubilant to see her.

"We have missed you!" Harry said, hugging her warmly. "Wulfhall isn't the same without you."

"You never were cut out to be a nun." Anthony smiled.

Mother was shaking her head as she embraced Jane. "I suspected you would have second thoughts." She smiled.

Jane kissed her, hiding her irritation. "I don't know. Maybe my future lies in some other nunnery. I will tell you about Amesbury. It is not perhaps the best place to test a vocation. I still want to become a nun." She would be glad to prove them all wrong.

Chapter 3

1527

Wrapped in a fur-lined cloak, Jane watched from the saddle as her hawk swooped on a doomed partridge. They would have a fine bag of birds for Mother's game pie. It was good to be out hawking, surrounded by the merry companionship of her grown-up brothers and fifteen-year-old Margery. She loved to watch her bird soar up high in the azure sky, then dive suddenly. The freedom of being on horseback in the fresh air was exhilarating, as was the thrill of a good catch.

As Anthony raced to retrieve the prey, Edward cantered down the hill toward them. He was Sir Edward now, having been knighted by the Duke of Suffolk, under whose command he had served in France four years earlier. This was one of the rare occasions he was at home, for these days he was often away, at court or in the north. He had spent much of the past two years at Sheriff Hutton Castle in Yorkshire, as master of horse to King Henry's bastard son, the Duke of Richmond, a boy of eight, the same age as young John. It was a coveted post, bestowed by the King himself.

"Bravo!" he called. "But we should go home now."

"Let's give it another half-hour," Thomas challenged. They still could never agree on anything.

"Mother will be waiting," Edward said, in a tone that brooked no argument.

"Then I suppose we must call it a day," Harry said. The brothers reined in their horses, Thomas scowling.

"Come, Margery!" Jane cried. Then they were off, galloping across the sweeping Wiltshire countryside toward Wulfhall.

As the house came into view, they slowed to a trot, and Jane moved ahead to ride beside Edward.

"I must speak with you," she said. "Catherine was in tears again this morning. I couldn't get any sense out of her. Edward, what is wrong with her?"

Her brother's mouth tightened. "It's a private matter."

Thomas was suddenly there beside them. "It's because of Joan Baker. Don't bother trying to look virtuous, brother. And I'll wager she's not the first."

Edward flushed. It took Jane a moment to understand Thomas's meaning. Joan Baker was a laundress at Wulfhall, a merry maid with blond plaits and a plump bosom. If Mother got to hear of this, she would send her packing, there was no doubt of it.

"I'll thank you to mind your own business," Edward hissed. Thomas grinned.

"But Edward, it becomes our business when we have to comfort your wife," Jane said evenly. "It's been plain to us all for a long time that she is unhappy. And she's not long out of childbed. This is when she should be especially cherished. Please show her some affection."

"By God, you take too much upon yourself, Jane!" Edward growled. "What do you know of what passes between a husband and wife—or rarely passes, in our case? You're going to be a nun."

"I only know that it grieves me to see her weep so often," Jane persisted. "As for becoming a nun . . ." She allowed her voice to trail off. She was nineteen now, and although the religious life still held strong attractions for her, Mother had been right: she had changed, and she was not now as certain of her vocation as she had been last year.

As they rode on in a frosty silence, she kept thinking about poor Catherine. Hopefully Edward, once he stopped sulking, would do something to cheer his wife. And maybe someone—not herself, but perhaps Mother—would remind Catherine to keep her husband happy in the marriage bed. Jane suspected that the root of their trouble lay there.

Back at the house, she hung up her cloak, changed her leather boots for soft slippers and went to her bedchamber to fetch her sewing basket. Edward had stamped upstairs ahead of her, and as she left her room, she could hear his voice raised in anger, Catherine's incoherent cries and the wails of baby Ned, their second child.

They all knew that the marriage had been foundering for a long time. The lengthy separations had not helped, and when Edward did make his infrequent visits home, he was restless and clearly eager to be away again. The family had rallied around to support Catherine—Father especially had been a tower of strength to her—but they could not mend Edward's indifference, nor her misery. Father had not hesitated to remind Edward where his duty lay and ordered him to look to his wife, but it had done no good. On the contrary, it had soured relations between father and son.

Of late, however, poor Catherine had become increasingly mournful and moody, taking pleasure only in her children. Mother thought she was breeding again, but Jane suspected now that Catherine had found out about Joan Baker—and the other wenches Edward bedded.

Lying in the tester bed that night, listening to Margery's even breathing, Jane thought back over her weeks at Amesbury, and wondered if Lacock Abbey, the other great nunnery in Wiltshire, might offer her what she had been hoping for. But the truth was that she was now undecided as to whether the religious life really was for her. And perhaps, she realized, she always would be.

"If in doubt . . ." Mother had said, leaving the sentence unfinished. "I've always said that, once a handsome young man presents
himself, you'll know exactly what you want in life."

But that was the trouble. No handsome young man had presented
himself. It was not that Jane lacked a dowry; Father could afford to
be generous. She feared that the reason no one had offered for her
hand was because she was too plain. No one had even made the most
tentative approach, and she was now beginning to resign herself to
spinsterhood. She would be the devoted daughter who stayed at
home and looked after her aging parents. Most of the time the prospect did not bother her too much, as she loved them both, and
Wulfhall. Marriage seemed to be something that happened only to
other people, and not always successfully. Look at Edward and Catherine. But sometimes she was fearful of a future without love, that
special love between a man and a woman, and children, which
Mother always said were God's greatest blessing.

She realized she was crying. Stifling the sobs, she buried her face
in the pillow. But Margery was awake.

"What's the matter?" she mumbled.

Jane sniffed. "Tell me truly, am I ugly?"

Margery reached across and patted her arm. "Of course not, dear
Jane. I think you are pretty. You are so fair."

"Too pale, you mean."

"Some girls would envy you. Your complexion is like alabaster,
and your eyes so blue. You look like one of the saints." She was trying to be kind.

"Then why has no man come courting?"

Margery sighed. "We live too quietly here. We rarely see anyone. And when we do get invited anywhere, the people are all old
and boring. They only talk about enclosure and taxes and how they
hate Cardinal Wolsey."

Jane sat up and stared at the dying embers in the brazier. "Do you
think that Father has been remiss, not finding us husbands?"

Margery harrumphed. "Why would he do that, when you've told
him for years that you want to be a nun?"

Jane had to concede that. "But you don't, and he hasn't bestirred himself."

"Maybe he likes having us at home. And I'm not in any hurry. I don't want to end up like poor Catherine, married to someone like Edward, who treats her indifferently. But you, Jane—you should tell Father that you want to be wed. Then he might do something about it. Now let's get back to sleep."

Jane settled down. Margery was right. She should speak to Father in the morning.

But when morning came, she was still undecided.

That May, Sir William brought Lady Fillol over from Woodlands to see their new grandson. They were greeted in the porch by Sir John, Lady Seymour, Edward, Catherine and the rest of the family, including a bevy of excited children, while the swaddled infant was proudly borne downstairs by his father to be inspected. After the birth of his second son, Edward had obtained leave from the Duke of Richmond, and ridden south from Yorkshire to spend some time with his wife and children. It was obvious to Jane that he was chafing to return.

As wine and sugared fruits were served in the Broad Chamber, with the evening sunshine streaming in through the windows, the families exchanged news. Jane was uncomfortably aware that Catherine said little, and noticed Sir William regarding his daughter with concern.

"You're looking a bit peaky, Cat," he said. "What ails you?"

Edward's face grew taut. Catherine ventured a smile. "Nothing, Sir. I am well, thank you."

"She's had a difficult time," Mother chimed in.

"It's true," Anthony murmured to Jane, "but not in the way Mother means." Aloud, he said, "I have some good news. I've been offered a post as secretary to my uncle, Sir Edward Darrell, at Littlecote House. I start in September."

Thus diverted, Sir William and Lady Fillol congratulated him, and the conversation took a less perilous turn. Catherine made an effort to be sociable, and Edward stopped glowering.

Mother had prepared another of her feasts. As the sumptuous repast was brought in, Jane was dismayed to see that Joan Baker had been summoned from the laundry to help serve at table.

"Mother cannot know what is going on between her and Edward," she whispered to Thomas, who had taken the space next to her on the bench.

He grinned. "Pray God he behaves himself!" There was nothing he'd have liked more than to see his brother discomfited.

Jane held her breath as Joan leaned across and placed a platter of fowl before her mother and Edward. The maid's face remained impassive, but as she drew back, her breast briefly brushed against Edward's cheek.

"Sorry, Sir," she said, a touch too familiarly, and walked away.

Edward looked furious, as Thomas stifled a chortle. Jane saw Father and Catherine exchange glances. She looked at their guests. Sir William was loudly praising the beef, but Lady Fillol was frowning.

Jane was still holding her breath, hoping that nothing else would mar what should be a happy occasion, and trying to think of something to say to lighten the mood. Mother had worked so hard to make their visitors welcome. But just as the board had been cleared, the cloth lifted and the last ewer of spiced wine was being served, Catherine suddenly burst into tears.

"What's this, then?" Sir William boomed.

Mother swooped to comfort the girl. Everyone crowded around, begging to know what was wrong. Edward patted Catherine's hand and tried to appear solicitous, but his eyes were cold and angry. Father looked embarrassed. Unhappiness in his daughter-in-law reflected badly on his son.

Lady Fillol beckoned her daughter. "Come, Cat, we will talk in private." And she led her away, into the chapel, and closed the door.

"Is she a little crazed after her lying-in?" Sir William asked.

"I have been wondering that myself," Edward said.

"Liar," Thomas murmured. "He knows full well what ails her."

"She has seemed a little distracted lately," Mother said, shaking her head. "We have done our best to cheer her."

"I do not doubt that, my lady," Sir William assured her. "I'll wager it is merely some woman's fancy; after all, she's not long out of childbed. Well, I'm retiring. My wife will tell me all about it when she comes up, I am sure. I bid you all good night."

After he had gone, the rest of them sat there for a while, listening to the indistinct sound of female voices beyond the closed door.

"Go to bed, all of you," Harry said, ever helpful. "I'll wait up and see that all is well."

"I'll stay with you," Jane offered, relieved that Harry was at home. He was often away at Taunton, where he was keeper of the Bishop of Winchester's castle, having been in the Bishop's service for some years now. "Mother, you look exhausted. You should get some rest."

"But I must know that Catherine's all right," Mother protested.

"I will stay up," Father said, in a voice that brooked no argument, the voice that had silenced many an importunate offender at the assizes. "Go to bed, all of you."

When they broke their fast the next morning, the atmosphere was tense. Mother was up first, ensuring that there was sufficient bread, meat and ale for everyone. Edward came downstairs with Jane and Margery. He had arranged a hawking expedition in honor of his in-laws, but looked as if he had barely slept.

"Good morning," he said. The Fillols barely acknowledged him, and Jane concluded that Catherine had told her mother about Joan Baker.

"Catherine is staying in bed," Edward explained. "She has a headache. But she has begged me not to deprive you of your sport. We leave after breakfast. The horses will be saddled and ready then."

"I regret very much that I am unable to join you," Father said. "I have estate business to see to and will be out all day. I assure you, I had far rather be going hawking with you on this fair day." He bowed to his guests and disappeared into the closet he used as an office.

Not a word was said about last night's little drama. Jane began to hope that nothing would come of it.

Mother had planned a spread for them to eat outdoors. When Jane emerged into the Little Court, where the horses were assembled, she saw a great cart laden with baskets, stools and a rolled-up carpet. The children were swarming around, dancing with excitement.

"Lizzie! John! Dorothy!" Mother called. "Get into the litter. You're coming with me." They were to spend the morning running wild in one of the wide-open spaces in the forest, while Mother set out the meal and kept an eye on them.

Jane mounted her horse, smoothed down the buff-colored skirts of her riding gown, straightened her feathered cap and pulled on her glove. Holding out her hand, she waited as Father's falconer brought her merlin falcon and attached her by the jesses to the glove. Trotting alongside Margery, she followed her brothers and the Fillols through the great gateway and along the path that led past the gardens. They broke into a trot as they reached the open track beyond and let the horses have their heads. It was good to be out in the bracing air, enjoying the freedom of cantering through the forest. Hopefully they would have good sport today. Heaven knew, they needed a distraction from the thinly veiled tension at home.

As they sat on the rug in the greenwood, eating the hearty fare that Mother had spread out over a vast white cloth, Lady Fillol seemed quiet. Sir William was exerting himself to be pleasant, but Jane was aware that he had not spoken to Edward, and that Edward had sat down as far away from his father-in-law as possible. It was as well that there were eleven of them, chattering loudly, to give the illusion that all was harmonious.

Jane was aware that Lady Fillol was toying with her food. Probably she was worrying about Catherine. At length, Lady Fillol laid down her plate. "I do apologize, Lady Seymour, but I feel quite unwell. I shall ride back to the house and lie down." She stood up.

"I do hope it's nothing you've eaten?" Mother asked anxiously.

"Not at all. I just feel a little light-headed."

"I'll come with you," her husband said. "Please excuse us."

Watching the couple walking back toward the tree where their horses were tethered, Jane could only feel relief. Sir William was all right, but his wife was hard work, and she was sure that something was amiss. She turned to Thomas.

"I think Catherine told her about Joan Baker," she murmured, under cover of the children's laughter.

"I have no doubt of it," he replied, ducking as young John thrust at him with his wooden sword. "Whoa there, sirrah! Mind that blade!" John skipped off, chuckling.

"I'll be glad when they've gone home," Jane said.

"So will Edward." Thomas grinned.

They returned to Wulfhall at four o'clock to find Sir William and Lady Fillol's litter standing in the Great Court, their baggage in the porch and the knight and his lady themselves waiting in the Broad Chamber.

Mother halted, bewildered. "Why are you leaving so soon?"

"Lady Seymour," Sir William said heavily, "I have witnessed something here this day that I had never thought to see in all my life."

"Dear Heaven, what?" she cried.

"On my honor, Madam, I cannot, for shame, speak of it. I am a guest in your house and you have been more than hospitable. It would not be fitting to mention so horrible a thing to such a gentle lady. But we cannot remain one moment longer under this roof."

"By God!" Thomas swore. "You go too far, Sir."

"Hush, Thomas. But Catherine—she will be so sad to see you go." In her distress, Mother put out a hand as if to ward off the Fillols' departure. "You cannot leave when your daughter is unwell."

"I have no daughter!" Sir William barked.

"I think you should explain yourself, Sir," Edward demanded, his hand on the hilt of his sword.

Jane could contain herself no longer. "Sir William, please. If something bad has happened here, in our home, it is an unkindness on your part to not say what it was."

He glared at her. "Mistress Jane, you must ask Catherine about that. Come, my dear, we are going."

Edward barred the doorway. His face was grim. "She told you about my fall from grace, then."

"I have nothing to say to you," growled his father-in-law. "Let us pass."

"Catherine has done nothing wrong! Why do you say you have no daughter?"

"Ask her!" And Sir William pushed past him, pulling his wife toward the waiting litter.

"Let them go," Anthony said. "Once they have calmed down, they will think more rationally. Whatever it is, they have probably got it all out of proportion." He turned to his older brother.

"This is none of your business," snarled Edward. "I must talk to my wife." He raced upstairs.

Mother was weeping. Jane and Margery hastened to comfort her, as Thomas shooed the children out into the gardens.

"What was he talking about?" she kept asking. "Wait till your father gets home. He shall hear of this."

Edward came downstairs shaking his head. "She won't say anything. She just keeps crying. I've left her with her maid."

An hour later, Sir John returned. Seeing them all gathered in the Broad Chamber, and noticing his wife's woebegone face, he wanted to know where Lord and Lady Fillol were, and what the matter was with everyone. Thomas was quick to tell him. Edward said nothing. Mother kept asking, "Why? Why?"

Father sat down heavily in his high-backed chair by the fire. He looked drawn, as well he might, coming home to all this after a day spent riding around his lands and dealing with his stewards and tenants. "Has Catherine said why her parents are so angry with her?" he asked.

"She will say nothing. She is too distressed," Edward told him, tight-lipped.

"I will speak to her," Father said. "Is she in bed?"

"No, she was sitting at the table in our chamber when I left her."

Father rose. "I'll go up."

Whatever Father had said to Catherine, he kept mostly to himself. Jane thought he was trying to spare Edward embarrassment. Mother, however, pressed him, after he had rejoined her and their older children in the Broad Chamber, the little ones having been sent off to have their supper.

"But why would Sir William say she was no daughter of his?" she persisted.

Father cleared his throat. "I have no idea."

"Does Catherine not know?"

"She seems as mystified as the rest of us."

Mother turned sharply to Edward. "What do you say to all this?"

Edward flushed. "Mother, I have not always been a good husband. Maybe Sir William assumed that Catherine gave me cause to stray."

Mother's face was puce. "You have strayed? God help me, if you were not a grown man, I'd beat you! That poor girl."

Edward had the grace to hang his head. Jane, seeing Thomas smirk, glared at him.

"Well, husband, aren't you going to reprove your son?" Mother demanded.

"I don't think Edward needs me to remind him of the shame and embarrassment to which he has subjected his wife and family," Father said. "He has to live with himself. That's punishment enough." His mouth set in a grim line.

The tower at Wulfhall was rarely used, except for storage. It was a relic from another age, a turning place from one wing to the next. But the children loved to play in the upper chambers, hiding and seeking each other amid the broken furniture and the detritus and dust of decades, if not centuries.

On the day after the Fillols left, John went missing. He was a cheeky, fair boy with a fine sense of adventure, and they were all sure he was hiding somewhere. Father James was waiting impatiently for him, so that he could begin the morning's lessons. But John did not like learning. Catherine, Jane and Margery went hurrying through the house calling for him.

"He'll be in the tower," Mother said.

"Just shout that I'll give him a beating if he doesn't show himself," Father muttered, but he was chuckling. He adored his grandson, and admired his escapades.

Jane checked the recess under the spiral staircase at the foot of the tower, then bunched up her skirts and ascended the stairs, calling for John as she went. He would not answer, she knew. She peered into the room on the first floor. It contained only a bed piled high with old bedding, and some ancient chests. John wasn't under the bed, but there was perhaps room in the chests for a small, wiry boy to conceal himself. Jane opened the first. It contained some moth-eaten furs, a leather jerkin and a rubbed velvet gown with a high waist and a wide collar embroidered with silver thread that had gone black. No John. There were ancient documents and manor rolls in another chest, broken toys and household stuff in a third and more clothes in the fourth. An old portrait stood against the wall, its paint cracked and flaking. It was of a woman Jane did not know, wearing a steeple headdress in the style of seventy years ago. She pulled it forward, just in case the naughty boy was hiding behind it. He wasn't. But there by the peeling wainscot was a handkerchief. Jane picked it up. It was embroidered with the letter C and an intricate design of knots, and blotched with yellow. She would have known it anywhere. It was Catherine's.

Jane pulled off the threadbare counterpane that covered the pile of bedclothes, half expecting to see John huddled beneath amid the bolsters and blankets. She stripped them from the bed too, just to make sure he wasn't there. And then she noticed the stains on the mattress—stains similar to those on the handkerchief. She dropped the latter in distaste, guessing what those stains might be. Maybe Catherine was being unfaithful too. She had certainly been here— but not with Edward, surely? Jane's mind reeled at the possibilities.

She heard a noise above her. John! Racing up the stairs to catch him, she resolved that she would say nothing for now. "Speak no evil," Scripture enjoined. Or, as Mother was fond of saying, "Least said, soonest mended . . ."

Sir John was away at the assizes in Salisbury and an uneasy peace had settled on the household when, two days later, a letter came for Catherine, brought by one of her father's servants. Jane, not far in her wake, recognized the livery, and waited as Catherine stood in the porch, breaking the seal and unfolding the paper. She heard the sharp intake of breath and saw her sister-in-law crumple, wailing, to her knees.

"What is it?" she asked, sinking down and putting an arm around Catherine, as footsteps sounded behind them.

Catherine was beyond speech; her mouth was working in distress. And then Edward was there, with Mother, Margery and the children behind him.

"Give it to me!" he commanded, taking the letter. As he read it, his face darkened. "By God, he'll answer for this!"

"What has he written?" Jane asked.

"Tell us!" Mother cried.

"He says he has made a new will, and that, for various causes and considerations, he has provided that neither Catherine nor the heirs of her body, nor myself, shall in any wise inherit any part or parcel of his lands. All he will leave her is forty pounds a year as long as she agrees to live virtuously in an honest house of nuns." As Catherine burst into fresh sobs, he recoiled from her. "It's outrageous. By God, I'll have this will set aside. None shall deprive me of what is rightfully mine."

"But Catherine is Sir William's co-heiress!" Mother protested, shocked. "Everything was to be divided between her and her sister. And when John was born, Sir William named him his co-executor with Catherine. Edward, I can perhaps understand why you have been excluded, but what of your wife and sons? It is John's right to inherit her share! Catherine, why would your father disinherit you in this way? My dear girl, what is all this about? You must tell us."

Jane thought immediately of the stain on the mattress, the handkerchief by the wainscot.

"Catherine?" Edward barked, glaring down at her. She was too distraught to answer.

"I will find out, I promise you!" he spat, his face like fury, and stamped off, leaving the rest of them to comfort his wife. Mother sank down on her knees and drew her daughter-in-law into her arms.

Thanking God that Thomas was away on estate business, and not here to make matters worse, Jane rose and went after Edward. She found him in the dining parlor, his back to her, staring out of the window. He was shaking with anger. She sat down at the table.

"She has betrayed me, I'm sure of it," Edward growled, "and it must have happened here in this house, on the day her parents left. They saw something. It couldn't have been one of our brothers—they were all out hawking with us. God's teeth, if I find that she's been bedding one of the servants, I'll carry her off to a nunnery myself, and be rid of her!"

Jane wrestled with herself. Should she tell Edward what she had seen? It was not conclusive proof that Catherine had been unfaithful, not cause enough to risk hurting young John and the baby.

Tears welled in her eyes. "Edward, what of those two innocent children? It would be terrible for them to lose their mother, and grow up in the knowledge that she was an adulteress. Talk to her reasonably. Get the truth out of her, and then think of your sons."

Edward turned to face her, his blue eyes blazing. "I am thinking of them! My concern is their moral welfare. If Catherine has been unfaithful, she is an unfit mother. And if so, are the children mine?" He was beside himself. Jane forbore to remind him that he was in no position to preach about morality.

She stood up. "If, Edward. If! Talk to her. You've just been made a justice of the peace, so you, above anyone, should know that under the law, the accused is innocent until proved guilty. Talk to her, for the children's sake—for Mother's sake."

"Very well," Edward muttered, and Jane followed him out of the parlor.

They found Catherine still weeping in the hall, being comforted by Mother, and the children peering in at the door. Jane shooed them away.

"Come," Edward said, "I want to talk to you." And he led his distraught wife upstairs to their chamber.

Within the hour, Edward emerged to tell Jane and their mother that Catherine had assured him, with many tears, that she had not betrayed him, and their sons were indeed his.

"But she will not agree to my contesting the will," he went on, "and so I don't believe her. I'm thinking of riding to Woodlands and demanding that Sir William tell me what happened that day."

"Is that wise?" Jane asked.

"It's the only thing I can do," Edward insisted. Just then a groom knocked and entered the room.

"Sir, my lady, a messenger from Cardinal Wolsey has arrived and is asking for Sir Edward."

They hastened to the hall. There stood a man in the Cardinal's livery. He bowed and held out a letter to Edward. "Sir, his Eminence requests that you make haste to Hampton Court, and attend him on an embassy to France." It was a command, but Jane could see that it was a welcome one. Edward was always ready to accept any task that could lead to preferment; and both he and Father knew that many men had risen high in Wolsey's service and gone on to serve the King.

"I thank his Eminence," Edward said. "If you will give me an hour's grace, I will pack my travelling chest and return with you. I must write a letter to my lord of Richmond too."

"He has been informed, Sir."

"Very good," Edward said. "My lady mother here will see that you are well refreshed." Mother was already instructing the groom to see that a good meal and a flagon of ale were brought for the messenger.

Jane ran upstairs with Edward.

"What will you do about Catherine?" she asked.

"It will have to await my return," he said.

"But you could be gone for weeks . . ."

"Thank God. I can't wait to get away. I need time to think and decide what to do. Now, Jane, if you don't mind, I need to prepare."

Jane left, feeling strangely unsettled, but her unease had little to do with the trouble between Edward and Catherine. No, it had been the unexpected excitement she had felt when she heard that Edward was to go to Hampton Court, mingled with disappointment at being left behind. It was the realization that the world was beckoning at last, and that she did, after all, want to experience every good thing it had to offer.

But there still remained that pull toward the cloister, that yearning to immerse herself in the quiet observance of her faith. How torn she felt.

Really, this indecision could not go on. If only she could find the answer in prayer.

She slipped into the deserted chapel and knelt down, fixing her eyes on the beauteous Madonna. One could live in the world and still be devout. She could think of many who did. The Queen, for example, whose piety was legendary—and Mother also. They had the joys of marriage and motherhood and worldly pleasure, and the consolation of their faith. There was no question that she too would always be devoted to God, but there were other ways of serving Him than in a cloister. She did not have to commit herself to the religious life.

She realized that her decision had been made.

"Thank you," she whispered. "Thank you for showing me the way."

Catherine did not come to the riding block to hand her husband the stirrup cup and say farewell. Mother had to perform that duty.

"God keep you, my son," she said, looking at him searchingly. "Write to us."

"I will," Edward promised, and rode away with the messenger as they waved him goodbye.

Wishing that she was riding up to Surrey with him, Jane returned to the house and knocked at Catherine's door. Receiving no reply, she lifted the latch and went in. Catherine was sitting rocking Ned's cradle, staring out of the window. Her cheeks were wet.

"Will you not confide in me?" Jane asked, taking the other chair. "I would never divulge anything you tell me in confidence."

"I don't want to talk about it," Catherine said. "Please leave me alone."

"You can't just stay in here moping," Jane protested. "Think of the children, if of no one else. Wash your face and come downstairs. There are tasks to be done."

"I will come down in a little while," Catherine promised.

When she finally appeared, joining Mother, Jane and Elizabeth in the kitchen, where supper was being prepared, she looked wan and said little. Over the next day or so, she trailed around the house like

a wraith, a ghost of her former self, or hugged her children posses-
sively, ignoring John's squirming. Even Harry's well-meant jests
did not rally her.

"This can't go on," Mother said one evening, after Catherine had
gone early to bed.

"Have you tried talking to her?" Jane asked.

"Of course I have. She will not open her heart to me, or to anyone.
You've tried, haven't you, Anthony?"

"She told me it was none of my business," he said.

"I've tried too," Harry chimed in. "I got short shrift as well."

"You know, I might ride to Woodlands myself and see Lady Fillol," Mother said. "We have to know what has caused this."

"It's fifty miles!" Harry reminded her. "And they wouldn't tell us
before."

"She may not even receive you," Jane worried.

"It's worth trying." Mother sighed. "We can't continue like this."

"No, we can't," echoed Margery, looking distressed. "It's making
everyone unhappy."

"I will ride to Woodlands tomorrow," Mother said.

"Then I will go with you," Harry promised.

Chapter 4

1527

Mother had hardly begun to make ready for the journey when the messenger arrived from Woodlands. Sir William was dead.

"He died of an apoplexy," the man told them, as Catherine broke down in tears.

They all made the sign of the Cross on their breasts. Jane wondered if Sir William's death had been brought on by anger. What a horrible time this was! Trouble heaped upon trouble. She wished—and could not believe it—that she could be away from Wulfhall, even for a short time.

"We will go to the funeral and pay our respects," Mother announced.

The messenger's cheeks flushed. "I beg your pardon, my lady, but my mistress would be grateful if you all stayed away."

"Well!" Mother spluttered. "I was only trying to do the decent thing, and I think that was a generous gesture, in the circumstances. But to have it thrown back in my face . . . It's an insult."

The man's face reddened further. "My apologies, my lady. I am only repeating what I was told to say."

"I'm aware of that," Mother replied. "Now you may go."

Her children stared at one another. Never had they seen her send a visitor away without refreshment. It was a measure of her rare anger.

Thomas came home, with Father hard on his heels, weary after a week spent convicting murderers and thieves. Sir John seemed more shocked when Mother told him about Sir William's will than at the news of his death.

"Edward is determined to contest it," Mother said, as they sat up later after supper in the parlor. Catherine had long since excused herself and retired, a sad little figure in her mourning gown.

"He must not! It would cause a scandal," Father said. "I have to think of my position."

Mother banged down her goblet. "Will you see Edward done out of his wife's inheritance? You ought to be thinking of those poor lambs asleep upstairs. Why should those innocent souls be cheated of their birthright?"

Father placed his hand on hers, looking chastened. "I think it is a case he cannot hope to win."

"But there is no proof or admission of any misconduct," Anthony pointed out. "What if Sir William misunderstood the situation? Should blameless children be made to suffer for it?"

Jane bit her tongue. Would what she had seen in the tower constitute proof? Ought she to say something? And what would happen if she did? It was probably best to keep silent. Again, she wished she could be away from all this unpleasantness.

"Husband," Mother asked, "why don't you ride to Woodlands and insist that Lady Fillol tells you what happened that day?"

"I doubt she would, and I would not wish to intrude on a grieving widow. I think the best course is for me to talk to Catherine. Until I have done so, let us speak of more pleasant matters."

"Father, I would appreciate your help," Jane said quickly, seizing her moment. "I have decided that, if it could be arranged, I would like to go to court and serve the Queen or the Princess Mary."

Father looked visibly relieved, and everyone spoke at once. "You, little mouse?" Thomas laughed.

"Oh, my dear child!" That was Mother. "How you do surprise me!"

"I would miss you!" cried Margery.

"The court is an envious place," Anthony observed. "You'd be a lamb among wolves."

"I can't understand why you want to leave Wulfhall," Harry said.

"I can," Thomas muttered.

"It's not that I want to leave you all," Jane assured them, aware that it was not entirely the truth. "But I felt envious when Edward went to serve the Cardinal, and it made me realize that I should like to go to court too, if it could be arranged. The Queen, as Father and Edward have often said, is a kind and virtuous princess, and the Princess is known for her learning and beauty. If there is a position, however humble, I would gladly fill it."

Father had heard her out, looking thoughtful. "So you're not going to be a nun, I take it?"

"No, Father. I think I knew that last year. Now I know for certain."

"Hmm." He stroked his beard. "There is much competition for positions in the royal households. Securing one is not a thing easily accomplished. You need to know the right people, and they may want a handsome consideration."

Jane sighed. Was the court now to be barred to her?

"Daughter, do not look so disheartened." Father smiled. "It might be contrived somehow. Young ladies in the Queen's service are well placed to find good husbands, and it's about time you were wed. I have long wanted to arrange a marriage for you, but you were set on the religious life. I need not say how pleased we are that you have reached this decision, eh, Margery?"

Mother nodded. "I've prayed that you would marry one day and have a family of your own."

Father thought for a few moments. "I think I know just the person who might bring this to pass. When I was at court, I became friendly with a distant cousin of ours, Sir Francis Bryan. You have heard me speak of him. He is vice-chamberlain to the Queen, and must have some influence. Leave this with me, Jane. I will write a letter to him."

Jane felt again that same excitement that had come upon her when the messenger had brought Edward the Cardinal's summons. Yet, she reminded herself, nothing was certain; she must rein in her hopes. But please God, let Sir Francis Bryan say yes!

Father had spoken to Catherine, but, he said, she had declined to talk to him. As those tense weeks of Edward's absence passed, and Jane hoped and prayed for a communication from Sir Francis Bryan, little more was said about the dark matter that hung over Wulfhall like a cloud.

Jane wondered why Catherine would not tell anyone what had happened to make her parents leave so abruptly. If, as she had told Edward, she had not been unfaithful, and the children were his, why was she holding back? Or was there nothing to tell? In that case, surely anger and a sense of injustice would impel her to seek redress, rather than shying away from doing so? But Catherine remained tight-lipped on the subject. It was like having a stranger in their midst.

And then, in the heat of August, Edward came home from France, earlier than expected. There was no loving reunion with his family; his face told them that something dire had happened and, at the sight of it, Mother sent the children to the chamber called the Old Room, where they had their lessons and played.

Jane wondered fleetingly if Edward had somehow displeased the Cardinal, but then she saw him recoil as Catherine came to greet him, and stare at his wife as if she were a piece of dirt to be brushed away. When he did not kneel for Father's blessing, but fixed him with that same look, Jane began to feel afraid. What was going on?

"Sir, I would speak to you in private, please," Edward said, his voice like steel.

Sir John nodded. "Of course. Come into my closet."

Catherine looked like an animal caught in a trap, staring at them both. Jane caught Mother's eye, but Mother looked as perplexed as she was. Jane thought guiltily of what she had seen in the tower. Should she have said something?

Father and Edward were in the closet for only a few minutes before Edward crashed out, slammed the door and stalked toward them. He pointed at Catherine.

"Leave this house," he commanded. "I will not have you under this roof a moment longer. You have dishonored me and my family, and I cannot endure your society any longer. Go and get your belongings."

Catherine's face had gone white with fear. With a great sob, she flung herself to her knees. "Edward, I beg of you! Please do not send me away. What of the children?"

"What of them indeed? You should have thought of them when you embarked on your evil deeds."

"Edward, what is all this about?" Mother cried.

He turned an anguished face to her, as Catherine's wails increased in volume. "Oh, God, Mother, I do not know how to tell you. This is the hardest thing I have ever had to say."

Jane was seized by a fit of trembling. She did not want to hear this.

Beside her, Margery was crying.

"You must tell me," Mother insisted, in the voice of authority that had quelled many an obstreperous child or servant. Catherine subsided to a whimper. Her eyes were dark pools of horror.

Edward closed his eyes as if he were in pain. "Father has been her lover these past nine years, almost since we were wed." He dragged the words out, his voice sounding strangled. "The boys are most likely his." Jane felt as if she had been punched. As Mother, poor Mother, sank down on a bench, she and Margery swooped to put their arms around her. "No," Lady Seymour said, in a broken voice, all her authority vanished in an instant. "No, no, no. Not Catherine, his own son's wife. I guessed long ago—God help me, I knew—

there was another woman, but I never dreamed of this. Oh, Blessed
Virgin, help us!" She collapsed in a torrent of weeping. Even Thomas
was blinking away tears.

Jane could not believe it. Not Father, their beloved father, who
had been as a rock to them all? Yet rocks could be made of clay. How
could he have done something so base, so vile? And kept on doing
it all these nine years? For if John was his son, this wickedness had
been going on since the year Edward married.

She tried desperately to recall any hint of what had been happening under their very noses, and of course, when she thought about
it, there had been signs, innocent in themselves, but now invested
with a new significance. This, surely, had something to do with the
Fillols departing so abruptly that day. Had they seen something
that aroused their suspicions, or had Catherine confessed to what
had been going on? Oh, God, it must have been her and Father in
the tower—and on more than one occasion, judging by those stains!
Her cheeks flamed with the shame of it. She could not bear to think
of Father in such a lewd situation. It was disgusting.

But it explained his constant kindness to Catherine, his anger
with Edward, and why he stayed up on the night Catherine's mother
spoke to her. He must have been anxious lest Catherine betray what
they had been doing. And when he had gone to talk to her himself,
it must have been to warn her to keep quiet. It was all so sordid.

And Mother—she had known that Father was being unfaithful
with someone. How had she stayed cheerful and gone about as if all
were well, putting everyone else first as usual? Such bravery was
humbling—and shocking. But of course Jane had known, in some
corner of her mind, that something was wrong. In her innocence,
she had put it down to Mother suffering the change of life.

"Now you see why she has to leave," Edward said. In response,
Catherine threw herself at him and clung to his knees.

"I beg you, do not send me away!" she screamed. "Please! Please!
I cannot leave my children! Edward, I beg you!"

He disengaged her, none too gently. "You will do as I order you,"
he hissed, his voice icy. "Get up. Go."

The world seemed to be turning upside down. Jane could not bear the thought of facing Father when he emerged from the closet, where he was no doubt hiding like a coward. And whatever Catherine had done, she could not help feeling some pity for her.

"I will take you to Prioress Florence at Amesbury," she said. "Harry, will you escort us?"

"Aye," Harry agreed.

"Margery, look after Mother," she urged. "I will be back as soon as I can. Catherine, please get up. We must gather your things."

Thomas and Harry lifted Catherine to her feet.

"I must see the boys!" she cried, struggling to evade their grip. "I cannot leave my baby! I must see them!" She was becoming hysterical.

"No," Edward said. "Someone, get her gear."

"I'll do it." Mother made for the stairs, looking defeated and suddenly much older. Jane could not stem her own tears. She could well imagine the pain of losing a child, and how John and Ned would feel when they realized that their mother was never coming back. And that would only be the beginning of it.

Just then, Mother stumbled and collapsed on the bottom stair. "It's no use," she wept, "I cannot . . . It's all so dreadful." Jane and Margery hastened to succor her.

Harry let go of Catherine and squeezed Jane's hand. "I'll take her to Amesbury," he said. "You stay with Mother."

Jane dabbed at her eyes, appalled to see Mother in such a state. "Maybe it would be best," she agreed. "I'll write a note to the Prioress."

"Please let me see my children!" Catherine begged, her eyes wild. She tried to push Edward aside, but he held her firmly, ignoring her cries. Jane fetched writing materials, but her hand was shaking so much that she could manage no more than an untidy scrawl.

"I have told Prioress Florence only that you have been an unfaithful wife," she said to Catherine. "I will not shame this family by telling the whole truth."

"That's very wise," Anthony observed, his voice hoarse, "and it's

what we should all agree to do. Let's not make this any worse than
it is. Imagine how the scandal would rebound on us if what has happened ever got out."

"You mean we should act among ourselves as if nothing has happened?" Mother said, rising unsteadily to her feet. "You believe I
can do that?"

Anthony's lean, handsome face flushed. "Mother, I am only trying
to spare you further distress. If we keep this matter in the family,
you will be able to look our friends in the eye, without shame. And
in truth, what else can you do? We are all bound to Father in loyalty
and obedience. If you abandon him, the world will censure you as a
faithless wife."

"We will discuss this later," Mother said.

She dragged herself upstairs and they sat there waiting for her,
the silence broken only by Catherine's sobs. Presently, Mother came
down carrying a bag crammed with clothes, with a groom in her
wake hauling a leather-bound chest. Jane could see from the resolute look on her face that she had recovered a semblance of her usual
composure and was doing her best to be strong. "Catherine, here are
your things," she said, her tone cold. "Harry, can you order the litter
to be brought round, and horses?"

"It's here," Thomas said. "I gave the order."

"You must go," Mother said, turning to face her weeping
daughter-in-law. "Edward has decreed it, and I will not gainsay
him. I hope, Catherine, that you realize the enormity of what you
have done, and that you are sorry for it. In charity, I will pray for
you."

"Please!" Catherine begged, her teeth chattering. "Please let me
see my children!"

"Get her out," Edward said, and as Harry hesitated, he pulled her
toward the door. She started screaming, but he slapped her face.
"Quiet! What must the servants think?"

Harry put a firm arm around Catherine and hurried her through
the door. Jane followed them and stood by as he bundled her into

the litter. When she leaned inside, Catherine stared at her, looking half crazed.

"Listen," Jane said. "If you respect our silence and never name my father as your paramour, I will do my best to ensure that you see your children. If you don't, I will think you the most ungrateful creature that ever lived, and do nothing more for you. Do you understand?"

Harry was looking at Jane with new respect. Catherine seized her hand. "I promise I will never speak of him! I give you my word, my vow. I'll do anything, if you'll bring my children to me or let me visit them."

"I will try," Jane promised. "God be with you." She stood in the Great Court, watching as the litter was borne off and Catherine's wails faded into the distance. Then she went to find Edward.

They were still in the hall, absorbing the enormity of what had happened.

"She has gone," Jane said. "Edward, you should be aware that a visit from the children may be the price of her silence."

Edward was slumped on a bench, his anger spent. "I don't want them seeing her. No good can come of it."

"Her discretion will come of it! Besides, I more or less promised her that if she keeps silence about Father, I will do my best to help her see the children."

"You had no right!" Edward barked.

"She has a lot of sense!" Mother riposted. "Do you want our shame trumpeted to the world? Word gets about, you know. Nuns love gossip. It'd be all over the county in five minutes. Think of me— and think of those poor children. They are going to miss their mother. They have never known a day without her."

"I will think on it," Edward growled.

"Then think quickly," his mother said.

"The thing I don't understand," Anthony spoke up, "is how you found out about Father being Catherine's lover." Jane saw Mother wince.

Edward hesitated. "You will find the truth hard to believe. When I was in France, I was racked with uncertainty about Catherine. I had to know if she had really been untrue to me, and if the children were mine. It was the worst time to be away from home, and it grieved me that there was no way I could resolve these matters until my return. I was losing sleep over it." He paused. "There was a gentleman in the Cardinal's retinue. When we were at Amboise, I heard him speak of a learned man in the town who was supposed to have great skill in magic."

"A warlock!" Anthony burst out.

Edward glowered at him. "Be grateful you weren't in my situation, boy. You know nothing of what you speak." He turned to the rest. "This man was reputed to be able to see visions and predict the future. I wondered if he could help me. I visited him in a house in a narrow street not far from the mansion where the artist Leonardo lived. At first, the man said it was forbidden to conjure visions, and if he did, he risked being accused of witchcraft or heresy. I swore I would tell no one. I offered sureties. In short, I begged and pleaded, because I was desperate to know the truth."

"But how did you know he was not a charlatan or fraud?" Harry asked.

"People at court spoke of him with respect, as a learned man, a man of probity. Only this gentleman of the Cardinal's had mentioned his magicking, and he assured me that he was as sound in that respect as in any other. And so I was happy to pay, handsomely, for his help."

Mother was shaking her head. "I cannot believe that a son of mine would involve himself in something like this. Father James would be appalled."

Jane herself was appalled, but also engrossed.

Edward stood up. "I can see that you don't approve of what I did, and I doubt you will believe it. There's no point in telling you what happened. I'm going to the stables."

"Wait!" Jane cried. "We'll hear you out. I'm sure you acted for the best reasons. Doesn't everyone agree?" Her gaze swept over the entire company.

"I will hear you out," Mother said, "but I've had shocks enough for one day."

Edward sat down again. "Mother, I gained no sense that this man was wicked; rather that he was sober and sincere. He understood my anxiety, and was sympathetic. He told me he would use a magical perspective to try to discover what was happening at home. He took me into a small room hung with black cloth, and invited me to sit with him at the table. On it were placed two silver candles and a bowl of what looked like cristallo, filled with water. He asked the water to let us see the truth about my wife, then he took five moonstones from his pocket and dropped them in the bowl."

Mother crossed herself, but held her peace.

"Nothing happened for a while," Edward recounted, "but then, to my amazement, an image began to appear in the water. It was of a woman in a green gown, like the one Catherine often wore, but . . . I will only say that there was a man with her, in a more familiar posture than befitted the honor of either of them. The vision lasted only for seconds, but I recognized him. It was Father."

"How could you be sure?" Thomas asked, incredulous.

"I had no doubt. But even if I was mistaken, or the man used trickery, it was no more than the truth, and Father has admitted it. Both of them have."

"So because of what you saw, you hurried home," Thomas said. "What did the Cardinal say to that?"

"I did not tell him the truth. I said my wife was crazed because her father had died, and I was in great fear for her. He was sympathetic, and gave me his blessing. I do not think he will hold it against me." He buried his face in his hands.

For a few moments, no one spoke.

"What will you do now?" Jane ventured to ask.

"If Catherine takes vows, you could easily obtain an annulment and marry again," Anthony said.

"You think I want to?" Edward asked, his tone bitter.

"You must give yourself time," Mother said. "We all need time to come to terms with what has happened." She was weeping again. "Your father is become a stranger to me. I know not how I shall cope. And what is to become of the children?"

Edward sighed. "I have thought long about this. I love them both. They may be mine, but even if they are Father's, they have the same blood. The law presumes that the husband is the father of any child of his wife, so there is no need to brand them with bastardy. Therefore I will do nothing to their prejudice."

Jane could see that Mother was as relieved as she was to hear that.

"As long as you do not withdraw your fatherly love from them," Mother said. "They are going to need that, especially John. And they are not to blame for any of this."

"I cannot stop loving them, even if they remind me of their mother and the wicked thing she has done," Edward replied. "But I do intend to contest Sir William's will; there is no reason why I, or her children, should be deprived of Catherine's inheritance."

Thomas looked up. "If you do that, brother, you risk angering Lady Fillol, who might have her revenge by proclaiming to the world that it was our father who tupped her daughter."

"Thomas!" his siblings chorused in protest.

"Have you no respect for Mother?" Harry snapped.

Thomas had the grace to look contrite. "I'm sorry, Mother."

"And I am sorry too, more than I can say." It was Sir John, standing in the doorway, looking like a broken man and searching their faces as if to see whether any semblance of love and respect remained. "Can you ever forgive me?"

His children rose to their feet, through the force of habit that had been drilled into them from infancy. All the obedience, deference and affection that Father had commanded throughout their lives could not be overturned in an instant. And yet already Jane found herself looking at him with new eyes. He was still the father she had loved, and yet he had become a stranger, a man revealed in all his sinful weakness. Her brain could not fully compass it.

"Margery?" Sir John said.

Mother would not look at him. Edward got up and walked out. "Margery, come into the Broad Chamber," Father said, and stood back so that she could precede him, his eyes wet with tears. Jane was shocked. She had never seen him weep.

Neither Father nor Mother ever revealed what had passed between them on that hot August afternoon, but it was clear that both were making an effort to go on much as before—except that nothing could ever again be the same. At supper, Father occupied his high chair at the head of the board, as usual, and Mother seated herself at the opposite end, as she always did. Between them, they kept the conversation going, and their children took their lead from them. It was not their place to censure their father.

Jane's heart bled for her mother. She was being so brave. Jane did her best to keep up the pretense that all was normal, but she was aware of her mother's pain and her father's shame, and was struggling to come to terms with both. Edward was sitting there like a furnace about to explode. The tension was palpable. No one was eating much of the good food that had been set before them.

"I had a letter from Sir Francis today," Father said, toward the end of the meal, as if it were something unimportant he had forgotten. "He writes that he will willingly sue for a place for you, Jane. He implied that I might ease his labors with the hope of a reward. Fear not, I will recompense him. It is the way of the court. Patronage was ever lucrative. I will send the money tomorrow."

"Thank you, Father," Jane said, her heart beating faster at the realization that she might really be going to court. But oh, how much more thrilled she would feel if this good news had arrived in happier circumstances! How could she leave Mother at this time?

"It will be a fine opportunity for you," Mother said stoutly, "and it may help you to a good marriage. I pray it comes to pass." Jane felt somewhat relieved.

At last, the interminable meal was over, grace was said and they could all escape to bed. Jane took a candle and went up with Margery. In the chamber they shared, with its low beams and wooden bedstead hung with embroidered curtains, they undressed without speaking, folded their clothes, pulled on their night rails and climbed into bed. Jane blew out the candle, and they lay there with the room bathed in the moonlight that shone through the open latticed window.

"I wish you weren't going to court," Margery said.

"I may never get there," Jane answered. "Nothing is certain yet. But if I do, I will ask the Queen if she has a place for you too."

"Would you?" Margery's voice was full of longing.

"Of course, dear sister. I love you so much. I will miss you dreadfully."

"But it's always easier for those who go to new places than it is for those who are left behind," Margery observed, with a wisdom that belied her fifteen years.

"Yes," Jane agreed. "And things won't be easy here for a long time, I fear."

"Do you think that Mother and Father will be able to put this behind them?"

"What else can they do? They are married. Father is an important man hereabouts. Mother will not risk any scandal. We have all agreed that secrecy is the best policy. And that begins at home."

"Well, I shall try to go on as normal," Margery declared, turning over in the bed, "and I pray that everybody else does. Good night, Jane."

Jane could not sleep. She lay fidgeting in the darkness, trying to curb the teeming thoughts in her head. At length, she got up, put on her night robe and tiptoed into the empty chamber next door, where there was a privy. When she emerged, she was wide awake, so she crept downstairs to the Old Room, where there was sure to be a book that would take her mind off all the tumults. Father James being a lenient tutor, the room was a jumble of hobby horses, dolls and spinning tops, with horn books and papers strewn across the desks. Jane smiled as she spied young John's untidy letters, then felt a pang as she thought of the loss that her unsuspecting nephew must soon face.

On a shelf there were some favorite books from childhood. Taking Chaucer's *Canterbury Tales,* she sat down and opened it. As she began to read, she became aware of a soft noise beyond the door at the far end of the room, which led to Father's closet. Was he up at this late hour?

She waited, wondering if she should make herself scarce, but then the door opened and Father walked through it.

"Jane! What are you doing?" He could barely meet her eye.

"I couldn't sleep, Father. I came to find a book."

"Alas, poor child, I doubt that any of us will sleep much tonight." He swallowed and came toward her. "My darling girl," he said, and folded her in his arms. "I am so sorry. What have I done?" His voice was muffled against her hair. His shoulders heaved. She did not know what to do or say.

"It's all right," she whispered at length. "You must give us all time."

"Try not to think too badly of me," he murmured. "I was a fool, fancying myself in love. Edward neglected her, and I took advantage of her misery." He released Jane and faced her, her big, strong father, weeping and looking strangely diminished. "Though she was willing, the blame was mine. I can never sufficiently atone."

Jane forced a smile. "I make no doubt but that you are forgiven in Heaven already, since you so truly repent. I forgive you heartily, and I will try to forget."

He drew in a sharp breath. "I do not deserve such charity, but I thank you, Jane, from the bottom of my heart. Your mother told me it was you who urged that we keep this within the family, and for that I thank you again. I am truly blessed in such a daughter." He had controlled himself now, and reached out his hand. Jane hesitated. More than anything, she wanted him back as he had been. Forgiving him was the first step toward that. She took his hand.

The letter from Sir Francis Bryan arrived a week later. Sir John came into the kitchen where Jane and her mother were baking pies, and read it aloud. "Jane, you are to go to court. The Queen has graciously consented to receive you as a maid-of-honor, and the King has signified his approval."

Jane's heart began thumping with excitement. "That's truly marvelous news! I never expected that it would come to pass." She could hardly focus on the list of things she would need for court, which threw Mother into a spin and mercifully distracted her from her unhappiness.

"You can only wear black or white, it says. No colors. We'll have to send to Marlborough for the mercer to come, and tell him to be quick, if you're to be at Greenwich by the end of the month. Why you can't just wear your best gowns is beyond me!"

Edward was standing behind Father, listening to the conversation—or rather, Mother's monologue. "Only the Queen and her ladies-in-waiting wear colors, Mother. All her maids-of-honor wear black and white."

"Why is that?" Jane asked.

"So that they do not eclipse her. Most of them are young, fair maidens, while the Queen—to be plain—is no beauty. But she is very stately and dresses sumptuously."

"What is Queen Katherine like?" Jane asked.

"I have never spoken to her, but I have seen her on many occasions. She is always gracious and smiling, even though she has many crosses to bear."

"Yes, she has no son," Father observed, sitting down in the chair by the hearth, "and she is past the ways of women."

Edward did not answer. Still he would not speak to his father. The atmosphere in the house remained tense, and Jane felt guilty for feeling relieved at the prospect of going away and leaving the rest of them to cope with it.

"Is the Queen beautiful?" eight-year-old Dorothy piped up.

"She was in her youth," Father told her. "Alas, she is no longer young. She is older than the King."

"I want to go to court," Dorothy insisted. "I want to wear pretty clothes and dance and sing and see the King."

"All in good time," Father said.

"As if I haven't enough to do fitting out one daughter for court," Mother huffed. "Jane, we must go upstairs and go through your chest, to see what can be used. You'll need new hoods, too. You can't wear your hair loose at court. When the mercer comes, we must allow extra for trains. And you can take my pearls—"

Edward interrupted. "I will escort you to court, Jane, before heading north to Sheriff Hutton. I am due back there soon." The hint of relief in his voice was unmistakable.

After supper, Jane and Edward walked in the gardens at Wulfhall.

"It's a solace to be out of the house," he said, his thin features drawn, dark eyes shadowed. "Our departure can't come soon enough."

"Won't you miss the boys?" she asked.

"They will do well enough with Mother."

"But they need you at this time."

"Jane, don't meddle!" Edward flared.

"If I meddle, it's because I care for them," she retorted, stung. "They have just lost their mother."

"And that's my fault? I didn't wallow in incest for nine years."

"Did she wallow?" Jane said slowly. "Or was she afraid to say no to Father? She was never happy, was she? A woman in love, who is indulging that love, must look happy. I cannot but think that the love was all on Father's side."

"The lust, you mean!" Edward growled.

"For nine years? I had heard that lust was quickly sated. No, Edward, I am certain that Catherine was more sinned against than sinning."

"You must remember how she conducted herself at the first," he snarled, bitter. "Older than Eve. Certainly she worked her wiles on me. She was no innocent; she knew what she was about. You do me wrong to take her part."

"No, Edward!" Jane cried, aware that she could not afford to anger or alienate him. Stiff-backed, cold and moralistic as he could be, he was yet her brother, and from next week he would be her only link to home. She touched his arm. "I am sorry for you both, but whatever Catherine's part in all this, she has lost her children, and that must be dreadful for her."

His shoulders slumped. "You are too soft-hearted, Jane. By her conduct, she has forfeited her right to her children's company. I cannot risk their being infected by her wickedness. She is no fit person to guide and rear them. And you might think of me. I have a wife— and no wife. I cannot remarry, unless Catherine takes vows, or I apply for a divorce, but that would be prohibitively expensive. It would take an Act of Parliament. So I must resign myself to being alone."

Or not so alone, she thought, but decided it would be wiser to bite her tongue. "I am truly sorry for you," she said, and linked her arm in his.

They strolled on in silence.

"What is the King like?" Jane asked, trying to break the mood.

"He's very handsome in person, or so the ladies say," Edward told her. "He's tall and magnificent, as a great prince should be, and he carries himself regally. Sometimes he's more of a good fellow than a king. He's not above sharing a jest with his inferiors, and I've even seen him playing at dice with the master of his wine cellar. Once, when an envoy was nervous at being in his presence, I saw him put an arm about the man's shoulders and talk with him familiarly, to put him at his ease."

"That's encouraging." She was rather dreading the prospect of meeting the King.

"He doesn't bite." Edward attempted a smile. "Don't look so frightened."

At last, everything was ready. As she said farewell, Jane clung to her mother. Father kissed her, then gave her his blessing and a purse of coins. Mother was putting on a brave face, smiling and bidding her to write often. Her brothers and younger sisters crowded around, with the children, to say goodbye. Jane gave Margery a special hug. "I haven't forgotten my promise," she said.

She climbed into the litter, next to the chest in which her new gowns had been carefully laid, with the hoods, wrapped in old silk, on top. There was a smaller chest containing body linen, furs and a winter cloak, and a small casket of jewels: Mother's pearls, which had been passed down from Grandmother Wentworth, three rings, a small pendant with a diamond, and a lozenge-shaped brooch of enamel depicting the Five Wounds of Christ. Tucked in beside Jane was a large basket containing food for the journey.

Edward mounted his horse, two grooms took up the rear, and slowly the little cavalcade passed out of the Great Court, through the Little Court and the gatehouse, and then took the road that led to Marlborough, Newbury and Maidenhead, where they would board a boat for Greenwich. Jane forced herself not to look back.

Part Two

A Place
of Pride
and Envy

Chapter 5

1527

The hosteler gave them a warm welcome at Hurley Priory, ringing the sanctus bell on the wall by the entrance to the guest house.

"Father Prior always likes to be told the instant that distinguished visitors arrive." He beamed. He was a rotund, apple-cheeked fellow, a merry monk in the mold of Friar Tuck, as Jane imagined him. The right man for the office. He showed them to their chambers, which were small and plainly furnished, but spotlessly clean, while the groom brought in their baggage. They were staying for one night only. Tomorrow, Edward and Jane were to take the boat at Maidenhead, and the groom would return home with the litter and the horses.

Prior Thomas was as jovial as his hosteler, yet there was steel beneath the charm, Jane suspected. At dinner, which they ate as his guests in the parlor of his house, he became quite heated about Cardinal Wolsey. "It's not fitting for a clergyman to own such wealth. He is Archbishop of York, but he has never been there."

Edward helped himself and Jane to more roast beef, placing slices on their shared gravy-soaked bread trencher. "People say it is he who rules England, rather than the King. I'm not sure that's entirely true. I've seen them together. They are great friends, and it seems that the Cardinal is almost a father figure to his Grace. There's no doubting that he is a very able man, but certainly he has too much power—and it is widely resented."

"Our Lord, whom he serves, was a humble carpenter. He did not own great palaces and vast wealth. I have seen Hampton Court and York Place. No churchman should enjoy such worldly riches."

Jane liked the Prior's sincerity. She was comparing the comforts enjoyed by Prioress Florence at Amesbury with the old table and chairs in Prior Thomas's dining room, his patched scapular and the simple wooden cross, the only object to adorn the walls. If the Prioress had been as holy as this good man, would she herself have stayed at Amesbury? She suspected that if she had, the world would still have beckoned her. She wondered how poor Catherine was faring there now. Edward had not mentioned her once on the journey.

"Wolsey is not the only prelate to pursue wealth and worldly advancement," her brother was saying.

"The Church is often the route to power," Prior Thomas observed, "and ever has been. But there is great corruption, and if the popes in Rome set a bad example, who will curb the excesses of a man like Wolsey?"

"The popes set a bad example?" Jane was shocked. All her life she had been taught to revere the Holy Father in Rome, who was Christ's Vicar on Earth and the fount of all spiritual wisdom and authority.

"I fear so," the Prior replied. "Surely you have heard of the excesses of the Borgias? Our present Pope Clement and the late Pope Julius both fathered bastard children, and . . . Well, I will not speak of the rest in your presence, Mistress Seymour. But popes are invested with Christ's authority to pronounce on moral matters. If they lack probity, what hope for the rest of us?"

"Father Prior, when we have the example of good men like you, who truly follow Christ and His laws, then there is much hope." Jane smiled. "I am an ignorant woman. I know nothing about the

Borgias, nor do I think I want to, but I'm sure there are many like me who try to observe our faith in quiet and humility. We always hear about the scandals of the few, but what of the goodness of the majority?"

Prior Thomas smiled at her. "My dear child, it may be that a simple maid like yourself has more wisdom than a disillusioned old man like me. I pray that the court will not change you. It is not for the faint in spirit. Guard your innocence well. At least you will be serving our most virtuous Queen. She is the mirror of piety, and a very gracious lady."

"Aye," Edward agreed. "She is much beloved. Alas that she has no son."

"It is a great tragedy." The Prior got up, fetched a bowl of fruit from the window ledge and laid it before them. "The Princess Mary is the King's only heir. No woman has ever ruled England before, and any one of the surviving members of the old royal House of York might challenge her title. We could see a return to the civil wars of my youth, when Lancaster and York contested the crown."

"Heaven forbid!" Jane breathed. The apple she was eating suddenly tasted sour.

"I serve the Duke of Richmond," Edward said. "There is talk at court that the King may get Parliament to legitimate the boy and name him his successor."

The Prior frowned. "But would the people of England accept a bastard as king? That would be the great test."

"Some think the people have such love for the King that they would prefer his bastard son to any sprig of the white rose of York. But there are traitors who call the Tudors usurpers and long for the return of the old royal line. Who knows what would happen?"

"It must worry the King greatly," the Prior sighed.

"Some say he should marry the Princess to one of the Yorkists and hope for grandsons," Edward opined.

"A wise idea." The Prior's eyes twinkled. "You should be advising his Grace, not Wolsey."

The conversation turned to the King.

"Jane desires to know all about him," Edward said. "I have been preparing her for her new position."

"Our sovereign lord is a very religious man, a true friend of the Church," the Prior informed Jane. "About six years ago, he wrote a book against the heresies of Martin Luther, and for that the Pope awarded him the title 'Defender of the Faith.' I have heard that he is assiduous in observing the offices of the Church, and that he creeps to the Cross on his knees, in humility, every Good Friday."

"His Grace is very learned in theology," Edward added. "He reads St. Thomas Aquinas and St. Augustine. The Gentlemen of his Privy Chamber say he likes nothing better than a good debate about religion."

"He sounds like a paragon," Jane said.

"We are blessed in such a king," Prior Thomas declared.

"And you will meet him very soon." Edward smiled.

It was exciting being on the river for the first time. Jane had never been on a barge before, and she found herself enjoying the gentle motion and the swishing of the oars through the powerful currents. The speed was exhilarating.

London was as marvelous as she had anticipated, with its skyline pierced by a hundred steeples and the fine mansions that lined the banks of the Thames. As they were rowed downstream, Edward pointed out Hampton Court, the great palace built by Cardinal Wolsey, and Richmond Palace, with pinnacles and domes that would not have been out of place in an ancient legend; and then, passing Westminster, she saw the great hall and the abbey, and after it the City itself, London Bridge creaking under the weight of its shops and chapel, with St. Paul's Cathedral dominating all.

Some way further along, Greenwich Palace sprawled along the River Thames like a great red-brick lion. It was vast, with huge oriel windows facing the waterfront and a great tower. Surrounding it were beautiful gardens with fountains, lawns, flowers and orchards. The scale of it all had Jane gaping. She had thought Wulf-hall large! How would she ever find her way around this place?

"Sir Francis Bryan should be waiting for us," Edward said, as the barge turned toward the shore. "Be wary. He's done you a great favor, and he might expect something in return."

"Surely not!" Jane felt the heat rise from her neck. "Father paid him for the favor."

"Be on your guard, that's all. He's not nicknamed 'the Vicar of Hell' for nothing. He's notoriously impious, and likes to make free with the ladies. But none can touch him, for he's a close friend of the King and a Gentleman of the Privy Chamber. His mother is Marga-ret, Lady Bryan, who is also held in high regard and was governess to the Princess Mary. Oh, and another thing. He wears an eyepatch. He lost his eye in a tournament last year."

"Oh, how awful!" Jane exclaimed.

Her stomach was churning like the water beneath her as she rose unsteadily to her feet. Gripping the bench in front for support, she smoothed the skirts of her new black gown and white kirtle, straightened the gable hood her mother had made, and gathered her train over her arm. She climbed the stone stairs to the quayside, her black veil flapping over her shoulder. At the top, they were chal-lenged by the King's guard in their splendid red uniforms, but when Edward explained that Jane was come to serve the Queen, and that Sir Francis Bryan was expecting them, a groom was immedi-ately sent off to inform him of their coming, and they were escorted into the tower and through an apartment of such splendor that Jane wondered if she had died and arrived in Heaven. Everything was gilded or painted in bright colors. The armorial glass in the oriel windows glittered in the sun's rays; huge tapestries hung on all the walls, and naked plaster cherubs gamboled along decorative friezes. There were carpets on the floor—Mother would have gone into spasms at the thought of people walking on them; her two Turkey rugs adorned tables, and woe betide anyone who got dirt on them.

Jane had to mind her train as they turned right into a long gallery hung with portraits and maps, and threaded their way through the press of courtiers waiting to see the Queen. A tall, dark-haired man was waiting at the far end. He wore an eyepatch and a fashionable short gown of fine gray damask above his doublet and bases, and he bowed courteously at their approach.

"Mistress Jane," he said, with a wolfish smile.

Jane curtseyed warily, keeping her distance, painfully aware that the low, square neckline of her court gown was revealing far more of her breasts than she would have liked.

"Welcome to court." Sir Francis beamed, his eyes raking her up and down. "You look most becoming. I take it your father is well?"

"Very well, thank you, Sir," Jane said. "In truth, we are all most grateful to you for finding me this position."

"It was my pleasure," he assured her. "Come. The Queen is waiting." She was feeling really nervous now. What place could a country girl have here in this mighty court? How would she avoid making a fool of herself? She could not believe that she was about to meet the Queen of England, and that that Queen was her new mistress. She might even meet the King today! She trembled at the prospect. She thought of turning around and running back to the barge. She hardly knew how she stopped herself.

Sir Francis led them into the Queen's lodgings, through two chambers of great magnificence, pointing out treasures and paintings with consummate ease and charm. Even on short acquaintance, Jane found his knowledge impressive, and feared she would find herself at a disadvantage if everyone at court was so learned. Listening to Edward conversing with Sir Francis, she realized she had not known her brother to be such a scholar. She began to feel even more inadequate.

The Queen's presence chamber was empty, save for the guards who stood at the doors. At one end, beneath a canopy of estate blazoned with the royal arms of England and Spain, stood a cross-frame chair upholstered in crimson velvet. To the far side was a door, where they waited for the usher to announce them.

"Her Grace is in the privy chamber beyond," Sir Francis told Jane. "Only the most privileged persons may enter, and now you are one of them." He gave her that wolfish smile, but there was warmth in it. "Have courage, mistress. The Queen is a gentle lady." Jane could see why women fell for him.

"This is where I leave you, sister," Edward said, kissing her and stepping back. "Good luck!" She was suddenly seized with fright and almost ran after him, but took a deep breath and reminded herself that he was not going far away.

They followed the usher through the door into a large apartment, as sumptuously furnished as the rest. Jane looked around. On the dais at the far end, the Queen sat in a great chair, her purple damask skirts spread wide about her. On her head she wore an ornate gable hood with biliments of gold, on her ample breast a pendant with three drop pearls. Her gorgeously attired ladies and a bevy of maids in black and white were seated or kneeling around her. They all looked up from their needlework as Jane sank into a trembling curtsey.

"Welcome, Mistress Jane," the Queen said, in a heavily accented voice that betrayed her Spanish blood. Jane rose and saw that she was smiling and holding out a plump hand adorned with sparkling rings.

"Kiss it," Sir Francis whispered.

She stepped forward, fell to her knees and did as she was bidden, thinking how old and sad the Queen looked. She was stout too—nothing like Jane had expected—and she had an overly prominent chin, yet there was a pleasing sweetness in her smile, her eyes were kind, and her dignified, gentle manner immediately set Jane at her ease.

"Sir Francis, I am most grateful to you for recommending Mistress Jane to me," the Queen said.

"She is most fortunate to be serving your Grace," he replied.

"It is a great honor, your Grace," Jane murmured, aware of the curious eyes of the women who would from now on be her daily companions.

"Mistress Elizabeth, please take Jane to the maidens' dormitory and look after her," the Queen instructed.

One of the ladies stood up, a young woman with dark hair, a rosy oval face and deep blue eyes.

"Come with me," she said.

Leaving Sir Francis and the Queen conversing, Jane curtseyed and followed the lady up a winding stair that led to a big chamber on the top floor, with gabled windows on both sides. Along the walls were long lines of pallet beds, each with a chest next to it, and pegs on the walls above on which to hang clothing. The room smelled of sweat, perfume, shoes and—faintly—bloody monthly clouts. It did not bother her, as she was used to sharing a room with Margery.

"I am Elizabeth Chambers, Mistress of the Maids," the young woman said. "Everyone calls me Bess. I am in charge of all the Queen's maids-of-honor, and responsible for their welfare. If you have any problems, come to me." She smiled. "I see you are wearing the requisite colors."

Jane was relieved to find her so friendly. "My mother has provided two other gowns, one of white, the other of black," she said, as two men in green-and-white livery entered the room carrying her baggage. "I will show you."

"There is no need," Bess Chambers told her. "You may have some time to dispose of your gear. The King always joins the Queen for Vespers, so you will need to be downstairs for six o'clock to attend her. Supper will be served in her privy chamber afterward, and the great ladies of her household join her at table, unless the King stays. We maids eat with the chamberers in the watching chamber with the officers of her Grace's household. After supper, we usually enjoy some recreation before attending her Grace when she goes to bed. You will take it in turns with the other maids-of-honor to sleep on a pallet bed in her bedchamber, in case she needs anything in the night. Is that all clear?"

"Yes, Mistress Bess," Jane said.

"In the morning, you will rise at six and make ready in time to help dress the Queen when she gets up. You will attend Mass with her and her household, after which breakfast will be served, which we take with her in her privy chamber. We attend her Grace as necessary during the day, depending on what she is doing. Often we sit with her working on our embroidery or making clothing for the poor."

It all sounded straightforward—and very pleasant. "I love embroidering," Jane said.

"Her Grace will be pleased." Bess paused for a moment. "Mistress Jane, forgive me, but I am instructed to say to every new servant of the Queen that virtuous and decorous behavior is required of her maids at all times. Precedence is always to be given to the great ladies of her household, for they are the wives of the highest peers of the realm. And when the King appears, as he may do without warning, you always curtsey low, and remain there until you are told to rise. Do not address him unless he speaks to you."

"No, mistress," Jane said, hoping she would remember everything.

"How old are you, Jane?" Bess Chambers asked.

"I am nineteen," Jane told her.

"And I am twenty-two. I have served her Grace faithfully since I was thirteen, which is why I now enjoy this position. You will find her a loving and kind mistress. We are all eager to do her bidding, not so much out of duty as out of love. And the King is a most gracious prince. He is friendly to us all. Oh, that reminds me—young gentlemen are always welcome in the Queen's apartments. She likes to see them, and she does not discourage them from paying court to us young ladies, so long as she considers them suitable company. But if anyone proposes marriage—or something less honorable— you must inform her at once, for she is in loco parentis, and any scandal would reflect upon her."

"Of course," Jane agreed.

"I will leave you now," Bess said. "I will see you downstairs before six o'clock."

Trying to still her beating heart, Jane waited with twenty-nine other maids-of-honor in the Queen's closet, an oak-paneled chamber fitted out as a chapel. She looked at her new companions, the girls and young women who would henceforth be part of her daily life. Some were staring at her appraisingly, some smiled at her, others seemed unaware of her presence. She hoped she would make a friend among them.

The altar was covered with a rich pall and frontal of cloth of gold, and the crucifix was encrusted with precious stones. In front of them stood the ladies-in-waiting. The Queen had seated herself in the smaller of the two chairs that faced the altar, her feet resting on a velvet cushion on the floor. Her head was bent over her missal.

There was the sound of approaching footsteps. A voice cried, "Make way for his Grace the King!" And there he was, the man who had wielded dominion over the kingdom for as long as Jane could remember: King Henry himself, the eighth of that name. He was everything she had expected: a personage of great height and assurance, his skin rosy and clean-shaven, his hair reddish gold, his shoulders broad beneath the rich damask of his gown. He had a Roman nose, hooked at the bridge, she noticed, and piercing blue eyes. He swept into the chapel, passing between the ranks of curtseying ladies, with his gentlemen and the Yeomen of the Guard following, and raised his Queen from her deep obeisance, taking her hand and kissing it. Then the two of them knelt and the Queen's chaplain began to say the divine office.

Jane knelt with the rest, hardly able to believe that the King of England was at prayer only feet away from her.

After the service, King Henry escorted the Queen back to her chamber, her ladies following two by two. Jane found herself paired with a pretty young woman with blue eyes and a dark wiry curl escaping from her hood. She smiled at Jane.

"I'm Margery Horsman," she whispered.

"Jane Seymour," Jane told her.

"Maybe the King will stay for a while," Margery murmured. "You might be presented to him."

Jane's heart began to beat very fast indeed.

"Mistress Jane Seymour," King Henry said, as she rose from her curtsey. He looked down at her from his great height, those steely blue eyes appraising her. "I trust you will do her Grace the Queen good service, and enjoy your time at court."

"I will do my utmost best, your Grace," Jane assured him.

The King nodded benevolently, and accepted a cup of wine brought to him by one of the ladies-in-waiting. Soon he was surrounded by admiring women, chatting and joking, as the Queen smiled at them from her chair. Jane stood there diffidently, next to Margery Horsman, waiting to be spoken to. But the King did not stay long. Putting down the half-full cup, he made his adieus, kissed his wife's hand and departed. The women exchanged glances, and the Queen looked downcast.

"She's missing again," Jane heard one lady mutter to another. "Such disrespect!" the other hissed.

It was astonishing to Jane that anyone would dare to show disrespect to the Queen. She wondered who had gone missing.

In their absence at Vespers, the table in the privy chamber had been set with four places and a dazzling array of gold and silver-gilt. The servitors were waiting with napkins and ewers. When the Queen seated herself, with three of her ladies, everyone else curtseyed and left the room, trooping through the presence chamber to the watching chamber beyond, where the officers of the Queen's household were waiting for them, standing at their places at the high table and at the head of the two boards set at right angles to it. Those ladies-in-waiting who had not been fortunate enough to be invited to eat with her Grace sat next to them, in order of precedence, then, at the lower end, the maids-of-honor and the chamberers. Margery Horsman told Jane that the grooms, ushers and pages always ate in the great hall with the rest of the lower servants of the household.

It was all rather overwhelming after her quiet life at Wulfhall, and Jane prayed she would give a good account of herself here. Out of the blue, she remembered Thomas once unkindly saying that she put people off with her prim expression, but her upbringing had been geared to maidenly modesty, to the downcast eye and demure bearing. She watched the other maids, decorous in their mien yet enjoying a lively conversation, with much laughter, and put on a brave smile.

She was seated next to twin sisters, who introduced themselves, in heavily accented English, as Isabel and Blanche de Vargas. They were olive-skinned and much older than she, but friendly.

"We come from Spain with her Highness twenty-five years ago," Blanche explained. "We have been with her ever since."

"She must be a good mistress to enjoy such devoted service," Jane said.

"She is the best mistress anyone could wish for," Isabel told her.

"And you, Mistress Jane? Where is your home?" Blanche asked, as platters of rabbit joints were laid along the table, followed by some kind of broiled fish. They all helped themselves. The food was well cooked and plentiful, but nowhere near as good as Mother served at home. At the thought of them all sitting down to sup without her in the Broad Chamber, enjoying the excellent fare, Jane suddenly felt choked, as homesickness swept over her in an engulfing wave.

"In Wiltshire," she said, unable to enlarge for fear of bursting into tears.

The very pretty girl sitting opposite leaned forward. "And your father? Who is he?"

Jane swallowed. "Sir John Seymour," she said, trying to summon an appetite for the food she had put on her wooden trencher but barely touched.

"Is he at court?"

"He was," Jane said, "and he has served the King well on his campaigns in France, but now he is sheriff and Justice of the Peace in Wiltshire. My brother Edward is master of horse to the Duke of Richmond."

The pretty girl looked impressed. "Joan Champernowne at your service, Mistress Jane," she said, extending a hand across the table. "And this is Dorothy Badby." She turned to the doll-like figure with the fair hair sitting next to her, who shook hands too and smiled.

"I have a sister called Dorothy," Jane told her.

She tried not to think too much about home as she chatted to the maids around her, swapping stories about their backgrounds and families. Like her, most of them were of the knightly class, except for the Vargas twins, whose father had been some kind of high officer at the court of Spain.

"Bess Chambers seems kind," she ventured.

"She's a good sort," Joan agreed. "Everyone likes her. She's fair and approachable. If you have a problem, you can always go to her."

Jane became aware of a rather strident young lady on the opposite table.

"Mistress Nan Stanhope," Joan said grimly, seeing Jane look across the room to see where the peals of laughter were coming from. The Vargas twins were shaking their heads.

"Her snobbery and pride are intolerable," Blanche fumed.

"She is impossible," Isabel muttered.

Nan Stanhope was a few years older than Jane. She had tawny brown hair, a determined pointed chin, cherry-red lips and wide-set eyes. She was attractive in her way, but no great beauty. She was giggling with a young man seated next to her, but when she saw Jane staring at her, she glared.

"She is not popular," Joan said. "Best not to cross her. She has a terrible temper."

"She looks as if she likes to be the center of attention," Jane observed.

"She's not the only one," Blanche murmured.

"Shush!" Joan hissed. "Not here!"

Jane tried another mouthful of the rabbit. She was intrigued. "Are you talking about the person who was missing earlier?" she asked in a low voice. "I heard the ladies talking as we left the privy chamber."

Blanche de Vargas spoke in her ear. "They were talking about a maid-of-honor who is absent tonight. Mistress Anne Boleyn."

Joan's mouth settled again into a grim line. "You'll meet her soon enough, Jane."

Jane stood watching as the ladies and maids moved deftly around
the Queen, unlacing, unhooking and removing her clothes, layer by
layer, then attiring her in a night rail of the finest silk embroidered
in black-work at the neckline and cuffs. When they had helped her
on with a damask nightgown fastened high at the neck, Bess Chambers ordered Jane to comb the Queen's hair, which, when released
from the confines of her hood and unplaited, was of a very great
length and the color of faded copper. As she carefully untangled the
rippling tresses, Jane saw that they were streaked with gray.

The Queen smiled at her. "You have a gentle touch, Mistress
Jane," she commented. "You must comb my hair again tomorrow."

Jane caught the fleeting scowl on Nan Stanhope's face, and the
smug, barely suppressed smiles of the others. Her heart sank. She
did not want to make an enemy on her first day.

She was exhausted when, at nearly midnight, she ascended the
stairs to the dorter, thinking that it could surely not have been this
morning that she and Edward had left Maidenhead. The last thing
she wanted was to find that Nan Stanhope's bed was only two away
from hers.

"Frideswide Knight sleeps between," Margery said behind her.
"She's a chamberer—and Nan's acolyte, always at her beck and call.
Would you like me to unlace you, Jane?"

"That would be a kindness." But as Jane stood there, Nan bore
down on her.

"Who do you think you are, little mouse-face, to look down your
nose at me at supper and then usurp my duty with the Queen?"

"I meant no offense," Jane defended herself.

"It was I who asked her to comb the Queen's hair," Bess Chambers said quietly.

"That is a privilege reserved for those who have long been in service, as you should know," Nan Stanhope snapped. "I have served
her Grace for sixteen years! I will not have my privilege usurped."

"In sixteen years you should have learned that you do the duties assigned you by the Mistress of the Maids," Bess retorted. "I was but giving Mistress Jane here the chance to show us what she can do— and if the Queen wants her to do it again tomorrow, and tomorrow, and tomorrow, I suggest you complain to her."

Nan's eyes flashed. "I might just do that. And I might also suggest to her that, having served longer than you, I have more right to be Mistress of the Maids."

"Heaven forbid!" Dorothy snorted. "Look at yourself and see why Bess was promoted!"

"Shut up!" Nan spat.

"Mistress Nan, I do swear you are more presumptuous than Lucifer!" Blanche de Vargas cried.

"Then you had best beware my pitchfork," Nan flung back. "Frideswide, give me my night rail."

"Just go to bed, all of you!" Bess commanded.

Jane said her prayers, doused her candle and lay down exhausted. It seemed she had escaped the conflicts at home only to be embroiled in more petty ones at court. Pray God it would not always be like this. At least most of the maids were friendly. She liked Margery, Joan and Dorothy. Bess Chambers was kind, the Vargas twins congenial. She wondered about the absent Anne Boleyn. There had not been a chance to ask anyone further about her. The only discordant note had been struck by Nan Stanhope. Jane made up her mind to avoid Nan in the future. Trouble found you, Mother said, if you went looking for it. At the thought of Mother, she quietly cried herself to sleep.

She was roused from her deep slumber when it was still dark by a noise close by. In the dimness she could make out a figure fumbling with clothing, then sliding into the empty bed next to her. The elusive Anne Boleyn, no doubt. She wondered where Anne had been, but the pull of sleep was too strong for her to speculate for long. She turned over and closed her eyes.

She woke with a start the next morning, wondering where she

was. She saw Bess shaking Anne Boleyn awake. A mass of dark hair streamed over the girl's pillow. Seeing that the others were hurriedly washing their faces and dressing, Jane struggled out of bed and padded across the bare boards to the row of basins on the table.

"Good morning," Bess said.

"Good morning," Joan and Isabel echoed, wiping their faces.

Anne Boleyn joined them, a sleepy-eyed young woman with sallow skin and a thin face.

Bess introduced them. "Mistress Anne Boleyn, this is Mistress Jane Seymour, come to be a maid-of-honor. She arrived yesterday, in your absence." There was the slightest emphasis on the last word.

"Good day, Jane," Anne said, and yawned. "Forgive me, I am so tired."

Bess pursed her lips, but said nothing. Behind Anne's back looks were being exchanged.

At a plentiful breakfast of cold beef, bread and ale, Jane asked Margery where Anne had been.

"With the King, of course," Margery muttered. "It's no secret."

"With the King?" Jane echoed.

"Aye. We don't mention it in the Queen's household, but it's all over the court that his Grace means to set aside our beloved mistress and marry another. Some say that the Cardinal went to France to arrange a marriage with a French princess, but nothing can go ahead because they are waiting for the Pope to annul the King's marriage. If you ask me, Mistress Anne has her eye on a crown."

Jane felt as if the world had gone out of kilter. "But how can the King even think of putting away the Queen? They have been wed for so long, and they have their daughter, the Princess Mary—"

"Yes, but no sons. A woman can't rule! The King needs a son to succeed him on the throne."

"But they seemed happy together last night." It was unbelievable.

"That is his way. He shows the Queen every courtesy, and to see them together no one would think he was contemplating divorce. She adores him, so she puts on a brave front, and I verily believe he does still love her in his way. But he loves another more." Margery glanced at Mistress Anne and lowered her voice. "This is how she repays the Queen's kindness, swanning in and out as she pleases, and doing her best to steal the King from her. And she was there, in June, with the rest of us, in the outer chamber, when his Grace went in and told the Queen that he wanted a separation. She heard her crying piteously. She was there when we tried to comfort our mistress afterward. She knows the pain she has caused."

Jane stared at Anne, feeling a wave of dislike. It was outrageous that a handmaiden could do such a great injury to so kind and gentle a mistress.

All around her was the excitement of the court. There were feasts, masques, dances, mummeries and banquets. Although the Queen's ladies were bound to behave with decorum, they were yet merry, and enjoyed their frequent diversions. There was much laughter in Katherine's rooms. Their days were often spent playing cards with the Queen or making music, and there were acres of beautiful gardens to enjoy, and outdoor pleasures such as archery, bowling and watching tennis.

The King was a regular visitor to his wife's apartments, although not as often as she would have liked, Jane suspected. She watched them unobtrusively, aware of the tension between them, although they were always courteous and friendly to each other. One common bond was their daughter, on whom they both doted, and they shared an interest in learning and music. Occasionally, she even heard them laughing together.

In those first weeks, as Jane became familiar with the ways of the Queen's household, and got to know her way around the court, she became aware of the swell of gossip about Mistress Anne and the King—and other tales of Anne's conduct. Some years back, she had attempted to betroth herself to the Earl of Northumberland's son, and been banished from the court for her presumption. Earlier still, she had been at the court of France, and there was fevered speculation as to what she had got up to there.

Anne herself seemed serenely oblivious to the gossip. Everywhere she went, she was the center of attention. Everyone was talking about her. Jane wondered how a girl who was really quite plain managed to inspire such adoration. For Anne was no beauty, being flat-chested and thin-faced, with an extra fingernail on one hand, which she tried unsuccessfully to hide with long sleeves. Yet she had eyes that sparkled with humor, that cloud of dark hair, and a flair for fashion. She drew all eyes in her cleverly designed attire, and whatever the maids said of her among themselves, they gave every outward appearance of basking in her favor, clustering around her like moths to a flame, as did the young gentlemen who frequented the Queen's chamber of an afternoon. Anne had only to flash her eyes at them and they were bewitched, it seemed, drawn to her wit and her talent. Her singing and dancing were incomparable, and she was skilled on the lute and in writing verse. Even the great Cardinal Wolsey, processing around the court with an ostentatious train of followers and a spiced orange pressed to his nose to keep away the smell of common humanity, seemed eclipsed by the growing celebrity of the new favorite.

But Katherine was still every inch the Queen, an example to be emulated. She was doubly royal, the daughter of the Spanish sovereigns, Ferdinand and Isabella, of whom she often spoke with deep respect and affection. She was learned and pious, charitable and gracious. She took a warm interest in Jane, as she did in all who served her, and was full of praise for her needlework. Jane soon came to feel that the Queen cherished her for herself. Katherine had become a substitute for the mother who was too far away. After just a month at court, Jane would have laid down her life for her.

She made sure she had as little to do with Anne as was compatible with courtesy and avoiding offense. She had seen the misery that came of infidelity, had seen how her own mother had been devastated by it. It was a crying pity that Katherine had no son, and Jane prayed fervently that God would grant her such a blessing, until Margery Otwell, one of the chamberers who looked after the Queen's linen, told her that their mistress had ceased to bleed four years ago. So her father had been right. There was no hope.

Fortunately most of her fellow maids-of-honor, even Nan Stanhope, were supportive of Katherine. There were three great ladies who were especially close to her: Lady Willoughby, a fierce, olive-skinned widow who had come from Spain with her when she was just eighteen; Lady Parr, another widow, who was pleasant and studious; and the young, black-haired and mettlesome Marchioness of Exeter, herself half-Spanish, who was stoutly loyal.

Bess Chambers told Jane that the Queen had another dear friend in Margaret, Countess of Salisbury, who was cousin to the King and the Princess Mary's lady governess. "But she is away from court at Ludlow, where the Princess is being brought up," Bess told her one day in September, as they hastened down to the kitchens to order a salad for their mistress's supper. "The Princess's absence causes the Queen great grief, as does Lady Salisbury's, but it is customary for the heir to the throne to be brought up at Ludlow. The princes of Wales have to learn how to rule their principality. As soon as the King learned that there would be no more children, he named his daughter Princess of Wales and sent her there. The Queen misses her greatly, but she knows her duty."

Jane was rarely privy to the confidential conversations between Katherine and her friends, but later that week she was tidying the outer chamber when the door from the privy chamber opened and Lady Exeter emerged. Behind her, Jane heard Katherine say, quite passionately, to someone in the room with her, "I will never agree that my marriage is incestuous and unlawful, and I will never do anything to prejudice my daughter's rights!"

Jane silently applauded her courage. It could not be easy taking a stand against the King, of whom everyone was in awe. But she was puzzled as to why the Queen's marriage was incestuous.

She asked Margery, snatching a moment alone together when they were in Katherine's bedchamber picking out garments for mending.

"Her Grace was first married to the King's older brother, the late Prince Arthur, who would have been king had he lived," Margery told her. "Apparently you're not supposed to wed your late husband's brother, but from what I've heard, it was no marriage, if you understand what I mean, so the Pope gave permission for her Grace to marry the King, or the Prince of Wales, as he then was. He granted them a special dispensation to do so."

"So you can't marry your dead spouse's husband or wife?"

"No, not if the first marriage was consummated. Her Grace insists that it wasn't. His Grace evidently believes otherwise. That's why he thinks their marriage is incestuous and against Scripture and the law of the Church. But"—she lowered her voice—"I know who I believe!"

Jane agreed. She could not imagine their devout, principled mistress telling a lie.

The gallants had not come chasing in Jane's wake, and she lacked the boldness to be forward and make eyes at them, as Anne Boleyn and Nan Stanhope did. Some of her fellow maids, like Joan Champernowne and Bess Chambers, were so pretty that they did not even have to try—the men came flocking. Sir Francis Bryan was among those who frequented the Queen's chamber, and Jane was touched when, after she had been at court for a month, he made a point of seeking her out to ask how she was faring. Uncomfortable at being an onlooker as others flirted and laughed, she was grateful for his interest. "I am settling in," she told him, "and I love the Queen, but I had never realized how full of intrigues the court is."

Sir Francis laughed. "You are shocked, little maid?"

How little he knows me, she thought, or suspects the wickedness to which I was exposed before I even came here. Aloud, she said, "I think it is human nature that shocks me, Sir Francis. That some people can be so ready to hurt others." Her eyes lighted on Anne Boleyn, who was laughing out loud at a jest made by her brother, George, a swaggering fellow with a good opinion of himself, and with whom—the maids had said, giggling—no woman was safe.

"Do not be so quick to judge Mistress Anne," Bryan said. "She is an extraordinary woman, a great thinker and a politician, and there are many of us who support her."

"What, in stealing her mistress's husband?" Jane asked. As Blanche de Vargas swiveled around to stare at her, she lowered her voice. "You have no idea of the misery that causes . . ."

Bryan frowned. "Shh! We cannot discuss this here. Let us walk in the privy garden."

Jane followed, a touch warily, as he led her down the staircase in the turret, and offered her his arm. They strolled along the graveled paths between neat, railed flower beds from which rose tall striped poles bearing brightly painted sculptures of royal heraldic beasts. Jane was thankful that they were not alone: two other couples were on the far side, out of earshot.

"You cannot condone what Mistress Anne is doing," she insisted. "Think how it grieves the Queen."

"No one admires and respects the Queen more than I do," Bryan protested. "I have great affection for her, yea, and pity. Her tragedy is that she has no son, for which cause her influence is diminished. She hates the Cardinal, but lacks the power to unseat him. Mistress Anne has that power, and she is determined that Wolsey shall go."

For as long as Jane could remember, Cardinal Wolsey had been the King's chief minister—king in all but name, many said. At court, she herself had seen the high pomp and ceremony that surrounded the great man, seen the King walking with his arm around Wolsey's shoulders, filial love in his eyes. She knew already that anyone with a petition or request made their first approach to the Cardinal, who—if he felt it fitting—would advise the King on whether to grant it. Wolsey was fabulously wealthy—he had the great palace of York Place near Westminster, and had built Hampton Court, which exceeded all the King's houses in magnificence—and he had twice come near to being elected pope.

"How could Mistress Anne ever hope to unseat him?" she asked, astounded. "And why would she wish to? If anyone can secure a divorce for the King, it is Wolsey."

"So many questions!" Bryan winked at her with his one sardonic eye and grinned. "And yet, sweet Jane, you have hit the nub of the matter. She can unseat him because right now the King's brain is in his codpiece, and when a woman has a man there, she can do anything she wants with him."

Jane laughed, feeling her cheeks grow warm. "She is bedding with the King?" she asked.

"Who knows? He is mad for her. But there is far more to it than bed sport, for her at least. Some years ago, the Cardinal mortally offended her. She was set on marrying the Earl of Northumberland that now is, but his Eminence would not have it, and he insulted her in the process. Now she is having her revenge. She publicly snubbed him when he came home from the French embassy. The Cardinal could have received no surer sign of her ascendancy."

Jane sat down on a stone bench with carved lions at either end. "She must hate him."

Bryan sat down next to her, watching a couple stealing a kiss under a shady tree at the end of an alley. "She has cause. She will use him to get what she wants, and then she will destroy him. He has too much power, and I, for one, will be glad to see him go."

His vehemence startled Jane. "You hate the Cardinal too?"

"I and many others." His face darkened. "There are two centers of power at court, Jane. One is the Cardinal, who is Lord Chancellor and holds God knows how many other offices. The other is the King in his Privy Chamber. The Gentlemen of the Privy Chamber enjoy great influence because they spend every day with him and have his ear. What they want is not always what the Cardinal wants, and he is jealous of their power. I was a Gentleman of the Privy Chamber. I was appointed many years ago with my brother-in-law, Sir Nicholas Carew, and honored with the King's friendship. But twice the Cardinal purged the Privy Chamber of its most influential men, alleging that the King was being led astray by young hotheads. Twice I lost my position. Since last year I have been at court only through the King's good favor, but the Privy Chamber is barred to me."

Without thinking, Jane laid her hand on his, as she would have done to one of her brothers. "But that is shocking. Surely the King has the power to order otherwise?"

"He is too much in thrall to the Cardinal," Bryan said. Suddenly he leaned forward and kissed her on the lips. No man had ever done that, save in greeting, and she did not know what to do. She was not sure that she even liked the sensation, and when he thrust his tongue against hers, she remembered what her brother had said about Bryan being called the Vicar of Hell, and drew away in distaste.

He smiled at her with those rakish eyes. "Forgive me if I was too bold, little cousin, but your kindness lent me encouragement."

"I am not sure that the Queen would approve," Jane said.

"She might, if my advances were welcome," he countered.

"And that might depend on your intentions." Jane smiled back, in command of herself again.

"Ah, so there is spirit in you, little cousin! Her Grace would be delighted if I found a lady I could love, I assure you. She has recently reproved me—as kindly as ever—for reaching the grand old age of thirty-seven without taking a wife."

"Then I must be even more careful, Sir Francis," Jane said, drawing away, "for it seems that your dealings with ladies have not always been honorable."

"A little dalliance never hurt anyone," he observed lightly, leaning back on the bench.

It was time to change the subject. She liked him, but she must be wary.

"I do see why you have no love for Wolsey," she said.

He sighed and regarded her ruefully. "That is why I and many others support Mistress Anne in whatever she can do to overthrow the Cardinal." His smile was wolfish again. "And now, sweet cousin, I think I should return you to your mistress."

They stood up and turned back toward the stairs, no longer arm in arm.

"Jane, will you kindly go and find Anne Boleyn," Queen Katherine asked, one morning in autumn as she seated herself at the breakfast table. "She should be here by now to serve me."

"Of course, Madam." Jane curtseyed and left the privy chamber. She looked in the dorter first, but it was empty. She ran down to the privy garden, but that too was deserted. She checked the chapel and the closets. Finally, she sought out the sergeant porter at the palace gatehouse. "Mistress Anne Boleyn?" he repeated. "She rode off home yesterday evening."

"Thank you," Jane said, and took the stairs slowly, anger burning in her. She wished she did not have to tell the Queen of this latest insult. At the very least, Anne should have done her mistress the courtesy of asking permission to leave court.

"She left for Hever Castle last night, Madam," she told Katherine nervously.

There was a pause as the Queen digested the news. "I see," she said.

"I wonder that her Grace does not dismiss Mistress Anne," Jane murmured to Margery as they fetched the embroidery tambours from the sewing closet.

"She will do nothing to displease the King," Margery told her. "She shows favor to that woman for his sake, because she loves him."

"She is a saint," Jane observed, remembering that her mother had shown a similar forbearance toward her father. "Maybe it is the best way, since a wife owes her husband obedience, and she has to live with him."

"Aye," Margery agreed, gathering up the tambours, "and—as the King's Great Matter proves—annulment is very difficult. Not that the Queen wants that."

Nor did her mother, Jane realized. At least her father had been discreet, unlike the King. "It is a scandal that a man may flaunt his mistress as his Grace does. Yet turn the tables, and imagine how far greater the scandal if the Queen were to take a lover!"

Margery's blue eyes widened. "I cannot ever imagine her doing so—but I take your point. Alas, men can commit adultery with impunity, but we poor women must be above suspicion, lest we foist bastards on our husbands!"

"That's enough idle gossip!" barked a strident voice behind them.

It was Lady Willoughby, on her way to the Queen's chamber. "Hurry along, ladies. I may agree with what you say, but it is not your place to say it!"

Jane shrank back against the wall, shamed. It was best to keep your head down in this court and say nothing.

Chapter 6

1528

Anne was back at court. She seemed to come and go as she pleased these days, much to the annoyance of the other ladies and maids. But the Queen never reproved her. She would do nothing to provoke her husband's displeasure.

Anne and Jane were among those in attendance on their mistress when the King burst without ceremony into her chamber one morning, greatly agitated.

"The sweating sickness is under our roof!" he announced.

The Queen paled and the ladies looked at one another in horror. "Three of my servants died during the night," the King went on, terror in his face and his voice. "It's under our own roof! We're leaving at once. I'm taking a reduced household to Waltham Abbey. Tell your women and Lady Salisbury to make ready with all speed. Hurry!" He bowed, remembering at last the courtesy due to his wife, but there was stark fear in his eyes, and he almost ran from the room.

Jane could remember people talking about the last outbreak of the sweating sickness; there had been a great visitation about ten years ago. She knew that it could kill with devastating speed, and that it struck people of all estates, high or low. Father James had once said that it was a manifestation of God's displeasure. It occurred to her that maybe the King was being punished for his wickedness, and his whole realm with him.

When the Queen commanded her to help Margery Horsman to pack her clothes, Jane's legs could hardly carry her into the wardrobe closet. She was trembling with fear. Had she come into contact with any of those who had died, inadvertently brushing against them in a gallery, or breathing the tainted air they exhaled?

Margery swallowed. "My grandmother died of this plague in the last epidemic, God rest her. I remember it as if it were yesterday. The physicians were useless; they knew of no cure. She died within four hours."

Jane was almost weeping with fear. "I am so sorry." It was all she could do to lift down the leather boxes containing the Queen's hoods from their shelves. Yet forewarned was forearmed. "What were the symptoms?"

"Grandmother had violent sweats and shivering fits, pains in her stomach, a vile headache and a rash—they all came on so fast. Then suddenly she broke out in a sweat. They say one can be merry at dinner and dead at supper, and in her case it was true. But the doctors told us that, once twenty-four hours have passed, all danger is at an end."

Joan Champernowne, Dorothy Badby and Nan Stanhope were being sent home. Even Nan was subdued. For all the hot weather, she had wrapped a scarf around the lower part of her face to avoid any contagion in the air.

Anne Boleyn, as usual, was absent, and when Jane arrived in the courtyard in the wake of the Queen, she caught sight of her standing with the King in the midst of his courtiers and household officers, all impatient to mount their horses and leave. She sensed suppressed panic, permeating the crowd like a miasma.

"Fear is the worst enemy," the Queen said. Throughout their hurried preparations, she had remained calm and smiling. "I do believe it is true what they say, that one rumor causes a thousand cases of sweat. More suffer from fear, I think, than from the sickness itself." Jane prayed she was right.

"There are forty thousand cases of the sweat in London," Katherine said, having gathered her women around her in her chamber at Dallance, the King's hunting lodge near Waltham Abbey. They had been there for four days now, and it was just past the dinner hour.

The Queen crossed herself. "We must pray for those poor souls, and we must pray for ourselves, for it is here, now, in this house. Mistress Anne's maid died of it last night!"

Jane was gripped with dread. Here. In this house. *Dear God, help us all!* The others were gaping at each other, terror-struck. Isabel burst into tears.

"Mistress Anne has been sent home," Katherine continued, "and the King is removing to Hunsdon at once. He has commanded that most of you go home too. Isabel, calm yourself. You, Blanche and Bess will stay with me and Lady Exeter. The rest must leave. You will be given money for your journey, grooms to escort you. Take only what you can carry. The rest of your gear can be transported with us, and will be waiting for you when you return. I will let you know when it is safe to do so. Now hurry, and make all speed to depart."

Jane bobbed a wobbly curtsey and ran up to the room under the eaves that served as a dorter for all the Queen's female attendants. She hardly knew what she was doing as she bundled up clothes and pushed them into the traveling bags that would be slung across her saddle. What if she had caught the sweat and it was at work in her already? She could be dead by evening!

She felt so alone, facing a long journey through miles of countryside, with only a stranger for company, and the plague lurking who knew where. Feeling a little faint, she somehow carried her luggage downstairs and went in search of the Comptroller of the Household. There was a queue of people waiting outside the closet he used as an office, all come, like herself, to collect the money for their journeys. To her comfort, she saw that Sir Francis Bryan was among them.

"Don't look so afraid, Mistress Jane," he said when he saw her. "We're the lucky ones—we're leaving. Are you bound for Wulf-hall?"

"Yes, Sir." Jane could hardly speak.

"Let me escort you there. I am going to my family's house in Buckinghamshire. I am happy to make a detour."

Jane could have wept with relief. Bryan might have a reputation, but he would hardly compromise her honor if he was taking her to her family. And she suspected he liked her. After all, he had secured her place at court, and at little advantage to himself.

With a scarf muffling her mouth and nose, Jane rode westward through Essex, with Bryan at her side and the groom following behind. They had a hundred miles ahead of them, and no idea of what they might meet on their way.

The land sweltered under the June sun. The tracks they followed were ridged with mud baked dry; the untended herds and flocks around them were lowing and bleating out their misery. In the first village they approached, they saw few souls abroad, only crosses daubed on the doors to warn of the pestilence within.

"We had best keep to the byways and avoid habitations," Bryan said, grim-faced, as Jane clamped her scarf to her mouth, and there-after they took a route through open countryside, where the air was hopefully purer. In the distance they could hear church bells tolling for the dead, and sometimes far-off cries and shouts, which sent them hastening in another direction. All their talk was of devising strategies to escape the sweat. Gone was the rakish Bryan, and in his place was a serious man concerned only for their protection.

North of London, they emerged from woodland and saw, in a val-ley below them, men throwing shrouded bodies into an open pit. The stink from it was on the breeze. Jane urged her horse on, des-perate to get away, and fretting in case they had been infected.

They were a little further on when she first felt a headache coming on.

"Dear God!" she cried. "I have it!"

Bryan peered at her in concern. "You are sweating?"

"No, but my head aches." She was trembling violently.

He reached across and felt her forehead. "You have no fever," he pronounced. "It's probably the sunshine or your fear that has caused it."

She attempted a grateful smile, near to tears. "Thank you, Sir Francis."

Already the pain was abating. She breathed deeply in relief.

The journey seemed interminable. They sought lodgings overnight at abbeys and priories, where they were not always welcome, for it was feared that they carried the sweat with them. At one nunnery, the porteress refused to open the door. When they were admitted, they found the rooms in the monastic guest houses bare of luxuries, but they were clean, and the plain food they received was welcome after hours in the saddle.

Bryan maintained his serious demeanor and a respectful distance. Jane felt safe with him, and even a little disappointed that he had not tried to flirt with her. Instead, they had become friends, united by their shared peril.

Near Newbury, they were overtaken by a traveler on horseback. Keeping their distance, they asked if he had any news of the sweat abating.

"No," he shouted back, "and I've heard that Mistress Anne Boleyn has it!"

Jane crossed herself.

"Pray God she does not die," Bryan muttered as they rode on.

But if she did, Jane thought, the Queen's troubles would be resolved overnight. It was wrong to wish Anne dead, but if God thought fit to take her unto Himself, He would be doing everyone a great favor.

"You don't agree with me," Bryan said, steadying his horse on the rough ground.

"I love the Queen," Jane replied. "I cannot bear to see what she suffers on account of the King's love of Mistress Anne, and this interminable wait for the Pope to give judgment. It's been a year now. The strain has been dreadful, and yet she is always cheerful."

"I love the Queen too," Bryan declared. "I have great respect for her. But the King needs an heir. As his friend, I can vouch for how long he has grieved over his lack of sons."

"But these doubts about his marriage—no one had heard of them until last year, and then it became clear that he was paying court to Mistress Anne. Do you think he really will marry her when—if—he is free? She is not royal; she cannot compare with Queen Katherine."

"No, but maybe she is what this kingdom needs right now. She is a forward thinker with radical ideas. The King lets her read banned books. Like many of us, she sees the Church as corrupt and presses for reform."

Jane looked at him sharply. "You mean she is a heretic? A Lutheran?"

"Some say, but I don't think so. At heart, I believe, she is as true a Christian as any of us. All she wants is reform."

Jane shook her head. "It worries me, at a time when the very tenets and traditions of Holy Church seem to be attacked from all sides, that someone like Mistress Anne has the power to influence change, even if it is for the better. It is the Pope who should do that, not a humble gentlewoman. Sir Francis, our faith is under attack. Those heretics who follow Martin Luther have rejected five of the seven sacraments! And there are those who want the Bible to be in English, to read and interpret it for themselves. I had never heard of such things before I came to court, and I have been appalled at the way everyone has an opinion on matters that are beyond a lay person's understanding. That is why Queen Katherine should be cherished. She is a truly devout daughter of the Church, and we should all seek to emulate her."

Bryan chuckled. "By God, Jane, you are become a politician

too—and a reactionary one! The King has need of voices like yours on his Council! But heed me." The smile vanished. "Keep your views to yourself. Those who criticize Mistress Anne rapidly fall from favor."

"I know my place," Jane assured him. "We are not at court now, there is no one to hear us but the birds, and you are my kinsman, whom I trust. I would not say these things at court, for all the world."

"No," he agreed, "you just stand there being discreet, but taking in everything that goes on. I've seen you doing it."

"Now you are mocking me," she laughed. Inwardly, though, she was disturbed by what Bryan had said about Anne Boleyn. All this talk of change threatened the faith she held dear—and that was something worth fighting for.

On the tenth day, they arrived at Wulfhall under a lowering sky. As they rode, weary, dusty and saddle-sore, down the road that led to the house, Jane could smell smoke. A bonfire was burning in the Great Paled Garden, where her father's groom was stoking it and throwing what looked like old clothes into the flames. Jane rejoiced to see her home looking as mellow and welcoming as she remembered it, if somewhat smaller in scale compared to the palaces she had grown used to.

Their arrival had been noticed. There was Lizzie, running out of the door to meet them, and there, not far behind, was Mother, with Father in her wake. They were all wearing black.

Jane slid down from her mount and ran toward them, her heart pounding in fear. Who had died? Pray God the sweat had not reached her beloved Wulfhall.

Mother and Lizzie clung to her as if they would never let her go, while Father shook Bryan's hand and Bryan explained how they had come to be there.

Mother was crying on Jane's shoulder. "Oh, my lamb, I am so pleased to see you! God has taken one daughter, but He sends me another. What a homecoming!" She was barely coherent, and when she finally disengaged herself, Jane saw that her face was ravaged with grief.

"Tell me it's not Margery!" Jane cried, as Thomas and Harry emerged from the house, both wearing grave expressions.

"The sweat took her three days ago," Mother blurted out, bursting into fresh weeping. Father left Bryan and cradled his wife in his arms. Shocked as she was by the news, Jane saw that it was as if nothing had ever gone wrong between them.

"No, no!" she protested, in tears herself. "Not Margery, please God. She was but sixteen." She recalled Margery on the last occasion she had seen her, her pretty, sweet sister with green eyes and a kind heart. It could not be! To die so young, and in such a manner, was beyond dreadful.

Thomas held her tightly for a moment. She could tell that he was shaken by their loss. "It was very quick," he said hoarsely.

"Frighteningly so," Harry added, embracing Jane in his turn. Then Father came forward, his face bleak, tears in his eyes.

"Jane!" he said, in a broken voice, and clasped her to him. It was as if Catherine Fillol had never been. He was once more the father she had loved and revered, and she took comfort from his strength.

The clothes on the bonfire had been Margery's. Mother had ordered that everything of hers should be burned, to limit the risk of infection. "All I have left of her is a gold locket that she had not worn since Christmas," she sobbed, taking Jane's arm and leading her into the house. Jane squeezed her hand, reflecting fearfully that she had fled the sickness only to find it in her own home.

They had sent a messenger north to tell Edward the news. "We wrote to you as well," Harry told Jane, as he helped her upstairs with her bag, "but we did not know where the court was in residence, with the plague being so virulent."

"The King is mortally terrified of the sweat," she said. "He was going to Hunsdon, with a greatly reduced household, when I left."

"We warned you not to come, but I am glad you are here." He attempted a smile. Good, solid, dependable Harry—he was always such a comfort.

"I would not be anywhere else," she assured him. "When was the funeral?"

"On the day after she died—of necessity. Father made the estate carpenter work all night making a coffin. She lies in the church at Bedwyn Magna."

"I will ride there and pay my respects," Jane promised, steeling herself to open the door to the bedchamber where she and Margery had slept, and blenching at the sight of the new bedclothes and curtains that had replaced those that had had to be destroyed. The windows were wide open, but there was still a strong smell of the vinegar and musk that had been used to purge the stench of the sweat from the room. She turned to Harry and hugged him. "I am so relieved that you are here."

He held her tightly. "Bishop Foxe is aging and blind, and relies more and more on those who serve him, but when he heard of Margery's death, he said that of course I must go home, and stay while I am needed—and until all risk of contagion is passed."

"It must be, surely, by now," Jane assured him, breaking away and opening her bag. "It strikes quickly."

"In truth, I should go back. The Bishop has been a good master, but the Cardinal is putting pressure on him to retire, as he wants the see of Winchester for himself. Therefore we must not give him occasion to complain to the King that the Bishop is incompetent. So I can stay only a couple more days. How long are you here for?"

Jane sat down on the bed she had shared with Margery, trying not to cry. Their chamber seemed so empty now, denuded of her sister and her possessions. "In truth, I do not know. The Queen said she would write when it was safe for me to return to court. I hope she will spare me long enough to see Mother a little restored."

"Margery's death has hit her hard," Harry reflected, "and indeed all of us. We sent to Anthony too, at Littlecote. Knowing him, he will come to us, despite the risk."

Jane rose. "Tell me, how have things been here? Father writes to me sometimes, but he says nothing of what happened."

"Much as usual. Mother and Father have put it behind them. They seem all the closer for it. But Edward has not been home since it happened."

"Is there any word of Catherine?"

Harry shrugged. "None that I know of."

Jane thought for a moment. "She must have suffered. Will you come with me if I visit her? I could take the boys." John had come dancing to meet her, his joy belying his black attire, and Ned was now an engaging toddler. Jane could only begin to imagine how their mother must be missing them, and she had not forgotten her promise.

Harry's blunt features creased in a frown. "Would that be wise?"

"She is their mother."

"Let's see what our mother says. If she agrees, I will accompany you."

Downstairs, Father was pressing Sir Francis to stay.

Bryan drained the cup of wine he was holding. "Sir, I thank you, but this is a house of mourning, and it would not be right for me to intrude."

"She was your cousin," Father said, "and for what you have done for Jane alone, you are most welcome. You have come so far out of your way."

"Well, I must confess, a night's rest and some of Lady Seymour's excellent food would be welcome after days on the road," Bryan said. "I thank you."

"By the north wall," Mother had said, "near your brother's brass."

Jane found the place easily, for it was marked by a large sheaf of fading roses. She knelt in the ancient church, still hardly able to believe that sweet Margery was here below her, buried with young

John and the dust of their forefathers. She tried to pray, but the words would not come. All she could feel was anger that an innocent life had been cut off in its prime—the kind of anger that many people, across all England, must be feeling now. She wished, how she wished, that she had told Margery how much she had loved her, and often. Now it was too late.

But it was not too late for Catherine to see her sons, or for her to let them know how much they meant to her, and she should have the opportunity. Thus resolved, Jane rode the five miles back to Wulfhall.

"No," Mother said firmly, kneading the dough for the pastry as if it needed punishing. "It will only unsettle those boys. John knows that his mother did something wicked and has to stay at Amesbury to repent her great sin. Little Ned has no memory of her. Leave them be."

Jane tried again. "I did say to her that I would do my best to let her see them, if she promised to stay silent about what happened."

Mother sighed. "I am thinking of the boys, not trying to punish her. Maybe there is a way for her to see them without their being aware of it."

"That may depend on whether Catherine can leave the abbey. Is she to enter the cloister?"

"No. It was arranged that she would board there and pay for her keep with her father's allowance, which was to be paid on condition that she entered a nunnery. She can go out if she wishes."

"Then," Jane declared, "I have the perfect solution."

Of course, it was unwise to go into Amesbury while the pestilence was still raging, as it continued to do all summer. During that time, Jane and her family stayed at Wulfhall, largely cut off from the world, and praying that the sweat would pass the rest of them by.

With the onset of autumn came colder weather, and reports reached them that the plague was at last abating in Wiltshire. Jane wondered if she should return to court, but there was no knowing if there was sickness further afield, and she felt that she should stay at home for a little longer, for Mother had taken Margery's loss very hard and needed her there. Queen Katherine would understand, she was sure.

Soon she and Harry judged it safe to go into Amesbury, where no cases had been heard of for some weeks. When they arrived, it was market day, although the crowd was much thinner than usual on account of the plague. While Harry took the boys off to look around the stalls, promising that they could watch the acrobats and jugglers later if they were good, Jane sped to the abbey and asked the porteress if she might see Lady Seymour. The porteress's face remained impassive. She rang a bell and a lay sister was sent to summon Catherine. Jane was asked to wait in a bare little parlor.

Five minutes later, Catherine appeared. She had lost weight in the past year, and her gray wool dress hung on her. A white coif covered her hair, and beneath it her pretty face bore faint lines, the scars of her sorrow. She stared at Jane as if she were an apparition.

Jane rose and took her hands. "I came to see how you are faring," she said. "I have been away at court this past year, serving the Queen, or I would have come before."

"How do you think I am faring?" Catherine's voice was bitter. "Does it please you to see how I suffer?"

"It was not me who forced you to come here," Jane reminded her. "I am sorry for you. I have thought of you often."

"I hate it here," Catherine muttered. "Edward strayed too, but he is not immured in a monastery. Have I not paid enough for my sin?"

"It was your father who laid that condition on you."

"It was Edward who ordered me out of the house! I had nowhere else to go, for I had no other means of support. Jane, can you speak to him? Ask him to take me back? I miss my children so much, it is torture."

"They are here," Jane said gently.

Catherine's face was transformed. "Really? Where? Can I see them?"

"Yes, that is why I brought them. They're at the market with Harry. But they must not see you. It would only upset them, and they have had much to cope with. Margery died in June, of the sweating sickness."

It was as if Catherine had not heard her. "But I am their mother! You'll never know how I have longed to hold them!"

"I'm sorry," Jane said, moved by her distress. "We all think it is for the best. It's either that, or not seeing them at all."

"I must see them!" Catherine cried. "Where are they?"

"Come with me." Jane led the way out of the porteress's lodge and they walked to the market, Catherine nearly running in her desperation to catch sight of her sons. Jane grabbed her arm and pulled her to a halt behind a stall selling hot pies. "Over there," she said, pointing to where Harry stood with Ned perched on his shoulders and John by his side, all laughing at the antics of a juggler.

Catherine clapped a hand to her mouth. "Oh, my sweetings," she wept. "Oh, they are so grown. I cannot believe it. Please, let me speak to them. Please!"

"Hush!" Jane bade her, wondering if this was as good an idea as it had seemed. "You'll attract attention to yourself. Think of them! They should not have you snatched from them all over again, just when John especially has grown used to being without you."

"You have no idea how cruel you are," Catherine flung back. "They are my children!"

Jane had to be firm. "In law, they are your husband's," she reminded her, "and Edward wants you to have nothing to do with them. I will speak to him, if I see him, but he is in Yorkshire." He had still not come home. "Mother, Harry and I have gone behind his back bringing the boys here so that you can see them. Please do not compromise us."

Catherine subsided and argued no more. She stood there a long time, gazing at her sons, yearning in her eyes. At length, the juggler ceased his play, and Jane saw Harry looking about him to see if it was safe to move from the spot. John was clamoring for something, jumping up and down. "Uncle Harry! Uncle Harry!"

"We must go now," Jane said. Reluctantly, Catherine tore herself away, and on the way back to the abbey she cried so hard that Jane felt choked herself.

"I will bring them again," she promised.

"But you will go back to court," Catherine wailed. "When will I see them?"

"I will come whenever I can, that's all I can say," Jane tried to reassure her.

They had not been home for an hour when one of the Littlecote grooms came riding into the Great Court with a letter for Sir John from Sir Edward Darrell.

Anthony was dead of the sweating sickness.

This time, Edward did come home, arriving two weeks later. A devastated Mother threw her arms around him and would not let him go, until Father stepped forward and gently disengaged her.

"It is the will of God," he said, his voice tremulous. "His soul is with the saints in Heaven. Take comfort in that, as I do."

Jane watched as Edward knelt for Father's blessing. His eyes were cold, and Father looked abashed as he placed his hand on his son's head and croaked the words. Never again would the two of them have the easy, congenial relationship they had enjoyed before the affair of Catherine had come to light.

After all the subdued greetings and expressions of grief were behind them, the family gathered at the supper table in the Broad Chamber, which had been rendered gloomy with black hangings. Over cold beef cuts, they reminisced about Anthony: how brilliant he had been, how kind, and what a promising future he had had, now never to be realized; then they wept again, for the tragic loss of two of their own.

"I think I will never be merry again," Mother sobbed.

Father tried to lighten the mood, telling them how a woman brought before him on a charge of theft had pleaded her belly. "She was seventy at the least!" he added.

"Why did she plead her belly?" John asked, his eyes wide with curiosity.

"A woman who is with child cannot hang for her crime, my boy, because the child is innocent."

The talk drifted to the King's Great Matter. "The whole country is talking of little else," Edward said.

Mother snorted. "It's a disgrace when a man thinks he can just set aside his old wife for a young chit of a thing!" She glanced at Father.

He swallowed. "I think there is much more to it than that, my dear. And the King is not just any man. He needs an heir."

"He should wait until the Pope speaks before going chasing after Mistress Anne Boleyn! Jane doesn't think much of her."

"I hardly know her," Jane said. "I keep out of her way. But it grieves me to see her lack of love and respect for the Queen. She seems not to care how much she is hurting her."

She felt Edward tense beside her. This was too close a subject for comfort. While the others voiced their opinions, she bent close to his ear. "I have seen Catherine," she said.

He stiffened. "I want nothing to do with her," he muttered. He had changed in the past year; there was about him a hauteur and reserve that had not been there before.

"She is desperate to see the boys."

"She should have thought of that before she played the whore," he whispered. "I will not allow it."

"Edward, she has changed. She is a husk of her former self. I truly believe she has repented."

"I care not, and I'll thank you not to interfere."

Jane clutched his arm. "It will kill her, not seeing her children. It's all she lives for. Please reconsider of your charity."

"No." He drained his cup. "I'm coming home," he said suddenly.

"You are?" They all turned to look at him.

"That was why I was delayed in coming south. As soon as I heard about Margery, I wrote to the King and asked if, in the circumstances, I could be assigned a post locally, and his secretary responded, appointing me to offices in Dorset." He grimaced. "The Duke of Richmond was not pleased. He's nine now, and likes his own way. He wanted me to stay, but my place is here."

"I am right glad to hear it," Sir John declared. Edward nodded, unsmiling.

"Oh, my son!" Mother cried.

"Will Dorset be enough for you?" Thomas almost sneered. Clearly it peeved him that Edward had simply asked the King for something and been granted it, while he, who was desperate to enter royal service, had so far been—as he saw it—snubbed.

"I am content," Edward said, not rising to the bait. "I shall be able to read all the books I've not had time for. I've not even read Sir Thomas More's *Utopia.*"

"It will be good to have you home," Mother said. "God knows, we need some cheer."

Jane thought of the letter in her pocket, the letter bearing the Queen's seal, which had been waiting for her on her return from Amesbury. Soon, she would have to break it to Mother and the rest that she was leaving them once more, for she had been summoned back to court.

The talk at Greenwich was all of the legate who had come from Rome to try the King's case with Cardinal Wolsey. Mistress Anne Boleyn, miraculously restored to health, was riding higher in the King's favor than ever before, to Jane's dismay. She was relieved to learn that she would have to suffer Anne's daily presence no longer, though, for the King had assigned his sweetheart an establishment of her own, at Durham House on the Strand, near London. Jane could not have borne much longer to see the Queen so slighted by her rival, and courtesy had its limits. Even so, it was galling to hear that Mistress Anne kept as much state there as if she were queen already. Everyone said it would come to pass. Meanwhile, the Queen showed herself as patient and saintly as ever, and the Cardinal was going about with a harassed look on his red-veined face.

Jane was pleased to hear from Margery Horsman that Bryan had been restored to the Privy Chamber. They were in the dorter, unpacking the chest containing Jane's gear, which had been awaiting her arrival.

"He deserves it," Jane said, and told Margery about his kindness to her.

"It is the Queen who needs kindness just now," Margery said. "She has been warned that she stirs up the King's subjects against him, and that she is too cheerful. If only they knew what it costs her to look cheerful!"

"She loves the King too much to stir up anyone against him," Jane protested, shocked.

But Katherine was taking the warning seriously. Jane soon found that life in her household had changed. The Queen never left the palace unless she had to. She adopted a grave demeanor and dressed in sober colors, so as not to draw attention to herself. No longer did she spend time making merry with her ladies; instead, she was to be found in her chapel, in prayer. Jane and most of the Queen's women were fervently praying that the Pope or the legate would speak in her favor, and soon. Their existence was dull and somber. The real, exciting life of the court revolved around the King and his favorite at Durham House. Jane feared that it would not be long before England had a new queen.

The King kept Christmas at Greenwich, laying on jousts, banquets, masques and disguisings for the court's entertainment. But Jane could not take pleasure in the festivities when the Queen showed no joy, and it was plain in her face how troubled she was. Katherine's only comfort was in the company of her daughter, the Princess Mary, who had come to court for the Yuletide season.

Jane was one of those whom Katherine asked to keep watch over Mary, and she was touched by the trust her mistress reposed in her.

She was much taken with the Princess, a sweet, loving child of twelve, with her father's red-gold hair and her mother's features. Yet already those features were clouded by anxiety. For all that she had been away from court, Mary was aware of the tensions between her parents, and of the unseen presence of Anne Boleyn, who was keeping to her apartments but making all welcome. Even as they played Hoodman Blind, Fox and Hounds and ninepins, Jane saw that the Princess was a very unhappy girl indeed. She clung to her mother the Queen, and was reserved to the point of sullenness with her father, even though he tried his best to make merry with her. God grant that the King's Great Matter would be decided soon, Jane prayed, if only for the sake of this poor child.

Chapter 7

1529

A court had been convened in the monastery of the Black Friars in London. Cardinal Wolsey and the Papal legate were to preside and hear the King's nullity suit. It was no secret that his Grace was hoping for great things. It was even being said that he was planning his wedding to Anne Boleyn.

Queen Katherine stood in her lawn smock as her ladies and maids clustered around her, attiring her in a kirtle of yellow brocade. Lady Willoughby and Margery Horsman entered her chamber, carrying the sumptuous gown of crimson velvet edged with sable, fitting it on her and lacing it up at the back. Nan Stanhope brought the fur oversleeves, while Jane fastened a gold pomander around the Queen's waist. Finally Lady Exeter hung the rich collar winking with gems around Katherine's neck, and the Vargas sisters placed a hood lavishly adorned with goldsmiths' work on her head. Beneath it, her face was pale and lined with care, but she looked every inch a queen.

"Now I am girded for battle," she observed, attempting a smile. "They must understand that I do not recognize this court they have set up. I can hope for no fair trial of my marriage in England. The King's case must be heard in Rome!"

Jane was impressed by her courage. It was no mean thing to stand up to the King, whose rages these days could be terrifying.

The Queen was ready now, as were the four ladies who were to attend her. Jane and the other maids were to stay behind in Bridewell Palace and await her return.

Dorothy Badby burst through the door. "Your Grace, there are crowds outside the Black Friars, all shouting for good Queen Katherine and wishing you victory over your enemies."

Katherine's eyes clouded. "The King will not be pleased. But he values the love of the people; he must heed them and come to his senses."

She had been saying that for as long as Jane could recall. "Let us go," the Queen said.

It was quiet in the vast ornate rooms of the palace. Jane and the others tried to busy themselves, but they were all wondering what was happening in the great hall of the monastery on the other side of the River Fleet, and were alert for any sound that heralded the return of their mistress.

"Imagine, an English king and queen summoned to appear in a court!" Isabel reflected. "It would never happen in Spain!"

"I cannot believe that this Great Matter has now dragged on for two years," Bess Chambers said, shaking her head.

"How much longer can the Queen stand it?" Jane asked, her heart grieving for Katherine.

"Hopefully it will soon be resolved," Nan Stanhope said. "I did not come to court to lead such a dull life. We go nowhere; we do nothing; we're shut away with the Queen like nuns."

"Would you rather serve Mistress Anne, then?" Bess asked sharply.

"If I had a choice, yes. She is queen in all but name, and everything revolves around her. Katherine's day is done."

Blanche de Vargas grimaced in distaste. "You might be singing a different tune before this day is out!"

"How can you be so dismissive of a loving mistress?" Dorothy asked.

Nan shrugged. "How are we to find husbands or gain preferment if the Queen has no influence? She's supposed to help us make good marriages, but in all the years I've been here, she's done nothing for me. I've had several suitors, but nothing has come of it. I'm nearly thirty, and I'm sick of waiting."

"Some of us have devoted our lives to the Queen," Isabel de Vargas said. "We did not look for anything else."

"Well, I do!" Nan snapped. "If things go against the Queen, I shall write to my father and insist that he make suit to Mistress Anne for a place for me. And if he will not, I shall do it myself!"

Blanche flared. "None of us would so lower ourselves! There can be only one queen in England, and I for one will never recognize any other than our good mistress. And I think I speak for us all."

Everyone, apart from Nan, fervently agreed.

"I could never serve Anne Boleyn," Jane declared. "I hate her and everything she stands for. Any woman who sets out to steal another's husband, let alone the husband of her mistress, is beyond redemption."

"But the King says he is not the Queen's husband, and that the Pope was wrong to allow their marriage," Nan was pleased to point out, "and Mistress Anne is of the same opinion, so how can she be stealing another woman's husband?"

"The King was married to her Grace for eighteen years without complaint," Blanche cried, "and then he fell in love with Anne Boleyn, and suddenly his conscience is troubling him!"

"He needs an heir, and that she cannot give him!" Nan countered. "He may well be right to see in that the judgment of God."

"If the King has doubts, it is best that he seeks reassurance from the Pope," Jane said. "But until his Holiness pronounces him a free man, Mistress Anne has no business to be encouraging his addresses."

"Wake up, little innocent!" sneered Nan. "The King loves her inordinately and wants to make her queen. She comes from an ambitious family for whom preferment is all. Do you really think she is going to pass up such an opportunity? I wouldn't!"

Jane reined in a rare flare of temper. "It is not a question of ambition, nor opportunity, nor what she and her family want. What she is doing is morally wrong. Even Martin Luther himself would not condone it."

Nan was just about to deliver a tart reply when Bess Chambers looked up from her embroidery. "I don't think that Mistress Anne is encouraging the King at all. Look at all those times she's taken herself off home to Hever and stayed there. She's there now."

"She is playing a clever game," Isabel sniffed. "The King is mad for her, so she keeps her distance to inflame his ardor the more."

"I think she went to Hever last year to bear his bastard," Blanche opined.

"That would not surprise me," her sister said.

"On the contrary, the word is that she is holding out for marriage," Margery countered.

"What will happen to us if the Queen is set aside and the King does marry her?" Dorothy fretted.

"I would go home rather than enter Anne Boleyn's service," Jane said.

"I am sure that the King will see the Queen well provided for and served," Bess tried to reassure them. "We'd be retained."

"Oh, I do wish I knew what was happening! It's hard to settle to anything." Margery sighed.

They sat there in silence, heads bent over the altar cloth and frontal on which they were working, listening to the chimes of the clock, the song of the birds in the trees outside the open window, and the sound of their own breathing. Presently they heard distant shouts and cheers, and stared at each other.

"The sentence must have gone in the Queen's favor," Margery whispered. "They would not cheer so if she was to be repudiated."

Soon came the tramp of footsteps in the gallery, and then the door was opened and in came the Queen, leaning on the arm of Master Richards, her receiver general, with her ladies behind her. She sank into her chair, her face drained of color, her breathing heavy.

"Quick, fetch wine and something to eat!" Lady Willoughby ordered, as the maids rose from their curtsey. "Jane, bring her Grace's slippers."

When Katherine was settled, sipping from her goblet and looking somewhat restored, they all clustered round, eager to hear what had happened.

"Have they declared for you, Madam?" Blanche asked, forgetting that the Queen should speak first. "We heard the cheering."

Katherine smiled faintly. "No, my dear. They have declared nothing at all. But I did what I went there to do. I said that it was no impartial court to me, and that I would not attend it." She rested her head back against the chair. Clearly the effort had been great.

"Her Grace was magnificent!" Lady Exeter said. "When she was summoned, she fell on her knees before the King, in front of that crowded assembly, and begged him to spare her the extremity of the court, and she made so many heartfelt pleas to him that we were all near to tears."

"And did he respond, Madam?" Bess asked.

There was a prolonged pause. When Katherine spoke, her voice was broken. "No. He said nothing at all. He would not even look at me."

In the third week of July, to Jane's surprise and pleasure, Edward appeared in the Queen's chamber at one of the afternoon gatherings that had used to be so crowded but were now far less frequented, for most ambitious young men had abandoned Katherine's staid court for the grand lodging of Mistress Anne. But here was Edward, bowing courteously to the Queen, and looking very tall and elegant in his fine black clothes, with his red beard trimmed to a point and a feather in his black cap. There was about him, still, that new reserve and proud demeanor that Jane had noticed at Wulfhall the previous autumn, but he greeted her kindly, and gave her the glad news that he had been appointed Esquire of the Body to the King, thanks to the recommendation of Sir Francis Bryan.

"We owe him so much," Jane said, as they sat down in a window embrasure.

"He is our kinsman," Edward replied, "and I think he likes us for ourselves. I must confess I did wonder if he would ask for your hand. He is not married, and it would be a good match."

Jane recalled Bryan's bold advances. "There was a time when he showed an interest in me, but you had warned me of his reputation with the ladies, and I put him off. Later, on that long ride from Waltham, I got to know him much better—as a friend, you understand—and I saw that there was more to him than the name Vicar of Hell leads people to believe. But I do not think he is the marrying kind."

"I might sound him out on that point," Edward said. "From now on, serving in the privy chamber, I will see him every day."

"Please don't do so on my behalf, or mention my name," Jane insisted.

Edward raised his eyebrows. "Why not? Marriages are brokered all the time. Mine was." His voice was bitter.

"Just don't say my name," Jane pleaded. "Let that come from him—although I doubt it will. And Edward, I am not sure if I want him for a husband."

"You could do a lot worse; at least you like each other. But I'm not sure if we can afford him. Father has money set aside for dowries for all you girls, but there are three of you, and Sir Francis told Thomas at Wulfhall last year that he was hoping to find a rich bride."

Jane was taken aback. "You don't think that was a subtle way of finding out if I was a rich bride?"

"Well, Father had asked him if he was ready to settle down yet. It was all light banter. But he and Thomas thought you might have been the object of the exchange, even though your name was not mentioned."

"I would have liked to be consulted before they broached the matter!"

Edward shrugged. "I'm sure you would have been, had they agreed to anything."

"And it sounds as if Sir Francis was putting Father off."

"Jane, you are making too much of this."

"Possibly," she countered. "And don't think I am disappointed. I like Sir Francis, but I do not love him."

The next day, as Jane was returning to the palace, having seized the opportunity for a quiet walk in the gardens, she looked up and saw Edward hurrying across the covered bridge that spanned the River Fleet and linked Bridewell Palace with the Black Friars' monastery. He noticed her and waved. Men were crowding behind him, making for the court. When he caught up with her, he was breathless with excitement. "The legate has revoked the King's case to Rome. The Pope himself will pass judgment."

"Thank God!" she breathed. "Now the Queen has a fair chance of a just sentence."

"The King is furious. You should have seen his face!"

"I'd like to see Mistress Anne's! She was very confident that the crown would be hers. Oh, Edward, this is encouraging news. God may yet lead the King to see the error of his ways."

"It will curb Mistress Anne's ambitions," her brother said, taking her arm and steering her away from the advancing crowds of courtiers. "Only this morning she was in the King's privy chamber, telling us all what would happen when she became queen. She will have the Bible made into English, for a start. By God, she is hot for reform of the Church! She was scathing about the Pope—and Cardinal Wolsey."

"She is very determined—and she is leading the King to perdition," Jane murmured, "and if she has her head, we'll all go down with him. It frightens me. Must we lose our immortal souls for a light woman and her dangerous ideas?"

Edward smiled at her. "Do not be so disheartened, sister. Reform of the Church can only be a good thing. There are abuses that need to be corrected. I for one would like to see the sale of indulgences by priests stopped. Why should the rich be able to buy their way into Heaven? And why should we not read the word of God in our mother tongue? These things cannot endanger our souls."

"But it is the priests who are ordained to interpret the Scriptures for us."

"Jane, not all priests are as devout as Father James, and some are barely literate. How shall they interpret the Latin Scriptures for their flock? No, I want to see the Church reformed, as it should be."

Jane was suddenly aware of someone watching them. She looked up. It was Nan Stanhope, who was regarding Edward with undisguised interest.

"This is a serious conversation to be having with such a handsome suitor," she said lightly.

"He is not my suitor!" Jane exclaimed. "Mistress Nan Stanhope, may I present my oldest brother, Sir Edward Seymour. He has just been appointed Esquire of the Body to the King."

Edward bowed. When he raised his head, Jane saw him looking at Nan as if she were an object of wonder, and his eyes, so cold of late, were warm.

It could not be, Jane thought furiously, as sleep eluded her and she tossed in her bed. Edward could not be in love with Nan Stanhope. Of all the girls to choose! Why could he not have fallen for the lovely Joan Champernowne, or Margery, or Bess? Why was he pursuing one who was so sharp-tongued, so volatile and so unpleasant? Not that he was actually doing much pursuing, for Nan had been throwing herself at him for two weeks now, all through the summer progress—or that part of it in which the maids-of-honor had participated, after the King begrudgingly summoned the Queen to join him and the court, and Mistress Anne, at Woodstock. It sickened Jane as much to see Edward dancing attention on Nan and caressing her openly as it did to witness the King's displays of devotion to Anne Boleyn.

Now it was September, and the court was crammed into the small hunting lodge at Grafton, with the maids cramped together in a tiny attic. The cardinals had arrived that very day, for the legate to take formal leave of the King, and everyone had thought that Henry would refuse to receive Wolsey—but no, he had welcomed him with open arms and great emotion. It was as if nothing had gone wrong between them, and the court had been buzzing with speculation that Wolsey was about to be restored to his former eminence. Mistress Anne and her party had gone about with glowering faces, leaving no one in any doubt that she would discountenance the Cardinal if she could.

The next afternoon, Henry and Anne rode out to the chase. From an open window overlooking the courtyard, Jane watched as the King bade a smiling farewell to the cardinals, who were due to leave for London later that afternoon, and heard him say he would see Wolsey on his return. She noticed the sly expression on Mistress Anne's face, and was not surprised when the hour for the cardinals' departure arrived, and still the King was not back. Jane and the other maids were in attendance on the Queen as she did her best to entertain them. She saw the grim disappointment in Wolsey's lined, careworn face, and the defeat in his eyes. Eventually, he had no choice but to take his leave, for dusk was falling and they had to be on their way.

Jane was in bed when she heard the hunting party return, some hours later.

Jane stood watching as the new Imperial ambassador presented himself to the Queen. The last one had been a great support to Katherine, who had been sorry to see him leave, but it was obvious from the warmth in her expression that she liked what she saw of this new man, who had been sent by her nephew, who was Holy Roman Emperor and King of Spain, and the most powerful ruler in

Christendom. Jane took to Messire Chapuys too. She guessed he was in his late thirties, and found herself arrested by his angular, sensitive face and the sincerity and admiration in his eyes when he spoke to the Queen, assuring her of the Emperor's love and concern for her interests. Jane hoped her instincts were right, and that this new ambassador would champion Katherine's cause as vigorously as his predecessor. Certainly his assurances suggested that he cared about what was right and just. She sensed the strength and wisdom in him, and passion even. When he had gone, the Queen looked a hundred times happier.

God knew, she had need of good cheer. The King had begun to persecute her with petty unkindnesses and wild threats. Her daughter would be taken from her care; she would be banished from court; he would bring down the full force of the law on her. They heard him shouting behind the closed door of her closet. And Anne Boleyn was now omitting the courtesies due to the Queen, spitting venom and dropping dark hints of vengeance. For Jane's good mistress, life had become a nightmare, yet she bore it all with patience.

They had not been back at Greenwich for long when Edward came looking for Jane. Usually Nan was with him, weaving her coils around him, but today he was alone. Taking advantage of weather that was unseasonably mild for December, brother and sister took a stroll in the palace gardens, and sat down on the stone rim of a fountain.

"You've heard that the Cardinal has been stripped of his office of Lord Chancellor," Edward stated. "He was adjudged guilty of allowing the Pope to interfere in English affairs."

Jane was shocked. She had not heard. The news must be very fresh. "Are not England's affairs the Pope's lawful concern?"

"Not any more, apparently. Jane, this is cause for rejoicing. Wolsey's fall is a victory for those of us who want to see the Church reformed. Nan agrees with me." He recalled what details he knew.

What victory was there, Jane wondered, in an old, broken man being stripped of all his lands and goods, and banished to the country? It was hard to believe that this was the once-mighty Cardinal, whose word had been equal to the King's. She had not liked Wolsey much, or approved of his worldliness and greed, but he had represented everything that was stable in the Church, and the traditions that were steadily being undermined.

"The King has seized Wolsey's house at Westminster, and is having it refurbished as a palace for Mistress—sorry, the Lady Anne." Yes, they must all now call her that, her father having lately been created earl of Wiltshire and Ormond. Anne was now queen in all but name, and Jane was burning at the injustices done to Katherine.

Edward was no comfort. It was no secret where his loyalty lay. Jane knew it was futile to try to bend his opinions, so she always avoided discussing the matter on the few occasions she saw him.

"I didn't actually come just to tell you about Wolsey," he said, his cheeks flushed. "There's something else. I wish to marry Nan." It was the last thing Jane wanted to hear, but it was no surprise. "I've been home. I saw Catherine. I tried to persuade her to become a nun and set me free, but she refused. By God, now I know how the King feels!"

What could she say that would not make things worse? He had dealt severely with Catherine, and now he was reaping the harvest of his cruelty. "I know what you're thinking," he said. "But she betrayed me, Jane. It was unforgivable."

"It is two years now," Jane said, wishing—as she often did—that she had been able to do more for Catherine in that time. "Can you not find it in your heart to forgive her? Mother forgave Father. And the boys need a mother."

"And they shall have one, in Nan, as soon as I am free."

"Nan?" Nan would have those boys disinherited as soon as she could snap her fingers. She was selfish and ambitious; she would be thinking of her own sons.

"Aye, Nan. I know you don't favor her, Jane, but she has been a great support to me. It was she who made me go to the King and ask him to restore Catherine's inheritance."

"You did not tell him the whole truth?" Pray God he had not told Nan either!

"I spoke to his Grace in confidence. He was most sympathetic, and said it was not right that I should lose my wife's inheritance on account of her misconduct."

"It was on account of your misconduct too, Edward!" Jane could not stop herself from reminding him. "And you have shamed Father by telling the King! I cannot believe you could have done it."

"Jane, a lot of money is at stake, and I needed the King's help. I told him we have resolved never to speak of what happened, and he has agreed to lay the matter before Parliament on the grounds that I was deprived on account of my wife's adultery. No man is named."

"Before Parliament! Then the whole world will know that Catherine betrayed you."

"Yes, but they will never know that it was with our father. I assure you of that, as the King assured me."

"You told only the King? Not Nan?"

He looked away. "Of course she has to know, if we are to be married."

Jane stood up. "You have told her, then?"

"Yes."

Jane sighed. "You fool. She is the last person you should have told. She will never keep it a secret."

Edward spoke through his teeth. "She has given me her promise not to utter a word about it. And I ask you to be friendly to her, as my future bride."

"You ask too much!" Jane cried. "She has a poisonous tongue. No one likes her. And Catherine is young yet—you may not be a free man for years, and praised be God for that!" In a rare passion, she walked away, shaking.

Edward came after her. "She is the woman I love, and I intend to wed her if I have to wait till my dotage to do it!"

"I pray you do!" Jane flung back. "And if she dies first, you will have had a lucky escape!"

Chapter 8

1530

That winter, Parliament passed an Act setting aside the terms of Sir William Fillol's will, and overnight Edward became a man of substance. Nan Stanhope went about with a smug smile on her face, and Jane did her best to avoid her.

But Nan would not have it. It seemed that she sought Jane out at every turn—at meals, during the gatherings in the Queen's chamber, where she was always hanging on to Edward's arm, or as the maids formed a procession to attend their mistress to hall or chapel. Her approaches were friendly, but there was always a barb to them.

"How I look forward to meeting your father," she would say, or, "I have heard say that your father has an eye for the ladies," or even, "I dare say I shall find your father as handsome as his son!" It was infuriating, and Jane went in dread that someone would overhear her remarks and guess the truth.

She hated confrontations, and avoided them if she could. In the end, she decided to ignore Nan's insinuations, in the hope that Nan would tire of them landing on deaf ears. But Nan seemed to sense her discomfort, and gave her no peace.

Jane complained to Edward. "You must stop her!" she cried. "She keeps taunting me with what she knows, and I can't bear her malice anymore." Edward sighed. "I will speak to her," he said. "But maybe you perceive malice where none is intended. I know you don't like Nan, but please try to get on with her."

The injustice of this stung. "You might well ask her the same! I'd be happy if we could just keep to the courtesies."

Whatever Edward said to Nan, it bore fruit. The barbs ceased and she kept her distance. And soon there was much to distract both her and Jane, for in the spring, the Princess Mary paid a rare visit to court. They were at Windsor Castle, the most ancient of the King's residences, where the Queen's chamber in her lodgings in the Upper Ward had a ceiling studded with tiny mirrors, and windows overlooking gardens and a vineyard. Jane felt quite emotional as she watched Katherine embrace the beloved daughter she saw all too rarely. She believed that the King kept them apart on purpose, to punish Katherine for denying him his freedom and for infecting Mary—as he would see it—with her opinions. For Mary had openly said that she would accept no one for queen except her mother, and she made no secret of her hatred for Anne Boleyn.

Jane felt sorry for the Princess, who was now a small, slight fourteen-year-old with wary eyes and all kinds of ailments brought on, she was sure, by unhappiness. She herself had known what it was to suffer helplessly through the infidelity of a father. Watching mother and daughter together, her heart bled for them, especially as the King was riding out hunting with Anne Boleyn nearly every day, leaving the Queen to her own devices.

"I cannot believe that my father has brought that woman here with him," Mary said, as they sat sewing with the Queen's women. Jane heard the bitterness in her voice, a bitterness Katherine never expressed.

"Do not let it upset you," Katherine soothed. "One day soon, his Holiness will speak, and then his Grace will return to me, and the Lady Anne will be sent away."

Jane saw the doubt in Mary's eyes. What great grief infidelity could bring in its wake. Look at her own motherless nephews—or half-brothers, if you believed Edward. Didn't anyone think of their children when it came to gratifying their illicit passions?

"I hear that the Cardinal is proving himself a devout shepherd for his flock in York," the Queen said. "Exile, it seems, has awoken him to his spiritual responsibilities. Messire Chapuys told me that the Lady Anne would have had him arrested for treason, yet the King refused to proceed against him. I think his Grace still has a deep affection for him. But the Lady has not ceased to work against the Cardinal, and I doubt we shall ever see him restored to favor. He is not a well man. I never thought to feel sorry for Wolsey, but I do now."

Jane felt pity for him too. Harry had been in his employ since Bishop Foxe died and the Cardinal had been made Bishop of Winchester in his stead, and had found him a fair employer; Wolsey might not have spent much time in his diocese, but he knew all that went on there, and took an interest in his servants. Whatever his failings, he had worked tirelessly to secure a divorce for the King, and it was not his fault that the case had been revoked to Rome. That had been more than a year ago now, and still the Pope had not spoken.

News that Sir Francis Bryan had offered Thomas a post in his service had been the only cheerful tidings in recent weeks. Bryan was going to France, as England's ambassador, and Thomas was to be his messenger. "I'll be going to and from the King," he told Jane excitedly when he arrived at court and came with Edward to see her in the Queen's chamber, looking as charming and handsome as ever. "I'll be reporting personally to his Grace. That should get me noticed!" He was desperate for preferment.

"Assuredly it will." She smiled.

Edward raised his eyebrows. "So long as you behave yourself, little brother."

"Sir Francis has again been very good to us," Jane said quickly. "Does he really do it without hope of reward? That is rare for a courtier." She had been at court long enough now to know how things worked.

"Oh, he will reap a reward," Edward said. "He is high in favor with the King, and his Grace is appreciative when his gentlemen recommend able and apt persons for royal service. And in gratitude, we may do Francis good service in time to come."

"Then he has advanced us for his own profit?" Jane asked, disappointed. "I had thought he liked us."

"I have no doubt that he does," Edward said. "I don't think it's all about self-interest. He likes you especially. He often speaks of you."

That was unexpected.

"Ah, now we get to the nub of the matter." Thomas smirked.

"You have not encouraged him, I hope!" Jane cried. The last thing she wanted was for Bryan to think that she was pressing her brothers to arrange a marriage. Her cheeks burned at the thought.

Edward paused. "I did, but he did not take the bait. I said you were twenty-two and that Father is hoping for a good match for you. Francis said you deserved it, and he himself would keep an eye open for someone suitable."

"Then he is not interested," Jane said, knowing she had no right to feel spurned.

"He's forty, and not yet wed," Edward said. "He ought to settle down soon."

"The eternal bachelor," Thomas observed. "I don't believe he's waiting for a rich wife to come along. But I am!"

"Don't heed him," Edward muttered. "It may be, Jane, that a seed once planted takes root. It would be a good marriage. Don't hope too much, though."

"I hope for nothing," she replied, with a touch of bitterness. "None of the other maids-of-honor are spoken for, so why should I complain?"

Edward flushed. He would not speak of Nan Stanhope in front of Thomas.

"Have you paused to wonder, sister, if that is because you all serve the Queen, and she is out of favor?" Thomas asked, lowering his voice, for Katherine was only feet away from them. "Few now ally themselves with those who are associated with her."

"Young gentlemen still gather in her chamber," Jane said.

"Aye, but not in such numbers as they did," Edward put in.

"I will not leave her service!" Jane hissed, fierce. "No one could have a better mistress. And I would never serve the Lady Anne, if that's what you're hoping for."

"All right, sheathe your claws." Thomas grinned.

"You never take anything seriously!" Jane chided him.

"Believe me, I take my family's interests very seriously," he declared.

"More like your own," Edward muttered.

"That's enough," Jane told them. "Believe me, I am content to wait until a suitable husband presents himself. And if he does not, well then, I am happy serving the Queen, and if the worst comes to the worst, I can yet become a nun!"

Chapter 9

1531

Jane had told herself that she had no great desire to be married, but at heart she wondered if that were true. She was more upset than she would admit about Bryan's lack of interest, and it had long disappointed her that not one of the gallants who came to the Queen's chamber had ever done more than make polite conversation with her. Plain Jane, Nan had once called her, in spite, yet it was true. Maybe she should have entered a convent after all.

She had always thought that, as the oldest daughter in the family, she would be married first, so she was shocked to receive a letter from Father telling her that Lizzie was to be wed to Sir Anthony Ughtred, a widower whom Sir John had known in his fighting days, and a soldier who captained the King's garrisons at Berwick and on the Scottish border. As well as his military duties in the far north, Sir Anthony had mercantile interests in various counties, and while visiting Wiltshire, he had spent two nights at Wulfhall, seen Lizzie, been smitten and asked for her hand. Just like that.

The wedding was to take place without delay—Mother was in a fluster getting everything prepared—and after the ceremony Sir

Anthony would bear his bride north to Yorkshire, where she would be mistress of two great houses, Kexby Hall and Leppington Manor. The King himself had granted Kexby to Sir Anthony, whom he much favored; it was one of the properties confiscated from the late Cardinal Wolsey, who had died last November on the way south toward the Tower to face charges of treason.

Jane laid down the letter. She was pleased for Lizzie, who had done so well for herself by this marriage, but the news brought home to her how much she did want a husband and babes of her own, and the kind of household in which she had grown up. To be another such as Mother would not be a bad way to spend one's life.

What hurt most, though, was that Lizzie would be married first. She was not yet thirteen! It was as if Father had faced the fact that she, Jane, was unmarriageable, and given up on her. But then, she consoled herself, Sir Anthony had seen Lizzie and asked for her hand. What father would have refused such a good match?

She wrote sending her congratulations and wishing Lizzie every joy in the future.

The Queen gave her leave to attend the wedding, and she traveled home with her brothers for the festivities. The whole family and a host of Ughtred relations gathered in the great tithe barn for the bridal feast. Mother had excelled herself: among the dishes there were baked meats, raised pies, savory tarts, salmon in sauce, capons in wine, blancmanges and berries in season. And at the head table, presiding over all, sat the genial Sir Anthony and his little bride, who was wearing a yellow gown she had embroidered herself. Jane was happy for her sister, and joined in the laughter and banter, but she could not help feeling envious. It should have been her sitting there in her bridal finery. She was twenty-three now—almost an old maid.

There was dancing after the boards had been cleared and the candles lit. The minstrels struck up a brawl—or a branle, as Jane had learned to call it at court—and the newlyweds took to the floor as everyone clapped. Jane was on her feet for much of the evening, mostly dancing with her brothers, or John or four-year-old Ned; but none of the other young men who partnered her asked a second time.

She sat down for a space, drinking hot spiced wine to stay warm. The braziers in the barn did not quite dispel the January chill, and she was glad of her fur oversleeves and rabbit-lined gown.

Lizzie sat down beside her. "I'm so glad you were able to come home for the wedding, Jane," she said, her pretty face flushed from exertion. "It seems strange that in a few days I will be going to live in Yorkshire . . ." Her voice faltered. "I shall miss you all, and Wulfhall."

"Your husband seems a kind man," Jane reassured her. "He looks so proud of you. I'm sure you will be happy. I was homesick when I went to court, but I got over it. There was so much to distract me. It's Mother who will miss you dreadfully. With Edward, Thomas and me at court, and Harry in Taunton a lot of the time, she'll have only Dorothy for company. The house will seem empty."

"Can I ask you something?" Lizzie was blushing. She bent to Jane's ear. "Mother said that on my wedding night, I must let Sir Anthony do whatever he pleases, so that we can have children. I asked her what she meant, and she said the man must put his member inside the woman to give her the seed from which life is made. She said it hurts a bit the first time, but that pleasure comes afterward. But one of the maids said it was really painful. Do you think that's true?"

Jane swallowed. How could she know of such things? No man had shown enough interest to kiss her, let alone bed her. She shook her head. "I have no knowledge of men or love. One of the Queen's ladies said her wedding night had been wonderful, but she did not elaborate. Why don't you tell Sir Anthony of your fears? He looks kindly. I'm sure it will be all right."

And it was, apparently. After being put to bed with her bridegroom with many jests by the company, and lying there looking petrified, Lizzie emerged the next morning with a broad smile on her face.

Before she returned to court, Jane made the journey to Amesbury, taking Harry and the boys with her. Harry had been once without her, taking a nursemaid to stay with the boys while he fetched their mother, but Catherine had been too ill with a fever to see him, the porteress had said.

Today Catherine was helping in the kitchens when they arrived. When she was brought to the porteress's lodge, Jane was shocked by the change in her. She was gaunt, her skin stretched tight across her cheekbones, her eyes wild. Worst of all, she did not seem to know who Jane was.

"Catherine? It's me, Jane! I've brought John and Ned. They're in the market with Harry."

"Who are John and Ned?" Catherine asked, her eyes vacant.

"Your sons."

"I have no sons. They were taken away after they found us together."

"Who found you?" But Jane already knew the answer.

Catherine's voice was almost a whisper. "They found us in the Old Room. We were naked, for shame. I was in his arms."

Jane did not want to hear more. Her cheeks were burning. "Your sons are here!" she repeated. "Come and see them." She reached for her sister-in-law's hand. It was thin, like a bird's claw.

"No!" Catherine cried, pulling it away. "Let me alone!"

Jane turned to the porteress, who was hovering, praying she had not heard what Catherine had said. "What ails her?"

The nun shook her head. "I do not know. Would you like to speak to the Prioress?"

"Yes, indeed," Jane answered.

They waited, and presently Prioress Florence's hawklike face, much aged now, appeared at the grille between the parlor and the convent proper. "Jane Seymour!" she said. "How good to see you. I am sorry that you find Lady Seymour in a poor case. Alas, the physicians cannot say what is wrong. She has never been very happy here.

She confided to us the reason for her coming, and even if she had not, we would have learned of it from her ramblings. We do not judge or condemn. God has forgiven her, for she has truly repented, but I fear that her sorrow was so great that she has retreated into madness."

"Madness?" echoed Jane. She looked at Catherine, sitting there fiddling with her rosary, oblivious to what was being said.

"She has lucid periods, but remembering is too painful for her, so we lose her again."

"I have brought her sons, so that she can see them," Jane said.

"It's probably best that she doesn't," the Prioress said. "We don't want her upsetting herself. It's all we can do to make her eat. She's better off in her own world."

"Mother Prioress, I am grieved to see her so," Jane said, fighting tears. "This is a very sad situation. What can I do to help?"

"Pray for her, my child. She is in God's hands. He will comfort her."

"I will do that," Jane promised. "Will you write to me if there is any change?"

"I will," Prioress Florence promised. "It's best to let her be, Jane. Any reminder of her old life can only cause distress."

Jane understood that she was being warned not to come again. She felt in her purse and laid some coins on the ledge. "For her comforts," she said. "I will send more when I get my next quarter's wages." Then she watched as Catherine was led out of the parlor by the porteress, wondering if she would ever see her again.

Five days later, she took the road that led to London, accompanied by a maid and a groom. Her first stop was at the church at Bedwyn Magna, where she knelt by little John's brass to pray for her lost siblings. She knew she would always miss Margery's gentle presence and Anthony's learning and wisdom.

As she stood up, she saw that someone else was in the church. It was the priest, sitting in a pew with his head in his hands, his shoulders heaving.

"Father?" She hastened to him. "What is wrong?"

He raised a tearstained face. "Oh, my daughter, that I should see this day. We are all lost. Convocation has bowed to pressure and named the King Supreme Head of the Church of England. The Pope's authority is swept aside. This kingdom is in schism, and our souls are all at risk of damnation." He broke down afresh, as Jane sank to her knees beside him, unable to comprehend the enormity of what she had just heard.

The priest gripped her hand. "The King is to be Supreme Head so far as the law of Christ allows. Well, I say to you, kind mistress, it does not allow!"

It was as if the world she had known were crumbling about her. "His Holiness is Christ's Vicar on Earth, the rightful successor to St. Peter," the priest said. "Did not Our Lord himself address his disciple Peter, and tell him, 'Thou art Peter, and upon this rock I will build my church; and the gates of Hell shall not prevail against it'? Only the Pope can be head of the Church; no king can usurp his power."

We are at the gates of Hell, Jane thought wildly. No man, be he king or emperor, can abjure the authority bestowed by our Savior.

It was sheer wickedness and presumption, and it could never be lawful. "I am in dread to hear this," she said. "I serve the Queen, and I know how greatly this will distress her."

"She is a courageous lady, and much loved. I pray that the Pope speaks for her soon. It is the only remedy for this madness."

A terrible thought struck Jane. "Will we all be excommunicated?"

"The King may well be, and those clergy who offer him their allegiance. And then where shall we be, cut off from the sacraments for no fault of our own?" It was a prospect to freeze the blood.

The talk in the abbey guest houses along the route was all of the King becoming head of the Church. Generally, people were disapproving and worried, but some thought it a good thing. "Why should we pay taxes to Rome?" they asked. "Why should the Pope interfere in English affairs?"

When Jane got back to court, she found Katherine calm, as usual. "The King will never break with Rome," she assured her ladies. "At heart, he is a good son of the Church, but he is angry that his Holiness is taking so long to give sentence on his case. I know him well. This is mere defiance, a rattling of swords, as it were."

Jane wished she could believe it.

There was also talk of a plot to poison the good Bishop Fisher, a stout supporter of the Queen. Some had died at his table, but he, being abstemious, had escaped. In most people's opinion, the Lady Anne was responsible. Jane found that hard to believe too. Anne could be vicious, and she was certainly vengeful, but Jane could not see her stooping to murder.

Summer came, and the court was at Windsor again. Still there was no word from Rome, and even the Queen's patience was wearing thin. At least the King had begrudgingly agreed to allow the Princess Mary to visit her again. Mary was fifteen now, a sad little figure who was still too small and thin for her age. She had been ill, and looked pale, and Katherine was assiduous in seeing that she ate well and got plenty of fresh air. Everyone was to be cheerful, for the Princess's sake.

To the relief of all, the King took Anne Boleyn to Hampton Court for a few days. Katherine clearly enjoyed the respite from the tension. She went for longer and longer walks in the Great Park with her solemn-faced daughter, and tried to divert her with music and dancing in her chamber. Jane was becoming adept on the lute, and Mary, who had been an expert musician from childhood, taught her a more complicated piece.

"You have mastered that well, Mistress Jane," she said in her gruff little voice, as a hint of a smile played about her buttoned-up mouth. "Shall we dance a pavane?"

"I should be honored, your Highness," Jane said, rising, as the Queen signaled for the players to begin.

Jane had mastered most of the dances that were fashionable at court, but the pavane, with its two beats to a step, was challenging. Always she wanted to go faster.

"No!" the Princess cried, tossing back her long red hair. "You must stay in time!"

Jane tried again, and still managed to stay ahead of everyone else. In the end, they all collapsed in giggles. It was heartening to see Mary's serious young face crumple into laughter. The Queen was plainly overjoyed at the sight.

During the days that followed, the Princess began to relax more, and to revel in the company of the maids-of-honor, playing Hoodman Blind in the deserted galleries and tag in the gardens. But when the King returned with Anne Boleyn, Katherine forbade her daughter to leave her apartments. Yet Mary was all too aware of her father flaunting his mistress in the court beyond the door, and her face grew pinched again.

Preparations were in train for the King's annual summer progress, and Jane expected Mary to be sent back to Hunsdon in Essex, where she usually resided, but no order came. They were due to leave Windsor for Woodstock in the middle of July, and she and the other maids and chamberers were busy packing.

On the morning they were to leave, Jane was up early. She attended the Queen at Mass, as usual, and helped serve her at breakfast.

The Queen laid down her knife. "Do you not think it is quiet here, ladies?" she asked. It was true. There was none of the commotion and bustle that was normal when the court departed on progress, no running feet or shouts from below. Katherine rose and looked out of the window. Jane heard her intake of breath.

"The wards are empty," the Queen said. The women crowded around. There was no procession forming, and no sight of any carts or sumpter mules.

"Maybe I am mistaken, and it is not today," Katherine said. "'No one tells me anything these days." She gave them a weak smile, and sent her chamberlain, Lord Mountjoy, to find out when the court was leaving.

He returned with a pained expression.

"Madam," he said, "the King left for Woodstock early this morning."

It took a while for them to understand the significance of what Henry had done. The Queen merely nodded and continued with her breakfast. Jane thought this must be some new ruse of Anne Boleyn's, intended to slight and discourage Katherine; it was much the same trick she had played on Wolsey at Grafton. Because of it, the King had never seen Wolsey again. Jane caught her breath. What if Anne had a similar intention this time? No, surely even she would not go so far. The Pope had not yet given sentence.

Katherine was eating and conversing with her daughter. Jane glanced around at the ladies and maids standing in attendance. She caught Margery Horsman's eye. Margery looked concerned too.

As Jane was helping to remove the silver-gilt plate used for the service of the Queen's breakfast, a groom in the King's livery was announced. He bowed to Katherine, but addressed a point beyond her shoulder.

"Your Grace, I am to inform you that it is the King's pleasure that you vacate Windsor Castle within a month," he said, and swallowed.

The King had left the Queen without saying goodbye; he had abandoned her without a word, the woman who had been his devoted wife these twenty-odd years and borne his children.

Jane watched Katherine struggling to preserve her composure. The Princess was looking at her, bewildered. Then Katherine spoke, her voice firm. "Go where I may, I remain his wife, and for him I will pray."

"I am to be sent to Easthampstead," the Queen informed her assembled household, one hot August afternoon. "It is a fair house, with space for everyone. You are all welcome to come with me. No one will be turned away. The King has most generously agreed to pay wages to everyone."

Jane had already made up her mind to stay if she could. She had grown so devoted to the Queen that she could not bear the thought of leaving her. Evidently most of the others felt the same. Joan Champernowne left, but only because she was to be married soon.

Easthampstead Park was a hunting lodge in the middle of Windsor Forest, ten miles from the castle. On the way, the Queen told them she had stayed there several times in earlier years, and it was a fine house. Her smile was unfailing. Jane was moved to see how the people cheered her as their procession passed.

When they clattered through the twin gatehouses, crossing the drawbridge in between, Jane had the sense that they were entering a prison, but the mansion that stood before them looked more like a palace. Katherine's small court was lodged in the central of the three wings that surrounded the courtyard; its dorter windows looked out onto the moat.

The King had indeed been generous. Soon after their arrival, two hundred and fifty new maids-of-honor were sent to attend the Queen, and she received such handsome provision that she was able to maintain the magnificence to which she was accustomed. Jane hoped that his Grace's conscience was troubling him.

The new maids were accommodated in the other wings, and were strictly ruled by their own mistresses. They appeared only when the Queen received visitors, no doubt so that none should say that she kept less state now that she was separated from the King.

It was a comfortable existence, but to Jane it felt as if they had been exiled. The Princess Mary was forbidden to visit, as were the Queen's staunch friends, Lady Exeter and the Duchess of Norfolk. The Duchess was estranged from the Duke, who was Anne Boleyn's uncle. He supported his niece, and she the Queen. At least Lady Willoughby and Lady Parr had been allowed to remain, so Katherine did not lack for friends of rank. And Lady Exeter had sent her own maidservant, Eliza Darrell, to wait on the Queen as a maid-of-honor and act as go-between for them. Although they were cousins—Jane's grandmother had been a Darrell—Jane had never met Eliza, but liked her on sight. She was nineteen, a beautiful girl with fair hair and green eyes, and she won the hearts of everyone but Nan Stanhope. Nan was in a foul mood these days. She hated being apart from Edward, and she was desperate to return to court.

Jane was present with Lady Willoughby that autumn when a deputation of lords of the Council came to Easthampstead to see the Queen.

Their spokesman was the Archbishop of York. He informed her that all the universities of Europe had determined that the Pope had had no authority or grounds to issue the dispensation permitting her marriage to the King, and that it was worthless.

Jane was appalled to see the Queen fall to her knees and raise her hands in supplication.

"I am the King's true wife!" she insisted. "He has yielded to mere passion, and I cannot think that the court of Rome and the whole Church of England will consent to anything that is unlawful and detestable. But still I say I am his wife, and for him I will pray."

The lords were implacable. "It is our duty to warn your Grace of what the King might do to you if you persist in your defiance," the Archbishop said.

"I will go even to the fire if the King commands me!" she cried.

"It may yet come to that," the Archbishop snapped, and they departed, leaving her shuddering and unable to rise, and her ladies and maids swooping to succor her. As Jane fetched a damp cloth to mop her brow, she was trembling with indignation at the way her beloved mistress had been treated. It was the Pope who should rule on the royal marriage, not the universities!

A few days later, the command came from the King: the Queen and her household were to remove to the More, a house near Esher

once owned by Cardinal Wolsey. It was a magnificent mansion and,
as before, Katherine kept great state there. Visitors came, among
them the Venetian ambassador and his suite of thirty elegant gentlemen, and Jane was one of the eighty maids-of-honor in attendance when they came to watch the Queen dine. Jane had always
wondered how royal persons felt about eating in full public view,
almost as entertainment. I could never do that! she thought. I would
not be able to eat a thing, I'd be so embarrassed.

Afterward, when hippocras and wafers were served, and the company mingled, a young man with dark eyes and olive skin appeared
before Jane.

"*Bella signorina!*" he addressed her, kissing her hand. "You English ladies are so beautiful and fair."

Jane did not quite know how to respond. It was astonishing to
have a young man address her so enthusiastically—and very pleasant! "I thank you, Sir," she said. "I hope you are enjoying your visit
to England."

"We are seeing many marvels," he answered, "but never anything
as *magnifico* as all you lovely ladies! Tell me, you serve the Queen?
She is nice lady?"

"She is a most gracious lady," Jane said. "Where do you live in
Italy?"

"In Venice, *signorina*—La Serenissima! You must visit one day.
She is beautiful city. I take you there, eh?" He gave her a meaningful
look. But just as Jane was seeing herself in Italy, the mistress of a
palazzo, with her handsome Italian husband at her side and a brood
of olive-skinned children, to her surprise, the young man bowed
and moved on, patting her backside as he did so. She spun around
in indignation, but he was gone from her reach.

"He did that to me too!" Dorothy fumed. "The nerve of him!"

"The first man in years who shows an interest in me, and he dis-
appears after two minutes—and insults me!" Jane exclaimed. Then
suddenly they both found themselves laughing. "It was good to be
called *bella signorina,* even if he didn't mean it," Jane said.

———

Gloom descended on the More in early December when Lady Parr died. The Queen had loved her, and was much broken by her death.

Now she had only Lady Willoughby to confide in. Lady Willoughby's loyalty was steadfast, but her manner was bracing and she had a fierce Spanish temperament. She nagged rather than coaxed, and Jane felt that Katherine needed someone gentler at this time. She wished that she herself could comfort her, but the Queen did not confide in her maids.

A ray of light in the gloom was a letter from Thomas, informing Jane of his return to England. He had enjoyed his time in France, but although King Henry had been unfailingly courteous to him, he had not offered him preferment, so Thomas was going to stay in Bryan's service. Thank goodness for Bryan, Jane said to herself. We all owe him so much. She no longer hoped that he would ask for her hand; he could never do it now, even if he wanted to. No man so close to the King would look for a bride in the fallen Queen's household.

They spent a mournful Christmas at the More. The King had again refused Katherine's request to have Mary with her, and he had forbidden her to communicate with Ambassador Chapuys.

Jane had a letter from Lizzie, who was enjoying life in Yorkshire, although she missed everyone very much. Sir Anthony was an indulgent husband, and she was growing to like him. At his behest, she had made the King a fine shirt with a high collar, and sent it to him as a New Year's gift.

Father wrote, sending Jane the greetings of the season, which made her wish herself at home, and Edward sent a gift of venison. Jane presented it to the Queen, along with the silk purse she had made her, and was heartened to see Katherine smile.

The Yule log was brought in on Christmas Eve, and there were feasts on Christmas Day, New Year's Day and Twelfth Night, but they were sad affairs compared with what would be going on in their absence at court, and at Wulfhall. Katherine put on a cheerful front, but Lady Parr's absence made everything seem sadder still. Jane was glad when the maids-of-honor organized a treasure hunt, and they all ran shrieking around the house.

Chapter 10

1532

Eliza Darrell had helped to smuggle in a letter from Messire Chapuys. The Queen read it as she sat in her chair by the open window, where she could enjoy the May sunshine. Her ladies and maids were with her, listening to Bess Chambers reading aloud an old romance.

Jane, watching Katherine, saw that the news was of some grave import. The Queen looked up from the letter, her expression pained.

"The clergy have renounced their authority to make new Church laws without the King's consent. That is bad enough, but there is worse. When the bishops were gathered in convocation, his Grace addressed them, and said he had thought that the clergy of his realm had been his subjects wholly, but he had now perceived that they were but half his subjects, for they had all made an oath to the Pope, contrary to the oath that they made to him. So they have had no choice but to renounce their allegiance to Rome. Henceforth, they will answer to the King only, not the Pope." Her voice was choked.

Jane felt sick to her stomach.

"Does this mean that the King has broken with the Pope?" Lady Willoughby barked.

"I fear it does. I cannot believe he has gone that far." So great was Katherine's distress that she had failed, for perhaps the first time in her life, to give the King his due title in front of his inferiors. "That is not all. Sir Thomas More, who has been a stout friend to me, has resigned as Lord Chancellor. He cannot countenance these changes. If only the Pope would speak! I know that my husband wants to return to the fold. He does not want to be cut off from the rest of Christendom, or risk excommunication."

The women expressed their shock at the news. Only Nan Stanhope stayed silent.

"Of course," Katherine said, "the way will now be clear for Master Cromwell to push through his reforms unhindered." Jane had been hearing a lot about Master Cromwell lately. Enforced exile was breaking down the barriers between the Queen and her faithful maids, and she had begun to express her views more freely to them, and keep them informed of what was going on.

People sneered at Thomas Cromwell, for he was the son of a blacksmith who had made good as a lawyer. But they did not do so to his face. He had long been in Cardinal Wolsey's service, but had transferred to the King's after his master's fall, and since then, he had made himself indispensable; the Queen had said it was because he was ready at all things, evil or good.

She had told them of Ambassador Chapuys's warning that Cromwell had risen above everyone save the Lady Anne, and now had more credit with the King than even Wolsey had enjoyed. It was no secret that Cromwell was hot for reform. He supported the King's supremacy. Like Anne, he wanted the Bible in English. Like Anne, he was opposed to the Queen and everything she stood for, including the Church of Rome.

Jane shivered, fearful for her mistress. If Cromwell was as ruthless as people said, the future would be bleak indeed.

That month they were ordered to move to the palace at Hatfield, a red-brick house ranged around a courtyard amid lovely gardens, which were all in colorful bloom. Jane could have thought of worse places to sit out one's exile, as she walked in the surrounding park, admiring the scenery, or danced in the great hall with the other young ladies for the Queen's pleasure.

One day, strolling alone in the park under a blazing sun, with not a soul in sight, she sat down to rest in the shade of an old oak tree. Suddenly she felt a slight frisson of—she knew not what! It was not fear, certainly. Rather, it was a sense of import, of triumph even. She got up and walked away. The feeling ebbed. When she returned, she felt it again, undeniably. And then, although the words were not spoken aloud, she heard them, in her head. *This is the Lord's doing; it is marvelous in our eyes.*

It seemed to be a woman speaking; she could barely tell. What she did experience was a rush of joy, for there was no doubt in her mind what it portended. The Queen would be vindicated: the Pope would speak in her favor. What she herself had just felt and heard had been prophetic, and that God had vouchsafed her, His humble servant, such foreknowledge was thrilling indeed.

Hurrying back to the palace, she slowed her steps. Maybe it would be best not to say anything of it to the Queen for now—just in case she was wrong. It would be cruel to raise Katherine's hopes. But when she returned, she almost changed her mind, for there was her good mistress being comforted by Margery and Bess.

"The King has dismissed Lady Willoughby," Isabel told her. "He is a bad man, a wicked man, for he thinks she plots with the Queen! And now she has no great ladies to talk to, only us maids."

It was as well, Jane thought, that Katherine had allowed them to draw closer to her. Aloud, she said, "I am sure the Pope will speak soon and that all will be well. It's nearly three years since the case was revoked to Rome, so it cannot be much longer. And then right and good order will be restored, you'll see."

"I do pray so," Isabel said fervently.

August brought a visit from Thomas, a welcome diversion for the maids. Jane was astonished and delighted to see him as he bowed before the Queen, looking so handsome with his fine eyes, the hint of humor in his expression, and a luxuriant chestnut beard. The King, he said, had appointed him master forester of Enfield Chase, and seeing that Hatfield was nearby, he had come to pay his respects to her Grace and visit his sister. The post was a minor one, Jane knew, but by the way Thomas had announced it, you would have thought he'd been made Lord Chancellor. She suppressed a smile. She had long grown used to his inordinate ambition and sense of entitlement. She was surprised that he was willing to visit the Queen, but of course he had wanted to show off.

He stayed for only an hour or so, and they spent most of that time walking in the gardens and catching up on family news.

"Mother and Father are well," he told her. "The boys are shooting up. Harry likes working for Bishop Gardiner, who has replaced Wolsey at Winchester. And Lizzie's husband has left for Jersey. He has been appointed governor, and he and Lizzie will be living in a royal castle! But she is not to go until it is ready to receive her." He paused. "You will not like this, Jane. Because she did not want to stay alone in Yorkshire, they closed up their houses and Sir Anthony obtained for her a place in the Lady Anne's household."

Jane did *not* like it. She walked on, shocked.

"You should sue for a place too," Thomas said. "I am sure Sir Francis will be pleased to help. I still work for him. I could ask him."

Jane turned on him. "How could I serve a woman who is the scandal of Christendom, and who has done her utmost to break the Queen's marriage?" she flared. "I could never betray my good mistress thus."

Thomas was unmoved. "It would be a wise course, sister. Perhaps you have heard that Archbishop Warham has died." Jane had. Katherine's chaplain had given them the sad news, and the Queen had been very worried about who would take Warham's place. "As you know, he was against the divorce," Edward went on, "but this new man who is to replace him, Thomas Cranmer, is for it, and a passionate advocate of reform. He was chaplain to the Boleyns. I think there will be great changes, very soon, and you would do well to prepare for that."

"Only the Pope can pronounce a divorce," Jane pointed out, chilled at the prospect of what Cranmer's appointment would mean for the Queen.

"It was Dr. Cranmer's idea to canvass the universities. With learned opinion on the King's side, he may not wait for the Pope to give sentence. The word is that Cranmer will do it."

Jane stared at him, horrified. At length, she found her voice. "He has not the authority. It would not be lawful."

"Sweet sister, where have you been these past years?" Thomas was losing patience. "We are in the process of another divorce, between England and Rome. It is all but complete, and lacks only the ratification of Parliament. Believe me, this marriage will go ahead, and soon."

"Then I shall stay with the Queen—the *rightful* Queen!" Jane could not hide her distress.

"That would not be wise, and it would reflect badly on our family. These are dangerous times. The Lady Anne rules all. Any who favor the Queen are her enemies. She has even made threats against the Princess. You would do well to consider your position. Think of the rest of us. The King is taking the Lady Anne to France, and Father will be in attendance on his Grace, to show where *his* loyalties lie. Lizzie is going, and Edward. I hope to go too, if Sir Francis permits. Think of your future, Jane. There will be no advantage in remaining with the Queen—quite the contrary!"

"No," Jane said. "I will not compromise my principles for anyone."

Thomas snorted in exasperation. "You are a fool," he told her, "and I will not let you persist in your stupidity."

Soon afterward, Jane received a letter from Bryan. The Queen looked at her questioningly as she handed it to her. Why would Bryan write to her?

She read the letter with dismay. He was proposing a marriage with William Dormer, the son and heir of Sir Robert Dormer, the Member of Parliament for West Wycombe.

"Lady Dormer was Jane Newdigate, and is descended from King Edward III through the Nevilles," Bryan had written. "The Dormers cannot but approve of you, and you of them. They are staunch Catholics, and Sir Robert prefers to live a quiet life in the country because he despises and fears the power and ambition of those who are in command at court, and is in grief over the break with Rome. William is twenty years old, and will inherit goodly estates."

"Who is the letter from, Jane?" asked the Queen, as was her right and duty, for she was in loco parentis to her maids. Jane showed her. There was nothing in it of which she could disapprove.

"It is an honorable proposal, and a good match for you," Katherine said. "I shall be greatly saddened to lose you, dear Jane, but you cannot let an opportunity like this slip. How old are you now?"

"Nearly twenty-five, Madam."

"It is a good age to be wed. I was about your age when I married the King."

"But William Dormer is five years younger than me, Madam."

"His Grace was five years younger too." The Queen smiled. Yes, Jane thought, and look what happened when you grew old and he did not. "Sir Robert is clearly of the true faith, and it sounds as if he does not support the King's desire for a divorce," Katherine said approvingly. "But it surprises me that Sir Francis Bryan, who is all for reform and bends with the wind to retain the King's love, has suggested a match with a family that cleaves to the old ways."

It did not surprise Jane. This was Thomas's doing, all part of a clever plan to detach her from the Queen. "He is my kinsman, Madam," she said. "He has ever been helpful in advancing my family, and he knows that I too cleave to the old ways, and that I am utterly loyal to your Grace. He has chosen well, but Madam, I do not want to leave your service."

"Nonsense, Jane!" the Queen replied. "You are dear to me and have served me well; yet when your father placed you with me, it was surely in the hope that I would help you to make a good marriage. Why do you think I invited all those young gentlemen to my chamber? It was for you maids. So you should accept this marriage, especially since Sir Francis states that your father gives it his blessing."

Jane felt trapped. "Yes, Madam." Bryan had presented her with a fait accompli. It would have been nice if she had been consulted too. She looked at the letter again. "If I am agreeable to the match, I am invited, with your Grace's permission, to visit Sir Robert and Lady Dormer, to meet their son. They live at Wing, near Aylesbury."

"That is a very good idea," the Queen said, "and of course you should go. I think it is not far away."

"Aylesbury is about thirty miles from here, Madam," Nan Stanhope said, looking at Jane with envious eyes.

"You must take one of the grooms with you, and Margery will accompany you." Margery looked pleased at the prospect. They had so few diversions in their lives. "I myself will write to Sir Robert Dormer, signifying my approval," the Queen added, "and we shall arrange a date. In the meantime, Jane, respond to Sir Francis and tell him you are well content with this marriage, and that you look forward to visiting the Dormers soon."

"Yes, Madam," Jane replied, aware that she hadn't said she was content.

It was all happening too fast. This morning she had been going about her daily duties without a thought for the future, and now, suddenly, she was to be married. She would willingly have poleaxed Thomas, if he had been within striking distance.

The manor house at Wing was set in the midst of a beautiful country estate; it was an ancient stone building plastered white, with a tall oriel window in what Jane realized must be the hall, and a stout oak door set in a pointed archway. It bespoke wealth and good management.

Their approach had been noticed. Suddenly the door opened and a man and a woman emerged, and stood there waiting for them to dismount. The man—Sir Robert Dormer, Jane guessed—looked to be in his middle forties, and wore a black gown of good quality; his wife was in black too, wearing a gable hood and a white partlet covering the neckline of her dress. He was smiling; she was not. In fact, she looked disapproving. There was no sign of William Dormer.

Jane had an idea that this meeting was going to be an ordeal. "Welcome, Mistress Jane," Sir Robert said, executing a slight bow. "And you must be Mistress Margery?"

"Yes, Sir Robert." Margery smiled.

"Welcome," Lady Dormer echoed, stone-faced. Jane dropped a curtsey. "Pray come in. You"—she looked at the groom—"may go through that door to the kitchen and have a cup of ale."

A copper-haired young man of middle height was waiting in the hall, a lofty room with a vaulted ceiling and two fine tapestries on the walls. So this was William Dormer. He was looking as nervous as Jane felt. Her second impression was that he was very handsome. Those cheekbones! And those blue eyes and full lips! Suddenly wedlock did not seem such a dismal prospect after all.

William Dormer bowed lower than his father had, and Jane curtseyed again. He gave no sign that he found her as attractive as she did him. In fact, he spoke not a word. Sir Robert signaled that they should sit down beside the vast hearth, in which flowers had been tastefully arranged, and Lady Dormer beckoned a manservant. "We will have refreshments now, Walter. Please see they are brought promptly."

Wine was brought, and wafers and sugared fruits, as for a special occasion. The cloth that covered them was snowy white. It was clear that Lady Dormer ruled her household efficiently, and probably strictly too. Jane wished she would unbend a little and smile. She felt daunted at the prospect of having to live here under this woman's rule. You could not compare it with the happy household presided over by Mother at Wulfhall.

It was Sir Robert who tried to put them at their ease, asking if they had had an easy journey, and if the inns at which they had stayed had been satisfactory. He told them that Wing Manor had been built more than two centuries before, and that he had bought it soon after his marriage. "It is my wife who has made it what it is today," he said, inducing a slight lifting of Lady Dormer's lips.

Dinner was served in the parlor. The conversation continued with awkward pauses, filled hastily by Sir Robert, who spoke of the good hunting hereabouts, and the new wing he was planning to build. Nothing was said of the marriage. William contributed little, but Jane was aware of his eyes on her. He seemed to be in awe of his mother, and kept looking at her, as if he needed her approval.

"How does the Queen?" Sir Robert asked.

"She is in fair health," Jane told him, taking care to eat daintily, "but weighed down by sorrows."

"Alas, poor lady," he said. "We feel for her."

"She is a good mistress, and we all love her." Jane looked at Margery, who nodded agreement. "She does not deserve her misfortunes, yet still she stays cheerful, taking all patiently and with great faith."

Lady Dormer looked up from her plate. "Does it please you to be away from the court, Mistress Jane?"

"I do not miss it, my lady. I wish only to serve my gracious mistress. There are things that go on at court of which I could never approve."

"That is why *I* stay away," Sir Robert said. "It is better thus. All of us here are for the Queen—and the Pope."

"The court is a wicked and godless place," Lady Dormer barked. "My brother, Sebastian Newdigate, was a Gentleman of the Privy Chamber to the King, and much favored by him, but when this vile divorce business broke out, I warned him not to stain his soul and honor with such dangerous and pestilent contagions as the bad example of his master might lead him to. Fortunately, my brother had already had a calling to the religious life, and two years ago he became a monk at the London Charterhouse. So, Mistress Jane, if you marry my son, we would not want you to return to court unless the Queen is restored to her place."

"I would not contemplate it," Jane said. "I could never serve the Lady Anne." She was disconcerted at the way Lady Dormer had said "if," and annoyed that William had nothing to say to her. This meeting was becoming increasingly uncomfortable.

Lady Dormer dabbed at her mouth with her napkin. All her movements were economical, although there was a certain grace about her—the kind that Jane had seen in the nuns at Amesbury. She wondered if Lady Dormer had once been a nun.

That lady turned to her. "I am determined to arrange a suitable marriage for my son," she said. "When I saw the corruption of the state of this kingdom, I decided that I would marry him to some virtuous gentlewoman of equal rank. Sir Robert was in agreement, and he asked me to take charge of the matter, wishing me to resolve it before the King hindered our intention by commanding a marriage we did not like. For, William being our only child and heir to a great patrimony, many courtiers have sought to marry their daughters and kinswoman to him."

"Sir Francis Bryan's but one of them," Sir Robert said.

"But he is a notorious favorite of the King, and we think he is only pretending to favor this match," his wife put in. "He supports the Lady Anne Boleyn. Why would he interest himself in us, who are of the opposite party?"

Jane was sitting there in mounting astonishment. "But Lady Dormer, why would Sir Francis sue for this marriage if he did not intend for it to take place?"

"I think it is to put off someone who could have offered us a better match," the woman said bluntly. "Whatever the reason, I would never trust the man or his motives. I detest him!"

"Then why did you agree to my coming here?" Jane asked.

"Sir Francis enjoys great influence as one of the King's intimates," Sir Robert said. "We are in a precarious position, and we thought it prudent to concur. After all, he seemed serious when he treated of this marriage with us."

"And he *is* serious," Jane declared. "He wishes to see me married well, and approached you at my brother's instigation. They both want me to leave the Queen's service. Sir Francis proposed William as my husband because he is of like mind to me, and loves the Queen and his Holiness."

"This is not about you yourself, my dear," Sir Robert replied. "You seem a devout and modest young lady, and I like you. I am sure William does too." He looked at his son, and William made what passed for a nod of agreement. "But we would rather not have dealings with someone so close to the King as Sir Francis, whose reputation is not of the best."

"So what is to happen?" Jane asked, bewildered, for nothing was making sense.

There was a short silence. "Fear not, we will treat again with Sir Francis to make sure that he really is sincere," Sir Robert said. Lady Dormer's mouth tightened in a disapproving line.

Fortunately they had nearly finished eating, and could soon be on their way back to the inn at Tottenhoe where they had lodged the night before. Jane suspected Lady Dormer would do everything in her power to prevent William from marrying her. Inwardly, she sighed. Bryan had been the cause of all this, *and* her meddling brother Thomas, and they could deal with the matter. She desired no part in it, and she was convinced of the wisdom of that when, on parting, William Dormer did not even bow, but gave her a haughty stare that told her unequivocally that he did not want her.

She knelt beside the Queen and told her what had happened. Katherine patted her shoulder.

"You may have been mistaken, Jane. Why would they not want you as a bride for their son?"

"I cannot think, Madam." She could hardly tell the Queen how much the Dormers hated Bryan. It was cruel that his kind gesture in brokering a betrothal had been the thing that might wreck her prospects. She felt tears brimming. On seeing William Dormer, she had thought that happiness could be hers, and then, so rapidly, she had been disillusioned. The Dormers did not approve of the match, and William's indifference had stung. Her one chance of marriage was going to end in humiliation.

She got up and fetched her lute. She must not brood like this.

Bryan wrote again, his tone indignant. He was sorry to tell her that William Dormer was betrothed elsewhere, to the daughter of Sir William Sidney, a prominent courtier.

"Lady Dormer took the whole business, and the blame, upon herself," Bryan had written, "assuring me she had negotiated the matter before with Lady Sidney and could not go back on her word. I have told her that they will see you just as well bestowed in life. I promise, Jane, that I will find you a better marriage."

So there had been another match in mind. Lady Dormer had wasted no time. She had hurriedly made an overture to Sir William's wife, offering William as a husband for his eldest daughter, and Lady Sidney had evidently been well pleased. Bryan told Jane that Lady Dormer had ridden up to Sir William Sidney's house in London with her son, and there the two mothers had concluded the betrothal.

Try as she might, Jane could not but feel spurned, for the second time in her life. The whole business had been utterly distasteful. Her resentment simmered.

When she told the Queen what had happened, Katherine displayed rare anger. "But there was an understanding," she said, clearly appalled.

"I knew that Lady Dormer was against it, Madam. I must confess, I *am* upset about it. Clearly I was not good enough for her son."

Katherine put an arm around her, something she had never done before. "Well, Jane, if you are good enough to serve me, you are too good for William Dormer." That did make Jane feel happier. She was much better off here, in exile with a loving mistress, than she would ever have been at Wing Manor as William's unwanted wife.

As Christmas approached, and the maids occupied themselves with making gifts for the Queen and each other, Jane received another letter from Bryan.

"You will not credit this," it read, "but William Dormer has entered the service of Master Cromwell." Jane was staggered. Cromwell was surely the last person of whom Sir Robert and Lady Dormer would have approved. But self-interest had evidently overridden all other considerations, because such an appointment was assuredly an advantageous step to advancement. What hypocrites these people were!

And had Thomas and Bryan known that this might happen? Was it this that had led them to suggest a marriage that would have placed Jane advantageously in the reformist camp?

Part Three

Rivals

Chapter 11

1533

The order came in February. The Queen was to move to Ampthill Castle, and her household was to be reduced. The vast train of extra maids-of-honor had been dismissed, and fewer than thirty had been retained. Jane was praying that she would be allowed to stay. She could not bear the thought of leaving Katherine, especially when it was clear that Ampthill Castle would be more of a prison than a house of retirement. Already they had been warned that new rules and restrictions would be imposed. They would not be allowed to leave the castle precincts, for a start. Exile alone not having worked, the King was further punishing his wife for her defiance. But Jane would willingly have endured any privations to stay with the Queen. It was unthinkable that she leave her at this time, with Katherine so low in spirits.

The Queen appeared composed when she summoned her household, but her voice shook as she dismissed those who were to be let go. Jane waited, holding her breath, watching the women who were to leave break down in tears or kiss their mistress's hand with emotion. She felt choked, for they had been her daily companions and friends; she shared a special bond with them. But her name was not on the list. She exhaled in relief.

They were preparing to depart for Ampthill when Lord Mountjoy brought a letter for Jane. She could have wept when she read it.

"Is it bad news?" Katherine asked, her face filled with concern.

"Yes, Madam." She could hardly speak. "My father commands me home without delay. He says that he has written to the King and found me a place at court, and has bought it dearly for me."

"With the Lady Anne?" Katherine's voice was gentle.

Jane could not bear the thought. Indignation rose in her breast. She was sure her brothers had urged this, out of self-interest, and Father had complied—anxious, no doubt, to win favor with Edward, she thought bitterly—and she must pay the price. No doubt Bryan had played his part too!

"I fear so, Madam." She found herself weeping uncontrollably, and fell to her knees by the Queen's chair. "Let me stay, your Grace! Oh, do let me stay! You could write to my father and command it—"

"Hush, child, do you think my word would carry any weight? Besides, it is more to your benefit to be serving one who is in favor than one who is not. Your father is wise; he sees this."

"But I cannot serve her. I hate her and all she stands for!"

"I am very sorry," Katherine said, "yet there is no remedy. You must obey your father and go home—but you go with my blessing."

At that, Jane wept afresh. "I will never have such a kind mistress," she sobbed. "I wish—I so wish—your Grace and the Princess a happy ending to your troubles."

In streams of tears, she dragged herself to her feet and went to pack her things, while Lord Mountjoy arranged horses and an escort to take her on her way. She clung tightly when Katherine embraced her and bade her farewell.

"Your Grace knows that I am not going willingly!" she cried.

"I know that," Katherine soothed. "May God be with you always." One final curtsey, and Jane's service was ended.

Wulfhall slumbered as it had for centuries in its winter-wrapped valley. Sunk in misery and resentment, Jane was pleased to see it, and to be held against Mother's ample bosom and have her tears dried. Mother was the same as ever, and here was Dorothy, fourteen years old now and very grown up, come to help her carry her bags up to her chamber. Otherwise the place was quiet, no longer the teeming household in which she had grown up. Father was at the assizes at Salisbury, Harry away at Winchester. They had had a letter from Lizzie, who was expecting her first baby.

"She's too young," Mother said, as Jane joined her in the kitchen, where she was cutting pastry leaves for a pie. "I was nineteen when I had my first. Lizzie's only fifteen. I pray that all will be well. She is looking forward to the time when she can leave the Lady Anne's service and go to Jersey. I don't think she's enjoying herself very much, but then we all have to make the best of things. There was something she wrote in her letter, though . . . Dorothy, fetch it, please. My hands are all floury."

The letter was duly brought and Jane perused it. The Lady Anne, apparently, kept a lively court, with lots of dancing and merry pastimes, and the young gallants flocked to it. Yes, thought Jane, but she has no right to be keeping court at all!

"I do not want to serve the Lady Anne," she said.

Mother made a face. "He must needs go that the Devil drives," she observed. "But that wasn't what I wanted you to see. Read on."

Jane read—and read again. Lizzie had written that there were rumors at court that the King had already married Anne. She looked up, horrified. "That cannot be true! The Pope hasn't spoken, has he?"

"No," Mother said, "nor Archbishop Cranmer, to my knowledge."

"It's probably just gossip," Dorothy opined, sneaking a sugar plum and cramming it in her mouth.

"Knowing the Lady Anne, she will want a big state wedding with all the pomp and pageantry there could be," Jane said. "She's the last person who would consent to being wed in secret."

She could not go to court and serve that woman, even if she were queen. It would not be right. She would tell Father when he returned home.

"No, Jane," Father said emphatically, from the great chair he used as master of the household. "It is all arranged, through the good offices of Sir Francis Bryan, and if you do not go, it will give offense—and I will be out of pocket."

"I thought Sir Francis might be involved somehow," Jane said, bitter. "I wish he would stop meddling in my life. Look at the Dormer fiasco."

"That was not his fault," Father said. "It seemed a good match for you. And he himself offered to find a place for you at court to compensate for the disappointment. He smoothed the way." He looked weary after his long ride. Mother handed him a goblet of steaming lambswool to warm him.

"I know he has good intentions, but he does these things without even consulting me!" Jane complained.

"He consulted me, which was more important," Father said. "I made an approach to the King, and Sir Francis did the rest. I paid for the privilege. If this family is to prosper, we have to move with the times. The Lady Anne will soon be queen. Sir Francis was lucky to secure a place for you, and you will accept it and do your duty graciously. I would not offend the King for anything." It was not like Father to be so severe, but he had been dealing with malefactors for days, and clearly accounted his daughter one of them.

He regarded her fiercely. "Jane, what happened with the Dormers brought home to us the need to remove you from the Queen's service. We have our pride, and I will not have you rejected again when another suitable match presents itself. The Lady Anne has been told that you came home of your own free will—"

"I did not!" Jane interrupted. Father raised a finger.

"It is best that she thinks you did. Even with Sir Francis's recommendation, she could hardly be expected to accept someone who is overtly sympathetic to Queen Katherine. I am ambitious for my children, Jane. Lizzie has married a man high in royal favor and done well for herself. Edward and Thomas are making a success of their lives and look set for advancement. Placed in the Lady Anne's household, you will have every opportunity of making a good marriage. Be pragmatic, girl. Think of your family."

Jane bit her tongue. She was wondering how she was going to be civil to the Lady Anne, let alone bring glory on her own family. There had been no conflict of loyalties in Queen Katherine's household, only a sense that she was doing the right thing.

"You will go to court, and that's an end to it," Father decreed, and she knew herself defeated.

Mother shook her head as she inspected Jane's gowns, holding them up one by one and frowning. "These have seen service for some years and need replacing," she decreed. "Look how that silk has rubbed. The Lady Anne is a leader of fashion, and you must be provided for accordingly." The tailor and the mercer were summoned, and Jane stood impatiently while Mother hummed and hawed, finally choosing several bolts of material and ordering ribbons, braid, pins and Holland cloth for shifts.

"These hoods could be refurbished," she pronounced. "No, they are too worn. Shall we order you French ones?"

The Lady Anne favored French hoods. Jane briefly imagined herself wearing the halo-shaped headdress that daringly exposed the hair. She did not want to be identified in any way with Anne.

"I prefer English hoods," she said, picking up a gable-shaped example in black velvet and admiring it.

"Very well, we'll have two of each," Mother told the tailor.

Jane looked on, too weary to protest. The last week had been deeply distressing. She missed Queen Katherine and the other maids-of-honor, who had been her close companions for years, and she was worried about what the future held for the Queen. Going to serve the woman who was determined to supplant her made Jane feel that she was contributing to Katherine's misfortunes.

The weariness persisted. One day she fell asleep as she sat with Mother and Dorothy stitching the body linen she would take to court. Mother shook her awake and felt her brow. She frowned.

"You're burning up, child! You had best get to bed. I'll bring you a hot posset with some feverfew. Help her, Dorothy."

Jane was grateful to slide between the sheets and sleep. When she awoke, she had a rasping sore throat, she ached all over and there was a strange pain in her eyes.

Mother was sitting beside her. "You've slept for six hours," she said. She rested her hand on Jane's forehead. "Still hot. I've sent for the physician."

He came that evening with his leeches and bled Jane from her arm—"To remove the bad blood and balance the humors," he said to Mother. He gazed at her urine for a long time, then examined her throat and neck. "Her glands are swollen," he said. "You must reduce the fever. Keep her warm, but not too warm. Continue with the herbal essences and give plenty to drink. I will return in a week to see how she does."

Lady Seymour went into action. When Jane was not asleep or wandering in her mind, which she was for much of the time, she was aware of Mother moving silently around the bedchamber, stoking up the fire, sponging her down, lifting her up to sip drinks, spooning down honey to ease her throat, or just sitting watchfully beside her. Sometimes Dorothy took over, so that Mother could get some rest, and one evening Father sat with Jane and read to her from an old bestiary she had loved as a child. It soothed her to hear once more the old legends about lions, unicorns, gryphons and panthers. It took her back to a world that was less complicated, in which there were no impossible moral choices.

Father told her she must not worry; he had written to inform the Lady Anne of her illness, and received a gracious response telling him that Jane was to come to court only when she was fit enough to do so. Jane prayed that would not be for some time—and it seemed that God heard her, because although the fever and the sore throat abated within three weeks, she could not shake off the debilitating fatigue, and had to keep to her bed. Mother sought to build her up with heartening food and her own special cordials, but Jane's recovery was slow.

In the spring, there was momentous news. Father heard it proclaimed by the King's own heralds in the marketplace at Amesbury, and came cantering home to tell them. Archbishop Cranmer had ruled that the King's marriage to the Lady Katherine was null and void. The King had married the Lady Anne, and that marriage was good and valid. The Lady Anne was now queen of England.

Jane wept into her pillow, crying for Katherine, to whom this would be heavy tidings indeed, and for herself, for in serving Anne as queen, her betrayal of Katherine would be the greater. She was appalled that the King had gone ahead and done all this without the Pope's sanction. It was sheer wickedness. Surely his Holiness would speak now!

But Father was jubilant. "It will be a much greater honor to serve Queen Anne now than it would have been before," he exulted, ignoring Jane's wan disapproval, and hastened away to write again to the new Queen to assure her that her maid-of-honor was on the mend and eager to attend her.

"It's wrong, and I don't want any part in it!" Jane said weakly.

"Hush, child." Mother was sitting beside her. "These are weighty matters, beyond the understanding of us women."

"Oh, I think Anne Boleyn understands them very well. Certainly the good Queen does." Jane's heart was pounding sluggishly. This was not doing her any good.

Mother patted her hand. "Just leave the arguments to those who are qualified to judge, and keep your private thoughts to yourself. You must think of your father's position."

Normally, when Mother spoke thus, it was enough to quieten her children, but Jane had to say what was on her mind. "Mother, for-give me, but I cannot forget my loyalty to the true Queen, who was a kind mistress to me, and is patient and good. I can never accept Anne Boleyn in her place. I may be a woman, but I know God's law, which is that a man may have but one wife at a time."

"Enough!" Mother chided her. "I'm sure we all share your senti-ments, but it is folly nowadays to speak thus. None of us has the power to change things. Keep your true allegiance in your heart, and utter no word of it. That's wise advice I'm giving you."

Jane subsided and closed her eyes. Mother was right; and the way she felt now, she needed no more heavy matters to cope with.

Lizzie wrote from Jersey, whither she had traveled while Jane was in the depths of her delirium. She had been safely delivered of a son and named him Henry, in honor of the King. He had been born in the castle at Mont Orgeuil, where Lizzie was settling in happily, in great state, as wife of the Governor. Mother and Father were thrilled to be grandparents again, and Mother immediately set to work to make some garments for the baby's layette, for dispatch to Jersey.

There was good news from Harry, too. On the recommendation of Bishop Gardiner, he had secured a post at court, having been ap-pointed sewer extraordinary in the King's Privy Chamber, where his brothers were serving.

"What's a sewer?" Dorothy asked, when Mother and Father came, rejoicing, to Jane's chamber to impart these glad tidings.

"A gentleman who waits at the King's table," Father said proudly.

But the news was not all good. Soon afterward, Edward wrote to say that Queen Katherine—or the Princess Dowager of Wales, as she was henceforth to be called—had refused to accept Archbishop Cranmer's ruling, or to relinquish her title.

"She still maintains that she is the King's true wife, and will abide by no decision save that of the Pope," Jane read, after Mother had brought her the letter. She lay there trembling. How could she ever bring herself to call Katherine "Princess Dowager"? To Jane, she would always be the true Queen. Her soul seethed in anger against the upstart who had taken her place.

By June, when Edward and Thomas sent home enthusiastic accounts of Anne Boleyn's coronation, Jane was well enough to sit up in a chair for short periods. She was shocked to read that the new Queen, six months pregnant, had brazenly gone to her crowning in a white gown that symbolized virginity. She must have been with child already when the King married her, or maybe they had married in January, as gossip had hinted. Even then, she must have conceived before . . .

Father had done the arithmetic, but he took a more pragmatic view. "The King desperately needs an heir," he said, taking his seat by the bed. "That's what this Great Matter is all about—getting a son. Maybe his Grace wanted to be sure she could breed before marrying her, after all the to-do."

"But to go to her crowning all dressed in white—for shame!"

"Jane," Father exhorted, "you must understand that, in a queen, white symbolizes moral purity, as does loose hair. Edward says Queen Anne sat on hers, it is so long."

"Forgive me," Jane could not help herself, "but I cannot associate Anne Boleyn with moral purity."

"Enough!" Father said. "That's treason, and I will not have it spoken in my house. I fear your illness has crazed you."

Jane lay back on the pillows and closed her eyes. "It seems to me it is the rest of the world that is crazed," she murmured.

"Hush," he reprimanded, more gently. "We must all make the best of things."

Only when summer was at its height did Jane start to feel stronger and begin to put back on the weight she had lost. She spent a lot of time sitting in My Young Lady's Garden, enjoying the fresh air that

Mother deemed so healthful. She reread the romances she loved, practiced on her lute and did some embroidery. There was no need to work on her court attire: Mother had it all finished and stacked away in a traveling chest, ready for Jane's departure.

By September, Jane was fully restored to health, but by then Queen Anne had gone into confinement at Greenwich, and all England was poised to hear news of the birth of a prince. A Mrs. Marshall, Mistress of the Maids, wrote to Jane to say that she should come to court after her Grace had been churched and returned to public life.

The King had commanded that prayers be offered up throughout the land for the Queen's safe delivery. On her knees in the family chapel, Jane joined in through gritted teeth, although she could not wish ill on an innocent babe. She suspected that Father James, old and creaking in the joints now, felt the same, but he dissembled well. Father, however, was hearty in his supplications to the Almighty.

And then God spoke and made His displeasure at the King's marriage clear. The child was a princess.

Jane's departure for the court could be delayed no longer. In vain did she protest that she was still suffering from fatigue. Sir John, knowing her to be recovered, refused to listen. On a chilly morning in early October, Sir Francis Bryan arrived at Wulfhall, having offered to escort Jane himself to Greenwich. Reluctantly, she bade farewell to her family, and soon they were on the road toward London.

Bryan had changed. There was a new gravitas about him that rode well with the lines that had appeared on his weather-beaten face. His one eye was as sardonic as ever, but he was more serious now than he had been wont. As they rode together along lanes bordered by trees aflame with autumnal glory, he asked Jane if she was looking forward to serving the Queen.

She paused too long before she opened her mouth to answer.

"I can guess what you would like to say," he said. "In truth, she is not popular, neither with the people, nor at court. Oh, they all fall over themselves to fawn upon her and seek her favor, but they do not like her. Some would declare their allegiance to the old Queen, if they dared, but they have been silenced for the most part." He glanced behind him, ensuring that their two grooms and Jane's maid were out of earshot.

"And what do you think of Queen Anne?" Jane asked, feeling distaste at calling the woman by that title.

"I was one of her earliest supporters, as you know," he said. "I was also one of her chief favorites. But I cannot say I have much love for her now. She is become a shrew, with her overweening pride, and she knows not how to behave like a queen. People are drawing unflattering comparisons behind her back. I think even the King has his concerns, but he is still determined to do everything for her. He's gone so far, he cannot lose face."

This was news indeed. "But he turned the world upside down to marry her!"

"And he has since found out that all cats are gray in the dark," Bryan said grimly. "He was unfaithful while she was pregnant, and when she upbraided him for it, he told her she must shut her eyes and endure as more worthy persons had done."

Jane's eyes widened at that. She should have guessed that it would be only a matter of time before the King compared his second wife to his first, and found Anne wanting.

"Sometimes I think he is still in thrall to her," Bryan continued. "At others, I wonder. If she gives him a son, her position will be assured; if not . . ." His voice tailed off. "His Grace put on a brave front when the Princess Elizabeth was born, but in private he showed himself deeply disappointed and frustrated. I, for one, would not be saddened if Madam Anne were to fall."

"Nor I," Jane murmured. "My dearest wish is to see the Queen restored."

Bryan shook his head. "That will never happen, I promise you."

Jane walked through the Queen's apartments at Greenwich looking around her in astonishment. They were so altered—and so much more magnificent than in Katherine's day. Gold leaf gleamed from ceilings and woodwork. Fabulous tapestries lined the walls. The hearths were laid with costly Seville tiles, and the rich furnishings were in the antique style. Henry had been lavish. Servants wearing Queen Anne's livery of blue and purple, their doublets embroidered with her motto, "The Most Happy," were going importantly about their business, and one ushered Jane and Sir Francis to her privy chamber. As they crossed her empty chamber of presence, with its rich chair and canopy of estate bearing the arms of England on a dais at the far end, they caught up with a small procession of women.

"My lady mother!" Bryan exclaimed, and the lady at its head turned around. In her arms she cradled a tiny swaddled baby wrapped in a rich robe, and wearing a bonnet banded with cloth of gold. Bryan bowed. "Jane, this is the Princess Elizabeth." At his urgent nod, Jane dipped in a hasty curtsey. "Mother, may I present Mistress Jane Seymour, who has come to serve the Queen?" Jane bobbed again. "My mother is the Princess's lady mistress, Jane, and governs her nursery."

Lady Bryan smiled graciously. She had a fine-boned face with twinkling eyes and an air of serenity about her, and when she greeted Jane, her diction bespoke breeding. It was easy to see why the King had appointed her. Jane remembered that she had once been lady mistress to the young Princess Mary.

She peered at the infant. It looked much like any other baby, with its chubby cheeks and dimpled mouth, its blue eyes and fair lashes. It was hard to believe that the King had put the souls of all his subjects in peril for this tiny scrap of humanity.

"Her little Grace is going to visit her lady mother." Lady Bryan smiled as the doors to the privy chamber opened for her.

Jane and Bryan followed her in and waited to be announced. The privy chamber was sumptuous: the ceiling was decorated with gilded bosses between a lattice of white battens; costly tiles had been laid in the fireplaces and alcoves, and everywhere there was ornate gilded furniture and vast tapestries graced the walls.

Jane saw Anne Boleyn seated amid her ladies and a great gathering of courtiers. Lady Bryan was placing the babe in her arms, and she bent to kiss its head. Her attendants and courtiers crowded around, cooing at the child and praising it to the skies. Then Anne saw that Jane and Bryan were waiting, and ordered that the babe be laid on a large cushion at her feet. She nodded for them to come forward.

In the two years since Jane had last seen her, Anne had grown hard-faced and her eyes—once her chief claim to beauty—were now shadowed and watchful. Her sumptuous crimson gown, rich furs and satin French hood could not compensate for the loss of her youth and the lines of discontent around her mouth. And yet the men flocked around her.

Anne smiled as Jane curtseyed and Bryan bowed, but the smile did not reach her eyes. "Francis, welcome." She inclined her head regally. "And Jane Seymour—I remember you from the days when we both served the Princess Dowager. Welcome back to court." She held out a beringed hand. Jane bent her lips to it, hoping that Anne could not perceive the hostility she had aroused by giving Katherine that hateful title. She rose, keeping her eyes demurely downcast.

"My chamberlain will administer your oath of allegiance when he returns this evening," Anne told her. Her manner was friendly, but there was a brittleness about her, and no wonder, for after all that had passed, she had not borne the hoped-for prince. "This is a godly household and a religious one," she said. "While you are in my service, you will show a virtuous example, and eschew infamous and lewd persons, on pain of instant dismissal."

"Yes, your Grace," Jane murmured, keeping her eyes lowered and wondering how it was possible that a woman like Anne Boleyn could be exhorting her to virtue.

"Mistress Marshall," Anne said. A woman in dove gray stood up. "Take Mistress Jane to the dorter."

Before Jane was out of earshot, she heard the Queen laugh. "She never did have anything to say for herself, the little mouse!"

Her resentment deepened. And then it was banished, for waiting in the maidens' dorter to help her unpack was Margery Horsman. What a relief it was to see a friendly face among so many new ones.

"I was summoned home too," Margery explained, as Jane sat down gratefully on the bed. It was the same one she had occupied when Katherine was queen, while the dorter looked no different; it was as if the past two years had never been. "My family did not want me serving the Princess Dowager. I look after the Queen's wardrobe."

"I loathe that title they have given our good mistress," Jane said. "She is the true—"

"Hush!" Margery hissed. "As you value your position, never refer to her as queen. It is utterly forbidden."

"Then I will say it and go home," Jane retorted. "I did not want to come here."

"And then your kinsfolk will suffer." Margery took her hands. "Oh, Jane—who are we to question? Our families make our moral choices for us."

"That's true," Jane said bitterly. "My family insisted I come to court. At least you are here, which will make it bearable. Tell me, what is Queen Anne like as a mistress? Does she always ridicule people in their hearing? She called me a little mouse!"

"She always has a jest on her lips," Margery told her, "and often at someone's expense. She tells us all we must be virtuous, but she flirts like mad with the gentlemen who frequent her chamber. I must say, though, I do enjoy the pastime there is to be had in her household. There is much dancing and music and pleasure, unlike how it was with the poor Princess Dowager. I am never bored. There is always some diversion."

That, Jane found, was true. If the Queen's ladies were not planning or ordering the latest fashions, they were dancing in her chamber, or reciting poetry, or putting on interludes, or playing at bowls or shooting at the butts. The afternoons and evenings were busy with courtiers visiting, there was much banter and love-play and the King sometimes joined in the revelry too. He was attentive to the Queen, but not in the way he had once been; of course the hunter had caught his prey, and no longer had need to exert himself.

He noticed Jane at once, the first time she was in attendance during one of his visits. It was what made people love him: he had the common touch.

"Mistress Seymour! It pleases us to see you back at court." He must be over forty now, but he was still an overpowering presence, tall, broad and full of vitality, with fine features, a bullish neck and red hair combed over his ears; yet all too often, Jane saw, those narrow eyes and pursed mouth tightened in imperiousness or anger, and there was cruelty in his gaze. She found him terrifying, this man who was now king and pope in his own realm, who had the power of life and death over all his subjects—and who would, it seemed, take possession of their very souls.

She curtseyed low, but he raised her and smiled, and in that instant she could see the eager young man he must have been beneath the worldly, authoritative countenance. His eyes lingered on her for several heartbeats.

"Your Grace," she whispered, bowing her head.

"I trust you will be happy here and serve the Queen well," he said. "Your brothers are doing me excellent service. Pray send my good wishes to your parents." And then he had moved on, and was greeting Anne's sister, Mary, whom he evidently liked well.

Jane did her best to perform her duties efficiently. She did not want the Queen to take particular notice of her, so she was careful to conduct herself with circumspection and decorum, keeping her eyes downcast and her presence unobtrusive. Anne was friendly, but she soon stopped making an effort when she saw that Jane was not interested in cozening favor from her.

Jane quickly realized that if she was to have any sort of life in the

Queen's household, she must accept the fact that most of those who served in it were there because they were of the Boleyn faction and affinity and exulted in Anne's advancement. She learned not to let the title of queen stick in her gullet when she addressed Anne or spoke of her, and to hide her affection for Queen Katherine. Once she had come to terms with all this, she began to make friends among the maids-of-honor. She grew fond of Anne Parr, the daughter of the Lady Parr who had served Katherine. Anne had been distraught at her mother's death, and Jane was glad to see her looking so much happier now.

The Queen's beautiful cousin Madge Shelton was rivals with pretty Anne Saville for the attentions of Sir Henry Norris, head of the King's Privy Chamber and a frequent visitor to the Queen's apartments. Yet the personable Norris, a widower whose daughter, Mary, also served the Queen as maid-of-honor, seemed to have eyes only for Anne, who either encouraged or put him off, according to her mood. The two Marys—Mary Norris and Mary Zouche—were amiable and friendly to Jane, as was another Mary, the Queen's old nurse, Mrs. Orchard, who served her as a chamberer.

Jane could not help liking Elizabeth Holland, who had served Anne Boleyn as a maid for many years.

"It's an open secret that Bess is the Duke of Norfolk's mistress," Margery informed Jane. "He's uncle to her Grace, as you will know, but"—her voice sank to a whisper—"they don't get on." This had already become apparent to Jane, who had overheard the brusque, charmless Duke sparring with his niece. But Bess Holland was a cheerful soul, and popular. The only person she had a bad word for was the Duchess of Norfolk, who now lived apart from her husband on Bess's account.

"She takes the greatest of pleasure in telling people that I was a washerwoman in her household," Bess told Jane, as they laid out the Queen's gown one evening. "But I was no washerwoman! I was put in her children's nursery to teach them. My uncle is Lord Hussey! She says I sat on her chest till she spat blood, but that's a wicked lie. She'll say anything to discredit me. But my friends know the truth."

Jane was glad to be included among Bess's friends, even if she did have reservations about Bess's anomalous position. Again, she had seen how infidelity could lead to trouble and conflict. Yet she could not but be drawn in by Bess's warmth.

Madge Shelton, the object of so much male attention, was working on a book of poems with two of the Queen's ladies. One was Lady Margaret Douglas, the King's own niece, and daughter of his sister Margaret, who had married the King of Scots and then the Earl of Angus. Lady Margaret was the chief lady-of-honor, by virtue of her royal birth, and a great beauty, with red-gold hair and a soft loveliness about her. Jane soon learned that the softness belied a lively and headstrong spirit.

She was flattered when the Lady Margaret asked, in her pretty Scots accent, if she would like to contribute to the book.

"We write poems, and we collect them," she explained. "There are some of these books already circulating in the court, but they are all by men. We thought it would be a novel thing if women were to express themselves in verse, or choose those verses that best please them. We have included some by Sir Thomas Wyatt and the Earl of Surrey." Surrey was Norfolk's son, a roistering young gallant who often joined the Queen's gatherings, and was newly wed to one of her youngest ladies, Frances de Vere. "Tell me, Mistress Jane, do you write poetry?" Margaret asked.

"Alas, no, my lady," Jane confessed. "I have never tried."

"Then sit with us and see what you can do," Mary Howard invited. This beautiful, dewy-eyed young woman was about to be married to Edward's former master, the Duke of Richmond, and might yet be a very great lady indeed if the Queen bore no son, for there was still talk that the King meant to name Richmond his successor.

The three of them invited Jane to sit down with them at a table near the window, and Madge pushed a sheet of paper toward her. "Go on, try!"

Jane dipped a quill in the inkpot and thought for a few moments. She was overwhelmed at being asked to join such great ladies in their pastime, and daunted after reading some of their work. They were so accomplished! She could never hope to write verse of that standard.

Groping about in her mind for inspiration, she thought suddenly of William Dormer, and then found she was able to put pen to paper:

> *Fancy framed my heart first*
> *To bear goodwill and seek the same,*
> *I sought the best and found the worst,*
> *Yet fancy . . .*

At that point, inspiration dried up, and she could not think of anything that rhymed or scanned.

"It's pathetic," she said, and showed them. They began laughing, but not unkindly.

"Think about it for a space," the Lady Margaret advised. "It'll come to you."

"We'll include it anyway." Madge Shelton smiled. "And if you like, we'll help you to write more verses."

Gradually, Jane realized, she was becoming accepted, and liked for her own sake.

Christmas was approaching. Jane noticed a new tenderness between the King and Anne when he came to visit her. The ladies-in-waiting were giving each other significant glances.

"She is with child, I'll wager," Margery murmured, as they sat in an alcove watching Henry and Anne having an animated conversation. Anne seemed her old witty self. She was flirting with her own husband!

"So soon?" Jane was astonished.

"It does not surprise me. He was back in her bedchamber as soon as she was churched. She wanted to feed the Princess herself, but he would not hear of it. He wants an heir, and he has no time to waste."

Margery was right. Jane guessed that Anne was with child when she was deputed to attend the Queen in the mornings and witnessed her vomiting regularly. Pale and drained, she would rest on her bed, but be her normal self by afternoon.

One morning, as Anne lay on her rich counterpane, and Jane was tidying the bedchamber, Lady Worcester came to sit with her. They were close, those two, and Lady Worcester was well connected, being married to a cousin of the King, while her half-brother, Sir William FitzWilliam, was treasurer of the King's household.

Jane heard Anne complaining bitterly—not for the first time—of the obstinacy of the Princess Dowager.

"Still she insists on calling herself Queen! Well, she shall suffer for it." The venom in her voice was chilling. "As you know, she complained that Buckden was damp and unhealthy, and when the King commanded her to move to Somersham, she refused to go, saying it was an evil place. So he ordered her to go to Fotheringhay Castle instead, and—would you believe it?—still she refuses to budge, insisting it is an even unhealthier house!"

They were hounding her, Jane realized, to break her resolve. She was so appalled that for a moment she had to stop what she was doing. Then, fearing they might realize she was listening, she resumed folding the Queen's clean towels, brought up by her washerwoman earlier.

"Madam, I think she is right, and that the King has been misinformed about the state of those houses," Lady Worcester said, after a pause. "My husband says they are both in poor condition."

Anne bridled. "I care not what state they are in! She is in no position to defy the King. If she is his true wife, as she claims, she is bound to obey him."

Jane curtseyed and left the room, anger rising in her. She was in no doubt that those houses had been chosen on purpose to bring the good Queen to heel, or even—God forbid!—to make an end of her, which the damp at Buckden had failed to do. It was sheer wickedness, what they were doing. Had Katherine not suffered enough?

———

"Have you heard?" young Lady Zouche trilled, seating herself at the dinner table with the other ladies and maids. They were all eating together today, since the Queen could not face food and had kept to her bedchamber with only her sister for company.

"Heard what?" Lady Rutland asked.

"You all know that the Duke of Suffolk was sent to Buckden to convey the Princess Dowager to Somersham. Well, according to my husband, who had it from a servant of Ambassador Chapuys, she locked herself in her chamber and refused to leave it. Neither threats nor entreaties could persuade her. The Duke was reduced to standing outside her door and pleading with her to come out. But, against all reason, she refused, daring him to take her by violence."

"She is the most obstinate woman that may be!" exclaimed Lady Boleyn, Anne's aunt.

Jane said nothing; the maids-of-honor did not join in the conversations of the ladies-in-waiting unless they were invited. But she had lost all appetite for her food.

Anne was full of plans for the great household that was being set up at Hatfield for the Princess. Elizabeth was to be conveyed there in great state that month.

"She is being carried by a roundabout route so that more people can see her," the Queen told her ladies. She did not seem upset at being parted from her daughter. To Jane, that seemed unnatural, but she knew it was no great matter for royalty or the aristocracy, whose children were raised by servants and wet nurses, and then sent away to some great household to learn manners and anything else that might befit them for a glorious future. It was the first step to preferment. Even so, Jane did not like the practice. She was profoundly grateful that she had been brought up in her family home, and had benefited from her mother's example. And by that yardstick, she had no great opinion of Anne as a mother. Anne had kept her child by her in the few weeks since she had borne her, and showed her off almost defiantly, but Jane had not seen her display much tender motherly affection.

She had been more preoccupied with wreaking vengeance on her stepdaughter, the Princess Mary. At Anne's insistence, Mary was to go to Hatfield too, to wait upon her half sister, Elizabeth. It shocked Jane that such humiliation should be heaped upon that unhappy girl, who had been forbidden to see her mother for nearly two years now. But Mary had made her support for Katherine clear, and now she was being punished for it.

"I marvel that the King allows it," Jane murmured to Margery one day, when, with Christmas nearly upon them, they were out in the park hunting for sprigs of holly. "To treat his own natural daughter thus!"

"He will have her bend to his will, come what may," Margery said, stamping her feet in the cold. "And he will deny the Queen nothing while she is carrying his child."

"I cannot bear to think how the Qu— the Princess Dowager will feel when she hears of it," Jane said. "My heart bleeds for them both."

"And mine," Margery agreed, pulling a branch off a holly bush. "But we must not think or speak of it."

Thanks to Ambassador Chapuys, it was known all around the court that a hostile crowd of farmers and yokels, armed with scythes and billhooks, had encircled Buckden and stood there, watching menacingly, lest the Duke of Suffolk attempt to take the good Queen by force. Jane silently cheered them, as she prepared for Christmas. Anne was determined that her first Yuletide as queen should be celebrated magnificently, and her women were busy making wreaths and garlands of holly, bay and mistletoe to decorate her apartments. Jane could not help comparing the warmth and festive splendor of the court with the bleakness of Buckden, where the poor Queen huddled behind her locked door. She could take no pleasure in the revelry, and she took even less when Mary Howard, now Duchess of Richmond, told them all how her father, the Duke of Norfolk, had threatened violence to the Princess Mary when she refused to go to Hatfield.

"He said that if she were his daughter, he would knock her head against the wall until it was as soft as a baked apple," she said, grimacing. "But I think he only said it to stay in good credit with the King. He was strict with us, but never cruel."

Yes, Jane thought, but how terrifying for poor Mary, being spoken to like that.

Margaret Douglas looked sad. "I served the Princess," she said. "She is a sweet lady and does not deserve to be unhappy." Jane wondered how Margaret must feel, serving the woman who was the cause of Mary's troubles. She too must be finding her loyalties cruelly divided. She guessed that Margaret was as grieved as she herself was when word spread that, on Christmas Day itself, Mary had been forced to go to Hatfield. But Margaret said nothing; she remained tight-lipped, though her eyes were bright with unshed tears. That is the trouble, Jane thought; we all stand by and do nothing. Even the feisty Margaret, the King's own niece, whom he loved like a daughter, dared not speak out.

She was pleased to see the Duke of Suffolk back at court before New Year, and to hear that Katherine had been left in peace at Buckden.

"Probably the King fears that the Emperor will declare war if his aunt is mistreated," Margery said, as they were getting undressed one night. Jane was aware that the Emperor was the most powerful sovereign in Christendom. Surely, she thought, as she got into bed, he would do something to protect the rights of the Queen and her daughter?

Chapter 12

1534

On New Year's Day, the traditional exchange of gifts took place in a glittering ceremony in the presence chamber. It was customary for every courtier and servant to give the King a present, and if they were lucky, they might receive one in return. Jane had agonized over what to offer his Grace. What would he like? More to the point, what could she afford? She had other people to buy for, and she had already sent home gifts—a leather belt for Father, some velvet slippers for Mother and a pretty silver ring for Dorothy. Above all, did she want to buy Henry a gift, after the way he had treated poor Queen Katherine? Yet what choice did she have? All the other maids-of-honor would be giving him something, and there was much competition to outdo each other.

In the end, she decided that a set of silk handkerchiefs embroidered by herself in gold thread would be most acceptable. The King would surely appreciate the trouble she had taken. And secretly she hoped he would find her embroidery pleasing.

Wearing their best gowns, the maids went in procession after the Queen to the royal apartments, where King Henry was enthroned beneath his canopy of estate, surrounded by a throng of gentlemen and courtiers. The court cupboards and buffets standing against the walls creaked under the weight of the plate and other gifts given to his Grace that morning, which would be left on display for all to see.

He rose and greeted his wife, then waited as her gift to him, a bulky shape covered with a rich cloth, was carried in and placed on a table. Anne herself removed the cloth to reveal an exquisite diamond-studded fountain encrusted with rubies and pearls. When she turned a handle, water sprayed from the nipples of three solid-gold naked nymphs.

The King's delight was plain. He kissed Anne heartily and thanked her, then signaled to her ladies to come forward in order of rank with their gifts, acknowledging each graciously, as a secretary listed them in a book. Soon it was Jane's turn. She curtseyed and held out her offerings. She could see at once that the King was impressed.

"It is gifts like these, made with such care, that mean the most," he said, smiling down at her. Then she remembered how cruelly he was treating his wife and daughter, and all her pleasure in his appreciation, and in the present he gave her in return—a small silver cup—was spoiled. She murmured her thanks and stepped back, glad to give place to Anne Saville.

Afterward, she found her brothers among the throng who were moving slowly around the vast chamber, admiring the King's gifts, and showed them her cup. They had similar ones.

"I have gifts for you too," she told them. "I will give them to you at the feast tonight."

"Harry is wishing he was at Wulfhall," Thomas told her.

Harry looked shamefaced. "I keep thinking of Father and Mother and Dorothy, just the three of them alone, and what it used to be like with all of us there making merry."

"I've been wishing I could be there too," Jane told him, "but our parents want us to be here at court, so take comfort in that."

Edward was saying little; he seemed preoccupied. When Thomas and Harry were drawn into conversation with a noisy group of young gentlemen, she asked him if all was well.

"Catherine has died," he told her. "I had a letter from the Prioress."

"I am sorry to hear that." Jane crossed herself. It had weighed on her conscience that she had not seen Catherine for so long. But Prioress Florence had effectively told her to stay away. Perhaps she should have insisted on visiting, even though it would have been difficult from the court. Should she have gone last year, after she had recovered from her illness?

"She is to be buried at the church at Horton, near Woodlands, with her forefathers," Edward told her. "Her mother will be chief mourner." He was not wearing black, but a rather splendid gown and doublet of a coppery color. His bitterness was still evident.

"Do the boys know?"

"Not yet. I will tell them when I go home." He paused. "Fortunately, they will have a new mother soon. Nan and I are to be married."

Jane tried to hide how unwelcome this news was. She had been glad to leave Nan behind in Katherine's household. Nan was too prideful, too domineering, and she would rule Edward with ease. Even after four years, he was too besotted to see it. As for her being a good stepmother to John and Ned, Jane would not count on it.

"Congratulations," she said, forcing a smile. "When is the wedding?"

"In March, at Rampton in Northamptonshire," Edward said. "Nan's family live in the manor house, and she returned there when the Princess Dowager's household was reduced last spring. Afterward, Father is allowing us to reside at Elvetham."

Jane wondered how Nan would get on with Mother. They were opposites in nearly every way. She could see why her father had placed Elvetham, his Hampshire property, at Edward's disposal. It meant that Edward would not have to live with Father; and Mother would not readily give place to any daughter-in-law, let alone a domineering one. Wulfhall was her domain.

"I am pleased for you," she said, and smiled at Edward.

"You should be," he replied. "I have been badly used."

Spring was approaching when Jane was chosen, with Lady Cobham, Lady Parker and Anne Parr, to attend the Queen when she visited the royal nursery at Hatfield. The baby Elizabeth was duly admired and petted, but it was clear that Anne was more preoccupied with planning apartments for the Prince she hoped to bear. She was in her fourth month now, and already they had loosened the laces on her bodice.

Jane heard her ask Lady Bryan where the Princess Mary was— although she called her the Lady Mary, for that her mother was not supposed to have been lawfully married to the King. Only Elizabeth might be called princess.

Lady Bryan ushered the Queen into the schoolroom and closed the door behind her. Then she set down the Princess Elizabeth on a quilted mat on the floor. She was a lively flame-haired charmer who was already trying to pull herself to her feet. Jane and the other maids knelt down and offered a silver rattle and a ball, both of which she tried to cram in her mouth. Her dark eyes were everywhere, full of curiosity. As she played with the baby, Jane wondered what was being said within. She feared for Mary, if she persisted in her defiance. She was so good, so loving and devout—her mother's daughter in every way.

The door burst open and Anne emerged like a tempest. A woman came hastening after her.

"Your Grace, she is not a bad girl at heart," she cried. "She is confused and frightened, and deeply grieved at being separated from her mother. And she is at a difficult age, when the young are wont to be rebellious. She should never have spoken to you like that, but she is her own worst enemy."

"I care not!" Anne stormed. "I'm washing my hands of her."

They left soon afterward. The Queen was clearly in no mood to waste time prolonging the pleasantries.

Jane fetched the cambric for the smocks that Anne had asked her maids to make for the poor and needy. Anne was already at work, sitting with her brother's wife, Lady Rochford, an edgy woman with a heart-shaped face and a barbed tongue, who rarely smiled. As the maids took their places, Jane noticed that Lady Rochford was looking especially downcast today.

They spoke of their work for a few minutes, then Anne summoned her musicians to entertain them as they sewed.

"You look sad, Lady Rochford," Lady Berkeley said suddenly.

Jane Rochford looked up, her eyes on Anne. "I received some sad news today," she said. "Bishop Fisher has been attainted in Parliament."

Anne glared at her. "He treasonously supported the Nun of Kent, who has herself been attainted for treasonously inciting people to oppose my marriage to the King. The woman is mad, but he encouraged her—and he will not recognize me as queen."

Jane had heard—who hadn't?—of the Holy Nun of Kent and her visions, and how she went about the county warning of what would happen if the King set aside his lawful wife. It was madness, but she was more to be pitied than condemned. No sane person would persist in such folly.

"The Bishop is a devout and good man," Lady Rochford countered, "and a great friend of my father; they share a love of learning, and they both served the King's grandmother, the Lady Margaret, who was herself a holy woman. My father was present when she died during a Mass celebrated by the Bishop. So perhaps your Grace can understand why I am shocked that such a saintly man has been attainted."

"He may be saintly, but he is misguided at best," Anne retorted, "and because he is saintly and people revere him and respect his opinions, he is dangerous. If we make an example of him, our enemies will be forced to see the error of their ways."

Lady Rochford had blenched. "How do you mean, make an example?"

"A spell in the Tower should be sufficient," Anne said coldly.

Jane doubted that would turn the good Bishop from his convictions, God save him. These were sad times indeed, when men like him were thrown into jail for standing up for what was right.

The King would brook no further defiance. That spring, Anne gathered her household in her presence chamber and announced that Parliament had passed an Act vesting the succession to the crown of England in his children by Queen Anne, and confirming the bastardy of his daughter Mary. Jane was deeply perturbed, because all the King's subjects, if so commanded, were to swear an oath acknowledging the King's supremacy, his lawful matrimony to Queen Anne, and the Princess Elizabeth as his legitimate heir. Those refusing to swear would be accounted guilty of abetting treason and sent to prison.

As they all left the room, Jane found she was trembling. What would she do when she herself was required to swear the oath, which would be required of everyone in royal service? It went against everything in which she believed. It was her beliefs, her sense of right and wrong, that gave her integrity and made her what she was. Could she deny all that by taking the oath? How could she bring herself to repudiate the sacred authority of the Holy Father in Rome, and all that he stood for? She could not perjure her immortal soul, or betray the true Queen and Princess. And yet what might happen to her if she refused it? She would be dismissed in disgrace, and imprisoned. Her brothers would fall from favor; her family might suffer. She could not do that to them.

Would it be possible to take the oath with reservations? She was terrified of going to prison. She could feel the walls closing in on her . . . As soon as she was free, she sought out her brothers and asked for advice, but they were all ready to swear the oath, and told her to set aside her concerns. She asked Bryan, who advised her to bend with the times. She asked Margery and Anne Parr and Lady Margaret Douglas.

They all said it was best to bow to the King's will.

But what was it that Scripture enjoined? "Render unto Caesar the things that are Caesar's, and unto God the things that are God's." This, surely, was a matter for God, for it was His Son who had instituted the Papacy and Holy Church. Dear God, she prayed ceaselessly, what shall I do?

God, speaking through the Pope, had pronounced sentence at last. The King's marriage to Queen Katherine was good and lawful, and he must put away the Lady Anne and restore his wife to her proper place.

Jane had heard the news from the King himself when he had come charging into the Queen's chamber like an enraged bull and shouted it out. Anne had been visibly shaken, and her hand had gone instinctively to her belly—and no wonder, for what would happen to her now?

But the King was adamant. "This Pope—this Bishop of Rome—shall learn that his sentence no longer carries any weight in England!" It chilled Jane to hear him. This momentous news was what she and all England had been waiting for, but now she feared that nothing would change.

"I will never forsake you," the King told Anne. Jane recalled Bryan saying that Henry had gone too far to turn back, but she wondered what would happen if the child Anne was carrying turned out to be another daughter.

On Easter Day, after Mass, Jane listened in horror as the Queen's chaplain informed his flock of the wickedness of Pope Clement, and exhorted all true subjects to pray every Sunday for King Henry VIII as being, next unto God, the Supreme Head of the Church, and Anne, his wife, and Elizabeth, their Princess.

The Queen's strident aunt, Lady Boleyn, whom Anne tolerated only because her beloved uncle James was her chancellor, took pleasure in telling her that there had been celebrations in several places in anticipation of the Princess Dowager's return to favor. Anne gave her a withering look.

The King's officers came to the Queen's apartments and all her servants lined up to take the oath. Jane took her place with the other
maids-of-honor, her heart racing. The previous evening, when she
had learned what would be required of her this day, she had gone to
the chaplain who usually shrove her, and blurted out, under the seal
of the confessional, all her fears. Was it a worse sin to follow her
conscience and disobey the King, with all the consequences that
would result, than to take the oath without meaning it?

There was a silence from behind the grille. "My child, the King's
Highness is Supreme Head of the Church, with authority over spiritual matters. What makes you so certain that your conscience is
leading you in the path of righteousness? Is your understanding
better than his?"

Jane was about to answer truthfully, but she paused. This priest
was a royal chaplain in the Queen's employ, and might be a reformer
like her. Could she trust him?

"It is because I fear that I have not perfectly understood that I
have come to you," she said carefully. "It is hard to change the beliefs and certainties you have held all your life." She did not add that
she was as sure of them as she was of her own existence, and that she
could never change them. Already she knew that this confession had
been a mistake.

"Indeed," the chaplain said. Then he surprised her. "Remember
that God hears what you are thinking, whereas humans hear only
what you say. Therefore, your duty as a Christian is to tell the truth
to God. Reserving some of that truth from the ears of human hearers
is a moral act if it serves a greater good."

It was as if the weight of the world had slid from her shoulders.
"Thank you, Father," she murmured.

He had given her a light penance for all her small venial sins, and
dismissed her. She left the chapel wondering if he himself had reservations about the oath.

Now she was next in line. She stepped forward, placed her hand on the Bible, fixed her mind on God and read aloud what was written on the document given to her: "I, Jane Seymour, swear to bear faith, truth and obedience to the King's Majesty, and to his heirs of the body of his most dear and entirely beloved lawful wife Queen Anne, begotten and to be begotten. I do utterly testify and declare in my conscience that the King's Highness is the only Supreme Governor of this realm, as well in all spiritual or ecclesiastical things as temporal; and that no foreign prince, person, prelate, state or potentate has, or ought to have, any jurisdiction within this realm. And therefore I do utterly renounce and forsake all such powers or authorities, and do promise that from henceforth I shall bear faith and true allegiance to the King's Highness, his heirs and lawful successors, so help me God."

It was done. She told herself she had made the right decision.

That afternoon, being off duty, she walked in the gardens, enjoying one of the first really warm days of the year. She had arranged to meet Edward. He was newly arrived back at court, and she wanted to hear about the wedding.

He was infinitely more cheerful than when she had last seen him, and gave her a brotherly hug. They strolled together between the flower beds.

"It was a fine occasion," he told her. "Father and Mother came with Dorothy and the boys, Lizzie sent a gift, and there were a whole host of Stanhope relations. Nan's parents had spared no expense. It was a lavish feast."

"And Nan? Did she make a beautiful bride?" Jane asked.

"Nan would look beautiful in anything," Edward said, still clearly besotted.

Jane smothered her resentment. "And has she settled in happily at Elvetham?"

"Yes," Edward said, but without conviction. "The truth is, she longs to be at court. Alas, it seems there is no place available. We asked Francis to speak for her, but he said his credit with Queen Anne is not what it was."

Jane was secretly relieved that Nan would not be joining the Queen's household. One shrew was enough! Anne's temper had been very uncertain lately.

"And the boys? Do they like her?"

Edward hesitated. "Alas, no. She has not taken to them, and they know it. I've left them at Wulfhall. She wants me to disinherit them."

It was exactly what Jane had feared. "But you will not, will you?"

"In faith, I do not know, Jane. Nan tells me it is the right thing to do, for their legitimacy is dubious. She says the way must be clear for our sons to inherit."

"But the law presumes that John and Ned are your lawful sons."

"Yes, but we know that they might not be. And Nan is adamant. So I have said I will think on the matter."

Jane reflected that, for all his ability, his learning and his air of authority, her brother was malleable and weak. Already, it seemed, the strong-willed Nan ruled him. But if it lay in her, Jane would not let those young boys be disinherited. They had suffered enough through the loss of their mother.

"Think very carefully," she enjoined. "Do what is just." He looked away.

They walked on toward the tennis courts. A burly black-haired man in a long black gown was coming toward them. Jane recognized the heavyset face and shrewd eyes of Master Cromwell, one of the most powerful men at court. Since the disgrace of the Cardinal, he had risen to become the King's chief adviser. He was a supporter of Anne, and Jane had seen him several times when he had been a guest in the Queen's apartments.

"Sir Edward." He gave a slight bow.

"Master Cromwell. May I present my sister Jane, who is maid-of-honor to the Queen?"

Cromwell bowed again and gave Jane a charming smile. She smiled back.

"May I congratulate you, Master Cromwell, on being appointed principal Secretary to the King?" Edward said.

"I thank you," Cromwell said. "It is a great honor, and I trust I will repay his Grace's trust." He nodded and walked on.

"There's no doubt of that," Edward muttered. "No one has a better grasp of affairs; even Cardinal Wolsey could not match Master Cromwell for genius. He has a finger in every pie. Privy Councillor, Chancellor of the Exchequer, Master of the Jewel House—and now principal Secretary!"

"He seemed affable," Jane said.

"Yes, he's of good cheer, gracious and generous, and keeps a convivial table. He has a host of admiring friends and clients. But I sense a ruthless pragmatism there; hard steel beneath the charm. They say that Master Cromwell is the King's ear and mind, and that his Grace entrusts to him the entire government of the kingdom."

Jane had heard talk of that. "Surely it is the King who rules?"

"Ah, but what he decides, Master Cromwell puts into effect. It was the King who decided to break with Rome, but it is Cromwell who is implementing the changes."

They descended the steps to the river and continued along the quayside. Further ahead, they saw the King emerge from his barge and enter the palace, with courtiers descending on him like locusts, each with his own petition.

"Do not underestimate Master Cromwell," Edward said. "The word is that his spies are everywhere."

"The Queen's ladies do not like him."

Edward shrugged. "That does not surprise me. The nobility disdain him for his humble origins, but they envy and fear him too."

"The Queen favors him. She calls him her man."

"Of course. They support the same causes—the royal supremacy, religious reform, the translation of the Bible."

They retraced their steps to the gardens, and Edward left Jane at the door to the Queen's apartments. "Say nothing of what we have discussed," he said.

"As if I needed telling." She smiled. "After all, there might be a spy hiding in a bush or behind a tapestry!"

The King's commissioners had gone out to every part of the realm to administer the new oath to all who held public office—and no doubt anyone whose loyalty was in question. Jane saw that the Queen was tense, lest there be reports of disaffection or demonstrations, but for the most part there were no protests.

Only a few refused to take the oath. It was no surprise that Bishop Fisher was among them, while Sir Thomas More, that good, wise man, had refused it twice. Both were now in the Tower, and there was much anger among the people, and fear too. Anne had been right: the punishment meted out to Fisher and More had silenced tongues that might have spoken in protest at what was happening. No longer did Jane feel she could confide her opinions or her deep-felt concerns to anyone, even her brothers or her friends. The court was a dangerous place, for who knew who might be listening?

But some were not as feeble as she. Her heart sang when she heard that Katherine had refused the oath—until it dawned on her what this might mean for her beloved former mistress. Every day she prayed that the King would not send Katherine to the Tower. By all reports, the good Queen was in indifferent health, and might not survive imprisonment—but that was what the King wanted, wasn't it? Had he not already immured her in a damp, unhealthy house?

After several weeks of worry, Jane began to hope that Katherine would not be punished severely. At the height of summer, the good Queen was sent further away from London, to Kimbolton Castle, which Lady Rutland said was a well-appointed house. Even if she was to live there under house arrest, she would be comfortable. That was something, and God willing, it would be beneficial to her health.

But the noose was tightening. Anne took the greatest of pleasure in informing her ladies that henceforth, anyone saying or writing anything to the prejudice or derogation of the lawful matrimony between her and the King, or his lawful heirs, would be guilty of high treason. "For which," she concluded triumphantly, "the penalty is death."

Jane kept her eyes downcast. It was folly to betray even by a shift of expression that you did not approve of the King's marriage or his supremacy. She did not have the courage of Fisher or More or Katherine. Anyway, what difference would the opinion of a country maid—for that was all she was, really—make to these momentous changes that England was being forced to suffer?

Anne was big with child now—and nervous. She spoke often of her conviction that it would be a boy, the living image of his father. The King came often to see her, and fussed over her as if she were made of glass. All his expectations were focused on her bearing him a son.

One warm July afternoon, Anne stood up and rubbed her back. "I think the Prince is on his way," she said, and gave her ladies a weak smile. "It's earlier than I expected. I should have taken to my chamber ere now."

"Your Grace should lie down," advised her old nurse, Mrs. Orchard.

"I would that my sister were here," Anne said. Mary Carey had gone home to be with her young children for the summer, and was tardy in returning. "And my mother. Ooh, there it is again!" She winced. "Yes, maybe I should go to bed, although last time the pains were easier to bear standing up. Ladies!"

All the ladies-in-waiting stood up and followed the Queen to her bedchamber, while Margaret Douglas hurried away to inform the King what was happening.

Jane and her fellow maids-of-honor stayed where they were. As unmarried women, it was not thought fit that they attend the birth. But they could hear Anne's cries increasing in volume and urgency as the afternoon wore on. The Lady Margaret sat with them, being unwed herself, and they all looked at each other nervously, knowing that one day, it might be one of them suffering the pangs of travail.

"The King said he would wait in his privy chamber for news," Margaret said, for the third time. No man, even a physician, would be allowed near the Queen while she was in labor, and Jane thought it a very wise rule, because what woman would want a man to see her at such a time?

The cries ceased. They looked at each other again. It had not been two hours! And then they heard a terrible wailing, like a vixen in distress. It was the Queen. Jane froze.

"Should we send for the King?" Margery asked nervously.

"I will go," the Lady Margaret said, and sped away. Still the howling and keening continued. They waited in trepidation, knowing that something dreadful had happened.

Anne's cries were subsiding when they heard footsteps approaching. The doors from the antechamber were flung open and an usher announced, "Make way for the King's Highness!"

"The King! The King!" cried the ladies within.

Hurriedly the maids curtseyed as Henry strode in, swept past them and himself opened the door of the bedchamber. There was a silence before it closed behind him.

Jane crossed herself. The child was lost or deformed, there could be no doubt of it. Detest Anne as she did, she could yet feel a sisterly pity for her. It was tragic for a woman to endure months of the discomforts of pregnancy, only to lose her babe at the end of it. It was so easy for the King—or any man—to demand sons; they did not have to undergo the bearing of them.

No one spoke, but no one was doing any sewing either. The midwife emerged carrying a little cloth bundle, and hastened away with it. The maids stared after her, horror in their eyes. And then the door opened and the King came out, his face ravaged, his blue eyes brimming with tears.

"You will not speak of this to anyone," he commanded. His voice broke and he sank into the Queen's empty chair. No one moved. And then Jane, plucking up courage from nowhere, stepped forward and placed her hand on his heaving shoulder. The others gaped; one did not presume to touch the Lord's Anointed unless he himself invited it. But the King was also a human being, and he was in deep distress.

"Take comfort, Sir," she said. "Her Grace bore a healthy princess last time. You are both of meet age. Other children will follow." She reached into her pocket, drew out her handkerchief and gave it to him, thanking God it was clean. He dabbed his eyes and mastered himself with a visible effort.

"Thank you, Mistress Jane," he murmured. "You have a kind heart."

With that, he stood up, bowed to them all and departed, taking her handkerchief with him.

Anne emerged from her confinement defeated and sunk in misery. She could take no pleasure in anything, mourning for the boy she had lost, and convinced that she had forfeited the King's love, for he came only rarely to see her, and when he did, it was with an air of injury. She poured out her heart to her women, over and over again, ranting and weeping, forgetting the dignity a queen ought to observe.

Her ladies tried to rally her. They exhorted her to make an effort to be her old self, the one who had captured the King's heart; she should be witty and charming and stimulating company. She tried, when Henry gave her the opportunity, but failed miserably. She was too mired in grief, anger and fear that he might do to her what he had done to Katherine.

Jane watched and listened with mixed feelings. She was at war with herself. Anne had stolen her mistress's husband, robbed her of the title of queen and been venomous toward Katherine and Mary; therefore it was to be expected that God would exact vengeance on her, which she fully deserved. And yet Jane could not but be moved by Anne's distress, her fear and the tragedy that had befallen her.

With the falling of autumn leaves came whispers that the King had a new mistress, who was said to be very beautiful. Jane wondered who it could be, glancing around the privy chamber at the ladies and

maids. Most were beautiful in their way. But then she came upon
Harry one day, enjoying his afternoon off in the bowling alley, and he
told her it was well known in the privy chamber that it was Joan
Ashley, a maid-of-honor who had joined the Queen's household the
previous winter. "This augurs well for the Princess Dowager and the
Lady Mary," he said, keeping his voice low as they stood to one side,
watching the courtiers competing. "Mistress Ashley is greatly attached to them. She may influence the King in their favor."

"I rejoice to hear it," Jane whispered, and began to take more
notice of Joan Ashley, who was fair-haired, demure, rather vacantly
pretty and only seventeen years old—the very last person she could
have imagined dallying with the King. But yes, Joan was mysteri-
ously absent on occasion, just as Anne herself had been all those
years ago. And soon the other ladies got wise to what was afoot, and
gossiped behind the Queen's back. Jane was convinced that Anne
knew what was going on. Certainly she did after the King openly
paid attention to Joan at a feast for some French envoys with everyone looking on.

That was the evening when Anne's sister, Mary, returned to court
with a high belly, with all eyes upon her, some shocked, some mali-
cious, some exultant that the Queen had been publicly discomfited.
Anne swept her out of the privy chamber, and the King stomped
after them. The next morning, Mary had gone.

Of course, the court was abuzz with speculation, delighted at this
whiff of scandal.

"Mary has made a most unfortunate marriage," Lady Rochford
sniffed, as the ladies crowded around her the next morning to find
out what had been going on, and the maids pricked up their ears to
listen. "He has no title, no money and nowhere to live; he is just a
soldier in the Calais garrison. But she loves him." She said the word
with scorn. It was no secret that her own marriage to George Boleyn
was unhappy, or that they despised each other.

The gossipmongers were in their element. The talk was all of
Mary Carey's misalliance or Joan Ashley. And then, one evening

when Anne was dining with the King, Lady Rochford entered the fray again.

"I hear that the King's sweetheart is over-free with her favors and that he has competition!" she said, looking pointedly at Joan. "He won't be very pleased about that."

Joan colored, but said nothing. Among themselves, they were keeping up the pretense that they did not know who the King's sweetheart was. But Jane still found it hard to believe that Joan was promiscuous.

Lady Rochford was warming to her theme. "And if the Queen learns of it, of course, there will be trouble. Instant dismissal, I'll warrant."

But it was Lady Rochford who got into trouble, and with the King himself, for making up calumnies about Mistress Ashley. Jane went into the dorter one day and found Joan sitting on her bed hugging herself, all alone. Tears were pouring down her cheeks.

"I had to come up here to calm myself," she said. "That vile woman has gone, thank God. She's been sent home. I think you know it was me she slandered."

"We all know," Jane said, sitting down next to her.

"It wasn't my fault," Joan blurted out. "When the King pursued me, who was I to gainsay him?"

Oh, weak little fool! Jane thought, then pulled herself up, wondering what she would have done had she been in the same situation. It would take great courage and resolve to say no, and this girl was little more than a child.

"She said some awful things about me," Joan said. "I don't know where she got the idea that I was wanton. The King has been my only lover. And now he has ended it!" She burst into fresh weeping.

Jane could well imagine whence had come the slurs on Joan's character. Who else would have had a burning desire sufficiently to tarnish her reputation so that the King spurned her? And Lady Rochford, with her love of intrigue, had been the Queen's willing tool. She comforted the girl as best she could.

"It is for the best," she said, "and now everyone will know that you have been unjustly slandered."

"But I had so hoped to do something to mitigate the plight of the good Queen and her daughter," Joan sobbed.

"Shh! Do not call her by that title here!" Jane hissed, even as she inwardly applauded the girl's motives. "That would get you into even more serious trouble. You can do no more. Put this behind you and act as if nothing has happened. The scandal will die down, I promise you."

Jane did her best to conceal her shock when, in November, news came that the Nun of Kent and her followers had been barbarously executed at Tyburn. She shuddered when she heard the women speaking of it; some had husbands or brothers who had been in the crowds that witnessed the savagery of their ends. The Nun herself had been lucky; she had been hanged until dead before being beheaded. But the five men who died with her, four of them priests, had suffered the horrors of a traitor's death. They had been drawn to their execution on hurdles, traitors being unfit to walk upon the earth, and hanged until they were nearly dead, then revived and stripped for the butchery to come: castration and disemboweling, followed by the drawing of their hearts from their bodies. If they were still conscious—and it was hard to imagine that anyone could survive such agonies and still be sentient—they would have seen their vital parts thrown into a fire before they suffered the merciful release of beheading. Even then, the carnage continued, with their bodies being quartered. The quarters would be displayed in public as a warning of the terrible fate that awaited those who defied the King. The Nun's head was now on a spike above London Bridge.

It was not just the cruelty of their deaths that appalled Jane, but the realization that the King had reached the point where he was ready to spill the blood of those who opposed him. It was a terrifying world she inhabited, and suddenly she wanted with all her heart to go home, to a place that was safe and normal, where the old ways

mattered and good people did not suffer for following their consciences, and where you could observe your faith in the time-
hallowed ways.

It was, she knew, a fantasy. Even Wulfhall was no longer such a
refuge. They were all bound by the new laws, Father James too. If
she had taken the veil at Amesbury, not even the authority of the
Prioress could have protected her. Nowhere, least of all this glittering, teeming court seething with intrigue, was safe.

Chapter 13

1535

It snowed in January, and the maids-of-honor enjoyed snowball fights in the Queen's privy garden, by the light of torches. One evening, Jane spied the King and Queen watching them from a window. Through the latticed panes they appeared to be smiling. When they went indoors, Henry had gone, and Anne was in a thoughtful mood. They were preparing her for bed when she told them what was on her mind.

"There have been reports of irregularities in the monasteries," she said, sitting straight-backed in her black satin nightgown as Jane combed her long dark hair. "Master Cromwell is to look into the matter. Naturally, his Grace and I are concerned to root out abuses within the Church."

No doubt you will do it thoroughly, Jane said to herself. Nothing is safe from your meddling. But she soon forgot the remark, and it was only much later that she remembered what Anne had said, and its significance. In fact, they were all far more interested in the King's amours.

Always there was speculation that he was pursuing one lady or another, but this time, there really were grounds for it. The young lady in question was the Queen's own cousin Madge Shelton, and Margaret Douglas reckoned that Anne had put her up to it.

"That would not surprise me," Lady Boleyn said. "Better to keep such things in the family, to avoid any malign influences." She looked pointedly at Joan Ashley. "There are some whose sympathies lie where they should not."

Jane looked down at her tambour, praying that no one had guessed where her own sympathies lay. Margery probably still shared them, but they did not speak of such things these days.

Anne was as friendly as ever to Madge, but it was easy to tell that she was miserable. When Frances de Vere, the young Countess of Surrey, was at last permitted to consummate her marriage to the Earl, and was full of the joys of the nuptial bed, Jane saw the Queen look away and bite her lip. But whatever had passed between the King and Madge Shelton, it did not last. And soon, other matters of greater moment seized everyone's attention.

More brave souls had refused the oath. They had not only denied the royal supremacy, but also protested their allegiance to the Pope. They were either courageous or foolhardy, Jane thought, remembering the fate of the Nun of Kent and her associates.

In May, the Prior of the London Charterhouse, two Carthusian priors and a monk of Syon were hanged, drawn and quartered at Tyburn, as joyfully—word went around—as bridegrooms going to their marriages.

Anne, stabbing her needle into her embroidery frame, was merciless. "They got what they deserved!" she snarled. "Maybe Bishop Fisher and Sir Thomas More will learn a lesson from their fate and swear the oath." She was determined that these two in particular would comply, and the King had the oath put to them once more in the Tower. Again they refused to take it.

"They are traitors and deserve death!" Anne raged. Her emotions were all over the place these days, veering from an almost desperate gaiety to seething anger. And then the reason for it became apparent. She was with child again.

The King's joy at the news did not mitigate his wrath at those who defied him. As Anne presided over celebratory feasts and revelry, ten Carthusians monks were chained to posts, standing upright, and left to die of starvation. Among them, Jane heard, was Sebastian Newdigate. She spared a thought for his sister, the redoubtable, devout Lady Dormer, who would be grieving deeply, even as she exulted that her saintly brother had been vouchsafed a martyr's death.

It was a terrible summer, full of horrors. In June, Bishop Fisher was condemned as a traitor and beheaded, and three more Carthusian monks were hanged, drawn and quartered at Tyburn. The execution of the Bishop was especially shocking, for he had just been made a cardinal by the Pope; it was a chance for the King to demonstrate his contempt for the Church of Rome.

With a prince in her belly—everyone said it would be a boy—Anne was invincible. Her every wish was the King's command. Now—and she made no secret of it—she was urging him to send Thomas More to the block. Jane had barely known More, and then only by sight, but she was aware of his great reputation as a scholar and a man of faith and integrity. He was a champion of the true faith, and his opinions counted, so respected was he throughout Christendom. Moreover, he had been the King's friend. Jane could not believe that Henry would ever put such a man to death.

She began seriously to think of resigning her post and going home.

She could always plead ill health; no one would guess the truth.

She arranged to meet her brothers down by the river, where they could be private, and told them what she was contemplating. Edward and Thomas thought it was folly. Only Harry was sympathetic.

"I wish I could go home too," he said, "but alas, my living is here, and as it was Bishop Gardiner who secured it for me, he would think me ungrateful if I returned to his service."

"Don't brood so much on things, Jane," Thomas advised. "Who cares who is queen or not, or about oaths and supremacy, so long as we can get on in the world?"

"There is such a thing as conscience," she reminded him. "Every day I have to serve the woman who supplanted my good mistress, and I do not like myself for it."

"We all have to dissemble in one way or another," Edward said. "I don't like her either, but queen she is, and we must make the best of it. If you go home, you can say goodbye to your chances of a good marriage and all that the court can offer. Nothing happens in Wiltshire."

"I said goodbye to a good marriage long ago," Jane retorted. "I'm twenty-seven, and no man has ever been seriously interested in me." She thought of William Dormer and winced, and of Sir Francis Bryan, and how some men were just not made for marrying.

"Stay, for my sake," Harry pleaded. "Your presence at court lightens my days."

"Aye," Thomas agreed. Edward nodded.

"Very well," she sighed. "But if things get any worse, I will think again."

By the third week in June, Anne's child had quickened and her gowns needed to be unlaced. She was feeling extraordinarily well, she said. It looked as if this pregnancy would have a successful outcome. But just three days after Fisher's execution, she stood up after dinner and screamed suddenly, pointing speechlessly at blood on the floor, great clots of it. Sickened at what she had seen, Jane ran for the physicians, as the other ladies leapt to assist their mistress. The world seemed to be running with blood these days, and somehow Anne's blood, which was no doubt that of her child also, seemed to be linked to that of the martyrs. For martyrs they were, Jane was in no doubt: they had died for a holy cause, and God was punishing Henry and Anne for it. Blood for blood: a life for those other lives.

It was all over very quickly. The Queen's child was stillborn. It had been a boy. Again the King came, weeping and perplexed, to commiserate with her. This time, though, he was tight-lipped when he left.

Anne made a quick recovery, but she appeared pale and wan when she emerged from her chamber, and more highly strung than ever. It did not help that the King now rarely came near her. Once he had done nothing but what pleased her, or was to her comfort. Now there were rumors aplenty that her star was about to fall.

Convinced that she needed to make greater efforts to win God's favor, she had all her ladies busier than ever, assisting her in good works. They made clothes, hemmed sheets, rode out with her when she dispensed alms, and made up baskets of food for the poor. Jane did not mind, for this was what a queen should be doing. Anne also believed that ridding the monasteries of corruption and having the Bible translated into English would be pleasing to the Almighty. Jane was weary of hearing how a reformer called Miles Coverdale was undertaking that task, and that his work was going to be dedicated to Anne and Henry. Jane and Margery had been ordered to make smocks for the poor.

They were sitting on a window seat in the Queen's chamber at Windsor, bored with their task and distracted by the love play between Lady Margaret Douglas and Lord Thomas Howard, who were cosily ensconced in an alcove, oblivious to everyone else.

"There is no hope for them," Margery murmured. "The Lady Margaret is third in line to the throne. One day the King will arrange a great marriage for her. Lord Thomas is a younger son with no fortune."

"She is in love with him," Jane said.

"She is a fool! Remember, Mary Carey was banished from court for marrying such a one."

"The King loves the Lady Margaret like a daughter. He would not banish her."

Margery shook her head. "He loved Mary Carey once," she whispered.

"What?" Jane was astounded.

Margery kept her voice low. "Yes, some years before he courted the Queen. Didn't you know? She bore him a daughter. Of course, it was all hushed up, and the child was passed off as her husband's, but several people in this household know about it, and I've been told that the little girl is the very image of the King."

Jane struggled to take it all in. "You are saying that the King had a child by the Queen's sister?"

Margery nodded, looking warily in the Queen's direction, but Anne was laughing with Sir Henry Norris and some other gentlemen.

"Then," Jane said slowly, "his marriage to the Queen must be as incestuous as his marriage to Queen Katherine."

"How do you mean?" Margery asked, her eyes widening.

Jane lowered her voice to a whisper. "The Queen was married to Prince Arthur before she married his brother, the King, but her first marriage was not consummated, so the Pope allowed her a second. The King had a child with Mary Carey before he married her sister. There was no dispensation. If the King's first marriage was invalid, as he says, then by the same token, his second must be too." And he is either stupid or a hypocrite, Jane thought—but of course she did not say it aloud.

Margery drew in her breath. "I never thought of it in that way. But for God's sake, Jane, never say that to anyone else. You know well it's treason to deny the King's marriage to Queen Anne."

Jane was staggered. To think that this Great Matter, all these religious changes, even the King's supremacy, had been built upon a lie. It did not matter whether the old Queen had been fully Prince Arthur's wife or not—Anne had been forbidden to Henry on account of his fruitful liaison with her sister. But people had died bloodily in the interests of perpetrating that lie. It was sheer wickedness. No wonder the King had tried to keep his affair with Mary Carey a secret. And no wonder God had denied him sons.

Again, Jane thought she should go home. She wanted no part in the whole evil business. In serving Anne as queen, she was effectively condoning it. She did not think her conscience could bear it any longer. She was almost resolved upon leaving Anne's service when it was announced that the court was shortly to go on a great progress to the West Country.

"We will be visiting Berkeley Castle," Anne told a delighted Lady Berkeley, "and staying at Wulfhall and Elvetham." She smiled at Jane. Those two visits would be a signal mark of royal favor toward the Seymours, but they put paid to Jane's plans. If she resigned her post now, it might jeopardize the royal visits to her family, and she would not for the world deprive her mother of the chance of entertaining the King. How proud she would be at the prospect!

Moreover, during the royal visit, she, Jane, would be able to seek the advice of her parents and Father James as to what she should do. At Wulfhall, her future would be decided.

They were plunged into a flurry of preparations. The Queen's rich gowns had to be folded and laid carefully in her great iron-bound traveling chests; her hoods went on wooden stands in boxes; her linen was packed in cloth bags. Jane herself had six gowns now with as many kirtles, and she decided she would need them all.

Finally, everything was ready: the royal furnishings, the rolled-up tapestries and carpets and the chests of plate were all stowed on carts or sumpter mules, and on 5 July, the King and Queen mounted their horses and the long procession set off for Reading. Jane, riding behind with Anne's other attendants, could see that his Grace was in an unusually good mood, laughing and jesting with Francis Bryan and his other gentlemen. It was well known that he enjoyed touring his realm and being seen by his subjects. They came running to hail him as he passed, with their shouts of praise and their grievances, and from time to time he would pause to talk to them.

At Reading Abbey, where Jane was one of the ladies who stood unobtrusively in attendance while the King and Queen dined, Henry was full of the good hunting he expected to have on the morrow. But there was an edginess to him that belied the holiday mood. It was clear from what he said that this progress was intended to drum up support for his religious reforms.

"I mean to honor both those who have supported me and those I need to win over with visits," he said, breaking apart the manchet bread that lay by his plate. "Fear not, Anne, we will have everyone on our side in the end."

Anne smiled. There was a new kindness between them. Maybe it was the prevailing holiday mood. Yet Jane could sense an uneasiness too, and it was not all on Anne's part.

The King went hunting on the way to Ewelme Palace, while the Queen traveled there by litter and the court made its leisurely, cumbersome progress through the pleasant Oxfordshire countryside. The next night they stayed at Abingdon Abbey, and it was while they were unpacking that Lady Boleyn came in and announced, with some satisfaction, that Sir Thomas More had been beheaded the day before.

Now Jane knew why the King had been on edge. He had known that while he was out hunting, his old friend would go to the block. She found herself trembling, shaken by the news. She bit her lip and kept her eyes downcast, then worried in case that gave offense. Lady Boleyn had an eagle eye, and if she thought that a lack of positive response to the news signified disapproval, she might pounce. Fortunately, several other ladies were saying that it served Sir Thomas right and he had only got what he deserved, so Jane's silence went unnoticed—she hoped.

She longed to be at Wulfhall, back with her family, and comforted herself with fantasies of staying there when the court moved on. But they would not be there for several weeks yet.

From Abingdon, they traveled to the ancient palace at Woodstock, and sojourned there for a time. Jane was intrigued by a local legend about Fair Rosamund. Anne Parr's mother had told her the tale, and she recounted it to the maids-of-honor as they took the air with the Queen in the great park that surrounded the palace.

"Fair Rosamund was the mistress of a king who lived long ago," she related. "He built a bower for her, where he could visit her and keep her safe from his evil Queen. But the Queen—I think her name was Eleanor—discovered where she was, so he built an intricate maze around the bower to prevent her from finding Rosamund. But Eleanor was so wily that she found out the way, and left a trail of thread so that she could make her escape afterward. She murdered Rosamund by giving her a poisoned cup to drink from. The King was so angry that he shut Eleanor up in a castle for as long as he lived."

"Weren't all those stone crosses built for Queen Eleanor by her husband after she died?" Mary Zouche asked.

"That was another Eleanor," Queen Anne told them. "Her husband loved her dearly, and was so grieved at her death that he built a cross everywhere her body rested on the way to Westminster Abbey. I've seen her tomb there." She looked wistful. Jane doubted that the King would ever be building crosses for Anne; he no longer loved her enough.

"Is the bower still here?" she asked.

"I don't think so," Anne Parr said. They returned to the palace and found the steward. He didn't know either, so they went searching, walking for what seemed like miles before they found the remains of a little stone house and cloister set in a ruined garden.

"This may be the place," the Queen said.

"It's eerie," Lady Rutland commented. Jane shivered. She felt it too. She could almost sense the shade of Rosamund crying out to be avenged. Maybe she really had been murdered here in this isolated spot.

"Poisoning is a horrible way to kill someone," Mary Norris said.

"Women use it because they don't have the strength of a man," Lady Boleyn answered.

Jane stole a glance at the Queen, who was gazing at what was left of the house, as if imagining the long hours Rosamund had spent alone there, waiting for her King, perhaps terrified that the Queen would find her. Anne's face gave nothing away. Jane thought of her threats against the Princess Mary. She had repeated them more than once, and there had been a time when they could have had no more import than someone saying, "I could kill you!" But in the wake of the summer's executions, Anne had grown more vehement in her hatred of Mary and Katherine. If she had persuaded the King to send More to the scaffold, as everyone believed, what else might she demand of him? Or would she stoop to more underhand means of ridding herself of her enemies? It was not such a far-fetched notion as some might think, Jane reflected, as she wandered around the ruins. She remembered people blaming Anne for that attempt to poison Bishop Fisher. The Bishop had been more vociferous than most in opposing the King's divorce. Certainly someone had wanted to silence him. Jane looked across at the Queen, who was making her way along the crumbling cloister, her black veil flapping in the breeze. Anne could be ruthless when provoked; and she had been unmoved when told of the suffering of the Carthusians.

Yet was she capable of murder? It worried Jane that she could not answer that question. But who knew the secrets of people's hearts?

They gathered in what had once been the garden. None of them wanted to linger for long, and Jane was glad when they got back to the palace.

From Woodstock they moved to Langley, and from there progressed to the pretty town of Winchcombe in Gloucestershire. Just beyond it lay the King's castle of Sudeley, where Henry and Anne were to stay for a week, with their households. Everyone else was accommodated at nearby Winchcombe Abbey.

The King spent a lot of the time at the abbey in conference with Master Secretary Cromwell, who had just arrived from London. Jane was concerned to hear the Queen telling her ladies that Cromwell had come to arrange for the King's commissioners to visit and report on all the religious houses in the West Country.

Disquieted though she was, Jane loved Sudeley. Its soaring royal apartments boasted magnificent chambers, tall windows and a fine banqueting hall, all set amid glorious countryside. She took pleasure in exploring its gardens and courts. But then Anne announced that, first thing on the morrow, she would be riding to Hailes Abbey, and all her officers, ladies and maids were to attend her.

"This must be an important visit," Margery muttered. "She means to make an impression."

"Hailes is a royal foundation," Anne said, "and we are going to see its famous relic, a vial of the Holy Blood of our Savior."

Jane had heard of it, of course, for Hailes Abbey was a renowned place of pilgrimage, but she had never visited, and was thrilled to have the chance to do so. To see the actual blood of Jesus, shed at Calvary and miraculously preserved over the centuries, would be a truly wonderful thing. Many miracles and cures had been attributed to it over the centuries, and even the very sight of it was said to put pilgrims in a blissful state of salvation.

It was not a long ride—about three or four miles—and presently they saw the great abbey in the distance. Waiting to receive the Queen's party were Abbot Stephen and a tall, hook-nosed cleric in severe black robes, whom Anne greeted affectionately. Behind them stood a group of officers wearing the King's badge.

A voice behind Jane murmured in her ear, "That's Hugh Latimer, a fiery reformist. The Queen's influence has just secured him the bishopric of Worcester."

She turned to find Sir Francis Bryan grinning at her.

"They're thick as thieves, those two," he said. "Hailes is within his diocese, so it is only meet that he come to attend the Queen." His tone was sarcastic. "And those black crows are Cromwell's men, sent to find fault with the monasteries."

Jane's eyes widened. "I thought—"

"Later," Bryan muttered. "We're going in."

Jane followed the Queen, troubled by what Bryan had said. Surely they could not be targeting the blessed abbey of Hailes?

As Abbot Stephen escorted them through the beautiful church to the ornate shrine where the precious Holy Blood was housed, Jane became aware of a certain tension between him, the Bishop and the King's officers.

The shrine stood at the center of the apse, with five chapels surrounding it. A long queue of pilgrims was waiting in the side aisle, behind a rope barrier guarded by a monk holding a wooden money box.

"They flock here every day, your Grace," the Abbot told Anne. "We have asked them to wait until you have worshipped at the shrine."

Anne looked about her at the mighty pillars, the stone carvings, the tiled floor. "It has brought you great wealth," she observed.

He nodded. "We charge pilgrims eighteen pence to see the Holy Blood. Some give more, of course. We are most fortunate to have such a miraculous relic."

Anne nodded. She and Bishop Latimer exchanged glances. "We shall all see the Holy Blood," she said.

"Gather round, good people." The Bishop addressed the waiting queue. The Abbot opened his mouth to protest, but Latimer held up a hand. "Father, you can surely forego your eighteen pence for one day, in the Queen's honor." The Abbot bowed, his protest quelled.

The people came forward, bringing the odor of unwashed bodies. Jane found herself pushed against a pillar, but she had a good view. She folded her hands in prayer, holding her breath in awe as the elderly monk in charge of the relic parted the red curtains that concealed it to reveal the golden shrine, encrusted with jewels, containing a vessel of green beryl, shaped like an orb and banded with silver. The monk leaned in and opened it, as a collective sigh was offered up by the crowd. Jane saw a glister of red, thick and viscous. She could not take her eyes off it. The very blood of the Lamb, given for her, and for all mankind. Her heart sang as her soul rejoiced. She was lifted up, transcendent, lost in a rapture she had never before experienced, not even when she'd had that long-ago dream that she thought had been a calling to the religious life. Maybe this was the calling, and she should heed it. It might have been God's purpose for her all along; it might be a miracle, worked by the Holy Blood.

Her thoughts were interrupted by the Queen's voice. "Pray, Father Abbot, remove the vessel from the shrine and let us see it more closely." There was a pause, then the Abbot nodded to the monk, who reached into the shrine again and brought out the relic. In the light, the blood appeared lighter, almost honey-colored.

Anne looked at the Bishop, then turned to the Abbot. "Father Abbot, my brother, Lord Rochford, who came to see you three days ago, has informed me that this is the blood of a duck, renewed regularly by this monk here. I was so shocked that I had to come and see it for myself."

Jane was not the only one who gasped aloud. "No!" a woman screamed.

Anne nodded at the old monk, who was looking very distressed. "Is this not what you told Lord Rochford and the King's commissioners over there?" she asked. He nodded, tears in his eyes. Jane was so appalled she did not know what to think. Could that long line of pilgrims, stretching back over the ages, have been hoodwinked, cheated?

The Abbot had gone pale. "Your Grace, I had no idea. Brother Thomas has been looking after the shrine for forty years, longer than I have been here." He turned to the monk. "Is this true?" he barked.

"Father, may I speak with you in private?" Brother Thomas quavered.

"Is it true?" the Abbot repeated.

"That is what I said." The old brother hung his head.

"Let's have no equivocation. Is this relic here the Holy Blood of Christ, or is it the blood of a duck?"

Jane held her breath as the monk struggled with himself. "It is the blood of a duck," he said at length, in a strangulated voice.

She did not, could not, believe it. They had put him up to it, put the words in his mouth. There was no end to their wickedness.

"So this is nothing but a vile fraud," Anne pronounced. "Good people, you have seen here today how the godly are fleeced and deceived. Father Abbot, I shall be informing the King of this trickery. In the meantime, you will remove this false relic."

The Abbot bowed his head. Behind her, Jane heard angry protests raised in the crowd.

Bishop Latimer's voice rang out. "Go home, all of you. Tell everyone what you have witnessed here today. Pray that true religion will flourish."

"Amen!" the Queen said.

As they rode back to Sudeley Castle, Jane was silent, thinking how Anne must have known beforehand what the monk had said to the King's commissioners, and planned to humiliate the Abbot publicly. And that monk had clearly been coerced into denying that the blood was Christ's. But how could such a holy and famous relic, revered for hundreds of years and seen by many wise and learned men, be a fake? She would not believe it. No one could have experienced such rapture as she had this day in the presence of the blood of a duck!

When they arrived at the castle, Sir Francis Bryan dismounted and handed her down from her saddle. "Well, that was timely!" he said, as they strolled back to the royal lodgings.

"How did they know it was a duck's blood?"

"They didn't. How could they? They just wanted to prove the relic a fake. It suits their purpose."

"So this is what you meant about the commissioners being sent to find fault with the monasteries?"

"It is."

Anne Parr and Mary Zouche had gone ahead to attend the Queen, so Jane leaned for a moment against the wall of the great banqueting hall. From the kitchens below, the smell of roasting meats wafted up. It would soon be dinner time.

Bryan lingered. "There is talk of the King closing down some of the smaller houses. Master Cromwell has been telling him that he will make him the richest sovereign on earth. The Church has untold wealth. It will be plundered to fill the empty treasury."

Jane had rarely felt so angry. "But that's wicked! They are God's houses."

Bryan shrugged. "Master Cromwell would have us all believe that they are either inefficient or too worldly, or that they are hot-beds of popery or bawdy houses—saving your presence, Jane. The commissioners have their instructions."

Jane was twisting her rings in distress. "I cannot believe that they would even contemplate such a thing. The King is a devout man. How can he sanction it?"

"The King will find a moral pretext for anything he wants to do, Jane. Believe me, I know him. Once the royal conscience has been outraged, it must be satisfied."

"What of the consciences of the rest of us? There are several reli-gious houses near where I live, and no scandal has ever touched them. Those who serve God in them are good people. They do no ill." Then she remembered the Prioress of Amesbury and realized that was not quite true.

Bryan gave her a long look. "You're an innocent, Jane, and that's why people love you. Mark me, you'll see this come to pass, and maybe, in time, the bigger houses will go too."

"But that's the worst kind of sacrilege. What of all those poor souls with vocations?"

"I think the plan is to pension them off or find places for them in larger monasteries."

"The people will not stand for it!"

"The people, may I remind you, sweet Jane, have stood for a good deal—for the putting away of the Princess Dowager, the disinherit-ing of her daughter, the King's supremacy, the Act of Succession, the executions of good men—and Anne Boleyn, whom they have to thank for the loss of their lucrative trade with the Empire. I hardly think they will rise now, for the sake of monks and nuns."

"All the same, it is utterly wrong and wicked," Jane insisted. "The world, I think, has gone mad."

In bed that night, in a room at the top of Sudeley's tower, she lay wakeful. What Bryan had told her was preying heavily on her mind.

It had brought home to her what she most disliked about the court—the sheer absence of morality, humanity and rightness. All was self-seeking and riding roughshod over the sensibilities and values of others. And it was dangerous to disagree or show any disapproval. Add to that the gossip, the backbiting, the intrigues and the perils of being at the center of events—and you could see the abyss opening up before you. Here, in the shires, news came late and sometimes garbled. Her father had rarely discussed political matters with his womenfolk. Jane had been amazed to discover that she had the ability to grasp them; she had grown up thinking it beyond her. But increasingly she wished she had remained in blissful ignorance.

In August, having traveled via Tewkesbury and Gloucester, they stayed for six days at Berkeley Castle, as guests of Lord and Lady Berkeley, who took great pleasure in showing them all the grim little cell where the deposed Edward II had been imprisoned and murdered two centuries before, on the orders of his wife and her lover.

The King frowned. "For that, they both deserved the severest punishment," he said sternly. "For a queen to betray and murder her lord the King is the worst kind of treason."

"Regrettably she died in her bed," Lord Berkeley told him. "But her lover was hanged."

"He deserved worse," Henry declared, "especially considering what was done to the King."

Jane winced as Lord Berkeley told everyone how Edward had been killed by a red-hot spit thrust into his bowels. "People say that his screams echoed beyond the castle walls," he added darkly. After that, Jane was eager to leave Berkeley; she was convinced that the sufferings of poor King Edward were imprinted on its ancient stones, and fearful lest his soul might not be at rest.

But it was not the murdered King's ghost that prowled the turrets and staircases at Berkeley by night. Coming up from the hall one evening, having retrieved a pearl the Queen had lost from her hood, Jane passed through the chapel, which was lit only by the lamp next to the altar; and there, in the shadows, she saw Thomas Howard and Margaret Douglas in a passionate embrace, oblivious to anything but themselves. She hurried on, thinking how unwise it was of Margaret to involve herself with a man who could offer her nothing. The King was hardly likely to approve their marriage, even if the Queen wanted it. She wondered if Anne knew how close the couple had become. But Anne was preoccupied, simmering after hearing from Master Cromwell that the monks of Hailes had restored their relic to its shrine, where the faithful were still flocking to see it.

Thornbury Castle, their next stop, seemed to be haunted too. It had belonged to the Duke of Buckingham, a distant cousin of the King, who had plotted to seize the throne and been beheaded some years before. All his property had been forfeited to the Crown. The Duke had left Thornbury unfinished, but enough had been completed to afford luxurious lodgings for the King and Queen and their attendants. The maids were accommodated in an attic up a steep stair, but the views from high up were glorious. Yet Jane could not stop thinking about the man who had planned the castle on such a dangerously grand and pretentious scale, how he had laid out the lovely gardens—and how he had met his end. How could he have borne to leave behind his beautiful house? Or had he never really left it? Was his spirit still here? There seemed to be shadows in every corner.

Two of them were Margaret Douglas and Thomas Howard, whom Jane glimpsed stealing into the Duchess of Richmond's chamber. The door closed. As she passed, Jane heard the Duchess's voice from within, and was relieved to know that the couple were not alone. It was no surprise that Mary Howard was encouraging the match: Thomas was her uncle.

The progress afforded many opportunities for dalliance. Margaret and Thomas were not the only ones. Maybe it was the prevailing holiday mood, or the sense of freedom that travel induced, which gave impetus to snatched kisses and secret meetings. Jane heard the other maids whispering about their flirtations in the dorter at night. Her brother Thomas made no secret of his conquests. But no one had come seeking her favors, and she doubted they ever would.

Jane loved Acton Court, where Sir Nicholas Poyntz had built a fine new wing especially for the King's visit. She marveled with everyone else at the antick friezes and murals in the royal lodgings—and that Sir Nicholas had gone to such trouble and expense for a visit that was to last for only two days. Henry and Anne were suitably impressed, not only by Sir Nicholas's extravagance, but also by his overt loyalty, which to him was doubtless worth the outlay.

From there, the court moved on to Little Sodbury, and soon they were entering Wiltshire, to Jane's joy and relief. Soon she would be home!

On the fourth day of September, they rode eastward from Bromham Hall to Wulfhall, where the King was to stay for three nights. Jane could hardly contain her excitement. She could only imagine what her mother was feeling.

Chapter 14

1535

The hunting horns had sounded their arrival, and Father and Mother were waiting in the Great Court, with their entire household gathered behind them. The cobbled enclosure was packed with men and horses, for the local gentry had come to pay their respects to their sovereign and make up the party for tomorrow's hunt. Dorothy, who had blossomed into prettiness, waited beside her. Edward, having ridden ahead with Thomas and Harry, was standing, tall and elegant, beside Nan, whose low-bodiced gown was of tawny silk. With them was John, who had shot up in height and was now quite the young man at sixteen, and Ned, a robust eight-year-old, nearly jumping up and down with excitement. Sir John, resplendent in scarlet, with a sprightliness belying his sixty years, had a hand firmly clamped on the boy's shoulder. Mother was stately in plumcolored damask and sable, with a startling yellow kirtle and matching hood. They looked so pleased and proud to be welcoming their King. You would never have thought that infidelity and scandal had nearly riven this family apart. But that had been eight years ago now. The wounds had healed, Jane hoped, and poor Catherine had atoned with her sanity and her early death.

"Welcome, Sir, to our humble home," Father beamed, approaching his sovereign's splendid black charger and handing the stirrup cup to the King. "It is a great honor to have your Graces here."

He knelt, and everyone else made deep reverences. The King and Queen dismounted. King Henry dominated the scene, seeming to dwarf every other man present. His doublet and gown were of green damask slashed with cloth of gold and aglitter with gems. Costly furs lined his sleeves and an enormous ruby was pinned to his black velvet bonnet. His fingers were laden with rings. It struck Jane that he was still a handsome man, for all that he must be forty-four now; there was no gray in his red-gold hair, and his fair skin was tanned after weeks of hunting in the sunshine. Truly he was the epitome of a king—and he was smiling broadly.

"Sir John, we are well pleased to see you," he declared, raising Father and clapping him on the back. "And Lady Seymour, we have heard that you keep a table unrivaled in Wiltshire!" He took Mother's hand and kissed it jovially, and she blushed a deep red from her bosom to her hairline.

"It is a pleasure to entertain your Graces," she stuttered. Then she caught sight of Jane and smiled a welcome.

Jane joined her family as the King greeted them. Henry's gaze rested a second too long on Nan's comely bosom, and he had Dorothy blushing when he praised her sweet face. Then he was standing in front of Jane. Instinctively she lowered her head, not wishing to appear bold, but he raised her chin with his finger and she was forced to look into those piercing blue eyes. She could read nothing in them but kingly interest.

"Mistress Jane." He smiled. "Sir John, we shall have to find a husband for this fair young lady."

Jane winced. But the King was passing on. She curtseyed low to the Queen, who had followed in his wake.

"Yes, we shall," Anne said, inclining her head graciously.

Bryan, who was among the crowd of courtiers clustering behind her, winked at Jane. She smiled, appreciating his attempt at commiseration. She did not want a husband of Anne Boleyn's choosing.

"Let me show your Graces to the lodging we have prepared for you," Father said.

It would be the master bedchamber, Jane knew. They had no finer one.

Joining the other maids who had been deputed to attend the Queen, she watched her father proudly showing the King the long gallery he had had built, and the chapel, which had been new-hung with tapestries in his Grace's honor. Everything looked polished and gleaming. She saw Anne glance about her and smirk at Lady Worcester. Let her sneer, Jane thought. Her ancestors were in trade! She would not let her mistress's snobbery mar her pleasure in being back home at her beloved Wulfhall.

As Sir John left the bedchamber, having ensured that his royal guests had everything they could possibly need, he gave Jane a warm hug. "It is good to see you, daughter," he said, "and it is good to have my family all together."

"It is good." Jane kissed him, feeling a pang for Margery and Anthony. Still there were yawning empty spaces here.

The Queen desired to rest, so Jane hurried down to the kitchen to be clasped in her mother's distracted embrace. Orderly chaos reigned, as servants scurried hither and thither to prepare for tonight's feast, and the bench was laden with an array of tempting dishes and puddings.

"Your father has gone to the barn, where we're accommodating the King's retinue," Mother said, mopping her brow. "This visit is a great honor, but I'm fit to drop, and God only knows what it's all costing. Dorothy, fetch some parsley from the garden." She turned to the scullion, sweating by the turnspit. "Look sharp, boy—how is that meat doing? Where's Nan? That girl is useless, too grand to get her hands floury. Jane, will you help me with this pie?" A bowl of peeled apples stood ready, and a dish of custard. Jane fetched an apron and tied it over her traveling gown.

Soon they were up to their elbows in flour and sugar, making pastries and even a subtlety in the shape of a crown; it was as if the honor of their house rested upon their culinary skill. Mother was determined that the King, in days to come, should have cause to look kindly upon the Seymours, if only because he had eaten so well under their roof.

Now was not the time for a conversation about Jane's future—and if things continued in this vein, there would not be time in the three days ahead of them. Again she toyed with the idea of staying behind when the court moved on.

John came in from the courtyard with Ned in tow. "Grandfather says do you want to serve wine in the garden before the feast?"

"Tell him yes," Mother replied.

"How are you faring, boys?" Jane asked. "I think of you often."

"We are in good health, but our tutor works us too hard at our lessons." John grimaced.

"They're doing very well!" Mother said.

"And your new stepmother?" Jane asked.

"She doesn't like us," John muttered.

"Of course she does," Mother put in, rolling out the pastry as if her life depended on it. "It's just her manner." But her eyes met Jane's and she made a face.

When Mother was satisfied that all was ready, they went upstairs to change for the feast, and Jane put on one of her fine black court gowns, leaving her fair hair loose. Taking advantage of the lull while the royal guests took their ease, and grateful that Margery and Mary Norris were attending the Queen, she made for the chapel.

Father James was lighting the candles, as dusk was falling. He looked up with pleasure at the sight of her, and she knelt for his blessing, thinking sadly that he had grown old in the years she had been away.

"And how is life at court?" he asked.

"Difficult, Father," she told him. "I do not know how much longer I can endure this conflict of loyalties, or what is being done to those who oppose the King. My heart bleeds for the old Queen."

Father James looked nervously about him, as if Master Cromwell might be concealed beneath the wall hanging. He lowered his voice. "Have a care, Jane. It is now treason to refer to her by that title."

"There is no one here, and as far as I am concerned, Queen she is, and Queen she will be until she dies. I can never take Anne Boleyn for Queen in my heart." Months of pent-up resentment were clamoring for a voice.

The old priest crossed himself. "We who hold to the true ways must keep silence," he whispered. "I am no Thomas More and you are no Nun of Kent. Like most people, I took the oath, for I do not seek martyrdom. Yet it grieved me to acknowledge the King's supremacy and his heirs by Queen Anne, who can be no true wife to him while Katherine lives. It stuck like bitter gall in my throat. But today we must not dwell on such matters. It will not do to present a gloomy countenance to the King. I find myself, despite everything, liking him."

"I like him too," Jane admitted, "even as I hate him for the evils he has wrought. It is this Anne who has led him from the true path, with her wiles and her cozening. She has used religion as a weapon in her greediness for advancement, and now we must all believe as she does. It is wrong, so wrong!"

"Calm yourself, my child." Father James touched her sleeve. "It will soon be time for the feast. For this evening, let us enjoy ourselves. I am sure God wishes it. He is aware of the moral burden you bear."

Seated at the center of the high table in the Broad Chamber, the King was very merry.

"I rejoice to hear there's good hunting to be had hereabouts!" he beamed, helping himself to another custard tart. "These are excellent, Lady Seymour." Mother's cup was quite clearly full. He had lavished praise on every dish that had been placed before him, and from the way he tucked in, it was unfeigned.

"We're in for a good season, Sir," Father said. "We'll ride out tomorrow and show your Grace some lively sport. But I fear that's all that's lively in these parts. This year's harvest has been ruined due to the bad weather."

"So I heard," the King replied, frowning. "I trust things will improve soon."

Father was watching Jane, who was sitting further along the table between Harry and Father James. He turned to the Queen. "Your Grace, I trust that Jane is giving satisfaction."

Anne nodded and smiled at Jane. "I have no complaints." Praise indeed!

"You have a fine family," Henry told Mother, looking wistful.

"Ten I've borne, Sir, and buried four, God rest them." She swallowed. "We count ourselves lucky."

"Oh, to be a country gentleman and have a houseful of children and a good table like this!" The King sighed.

"Your Grace is made for greater things," Sir John said.

"Aye, indeed," Henry replied. "But it's men like you country gentlemen who are the backbone of this realm. New men, who serve me well, and support my reforms."

Anne smiled again. Beside her, Jane sensed Father James stiffening. She was also aware that although the King was a jovial guest and had made them all feel at ease in his presence, beneath the bonhomie he was not a happy man. She had seen his eyes resting on her brothers, and imagined him thinking that, at his time of life, he should have healthy sons like them. Had the good Queen given him such, she would be sitting here at his side today, not languishing in Kimbolton Castle.

After the dishes had been cleared away, hippocras was served, and the King lingered at the high table discussing local politics with Sir John, while the other men sat around playing at dice or cards. Anne thanked Mother and retired to bed. Clearly she had no desire to enjoy a domestic tête-à-tête with her, and anyway, poor Mother was fighting to stay awake. Even the King noticed, and bade her go upstairs, thanking her heartily for the excellent feast she had served.

"You're a lucky man, Sir John, having such a good woman to wife," he said, watching her depart. "Meek, well bred and, above all, fruitful." He sighed. "You are blessed indeed."

"I know, Sir," Father said, and there was a world of meaning in his voice. The King looked at him speculatively, but said nothing. After a pause, he spoke of the price of corn.

Dorothy followed her mother to bed, and Bryan came over to join Jane, as she sat alone near the fire, working on an embroidered pillow cover that was to be a gift to the King. "A splendid evening," he said, regarding her with his single, sardonic eye. "But his Grace is not happy."

"I hope it is nothing we have done?" Jane asked, alarmed.

"No." Bryan lowered his voice. "It's that accursed woman. Did you hear her on the way here, railing at him like a fishwife?"

Jane glanced nervously at the King, but he was deep in conversation with her father. "And did she have good cause for complaint?"

"Oh, yes." Bryan grimaced. "The Emperor wants the Lady Mary restored to the succession. Needless to say, Madam Anne was up in arms about it. I think she fears the King will do it, and he may have to, if she bears him no son. Elizabeth is too young to rule." He leaned closer, so that their foreheads were almost touching. "But how can she get a son if the King does not go near her?"

Jane shook her head almost imperceptibly. This was dangerous talk. "You are wrong, Sir Francis. The King has visited her bed several times on this progress, to my knowledge."

"Ah," he replied, and winked. "I wonder what she did to lure him back."

Jane shrugged. "What she usually does, I suppose. She still has some kind of hold on him."

"She knows well how to rule him!"

"Yet he does not always heed her. He can be quite brutal sometimes."

Jane became aware that people were looking at them, and realized that they might be mistaking sedition for dalliance. She sat up.

"I must go," she told Bryan. "We have attracted attention. People may be drawing the wrong conclusions."

He looked uncomfortable. "I like you well, Jane, but you must know that I am not the marrying sort. I don't have it in me to stay faithful, and my life is at court. You deserve better."

She forced a smile. If some rich heiress loomed into view, he would doubtless find that he was the marrying sort after all. *I like you well.* It had sounded like a death knell. More and more, she was becoming convinced that she was unlovable; that there was something in her that men found repellent.

"I will always be your friend," Bryan assured her.

She rose. "I must go to bed."

"I have offended you," he said, looking genuinely concerned. He stood too. "Listen, Jane. I am trying to do the honorable thing. I'd bed you now, if I could—but I would not dishonor you by suggesting it."

Jane felt her cheeks flush, and hoped that anyone watching might think it was the heat from the fire. "I hope, Sir Francis, that one day, some truly honorable man will refrain from hinting that I'm good for bedding but not for marrying." She curtseyed to the King and walked away. Bryan caught up with her just outside the door.

"I did not mean that, Jane! It's that I'm not good enough to marry you."

"Oh, Francis, stop tying yourself in knots!" she cried, exasperated, and left him standing there.

Jane slipped outside. It had been hot and smoky in the Broad Chamber, and she was greatly agitated. She needed some air. It was peaceful in My Old Lady's Garden, and the scent of late roses hung delicately in the nighttime breeze. The moon was a perfect crescent, and Jane gazed at it for a time, trying to make out a face, as she had done in childhood. She could not leave this beloved place. She would not go with the court when it left Wulfhall. She did not want a marriage arranged for her, and she could not bear the prospect of other men rejecting her. She would plead illness. In a way, that would not be an untruth, for she was sick to her soul of living a lie and of all the petty deceptions she was forced to practice. She could not compromise her conscience anymore. She would stay here and help Mother and be a companion to her parents as they aged, and then, when her time was done, she would lie with her siblings in the church at Bedwyn Magna.

Her decision made, she felt a calmness descend on her. Forget . Bryan, she told herself. You don't really want him. He'd be no good to you.

She sat down on her favorite bench, enjoying the peacefulness of the garden. In the woods nearby, an owl hooted. And then, just as she was thinking that she ought to get some sleep, for tomorrow would be another busy day, and they must be up early to prepare a good breakfast before the royal party departed on the hunt, she heard a door click. Someone was approaching, taking their time. She turned around, and there was the King, all alone, emerging from behind the hedge, looking as if he had the cares of the world on his shoulders.

Instantly she was on her feet, curtseying. "Your Grace!"

"Mistress Jane!" He looked startled.

"I was just taking the air, Sir. It was hot indoors. But I will leave you in peace now."

"Stay." Their eyes met, and she could see that he was troubled.

"You were kind to me once," he said, sitting down heavily on the bench. "I have not forgotten that. It was a simple gesture, but I knew it was well meant. People do not always treat kings like human beings." He smiled at her. "Sit with me awhile. Don't look so afraid. I don't bite."

She sat down, smoothing her silk skirts. It was growing chilly. "What a beautiful garden," the King observed, looking around him in the moonlight. "So peaceful. There's a sense of timelessness here.

This is the true England; its essence does not lie in courts or cities. Do you understand what I mean, Jane?"

"I think I do, Sir." She nodded. It seemed so unreal, sitting alone with the King, whom never she had seen unattended. "I love it here."

"You prefer it to the court." It was a statement, not a question.

"It is my home, Sir," she said, wondering what he would say if she told him she was planning to leave the Queen's service.

"It is rare to find someone who leans toward a quiet life," he said. "Sir Thomas More was one such. I envied him his happy home, his family and his leisure to study."

Jane was amazed that the King would even mention More to her. *Yet you took him away from all that and shut him up in the Tower!* she wanted to say.

He swallowed. "I loved and respected him."

Jane remained silent, not sure that she was supposed to express an opinion.

"The world knows who was the cause of his death!" he blurted out, his eyes steely. She was in no doubt as to whom he was referring, but whatever he said now, he had signed the death warrant. He was responsible.

She looked up at him. There were tears in his eyes.

"He defied me," he said. "He was my friend, but he defied me, and people think the worse of me for it."

Jane found her voice. "I am very sorry for your Grace," she said quietly.

He drew in his breath, closing his eyes. "So am I, Jane, so am I. All I have done, all that blood spilt, has been for nothing, for still I have no son to carry on my great work of reformation."

"Her Grace may yet bear you a son," Jane ventured.

"I pray for it daily! The Emperor demands that I restore the Lady Mary to the succession, but he's a fool. Set a woman upon the throne, and if she marries a subject, there will be jealousies and factions warring at court. Let her marry a foreign prince, and what then of

England? This great realm reduced to a dominion of France or
Spain! Loyal, true-born Englishmen must shrink from the prospect.
I could weep when I think of it." He looked to be on the brink of it
now. "Jane, I need a son!"

"I pray for it daily too, Sir," she declared. He nodded. She realized
he was too choked to speak.

They sat there for a while in silence. She wondered if he had regretted his outburst. It seemed extraordinary that he had confided
in her; it was probably a measure of how distressed he was. Maybe
he had gone too far with his reforms to turn back, and now repented
of it. He seemed to be at war with his conscience over More. He
could not see that his problems were all of his own making. He
could have married his daughter Mary to some great prince and
got a grandson to succeed him. But no: he had put away his devoted wife and taken, in her place, a shrew. In his blind infatuation,
he had not seen things clearly. Now he was reaping what he had
sown. And others, Anne and Cromwell among them, had made him
cruel and ruthless, pushing him ever further along the path to
damnation—and no one dared speak out in protest.

"Your family has lived here a long time," the King said suddenly,
mastering himself.

"Yes, Sir. Seymours were living in Savernake Forest back in the
fourteenth century."

Henry nodded. "I like your father and mother. They are genuine
people. That is a rare thing."

"I know, Sir," Jane agreed. She shivered. It really was cold now.
Autumn was almost upon them.

"I have kept you out too long," the King said, rising to his feet.
"Forgive me. There is a gentleness in you that induces confidences,
Jane."

Jane had risen too. "We all need someone to talk to sometimes,
Sir."

"Would that I could talk to you more often," Henry said, looking
down at her intently. There was something in his gaze that arrested
her.

No man had ever looked at her like that before. She was stunned.

"I-I am always ready to listen, Sir," she stammered, and began walking toward the house before realizing that she should have waited for him to precede her. But she had been desperate to get indoors and be alone with her thoughts. At the door, she dropped a quick curtsey, not meeting his eyes, for she did not want to see again what she had seen there earlier.

"Good night, Jane," he said, in that high, mellow voice.

"Good night, Sir," she murmured, and fled upstairs.

She could not sleep. Having crept into bed and squeezed herself into the narrow space left by Dorothy, she lay there going over and over what had happened in the garden. It had been innocent, on the face of it; anyone overhearing the conversation would not have detected any amorous interest on the King's part. And yet for all her inexperience, she had recognized the desire she had seen in his eyes for what it was.

Of course, she would never permit him any liberties. It was notorious that he tired of his mistresses all too quickly, and no decent man wanted another's leavings, even the King's. No, she would not let him spoil her for marriage. Besides, he was married himself. Not that she would have any qualms about betraying Anne, for Anne was not, and never could be, his lawful wife. But Katherine, his true Queen, lived, and Jane would never be disloyal to her. Her dearest wish was that the King would return to her.

She could not deny that he had a certain physical attraction. But she must not forget that he stood perilously close to eternal damnation, and that he had the blood of good men on his hands. Look how cruelly he had treated his adoring wife and child! No sane woman would want to entangle herself with such a man.

But she, Jane, had seen the vulnerable soul beneath the kingly magnificence, had perceived the doubts and fears behind the air of assurance. He did have a conscience; he was not beyond redemption. Suppose—she was really running away with herself here, for after all, it had but been one meaningful look—suppose God intended for her, someone quiet, humble and insignificant, to bring the King back into the fold and set him on the road to salvation? "The meek shall inherit the earth," Christ had said.

Nonsense! she told herself. And yet the King, the Lord's Anointed, who had been invested at his coronation with a wisdom denied to ordinary mortals, had unburdened himself to her, a simple woman. He had spoken of great matters, trusting in her understanding. And if he ever did so again, she might have an opportunity to do some good on behalf of those she loved—although he might expect more than gratitude in return! And how could she refuse him?

By the time the sky began to lighten, she was resolved, strengthened. She would warn Father and Mother that she would be in moral danger if she returned to court. Then they would surely back her decision to stay at Wulfhall.

The next morning, the King gave no indication that Jane meant any more to him than any other person under Wulfhall's roof, and she was glad. She had inferred too much from what she thought she had seen the night before.

They rode out to the forest for a day of excellent hunting, leaving the Queen behind. It was her time of the month, and she was in a foul mood because her hopes of a pregnancy had been dashed. Complaining of cramps, she stayed in bed, with Mother torn between fussing over her and giving orders for the loading of the vast repast that was to be eaten in the open air.

Three hinds had been downed by the time they gathered in a clearing to enjoy it. The King ate heartily, wolfing down the game pasties that Mother had heard he loved, and entertaining the company with tales of previous hunts.

"You mean the Abbess actually warned your Grace off her land?" Bryan asked, gaping.

"The good woman did not know who I was," Henry chuckled. "You should have seen her face when I told her!"

"He's enjoying himself," Edward murmured in Jane's ear.

"So are they," Nan said, nodding in the direction of Sir Henry Norris, who was stealing a kiss from Madge Shelton. She leaned across and took a slice of venison pie. "The word is that he wants to wed her."

"He's unhappy," Jane said.

"Who, Norris?" Nan asked.

"No, the King." Jane kept her voice low.

"He has much to be unhappy about," Edward said. "There is talk that the Emperor may invade England to secure the rights of the Lady Mary."

"No!" Jane cried. War, with all its horrors, was not the right way forward.

"At present he is fighting the Turks on his eastern border, but he seems set for a victory. The King is looking to his coastal defenses. They were discussing it at Bromham."

"Do you think the Emperor really will come?"

Edward shrugged. He did not look too alarmed.

"He won't come on the Princess Dowager's account," Nan said. "She is too old and ill. He'll not fight for her now."

"But he will for the Lady Mary!"

"Possibly." Edward refilled their goblets with the good wine Mother had provided. "Remember, not once in all those years of the Great Matter did he bestir himself. Why should he do so now? Don't worry, sister. Look, the King is rising. We should attend him."

They all got to their feet and went to fetch their horses. The sun was high in the sky. There would be good sport this afternoon, but Jane was aware that the clouds of war were threatening, and felt afraid.

That evening there was another feast for the King and Queen and the family in the Broad Chamber. Everyone else was enjoying roasted meats and ale in the great barn. Jane was surprised when, after a roasted swan redressed in its plumage had been presented and duly admired, Father turned to the King.

"Your Grace, Clement Smith, a gentleman of Essex, has asked for the hand of my daughter Dorothy," he revealed. "His brother is employed in the office of the Lord Treasurer's Remembrancer. He himself is a widower. He is a friend of my son Harry, who suggested the match."

Dorothy was listening wide-eyed, but Jane nearly choked on her meat. Was another younger sister to be married ahead of her? What must it be like to be married at sixteen and have your whole future settled? Lizzie had been only thirteen . . . Again Jane wondered why there had been offers for her sisters but not for her. It must be obvious to the King that no man had asked for her. Her cheeks burned with the shame of it.

The King beamed at Harry. "It will be a good match for her. I approve." He smiled down at Dorothy. "But Sir John, why is it that your eldest daughter, the fair Jane here, is not yet betrothed? It seems strange that her younger sisters have been married first." His gaze rested on Jane, who was wishing that a hole would open up in the floor and swallow her.

"It does seem strange," Queen Anne echoed, her tone suggesting that it was anything but.

Sir John frowned. "When Jane was young, Sir, she wanted to be a nun. A foolish girlish fancy, you understand. But we let her test her vocation, and she decided that the religious life was not for her. Thus for some time I was not seeking a husband for her. Then Sir Francis Bryan tried to arrange a match with Sir Robert Dormer's son, but for reasons of her own, Lady Dormer was against it. Since then . . . May I speak freely?"

It was infuriating being discussed like this, as if she were not present. *I'm here!* Jane wanted to say. *I can speak for myself.* But she remained dutifully mute, wondering what Father was going to say.

The King, helping himself to another plateful of meat, signaled for Sir John to go on.

"Sir, I have been led to believe by Sir Francis Bryan that he might offer for Jane's hand."

Jane could keep silent no longer. "Father, you have been led astray. He has made it quite plain to me that he does not intend to wed. He is a friend, nothing more. And I would not have him, for I believe he can make no woman happy."

They were all staring at her—Father and Edward in dismay, Mother as if a mouse had roared, Thomas with a grin, Anne with astonishment and the King with blank admiration. "Well said, Mistress Jane," he complimented her. "Exactly my own view of Sir Francis. Likable he may be, but he is a rogue. Well, we shall see if we can find a good match for you. I am sure there is some fine fellow who will appreciate so fair and spirited a wife." His eyes rested upon her for a second longer than was comfortable.

On the third and last day of the visit, when the King was receiving local petitioners in the Broad Chamber and the Queen, making no secret of her boredom, was resting with a book, Jane escaped to My Young Lady's Garden to weed the herb bed she had herself planted some years before. She was kneeling there, wearing her everyday dress of dove-gray worsted, her long hair rippling around her shoulders, and her task was nearly completed, when she became aware of a pair of feet in white hose and splayed velvet shoes standing next to her. Only one person she knew wore such shoes. It was the King.

She jumped up, smoothing her skirts, and curtseyed.

"Good morning, Mistress Jane," Henry said, breathing in the sharp, heady scent of the garden. "It's good to be out of doors enjoying this fine weather. I doubt it will last much longer."

"It is unseasonably warm, Sir," she agreed.

"You do your own weeding?" he asked.

"Yes, Sir. I made this bed myself. It contains herbs my mother needs for her still room."

"It is very neat. I imagine your mother makes physick as well as she cooks." He crouched down on his haunches, examining the plants and pulling off a leaf here and there. "Marjoram—good for headaches. I make it up myself with sage and lavender," he murmured. "And chamomile is efficacious for the stomach. And feverfew is essential." As he worked his way around the plot, Jane was surprised at the extent of his knowledge.

At length, he stood up. "I've always had an interest in medicine," he told her. "I like to make my own remedies. My physicians don't always approve, but they dare not say so!"

Jane showed him the other beds of herbs, and then she noticed, out of the corner of her eye, that they were being watched. It was the Queen, standing at the window above. She could not make out Anne's face, as the sun was on the panes, but she worried what her mistress was making of her being all alone here with the King. Not that they were doing anything amiss, but Anne was always suspicious of Henry paying any attention to other ladies. God knew, she had cause!

Jane was saved by the dinner bell. The King gave her his arm, and they strolled into the house as his attendants came running. At table, he was full of the garden and the herbs he had seen, and Anne seemed slowly to relax.

That evening, after a delicious supper, the King and Queen remained at the high table, playing cards with Jane's parents. Jane and Dorothy fetched their tambours, and sat sewing as they chatted with Lady Worcester and Lady Zouche by the fireside. The game ended, and the King strode across. He leaned over Jane's chair.

"That's beautiful embroidery," he said. "I like the way you have rendered the unicorn. What is it for?"

Jane looked up. She saw the Queen watching them. "A pillow cover, Sir," she said, and smiled. "It was meant to be a secret. I am making it for you, Sir. I have the other one, with the lion, here."

He smiled down at her. "A pretty conceit, and a fine gift." He bent low by her ear. "When I rest my head on these at night, I will think of you, sweet Jane."

Oh, no! Just because she was plain and no man had wanted her, he must not think that she was fair game. "Sir, you might think on my mother too, for she made the one with the lion."

He stood up. "I will thank her," he said, a touch stiffly.

Jane was relieved when he had gone to bed. This was the last opportunity she would have to speak to her family about her future, for the King was to depart in the morning. They would all see him again when he visited Edward and Nan at Elvetham. It was another great honor, and her parents and brothers were bursting with pride, for everyone would see, if they had not realized it before, that the Seymours were a family of standing, and upcoming in the world. But the visit was only to be a short one, and there probably would be no opportunities for serious conversations.

Father and Mother were about to retire, but she stayed them. "Please sit down. There is something I must tell you," she said. "When the court goes tomorrow, I am remaining here. I have had my fill of it."

They all stared at her as if she were mad.

"No," Father said. "To leave your post, which was bought dearly for you, and which many would covet, is utter folly. It would give great offense and lose us the King's favor, for which we have all worked so hard, especially these three days."

"You're a fool," Edward snapped. "The very idea! It would rebound on me and Thomas too."

"She has taken leave of her senses," Nan sniffed.

"Why on earth would you want to rusticate down here when you could be at court?" Thomas asked, incredulous.

"Don't even think of it!" Mother ordered.

"Jane, why have you had your fill of the court?" Harry asked gently. "Is it because of Sir Francis Bryan?"

Jane turned gratefully to him, thinking that he was the kindest and most understanding of her brothers. She was near to tears. "Partly," she said. "But the life there is so superficial, there is much envy and viciousness, and I am endlessly having to compromise my principles. These changes we are seeing now"—she lowered her voice—"I cannot countenance them. I serve a woman who pretends to be queen. It goes against everything I believe in to call her such."

"Enough!" Father growled. "That is treason, and I'll not have it uttered under my roof, especially with the King sleeping upstairs. If you were overheard, they would hang you! Keep your scruples to yourself."

Jane was in despair. "There is something else," she whispered. "The King has been showing an interest in me. I do not—"

"The *King* is interested in you?" Edward's face lit up. Father's eyes gleamed and Thomas cried, "By God, Jane, you're a clever girl! That is the most marvelous news."

"What? It's marvelous that he wants to seduce me?"

"It is! But you won't let him, of course."

"Of course I won't!" Jane's blood was up. "What do you take me for?"

"Where are your brains, sister?" Edward retorted. "Our sovereign lord wanted to seduce Anne Boleyn, and now she is Queen. Even before that, there was nothing he would not do for her. Think about it."

"Edward, you are being ridiculous!" Jane snapped. "The King has seduced many young ladies in his time, and all but one have been discarded."

"And that one said no to him," Nan put in.

"*I* will say no to him, if it comes to it," Jane declared, "but that he might make me Queen is stretching the imagination much too far."

Sir John banged the table.

"Hush," Mother hissed. "You'll waken everyone!"

"Jane, heed me," Father said. "Our family has striven for preferment for a long time. Little by little, we have gained an office here, a privilege there. It took long enough for your brothers to get places in the Privy Chamber. Now we have a golden opportunity to make our way in the world, and you can help us to do it. While the King is interested in you—and *I* am not suggesting that he might make you Queen, or that you should compromise your virtue—we can all prosper and gain influence. Do you understand me?"

Jane nodded reluctantly. She did not like the idea of being used, but was that not what fathers normally did? They used their children for their profit and advantage. The chances of the King wanting her, plain Jane Seymour, as his queen were as remote as the likelihood of her marrying the Pope! And while he was courting her—if, indeed, he really was—she might do some good, to her family and to others.

Edward, however, was on a mission, speaking urgently in low tones. She had always known that he was ambitious. "Anne Boleyn got a crown because the old Queen failed to bear the King a son," he said. "Now she herself has failed in the same respect. Think about it. When you go again on progress tomorrow, Jane—as you will do, and we'll have no arguments about it—you will encourage the King's advances, but keep your distance. It is your privilege."

"Aye," said Thomas. "His Grace well knows the rules of courtly love; he has played the game often enough. Treat him as your servant, and remain tantalizingly out of his reach. He does not value what he obtains easily."

"Above all, preserve your virtue," Mother enjoined. "He cannot but admire that in you. Tell him you are saving yourself for when the right husband comes along. See if he takes the hint."

Jane rounded on them. "I can't believe what I'm hearing. You are all running away with yourselves. A light flirtation and you have a crown on my head. He will probably forget all about it, for I have already put him off."

"That's a good start," Edward said, smiling.

Chapter 15

1535

Why, she asked herself, should she feel so unsettled, nay, excited, by the King's attentions? She had seen and spoken with him many times before this visit. It was being singled out for special attention, she supposed. It had not been what he said so much as the look in his eyes when he said it, a look that had conveyed unmistakable interest.

It had meant nothing, she told herself firmly, as she rode away with the court the next morning. It had been a passing interest, born of the moment. He had been toying with her, to see if she was willing, and she had made it clear that she was not. Probably he was offended. He had not spoken to her since, or given any sign that he was aware of her presence in the crowded courtyard. But Queen Anne had been cool to her.

It had been a wrench to leave Wulfhall, and she wished desperately that she could have stayed, but that had been impossible in the face of her family's protests. Even Mother, who should have understood why Jane wanted to be at home, had been dazzled by the ludicrous suggestion that her daughter might wear a crown. No one had even thought to ask Jane if she actually wanted the King's attentions. They had simply taken it for granted, and assumed she had it in her to win his love. Heavens, she would hardly know where to start, even if she had the opportunity! She was so distracted by her family's reactions that she had found it hard to focus on how she herself felt about the King. He was undeniably attractive, and in his overpowering presence she had seen how easy it would be to succumb to his charm. It was the gentlemanly courtesy that drew you in, and his extraordinary condescension, that innate common touch that put people at their ease.

Entangling herself with him would be fraught with perils. She knew of the cruelties of which he was capable. He had already discarded one wife and been repeatedly unfaithful to her supplanter. She had witnessed the sufferings of both. It was so easy to be beguiled by his majesty and his magnetism; and it would be utterly foolhardy. Moreover, he was married and out of bounds. In the long view, he was unlikely to want to go through the complications of another divorce. He could offer her nothing but the loss of her good reputation. That decided her. Whatever her family said or wanted, she would not encourage the King's advances.

It was October, and the countryside was a blaze of greens, golds and reds when the court came to Winchester. The King and Queen were in a merry mood, and rode out hawking daily. Gowned in very fine rose damask, Jane was present in Winchester Cathedral when three bishops were consecrated. Queen Anne looked on triumphantly, and no wonder, for they were reformists whom she herself had advanced. If she had her way, Jane knew, the Church of England would be run entirely by men like these. It was a bleak prospect.

Afterward, there was a reception in the great hall of the castle. Jane was captivated by the sight of King Arthur's Round Table, which was hanging up high on the wall. It was painted in bright colors, with the names of the famous knights in fine script around the circumference, and the picture of Arthur enthroned at the top.

"It's magnificent, is it not, Mistress Jane?" said a voice behind her, and she turned to see the King smiling down at her.

"It is, your Grace," she agreed, grateful she had not offended him over the pillow cover, but praying that this was mere friendliness.

"That's my father up there," he told her. "He had himself painted as King Arthur when the table was restored. We Tudors are descended from Arthur, you know. My brother was born here in Winchester. He was called after him. When I was a boy, I fancied myself as one of the Knights of the Round Table."

"Your Grace has read Sir Thomas Malory's *Le Morte d'Arthur*? I loved it as a child."

Henry's smile broadened. "It was one of my favorite books too. We have an original copy in the royal library. I will show it to you, if you wish."

"That is very kind, Sir." She noticed that people were looking at them, and glanced around to see if the Queen was watching. Fortunately Anne was deep in conversation with *her* bishops, as she liked to call them. The King led Jane to a table where wines and sweetmeats had been laid out. She noticed that he was limping slightly.

"You must try these," he said, himself serving her with a plate of gilded shortbread. "They are delicious." He handed it to her with a slight bow.

"I thank your Grace," she said.

"In that gown, and being so fair, you are a perfect English rose," he murmured. There was a pause, a heartbeat.

"Sir, you flatter me!" She felt herself blushing.

"To me you are fair—and beautiful." He leaned in as he said it.

"Sir, it is well known that the Queen's beauty eclipses that of all other ladies. I could not presume to compare with her."

His smile vanished. "Jane, you have little idea of what makes a woman beautiful to men. It is not just a matter of face and form. If her heart is pure, it shines forth. If she be modest and virtuous, yet kindly withal, it is written in her face. But if she is shrewish, complaining and unkind, be she never so lovely, she cannot be beautiful."

She was astounded at his candor, and did not know how to answer. She was aware of her brother Edward watching them with ill-concealed interest.

She was saved by the King's sharp intake of breath. "Forgive me, Jane, I must sit down. This old wound in my leg is paining me. Do help yourself to some wine." He bowed and left her, making slowly for his chair of estate on the dais. She curtseyed to his back, glad that he had not prolonged the conversation. She did not want people thinking that he was singling her out. She knew how fast gossip spread throughout the court.

But Thomas had noticed. "Good work, sister," he murmured, as he sidled past her. She glared after him.

That evening, there was a feast in honor of the bishops, and afterward Anne's ladies and some of the King's gentlemen gathered in her chamber. Jane settled down to a game of cards with Margery, Thomas and a pleasant young knight, chestnut-haired and handsome, called Francis Weston, a great favorite of both the King and Queen. A man was sitting in the window, playing the virginals. Jane had seen him several times, when he had come from the King's privy chamber to play for Anne. He was dark, like a gypsy, and always finely dressed for a humble musician; she thought him affected in his manner, as if he was trying too hard to ape his betters, but there could be no denying that he was gifted at music.

As Jane waited for Weston to lay down his cards, she noticed the musician's eyes on the Queen; he seemed entranced by her. Clearly Anne was aware of it too, and none too pleased about it, for after a short while, she abruptly dismissed him.

"Smeaton is getting above himself," Weston observed. "He thinks himself in love with the Queen. Of course, we all are, but she would never condescend to notice one so lowly."

"He is insufferably proud," Thomas snorted. "And he hates Norris."

"Why?" Jane asked.

"Norris loves the Queen, always has," Weston told her. Of course, it was no secret. "He's going to marry Madge Shelton, but his heart isn't in it."

"Do you think the King knows how Norris feels about the Queen?" Jane wanted to know. She had seen Henry show warmth and affection to Norris, who was widely liked and respected.

"I doubt it! But"—he kept his voice low—"does the Queen love Norris?"

"No." Jane was certain. "She loves to flirt with the gentlemen, but that's as far as it goes. If she likes anyone, it is her brother." Lord Rochford was a frequent visitor to the Queen's chamber, and was jesting with her now. "They are very close."

"But she loves the King more," Weston told her.

"Of course," she agreed. "Your turn, I think."

The next day, the court rode out to the hunt, but the kill was interrupted by the arrival of a party of horsemen led by Master Cromwell. Jane watched as he dismounted and knelt before the King. As he spoke, Henry's face darkened, and Anne, standing beside him in a green velvet riding habit, looked stricken.

Sir Francis Bryan came over to where Jane waited with some of the Queen's attendants. "The Emperor has crushed the Turks," he said. "They can no longer threaten the eastern reaches of the Empire. That means he is free to make war on England."

The ladies gawped at each other, openmouthed. Jane felt a tremor of fear.

"Do you think it will come to war?" she asked.

"We must pray it will not," Bryan said. "All England's might could not resist the forces of the Emperor."

The King and Queen put on brave faces. As the progress wended its way through Hampshire, they made merry and gave every appearance of being happy together.

At Portsmouth, the King took especial pride in reviewing his ships and ensuring that they were all fitted out for battle at sea. Jane stood on the deck of the *Mary Rose*, watching him give orders for the reinforcement of her structure. She was a fine ship, well armed with cannon, and adorned with colorful banners that flapped in the wind. The King was in his element. While Anne was talking to the young Duke of Richmond, who was Lord High Admiral, Henry came over to the ladies and invited them to join him for a tour of the ship.

"Mistress Jane, we will lead," he said, taking her hand. Jane was startled; she could sense the others' eyes on her as the King escorted them across the decks and took them high up on the forecastle. She struggled with her skirts on the narrow stairs, and tried to raise enthusiasm for the marvels that he was so enthusiastically pointing out; she was embarrassed at being singled out above the other ladies. Now tongues would wag.

As she stood at the bow, looking out on the harbor and the sea beyond, the King was suddenly beside her, leaning on the ledge.

"I love the sea," he said. "It's in my blood."

"Your Grace has a fine navy," she told him. If she kept him talking about ships, he might not progress to less welcome matters.

"I've built it up over many years," he told her. "We're an island nation, and our strength is in our sea power. This is the greatest navy England has ever had." He turned to her. There was no mistaking the hunger in his eyes. "Jane, you must know that I would be your servant. Can we talk, properly, in private, rather than my contriving to speak to you when all eyes are upon me?"

What should she say to him? He had taken her unawares. Her mind raced. "Sir," she said humbly, "forgive me, but it would not be proper for us to meet in private."

"Then walk with me in the garden at Portchester tonight. Bring a maid with you and ask her to follow at a discreet distance. Tell her we are discussing your marriage, and that of your sister."

How could she refuse him? He was the King. "Yes, Sir," she said.

"Nine o'clock," he told her, and turned back to the others. "Time to leave, ladies," he called.

She realized she was on the brink of wading into deep water. She was
tremulous, but resolved. If the King showed her favor, she would
take it for an occasion to sue for kinder treatment for the true Queen
and the Princess. But whatever he asked of her, she would not compromise her honor.

After supper, she beckoned to Anne Parr, and they slipped away,
creeping through the old royal palace within Portchester Castle, and
descending the spiral stairs to the bailey. Below the King's windows
in the great chamber range lay a garden, surrounded by a high hedge
of box. Jane paused at the gate.

"Stay here," she bade Anne. "If I call, come at once."

She opened the gate, and there was the King, striding along the
path between the flower beds.

"Jane!" he said, and executed a courtly bow as she made her obeisance. "Thank you for coming. You must think it bold of me to
presume on your kindness, but since we talked at Wulfhall, I have
not been able to banish you from my mind." He reached for her
hand.

"Sir," she said, drawing it away and summoning up her courage,
"I am sorry, but there cannot be more than friendship between us.
Your Grace has a wife. I would not betray her." She was not speaking of Anne, but he could not know that. She had barely given Anne
a thought.

Henry looked distressed. "I no longer love her," he said. "You
know how she is. It's like living in the midst of a tempest. In you, I
find such quietness, such peace, that I think I am in Heaven."

"But Sir, you hardly know me."

His eyes were intent. "I know enough to be convinced that with
you I could be a happy, contented man, at peace with myself. I no
longer want a wife who flirts with others and mocks me in what
passes for wit. I want a loving woman with an even and constant
temper. I like your gentleness and I admire your virtue, for I know
that neither is feigned. Anne is too bold; she must have her own
way. I do not think you are like that, Jane. You are kind."

"Sir, I do not know what to say to you," Jane said, her mind reeling. "I would be a friend to you, of course. It is my duty and my pleasure. But I cannot be more."

He seized both her hands before she could stop him, gripping them fiercely. "Help me, Jane! I have so many cares. The Emperor may invade us. If I am killed in a war, there will be no one to succeed me and defend this realm. England will be plunged into civil strife. I cannot sleep for thinking of it. And then there is Anne. It seems she cannot give me a son. Is God frowning on this marriage too? Two boys she's lost. I am forty-four! I have no time to waste in hoping and praying."

"I know that the Queen prays daily for a son," Jane said. "It is her dearest wish, and she grieves for the loss of those babies as much as your Grace does."

"Help me, Jane," Henry pleaded, squeezing her hands.

She tried to pull away. "How can I help you?"

"Show me some kindness, I pray! Consent to be my acknowledged mistress."

"Your leman, you mean!" She pulled away from him, shocked.

"No, sweet Jane! If you could love me in your heart, I would place you above all others and serve you only."

"And what would the Queen say about that? My position would be untenable."

Henry's gaze hardened. "I hardly think that she, who pushed her own cousin in my path, could object."

Jane drew her cloak more tightly around her. The night air was chilly. "Your Grace should know that she frets constantly lest you are unfaithful. If she encouraged Madge Shelton, it was because she knew that Madge would not intrigue against her."

"But you would not do that either." The pleading look was back in the King's eyes.

"No, Sir. But I cannot be your mistress. I am sensible of the great honor you are doing me, but when I have a husband, I intend to go to him with my reputation unstained."

"Jane!" Henry's voice shook. To her amazement and horror, he sank, rather stiffly, to one knee. "I cannot let you go. See, I am beseeching you, not as your King, but as a humble suitor."

She could not believe it. The King of England was abasing himself before her. She had not dreamed that his feelings for her went so deep. Or was it lust that drove him? She realized she knew too little of men.

"Sir, I beg of you, give me time to consider," she gasped.

He stood up and clasped her hands again, gently this time. "Then I may hope?"

"I cannot say." She lowered her eyes. "I should go, Sir. I might be missed."

Henry extended a finger and tilted her chin upward. His eyes were tender, yearning. "Good night, then, sweet Jane. I pray you will think kindly on me."

She curtseyed and hastened away.

"Well, are you to have a husband?" Anne Parr asked, following in her wake.

"I have no idea!" she answered.

At the Vyne, Sir William Sandys's fine house in Hampshire, Jane did her best to avoid the King, but he sought her out quite openly, urging her to give him an answer. She feared she would soon be running out of reasons for not arriving at a decision. One day she hid from him in the antechamber to the chapel, but he came after her, so she stole into the chapel itself. It was dark in there, with long hangings covering the windows. The door opened, and Jane slipped behind the thick material, praying he could not see her.

"Jane?" he whispered. She said nothing. She did not want to be alone with him.

He pulled aside the hanging and light streamed in. "I knew you were here," he said, grinning, and then he looked up and his smile faded. Jane turned and saw above her the most beautiful stained-glass image of a young woman kneeling. She drew in her breath. It was Queen Katherine.

Henry frowned. He pulled aside the next curtain, and there, behind the altar, was his younger self at prayer.

"What a glorious window that is, Sir," Jane ventured.

Henry nodded. "I remember these being made. My sister Margaret is in the other one. I can see why Sandys did not want me to see them. He's loyal, my Lord Chamberlain, there's no doubt of it, but he's also a connoisseur of art. It would break his heart to destroy this one." He gestured at the figure of Katherine.

"Maybe it should be altered to look like the Queen," she suggested.

"No, maybe it should not," Henry said brusquely. "We will let Sir William keep his hidden treasure. And now, Jane, will you walk with me in the gallery?"

Edward and Nan had ridden ahead to see that all was ready to receive the King at Elvetham. As the royal procession approached along the avenue through the hunting park, Jane took pleasure in the sight of the stately old house ahead of them, and again, family considerations warred with her conscience. They could have so much more if she consented to become the King's mistress. She felt she owed that to them. But it would come at a price, and the price would be her honor. She was not rich; it was all she had. And Queen Katherine had been betrayed one time too many already. She knew what her decision must be.

After Edward had welcomed the King and Queen, and they had been taken to their lodging, he and Nan showed Jane and the rest of the family around the house. Nan, still bitter about being kept from the court, was diverting herself by carrying out extensive improvements. To hear her talk, everything at Wulfhall was outdated and undesirable, although she did not say so in as many words. Jane was angry, hurt on her parents' behalf. They had welcomed Nan into their home, given her the finest it had to offer, and she was repaying them by belittling it all. Edward seemed unaware of the unfavorable comparisons that were being drawn. He too was eager to make Elvetham a show house, a place to which the King would want to return, and which would be the envy of neighbors for miles around.

When the tour was over, and the house and plans had been duly admired, he asked Jane and their brothers to join him in the parlor.

"I have news from Jersey," he told them, his expression grave. "Sir Anthony Ughtred has died of a fever. He left our sister great with child, and she has just given birth to a daughter, whom she has named after Mother."

"Oh, poor Lizzie!" Jane cried. "She is so young to be widowed. What will she do?"

"She cannot stay on at Mont Orgeuil," Edward said. "She says that now the babe is born, she will return to Yorkshire with her children, for young Henry has inherited his father's property."

"She will be lonely," Jane said.

"She has her son and daughter to think of," Edward replied, making it sound like a reproof. "We must pray for her, and for the soul of Sir Anthony." He paused. "How goes it with the King?"

Jane felt her cheeks growing warm. Thomas raised his eyebrows.

"If there is anything to tell, you will all be the first to hear it," she said firmly.

At Elvetham, Jane realized that people were talking about her. She could not but be aware of the stares and the whispered asides. When she entered the guest bedchamber to help prepare the Queen for bed that night, Anne gave her a frosty stare and would not speak to her. Others followed her lead, but many people were suddenly friendly. She realized that they assumed she had influence and could procure favors for them. When they approached her, she put them off, feigning ignorance of why they thought she could help them.

This could not go on. She must speak to the King.

Toward the end of October, the court returned to Windsor, and the great progress came to an end.

Two days after they arrived, Jane received a summons to the royal library. Waiting for her there was Henry. He held out his hands to her before she could make her reverence.

"Jane! I promised I would show you this." He led her to a table, on which lay a manuscript in red and black ink, with fine illuminated columns on either side of the page. It was *Le Morte d'Arthur*. She turned over the leaves, but could take no pleasure in it, for she knew that what she was about to say to Henry would anger or grieve him.

"Sir," she ventured, suddenly resolved, "this is wondrous, and I thank your Grace for showing it to me. But there is something I must say. I have thought long and hard, and my conscience tells me that I cannot be your mistress, however sensible I am of your favor."

He looked as if the roof had fallen in on him. "Jane, please . . ."

"Please do not press me, Sir. I value my honor beyond price, and I pray that your Grace will too." She curtseyed and left him standing there, dismay and incomprehension on his face.

She waited for the sky to fall, to be dismissed, or worse still, to hear of her brothers' fall from favor. Nothing happened. When the King visited the Queen's chamber, he acted as if Jane were invisible. He did not seek her out. She concluded that he was doing as she had asked, that he respected her decision. He must have realized that it was for the best. By the end of November, she knew for a certainty that she had done the right thing. The world did not know it yet, but Anne was pregnant again.

In the middle of December, Jane went walking in the gardens at Greenwich, making the most of the sunny, crisp weather in her free time. Tonight there would be another feast, and the Queen must be splendidly arrayed, but she was resting now, as she had taken to doing in the afternoons.

Jane saw Edward and Thomas coming toward her, with Bryan and two other finely dressed gentlemen, all deep in conversation. She recognized the Imperial ambassador, Messire Chapuys, and Bryan's brother-in-law, Sir Nicholas Carew, the King's Master of Horse and a champion jouster, whom she had seen in action several times. Muscular and handsome, with a brown beard and a military bearing, he was as close to the King as Bryan was. Bryan had told Jane, grinning, that his sister, Elizabeth, Sir Nicholas's wife, was close to the King too—and sometimes more than she should be!

"Mistress Jane!" Bryan called. "We were just talking about you." Jane stopped in her tracks, startled.

"It's all right, sister, we have told these gentleman about your friendship with the King," Thomas blurted out.

"It is not all right," she retorted. "It is my private business."

"Mistress Jane, the whole court knows about it," Bryan told her, "and these gentlemen are your friends. May I present Messire Chapuys?" The ambassador bowed. His shrewd eyes were appraising. She felt diffident in his presence.

"These gentlemen would like to talk to you," Edward said. "You know Sir Nicholas Carew, of course." Jane dipped a curtsey, wondering what this was about.

Carew's gaze scanned the deserted garden. "I am glad we have found you here alone, Mistress Jane. Your brothers have confided to me and Messire Chapuys that you are a friend to the Queen and the Princess."

"His Majesty the Emperor is working to have the Princess restored to her former position in the succession," Chapuys said.

"We are hoping that you might kindly use any influence you have with the King on her behalf," Carew added.

"I wish to do so, sirs," Jane hastened to assure them. "It was the reason why I welcomed the King's interest. But it was a passing fancy. I am not sure how much influence I actually have."

"More than you think, I am sure, and deservedly," Carew said, gallant as ever.

"Then I must choose my moment," she replied, wondering how she might broach the subject with Henry, and if she would ever have the opportunity.

"We all support the true Queen," Bryan declared. "I think you know, Jane, that my sympathies have secretly been with her and the Princess for a long time. Since I realized how far short of Katherine's example the Lady falls as queen, I have distanced myself from her faction."

"He even picked a quarrel with Lord Rochford, to make that point," Carew said.

"Mistress Jane, you are in a position to do much for so many," Chapuys said gravely. "Through your influence, the Lady's position may be undermined."

"But she may soon bear a son," Jane pointed out.

"Then she will be invincible, more's the pity," Bryan fumed. "For my money, the odds are against it. Two boys she's lost. Jane, you have your foot in the stirrup now. Ride the King to your advantage!"

Jane bridled. "What *are* you suggesting, Francis?"

Bryan made a self-deprecating gesture. "Forgive me! I did not mean it in that way. I know you for a virtuous lady—none better." He winked at her. "I think you have no idea of how important you've become. The King's interest in you has opened up all kinds of possibilities. The petitioners will be queuing at your door before you know it."

Jane suspected that Bryan, like her brothers, was looking to her to obtain favors for him. He was calling in their debts, and it was true, there were many. But she was in no position to seek favors for others.

"I too have privately adhered to the Queen and the Princess, ever since the legatine court six years ago," Carew told Jane. "My wife has for some time secretly been in touch with the Princess, assuring her of our support and keeping her informed." He emitted a sigh of exasperation. "I bitterly regret now that I once encouraged the Lady, but she is my cousin, and I thought she would make a good queen. I was wrong. I soon came to deplore her overbearing ways, especially her appalling treatment of my friend, the Duke of Suffolk, and others. I am of the old faith, and I cannot countenance the religious changes she has brought about."

They were speaking treason. It was the truth, but they could all die for uttering it. Jane was profoundly thankful that there was nowhere nearby where anyone could be concealed.

"I am for reform," Edward said, "but I have never liked Queen Anne, and she certainly doesn't like us Seymours. Jane, we are all united in our resolve to join Messire Chapuys in working for the restoration of the true Queen and the Princess Mary. Will you help us?"

They were all looking at her hopefully. "If the Lady fails to give the King a son, he may be convinced that his so-called marriage is in error, and may even be persuaded to take back his lawful wife and daughter," Chapuys said.

If Katherine lives so long, Jane thought.

"Will you assist us by interceding with the King for them?" Carew asked.

"I will try, I promise," she said doubtfully.

Bryan was eyeing a point beyond her. "We are being watched," he muttered. "The Lady has seen us from her window."

"She knows us for her enemies," Carew said.

"She certainly thinks I am one," Jane offered. "She barely speaks to me, and reproves me for the slightest fault."

"She's jealous," Thomas observed.

"I had better go," Jane said. "Now she's up, she will expect me to be in attendance."

"I think you should stay," Bryan said. "Look who draws near."

Jane turned and saw the King coming toward them, wrapped in furs against the cold, his gentlemen following.

"We will leave you now," Carew said, and bowed.

"She's still watching," Edward warned. "Be careful."

The men all bowed low in the King's direction and withdrew as Henry approached. Aware of Anne's eyes on her, Jane curtseyed, but he raised her, took her hand and kissed it heartily. Jane almost snatched it away.

"Your Grace, the Queen is at the window," she hissed. "I must go." She curtseyed again, and hastened back toward the palace, fearing that she might have offended him but aware that she could have done nothing else. Oh, why did she always feel that she had to be weighing everything she did?

With the interests of her coming child to protect, Anne grew vehement against the Princess Mary. For a long time, she had wished her and Katherine dead. Jane was present when she railed against Mary to the King, not caring who heard.

"I cannot tell you how it terrifies me to think that, if we are invaded, our children might be excluded from the throne for the sake of the Lady Mary," she cried, as he sat there glowering. "Because, if the Emperor has his way, that is what will happen."

"You must stop worrying, Anne," Henry comforted her. "If he invades these shores, we will be ready for him." Jane, her head bent over her sewing, thought his bravado sounded a little forced.

"Sir!" Anne sounded desperate. "The Lady Mary will never cease to trouble us. Her defiance of your just laws has only given courage to our enemies. I pray you, let the law take its course with her! It's the only way to avert war."

Jane held her breath. She was aware of Henry hesitating. "You are asking me to send my own daughter to the scaffold."

"She is a traitor, and a danger to you," Anne persisted. "While she lives, our son will never be safe!"

"Maybe my *threatening* to have her executed would serve as an effective warning to the Emperor," he said heavily. He paused, then spoke again. "You're right. I am resolved. It shall be done!"

Jane stifled a gasp, and the other ladies exchanged horrified glances. Surely the King would not sanction the execution of his own daughter? That poor, sweet girl, who had suffered so much on account of her father's actions, and committed no worse crime than supporting her mother . . . it was horrible. Jane did not sleep that night for worrying. She lay awake, resolved to get a warning to Chapuys.

The next day, the King visited Anne before dinner.

"I have just come from the Privy Council," he announced. "I declared to them that I would no longer remain in the trouble, fear and suspicion that Katherine and Mary are causing. I said the next Parliament must release me by passing Acts of Attainder against them or, by God, I will not wait any longer to make an end of them myself!"

Anne's eyes gleamed. "What did they say?"

"They looked shocked, but I told them it was nothing to cry or make wry faces about. I said that, even if I lose my crown for it, I would do what I have set out to do."

Would he? Jane was in an agony of apprehension.

"It was well done, Henry," Anne was congratulating him. "It is the only way to secure the future of our children."

"Yes, but, by God, at what a price!" he cried, turning away. As he did so, his eye caught Jane's. He looked anguished, and she guessed that already he was wavering in his resolve. But she glanced away in disgust. How could she ever have contemplated becoming his mistress?

When he had gone, Anne sat there brooding. "He said it only to placate me," she murmured. "I know him. But if *he* does not make an end of that cursed bastard, I will. If I have a son, as I hope shortly, I know what will become of her."

She meant it, Jane could see. In the days that followed, Anne became obsessed with the perceived threat from Katherine and Mary, and seemed to think of nothing but of how she might have them dispatched. It chilled Jane to the bone. Now that she might be carrying the heir to the throne, the Queen had recovered her ascendancy; her wish was law. It seemed that she ordered and governed everything, and that the King did not dare oppose her lest she become overwrought and lose the child. And yet, in private, Jane knew, he rarely saw her. He had the perfect excuse now for not visiting her bed.

Anne had been right. The King did not keep his promise. Parliament showed no sign of moving against Katherine and her daughter. But early in December, the news flew around the court: the Princess Dowager was gravely ill. A great sadness descended on Jane, for she had come to look upon Katherine as a second mother.

Anne was triumphant. "Now I shall soon be queen in the eyes of all," she crowed. But there was fear in her voice, and in charity, Jane could only conclude that her inhumanity masked insecurity. Anne was vulnerable, and she knew it. Everything—the King's love, her future as his consort—might rest on her bearing a son. For all her disapproval, Jane could not help pitying her.

A disturbing suspicion kept nagging at her. The old Queen had been ailing for some time, yet it seemed all too timely that she had taken a serious turn for the worse just after it became clear that neither the King nor Parliament would move against her and her daughter. Had Anne taken matters into her own hands? Was she really capable of that? Again Jane recalled the plot to poison Bishop Fisher.

She dared not speak of her fears to anyone. It would be treason. But she held her breath, waiting to hear the news she dreaded, and daily, in the chapel, she begged God to watch over the good Queen.

Christmas Eve was upon them when Edward came looking for Jane. He seemed unusually animated when he found her in the great hall with the other ladies, watching the Yule log being dragged to the hearth.

He pulled her aside. "I have some good news. The King has just given Dorothy a substantial dowry, with fair lands. It's double what Father could provide." He smiled at her. "I wonder why he should do that?"

Jane knew very well. By being generous to her family, Henry hoped to win her love, or at least to soften her resolve.

She thought of Katherine, and of Mary. Now, more than ever, they needed someone to protect them. If the King really was infatuated with her, perhaps he would listen to her pleas.

She looked up at Edward. "Will you tell his Grace that I, in particular, am deeply appreciative of his kindness?"

"You may be sure of it," he said.

"When is the wedding to be?"

Edward looked vexed. "Just after Christmas, which means that none of us at court can attend."

"Oh, I do hate to be missing it!" Jane cried, suddenly homesick for Christmas at Wulfhall and galled at the prospect of missing the excitement of the nuptial celebrations afterward. "Can we not ask for leave?"

Edward sighed. "I doubt it will be granted at this late stage, and those who have obtained permission to go home have already departed."

"Nonetheless, I will ask," Jane said.

But Anne took the greatest of pleasure in refusing.

At Midnight Mass, the Chapel Royal blazed with candlelight. The King and Queen descended from the royal pew that overlooked the nave, and made their offerings at the altar. Jane watched them as she knelt with the other maids-of-honor. On his way back, Henry paused for a second and gazed tenderly down at her. A hint of a smile played about his lips. She bent her head, but not before she had seen Anne's eyes flash with anger.

He danced with her during the Christmas revels, in front of the whole court, while the Queen glowered from her seat of estate; he had forbidden Anne to dance, lest she harm the child. Jane imagined that tongues would be wagging furiously. Certainly all eyes were on her, as she trod a stately pavane in her white gown edged with pearls.

"You look beautiful tonight," Henry said. He had not taken his eyes off her. "Tell me, has my fair ice maiden thawed a little?"

"A little, your Grace." Jane smiled. "But I must beg you not to dance with me more than once. The Queen is watching us, and so is everybody else. Already there is gossip."

"There is always gossip," he said dismissively. "Pay no heed to it."

"Yes, Sir, but it can damage reputations. And for your Grace to associate with a lady of dubious virtue would reflect badly on you."

"Very well, Jane. We will be discreet. I am yours to command. I will be in the chapel closet at eleven tonight. Please come, for I would talk to you privately."

There was a pause as they moved away from each other, then came back together again. "I will be there," she murmured, praying that she was doing the right thing. Surely he would not try to compromise her honor in a holy place?

He was waiting for her, tall, broad and bareheaded, in the dimly lit closet. He bowed to her, this big, powerful man who had a kingdom at his feet. She curtseyed, and he bade her sit with him on a bench.

"I am so pleased that you have come." He took her hand. "For such a favor, your humble suitor is filled with gratitude."

"Sir, I have not changed my mind. I cannot be your mistress. You are married, and it would be wrong. But I will be your friend."

"My friend?" Henry looked stricken. "Jane, I don't think you understand. I would be your servant. I would make no dishonorable demands of you. My sweet lady, I love you!"

Love? She had not dreamed of that!

She looked into his eyes and could read nothing there but sincerity and longing. Yet she had heard that men often mistook lust for love, or made declarations of love in order to have their way with women. She must be careful.

"Oh, Sir," she breathed, bowing her head. "I am not worthy."

For answer, Henry took her hand and kissed it fervently. "No one is more worthy of being loved!" he declared. "It is I, Henry the man, not the King, who makes suit to you, all unworthy."

She was not sure how to answer him. She knew that whatever she agreed to this night, it must remain a secret. She could not risk Queen Katherine ever hearing that she had betrayed her with the King. Katherine might not fathom her true motives. Jane could barely fathom them herself. They were not entirely altruistic: she was not immune to the King's charm, and she was aware of the benefits that would surely come to her family. And if she was completely honest, she relished having the power to put Anne's nose so far out of joint.

She returned Henry's gaze. "Sir, if we could meet like this and continue our friendship in secret, without risk of my honor being stained, then yes, I will be your mistress. But it must be in name only."

Henry rested his hand on hers. "It is all I ask for, to be with you like this. Thank you, Jane." And he bent forward and kissed her on the mouth, lightly at first, and then with passion. When she drew back, he was breathing heavily.

"No one has ever kissed me like that," she whispered.

Henry was delighted. "It is rare to meet with such innocence at court, sweetheart."

"I am not naive, Sir!"

He chuckled, and traced her cheek with his finger. "I meant it as a compliment. It comes as a refreshing change." He kissed her again, folding his arms around her. She stiffened.

"We should not get carried away, Sir." She had heard women whisper that in love play there was a point of no return. She had no idea what that meant, but she was not going to take any risks. "I think I should go. The hour is late."

"Of course." The King regarded her regretfully. "I am your servant, yours to command."

She took her leave of him, and he kissed her a third time. She wondered how long his restraint would last.

They met regularly after that, usually in the chapel closet, sometimes in the wintry privy garden, and once in the chapel itself, although Jane felt uncomfortable there, and shrank from physical contact. There was no doubting or deterring the King's ardor. To her, he revealed a gentleness and tenderness that few saw. He was avid for just a sight of her, he said; he sought her face everywhere. When she was not with him, he was half alive. Of course, he was never satisfied with snatched kisses and embraces, but Jane stayed firm. To her surprise he respected that. She was learning that he had a high opinion of himself as a knight, and that the habit of chivalry was deeply engrained in him.

She wanted to raise the matter of Katherine and Mary, and ask Henry to look on them with kindness—but as yet she did not dare. Her mastery over him was too new, too untested. She must start with small things. She did not like to think that she was using him. She was beginning to feel affection for him, and what she suspected was desire, for he was a most handsome man, and he had never been anything but kind to her. It was Anne who brought out the worst in him. Hopefully she, Jane, could counter that.

It could not last, she reminded herself. He would tire of her when he realized that she would never be his entirely. She had heard it said that he was fickle, and easily sated. She must never forget that few of his love affairs had endured for long.

Chapter 16

1536

When Jane arrived for duty in the Queen's chamber one bitter January morning, Anne was in tears. Lady Worcester and Lady Rutland were trying to comfort her. Lady Zouche turned and glared at Jane.

"He never comes near me!" Anne wailed. "His unkindness grows. And it's all your fault!" She flung a quill pen at Jane. The nib scratched Jane's cheek as it hit her. She put her fingers to the place and found them streaked with blood and ink. She stood there frozen, horrified at the vehemence of Anne's attack and the wound. All the women were looking at her.

"Has the witch's cat got your tongue?" Anne spat. "He's fucking you, isn't he?"

The ladies bristled. No queen—no lady—should use such language!

"No," Jane said, her chin held high.

"Lying little bitch!" Anne countered.

"Madam, calm yourself," exhorted Lady Worcester. "Think of the child!"

"Does he think of the child when he tups that whore over there?" Anne was nearly hysterical.

"Madam, I am no whore, and I resent my honor being impugned," Jane said, mortified.

"Oh, we're so high and mighty now that we're the King's leman!"

"You should know!" Jane retorted, before she could help herself. She was not having Anne, of all people, seizing the moral high ground.

Anne got up and slapped her hard on her injured cheek. "I could have you dismissed for that."

The blow stung, but Jane would not let anyone see she was in pain. "I would go home willingly," she said, "but I doubt his Grace will let me."

Anne stared at her, furious. "Get out!" she ordered. "I will speak to him, and then we shall see if you are going home or not!"

"What's that mark on your face?" Henry asked, as they strolled along his privy gallery the next day, admiring the paintings and maps that hung there.

Jane hesitated. She wanted him to know how Anne's jealousy was manifesting itself, yet she did not want to be seen as a tale-teller. "I scratched myself with my pen," she said.

Henry bent and gently kissed the place. "It will heal soon, darling. I want Master Horenbout to paint your likeness in a miniature, so that I can keep it with me at all times. And you shall have one of me."

Master Horenbout was one of the artists who worked for the King. The other, whom everyone thought superseded him in talent, was his former pupil, Master Holbein. But being painted by Horenbout was honor enough, for he usually only limned those of royal or noble blood.

"Your Grace is so kind to me," she said.

"And means to be kinder!" he declared.

Jane took her place with the other maids and ladies as Anne seated herself next to Henry on the dais in his presence chamber. He was receiving ambassadors and petitioners this morning, and the grand apartment was crammed with courtiers.

Chapuys was announced. He came wearing unrelieved black, his face gray and solemn. The room began humming with speculation.

"Your Majesty," he said, rising from his reverence, "I have great sorrow in telling you that the good Queen is dead."

Murdered. The word sprang immediately to Jane's mind as she absorbed the shock. It was what she had feared—and it was what Anne had threatened. She wanted to weep, and struggled to control herself. Poor Katherine. Her life had been so unhappy. She had not deserved to die alone, done to death probably, abandoned by the man who should have cherished her, and without the consolation of the presence of the daughter she had not seen in four years.

"Now I am indeed a queen!" Anne crowed triumphantly.

Sickened to hear her, Jane looked at Henry to see how he was taking the news, searching his face for any sign of guilt, but to her dismay it was transfigured with joy.

"God be praised that we are free from all suspicion of war!" he said loudly.

Was that all he could say? Even Chapuys's long experience in diplomacy could not conceal his disapproval. "I bring you this, her last letter," he said stiffly, and handed over a folded paper sealed with the arms of England and Spain.

Henry broke the seal and read, with all eyes upon him. Suddenly he was very still and a tear traced its way down his cheek. Jane heard him draw in his breath as he looked up. "God rest the Princess Dowager," he said. "I thank your Excellency. If you would leave us, please."

Chapuys bowed and withdrew.

"Thank God!" Henry said. "Thank God!"

Jane felt dangerously near to bursting into tears. She lowered her eyes. Surely a man who had committed murder would not openly rejoice thus? Even so, his reaction shocked her.

When he met her later in the holyday closet, he was in a testy mood. "Defiant to the last," he growled. "See how she signs herself!" He thrust the letter under Jane's nose and she saw, in the dear familiar handwriting, the words "Katherine the Queen." Before he took it back, she also glimpsed what was written above them: "Lastly, I make this vow, that my eyes desire you above all things." In the end, it had not mattered what he had done to Katherine; all the cruelties and the deprivations had counted for nothing: she had loved him till her dying breath. It was not often given to human beings to be the recipient of such selfless love and devotion—and he could not see it! He had thrown away a jewel for a gewgaw.

Henry slid the letter inside his doublet. "Jane, you realize what this means? I am free at last. Now no one can challenge my marriage, nor Elizabeth's right to be my heir. And I can make friends with the Emperor. There is nothing to stop me, for the cause of our enmity no longer exists. My subjects will be delighted."

He had overlooked one crucial thing, she realized. He was free! He was not lawfully married, since he had had a wife living when he had gone through that pretended ceremony with Anne, without even waiting for Cranmer to give judgment on his first marriage. And Cranmer's decision had no force against the Pope's dispensation.

There was no doubting it. The King was a free man.

"It's a pity the Lady Mary did not keep company with her mother!" The Earl of Wiltshire sneered.

Jane overheard him talking to Anne and Lord Rochford as she sat at the table sorting through poems with Margaret Douglas, Madge Shelton and Mary Howard; Thomas Howard was sitting on a window seat nearby, idly strumming a lute. Jane was appalled at the

Boleyns' callous disregard for the late Queen's sufferings, for which they were largely responsible, and kept tormenting herself with fears that they were to blame for far worse than that.

Why should I bow the knee to that woman? she asked herself, seething. Even if Anne was not a murderess, she was not the rightful Queen. She was a disgrace, and justifiably unpopular. Yet the King evidently did not see things that way, and if she bore him a son, no one could ever touch her. To ensure the child's undisputed legitimacy, all Henry had to do was go through a proper ceremony of marriage with Anne. But would it ever occur to him that he ought to do so?

No, of course not. He thought himself lawfully married in the eyes of this new Church of his, and he was of no mind to heed the Pope's judgment, so far had he fallen from grace. Therefore he would not see any need for a second marriage ceremony, unless, of course, he wanted to appease the rest of Christendom. He might just do it if he thought it would smooth the path to friendship with the Emperor. Then again, he might not wish to lose face in the eyes of the world, for to marry Anne now would be to admit that his first marriage to her had been of questionable legitimacy. But would he want to wed her now, if he had the choice?

Everything hinged upon Anne's bearing a son. If she did that, she would be unchallengeable, and Jane knew that she herself would have to leave court. She could not bear to stay and see Anne triumphant and back in power.

Jane could not bring herself to join in when Anne ordered dancing. This was a time of mourning! She was outraged when Anne bade them dress her all in yellow for the occasion. It was an insult to Katherine's memory! The King even joined them, eager to celebrate England's liberation from the threat of war, and he too was dressed entirely in yellow. How could they all rejoice so? Jane wondered. But Henry was in an ebullient mood, and had the Princess Elizabeth triumphantly conducted to Mass with the trumpets sounding, so that all should see his undoubted heir. After dinner, he joined Anne and her ladies in the hall and there was more dancing and demonstrations of joy. Jane had to join in, but she hotly resented being made to appear to condone the rejoicing.

Henry carried Elizabeth over to show her off to the ladies. He paused before Jane, who took the child's tiny hand and kissed it.

"Do you have a present for me?" demanded the two-year-old. She had a sharp little face and an imperious manner. They all laughed.

Jane felt in her pocket and drew out an embroidered handkerchief. "Would your Grace like this?" she asked, offering it to Elizabeth. The little hand reached out and took it; the sharp eyes regarded it with interest.

"What do we say?" Henry prompted.

"Thank you," Elizabeth responded. She gave Jane an engaging smile. Then the King set her on the ground so that she could join in the dancing. Already she was accomplished at it, and kept up very well.

Jane noticed that while the ladies made much of Elizabeth, Anne was more interested in socializing with the King's gentlemen. She rarely saw her child. Jane knew that her visits to the nursery household at Hatfield or Hunsdon or Ashridge were infrequent. Again it struck her that Anne seemed not to have deep maternal feelings. She was too focused on herself! If I had a little girl like that, Jane vowed, I would see her as often as I could.

That night, as they prepared the Queen for bed, she insisted that Jane comb her hair. Jane wondered why she would want her attentions, of all people, but Anne's manner made it clear that Jane was being put firmly in her place. Jane could not help feeling pleased to see one or two gray hairs in the long dark tresses.

Without warning, Anne burst into tears.

The women tried to soothe her, begging her to tell them what was wrong. Jane feared that her name might be mentioned. The King had danced with her four times.

"I am so frightened!" Anne blurted out. "Living, the Princess Dowager was my surety. I see that now. But she is gone, and if this child does not live, or is a girl, I fear they might do to me as they did to her."

"They?" Margaret Douglas echoed.

"Master Cromwell hates me. He is not the only one." Jane felt a frisson of trepidation: did Anne know that her enemies were uniting to restore the Princess Mary to the succession?

"But the King loves you!" Mary Howard reassured her.

Anne cried out, "You think so? Not in private. He hardly speaks to me. You know how rarely he comes here. In public, he makes a good show of affection, because he can never admit he was wrong to marry me. While Katherine lived, he would not have contemplated putting me away, for that would have been tantamount to admitting that she was his true wife. But now . . ." Lady Worcester put an arm around her heaving shoulders. "Oh, God," Anne wailed, "I fear that his rejoicing this week has been for more than one reason."

"Madam, calm yourself. You are with child. There is every chance that it will be a son. Then you will see how much the King loves you." But Anne was inconsolable. Lady Worcester looked at the other ladies and shook her head despairingly.

"All that stands between me and ruin is this child!" Anne sobbed. And she would not be comforted.

Her deep distress, which manifested itself again and again in the days that followed, made Jane uncomfortable. She could not but be moved by it. What must it be like constantly to be bearing children in fear that they would be lost or of the wrong sex, knowing that your happiness depended on having a son?

Was Anne suffering remorse for the way she had supplanted and hounded Katherine? Did she have an even worse sin on her conscience? Already there were rumors in the court that Katherine had been poisoned. Some blamed the King. Others said the old Queen had died of a broken heart.

Jane's thoughts were often with the Lady Mary, who must be bitterly grieving for the mother whose cause she had stoutly upheld.

She wished she could comfort the girl and tell her how much Katherine had loved her and spoken of her in the years in which they had been apart.

Now was her chance to speak for Mary. She seized it one evening when the King summoned her to the chapel and bade her sit beside him in the Queen's chair in the royal pew. She knew Anne would be furious if she could see her.

"I thought you would like this, sweetheart," he said, and gave her a little velvet pouch. Inside was a gold locket, encrusted with jewels, which opened to reveal a miniature of him. "I hope that you will wear it and that, when you do, you will think of me," he said humbly.

"It's beautiful, Sir." Jane unclasped her single row of pearls and put on the locket. "I have never had such a fine piece of jewelry. Thank you! I will indeed think of you when I wear it, which will be often. I think of you often anyway—and I think of another too, but with sadness."

He was all concern. "Can I help?" he asked.

Jane took a deep breath. "I grieve for the Lady Mary, who has just lost her mother," she said, watching to see how her words were received.

He frowned and sighed. "Jane, you have a kind heart, but you cannot know how deeply Mary has grieved me. She has opposed me in all things, and has stubbornly persisted in taking her mother's part."

"I thought only of her sadness, Sir. She must be missing her mother desperately—and her father."

He leaned back, looking vexed. "You should know that the Queen has tried repeatedly to bring about a reconciliation, but Mary will have none of it. This week, when her Grace offered to receive her at court with all honor, as an equal, if she would recognize her as queen, she sent back to say that that would conflict with her conscience. Tell me, what would you have me do? If it were anyone else, I would send them to the Tower." His mouth set in a prim line.

"I pray that your Grace would not so punish your own daughter," Jane cried.

"No, Jane, I would not." He sighed. "I have been truly forbearing, even though others would have me show severity to her."

That was reassuring. "Maybe, if you spoke to her yourself, you could bring about a reconciliation?" Jane suggested.

"I will not see her while she persists in opposing me." He was adamant. "If she wants my fatherly comfort, she knows what she must do."

Jane realized it was useless to persist further. All she could hope for was that the seed she had planted would grow and bear fruit.

Henry changed the subject. "I've had my secretary arrange your sitting with Master Horenbout. It will be tomorrow at three o'clock, in the holyday closet. Wear my locket!"

Jane went searching for Edward, whom she found playing dice with Thomas. She told them what the King had said.

Edward looked grave. "I do not think his Grace told you everything. Messire Chapuys has had a letter from Lady Shelton." Anne often spoke of her aunt, Madge Shelton's mother, whom she had appointed as governess to Mary. "The Lady wrote to Lady Shelton that when she had a son, she knew what would come to the Princess," Edward said. Jane trembled. It was exactly what she had heard Anne say to her ladies.

"But why did Lady Shelton inform Messire Chapuys?" she asked, astonished. "You would have thought he'd be the last person the Boleyns would want to know that."

"My information is that Lady Shelton turned against the Lady after Anne pushed her daughter Madge into the King's bed," Edward confided. "She thinks her daughter dishonored, and is also unhappy about the treatment of the Princess. Messire Chapuys is greatly disturbed. He fears what the Lady might do, and with justification, I think." He hesitated. "Is there somewhere we can talk privately?"

"The little banqueting house is deserted," Thomas said, pointing through the window at a small red-brick building on a hillock about a hundred yards from the palace. They walked there briskly in the cold breeze, and shut the door behind them. Inside, golden cherubs gamboled along a painted frieze, and two trestle tables were stacked against a wall. This was where the King privately entertained privileged guests. Their breath steamed in the biting chill as they huddled together on a window seat.

"Messire Chapuys told us that an autopsy was performed on the body of the late Queen," Edward revealed. "The findings were kept secret, which made him doubt that she had died of natural causes."

Jane was horrified to hear that others shared her suspicions. "You think she really was murdered?"

He regarded her gravely. "We all do. Her confessor, the Bishop of Llandaff, told Messire Chapuys that those who performed the autopsy confided to him a great secret. They found the corpse of the Queen and all the internal organs as normal as possible—except the heart. It had a black growth, hideous to behold, which clung closely to the outside. They washed it in water, but it did not change color. They had never seen anything like it, and drew the obvious conclusion."

Jane's hand flew to her mouth. "No!"

"What else could it have been?" Edward said. "It must have been poison."

Jane frowned. "The Lady made several threats during the weeks preceding the Queen's death. She was determined to do away with her, and the Princess."

"I can believe it of her," Edward stated. "What worries Messire Chapuys is that the Princess will be next."

"Heaven forbid!" Jane cried.

"We must all be on our guard," he enjoined. "The Emperor, thank God, is Mary's champion. He has deputed Messire Chapuys to watch over her, although that will not be easy, for he is not allowed to see her or communicate with her."

"But he says there are ways," Thomas added.

Jane stifled a sob. "It is terrible to think that the good Queen was murdered."

Edward's expression was grim. "Should they open her again, the traces will be seen."

Jane sat as still as she could for Master Horenbout, a grizzled Fleming with beetling brows and paint-stained fingers, who spoke in heavily accented English and carried himself as regally as the sitters he had painted. She had put on her best black gown with a neat gable hood, donned a single row of pearls and pinned Henry's locket to her bodice. She could not stop thinking about Chapuys's revelations. If he was right, Anne was dangerous. She might act on her threats to do away with Mary. Oh, blessed Mother of God, she might try to get rid of Jane as well! And if she bore a son, there would be no stopping her wickedness. For all her burgeoning feelings for the King, Jane began again to wish herself at home at Wulfhall, away from the perilous tumults of the court. If Henry persisted in his pursuit of her, Anne's wrath would only increase, and who knew then what she might do?

Chapter 17

1536

Jane had been keeping her head down for a week, trying to avoid the King and being noticed by Anne, when the Duke of Norfolk was ushered into the Queen's privy chamber.

"Good day, Uncle," Anne said, none too warmly, for they had fallen out and were not above trading insults. He had once called her a great whore, in Jane's hearing. But today he appeared agitated. "Madam, you should know that the King has taken a fall while jousting. He fell so heavily that everyone thought it a miracle he was not killed."

As Jane stifled a gasp, Anne's hand flew to her mouth. Her eyes registered terror. "Is he injured?"

"No, just a little shaken up," Norfolk assured her, as Jane sagged in relief. "He will live to joust another day."

"Not if I have anything to do with it," Anne said. "It's too risky." She was shaking, no doubt thinking of what might have become of her had Henry died and left her to fend for herself in a hostile realm, with a succession that would almost certainly be disputed and fought over.

Henry summoned Jane to his gallery that evening.

"Sir, I am so glad to see you unharmed," she said. "You gave us all a fright."

"It was nothing." His tone was dismissive. "Unfortunately the old wound on my leg has reopened and my doctors fear that an ulcer may develop. It's painful, but I'm not going to let it stop me riding or hunting—or doing anything else for my pleasure. Come, let me kiss you!" He held out his arms.

The whole court was to wear mourning on the day Queen Katherine was buried, by the King's order. Jane had been surprised to hear it, but Anne enlightened them all, sounding none too pleased.

"The late Princess Dowager was his Grace's sister-in-law. That is why the King is wearing mourning today. But it would be hypocritical of me to mourn one who was my great enemy. I am grieved, not that she is dead, but for the flaunting of the good end she made. I'm sick of hearing about it. Nothing is talked of but the Christian deathbed of Katherine! But we must perforce put on mourning, although I had rather wear yellow."

Jane stiffened. How dare Anne show such disrespect! No one had moved. She could sense that the others felt as she did.

"What are you waiting for?" Anne snapped. "Fetch my blue gown. I have a mind to accompany the King to the solemn obsequies that are to be performed today. It will give me credit in the eyes of the Imperialists and smooth the path to friendship with the Emperor."

Jane could not believe her ears. Margery Horsman beckoned her, and they hastened away to the wardrobe.

"She thinks the Emperor will be her friend?"

"She is deluding herself," Margery said, unlocking the door.

"And she's asked for a blue gown." It was a color Anne never wore.

"Blue is the color of royal mourning," Margery explained.

"She had done better to wear black, like the King," Jane retorted.

Little conversation was exchanged after the gown was brought and Anne was attired in it. Already the swell of her pregnancy was evident, and they had to unlace the stomacher a little.

"I have a fancy to eat fish," Anne said. "Jane, go and inform the privy kitchen."

As Jane sped on her way, she passed the door to the Chapel Royal, through which she could hear chanting in Latin; it would be the early Mass for the good Queen, the first of several that were to be said that day. Further down the gallery, she nearly ran into Chapuys, who bowed slightly. He was talking to a tall man with a grim face.

"I thought you would be at Peterborough for the Princess Dowager's burial," Jane heard the man say as she passed.

"No, Sir William, I am staying away, since they do not mean to bury her as queen," Chapuys said. Jane hurried on, wishing she could have congratulated him on standing up for his principles.

Her errand completed, she was returning along the gallery when the chapel doors were thrown open and the King emerged at the head of a procession of clergy, lords, officers and courtiers, all in black. He cut an impressive figure in his velvet robes, unrelieved by any color. Jane curtseyed low. He bent down and murmured in her ear. "I must see you. Come to my privy chamber at eleven." He straightened and walked on. Those following stared at Jane as she went on her way, her cheeks flaming.

The ushers and the King's guard stood impassively at their posts as Henry received Jane at the door of his privy chamber. It was deserted, he explained, for his gentlemen and grooms were all in the chapel, by his command.

"We safely have half an hour," he said. "The queen is at Mass." He led her into a small closet, furnished as a study. Books were piled on the desk, and there were scientific instruments on a shelf, next to a collection of physick bottles and a jumble of scrolls that looked like maps. Having closed the door, Henry clasped Jane to him and kissed her fervently. "I think I am in Heaven when I am alone with you," he whispered, and pressed his lips to hers again. She responded cautiously, fearful of inflaming his ardor too greatly. He could so easily get carried away and overpower her. She trusted that he would not, and that the chivalrous side of him would always conquer his carnal instincts, yet she did not want him thinking her light in conduct in consenting to be alone with him, and when his hand strayed to her breast, she removed it firmly.

"Oh, Jane, you are cruel!" His voice was plaintive, but he released her, and they sat down, he on his big oak chair and she on a cushioned stool that he had pulled out for her. As they talked, he held her hand and gazed into her eyes.

"I wish I could see you more often," he said.

"I would not upset the Queen," Jane murmured.

"That is wise," he sighed. "Much hangs on this pregnancy. I am counting down the weeks until the child is born."

"I pray it will be a son for your Grace," Jane said.

"By God, we'll have cause for celebration when he arrives!" Henry declared. "I've waited twenty-seven years for him. And I want everyone to see that God smiles on my actions."

Jane said nothing, and he went on to speak of other things, and then talk led to touching, and touching led to kissing . . . The minutes were ticking by, and all too soon the clock on the cupboard showed that it wanted but ten minutes to noon.

"I should go, Sir," Jane said, rising. Henry caught her hand and pulled her down on his lap.

"Stay a few moments more!" he begged, holding her tightly.

She giggled as he began kissing her once more. Again his hand closed over her breast, and she was just about to push it away when the door opened and Anne stood there, her eyes wide in shock.

"How could you?" she screamed.

Henry pushed Jane off his knee and leapt up.

"Go!" he said, and she fled without even curtseying.

"Darling, I am sorry," she heard Henry say to Anne as she left.

As she walked back to the Queen's apartments, her heart was thudding. This could mean dismissal—or worse. She wondered if she ought to flee now, before she had to face Anne's wrath.

But when Anne returned, she was in no state to censure Jane. She was doubling up with pain, and there was blood on her skirts. The ladies helped her to bed, asking each other where a midwife might be found, or whether they should send for the physicians. In the end, after much toing and froing, a competent woman who lived near the palace was procured through the good offices of Sir Henry Norris. By then, it was apparent that Anne was miscarrying. Jane sat in the outer chamber with the other maids, listening to the screams from beyond the door.

"It's enough to put you off ever getting married," said Margery.

"Indeed," Jane nodded fervently.

"It makes no difference who you are, queen or peasant," Margaret Douglas observed. "Childbirth is a hazardous business. Just listen to her, poor soul. It's like a wounded animal."

In the early evening, the screaming ceased, to be replaced by bitter sobbing. Presently the door opened and Lady Worcester emerged. She was crying—she who was normally so composed. "She has lost a boy," she told them, her voice breaking. "The midwife says it was of about fifteen weeks' growth."

Jane found herself pitying Anne, whose sufferings had ended in this tragedy, and whose future now looked perilously uncertain. She could not help wondering, though, if this was a judgment from God for Anne's part in the death of the Queen.

Her heart bled for the King and the death of his hopes. It would be a searing disappointment. But perhaps he would now see that this pretended marriage was cursed by God, and put Anne away. Jane was not cruel; she imagined a fine house somewhere far from court, in which Anne could live with her bastard, comfortably pensioned off and served with honor . . .

The King arrived, his face a mask of grief. He stumped into the bedchamber and closed the door. They could hear muffled shouts and Anne shrieking. When Henry emerged, only a few minutes later, he was weeping. Jane would have gone to him, to offer some comfort, but he departed before she had risen from her curtsey.

The young Duchess of Richmond came hurrying after. "He's gone? He cannot leave her like this! She is in the most extreme grief. She was crying her heart out when the King came to her, and he was relentless, bewailing and complaining about his loss—his loss, never mind hers! She was hysterical—she blamed his unkindness, which he took badly." The Duchess looked pointedly at Jane. "Do you know what he said to her? He said that she should have no more boys by him. He was implacable. And Mistress Jane, she told him he had no one to blame but himself for this disappointment, for it had been caused by her distress of mind over you!"

"I did nothing," Jane protested, feeling her cheeks burning. They were all staring at her, and many eyes were hostile.

The Duchess flared. "Then how come she said her heart was broken because he loved others? And how come his Grace looked chastened and begged her to pardon him?"

"I have done nothing wrong," Jane insisted.

"You are stealing the Queen's husband!" Madge Shelton cried. "Because of you, she is terrified that he will put her away, as he did the Princess Dowager!"

Jane bit her lip. She dared not say that Henry was not Anne's husband, and therefore it was no sin to accept his courtship. Nor could she say that Anne, in her day, had stolen another queen's husband.

"I have no desire to hurt her," she declared.

"You expect us to believe that?" Madge countered.

"Don't you care that she has lost this child on your account?" Lady Worcester asked angrily.

"I am sorry she has lost it," Jane said, "but I cannot think I caused it. This is the third son her Grace has miscarried. Maybe her constitution is not apt for bearing boys." And maybe God was showing His displeasure. "I am no threat to her Grace."

"You should be ashamed of yourself," the Duchess spat, and disappeared through the door to the bedchamber. Jane bent her head to her sewing, mortified. Margery came and sat next to her.

"Don't fret, Jane. She lost the child because she has been in a frenzy for most of her pregnancy, and not just about you. I don't think any of us are surprised. She has been living at the sword's edge. She knew how much rested on this child being a boy, and she agonized over it. Don't listen to them. They are her creatures, and they fear for the future."

Jane took Margery's hand. "Thank you, dear friend. I will try to ignore them."

Henry sent for Jane late that night. She came to him in the dimly lit chapel, and found him weeping in his pew, unable to control his distress. She took him in her arms.

"She lost my boy!" he sobbed against her shoulder, the bristles on his chin rough against her breast. "It is the greatest discomfort to me and all this realm." He raised a ravaged face to her. "I know I will have no boys by her. I see clearly that God does not wish to give me male children."

Jane held her breath. Was Anne's spell broken? Could he at last see the truth?

"Oh, Jane, help me!" he begged. "I am in great fear that I have again incurred the wrath of God. Those miscarriages did not occur without good reason: they were manifestations of His displeasure. I think my marriage with the Queen is as displeasing to Him as my unlawful union with Katherine."

Jane had never thought to hear him say it. Into her head there came, unbidden, an image of herself seated in a great church, wearing a crown. It was what her family had envisaged, and she had put it down to fond ambition, but with a heady rush of fear and excitement she now saw that they had perhaps been prescient. If Henry set Anne aside, what was there to stop him from marrying her? She was of similar rank and lineage to Anne, and he loved her. That had been sufficient to secure Anne a crown.

Visions of the future flashed, unformed, through her head, but she knew she needed time to think. For now, she must choose her words with care, for what she said might prove crucial. "Alas, Sir, I wish that I could help you, but I am not learned in these matters, and I fear that you might take amiss any humble opinion I might express."

Henry sat up and looked at her with new interest, tears still staining his cheeks. "If you have something to say, you may utter it without fear, sweetheart."

Even with this reassurance, Jane dared not suggest that his marriage to Katherine had been a true one, which was why God was angry. Nor was she about to mention Mary Boleyn by name. "Sir, could there have been some impediment to your union with the Queen? Some affinity or consanguinity that was inadvertently overlooked?"

She knew by his face that he understood what she was talking about.

He looked embarrassed.

"What have you heard?" he pressed her.

"It was just gossip, Sir. Something about your Grace and the Queen's sister."

Henry's fair skin flushed. "It's true, but it was a long time ago. I was aware of the impediment it created, so I obtained a dispensation from the Pope, sanctioning my marriage with Anne. But two years ago, Parliament passed an Act that rendered Papal dispensations unlawful if they were contrary to the will of God. Jane, Cranmer confirmed my marriage. He has never expressed any doubts about it. Thus I have always believed that it was not contrary to the will of God. But maybe that impediment was insurmountable. I must talk to Cranmer."

Jane wondered if Cranmer would be willing to unmake the marriage he had so sensationally declared to be true and valid. But she had heard him described as the King's puppet. People whispered that he would find a theological precept for doing Henry's bidding, whatever it was. If Henry went to Cranmer with good reasons for wanting an annulment, Cranmer might well be amenable.

She gathered her courage. "Sir, has it occurred to you that putting

away the Queen might restore your credit with God? It would leave
you free to make another marriage, to a wife who could bear you
sons."

To her amazement, Henry was nodding. "I am aware of that, darling. It would also ease the way to friendship with the Emperor and
silence my opponents. Anne is not popular. She is a constant storm
center, which is why I love the peace and quietness I find with you.
I will tell you, I made tentative inquiries about an annulment last
year, before the Princess Dowager died. My advisers were of the
opinion that it would be seen as an admission that I was wrong to
put Katherine from me. I would be expected to return to her, and
any new marriage would also be controversial, because half Christendom held her to be my lawful wife."

This was news indeed, that he had already considered divorcing
himself from Anne.

"I'm no longer young, Jane," he said. "I can't afford to wait much
longer for God to send me a son. I must talk to Cranmer." He took
her hand. "You give me sound advice. I do so love you, Jane. Look,
I have a gift for you." He reached into his pocket and drew out a roll
of velvet, which he placed in her hands. She unraveled it to find an
emerald pendant and a matching ring with a great stone. She drew
in her breath. That he should offer her such costly gifts!

"Emeralds stand for purity and faith," Henry said.

"I do not know how to thank your Grace. They are gorgeous. You
are so good to me. I have not the words to show my appreciation."

He bent forward and kissed her gently on the lips. "I would give
you the world," he said. "And when we are alone together like this,
Jane, you should not be calling me 'your Grace' or 'Sir.' I am Henry,
your humble servant."

Jane wound her arms around his neck. "Yes, Sir—I mean Henry."
They both laughed, but his eyes remained sad.

"What can I do to make you feel better?" she asked.

He gazed at her with yearning. "Comfort me," he said. "Help me
to blot out the pain I feel."

Her defenses melted. It came to her that she might bind him

closer to her by showing him kindness now rather than holding herself aloof. She tightened her arms around him. "How can I do that?"

For answer, his mouth closed on hers needily. "Come to bed," he murmured.

Some years back, she had asked her mother what would happen on her wedding night.

"I mean, I know what happens, but I worry that I won't know what to do," she had admitted.

"You won't have to do anything," Mother had told her, looking embarrassed. "Your husband will know what to do, and you will take your lead from him."

"Does it hurt?" Jane had asked.

"A little, at first, but that soon wears off. Don't worry, child. All will be well."

As Henry dismissed his impassive-faced guards and led Jane across the frosty privy garden, through the door at the bottom of a turret and up a secret stair to his bedchamber, she recalled that conversation and smiled. What she had not realized then was that instinct and desire dictated what passed between a man and a woman. She had known, as she sat entwined with Henry in the chapel, that now was the right time to give herself to him, and it was that knowledge that had impelled her here tonight.

Closing the door, he turned and cupped her face with his hands, kissing her lips hungrily. "Darling, you cannot know what this means to me. I thought myself in the pit of Hell, and that there was no way out—and then you lighted my way. Oh, Jane! Was ever man so blessed?" He pressed her to him.

Cradled against his chest, she felt safe and loved. Needs she had suppressed for years burgeoned in her. "I fear I am innocent of the ways of lovers," she whispered.

He tilted her face up toward his. "There is nothing to fear, Jane. I assure you, it will be a great joy to us both. Come, let me act as your tirewoman." Deftly he helped her unhook her gown and unlace her kirtle, then he bade her lie on the bed as he drew off her stockings, caressing her legs as he did so. She lay there in only her smock as he divested himself of his own clothes, and she caught a glimpse of him naked, muscular and virile in the candlelight. Then he was in bed with her, holding her tightly, his need overtaking him. As she felt him thrust inside her, there was a stabbing pain, but soon all her fears were swept away on a great tide of pleasure as she finally learned, at the great age of twenty-eight, what rapture it was to surrender herself to the man she desired. And when it was over, he lay in her arms, weeping tears of mingled grief and joy.

Chapter 18

1536

She awoke before dawn to Henry's mouth on hers, and his body, demanding, insistent, taking possession of her. He was strong and powerfully built, and she was small and slender; again it amazed her how perfectly they fitted together. She gave herself up to his embrace. Last night he had come to her in his terrible need, and making love had been an intensely emotional experience; but this morning, he was back in command of himself, his grief under control, and his mastery thrilled her.

Afterward, as he lay sleeping beside her, doubts began to creep into her mind. She had been so certain last night that this was the right thing to do. There had been nothing calculated about it; she had seized the moment. It had not felt like a surrender, but a mutual coming together. But now, she felt nervous about it. Would Henry discard her like he had all those other women? How she would be shamed in the eyes of those whose hopes were invested in her! And what if she were with child? The realization that this was a genuine possibility made her catch her breath. She saw herself going home, dishonored, to Wulfhall and a life of ignominy.

She was beginning to regret giving way to her loving impulse when Henry stirred and reached for her hand. "Thank you, Jane," he said. "You have made me feel whole again." He raised himself on one elbow, bent down and kissed her tenderly. "You know, it's like buying a suit of clothing in the most glorious color, then seeing the same suit in another shade, one that would not have been your first choice, and discovering that you like the second one best because you never realized that it would suit you better. I've known you for years, darling, and yet I never really saw you until that day when you did not think twice about comforting me after Anne lost her child. And last year, at Wulfhall—I knew."

"Knew?" she murmured, feeling greatly reassured.

"I knew that I could love you, and that this love would be pure and wholesome, not tainted and volatile. I knew that with you I could find peace—as I have this night, darling, which has been the greatest comfort to me. Oh, Jane, never leave me!"

She gazed up at him. "As if I could, Henry," she said. Whatever he had done, whatever he was capable of, she knew that her feelings for him were true. Being loved, being made to feel cherished and safe meant everything to her.

Anne lay in her chamber, looking ill, as her ladies seated themselves around her with their sewing. The loss of her son had aged her, and her mien showed little trace of the temptress who had enchanted the King. But she put on a brave face.

"It was all for the best," she told them, "because I will be the sooner with child again, and the son I will bear will not be doubtful like this one, which was conceived during the life of the Princess Dowager."

So she knows her marriage is a pretense, Jane thought, sitting in a corner, as far as she dared from her mistress, trying to look invisible and treasuring the memory of the night. Anne had studiedly ignored her, but her bravado did not last. Soon she was in tears again. "I'm scared," she admitted. "I should not have reproached the

King." She gripped Mary Richmond's arm. "He might think I am as barren of sons as Katherine, and find a pretext to have our marriage annulled and Elizabeth declared a bastard." She was beside herself, and with good reason, Jane now knew. She felt no guilt, but she could not but feel sorry for Anne.

"Who will be my champion?" Anne cried. "When Katherine fell from favor she had the might of the Empire behind her. But who will speak for me?"

"Archbishop Cranmer for one, Madam," Lady Zouche reassured her.

Jane wondered if Henry had spoken to Cranmer yet.

"And your bishops," added Lady Rutland.

"Your father and your brother support you staunchly," Madge said.

Anne dabbed at her eyes. "But if I lose the King's favor, they might all abandon me, and I shall have no one!" She was becoming overwrought again. "There are those who seek my downfall, and without the King's protection, my enemies will destroy me."

"Madam, calm yourself," Lady Worcester exhorted her. "The remedy for your fears lies in your own hands. Concentrate now on getting well, then allure the King as you used to. Dress to please him. Dance, sing and display the talents he admires. Be witty company, and do not dwell on your woes. Be the woman he fell in love with. The rest will follow."

"I can't . . ." Anne's voice was plaintive.

"You can!" Mary Richmond insisted. "Woo him back. Remind him why he married you."

Anne looked at them doubtfully. The fight had gone out of her. She was too beaten down with misery. Again Jane was moved to sympathy. Could her conscience permit her to add to Anne's sorrows? Even if Anne was in the wrong, true happiness was not attained through another's suffering.

———

Edward and Bryan waylaid Jane in the gallery.

"The whole court is talking about you, Jane," Bryan told her, a gleam in his one eye. "Rumor has it that the King will seek a divorce from the Lady and remarry."

Edward looked at her intently. "No longer do people see you as just another of his Grace's passing fancies. They say he means to marry you. You have done well."

Bryan leaned closer to her. "He has certainly considered an annulment. Master Secretary told me. And who else would he marry?"

"A princess with a rich dowry, I imagine."

"But it's you he loves." Bryan smiled. "Why would he look elsewhere?"

"I told you at the outset that you could be Queen," Edward reminded her.

"That is wishful thinking!" she countered.

"But you would like to be, would you not?"

"I don't know!"

"Then you have thought about it?" Bryan persisted. "And the King has given you cause to do so."

"Listen. He loves me. He told me so."

Their faces lit up. "It looks hopeful," Edward said.

"Brother, you are jumping to conclusions!" she reproved him. She told them what Henry had said. "I do not know if the King has spoken with the Archbishop. Besides, I am not sure that I want to be Queen."

"It's not about what you want," Bryan said. "It's about what is best for you, for your family and friends, and for England at large. The Lady is vulnerable. Now is our chance to topple her. Say you will do all you can to help."

She was saved from answering at once, for two grooms in livery came hurrying along the gallery. She waited until they had gone, trying to collect her thoughts, and then suddenly she saw her duty clearly. Bryan's words had brought it home to her. He was right. Anne must be removed, if only for Henry's peace of mind. She was the source of all the ills that had befallen the kingdom, the rightful Queen and the Princess. Because of her, good men had died barbarously, innocent blood had been shed and good order overturned. The English Church was in disarray and heresy was flourishing. Was it presumptuous to wonder if God had appointed her, Jane, to put an end to these ills? He had chosen a simple maiden as the mother of His Son; why should He not choose another, pure in heart, to save England and its King from damnation? It was a daunting prospect, but the King loved her. She had stout friends, and might through Chapuys's influence win the support of the Emperor. By her means, true religion might be reestablished, and the rights of the Princess Mary recognized. And supplanting a mistress who had no right to be queen was no sin. Pray God Henry would tell her soon what Cranmer had said.

Edward and Bryan were watching her, impatient for her reply. "I will do my very best," she told them.

"Well said!" Bryan grinned.

"You will not regret it," Edward chimed in. "Great good may come of this."

"I do not seek a crown, but if one comes to me, I will thank God for it," she declared.

"I think it will," Edward said, "but you have to play your cards cleverly. There must be no more secret meetings with the King. Insist that he sees you only in the presence of your family."

Not to see Henry alone again. Not to lie in his arms and experience the sweet delights they had shared last night. She did not know how she would bear it, her life being otherwise so miserable. She wondered what Edward would say if she told him the truth.

She stalled. "That won't be difficult, for he departs for London tomorrow for Shrovetide, and you are going with him, are you not? I will not see him for some time, or at least until the Lady is fully recovered. We are to stay behind and attend on her. She would send me away if she could, I know, but she probably fears to provoke the King."

"Well, when you do come to court, heed what I say." Edward was stern. "It's one thing to act virtuously, and another to be seen to be virtuous. He's given you very valuable presents, hasn't he?"

Jane thought of the emeralds, locked away in the bottom of her traveling chest.

"Who told you that?"

"Our friend Cromwell is Master of the Jewel Tower. He knew that the King was going to give them to you."

Was nothing secret? "But I have hidden them. I cannot wear them; they are too grand for a knight's daughter. Everyone would know who gave them to me, and the Lady would have my hide."

Edward was severe. "Jane, you should never have accepted them in the first place. A virtuous woman does not receive gifts from a man unless they are betrothed or wed. You should know that. Promise me that, in future, you will return any presents the King offers you."

The rebuke stung. "But I did not know that! How could I? The occasion never arose. And the King did not think any the worse of me for it. He did not demand favors in return."

"Nevertheless, you will be more circumspect in future and be guided by me. If Father were here, he would say the same."

"Edward is right," Bryan said.

"I would not dream of accepting any more of the King's gifts after what you have said," Jane bridled.

Henry sent for her that evening, requesting that she come to the holyday closet.

She went, in defiance of Edward. She would not deny them this last opportunity for loving each other before they were parted. Her only concern was the risk of pregnancy, but desire overrode that. This time it was even more blissful than before. She had not known that such pleasure was possible. When she stole away in the middle of the night, so that none should suspect what she was about, she hurried through the sleeping palace as if on wings.

She saw Henry the next morning, coming out of the chapel after Mass, wearing his riding clothes.

"Good morning, Mistress Jane," he said, his eyes searching hers with a secret, knowing look.

"Good morning, your Grace," she replied, curtseying, aware of the gaze of his gentlemen upon her.

"I have something for the Queen," Henry said. "Come, I will give it to you to take to her." He took Jane's hand and led her to his lodgings, not caring who saw. It saddened her to see his privy chamber empty, stripped of its tapestries and furnishings, which had been sent ahead to York Place. She felt sick at the thought of his leaving. He led her to a door in the corner and up the spiral stair that led to the Queen's lodgings. Halfway, he turned to her, bent down and took her in his arms, holding her tightly as if he would never let go. "Jane! Jane! I do not know how I will bear being parted from you." His breath was hot in her ear.

"I will miss you too, Henry."

"I love to hear you call me by my name!" He looked down at her joyously. "I will write to you, and I beg you will write in return."

"Of course I will," she promised. "But I must go. I will be missed. Pray give me the thing you have for the Queen."

"I have nothing for the Queen," he admitted. "I just wanted to say goodbye to you properly. Oh, my love, how the time will drag until we meet again." He bent his lips to hers and kissed her longingly.

The great palace of Greenwich was echoing and deserted. Apart from the steward and a few necessary servants, only the Queen's household remained in residence. Jane wandered through the empty galleries and magnificent chambers, glad to get away for a space, because Anne was sunk in wretchedness. The Queen hated being confined to her chamber, she was hurt that the King had gone to London without her, and she was fearful about the future. Her temper was volatile, and she was prone to lashing out for the slightest reason. Jane had been slapped today, ostensibly for tugging too hard on Anne's hair, but she knew well that Anne gained great satisfaction in chastising her. The galling thing was that she had no redress. It was the privilege of any mistress to punish a servant who gave offense.

When she returned to the bedchamber, Anne was lying in bed, propped up on her pillows, and her female fool, a plump woman with a merry wit, was doing her best to rouse her from her misery. "Which are the most profitable saints of the Church?" she asked. The ladies shook their heads.

"Those painted on the glass windows, of course! They keep the wind from wasting the candles."

That raised a faint smile from Anne. The fool waved her stick, jangling the bells attached to it. "Which are the cleanliest leaves among all other leaves?" No one knew. "I'll tell you, then, it is holly leaves, for nobody dares wipe his arse with them!"

The ladies snickered.

"Have done," Anne said peevishly, and began weeping. "He could have celebrated Shrove Tuesday here at Greenwich, but no, he could not wait to get away from me," she lamented. "Once he could not be without me for an hour." She was working herself up into another frenzy. Raising herself on one elbow, she pointed a finger malevolently at Jane. "My only consolation is that he has been unable to take that bitch Seymour with him. He has had to leave her here for propriety's sake. No doubt, Madam Jane, you think he will abandon me and marry you, you whey-faced cow! Well, he will not, I promise you!"

Jane stood there, profoundly embarrassed, aware that everyone was looking at her.

"I suggest you leave," the Duchess of Richmond said coldly.

"With pleasure, Madam," Jane replied, and walked out, holding her head high.

"The King will surely send for me now that I am well," Anne assured her attendants. Jane, standing at the back of the group of women, as far out of sight as possible, rather doubted it. But daily Anne was eagerly awaiting a summons to York Place. When the hours passed and no word came, she was plunged once more into despair, and then the next day she would be hopeful again, and so it went on, made worse by the fact that riders in royal livery regularly brought messages from the King for Jane, to Anne's overt disgust.

Jane hid them in her sleeve, and read them in private. He loved her; he was missing her; soon they would be together. In the meantime, he was busy with the business of Parliament, but as soon as he was free of it, he would send for the Queen, and then he and Jane would be reunited.

She kissed his letters, and kept them in her bodice, next to her heart. She was missing him more than she could have imagined. She wished he was there to protect her from Anne's venom, and that he would tell her what had passed between him and Archbishop Cranmer—but maybe he would do so when he saw her. It might not be the kind of thing he would write in a letter.

Anne was becoming violently jealous. She watched Jane continually, her eyes dark with anger and suspicion, and picked fault with everything she did, slapping or pinching her for the slightest misdemeanor. Once she deliberately pinched Jane's hand with her fingernails, drawing blood.

There came the day when Jane had had enough. Always she wore the locket with Henry's picture, which made her feel close to him. It was usually concealed by the partlet she donned over her low-necked stomacher. But as she bent forward to retrieve a brooch Anne had dropped on the floor, the locket swung loose.

"Is that a new locket?" Anne asked sharply.

"Yes, your Grace." Jane prayed she would not ask her to open it.

"It's a costly piece. Let me see it."

"Why?" Jane asked.

"Because I command it!" Anne rose and faced her. Jane's hand flew to the jewel.

"Open it!" Anne shrilled.

"No." Jane would not be bullied.

Anne lost her temper. She ripped the locket from Jane's neck so violently that her hand was dripping blood, and fumbled with the clasp. Her eyes flashed with anger when she saw the portrait inside, and she thrust the locket back into Jane's hands. "Take it—and him! You are welcome to him!" But then, just as Jane was bracing herself for the blow that would surely follow, Anne's face crumpled and she sank to the floor, weeping. "If I could dismiss you from my service, I would do so with pleasure," she sobbed.

Margaret Douglas and Mary Zouche came running when they heard the cries. Jane deemed it best to leave her to their ministrations, and fled to the maidens' dorter.

She did her best to keep out of Anne's way after that, but it was not easy, for Anne made a point of singling her out. Fortunately, Anne's spirits had soared when she learned that Parliament had granted her two manors.

"It must have been done with the King's approval," she declared. "He still loves me above all others. Mistress Seymour, you are no more than another passing fancy. I doubt he will send for you again."

Jane was growing used to these barbs. It was best to ignore them and avoid engaging in an unseemly quarrel, so she had made it her policy just to stand there, eyes lowered, saying nothing.

Edward came secretly to see her, riding downriver in a hired boat and sending word of his coming ahead. She waited for him, shielded by a clump of trees in the park.

He embraced her hurriedly. "I dared not write," he explained, "but I have wished that you could be at court. The talk there is of nothing but the estrangement between the King and Queen. Many are of the opinion that the Lady is unable to conceive a child, and some even say that the Princess Elizabeth is a changeling, and that the miscarriage the other day was a pretense. I have heard it said that the King would marry you if he could. Messire Chapuys is contriving to befriend those who want the Lady removed. He is hoping that her enemies at court will unite to overthrow her. The King may send for her soon, and I will look to see you at court. Remember the advice I gave you, dear sister. We are all counting on you."

He left Jane in a turmoil, hurrying away as soon as he could, so that no one should see him. *The King would marry you if he could.* The words went round and round in her head.

In the third week of February, another royal messenger arrived at Greenwich, asking for Jane. Ignoring Anne's glowering gaze, she went into the antechamber, the women staring after her, and stood there cringing as he placed in her hands a letter bearing the King's seal and a heavy velvet purse. When she opened it, she saw it was full of gold sovereigns.

She must not accept either. Edward would be furious, and there was all the more reason now for her to be seen to be virtuous. Anne's ladies were watching, hostile, and this young man in livery would tell the King how she had received his gift. He would talk to his friends, and gossip would spread, and all would know how the King's sweetheart conducted herself.

She did not open the letter. She kissed it, as reverently as a subject would kiss the monarch's hand, and returned it, unopened, with the purse to the messenger. Then she fell to her knees. "I pray you, Sir, entreat the King in my name to consider that I am a well-born gentlewoman, the daughter of good and honorable parents, and without blame or reproach of any kind. Tell him there is no treasure in this world that I value as much as my honor, and on no account would I lose it, even if I were to die a thousand deaths. If the King wishes to make me a present of money, I ask him to reserve it for the time when God will be pleased to send me an honorable marriage."

The messenger looked at her curiously, but he thanked her and departed. She wondered how Henry would take her message. Would he understand why she had spoken thus? Pray God he would not be offended! She began to worry that she had done the right thing. But what else could she have done?

There was little time to wonder, for soon afterward the Queen was summoned to London and they were all plunged into a flurry of packing and preparing for the journey. A triumphant Anne was proclaiming to everyone that she had known the King would send for her as soon as she was well, and that he wanted her with him so that they could celebrate the feast of St. Matthias together.

"How appropriate," Margery muttered to Jane, folding towels. "He's the patron saint of hope!"

Chapter 19

1536

Jane wondered if Henry would seek her out when they arrived at York Place, but he did not. Her spirits, which had risen in anticipation of their reunion, fell. Maybe Anne was right, and his love for her had not survived the test of absence—or he was feeling rebuffed. She attended the Queen to chapel for the Mass in honor of St. Matthias, and Henry walked right past her when he went to make his offering at the altar, but did not acknowledge her. How she stopped herself from weeping she never knew. How would she face her brothers, or Bryan, or Carew, or Chapuys, if he forsook her? She did not think she could bear it. And what if she were with child?

At the feast in the hall that evening, she was seated with the other maids-of-honor at a table at right angles to the one on the dais. She watched Henry chatting with Anne and giving every appearance of being an attentive husband. Not once did he look in Jane's direction. And when the dancing began, he led Anne out and partnered no one else all evening. Jane went to bed disconsolate and fighting tears.

There was no word from him the following day. Anne was going about with a satisfied smile on her face. She sent for her mercer and her tailor and ordered satin for caps, and other pretty things, for her daughter. She laughed loudly with her brother when he came to visit her, and it was with a sinking heart that Jane heard them exulting that the Boleyns were still supreme at court.

By evening, when the summons came, Jane was ready to climb the walls in desperation. Whatever Edward said—and now that she was back at court, she must take care to be circumspect—all she knew was that she longed to see Henry alone, for one last time. After that, he must keep an honorable distance.

As soon as Anne was safely in bed, Jane sped as if on wings out of the palace and past the guards into the privy garden, where the moonlight cast long, mysterious shadows. Henry was sitting in an arbor, waiting for her. When he saw her, he sprang to his feet, enfolded her in his arms and whirled her around. "Jane!" he whispered. "Jane! How I have missed you!"

"Oh, I have missed you too, Henry!" Her unwonted boldness surprised her, and him too, evidently, for he kissed her more passionately than ever before. How could she have thought he had forsaken her?

"I had wanted to welcome you back long ere this," he told her.

"I thought you no longer loved me," she admitted, as he drew her down on the bench beside him.

"I feared that," he told her, gazing at her as if she were the Blessed Virgin herself. "But I have a duty to the Queen. This affair between us has distressed her, I know, and I promised I would not seek your company on the feast day."

She felt as if she had been slapped. He had a duty to the Queen? The last he had told Jane was that he was contemplating putting Anne away, and had been going to seek the advice of Archbishop Cranmer about it. Had he spoken to Cranmer at all?

"I was wrong to come here," she said, drawing away.

"Why?" Henry was astonished.

"I would not distress the Queen further." She looked away, trying to hide her tears.

"Jane," he said, "my duty is not only to the Queen, but to this realm. I need an heir, and a woman who is torn by jealousy is not like to conceive."

It took her a moment to understand what he was telling her. The realization hit her like a blow. He had not only had a stupendous change of heart, but he had returned to Anne. He had slept with her! It explained Anne's being so pleased with herself. She burst into tears.

"Darling, please!" Henry drew her into his arms. "I need an heir. It does not change how I feel about you. I love you."

She shuddered and disentangled herself, feeling as if she were dying inside. "I have no right to your love, Sir. It is wrong, what we are doing."

"Jane!" he protested, a look of anguish on his face. "Do not leave me! I have taken you for my only mistress. I was much moved by the message you sent when you returned my letter. You behaved most virtuously. It is rare to find that in my court. I only loved and desired you the more for it. I beg of you, stay tonight! I cannot bear the thought of losing you."

"If only you knew how it grieves me too," she murmured. "And it breaks my heart to know that I must share you with her."

"It is my duty," he declared. "Think of it as a matter of state."

She took his hand, realizing that she loved him, come what may. But if Anne became pregnant again, her own position would become more untenable than it already was. No one must know that she and Henry were lovers.

She stiffened. "I should not have come here. The very walls in this court have ears. There is too much gossip already, and if we were seen together like this, people would suspect the truth, and my reputation would be ruined."

Henry squeezed her hand. "Darling! I will ensure that never happens. To show the world that I love you honorably, I will not henceforth visit or speak with you except in the presence of one of your relatives. Will that satisfy you?"

"You know it will not. But it is the only way."

She feared it might lead to her losing him, but his eyes were filled with yearning. "Then it must suffice," he said. "We must hope that your family are not too vigilant."

She thought of Edward. He would be vigilant.

"One last kiss, I beg of you, before you go," Henry murmured, rising to his feet and taking her in his arms. When she broke away and ran along the graveled paths toward the Queen's lodgings, she wondered in despair where this love of theirs could lead. Nowhere, it seemed.

March came in. The daffodils were dancing in the wind and lifting their yellow heads to the sun as the court prepared to return to Greenwich. Edward found Jane in the Queen's garden and told her that Master Cromwell had most generously vacated his rooms in the palace so that he and Nan could occupy them.

She stared at him. "I had not realized you were become so important!" she exclaimed.

"If I am, it is because of you," Edward beamed. "These rooms are connected by a private gallery to the King's privy lodgings. Nan and I are being installed there as chaperones, so that the King can visit you in secret and preserve the proprieties. The fact that Master Cromwell willingly gave them up to us gives me cause to think that he takes the King's interest in you seriously."

"It is the King who has contrived a way for us to be together," Jane told him, exaltation in her heart.

Edward would not be gainsaid. "But Cromwell's assistance is significant, don't you see? He is actively supporting the King's courtship. And he hates the Boleyns."

"But he and the Queen are allies."

Edward put a finger to his lips and led Jane toward a deserted aviary. Behind the lattices she could see the caged birds hopping from perch to perch or pecking at their food. "They disagree on practically everything these days. She is an impediment to England's friendship with the Emperor, for which Cromwell and Chapuys are working hand-in-glove. Master Secretary is concerned about England's trade with the Emperor's dominions, for it has slumped since England and the Empire ceased to be friends."

"How do you know all this?"

Edward smiled, a trifle smugly. "Because Cromwell himself told me. He has made several friendly overtures lately. I do believe he is seeking my favor. I told you that the King's interest in you would bring advantages. Believe me, Jane, the reign of the Boleyns is coming to an end."

"What do you think the King will do?"

"Why, divorce the Lady! It's only a matter of time."

"That isn't the impression his Grace gave me. He spoke of getting an heir. And he did not speak to Archbishop Cranmer as he said he would."

Edward seemed unbothered by this. "Jane, you have much to learn about the King. He often says one thing when he means another. He even shows favor to those he intends to destroy."

Jane did not like hearing such things about Henry. "His concern about the succession is genuine. Maybe he has thought of marrying me," she said slowly, remembering his words of love and what he had said wistfully about her calming presence. "But the fact that he hasn't spoken of it makes me think he believes it isn't possible."

"Then we must make him believe that it is," Edward said, taking her arm and steering her along the path that led to the Queen's lodgings.

Two days later, Edward came to the Queen's chamber. The room was packed with ladies and gentlemen chatting, gambling, making music or flirting. Jane pushed her way through the throng to greet her brother. She could tell by his expression that he had momentous news. He looked more excited than she could ever remember seeing him.

"I am promoted to be a groom of the Privy Chamber," he told her proudly, "and it's been intimated to me that I am being considered for the post of master of horse." He lowered his voice. "And I have you to thank."

"Not at all," Jane said, impressed, for the office of master of horse was an important one. "You have achieved this by your own merits."

"No, Jane. This is what comes of the King's love for you. It's largely because of that that I stand in high favor with him. Others of equal merit have been passed over."

Jane saw that Anne was watching them malevolently, and guessed that she knew of Edward's promotion. "Someone does not approve," she murmured.

"She fears my having the King's ear," Edward said. "Jane, you cannot go on suffering her hatred. When we move to Greenwich and you lodge with Nan and me, you can resign from her service."

"Oh, that would be such a relief," Jane told him. "It has been a mortifying existence these past weeks."

Jane wondered how to broach her resignation to Anne. Should she write a formal letter? Or dare she risk telling her face to face? She shrank from the prospect. As the women unpacked and laid everything away, she pondered her dilemma, until, kneeling in front of the linen chest, she became aware of Anne holding forth to her brother. "Wholesale dissolution, that's what he's planning."

"It's just the smaller religious houses that are to be closed," Lord Rochford said, lounging on the window seat. He was a dark-haired fellow, handsome to some, Jane supposed, and he knew it.

"Mark me, Cromwell will close them all," Anne predicted. "Has he not promised to make Henry rich? All their wealth will go into his coffers, when some should be spent on education and charity. But Master Secretary's priority is to entrench himself in the King's good graces. God, how I hate that man! He has got so above himself. Do you know what I found out, brother? Last year he discussed with Chapuys the desirability of restoring that brat Mary to the succession."

Rochford raised his eyebrows. "Indeed."

"I'll see his head cut off first!" Anne fumed. "He thinks my teeth have been drawn, but I am more powerful than he thinks." She glared at Jane. "Mistress Seymour, stop gawping and fetch me some wine."

Jane stood up and poured some Rhenish into a glass goblet. She found she was shaking at Anne's contempt. She would not put up with it a moment longer.

"Your Grace," she said, handing the goblet to Anne, "I would like to resign from my post."

Anne sniffed. "Nothing would please me more!" she declared. "And the sooner the better. In fact, get your things and go now."

"With pleasure, Madam," Jane retorted, and walked out, but not before she had had the satisfaction of seeing Anne's jaw drop at her boldness. In the dorter, she dragged out her traveling chest, piled her clothes and possessions into it, and sent for a groom to see that it was carried to Edward's apartment. On the way out, she met Margery Horsman, coming up the stairs.

"I'm leaving the Queen's service," Jane said. "I'm going to lodge with my brother. I can't stand it here anymore."

Margery hugged her. "I'm not surprised. But I will miss you."

"And I you," Jane said. "I value your friendship. If ever I'm in a position to reward it, I will do so." She kissed Margery, then sped on down the stairs to freedom.

The apartment vacated by Cromwell was spacious and beautifully appointed, with painted friezes, gold battens on the ceilings, and a fine carved mantelpiece. There were three rooms and a privy, and Jane had a bedchamber all to herself. In it was a solid oak tester bed with embroidered hangings. She threw herself down on it, exulting at not being at the Queen's beck and call any longer, and being free of her constant barbs.

Nan was in her element. She had longed to come to court, but had never dreamed of doing so in such opulent fashion. She bullied their two servants into keeping the rooms in pristine splendor, ready for when the King should come. She was not a little jealous of Jane, but the prospect of entertaining her sovereign at her own table seemed to be ample compensation.

The first night Henry visited Jane, he gave no warning. The door leading from his gallery opened, and there he was, looking handsome in green and gold—and there was Nan, in her brown dress, with her hair uncovered and unbound, sinking into a flustered curtsey before flying off to change and bring out some cold meats and a raised pie from the court cupboard. Henry grinned after her. "I've heard she rules here," he murmured.

Jane nodded, making a face. In anticipation of his coming, which she had expected for the last two days, she had worn a becoming gown the color of a dove's breast, and left her fair hair loose. The locket with Henry's portrait hung at her breast.

"I will eat here, just to please her," Henry said, taking Jane's hand and kissing it. "Then, I trust, she and your brother will retire to the next room, so that, if you scream that I am ravishing you, they will hear and come at once." He chuckled.

"I hope that is not your purpose." Jane smiled. "If so, I had better scream now."

Nan came back then, looking more presentable, and full of apologies. "It is but a humble meal, your Grace. My husband will have finished his duties soon, and will join us." As she spoke, she was serving the food on pewter plates.

"This looks good," Henry said. "A feast, Lady Seymour!" He sat down and tucked in with relish, his knee pressing against Jane's under the tablecloth. It was wonderful to be close to him again.

Edward returned, expressing pleasure at seeing his sovereign already arrived, and they passed a very merry hour together over the supper. But when the last crumb of apple tart had vanished, and Henry intimated that his hosts should leave the room, Edward demurred.

"Sir, I understood that this arrangement was made to protect Jane's reputation. Maybe the door should be left open."

Henry frowned. "Her reputation is safe with me, Sir Edward. I would do nothing to compromise her. You and your good lady being within earshot is protection enough. Am I not a knight who understands the rules of chivalry?"

"Oh, no, no, your Grace, I did not mean to imply otherwise," Edward hastened to assure him.

Henry clapped him on the back. "I know that. You must forgive me for being an ardent swain. I'm sure you felt the same about the fair Nan here." Nan preened herself at the compliment. Edward looked at her proudly.

"I still do," he said gallantly. "Come, Nan, we will withdraw into the bedchamber. I wish your Grace good night."

It was the first of many pleasant evenings Jane spent sitting with Henry in front of the fire, talking, listening to him playing on his lute or singing in his fine tenor voice, reading poetry, or doing what lovers do. Soon kisses would give way to caresses, and then he would pull her down on the hearthrug, where they lay together, giving and receiving pleasure, and Jane was enthralled by the miraculous new sensations in her body. Before long, they took to creeping into her bedchamber and making love on her bed. Again and again she set aside her fears of pregnancy. They had been lucky so far, which gave her courage. Besides, her feelings for Henry were deepening. Far from losing interest, he was growing ever more ardent. She felt they were friends as well as lovers.

There were times when the lover's mask slipped and she caught glimpses of the tormented man beneath. His desperate need for an heir was eating away at him, and when he mentioned Anne, he was tight-lipped. Jane felt sorry for him. He had turned the world on its heels to have Anne, and now he was reaping a bitter harvest.

"I can see why he loves you, Jane," Nan said. "After that shrew of a wife of his, you must seem like a lamb."

Early March brought warm spring weather, and Edward asked Jane to join him for a walk in Greenwich Park. They climbed the hill behind the palace, on top of which stood an old tower with the pretty name of Mireflore, though it was long abandoned and had an air of decay and neglect about it. They did not go in, but sat on the grassy slope before it, gazing down on the impressive vista of the palace below, with the wide river beyond.

Edward looked around. "Thank God there is no one nearby," he said. "I need to talk to you, Jane. There was a meeting last night, arranged by Messire Chapuys, at his house at the Austin Friars in London. He is drawing together all those who wish to see the Lady divorced."

"You were there?" Jane asked.

"Yes, with our brothers. Chapuys has been showing himself increasingly friendly toward us since last year. Now he believes it is the time for action. The Lady is hated at court and in the kingdom at large. She and her followers are blamed for the radical laws that have been passed recently. Some resent her for promoting what they see as heresy and for being the cause of religious change, and while I myself cannot deplore that, certainly I agree that she is responsible for the slump in trade with the Empire."

"I think she is unsuitable in every way to be a queen," Jane said.

"Many of the King's subjects would agree, especially the women, I hear. They hate her for usurping the place of the old Queen, who was much loved, and they hold her responsible for the executions of Sir Thomas More, Bishop Fisher and the Carthusians."

Jane shrugged off her cloak. The sun was unseasonably warm. "She has managed to alienate several of the King's friends and lords, and even her own uncle."

"I forbear to tell you what they say about her abroad," Edward said. "Mostly it's obscene. I tell you, Jane, there will be few to champion her if the King decides to put her away. Which brings me back to Chapuys and the reason he called us all together. He believes that the best hope of the Princess Mary being restored to the succession lies in your becoming queen. No, Jane, let me finish! You are known to love and reverence the Princess, and Chapuys knows you for a lady of great virtue and kindness."

That was gratifying. "But the King has dropped no hint that he means to divorce the Queen. Why do you and Chapuys assume that he will do so?"

"It is not just me and Chapuys who are in this," Edward replied, lying back on the grass. "There were several people at the meeting, all of whom are resolved to bring down Anne Boleyn and all her faction. Bryan and Carew were there, and Lord and Lady Exeter, with Lord Montagu and others of the Pole family."

Jane gasped. "But they are the King's own cousins!"

"Aye, and they all have claims to the throne, being of the old Plantagenet line. The King distrusts them, not only on account of their descent, but also because they are religious conservatives and supported the late Queen. They are reactionaries, but because of their royal blood they have influence."

"They would support me, a knight's daughter, becoming queen?" Jane could barely believe it. The Exeters and the Poles were haughty and grand, proud of their exalted descent.

"They were vociferous in your favor, believe me!" Edward assured her. "Lord Exeter said to Chapuys that he would not be among the laggards to shed his blood for the Princess."

"Lady Exeter loved the old Queen. She used to smuggle messages from Chapuys to her." Jane had been in awe of Lady Exeter, a spirited, resolute woman whose passionate nature reflected her Spanish blood, her father having married one of the maids-of-honor who had come with the late Queen from Spain.

"Carew is a friend of both her and her husband, as is Lady Salisbury, Lord Montagu's mother."

"Was she at the meeting?"

"Yes, she traveled up from her house in Hampshire to be there. She approves of you too."

"And the Princess herself? Does she know of this meeting and its purpose?"

Edward smiled. "Chapuys assured us that she approves. He keeps her secretly informed of events. Believe me, she will sanction anything to get rid of the Lady. She loathes her—and she has expressed great love for us Seymours." He looked at Jane intently. "It is clear that Anne's position as queen is now untenable. The King will surely see that soon, if he has not already. And then—Jane, think of it! You can expect great things, and a glorious future. Because what I have not told you is that there was another person at the meeting last night, one more powerful than all the rest put together—Master Secretary Cromwell himself!"

"Cromwell?" Jane echoed. "By all the saints!"

"He is a friend and neighbor of Chapuys, and is determined on this alliance with Spain. The Lady is an impediment to that, and he knows she hates him."

"I've heard her disparaging him to her brother," Jane said.

Edward sat up. "I'm sympathetic to Mary, of course, and ready to stand up for her rights—and I know you are too. But if you marry the King, your sons will displace her from the succession. That must be our ultimate goal: a Seymour king on the throne of England."

Jane knew she should have been jubilant at the prospect, but it unnerved her. It was not her brother's naked ambition that was disconcerting, for it was no more than she would have expected from him. It was the images that had leapt into her head, of Anne screaming in labor; Anne distraught at the loss of each dead son; Anne desperate to bear a prince. She remembered how Katherine too had failed in that duty, and how it had blighted her life. If she married the King, that might be her lot too, and one day her enemies might plot to destroy her. It was the first time that the all-too-real possibility of this had occurred to her.

Edward was watching her. "Why so glum? Most women would be ecstatic at the prospect of becoming queen."

"Supposing I can't bear him a son either?" she whispered.

"Nonsense! We Seymours are a prolific lot. Mother bore ten of us. Look at the family tree! We breed like rabbits. It's one thing that must recommend you to the King as a bride."

"You make me sound like a prize cow," Jane retorted, but she felt better.

Edward shrugged. "It's the way of the world," he observed. "Even the lowest peasant wants a son to inherit his pig!"

Jane soon realized that she was being treated with a new deference by Henry's courtiers. She felt her influence increasing daily. People came seeking favors from her, and several offered gifts as inducements, all of which she declined to accept. They must learn that she could not be bought, and anyway, she did not want Henry to think that she was using him to get privileges for her friends.

Lady Exeter smiled upon her whenever they passed each other in the court, and once she paused when they met in an otherwise empty gallery. "You are doing an excellent job, Mistress Jane," she murmured. "Keep up the good work. We are all counting on you." Then she swept on.

Her brothers also found themselves the focus of much interest. People gravitated toward them as the rising stars of the court, fawning upon them and craving their patronage. They were thriving upon it.

At night, Jane often lay wakeful, wondering where Henry stood in all this. He must be aware of public interest in her. Was he still contemplating ridding himself of Anne? He had said nothing more to Jane.

Edward and Thomas incessantly enjoined her to keep him at arm's length, stress her virtue and hold out for the ultimate prize. "You must by no means comply with the King's wishes except by way of marriage," they commanded. What, she wondered, would they say if they knew what was going on nightly in Edward's own apartment, or of how, in her own quiet way, she was binding Henry ever closer to her?

March was almost out when Edward came back to their lodgings in a state of what was for him great excitement.

"I've just seen Chapuys," he said, surprising Jane, who was arranging spring flowers in a bowl. "He'd come from Cromwell, who told him that he believes his Grace, who has always been one for the ladies, will henceforth live more chastely, and not change again."

Jane's scissors clanged as she dropped them on the table. "Then he means to stay with the Lady." Her heart plummeted.

Edward snorted and grabbed her by the shoulders. "No, Jane. Cromwell was grinning when he said it. He meant that the King will not change again now that he has chosen you. That's how Chapuys took it."

She exhaled in relief.

"We have the impression that Cromwell will now do anything to get rid of the Lady. She openly rebuked him for giving up his rooms to us. She's accused him of corruption, and threatened to inform the King that, under the guise of the Gospel and religion, he is advancing his own interests."

"Do you think it's true?" Jane asked, secretly rejoicing that Anne's conduct had further stirred up Cromwell against her.

"It doesn't matter. She is convinced of it. Cromwell told Chapuys that she would like to see his head off his shoulders."

"She would not go so far?" Cromwell was invincible, surely?

"I doubt her wishes carry that much weight with the King."

"But she is clever, Edward. Master Cromwell should be wary."

"I am sure that he, of all people, knows how to take care of himself."

When Edward had gone, Jane sat thinking. Unless Cromwell knew something they did not, they were all careering headlong on their course lacking one vital advantage. Since the winter, Henry had not given any sign of wanting to rid himself of Anne.

He visited Jane that evening. These days, she waited to see if he would give her any clue as to how he saw the future unfolding, but tonight he seemed preoccupied. And when Edward knocked on the door and inquired if they would like more wine, he gratefully accepted it and gulped it down.

"They brought me the Valor Ecclesiasticus today, Jane," he said. "It is the survey of the religious houses that Master Cromwell had drawn up. As you know, his commissioners have visited all the smaller houses."

Jane's heart filled with dread.

"Many are redundant in terms of numbers and income," Henry said, "and in several, morality is lax." He sighed. "I intend to have Parliament pass a bill for their dissolution."

Jane thought of all the poor monks and nuns who would be dispossessed. Most of these small abbeys and priories had stood for centuries, bastions of faith and the succor of their local communities. Now they were to be closed down, and England would be the poorer for it. It was incomprehensible that Henry could take such a step.

"I feel sorry for those who will be turned out," she dared to say.

Henry poured more wine. "They have a choice. They will be offered pensions if they want to return to the world, or they can enter some larger monastery." That, at least, was encouraging. He could not, after all, be intending to close all the religious houses. Maybe he was right, and these small houses were licentious or incapable of supporting themselves. Yet they could not all be corrupt or penurious! She wanted to protest that he was wrong, wrong, to be doing this, but the deferential habit of years was too deeply engrained.

"Don't look so woebegone, sweetheart," Henry chided. "The monasteries have been in decline for a long time. Do you know there were only two new foundations in England in the last century?" His eyes narrowed. "Some are still loyal to the Bishop of Rome, and I will not have that."

"I am sorry, Henry," Jane said. "It is just that I have always held our local abbeys in great reverence. The monks and nuns were not worldly or ill-behaved. In my poor understanding, I had thought they were all shining examples of faith." Even as she said it, she thought of the Prioress of Amesbury again, and knew that she was not speaking the whole truth.

Henry looked at her affectionately and took her hand. "You are naive, darling. My commissioners uncovered things I would blush to relate to you. I would purge the Church in my realm, purge it of all corruption and bad practices. You would not want to see things like that flourish, would you?"

"No," she agreed, "of course not. But when these houses are dissolved, who will look after the sick and beggars, or teach the children, or shelter travelers?"

Henry frowned, letting go of her hand. "I doubt these lax places are doing very much of that anyway. You are too soft at heart, Jane, although that is one reason why I love you. Let us talk of other matters."

She smiled and heeded his warning. "Of course. I was shooting at the butts today. I was going to tell you—I won!"

He bent forward and kissed her. "Clever girl!" he said.

Chapter 20

1536

On the first day of April, Jane was in the apartment with Nan, sewing a dropped hem and enjoying the warmth of the sun shining through the latticed window. Outside, the trees were in blossom, and the world looked new and inviting. Inside, it was not so inviting. Nan was the problem. She was not relaxing company. Jane thought she was jealous, for all her superior attitude. She never complimented Jane on her attire, although Jane often praised hers. She was a mistress of the art of the veiled snub, and she made a dispute of everything. If Jane said she liked a thing, Nan would disagree, purely on principle, it seemed, and she would argue the point until she won. Always she had to be right. Jane was fed up with her opinions being belittled, however subtly.

A lot of the time, Nan could be good company, for she had a wicked sense of humor. But today she was in an aggressive mood, and they had been wrangling on and off all morning. Jane decided to go out as soon as she had completed her task, and take some bread and cheese into the park, with a small flagon of ale. Then she would find some quiet place to sit by herself and work on her embroidery, away from Nan's barbed tongue, and those others who bothered her, the inquisitive and the petitioners.

How lovely it would be if she could be with her sisters instead. They wrote from time to time, and Jane was glad to hear how happy Dorothy was with Clement, although it worried her to read that Lizzie was struggling financially in Yorkshire. She wished she could do something to help. Maybe soon she would be in a position to do so. At least the children were thriving.

It was not just her sisters she missed, but her friends in Anne's household, especially Margery Horsman. Not wishing to come face to face with her rival, or go anywhere near the Queen's apartments, it was almost impossible for her to see them; and given that Anne hated her, it was probably difficult for them to make contact with her. Someone might see and report back.

Feeling sadly isolated, she laid away the gown in her chest, packed her basket and let herself out of the apartment, praying that Nan would not suggest coming with her. But Nan was expecting Edward back soon, and made no secret of her desire to spend some time alone with him.

As Jane walked through the orchards toward the park, she heard an imperious voice calling her, and turned to see Sir Nicholas Carew and Lady Exeter hastening toward her. "We have been hoping to see you, Mistress Jane. Might we have a word?" The Marchioness made it sound like a command.

"Of course, my lady," Jane said, bobbing a curtsey. "Do walk with me, and you, Sir Nicholas." Carew bowed courteously, and soon they were striding across open grass.

"It is no secret to you that we would see a certain person brought down," Lady Exeter said, having looked around to see that no one was within earshot. "We and your other friends are working to that end, in the hope of seeing you raised to that place where you ought to be, to the comfort of all."

"I am very grateful to you, my lady, and to you, Sir Nicholas." Jane wondered what was coming next.

Lady Exeter smiled bountifully. She was a big-boned woman in her mid-thirties, with large black eyes and a determined chin. Her gable hood was encrusted with precious stones, great ropes of pearls adorned her black velvet bodice, and a long court train trailed behind her. Her fingers glittered with rings. There was no mistaking that she was of the highest ranks of the nobility.

"My husband the Marquess and I hosted a supper last night for Messire Chapuys. Lord Montagu was there, and others who share our views, including Sir Nicholas here. Chapuys told us in confidence of a report he had just received from France, that King Henry is soliciting in marriage the daughter of King François."

All Jane's pleasure in the day vanished. That was what Cromwell had meant when he said that the King would not change again. These good people were building castles in the air. Jane found herself trembling. It explained Henry's silence. Of course, it made sense that he would want to marry a princess—but Anne had not been a princess, and he had married her. And he loved her, Jane; she could not doubt it.

"It's probably mere gossip," Carew chimed in, looking at her with concern, "but we need your help."

Jane swallowed. "What would you like me to do?"

"We need you to bring the King to a decision about his marriage," Lady Exeter said.

Jane shook her head. "Alas, my lady, that is a delicate subject. He never mentions it, and I do not wish to be seen to be fishing for my own ends. And if this French match is being negotiated, it's no business of mine." She heard herself sounding bitter.

"It's everyone's business," Lady Exeter said stridently, "and you are best placed to help. It may profit you immeasurably, but even if it leads only to a marriage with France, you will have done this realm a great service."

Jane was adamant. "I do not wish to discuss marriage with the King. It would be immodest and forward."

"Tactics, Jane, tactics!" Carew smiled. There was an almost feline grace about this tall, personable man who was closer to Henry than most, and an air of worldliness that gave Jane confidence. "You need to take a lateral approach. Tell his Grace how strongly his marriage is detested by the people, and that none consider it lawful."

"What, boldly, just like that?" She could not see herself doing it.

"Say you have been out, to market or wherever, and you heard things that concerned you. Say you fear that the people of England will never accept Anne as their true Queen. Tell him they deplore her heretical leanings. Above all, make sure you say these things in the presence of us, your supporters, and we will all promptly swear, on our allegiance to the King, that you speak the truth. Lady Exeter is giving a supper for his Grace next Saturday. I will be there, and Francis Bryan, and your brothers, so you will have moral support."

They were asking her actively to plot against Anne. She did not hesitate. A crown, a kingdom and the true religion were at stake. And it would mean everything to her to know exactly where she stood with Henry, and what his intentions were. "I will do it," she said. She wished no real harm to Anne, only that she was removed from her unmerited glory before she could do further evil.

"Excellent!" Lady Exeter beamed. "My dear, you are doing so well. Hold on to your resolve. His Grace respects you for your virtue, but he is the King, and many have succumbed to his persuasions. Be warned: most were quickly discarded."

"I am aware of that," Jane said. "Never fear, my honor is my most prized possession." She could feel herself flushing.

"If you continue in this vein, you may yet win a crown." Lady Exeter smiled.

"If it is God's will," Jane said, still feeling as if the ground were shifting beneath her feet. But maybe the French marriage was only gossip, as Carew had said. She must not place too much credence on that report. Foreign gossip was often wrong.

Lady Exeter's words about the King's fickleness had brought to mind Mary Boleyn, and she confided to her companions her belief that Henry's affair with Mary had rendered forever forbidden his marriage to Anne.

"Chapuys is aware of this," Carew said. "But you are telling us that the King is too, and that still he continues in his marriage?"

"He was going to discuss it with Archbishop Cranmer, but I don't think he did. He spoke of getting more sons with the Lady, and said he had no time to waste."

"By God!" Carew exploded. "So much for the famous conscience! Well, Jane, you have another matter to raise with the King, but this one had perhaps better be discussed in private."

"I think I will ask Messire Chapuys to my supper, so that he can endorse what Jane says," Lady Exeter put in. "I will send him a note at once."

When they had gone, Jane sank down under a great oak tree and tried to eat the food she had brought, but it was tasteless in her mouth. Lady Exeter's words about Henry's fickleness with women had disturbed her.

Had she been foolish to imagine that he might condescend to marry her? She went cold with shame when she envisaged him discarding her as he had the others. She loved him, and in her mind, he was hers. If he stopped loving her, she would be desolate.

After a time, she made herself take out her embroidery. She would not sit here and mope. She told herself firmly that Henry's love for her could not be doubted.

At about five o'clock, she was finishing a satin-stitch border on a coif when she looked up and saw Lady Exeter riding across the park toward her. She drew up and dismounted, then tied her horse to a nearby tree and sank down heavily beside Jane.

"I'm glad I saw you here," she said. "I have good news. Messire Chapuys is coming to my supper on Saturday. I saw him just now. He had not long arrived back from the Spanish embassy, where he had dinner with Lord Montagu. There is much to tell, but first and foremost, he assured me that he will support you whenever possible. Spain and France being enemies, he would do everything in his power to oppose a French marriage. He favors you because he knows that you can help the Princess, whereas no French princess would be prepared to stand up for her rights."

"This is good news," Jane said, "but was anything more said of the French marriage?"

"Much! Be patient, my dear, and do not worry! Lord Montagu said at dinner that he had heard talk of a new marriage for the King. He told Chapuys that we are all worried about the bad state of affairs in this country, and said that the Lady and Master Secretary Cromwell are on bad terms. Before I saw him, Chapuys had been with Master Cromwell, who told him that the Lady hates him—Cromwell, I mean—and would see him executed. Then—and this is important, my dear—he asked Chapuys how the Emperor would feel if the King remarried. Chapuys insisted that the world would never recognize Anne Boleyn as his Grace's true wife, but that it might accept another lady."

"But who?"

"No name was mentioned, but Cromwell is no fool. He knows that Chapuys would never endorse a French marriage. If the King wants the friendship of the Emperor, he had best not marry a French princess! I am certain that you can rest assured on that score."

Jane laid down her embroidery. She saw Lady Exeter looking at it admiringly. "So Chapuys was hinting to Cromwell that the Lady should be replaced."

"Oh, yes! He said he took care to point out that if it was true that the King was treating for a new marriage, it would be the way to avoid much evil, and the best way of preserving Cromwell from the Lady's malice. He said a third marriage could only be of much advantage to the King, who knows quite well that this marriage to the Lady will never be held as lawful. Chapuys also said that he himself would welcome the birth of a son to succeed the King, even though it would affect the Lady Mary's prospects. Now you must know, Jane, that what is said to Cromwell gets back to the King, so some groundwork has been laid for you."

"What did Cromwell say?" Jane asked, hope surging anew.

"He was all smoke and mirrors, as usual. He said that if Fate fell upon him as upon Cardinal Wolsey, he would arm himself with patience and leave the rest to God. Then he said—and Chapuys was sure he was being ironic—that the King would henceforth live honestly and chastely, continuing in his marriage. But in the next breath he added that the French might be assured of one thing, that if the King were to take another wife, he would not seek her among them."

Jane felt as if a great weight had been lifted from her shoulders. "Naturally," Lady Exeter went on, "Chapuys was relieved to hear that, as I am sure you must be too, my dear. And Cromwell hinted that there are moves afoot to remove the Lady, and also that he would not support her if that happened."

"I wonder what those moves are," Jane speculated.

"Who knows? Our job is to give the King a little push!" Lady Exeter rose to her feet and pulled on her riding gloves. "Now I must leave you, my dear, for I should keep our friends up to date. If you would tell your brothers, I would be most obliged."

"I'm going to tell them now," Jane said, springing up and grabbing her basket. "They will be delighted."

"I think the cat's in the bag," Bryan said, when Jane told him, her brothers and Carew what Lady Exeter had said. "Your parents should be informed that soon they shall see you well bestowed in marriage. I myself will write to them."

"Aren't you being a little premature?" Jane asked, trying to imagine the effect such news would have on Mother. She did not want to raise their hopes. "The King has said nothing to me."

"He will, never doubt it!" Carew insisted. "And if the King gets a divorce, it will effectively be an acknowledgment that his marriage to Queen Katherine was valid. The way will be clear for the Princess to be restored to the succession."

Jane saw Edward's smile waver and Thomas frown. Of course, they had other ambitions.

"Don't be too sure of that," Bryan warned. "It's what Chapuys is hoping for, but will the King want to admit publicly that he was wrong to put Katherine away, and that the Pope was right all along?"

Edward spoke up. "I think his Grace should put his first two marriages firmly behind him, and make a third, which will not be tainted by the rights and wrongs of the past."

"The Lady might fight back," Jane pointed out. "She could be a constant thorn in the King's side."

"Without him, she has no power," Bryan said dismissively. "While he loved her, she was invincible, but he loves her no more, it's plain to see. And when the ship sinks, all the rats will desert it, I promise you. What profit is there in supporting a fallen queen?"

Jane stood with her brothers and Nan near the back of the Chapel Royal. It was Passion Sunday, and the Queen's chaplain, Father Skip, was mounting the pulpit. Above their heads was the royal pew, where Henry would be sitting with Anne. Across the nave, some way ahead, was the portly figure of Master Cromwell, with Chapuys next to him.

"Which among you accuses me of sin?" the chaplain's voice rang out. "It is not I who have attacked the Church! A king needs to be wise and resist evil councillors who tempt him to ignoble actions. A king's councillor ought to take good heed of what advice he gives in altering ancient things."

There was murmuring among the congregation. People were glancing at each other, amazed that Father Skip should so publicly attack the King. Jane trembled for him. Henry would be furious, she could not doubt it.

But the chaplain was undeterred. "Look at the example of King Ahasuerus, who was moved by a wicked minister to destroy the Jews," he continued. "That minister was Haman, who had also tried to destroy Ahasuerus's queen, Esther. But after Esther exposed his evil plot and saved the Jews from persecution, Haman was justly hanged. And thus triumphed this good woman, whom King Ahasuerus loved very well, and put his trust in, because he knew she was ever his friend."

Jane winced. Anne was fighting back. No one could be in doubt that this had come from her as a warning to Cromwell, who was standing there with a half smile playing about his lips, looking for all the world as if he found it funny to be compared to a wicked minister. Effectively Anne had declared war on her most dangerous enemy. But who would the King support?

Skip pressed on perilously. "Among his evil deeds, Haman had assured Ahasuerus that eliminating the Jews would result in ten thousand talents being appropriated for the royal treasury, and for the King's personal gain.

"So, in our own day, we have cause to lament that the Crown, misled by evil counsel, wants the Church's property, and will have it. We can only lament the decay of the universities and pray that the necessity for learning will not be overlooked."

Anne might have said it herself. But was it not madness to provoke Henry thus, and in public too?

Yet there was worse to come. Skip was looking sternly on his flock. "But it is not only in fleecing the Church that corruption lies. Look at the example of Solomon, who lost his true nobility through his sensual and carnal appetite, and taking too many wives and concubines."

This really was going too far. Henry had proudly shown Jane an exquisite miniature by Master Holbein that depicted him as Solomon, the wisest of kings. She knew there could be no doubt in anyone's mind as to whom Father Skip was referring. And people were looking at her, Jane, because she too was implicated in the chaplain's diatribe.

When Henry came to see her that evening, he was still simmering with anger.

"I am sorry that you and I were insulted by that sermon, darling," he said, his eyes like steel. "I have had that priest censured for his slanders. He disparaged not only us, but my councillors, my lords and nobles and my whole Parliament."

Henry must know who had been responsible. But he did not mention Anne, and Jane did not like to criticize her directly. Yet here was the opportunity she had been waiting for.

"I feel sorry for Master Cromwell," she said. "To be publicly humiliated like that is dreadful. But the worst of it was the insult to you, Henry. No subject should even think of his or her king in such a way." She laid the slightest stress on "her." "Do you think he said those things of his own accord?"

Henry snorted. "I am aware of who put him up to it."

"How can a woman do that to her lord, whom she is bound to love and honor?" Jane wondered, shaking her head. "Especially when you have raised her so high and done so much for her."

Henry's eyes narrowed. He looked sorry for himself. "It seems I am fated to be unlucky in my wives. Katherine defied me, and now Anne shames me. She doesn't know when to stop. I am weary of her tantrums and her opinions. I shouldn't be saying these things to you, Jane. But you are so different from her, and when I think of this mockery of a marriage in which I am trapped, I want to weep and rage!" He balled his hands into fists; the knuckles were white.

"Henry, I am so sorry," Jane said, thinking that she had said enough for today. She reached out and placed her hand on his. "You can talk to me anytime you need to."

He relaxed a little and patted her hand in return. "You are like an angel," he told her. "I know that God has sent you to me for a good purpose."

Lady Exeter had gone to considerable trouble over her supper. Her table, laid with a gleaming white cloth, was weighed down with roasted meats, raised pies, capons in a sauce, and a great venison pasty, on which Henry's eye alighted greedily, for it was his favorite dish. The wine flowed freely, and the sumptuously furnished little apartment was soon filled with the sound of lively conversation.

Jane was delighted to find herself seated at Henry's right hand, while Lady Exeter was on his left beside Lord Exeter, a dignified auburn-haired man who bore some resemblance to his cousin the King.

Messire Chapuys was sitting next to Jane. Her brothers were placed with Bryan and Carew on the opposite side of the table. Inevitably the talk turned to Sunday's scandalous sermon and another in similar vein preached since by Hugh Latimer, one of Anne's reformist protégés.

"It is appalling that the Queen's own chaplain should preach such calumnies," Lord Exeter said.

"He will be holding his tongue in future, if he knows what is good for him," Henry growled, but half in humor.

Jane gathered her courage. "It is not just he who should be silenced, is it, Sir?"

He stared at her. The merry mood was rapidly dissipating.

"Your Grace, there is much talk that he did not act alone, but was encouraged to preach sedition," Lady Exeter said.

There was a pause. Henry speared another slice of beef on his knife. "I am sure of it," he said. "But the person concerned told me that the attack was aimed not at me, but at Master Cromwell."

"Sir, it did not come across that way," Bryan declared.

"I felt that some of it was aimed at me," Jane said. "I was most embarrassed. People were staring at me."

Henry took her hand in his. "I will not have you upset by this, darling."

Chapuys smiled at her. He had never said much to Jane beyond the courtesies so far, but his manner had been deferential. "Your Majesty, we all know who was behind this outrage. May I speak frankly, as a friend?"

Henry nodded, frowning slightly. "Go on, my lord ambassador," he said.

"Believe me, I speak only out of concern for your Grace," Chapuys said. "You know I have never approved of the Lady, for many good reasons, but she has gone too far this time. Your Grace's patience is admirable. It is the talk of the court."

He had given Jane an opening. "Sir, the talk is not just confined to the court. Yesterday, Lady Seymour and I visited the market by London Bridge. There was a man with puppets in the guise of your Grace and the Queen, and I was shocked to see that the Queen was beating the King over the head with a rolling pin." It was the truth.

Henry flared. "By God, I'll have him arrested!"

"But Sir, there is more!" Jane laid her hand on his. They were all watching her intently. "Among the crowd, I heard things that concerned me. People were clapping and jeering, and saying how much they detest your marriage to the Queen. Some openly said that they do not consider it lawful. If they represent public opinion generally, I fear that the people of England will never accept Anne as their true Queen."

"Such opinions are indeed widespread," Chapuys said.

"I've heard them expressed often enough," Edward added, looking at Jane with approval.

"And I've heard many deplore what they call the Queen's heretical leanings," Lord Exeter revealed.

Henry's cheeks were flushed. "You think I am not aware of this? Every week my Council receives reports of slanders against the Queen. If the offenders are caught, they are punished, but it seems I can't silence everyone."

Edward spoke. "It is said, Sir, that the voice of the people is the voice of God. Is it too presumptuous of me to suggest that your Grace ought to heed public opinion? Maybe it is telling you something." Jane held her breath at his boldness.

"Three months ago you would not have spoken thus," Henry said.

He was not as angry as Jane had feared, but rather thoughtful.

"Three months ago, her Grace was expecting a child," Lady Exeter pointed out.

There was another silence. When Henry spoke, his voice was

hoarse. "Yes, but she lost it. All my sons by her have been stillborn. Have I truly offended God by marrying her?"

Jane lowered her eyes, but she was listening avidly.

"If your Majesty is not quiet in your conscience, then perhaps you should seek a remedy," Chapuys suggested.

"Perhaps I should," Henry said, with an air of finality. He attempted a smile. "But this is not a conversation to aid the digestion. Lady Exeter, pray summon your fool to cheer us!"

He had changed the subject, but Jane was not disheartened. It was enough that he had not reacted with anger to the opinions expressed here tonight. On the contrary, she believed he appreciated the concerns that had been voiced by her and others. She had done rather well, she reflected, surprised at herself.

On Maundy Thursday, Henry invited Jane and her brothers to join him for a game of bowls. To her consternation, she saw Anne and her ladies returning to the palace. Anne glared at them, her face a mask of enmity. Jane was frightened that she would make a scene, but she swept past without a word.

"Her Grace is on her way to the chapel for the Maundy ceremony," Henry said in Jane's ear, looking as relieved as she felt. It was customary for the Queen to distribute money to beggars and wash their feet. Tomorrow would be Good Friday, and the King would be creeping to the Cross on his knees and blessing rings to be given to those suffering from cramp.

"Do they really work?" Jane asked.

"Well, kings of England have been blessing them all the way back to Edward the Confessor, so there must be some virtue in them," Henry chuckled.

After the game, which he won, they strolled through the gardens, the courtiers following just out of earshot. Henry tucked Jane's arm in his. His face was troubled.

"You know why I have doubts about my marriage," he said. "I have spoken to Cranmer. He wasn't happy, for he loves the Queen and shares her zeal for reform, and he fears it would look bad if he were now to annul a marriage that he confirmed just three years ago. But he has agreed to look into the matter."

Jane's heart began racing. Surely Cranmer would see that it had been no marriage at all. And if he did, he only had to pronounce it invalid, and then . . .

On Easter Saturday, while Henry was meeting with his Council, Jane was wandering along the riverbank. With no duties at court, she had a lot of leisure these days, and it was her great pleasure to be out in the fresh air.

She had had a letter from Father this morning, asking her what Bryan had meant about seeing her well bestowed in marriage soon. Clearly he felt he ought to be more fully consulted, and Mother, of course, was agog. Did Bryan really mean what they thought he was implying? he asked. What was going on? Should they come up to court? She had hurriedly dispatched a reply, saying that the King's love for her had increased, but that he had so far said nothing to her that indicated he wanted to marry her, although he did have doubts about his marriage. Bryan had jumped to conclusions of his own. There was no need for them to travel up to Greenwich.

On her way back, she met Margaret Douglas and Thomas Howard emerging from one of the banqueting houses. Margaret's face was flushed, her French hood slightly askew. It was obvious that they had been indulging in some dalliance.

"Good afternoon, Mistress Jane," Margaret said. "We miss you in the Queen's chamber, although I dare say you do not miss being there."

"It is a relief to be out of it, my lady," Jane admitted.

"You did well to leave. Her Grace's mood becomes more uncertain by the day."

"Does she speak of me?" Jane asked.

"Yes, you are her constant refrain. She blames you for the loss of her son, and for her present unhappiness. But you have friends in

her chamber, Jane. Even Lady Worcester has turned against her.
And Margery Horsman speaks well of you. They would love to see
you. They have been bidden to avoid your company, you know."

"I thought as much," Jane said sadly. "My lady, I would like nothing more than to see them."

"Then come to my lodgings on Thursday, at eleven o'clock. The
Queen should be in bed by then." As the King's niece, Margaret had
her own fine apartment in the palace. "I will look forward to seeing
you," she said, and walked on.

Chapter 21

1536

Jane stood next to her brothers in the nave of the Chapel Royal, waiting for the Easter Tuesday service to begin. She was aware of a hum of excited anticipation among the congregation, which seemed larger than usual.

"What is happening?" she asked.

A man in front turned round. It was the handsome Sir Francis Weston of the King's Privy Chamber. "Ambassador Chapuys was received by Lord Rochford at the palace gates this morning," he told them. "It seems that he has made peace with the Boleyns, and we are waiting to see if he acknowledges the Queen." He nodded toward the other side of the chapel, where Chapuys was standing near the foot of the stair that led up to the royal pew.

"He will never acknowledge her," Jane said, astonished and bewildered.

"If this new alliance with the Emperor is to go ahead, it may be expedient to do so," Edward murmured.

"She is not in favor with the King," Thomas said, "so it will profit him little to pay court to her."

"We shall see," Edward said. He hated it when Thomas challenged what he said.

A hush descended. The King and Queen must be arriving and taking their places.

During the service, Jane kept glancing at Chapuys. She thought he looked unusually tense. Surely he would not recognize Anne as queen? What of his promises to support her, Jane?

Presently, Henry appeared at the foot of the stairs, and proceeded to the altar to make his offering. Anne followed, with all eyes upon her. As she came through the door, Chapuys hesitated for a moment, then bowed. Jane was not the only one who gasped. That this man, who had been such a champion of Katherine and Mary, who had defied the King by calling them by their proper titles, and who had, for years, steadfastly refused to recognize Anne as queen, would do reverence to her was unbelievable. And now Anne was performing an elegant curtsey in exchange, before processing to the altar with a triumphant air. To Jane's amazement, Chapuys followed, and handed Anne two candles to use in the ceremonies. Jane was shocked.

Edward whispered in her ear, "He must be acting at the Emperor's bidding." But it was small comfort. It felt to Jane as if she had lost something very valuable. And then it occurred to her that Henry himself must have arranged or approved the encounter, for Chapuys had been placed in a position where he could not but have come face to face with Anne. Why would Henry want Chapuys to acknowledge Anne as queen if he was thinking of divorcing her?

She left the chapel despondent, thinking she might go home to Wulfhall, try to forget about Henry and the court, and ask her father to find some acceptable husband, so that she could be free of all the intrigues and uncertainties, and live out her days in peace and obscurity, surrounded by her children. When Edward hastened after her, she pushed him away and fled back to her bedchamber so that she could weep in privacy.

In the middle of the afternoon, there was a sharp rap at the door, and there stood Lady Exeter. She took one look at Jane's tearstained face and shook her head disapprovingly. "Battles were never won by weeping!" she declared. "Come! I have rallied the troops. We are going to pay a call on Messire Chapuys!"

Jane could not but be heartened by such resolve. Hurriedly she washed her face, put on her hood and followed Lady Exeter into the outer gallery, where she found her brothers, Exeter, Montagu, Bryan and Carew waiting for her. As they went to find Chapuys, they expressed their anger and astonishment at the deference he had paid to Anne.

They found the ambassador in the great hall, preparing to depart.

When Lord Exeter, as spokesman, confronted him, with Lady Exeter chiming in stridently, Chapuys looked abashed.

"Sirs, the mutual reverences done at the church were at the command of the Emperor—and of the King. His Imperial Majesty wants an alliance with England, and he is prepared to recognize the Lady as queen so long as the Princess Mary is restored to the succession before the bastard Elizabeth. My master is aware that moves are afoot to unseat the Lady, yet he does not wish to waste time, and he fears that the King is lukewarm about the alliance. Indeed, if I had seen in his Grace any enthusiasm for it, I would have offered two hundred candles to that she-devil!"

"But it did not look good," Lady Exeter pointed out.

Chapuys spread his hands self-deprecatingly. "You all know me, how I have fought for the Princess's rights, and for the true Queen, in her day. I am ashamed to think that you might believe I have betrayed you and the Princess. Indeed, I am resolved never to speak to the Lady again, and I shall tell the Emperor so. What happened this morning left me with a bitter taste in my mouth, and I did not attend the dinner she was hosting. Instead, I dined with Lord Rochford and the chief nobles of the court in the King's presence chamber. Politeness required such a courtesy."

He turned to Jane. "I can see that my ill-considered action has upset you, Mistress Seymour, and I am sorry for it. I am still your friend, and I will do my very best for you."

Jane smiled at him, feeling immensely relieved. "You were placed in an impossible situation. I understand how difficult it was for you."

She thought she understood too why Henry had forced Chapuys into making that obeisance. He would not lose face with the Emperor. He had made Anne queen in defiance of Charles and the rest of Europe, and he would have Charles's representative acknowledge her. Yet still there was some doubt nagging at her mind as she returned to the apartment. Anne, and no doubt many others, had seen the gesture as representing her return to favor, for it had been an overt move to win the King's approval. Would Henry really divorce Anne after securing the Emperor's recognition of her? It did not seem likely. All Jane had to cling on to was Cromwell's intimation that Henry meant to marry again.

That evening, Edward walked in with a grave face. "Master Secretary is in trouble," he told them.

"No!" Jane cried. "Surely not?"

He grimaced. "I was there. I saw what happened. The King was in an irritable mood this afternoon. He spoke harshly to Chapuys, and said he was not interested in an alliance with the Emperor against France."

"But what of Cromwell?" Jane wanted to know.

"When the King summoned Cromwell and Lord Chancellor Audley, Chapuys came over to where I was standing, and told me that Cromwell had clearly overreached himself in negotiating the alliance independently of his Grace. The King was sitting with Cromwell and Audley in the window, and we could see that he and Cromwell were angry with each other. I'm sure his Grace was furious with Master Secretary for exceeding his authority; apparently Cromwell agreed to the restoration of the Princess before seeking his approval."

"I wouldn't have liked to be in Cromwell's shoes," Nan remarked. "I've never seen him look so frightened. I think he was fast realizing that he had badly miscalculated, and that neither the King nor the Emperor would ever agree to each other's terms. Afterward, he was in despair."

This was terrible news to Jane. Cromwell had been her friend, and now he might no longer be able to help her at all. Henry would not lightly forgive such an infringement of his royal privilege, or being made to look a fool. And if Anne was indeed back in favor, as Jane feared, she might well take advantage of the situation and demand Cromwell's head. She had done as much with Thomas More, and she had made it clear that she would bring Master Secretary down if she could.

"If Cromwell falls, then the Boleyns will rule all," she said brokenly.

"Do not despair, Jane," Edward soothed. "Chapuys is still in hope of a good outcome. He thinks the King may be bluffing in order to secure greater advantages from the Emperor, and that he has made Cromwell his whipping boy. It is possible that that little charade was staged for Chapuys's benefit."

"I pray he is right," Jane said.

On Thursday evening, Jane was still fretting as she made ready to visit Margaret Douglas, and was pinching her pale cheeks to give them some color when Edward came in.

"Something is afoot, and you should know about it," he said, his expression serious. "Cromwell has just gone down to the country, to his house in Stepney. Ostensibly he is ill, and Chapuys is telling the Emperor that he has taken to his bed from pure sorrow. But there is more to it than that. Cromwell summoned me and Thomas before he left, and told me that he has been secretly meeting with various councillors and all our friends, who are more numerous than we think. He said he knows that the Lady is out for his blood, and fears that she may capitalize on the King's displeasure. He is determined to preempt her. Jane, you had best sit down."

Jane sank on to a stool, wondering what was coming. Edward

took another, and leaned forward, regarding her gravely. "Cromwell thinks we have all been naive in thinking that an annulment of the King's marriage would be sufficient to get rid of the Lady. She is clever and devious, and still has support in the Privy Chamber. He says that more radical action is called for. To that end, he has befriended those who would not normally be his natural allies, for he is no conservative or lover of the old faith. That is the measure of his determination to unseat the Lady!"

"But we all share a common aim," Jane observed.

"Yes, and that aim is to make you queen. Cromwell realizes that bringing that to pass offers him his best chance of survival."

"What did he mean, more radical action?"

"He has received certain reports from France against the Queen that offer a pretext for her removal. He was not specific, but he said that if we were happy to leave it to him, he would see that we achieve our purpose. He's a lawyer, Jane, and a clever one. We can rely on him. Chapuys is for it; he has already written to ask for the Princess Mary's approval. He says he is happy to unite with anyone who could help bring the Lady down, for they do a meritorious work that will prove a remedy for her heretical doctrines and practices."

Jane was perplexed. "I wish I knew what Cromwell intends. Aside from annulment, what other way is there of getting rid of her? Even if she has done something wrong, that is no pretext for dissolving the marriage."

"She could be immured in a nunnery. Then the King could be released from his vows. Or he could divorce her by Act of Parliament. That might well be what Cromwell is aiming at, and he may use these reports to discredit her in the King's eyes, so that he agrees to it."

"She has brought this on herself," Jane said. "God could never smile on her unlawful marriage." She could not feel any sympathy for Anne.

"God send that Cromwell moves quickly," Edward said grimacing.

Jane's head was spinning as she made her way to Margaret Douglas's lodgings later that evening. She had not seen Henry since the dramatic events of Tuesday, so she had no idea of what he was thinking about Anne or Cromwell—or even her own self.

Margaret welcomed her warmly. In her chamber, a visibly pregnant Lady Worcester and Margery Horsman were waiting. They embraced Jane with much affection and, she detected, a certain deference.

Margaret invited them to sit and called for wine. Sipping it, Jane was waiting to catch up on news and gossip, but there was a short silence, during which the others looked awkward.

"Something has happened since we met on Saturday," Margaret said at length. "You ought to know about it, Jane."

This was the second time something in that vein had been said to her that evening, and Jane was alarmed. What other ominous news was she to hear?

"It's about me." Lady Worcester looked shamefaced. "Foolishly I flirted with two gentlemen in the Queen's chamber, and my brother saw me and leapt to the wrong conclusions." Jane knew the Countess's brother by sight; Sir Anthony Browne was a member of the Privy Chamber, and she had seen him in company with Edward once or twice.

"What did he do?" she asked.

"He took it upon himself to admonish me. Whereupon I replied that yes, I had behaved lightly, and been wrong to do so, but it was little in comparison with the behavior of the Queen."

"The Queen?" Jane echoed.

"I told him what you must surely know: that she admits some of her court into her chamber at improper hours. And then, God forgive me"—suddenly she was crying—"I repeated something Mark Smeaton had confided to me, and I don't even know if it's true."

Jane was almost dumbstruck. She knew nothing of Anne's nocturnal activities. "That musician? What does he know of the Queen's affairs?"

"He is in love with her," Margery enlightened Jane. "I thought you knew. There has been gossip about it since last year's progress."

"I did hear something of it," Jane said. "It is not reciprocated, of course?"

"No, she spurned him quite firmly at Winchester, and never acknowledges him now," Lady Worcester informed her, dabbing at her eyes. "So Mark turned spiteful. He told me—and no doubt others—that the Queen was promiscuous, and that he could tell much more if he pleased."

"Is it true?" Jane asked, staggered.

Lady Worcester swallowed. "I do not know. But I told my brother and my half brother, Sir William FitzWilliam, what he had said. William once served Cardinal Wolsey, and has no love for the Queen, who brought his old master to ruin. Anthony hates her too. He and William urged me, on their allegiance to the King, to go to Master Secretary Cromwell and tell him what Mark had said to me. So I did. And now I wish I had kept my mouth shut. I used to be close to the Queen, but she is hard to love these days. Even so, I would not do her any injury." She looked deeply distressed.

Jane was wondering if this had anything to do with the French report that Cromwell had received. It didn't sound like it. "No one could take what Mark said seriously," she said, in an attempt to comfort Lady Worcester.

"But Cromwell has!" Margery burst out. "The Queen's chamberlain summoned me today and asked if I knew that the Queen was promiscuous. I told him she likes to flirt with the gentlemen, but then we all do, and it is an accepted thing. He asked if she was alone with men in her chamber late at night, and I said only with her brother on occasion; they like to talk privately together. But I assured him that I had never seen her behave improperly. He pressed me again, as if he wanted me to say she had, but I said I had told him all I knew, and that surely he had better things to do than to rake up scandals when there were none!"

A feeling of dread descended on Jane. Was Cromwell trying to make a case against Anne? If so, Anne could be in very serious trouble indeed. "What would happen to the Queen if Mark's allegation was true?" she asked.

"I don't know," Lady Worcester said. "The King would surely regard it as a very serious offense."

"It might be considered treason," Margaret said. "The succession could be compromised, even the legitimacy of the Princess."

Jane went cold. "Treason?" she repeated.

"Yes," Margaret said. "And the penalty, I fear, is burning."

"Oh, dear God!" Lady Worcester gasped. "I would I had never said anything!"

Jane was stunned. Of course, accusing Anne of treason would be the most effective way of getting rid of her. It was utterly abhorrent. She had envisaged a divorce, then obscure retirement, not this horror. She hated all that Anne stood for and wanted to see her unseated, but she would not wish such a fate on her worst enemy. Burning was the most dreadful of deaths.

"The trouble is, it's all too credible," Margaret said. "Many believe her to be a whore; her reputation is poor and she is unpopular. And she does flirt, she is indiscreet. I've seen her with Norris. There's something between them."

"I've noticed that," Margery added. "Maybe Mark has too and is jealous. But if she is being unfaithful to the King, how does she manage it? She enjoys little privacy. We're either sleeping in her chamber or within earshot, even when the King comes to her at night."

"Unless, of course, someone among her maids or ladies is helping her," Lady Worcester suggested, still looking distraught.

"But who? It would be hard to keep that a secret," Margery declared.

"All I pray is that they realize it was just malice on Mark's part," Lady Worcester said. But Jane trembled lest there would be much more to it than that. Cromwell had undertaken to get rid of Anne. Was this how he was going to do it? She did not want to be queen by means of Anne's agony.

"We must not speak of this to anyone," Margaret said. "A still tongue . . ." She looked sorrowfully at Lady Worcester.

As Jane walked back across the silent cobbled courtyard and through the deserted galleries, her mind was churning. Pray God they would see Smeaton's remark for what it was—unless, it occurred to her, there was substance in it. She paused in her steps. No, it would have been impossible. Anne had been preoccupied with trying to present the King with an heir and keeping his love. She had been almost constantly pregnant or recovering from giving birth, and she certainly could not have had an affair without someone knowing about it. She was never alone!

Even if it were true, she could not believe that Henry would condemn a woman he had passionately loved to such a terrible death. He would show leniency, she could not doubt it.

Crowding in upon these disturbing thoughts came guilt. If the worst happened, she would be to a degree responsible, for was it not partly on her account that Anne's enemies were conspiring to ruin her? Even if she said "Enough!" now, the damage would have been done. All she could do would be to try to ameliorate Anne's fate. She believed she had sufficient influence with Henry to do that.

Creeping into the apartment, she undressed in the dark and lay down. She did not sleep.

Three days later, Jane saw Cromwell in the court. She wondered what was in his mind. Still she had not seen Henry, and by now, after everything they had been to each other, it was hard to believe that all was over between them. It was heartrending, but maybe it was for the best. Her grief at the prospect was mingled with relief. She had involved herself in dangerous intrigues. When she had told her brother what she had heard in Margaret's lodgings, their jubilation had taken her aback and jolted her into a new awareness of how hazardous a place the court was, and how perilous the future of a queen who had failed to bear the King a son.

Now she was asking herself if she really wanted a crown and all the risks that went with it. Did she want to be anxiously looking for her flowers each month, and dreading the consequences if they appeared? Could she live with the constant threat of failure, in terror that her enemies would pounce? She loved Henry, but did she really want to embrace a future fraught with fear? Better to suffer the pain of losing him now than to endure worse suffering later on.

She thought with longing of Wulfhall and Mother. She would go home tomorrow. Edward and Thomas would not like it, but they had to accept her decision. And then she ran into Thomas in a gallery. His handsome face was flushed with jubilation. "Great news, Jane!" he cried, giving her a hug. "The King has just presided over the annual chapter of the Order of the Garter. The Boleyns are trounced! There was a vacancy for a new Garter knight, and the bets were on that Lord Rochford would be chosen, for the Lady had asked that he be preferred, but the King chose Nicholas Carew instead. I bet she is spitting with rage!"

"The King knows Sir Nicholas for my supporter," Jane said, somewhat cheered.

"And this proves that the Lady has not sufficient influence to get the honor for her brother. Chapuys says it means the Boleyns are falling from favor. And good riddance too, I say!"

"Amen to that," Jane said, but without conviction. She did not care about the Boleyns falling: it was how they fell that concerned her. She thought she might delay her departure for Wulfhall for a day or so, to see what happened.

Chapter 22

1536

She was overjoyed to see Henry at her door that evening. All her doubts and fears faded at the sight of him. He had come bearing a bunch of love-in-idleness, exquisite white violas that proclaimed his love for her. "They are beautiful," she exclaimed, burying her face in the soft petals and breathing in the scent.

"I knew you would not accept a jewel," he said, regarding her intently, "so it is flowers for England's fair flower. I am sorry for not coming to see you sooner. I have been much occupied with state affairs." His face clouded a little. Jane felt the first stirrings of dread.

She poured some wine, and offered him little cakes she had made using Mother's recipe and had asked to be baked in the palace ovens.

"These are good," Henry complimented her. "I should put you in charge of my kitchens." But there was little mirth in the remark. He leaned back in his chair. "Oh, Jane, what a day I have had. Anne is raising hell because I gave the Garter to Carew. But I promised King François years ago that I would remember Sir Nicholas, whom he loves, when a Garter vacancy arose, so I was bound to allow his name to go forward."

"I'm sure her Grace can understand that," Jane said.

"No, she doesn't. She railed at me like a fishwife." Henry closed his eyes. The quarrel had clearly upset him.

"Shall we play cards?" Jane suggested. Henry nodded, and she fetched the pack and dealt. They completed two rounds and then he threw his cards on the table.

"It's no good, Jane. I can't concentrate. Something else happened today, and I must speak of it."

She gazed at him in some alarm. "What is it?"

Henry hesitated. "This is in the strictest confidence, Jane. Promise you will speak of it to no one."

"I promise," she said.

"Thank you. Master Cromwell is better and back at court. Late this afternoon, he came to me with a deputation of the Privy Council. I was surprised to see them, for I could not think what they had come for. They were nervous, and no wonder!" His blue eyes narrowed. "Cromwell said that they had heard disturbing reports of the Queen's conduct. He told me that his suspicion had first been aroused by a horoscope cast in Flanders, which predicted that I would be threatened by a conspiracy of those who were nearest to me."

Jane began to shake. It seemed that her worst fears were being realized. "They were worried about a mere prophecy?" she asked. Probably Cromwell had inflated it for his own purposes into something sinister. He had a pressing motive, God knew. So any move against Anne should be on his conscience, not hers.

"No," Henry said darkly. "I would that were all, but they have depositions from some who have laid evidence about the Queen's misconduct, which suggest that she has been conspiring against my life."

Jane's hand flew to her mouth. This was worse than anything she had imagined. "But that is treason!" she whispered.

"Yes, and those who had been examining the witnesses were quaking at the danger as they knelt before me. They declared that, on their duty to me, they could not conceal it from me, and they were absolutely right not to do so. They were praising God that He had preserved me for so long from such evil designs. By the Mass, to think of how narrow an escape I might have had! It seems I have nurtured a viper in my bosom." He spat out the last words.

Jane was horrified. Infidelity was one thing; conspiring against the King wholly another. Surely Cromwell would not have gone so far as to invent a charge like that, even if he had made too much of Mark Smeaton's remarks.

"Are the proofs convincing?" she asked.

"The evidence I have seen was damning on the face of it, but it is not enough to enable us to lay charges. I have ordered further investigations and will wait to see what they uncover. If the allegations prove true, they will, of course, have serious implications for the succession. Oh, Jane!" He buried his head in his hands. She reached her arms out and held him.

"I am so sorry, so very sorry," she murmured in his ear.

He looked up. His eyes were like ice. "Even if there are no more proofs, I am resolved to be rid of her. Cranmer will have to find a way."

"I pray that you will need to do no more than that," she said.

"I will do whatever is necessary," Henry declared. "I cannot let treason go unpunished. It would be seen as weakness." He gave a deep sigh. "Once I would have been devastated to see this evidence, but now . . . I am wounded in my pride, not my heart. I am more angry than sad. But I must reserve judgment." He stood up. "I'm sorry, sweet Jane, I am not good company tonight. I don't want you embroiled in this, but I am very grateful for your sympathetic ear. You have a wise approach to life; you see the nub of the matter, and that helps me to see things more clearly."

"I am always here if you need me, Henry," she replied, taking his hand.

He bent and kissed her. "I will come again soon, and you will be mine again."

After he had gone, Jane was in turmoil. Part of her felt horror at this affair of the Queen; another rejoiced at the deepening understanding between herself and Henry. It gave her hope that when the time came—if it came—she might be able to plead for mercy for Anne. Hate her she might, but she could not have her blood on her conscience.

The usher wore royal livery. "Mistress Seymour, Master Secretary Cromwell asks that you attend upon him as soon as is convenient."

Jane was filled with trepidation. "I will go to him directly," she said. The usher nodded politely, and escorted her to the council chamber. The room was empty apart from Cromwell and Sir William FitzWilliam, who sat at the far end of the board with a pile of papers in front of them. Jane curtseyed as both men stood up and the usher closed the door behind her.

Cromwell smiled and indicated that she should sit opposite them. "This won't take long, Mistress Jane. His Grace is aware that you are here."

FitzWilliam spoke. He had a hatchet face and an abrupt manner. "We are investigating certain allegations made against the Queen, so everything said at this table is in the strictest confidence. Do you understand that?"

"Of course." Jane hoped they could not see how nervous she was.

"When you were in her Grace's service, did you see or hear anything that concerned you?" Cromwell asked.

"No, I did not," she said.

"No hint of unfaithfulness to the King?"

"No." Surely they would believe her; she, of all people, had good cause to wish Anne out of the way.

"Did she spend time alone with gentlemen in her chamber?"

"Not that I recall."

"Did she show special affection to any particular gentleman?"

Norris's handsome face came to mind. "No," she said.

"Not even in a way that you might have interpreted as mere friendship?"

"Her Grace is close to her brother, of course, and she favors many of the gentlemen in her circle, but not in an improper way."

Cromwell leaned forward. "When you say 'favors,' what do you mean?"

"She showed herself friendly and condescending to them. She played music and cards with them, and made merry. It was all innocent. There was nothing that struck me as inappropriate."

"Did she flirt with them?" FitzWilliam asked.

Jane was wary. "I'm not sure what you mean, Sir."

"Did she banter with them, or make eyes at them, or touch them?"

"She shared jests, quite openly, and sometimes made faces in jest, but she only touched them by the hand when there was dancing in her chamber."

Cromwell was beginning to look frayed. "Did she ever make any jests about the King?"

"No."

"Did she ever criticize his poetry or his clothes?"

They really were scraping the bottom of the barrel! "No." They looked at each other.

"Very well, Mistress Jane, you may go," Cromwell said, with less courtesy than when he had greeted her. She rose and left, glad to be out of what felt like tainted air.

Henry apologized that evening. "Cromwell thought you might know something, Jane. I'm sorry if you were inconvenienced. They are questioning all those who have served the Queen, and today the Lord Chancellor has appointed two Grand Juries to hear and judge the evidence. They will determine whether there is a case to be made against her, and whether it should proceed."

This sounded ominous. "Have you seen any new evidence?" Jane asked.

"Not yet, but Master Cromwell advised the appointment of these juries to assist in his investigation." He drew in his breath. "Darling, let us talk of more pleasant things. Come here!" He kissed her long and lovingly.

Two hours later, when the King had departed, Jane sat on her bed, pensive. Her flowers were overdue. The realization alarmed her, and she tried frantically to remember when she had last bled. She was sure it had been in the third week of March. Dear Mother of God, that meant she was a week late; she might be with child. But how would she know for certain? What other signs would she look for? She cursed her ignorance. She dared not think of the implications if she was pregnant. What would Henry do?

She was brooding on this when Nan knocked and came to sit with her. Although theirs had never been an easy friendship, she knew that Nan was on her side, and she approved of Nan's devotion to Edward, even if she did dominate him.

Nan was bursting with news. "Edward says that two Grand Juries have been appointed to investigate crimes in Middlesex and Kent. It's all around the court, for many gentlemen have been commanded to serve on them. He thinks it portends something of great moment, for Lord Exeter says it is rare for such juries to be appointed. Chapuys knows; he said Cromwell hinted to him that this concerns the Queen."

Jane feigned astonishment and crossed herself. "If so I fear for her."

"Whatever it is, she has probably brought it on herself," Nan retorted.

"What if they are making an occasion to get rid of her?"

"You should be grateful that the way might be cleared for you to become queen," Nan said.

"But I do not want to step over Anne's dead body to do so," Jane flared. "It is wrong to benefit from someone else's misfortune."

"People do it all the time." Nan shrugged. "And anyway, Chapuys thinks the King will just end up divorcing her. He said that Elizabeth will almost certainly be excluded from the succession, and that the Princess Mary might be restored, after any children you bear the King. Mary will be overjoyed."

"You're forgetting one thing," Jane reminded her. "The King has not mentioned marriage, still less children. You are all taking it as a foregone conclusion."

"It would not be appropriate for the King to offer you marriage while he still has a wife," Nan said.

"He did with Anne Boleyn!"

Nan would not be bested. "We shall see," she insisted. "Be grateful that Chapuys is using all means to promote the matter, with Cromwell and with others. He is determined to make you queen."

Sir Nicholas Carew seemed always to be looming on Jane's horizon these days. He was proving indefatigable in her cause, and she was grateful for that, given her mounting conviction that she was with child.

"Make an assault!" he urged her. "Capitalize on what is happening now. Surely you can remember something they can use against the Lady."

"I can remember nothing amiss," she said firmly. She could not wholly deplore his ruthlessness, since he was so entirely on her side, but she did her best to channel it. "There is no need for them to take this course!" she cried. "There are good grounds for an annulment. That's all that is needed, surely?" She could hear the fear in her voice.

Carew regarded her with his fine dark eyes. "Ah, but our friend Cromwell wants to make sure that she won't remain a nuisance after she has been put away."

"Her teeth will have been drawn. He has no cause to worry."

"But she has a daughter, and might fight for her rights as the old Queen did. Look at us: we still support Katherine and Mary, and we are working to bring down Anne. Cromwell is right to wonder if it might happen again."

Jane turned away. "So you would sanction her death, for that's what we are talking about?"

"For the peace of the realm, and your security, and that of your children by the King, yes!"

Jane breathed deeply. "And do our other friends agree?"

Carew nodded. "They do. Sir Francis Bryan and others in the Privy Chamber are doing all in their power to bring about your marriage. They see the necessity, and the Princess Mary agrees, I hear. I have written to her. I told her to be of good cheer, for shortly the Boleyns will put water in their wine. Jane, the King is as sick and tired of the Lady as he could be. Use your head. Take advantage of this, and make him declare himself."

"No!" Jane countered. "I will not have him thinking I am chasing him."

"Then threaten to leave him! That soon brought him running in Anne's day."

That, for reasons she could not tell him, was now unthinkable. "Nicholas, I appreciate your concern, and all that you are doing on my behalf, but I think I know by now how to approach the King. He would be unhappy if I treated him as she did."

Carew cheerfully conceded defeat. "Very well, Jane, have it your way. But it will not be the fault of this master of horse if the Lady is not dismounted!"

"Go gently, Nicholas," she urged. "For my sake, press for a merciful way of removing her."

Spring was flowering in all its glory as April drew to a close. The courtiers were preparing excitedly for the May Day festival, when traditionally jousts were held in the tiltyard. After that, the King was going to Dover to inspect the fortifications, and then overseas for a short visit to his town of Calais, and Anne was supposed to be going with him. Now that they were together as often as possible, Jane felt sad at the prospect of his being away, and feared that Anne might seize the opportunity to inveigle her way back into his favor; but then he would not be gone for long and, realistically, he was unlikely to succumb to Anne's wiles now.

She was trying not to panic at the growing probability that she was with child. She told herself that anything might have interrupted her courses. Losing her virginity and making love might well account for it. She was resolved to wait and see if she missed early next month before jumping to conclusions. In the meantime, she would endeavor not to fret.

The tournament and the summer progress were not the only topics of interest at court. They were overshadowed by rumors that the Queen's disgrace was imminent. Clearly not everyone questioned by Cromwell had respected the injunction to keep silent, Jane concluded; or else, which was worse, her own supporters had fed the speculation.

Chapuys told Edward he believed the King would just have his marriage annulled. Jane was thankful for that. It sounded as if Cromwell had not gathered enough evidence to proceed against Anne by other means.

"Certainly the King is determined to abandon her," Edward said at dinner one day. "It is bruited that she was secretly married to the Earl of Northumberland before he wed her, so he may have good grounds for divorce."

"Really?" Nan looked up. "I heard that Cardinal Wolsey forbade her to marry Northumberland and sent them both from court."

"Maybe they were already married," Edward said, munching.

"Please!" Jane begged. "We've been speculating for weeks now, and still the King hasn't said anything to me. Let be, please."

Edward raised his eyebrows. "I'm sorry, sister. This uncertainty must be wearying for you. I have no doubt that he will speak, and soon. Matters seem to be coming to a head."

"Just leave it!" Nan commanded. Jane smiled at her gratefully.

———

"The King is in Council," Thomas said, frowning, as he breezed into the apartment and made himself at home in the chair Henry used.

"On a Sunday?" Edward queried. "There must be some matter of moment to be discussed." They all exchanged glances.

Jane did not want to indulge in any more idle speculation, so she took herself off to Greenwich Park to enjoy the sunshine. Not far from the palace, she saw a group of people cheering and shouting, and realized they were watching a dog fight. Among them was the Queen. Anne saw Jane watching them and gave her an icy stare, then turned back to the entertainment.

Jane shrugged and strolled on. She would not let Anne bother her. Her footsteps took her toward the hill on which stood the old tower, Mireflore. It looked forbidding. She never went too close to it.

She found herself a shady spot and took up the pair of gloves she was embroidering. As the sun rose high above her, she stopped sewing and ate the cold pasty she had brought with her. Then she resumed stitching, every now and then breaking off to admire the view and the fine weather. The hours passed peacefully. Soon it would be suppertime, and she should go in, but she wanted to finish the gloves, and she was almost done. When she had completed her task, she lay back against a tree trunk and closed her eyes, drowsing in the warmth.

She woke to see the sun low down in the west and a group of Anne's ladies sitting on the grass on the slope below the tower. Not wanting to attract attention, she pretended to be asleep. When next she opened her eyes, she was surprised to see Anne emerge from the tower and run down the hill. The ladies followed her, and soon they were just tiny figures in the distance, heading back to the palace.

She wondered what Anne had been doing. Probably she had just been curious to see what it was like inside the tower. Dusty and creepy, Jane imagined.

She heard a door creak. Someone else was leaving Mireflore. It was Sir Henry Norris! Jane watched in surprise as he strode away down the hill, understanding dawning. He had been alone with Anne in that tower, which made a nonsense of all the arguments that she could have had no opportunities for an illicit affair. Jane remembered that it had been common knowledge among the Queen's ladies that Norris loved Anne; but she had never heard that it had been reciprocated. They had all thought him a hopeless case. Now it seemed they had been wrong. But heavens, had the pair of them any idea of the risk they had been taking? What if Cromwell, or one of his spies, had seen them? In the light of recent developments, it was very likely that Anne was being watched. How could she have been so reckless? Had she really been so foolish as to arrange a tryst with her lover in broad daylight, in a place where anyone could have come upon them, or seen them entering and leaving? Suddenly, Jane had to know.

She got up, gathered her things and walked up to the tower. It looked eerie in the fading light of early evening, but she suppressed her unease. There was a key in the great wooden door. She turned it easily. It was gloomy inside, and the menacing shapes of dark, sinister figures loomed at her from the faded murals. She shivered. It was chilly, too, and smelled of age and disuse. Cobwebs veiled the windows. She crept upstairs, and found a chamber containing an old bedstead. It was hardly the setting for a romantic tryst, with its ropes sagging and the floor covered in dust, but there were footprints in the dust leading to the topmost story. Jane continued upward, and was taken aback to find a beautifully appointed room furnished with tapestries and a luxurious bed. A rich Turkey carpet lay on the floor.

Here was evidence, if it were lacking, of why Anne and Norris had come here, and what they had been doing, and it plunged Jane into a dilemma. This was clearly of far more serious import than any evidence the Council seemed to have. Should she report what she had seen to Henry or Cromwell? Should she ask for Edward's advice? Or should she keep silent?

She did not want to stay in that room with its secrets and its air of illicit passion. As she hurried downstairs and out of the tower, she was realizing that if she said anything to anyone, Anne might well face death, and she, Jane, would have to live with the guilt. The prospect appalled her. No, she would say nothing.

When she returned to the palace, the candles and torches had been lit, and she found groups of courtiers crowding the galleries and halls, talking animatedly and looking about them. She saw Thomas with Bryan and Carew, and went over to find out what was happening.

"Why are all these people gathered here?"

"Where have you been, Jane?" Thomas asked. "The Council is again in session. Everybody is wondering what is going on."

"There can be no doubt that some deep and difficult question is being discussed," Bryan said, his saturnine features set in serious lines for once.

They waited—and waited. Jane saw people staring at her, whispering to each other. She thought she might go to bed. She hated being the focus of public attention. It dawned on her that that would be her life if she became queen.

She was about to leave when a distant clock chimed eleven, and suddenly word went round that the King had left the council chamber and the councillors were dispersing. Then one of the royal heralds came striding through the court, crying out that the King's visit to Calais would be postponed for a week.

"I wonder why," Carew said.

"They're not telling us," Thomas muttered.

"I think all will become clear soon enough," Bryan opined.

Her heart pounding, Jane bade them good night and returned to the apartment. Edward and Nan were there. They had heard the news, but Jane said firmly that it was idle to speculate, and retired to her bedchamber. She had just taken off her locket, hood and veil and shaken her hair loose, and was about to remove her oversleeves and unhook her stomacher, when there was a tap at the outer door that led to the King's gallery. There was no mistaking who it could be.

"I'll go," she called out, for Edward and Nan had gone to bed. She opened the door. There stood Henry, looking pained and drawn. "Jane," he said, "I have to talk to you."

She waited as he sank heavily into his chair, then poured wine for them both and drew up a stool facing him.

"I apologize that I am not dressed to receive you," she said, feeling a little guilty because of what she had resolved to conceal from him.

"You look beautiful," he said, distractedly. "Your hair is lovely." He touched it gently, feeling its silkiness. "Oh, Jane! That we could just be two lovers, free to enjoy each other, without a care in the world."

"That would be bliss," she agreed.

"Alas, I am weighed down with cares," Henry groaned, his eyes narrowing. "This matter of the Queen is serious. My Council has now questioned all her women and many other witnesses, and the matter now appears so evident that there can be no room for doubt."

"No!" Jane blurted out. She wondered if she alone knew how little doubt there was.

"She conspired my death!" he growled, looking thunderous. "She has taken lovers, and plotted with them to murder me so that she can marry one of them and rule England in Elizabeth's name. That is high treason, Jane, the most heinous of all crimes." He was seething, his fair skin flushed. Jane could well imagine the kindly Sir Henry Norris making covert love to Anne in the tower, but it was impossible to envisage him conspiring to murder the King, his close friend.

Henry's mouth tightened. "Today, in Council, we had no choice but to conclude that the Queen is an adulteress and regicide, and deserves to be burned alive."

"Oh, but Henry, that is a terrible death!"

"It is a terrible crime!" he snarled, and she recoiled, because this was not the Henry she normally saw. "Jane, you have a kind heart, but in this case your kindness is misplaced. Anne does not deserve your sympathy or anyone else's." He was implacable, and she found herself fighting back tears. "She has even betrayed me with a low-born musician."

"Mark Smeaton?"

Henry's eyes narrowed. "How do you know that?"

She must not reveal what Lady Worcester had told her. "I assumed it, because he was often hanging around her chamber. I thought she had rebuffed him. She never spoke well of him."

"It was a pretense, I am certain of it. He was arrested today, and has been taken to Master Cromwell's house for questioning, for it is believed he can tell us more."

Jane bit her lip. Even now, she was hoping that Mark would convince Cromwell that this was all a dreadful mistake. And yet, in her heart, she knew that it wasn't, and that Anne must be guilty, although probably not with Smeaton. Maybe she should tell Henry what she had seen, but she feared to do so because it might be the one piece of evidence that would tip the scales against Anne and send her to her death. And people would say that Jane had spoken out because she wanted a crown.

She took a gulp of her wine to steady herself. She felt she had to placate Henry, to let him know she was on his side. "I am more sorry than I can say that the Queen has committed these crimes," she said, reaching out a hand and hoping he would take it. "It is so hard to credit that anyone, let alone the person who is supposed to love you the most, could stoop low enough to do such dreadful things."

He grasped her fingers. "You must forgive me, Jane, for speaking roughly. I came here wanting to kill her with my bare hands, and I took out my anger on you." He downed the rest of his wine. "But I did not come here solely to rail against her. I had planned to come for another purpose entirely, though now is perhaps not the moment." He looked at her intently, then drew her to him, holding her tightly and kissing the top of her head. She could sense his need of her. "Or perhaps it is the right time," he murmured against her hair.

He drew back, still with his arms about her, and looked her in the eye. "When this is over, Jane, will you marry me?"

For all the speculation and predictions of the past weeks, it took her breath away. "Oh, Henry!" she gasped.

"I love you, Jane," he said, holding her gaze, "and this time it is a true, pure and honorable love, not the obsessive love I had for Anne. I was mad then, but I am older and wiser now. I know what is good and of value. I make suit to you not as your king, but as your humble suitor. Say you will have me!"

Jane hesitated. Every part of her wanted to say yes, but she was being asked to fill the shoes of a woman who might shortly die horribly to make room for her. Then she thought of the child that might be growing under her girdle—and of all the people whose hopes were vested in her, who had worked for months to bring her to this moment. She thought of the Princess Mary, and what she might be able to do for her if she agreed to marry the King, and she thought of the Church, and how she could right the wrongs that had been done to it—and of how she could work for the greater good.

The Queen was guilty, she was sure of it. She probably could not prevent Anne's death, but she might be able to influence the manner of it.

Henry was still holding her, still looking at her beseechingly.

"I love you," she said, and saw his eyes fill with tears. "And I will gladly marry you, but there is something I desire you to promise me first."

"What must I do?" he asked.

"Swear to me, I beg of you, that you will not send Anne to the fire. I should feel that it was on account of me, and whatever she has done, I could not live with myself knowing that her agony had made me queen."

Henry frowned, but his anger was dissipating. "Very well, Jane. Mercy is an admirable quality in a queen. I swear to you that she shall not be burned."

How terrible that they were having this conversation. It was coming to something when Jane was supposed to be pleased and grateful that Anne would not burn, for still she had to die to clear the way for Henry and Jane to marry. Did she really want to wed him on these terms?

She thought of the new life that was almost certainly stirring under her girdle. The choice had been made for her. "Thank you, Henry," she said quietly. "I will be your wife, and nothing could give me more joy." He crushed her to his chest and his lips closed on hers. He kissed her with even more ardor than he had shown before. In that kiss there was passion and longing, but there was also pain. It had been a strange proposal, in grim circumstances, and whether she had made the right decision she did not know, but she dared to offer up a fervent prayer that God would bless this marriage, even if it was to be made in blood.

"There could never have been a proposal more timely," she said. Henry was puzzled, uncomprehending.

"I believe I am with child," she told him, and saw his face transfigured by hope and joy.

"Are you indeed?" he asked in wonder.

"I am almost certain. Another week, and I will know for sure."

"Heaven be praised!" he cried. "A son to crown our happiness. A blessing from God." And he kissed her with renewed fervor.

They sat up late, talking and planning for the future.

"We must be wed as soon as possible," Henry said. "I cannot say when, but it will not be long, and certainly before you quicken. A son! I cannot believe it."

"I am ready," Jane said, realizing that the responsibility of bearing a prince was hers now. She felt a shiver of trepidation, and prayed again that God would smile on this marriage. "All I want is to make you happy. You deserve some happiness, Henry." It would make him a kinder man, a better king.

He kissed her. "You know, I can't remember Anne ever saying that to me. Bless you, Jane, for your sweet heart."

He told her that their marriage plans, and the proceedings against Anne, must be kept secret for now. It must never be said that he had set aside Anne only so that he could take another wife. However, Jane might tell her family, in strict confidence. And, he added, grinning, he himself should really seek her father's permission to wed her.

"I doubt he will refuse you!" She laughed.

He lay with her that night, but he did not love her. It might harm the child, he said, but there were other ways to be close. He caressed her and showed her how best to pleasure him. When he slept, she tried to calm her raging thoughts. He loved her, she could not doubt it now. He could have had his pick of all the princesses in Christendom, and yet he had chosen her. But she could not help tormenting herself with the suspicion that he had asked her in the heat of the moment, after hearing of Anne's crimes; that he was not prepared to waste time in negotiating a royal marriage, so had turned to her in the hope that, coming from a fertile family, she would give him sons; or that she was a means of his saving face, for soon the world would know how humiliatingly he had been cuckolded. The news that he was to wed again would go a long way toward wiping out any embarrassment. Yet how could she doubt his feelings, his need for her?

She had to admit that she too had a pragmatic reason for wanting to wed. Her fears about her condition had turned, in an instant, to happy anticipation. And yet that did not detract from how much she loved him.

She must face the unpalatable fact that Anne's removal was imminent and necessary. Jane had done what she could for her. She thought again of Anne's futile attempts to bear a son, and all for nothing. She had not needed to turn to other men in the hope of getting pregnant, for Henry was a virile and potent lover, as Jane herself well knew. No, if Anne had strayed, she had done it for her own gratification and ambition. Had it been Norris she had intended to marry after the King was dead? Jane could not think of anyone else it might be. Maybe Anne had sinned only with Norris— and perhaps Smeaton, although she was far from convinced of this. If so, she feared greatly for Norris. The penalty for men who committed treason was hanging, drawing and quartering; only in the case of noblemen was it commuted to beheading, and only then if the King was inclined to be merciful. She shuddered.

When she did sleep, she was troubled by a nightmare in which she was chained to a stake, watching with horror as the faggots were lit at her feet. Then the flames crept upward, and her gown was alight . . . She woke up, panting in terror, to see the sun shining in at the window. It was May Day.

That morning, she emerged from her room to find Edward and Nan in the outer chamber, both in their nightgowns, breaking bread and drinking ale. She sat down and helped herself to some breakfast, but she was so churned up with excitement and dread that she could barely eat. "I have something important to tell you," she said. "The King proposed marriage last night, and I have accepted."

Edward's eyes gleamed exultantly; Nan looked triumphant.

"By God, Jane, you did it, you clever girl!" Edward exclaimed, getting up and hugging her in an uncharacteristically exuberant way. "Our future is assured! We Seymours can now show the world a thing or two!"

Jane smiled at him, hardly believing it all. To think that she was to be the means by which her family prospered! She would not tell them yet of her hopes of a child. She would wait until she was certain, and safely wed.

Thomas and Harry were sent for at once. Thomas whooped jubilantly when told the news, although Harry was more cautious. "Are you very sure you want this, Jane?" he asked. "Don't feel you have to accept the King for our sake." Jane stared at him. She had thought him as avid for the marriage as the rest of her family. She should have realized that he was the one person who would never push her.

"Of course she wants it!" Thomas interrupted.

"I do," Jane assured them. "I love the King. He has always been so good to me. I just wish that I could be marrying him in happier circumstances."

"Jane, you have not betrayed the King or conspired against his life. It is Anne who has brought this upon herself," Edward said firmly. "The King has to have an heir. He will get rid of her and marry again, whether it is to you or someone else. Rest easy in your conscience about this. You have nothing for which to reproach yourself!"

"That's true," Harry said.

"Very well, I shall try not to feel guilty," Jane agreed. "But in common humanity, I cannot but pity her. Had his Grace merely had their marriage declared invalid, I would not have had a qualm. But I never anticipated anything like this."

"You mustn't brood on it," Nan insisted. "It's nothing to do with you."

"You have much to thank God for," Edward said, "and we must tell our parents the wonderful news. I shall send for them today."

"I would like to tell them myself," Jane insisted.

Edward nodded. "Then I will simply tell them that they should come to court for there is a matter here that will interest and rejoice them greatly."

"They'll guess!" Thomas sniffed. Edward frowned.

"Just say that I would appreciate their company and counsel at this time," Jane said.

"That's a good idea," Edward agreed. "We all want to see their faces when they hear the news. I'll get a messenger dispatched today. They should be with us in ten or eleven days."

Nan stood up. "It's growing late. We should get ready for the jousts," she said.

Chapter 23

1536

Jane sat in the stand with her brothers and Nan. Today's tournament was taking place in the tiltyard at Greenwich. She loved May Day, which this year had dawned warm and pleasant, and she had donned her damask rose gown for the occasion and left her hair loose. Pennants fluttered in the breeze as everyone crowded into their seats or behind the barriers. At the appointed time, Jane saw the King take his place at the front of the royal stand, which stood between the twin towers of the tiltyard. She thought how impressive he looked, tall and magnificent in black and gold, exuding power, his handsome face flushed in keen anticipation of the contest.

Anne sat down next to him, gorgeously gowned in cloth of silver. Jane could hardly bear to look at her, knowing what was in store. Again she was overwhelmed by a rush of guilt and dread.

When the jousts began, Henry and Anne gave every appearance of enjoying them, but Jane found it hard to focus on the knightly contestants running their courses, lances couched, armor gleaming. Lord Rochford was the leading challenger, while Sir Henry Norris led the defenders. At one point, Norris's mount became uncontrollable, refusing to enter the lists and neighing furiously. Henry leaned forward and called out to Norris, and minutes later Norris returned to the tiltyard on the King's own horse, the famous Governatore. The crowd leapt to its feet when Sir Thomas Wyatt won his course, displaying great dexterity, but all the knights, including Francis Weston, did great feats of arms, and the King cheered them on while Anne sat smiling encouragement.

The contest was but halfway completed when Jane saw a man in royal livery enter the stand and speak into the King's ear. Henry scowled, stood up and departed without a word, leaving Anne and everyone else staring after him. Jane looked at her brothers, wondering what this portended. Trembling, she turned back to the lists. There was a buzz of speculative conversation all around. The knights were still charging at one another, but the crowd's attention was elsewhere. Jane looked over to where the Queen was sitting. Anne had a fixed smile on her face. Norris was not yet out of the running, yet he failed to appear. Jane began to feel sick to her stomach. It was beginning.

When the jousts were over, she and her brothers were among the throng that returned to the palace, where Bryan and Carew were waiting for them.

"The King has left for Westminster," Bryan said. "He took only six persons with him, including Norris. He asked me to give you this." He handed Jane a sealed letter. It was brief and unsigned. *That which we have longed for will soon come to pass. M.S. has confessed all, and more.*

"What does it mean?" she asked, handing it to Edward as the others craned to read it. But she knew.

"It means that Smeaton has confessed to something and possibly incriminated others," Carew said. "I'll wager he did not enjoy his visit to Master Cromwell's house."

"This means that the Lady will soon be unseated," Edward declared. "And then . . ."

Jane could not bear to think of what would happen then. Yes, she was to marry the King, which was cause for great joy, but first there was this huge, threatening abyss to be overcome. She did not know how she would pass through it.

"The Queen has been arrested!" Nan cried, flying into the apartment and startling Edward and Jane. "It's all over the court! She was taken to the Tower this afternoon in broad sight of the people."

"What is she charged with?" As Edward leapt up, Jane started to shake.

"Treason, it is said. Some say adultery. But no one seems to know any details." Nan's eyes were glittering with excitement.

There was a brisk knock and Bryan burst in. "You've heard," he said. "I just saw Chapuys. He said to tell you, Jane, that you must not hold yourself responsible in any way, for this is divine vengeance on Anne for all the wrongs she inflicted upon the Queen and the Princess."

"So he believes she is guilty?"

"He is sure of it. I think we all are." He looked at Edward and Nan, and they nodded gravely. "He predicts that the outcome of the affair will be her execution."

Jane closed her eyes, not wanting to think about it.

Presently Carew and Thomas joined them. "I thought you would be here," Carew said to Bryan. "I came to salute my future queen." He bowed low to Jane.

"Amen to that!" Thomas beamed. "Why are you looking so miserable, sister? You will soon be wearing a crown."

"It is true," she said. She turned to Bryan and Carew. "Keep this to yourselves, as I am allowed to tell only family. The King has asked me to wed him, and I have accepted."

"By God!" Bryan and Carew exclaimed in unison, and embraced her in turn. "This calls for a celebration!"

"I had rather wait until this terrible business is all over," she said, tears welling in her eyes.

Bryan faced her. "Jane, you should be rejoicing with us that his

Grace has escaped this great peril and danger, and that you are going to marry him and be our queen. And when this she-devil is no more, any children you bear his Grace will be undoubtedly legitimate. So we all have several causes for rejoicing!"

Suddenly, from somewhere distant, there came a resonant boom. They all stared at one another. "That's a cannon," Thomas said.

"They're firing from the Tower to let the world know that someone of high rank has been imprisoned," Carew said. "They did it some years back when the Duke of Buckingham was taken there." There was a silence as they all recalled Buckingham's bloody death on the block—for committing treason.

"This change is long overdue," Bryan said. "A new queen on the throne, and the Princess restored to her rightful place."

"And sons for the King, by the grace of God," Edward added.

Jane turned away. Anne was not even tried yet. But of course, it was rare for anyone accused of treason to escape death, and Anne, she was sure now, was guilty. Everyone said so.

Jane did not want to show her face in the court. She could not face the prurient interest of the courtiers, or the sudden silences whenever she appeared. She stayed behind the locked door of the apartment and waited for news. Late that night, Edward came to tell her that Lord Rochford too had been taken to the Tower.

"He must have been involved in the conspiracy," he said. "Of course, the reformists are in shock. They fear that a change of religion is inevitable."

"As indeed I hope it will be," Jane said, envisaging the monumental task that lay ahead of her. She was not sure that she was equal to it. Oh, how she longed for Mother to be here, to lay her head on that ample warm bosom and confide her fears, knowing that Mother would not try to jolly her out of them, but would understand.

She was praying for some word from Henry to tell her what was going on, but there was nothing. She hated being left at Greenwich while he was at York Place. Edward said that he had not appeared in public since Anne's arrest.

At midnight, to her amazement, he came to her, cloaked and hooded. He was tense, restless and very angry. Edward and Nan quickly retreated into their bedchamber.

"Dear God, I have so longed to see you," Henry said, clasping Jane tightly to him. "I came by barge from Whitehall, and I must go back there soon. I cannot tell you . . . Do you have some of that Rhenish left?"

"Of course." Jane broke away, lifted the cloth off the ewer and poured him a full goblet. "Sit down and rest."

He downed half of his wine almost immediately. "Smeaton confessed to adultery with the Queen. After I raised him from nothing! And he said he was not the only one. He named Norris—Norris that was my friend and most trusted servant!" His face twisted in bitterness as everything fell into place, and Jane began wondering if she should tell him what she had seen at Mireflore.

"He incriminated Weston also, whom I have loved, and William Brereton of my Privy Chamber," Henry went on. "She has had to do with them all! And Jane, the worst of all—he named Rochford too." His face flushed. "Her own brother!"

"Oh, my God!" Jane cried, shocked to her soul. "It's—it's unthinkable that anyone could stoop to such wickedness."

"You would believe it, Jane, if you saw the evidence, which I hope you never will. The details are revolting." Henry drew in his breath. "And on top of her fornicating, she was plotting to have me murdered. Well, she shall pay for it! The law will take its course."

"You will not have her burned?" Jane begged.

"No, darling, I have not forgotten my promise. She shall have an easy death, if it makes you feel better. And she is being held in comfort in the Queen's lodgings. It is more than she deserves!" His mouth set in a grim line. "Well, I will be rid of her soon. And to make sure that there is no impediment to our son succeeding to the throne, I have today ordered Cranmer to find grounds for annulling my marriage. Elizabeth must be declared a bastard. My Council say there is no guarantee that she is mine, given that Anne has been unfaithful on numerous occasions throughout our marriage."

"Do you believe that Elizabeth is not yours?" she asked.

He sighed. "Of course not. You have only to look at her to see whose child she is. She has as much of me in her as she has of Anne. But I have been warned that speculation about her paternity can only undermine the security of the succession. The way must be clear for me to make a new, undisputed marriage."

Jane spared a thought for Elizabeth, not yet three, and so soon to be motherless and disinherited. The thought was almost unbearable. An innocent child . . . But there was Mary to be thought of, Mary who had been cruelly deprived of her birthright. She summoned her courage. "Henry, when I am queen, my dearest hope is to see the Lady Mary reinstated as heiress to the throne."

Henry shook his head. "Jane, you are a fool. You ought to be soliciting the advancement of the children we will have together, and not any others."

Stung, she leapt to defend herself. "I do think of them, but also of your peace of mind, for unless you do justice to Mary, Englishmen will never be content." Her hand flew to her mouth as she realized that she had dared to criticize the King's policy toward his elder daughter, which no wise person risked doing these days. She waited, head downcast, for him to explode.

"Jane, look at me," Henry said. She raised her eyes to see that he was not angry, but gazing at her lovingly. "Once again, you shame me by your kind heart. I'm sorry, sweetheart, I'm like an old bear at the moment, lashing out at everyone. It's this awful business with Anne that has put me in a foul temper. I will think about what's to be done with Mary, I promise you, but for now I have enough to deal with. And I came to tell you that I'm staying secluded in my privy chamber at York Place until all this is over."

"Then I will not see you?" she asked, dismayed. She needed his presence, and his conviction, to overlay her qualms about Anne.

"Yes, you will, darling, very soon. I can hardly bear to be without you, but it will not be for long." He kissed her, gently and longingly, then released her. "I prefer to remain in seclusion for now. This whole business is humiliating for me. I've given orders that I will see only Master Cromwell and a few of my councillors and secretaries. And you, when I can."

She understood. For a king who exuded such power and virility, it was shaming for the world to know that his wife had cuckolded him with his best friend, a lowly musician and her own brother.

"I will send for you as soon as I am able," he promised, and disappeared into the night.

Chapuys came to see Jane late the following afternoon. It was the first time he had ever sought her out directly or visited the apartment. Her brothers were all there, and looked suitably impressed.

Chapuys bowed low to her. "Mistress Jane, I came to tell you that I informed the Princess at once of the Lady's arrest, and she has sent back to say that I am to give you and Master Cromwell and all your friends every assistance in pressing for your advancement."

She hugged her secrets to herself. How she wished she could tell Chapuys that Henry had asked her to marry him. But Henry would tell him in his own good time, and that could not be yet. Still, it was encouraging to know that the Princess supported her. How jubilant Mary must have been to hear of her great enemy's arrest.

"When you write to the Princess, please send her my heartfelt thanks," she asked. "I have not been idle on her behalf." She recounted her conversation with Henry. "Once this is all over, I hope his Grace will look on her with more sympathy. I will not desist, I promise you."

Chapuys smiled. He really was a most attractive man, with that air of wisdom and compassion. "These arrests have shaken everyone. I hear there are now five men in the Tower with the Queen, and some gentlemen at court are in fear for their lives, lest they should be accused next. Even Sir Francis Bryan was questioned by Cromwell this morning, and he is known to be your man."

Jane's hand flew to her mouth. "Not Bryan?" She saw Edward blench. "No, I assure you," Chapuys said. "I saw him afterward, and he told me he made it plain that he was unquestionably the Lady's enemy and would profit from the fall of those accused with her. In all, he convinced Master Cromwell that he had abandoned her, so he has clearly been exonerated. He is a lucky man. Yet I am wondering if his going free was intended to give credence to the guilt of the others."

"Thank God!" Jane's heart was pounding.

There was a rap on the door. An usher in the King's livery stood there.

"I must leave you," Chapuys said. He bowed and departed.

The usher handed Jane a sealed letter and waited. She opened it and read, her spirits faltering.

> Darling,
>
> I will send for you as soon as I can, as I promised, but I think people will be the less suppositious and the more convinced of the matter in hand if you are not seen in public. Sir Nicholas Carew has offered his house as a refuge, and he will escort you there immediately. Take one of your brothers with you for company. The time will not be long, I promise.
>
> Written with the hand of him who loves you with a true heart. H.R.

She turned to her brothers. "He is sending me away, to avoid gossip and prejudicing the proceedings against the Lady," she said. "Nicholas Carew has placed his house at my disposal, and I am to go there today. I have no idea where it is, and I do not want to be sent away."

"If the King commands it, you must," Edward said sternly. "A lot rides on this."

"Nicholas has a house in the country," Thomas told them. "It's not far from London."

"It's at Beddington in Surrey," Edward said. "Who is to accompany you?"

"Sir Nicholas is to escort me there, but the King said I should take one of you for company."

"I am needed here," Edward said quickly. "Someone has to keep an eye open for what is happening."

"I am for Whitehall this afternoon," Thomas put in.

Edward glared at him. "What business have you there?"

"I too am keeping an eye open" was the rejoinder.

"I will come with you, Jane," Harry said. She looked at him gratefully. "I will help you pack," Nan offered.

Jane disliked Beddington Park on sight. It had been a long ride from Greenwich, more than twelve miles through the outlying villages of London, but after leaving the little market town of Croydon, they had entered a vast deer park, which Carew proudly informed them was his.

"Not far now," he said. Dusk was already deepening into darkness. Presently a church came into view. "The house is beyond." He pointed a finger. As they approached, Jane saw the forbidding black silhouette of a great mansion outlined against the sky. "My father built the hall and the two wings," Nicholas related.

All Jane wanted to do was to turn her horse and gallop away. The place looked so sinister. She took a deep breath as they approached.

It was now evening, and servants were awaiting them, holding torches aloft. Close to, she could see that the house was of red brick and set amid neat gardens, but it still felt forbidding. Carew helped her from her horse as Harry looked about him appreciatively.

"It's a fine place you have here, Sir Nicholas," he said.

"Wait till you see the great hall." Their host smiled. "It was the inspiration for the one at Hampton Court."

It was on a smaller scale, of course, but Jane had to concede that it was magnificent, with its hammer-beam roof, high windows and oak paneling.

"You will be tired after your journey," Carew said. "My steward will show you to your chambers." A man in livery came forward.

Jane's room was luxurious, more so than any at Wulfhall—the measure of Carew's success at court. The bed had a rich counterpane and heavy damask curtains, and there was a bench set with cushions and a solid oak table with turned legs. A fresh-faced maid in a clean gown and coif was waiting to unpack.

"I'm Meg, mistress," she said. "I will serve you while you are here. If there is anything you want, just ask."

"Thank you," Jane said, sinking down on the cushions. She was saddle-sore and weary, unusually tired—which might be down to her condition—and ill at ease, despite the luxury of the house. She was praying that Henry would summon her soon, for she did not want to stay here any longer than necessary. "I think I will retire, Meg," she said. "Stay with me. I do not like to be alone at night. Is there a pallet bed you could use?"

"There's one here, mistress," Meg said, pulling it out from under the tester bed. "I'll make it up."

Jane went downstairs to thank Carew for his hospitality and bid him good night.

"I'll be heading back to court first thing in the morning," he said, "but in my absence, my steward will supply anything you need. You'll find that my cook keeps a good table."

It was hard to sleep that night. Jane hated having the curtains closed, so the moonlight was streaming in through the lattice-paned window, casting shadows in the room. She closed her eyes so that she didn't have to see them, and thought of Henry, wondering what he was doing and thinking, and of Anne, immured in her prison in the Tower. She could only imagine her agony of mind. What must it feel like to be locked up there, fearing—and with good cause— that the only way out would be via the scaffold?

She thrust the thought away and made herself think of Mother and Father, who would hopefully be on their way to London soon.

She prayed she would be gone from here by then. It was so quiet in this vast, empty house, especially with Harry sleeping in the other wing. She was grateful for the presence of Meg, snoring softly nearby.

She heard the church bell toll three before she drifted off. It seemed that she got up and padded to the window, where she stood looking out on the church tower opposite. There was a light behind its windows, a pale moving light shaped like a disc, that suddenly became a disembodied face with a black beard and no body, or so it appeared. Then everything went dark and it was gone.

Blind terror gripped her and she woke up. She had known this house to be evil! Her first instinct was to run, but where should she go? Down into the darkness of the cavernous, empty hall? She could not face that, so she burrowed into her bed and pulled the covers over her head. She realized she was whimpering.

"Are you all right, mistress?" came a sleepy voice from the pallet bed.

"No, Meg, I am not," Jane confessed, peering out at her. "I had a nightmare. I dreamed that I saw a face at the window of the church tower—a face with a black beard."

"They do say that church is haunted, mistress," Meg said, a touch avidly, "though I've never seen anything myself. I reckon you dreamed of Old Scrat. My granddam used to say he showed himself roundabouts whenever something big were going to happen. It's a portent."

"Old Scrat? But that's the Devil!"

"Aye, and when he appears, there's Devil's work to be done, so my granddam told me."

Jane shivered. There could be no better way of describing this business with Anne. Devil's work. In the dread hours of darkness, the dream did indeed seem like a portent.

It was three days before she had a letter from Henry—three long, tedious, anxious days. He had gone to Hampton Court, where he was making preparations for their wedding. That cheered her, but she wanted to be there with him, involved in the planning. Had she been marrying anyone else, Mother would have been making the arrangements, and busying herself with baking meats and pies for the wedding feast. Alas, poor Mother would be deprived of that pleasure.

The rest of Henry's letter was written in more serious vein. The Queen was to be tried by a jury of her peers at the Tower on May 15, nine days hence. Jane did not think she could endure the suspense. But she had no choice.

She wrote back with good news; she could not contain herself until she saw him. She was with child; there could be no doubting it now.

She had been enduring Beddington for a week when she heard the clatter of horses' hooves in the forecourt. Hurrying to the window, she looked out to see Edward and Thomas dismounting, and behind them her parents, alighting from a litter. She flew to the door and opened it, crying, "Mother! Father!"

They hastened toward her and embraced her. It had been far too long—nine months—since she had seen them. Mother was the same as ever, plump and emotional, and Jane was so relieved to see her; but Father—she could barely hide her dismay. He looked shrunken and old, a shade of the man he had been, and there was gray in his thick brown hair. What had happened to him? A wave of guilt washed over her. She should have gone home and visited them long ere this.

"Edward says you have some news for us," Father said, after they had exchanged greetings and gone into the hall. Mother was looking up at the ceiling in awe.

"Yes," Jane said, seeing that her brothers were bursting to break the news themselves. She looked to see that the servants were out of earshot. "The King has asked me to marry him and I have accepted."

Mother screamed in delight and flung her arms around Jane. Father's eyes filled with tears of pride. "To think I should live to see my daughter a queen," he said. "Who would ever have dreamed such a thing could come to pass?"

"I do not know when I am to be wed, but the King assures me it will be soon," she told them. "I take it you know about this business of the Queen?"

"Mother and Father know that the Lady is to be tried for treason, and that her guilt is not in doubt," Edward supplied.

"If it had been, the King would never have asked me to wed him," Jane assured them, "and I would not have accepted. But he told me that the proofs are solid, and I have good reason to believe that is true." Seeing them all looking at her in astonishment, she added, "Do not press me on that. I just know."

Edward nodded. Mother regarded her with concern. "I wish you could be marrying him in other circumstances."

"So do I," Jane said fervently.

"And you cannot say where the wedding is to be?"

"At Hampton Court. The King is there now, making ready for it, so it cannot be long." Her voice faltered. "The Lady and her brother are to be tried on Monday."

"And her other accomplices tomorrow, in Westminster Hall," Edward informed her.

"Tomorrow?" Thomas echoed. "Shouldn't they be tried with her?"

"She is the Queen and they are commoners. She and Rochford have the right to be tried by her peers; the others will go before an ordinary jury."

"But any judgment given tomorrow could prejudice the verdict at her trial," Sir John observed.

"It will make no difference, given the proofs, so I am told," Edward said. Father looked dubious.

"Let us not talk of it," Jane said quickly. "Father, Mother, you must be tired after your long journey. Come and rest in the parlor, and I will send for refreshments."

"And we must talk about a wedding gown for you," Mother said.

"We ought to get one made up soon, and it will have to be something costly." She looked hopefully at Sir John.

"I think we should wait until the Queen's fate is known," he said.

"You can't make a wedding gown overnight!" she told him.

"I know you mean well, Mother, but it would not be right," Jane said firmly.

Mother subsided, vexed. "Well, I hope the King gives us enough notice," she muttered. "I wonder if he needs any help in planning the wedding feast."

Edward and Thomas rode back to court later that day. They were on tenterhooks to learn of the fate of the Queen's lovers on the morrow, and had promised to get word to Beddington as soon as possible.

Jane waited anxiously, unable to settle to anything. She was worried about her father too.

"Is he ill?" she asked Mother, catching her alone in the screens passage.

For a moment the mask slipped. "I don't know. He had a fever in the winter, and he's never quite recovered his appetite. He gets tired easily. This journey was a challenge for him, but he insisted on coming, and he claims there is nothing wrong."

"Have you asked him to see a physician?"

"Yes, and got my head snapped off for it. Father James tried too. You know your father: he hates to admit to any weakness."

"Shall I speak to him?"

"No, child," Mother said firmly. "You have enough to contend with. I'm sure he will improve soon, now that the good weather is back with us."

On the Friday evening, Edward's messenger arrived, lathered in sweat. As her family gathered around her, Jane read the message he carried and shuddered. Guilty of treason, all of them. They would suffer the grim fate of traitors. She could imagine all too vividly the rope strangling, the knife ripping, the butchery, the intolerable agony, the blood . . . She ran to the privy and was sick.

Back in the parlor, she could see in everyone's faces that they too were thinking of the terrible verdicts.

"There is no hope for her now," she whispered.

A letter from the King arrived the next day. He was back at York Place and missing her; he wanted her near at hand, especially at this difficult time. Beddington was inaccessible by river and he did not wish to be seen riding abroad in public and visiting her at this time. The indefatigable Sir Nicholas Carew had found her a new lodging where Henry could travel by barge to see her. Her parents and Harry could stay there with her, and act as chaperones.

She rejoiced to hear it. She could bear this house no longer, with all its unpleasant associations.

Chapter 24

1536

Carew arrived the next morning to find Jane and her family packed and waiting for him. He said it would be best if she traveled in the litter with her mother. "The King fears you will be recognized, and wishes to prevent a scandal. With the trial looming tomorrow, public feeling against the Lady is running high, but people are fickle, and if you are seen, they might turn against you."

"How would I be recognized?" Jane wanted to know. "They don't know me."

He shook his head. "Don't ask me. I fear his Grace is overanxious, but we must take no chances."

Jane did not look back as they rode away. She never wanted to see Beddington Park again. They traveled west to Carshalton, then north through Mitcham, Tooting and Clapham to the horse ferry at Lambeth, which took them across the Thames. After that it was a short hop to Chelsea.

The lodging chosen by the King was a grand one. Nestling amid gardens and orchards, it looked out on parkland stretching down to the river, and had stone medallions on its brick walls, not unlike the terra-cotta ones at Hampton Court, except that these had reliefs of Greek philosophers in profile. Harry enjoyed guessing who they were supposed to be.

At the imposing entrance, Sir William Paulet, Comptroller of the Royal Household, was waiting to receive Jane, with a large company of servants, cooks and some of the King's own officers, all wearing rich liveries and making their reverences. It brought home to Jane the reality of her situation, and the fact that soon she would be a queen and command such deference from everyone. Mother appeared ecstatic, and Father very proud; they were carrying themselves like royalty.

"Good afternoon, Sir William." Jane smiled. "This is a fine house indeed!"

"I hope you will be very comfortable here, Madam," he said, escorting her into the great hall, where sunshine streamed through the tall windows. Rich tapestries hung on the walls, and gold and silver vessels gleamed from the great buffet. A long table set with gilt candelabra ran the length of the room.

"His Grace ordered that the furnishings be brought out of storage," the Comptroller informed her.

"Out of storage?"

"Yes, the house has stood empty this past year. Did Sir Nicholas not tell you?"

Carew was pulling his riding gloves on, preparing to return to York Place. He looked uncomfortable.

"Tell me what?" Jane asked.

"This was Sir Thomas More's house," Paulet told her. "It belongs to the Crown now."

Jane looked around her at the beautiful hall built by the executed More. She had left one unhappy house for a worse one. She could see why people said he had hated to leave this place for the court, and why he had retired from public office when his position became untenable, but that had not saved him. More had chosen not to compromise his conscience rather than stay with his family, and he had died for it. She wondered what had become of his beloved wife and children, the clever daughters whom he had famously educated as if they were boys. She imagined them all sitting at this table at their lessons, or making merry at mealtimes. All that happiness, wiped out for the sake of their father refusing to utter a few words to please the King.

Harry was watching her sadly, Mother too. They must know she was wishing she could have stayed anywhere else. But the King had commanded, and she must obey. That was how it would be from now on.

Mother came with her to explore the house, trying to make the best of things for her, exclaiming at the sumptuousness of the bed-chambers that had been prepared for them, and admiring the fine paneling in the parlor. Then she hugged Jane and bustled off to in-spect the kitchens, while Jane wandered into the chapel where the devout Sir Thomas would have prayed daily. Trying to quieten the turmoil in her soul, she knelt at the altar rail, making her mind focus on spiritual things, and her eyes on the painting of the Virgin and Child on the reredos. She prayed for those men who had been condemned to a dreadful death; for Anne, who had to face her judges on the morrow; for Henry, that he might find peace of mind after all this was over, and for herself, that she would be a good queen—and a fruitful one—and that she would be given the strength and wis-dom to right the wrongs done to the Princess Mary and the Church.

There was little time to brood. The King had sent several ladies and maids to wait temporarily on Jane, most of them new to her, and they opened the chests in her bedchamber and showed her the rich fabrics that the King had bought for her, the bolts of silk and velvet in crimson and black and purple, and piles of fine linen—all fit for a queen.

"The tailors come tomorrow, Madam," she was told. From the piles of velvets and damasks that had been supplied by London mer-cers for inspection, it was clear that she was to be very richly adorned, as became Henry's consort.

Jane stood in her smock as her maids took her measurements. She was feeling self-conscious about her swelling breasts and slightly rounded belly, which she prayed were concealed by the folds of fine lawn. Mother was looking on, interested in the whole business of dressing a queen. Having borne ten children, she might well recognize the signs. Yet she was smiling with the others, fingering the gorgeous stuffs, and clearly appreciative of the maids' deferential attitude toward her.

But Jane found it hard to take pleasure in the magnificence that would soon be hers. She was all too aware of what was to happen on the morrow, and consumed by dread.

Afterward, Mother sat her down and sent everyone else away. "There is nothing you can do," she said, her eyes large with sympathy. "Even if you refused to wed the King, Anne would still die. And I do not think you have any choice but to marry him now. I'm not blind, child."

Jane wept on her shoulder. It was such a comfort to be in her mother's arms. "I was going to tell you, but I did not want you to think ill of me, so I was going to wait until after the wedding."

Mother kissed her brow. "Jane, I could never think ill of my good, sweet girl. I too was with child when we wed. A lot of women are. Once you are properly betrothed, there is nothing to stop you consummating your love."

"We were not betrothed."

"Hush! It matters not now. And the child you carry may be our future King. You are blessed indeed. We all are. Now, go and wash your face. Tomorrow will soon be over, and soon that unhappy woman will be at peace."

Jane hardly slept that night, and in the morning, when the tailors came to take her instructions, she was trembling so much that she had to lie down for a space, and they had to wait for her. But her parents and Harry seemed unmoved at the prospect of Anne's fate. They were eagerly awaiting the outcome of the trial, and were all of the opinion that the Queen deserved to die. Edward, who turned up to see Jane just before dinner time, was adamant about that too.

"Your friends at court are all demanding the death penalty," he said. "Chapuys still believes that Anne poisoned the late Queen and attempted to do the same to the Princess, and that for that alone she deserves to suffer. Left alive, she will remain a threat to you, Jane, and to any children you bear the King. I heard that her own father is to be among her judges. He was on the jury that condemned her lovers."

Sir John grimaced. "That he should be called upon to condemn his own daughter—and his son! How can he live with himself?"

"I think he does it to save his own neck."

"Do you think the trial will have begun?" Jane asked, increasingly agitated about the outcome.

"Probably," Edward said. "The Lady will be tried first, then her brother. I heard that people were queuing all night outside the Tower to get in."

"Ghouls, the lot of them!" Harry growled.

"When do you think we will know the verdict?" Jane asked.

Edward shook his head. "Who can say?"

They were interrupted by the arrival of a royal messenger with a note for Jane from the King. "I will send Bryan to you at three o'clock to inform you of the verdict," he had written. That was all.

She could not eat the beautifully prepared dinner that was put before her. She kept dropping stitches when she tried to sew. She picked up a book, but the words meant nothing to her. By two o'clock, she was pacing up and down, wringing her hands, heedless of her family's pleas that she should calm herself.

Three o'clock came and went, with no sign of Bryan. She began to wonder if Anne was putting up a defense that might just turn the tide and secure an acquittal. When she mentioned this to Edward, he frowned.

"It's very rare for people accused of treason to be acquitted," he said. "Lord Dacre got off a couple of years back, and the King was furious. I doubt it will happen this time."

Dusk was falling when at last, at long last, Jane, peering anxiously through her bedchamber window, saw Sir Francis Bryan riding at speed toward the house. She flew downstairs, nearly tripping in her haste, and was with her family in the hall when he burst through the door, his face triumphant.

"Burned or beheaded, at the King's pleasure!" he cried.

"Burned? No, he promised!" Jane wailed. "He promised!"

"Calm yourself," Edward soothed, grabbing her by the shoulders. "It is the penalty for women found guilty of treason."

"And too good for her," Bryan added, his expression grim.

"But the King promised me she should not be burned," Jane cried wildly. "I asked for that promise before I consented to marry him."

"Then I have no doubt that he will honor his word and commute the sentence to beheading," Edward said.

She was persuaded to sit down with them at the table, and Mother sent for refreshments for Bryan.

"She was found guilty on all counts," Bryan said. "They made a persuasive case against her, although some were saying afterward that the King had merely made an occasion to get rid of her."

"I do not believe that," Edward declared.

"How did she take the sentence?" Jane asked.

"Bravely. She said she had not always shown the dutifulness she ought toward the King, but she had never been unfaithful to him."

"Of course she would say that," Father put in.

"Then Rochford was tried, on many counts of incest, saving your presence, ladies. It was also objected against him that he had repeated that his sister had told his wife that the King has not the ability to copulate with a woman, for he has neither potency nor vigor."

"What?" Jane was aghast. It was simply not true, but she could not tell them how she knew.

"He wasn't openly charged with it, but it was shown him in writing, and he was warned by Master Cromwell not to repeat it aloud. But he did, showing great contempt for Cromwell and the King."

"By God," Edward fumed. "It sounds as if he said it more from envy and jealousy than out of love toward the King."

"You know what they were implying," Harry chimed in. "Witch-craft. In hinting that the King is impotent, they were implying that the Queen had worked some magic on him."

"But that's ridiculous!" Mother retorted. "I hold no brief for her, but why make him impotent when she was desperate for a son?"

Certainly it didn't make sense, unless they had been trying to show that Henry couldn't have fathered Anne's children.

That was Father's view. "I think they were offering a pretext for her infidelity. If the King could not give her a child, she had sought other men who could."

"But then the King would have known that he wasn't the father," Mother pointed out.

"None of it makes sense," Jane said, "unless they were just trying to demonstrate how Anne ridiculed him."

"It came from Lady Rochford," Bryan told them. "She deposed against her husband in regard to the incest. She hates him and his sister, and supports the Princess Mary. I very much doubt that Anne confided anything of the sort to her. It was said in pure malice, I'll wager."

His explanation was meant to reassure her, Jane knew, but he had not seen the flaw in it. This evidence had clearly been invented—so what of the rest? She began to wonder if the case against the Queen was as solid as Henry and everyone else had said. But she had herself seen Anne and Norris at the old tower. Could they have been there for an innocent purpose? What if this was merely a clever plot to remove the Queen so that the King could remarry and have a son?

Oh, God, she prayed silently, give me a sign that I am wrong. Let there be proof that she is guilty!

"What is it, Jane?" Father asked, regarding her with his weary eyes.

"Was it a just verdict?" she asked.

"Of course it was!" Edward and Bryan chorused.

"I've seen the indictment," Bryan said. "I was with his Grace when it was brought to him. He wept with anger when he saw it, and showed it to me. The evidence itemized in it was overwhelming—and it made for sickening reading. Never doubt her guilt, Jane!"

She was somewhat reassured. She had been right all along about that furtive tryst in the tower. She must stop doubting everything!

"You'll be pleased to hear that the King is coming to see you later tonight," Bryan told her. "His master cooks are already on their way here, to prepare supper for you both. But first he is going to dine at the Bishop of Carlisle's house."

It was after ten o'clock when the King's barge moored at Chelsea. From the house, Jane could see the twinkling lights of the torches that lighted its way, and hear the distant echoes of music. And soon, there he was, coming through the door and sweeping her into his arms. The first thing she noticed was that he had had his hair cropped and was growing a beard. It suited him. It was as if the cutting of his hair symbolized the severing of his marriage.

"Soon you will be mine," he told her joyfully. "Nothing can prevent that now. I do long for the day." There was about him an air of almost desperate gaiety.

"I was overjoyed to receive your news," he told her. "Are you well? I trust you are looking after yourself—and our son."

"I am very well," she told him. She did feel all the better for seeing him. His presence, so vital and so commanding, reassured her. It was wonderful to be with him again after more than twelve days apart. She had put on her best new gown, of deep green damask, with oversleeves and a kirtle of white tissue, and left her hair loose, the way he liked it. His eyes roved over her appreciatively.

Her family having discreetly retired to bed, Jane shared a late supper with the King, dining in the parlor on salmon and pork in delicious sauces. She had recovered her appetite a little, and was glad of the food, for she had begun to feel rather faint at the lack of it; and the good red wine heartened her.

"Are you comfortable here?" he wanted to know. "Do you lack for anything?" She marveled that he could think of domestic details on such a momentous day.

"It is a beautiful house," she said. "Thank you for lodging me here."

It was not until after a great bowl of fruit had been served that he brought up the subject of Anne's condemnation. "I have not forgotten my promise," he said suddenly. "I intend to commute the sentence to beheading, and I have sent for the executioner of Calais, out of pity. He is a renowned swordsman, and highly skilled. It will be very quick."

"Thank you!" Jane cried, thinking this was the strangest conversation she had ever had.

"Anne is lucky that you are so tender in your concern for her," Henry remarked. "I now believe that upward of a hundred men have had dealings with her. I had my suspicions; for a long time I expected something like this. Even before Cromwell alerted me to her crimes, I had composed a tragedy." Jane looked on, astonished, as he drew from his bosom a little book and opened it. There was the title, *The Tragedy about Anne*, written in his own hand. Jane thought he would give it to her to read, but he slid it back inside his doublet. "She only kept my love through practicing her enchantments," he said, his tone bitter. "She bewitched me. It's the only way I can explain my foolish passion for her."

He was a little drunk, Jane realized, and when he was drunk he always became garrulous. Surely he did not really believe that Anne had betrayed him with more than a hundred men? And if he had long suspected her of being unfaithful, why had he not acted on his suspicions before? No, he was blustering, to save face.

"You did not deserve it," she told him. "You made her a queen and honored her with your love; it was a treacherous way to repay you."

He stayed the night. Staggering from the effects of the wine he had consumed, he had to be helped to Jane's chamber, where his gentlemen, fetched from the barge where they had been idling away the hours playing dice, put him to bed. No other chambers being made up, Jane slept with the ladies who attended her, creeping into their room in the other wing and making herself as comfortable as possible on a pallet bed. They were shocked to see her there in the morning, but she explained that the King had been tired and she had felt obliged to give him her bed.

He emerged looking somewhat pale, but otherwise in command of himself, and apologized shamefacedly for putting her out of her room. She passed it off with a smile.

"And now I must see your father, to ask him formally for your hand," Henry said.

She loved him for his courtesy. He was the King, no common suitor. Father was summoned, and came hurrying downstairs, his bonnet askew, his gown looking as if it had been thrown on. He bowed low to Henry, who stared at his appearance for a moment, then threw an arm around his shoulders and led him to the parlor. "Sir John, I have a request to make of you," Jane heard him say. The door closed behind them.

Mother followed, in high excitement. "The King is still here? What did he want with your father?"

"He is asking for my hand in marriage," Jane told her.

"By all the saints!" Mother exclaimed.

Jane nodded. They waited. Mother fidgeted, looking very fine in her silk gown. Presently the door opened and Henry emerged, walking toward Jane with his hands held out. "Darling, your father has given us his blessing." He paused before Mother, as she bent low in a curtsey.

"Why, Lady Seymour, greetings!" he said, raising her to her feet. "Or should I call you my lady mother?"

"Oh, your Grace!" she fluttered. "This is such an honor. Jane is a good girl. She will make you an excellent wife." Jane blushed. Mother was babbling.

"I know that well," Henry said.

"We are all delighted, Sir," Father said. "I speak for my other children as well."

"Can I offer your Grace something to break your fast?" Mother asked.

"No thank you, my lady. I have some pain in my head." Henry
smiled ruefully. "I must be away to York Place, for there are matters
requiring my attention." His smile slipped. He had reminded himself of the grim matter of the Queen. "I bid you farewell." Jane
walked down to the jetty with him.

"When is it to be?" she ventured.

A pause; a heartbeat. "On Thursday, I think. Cranmer has to deal
with the formalities of the annulment first."

Thursday. The day after tomorrow. She did not know how she
would bear the waiting, and dreaded how she would feel afterward.
As for how Anne was coping, it was unimaginable.

They were nearing the barge now. The boatmen had raised their
oars in readiness for departure. Henry turned to Jane. "Do not brood,
darling. This will all be over soon. I will return tonight, and we
shall make merry. We need not waste any grief on that whore."

That afternoon, Jane was surprised to receive a visit from Lord
and Lady Exeter and Sir Anthony Browne of the Privy Chamber.

"We are hoping that congratulations will soon be in order," Lady
Exeter said, sweeping in grandly and looking impressed at the vast-
ness of the hall. Jane curtseyed, wondering how she would ever be
able to wield place over great ladies like this. She smiled and invited
the visitors into the parlor, sending for wine and some marchpane
delicacies she had baked herself.

"So, how are you enjoying Chelsea?" Lord Exeter inquired. Soon
it became clear that they had come to ingratiate themselves with the
woman whom they believed would be their queen, and to pump her
for confirmation of that, but she gave nothing away.

"The Lady Mary must feel vindicated by the verdict," Sir Anthony said.

"By all accounts, she has escaped great danger," Lady Exeter remarked.

"She must be feeling great relief," Jane replied. "My hope is that
the King will now restore her to the succession, and I shall not cease
to work for that."

"Then we shall all be indebted to you," Lord Exeter told her.

"I know you will not forget your friends, my dear," Lady Exeter said to her on parting. Her meaning was clear. *You owe us favors in return for supporting you.*

When they had gone, Jane leaned back against the door, mentally exhausted, and made a face at her mother.

She was grateful for the peace of the gardens. A brisk walk into the park would do her good. But when she got there and rounded the corner of a path, she saw that there was a crowd of people at the gate, presumably hoping to catch a glimpse of her. She smiled uncertainly, reminding herself that very soon, and for the rest of her life, the whole world would be watching her, but she was dismayed to see some hostile faces among the curious or eager ones. A man shouted out something; it sounded like abuse. Another threw a crumpled paper at her, which landed on the path. She picked it up and walked away, acutely aware of them watching her go. On the paper, verses had been crudely printed. It was headed: "A new ballad about our sovereign lord." Her face flamed as she read how she and Henry were supposedly wallowing in their swill, making the beast with two backs, while his wronged wife languished in the Tower awaiting death.

"It's horrible!" she whispered, screwing it up. "How could they?"

No sooner had she returned and shown her angry mother the verse than the doorbell rang again. She was relieved to see Carew and Bryan, come to inquire how she was settling in, and to ask after her health. Hard on their heels—to her astonishment—came Master Secretary Cromwell with Sir William FitzWilliam, all smiles and courtesy now. "We wish to pay our respects," they told her.

She invited them in, and they gratefully accepted refreshments. "This must have been a trying week for you, Mistress Seymour," Cromwell said.

"It has," Jane admitted.

"It has been no less grievous for those of us on the King's Council, who have had to deal with these treasons," FitzWilliam replied, looking pained. "Fortunately, justice has been well served, and will soon be meted out. Then we can all look to the future."

"Amen to that, Sir," she agreed.

"I understand that Lord and Lady Exeter were here earlier," Cromwell said, almost casually.

"Yes. They have been most kind to me."

He nodded, smiling. "And why should they not be? You are full of goodness. Tell me, do you know if they are in contact with the Lady Mary?"

A faint alarm sounded in Jane's head. "They mentioned her only in passing. They said she must feel vindicated by the verdict." Had she been right to tell him that?

"I imagine she does," he said, still smiling.

"Master Cromwell," Jane said, "this was thrown at me when I was walking in the park this morning." She handed him the scurrilous verse.

He frowned. "I have seen this, and I fear there are other copies in circulation. But do not fret. I intend to speak to the King and get them suppressed."

"I pray you do!" she cried. "I can never show my face in London if people think me so lewd!"

"Rest assured, we will find the culprits," he promised her.

Henry arrived at eight o'clock, in a barge festooned with streamers, with musicians playing in the gilded stern of the vessel. He himself came up to the house and invited Jane and her ladies to join him on board. In the cabin, there was a banquet laid out, with sweetmeats, sugared fruits, wafers and deliciously spiced hippocras. As they ate, they were entertained by the singers of the King's chamber.

Jane decided not to mention the ballad. She did not want to spoil the evening. Yet she was brooding about it all the same. She could imagine people she knew reading it, and laughing behind her back. What shameful images it would conjure up in their minds! She felt horribly embarrassed at the thought.

They were rowed upstream beyond Richmond, past the palace that soared above the river with its pinnacles and onion domes, to Syon Abbey at Isleworth, then on to Windsor.

Resting back on the cushioned bench, Henry told Jane of the preparations he had put in train for their marriage. "Anne's initials and badges are being replaced in all my palaces," he revealed. That would be no mean task, for they were everywhere. Jane imagined a small army of stonemasons, carpenters, painters, glaziers, embroiderers and seamstresses, all setting to work with a vengeance. "You need to choose a badge to use as your personal emblem when you are queen," Henry added.

Jane sipped her hippocras, thinking. "I have always liked the image of the phoenix rising from the ashes," she said. "Just now, it seems a symbol of hope and renewal." As a child, she had loved the tale of the magical bird, radiant and shining, setting its nest on fire and being consumed by flames every five hundred years, only to rise anew.

"The phoenix is also a symbol of Christ and His Resurrection, and of overcoming death," Henry added. "Might I suggest a badge showing a phoenix arising from a castle amid flames, with Tudor roses painted in red and white, surmounting a motto?"

"I like that."

"Then you shall have it. You need to think of a motto too."

Jane thought again. She wanted something that would distance her from Anne, whose motto, "The Most Happy," she had always felt to be rather self-centred. " 'Bound to obey and serve,' " she said. "Do you like that? It is how I see myself as your Queen."

Henry's broad smile proclaimed his approval. "It is perfect," he said. Then he bade her choose a heraldic beast, and suggested she opt for a white panther, because it could be easily overlaid on Anne's leopard. She liked the idea, for the panther represented procreation and rebirth, and it had long been accounted a royal beast.

It was midnight before they got back to Chelsea, and still there were a few people loitering by her gate. She watched them uneasily. Fortunately Cromwell had left a couple of stout fellows in livery, bearing cudgels, to guard it, which was comforting.

Henry was drunk again. Seeing her and the other ladies to the door, he stumbled through it and sat down heavily on a bench. The women looked at him uncertainly, and Jane waved them away.

"I signed the men's death warrants today," he said.

She did not know how to answer. What must it feel like, to have such power that, with a few strokes of your pen, you could condemn someone to execution?

"The traitors die tomorrow, on Tower Hill. I have commuted all the sentences to beheading."

"Even Smeaton?" she asked, amazed that his mercy should extend thus far.

"Even Smeaton. I knew that you would wish it."

"And what of the Queen?" she asked.

"They have drawn up the warrant. I will sign it tomorrow. She will die the day after. I've been thinking," he went on, his voice slightly slurred. "Anne was not only lecherous, she was cruel. She hounded Wolsey to his death; she was constantly demanding that I send the Princess Dowager and Mary, my own daughter, to the scaffold; she was ruthless against her enemies. I have no doubt that she was behind that attempt to poison Bishop Fisher. She made me send More to his death—and she plotted to do away with me too! She is a monster, and the world will be well rid of her. When I think of how narrow an escape I had . . ." A tear trickled down his cheek.

"She cannot hurt you now," Jane said firmly. "You are safe."

"I know, Jane," he said, looking up at her with a maudlin smile. "I will always be safe with you."

He left then, and she tiptoed through the sleeping house and sank into bed. Henry had lain here last night, she reflected. His head had rested on these same pillows. Soon she would be sharing a bed with him again. What a joy and comfort that would be.

She lay awake worrying in case anyone had seen her and the King enjoying themselves on the river. If word got around, it would sound ill in the ears of the people. But she understood why Henry had arranged their little trip. Having been publicly branded a cuckold, he was embarrassed and ashamed, and doing his utmost to bolster his pride. Making merry with a bevy of ladies made him feel virile and appreciated. Despite his belief in Anne's guilt, he must feel some qualms about destroying the woman whom he had once ardently loved, and who was the mother of his child. In seeking refuge in pleasure jaunts, he could distract himself.

The next morning there was a royal messenger waiting for Jane when she came downstairs. He presented her with a letter bearing the royal seal and a small velvet purse. Inside was a jeweled crucifix in the shape of the letter T, which Jane instantly recognized as one that had been owned by Queen Katherine. The old Queen had prized it, for this Tau Cross, as she called it, was in the true shape of the cross on which Christ had died.

It would be perfectly proper to accept such a special gift, especially now that they were to be married. Jane kissed it and fastened it around her neck at once. Then she opened the letter and read:

> My dear friend and mistress,
>
> The bearer of these few lines from your entirely devoted servant will deliver into your fair hands a token of my true affection for you, hoping you will keep it forever in your sincere love for me. There is a ballad made lately of great derision against us. If you see it, I pray you pay no regard to it. I am not at present informed who is the originator of this malignant writing, but if he is found out, he shall be strictly punished for it.
>
> Thus, hoping shortly to receive you into these arms, I end, for the present, your own loving servant and sovereign,
>
> H.R.

Feeling greatly cheered, she folded the letter and put it in her pocket. Soon it would go to join the others Henry had sent her in the small pewter casket in which she kept treasured things. And she would take it out and reread it when she was alone.

Henry did not come that day, and she spent it trying to divert herself from the dreadful awareness of what was happening on Tower Hill, and what was to happen the next morning. She thought of the men who were dying for sinning with Anne, mostly young men in the prime of life, their glorious futures snatched away from them. How foolish they had been to think they could get away with their wickedness!

She was horribly conscious that the last hours of Anne's life were ebbing away. Her parents and Harry understood. They suggested walks in the park, games of cards, or putting the finishing touches to a frontlet she was making for a new hood. In the end, she let Harry teach her chess, but made a poor showing, for her mind was elsewhere.

In the afternoon, she received a message from Bryan. The men had died bravely. Only Smeaton had admitted his offenses, but Rochford had hinted of deserving death for even worse crimes than those for which he was being punished. Jane immediately thought of the late Queen and Bishop Fisher. Had it been Rochford who had tried to poison the Bishop, and perhaps the Queen? She could believe it of him. He had been a nasty man and the world was well rid of him. But Norris she could grieve for. She had liked him. Even now, she found it hard to credit that he would have betrayed the King.

It would not be long now before Anne joined them in death. At supper that evening, Jane was so agitated that the thought of food made her feel nauseous, so she pleaded a headache and retired to the chapel, where she knelt until darkness had fallen, praying fervently for Anne's soul, and that God would give her courage on the morrow, and eternal peace thereafter.

———

In the morning, she was in such a state of agitation that Mother was worried. "There's nothing you can do," she told Jane, squeezing her hand. "You must try not to dwell on it. Keep telling yourself that justice is being done. Had she been left to carry on with her evil works, you might this day be mourning the death of the Princess, or even the King! Remember that—and think of the child you carry!"

"I will," Jane said, fighting back tears.

Dinner had just been served when Edward arrived.

"I come from the King," he said, as Mother served him with cold meats. "The execution is postponed until tomorrow."

"Why?" They were all agog, and Jane began to wonder if Henry would relent at the last minute and grant a reprieve.

"His Grace told me himself. Justice must be seen to be done, and in the face of the people. Everything has happened so quickly, and more time is needed to ensure that sufficient witnesses are present."

Mother frowned. "You'd think he would want it all over and done with."

"He may be concerned about how this looks in the eyes of the world," Father said. "I can't remember having heard of any queen of England who was put to death before."

"It must be terrible for her," Jane said. "It is bad enough for me, sitting here and building up to her execution. What must it be like for her, knowing she has to endure another day of dreading it?"

"I think the King is dreading it too," Edward said. "He seems much preoccupied. He said to tell you he will be coming to dine with you tonight. He bade me inform you that Archbishop Cranmer declared his marriage to the Lady null and void yesterday, and that he is now free to wed you."

He was free. "That is such a relief," Jane whispered. Could he not simply banish Anne to a convent, now that they were divorced?

"Nothing can prevent your marriage now," Edward said. "You will soon be queen. Are your new gowns ready?"

"Two of them," she told him. "The rest are to be delivered tomorrow."

"Then wear one tonight. Dress like a queen."

Henry arrived after dark, cloaked and hooded. Down by the jetty,
his barge displayed no lights.

"I do not want to be seen arriving here tonight," he explained, as
the front door closed behind him. "The crowd at your gate is growing in size. They are calling out for you. They seem friendly, but if
they see me here, their mood could easily turn." Despite his evident
tension, he was looking at her appreciatively. "Jane, you look wonderful. That gown so becomes you."

She had donned the purple velvet, which had been trimmed with
a border of pearls and pink roses. She was wearing the cross he had
sent her, and a silver filet over her loose hair, which Mother herself
had brushed a hundred times. Mother had also overseen the preparation of the supper by the King's cooks, who were by this hour no
doubt wishing themselves back at the palace. Yet the spread awaiting Jane and Henry was impressive. She counted twelve dishes and
then gave up. They sat down in the candlelit parlor, with the
diamond-paned window open to let in the balmy evening air, and
waited as the sergeant of the napery arranged their napkins over
their shoulders. Then the wine was poured and the servitors left
them alone.

Henry raised his goblet. "To us," he said, regarding her intently
with those piercing blue eyes.

"To us," she echoed.

"It is marvelous to be a free man," he said, "and to know that very
soon you will be mine. I wanted to be with you tonight. Your
brother told me you have been fretting about Anne. We must not
waste any tears on her. She would have killed me had she had the
chance."

"I know, Henry. I cannot bear to think of it. But out of pity and
common humanity, I cannot but shrink at the thought of what she
must suffer tomorrow."

He reached across the table and laid his hand on hers. "But she is prepared, I hear. The Constable of the Tower told Master Cromwell that no person ever showed greater willingness to die. And it will be quick. There will be no pain."

Jane was grateful to hear it. "I will pray for her," she said. "What will you be doing tomorrow?"

"Keeping to my privy chamber until it is over," he told her. "They will fire a gun from the Tower. When you hear it, you will know that she is no more. Then I will come to you as soon as I may. We will be betrothed first thing on Saturday."

"On Saturday?" She was shocked.

"I know it is only the day after the execution," Henry said, downing his wine, "but darling, I cannot afford to wait. The Privy Council has petitioned me to marry again, pleading the utmost urgency because of the uncertainty surrounding the succession. We must be wed as soon as possible."

Jane felt a sinking feeling in the pit of her stomach. God send that the child she carried was a son.

"Does Elizabeth know what is to happen to her mother?" she asked.

"No." Henry looked distressed. "Thankfully she is too young to understand the change in her status, and I intend to ensure that she will not suffer on account of what Anne has done. She must be shielded from any scandal."

"And the Queen agreed to the annulment without protest?" She could not imagine Anne, who had been so fierce to uphold her daughter's rights, willingly agreeing to Elizabeth being bastardized and disinherited. Had two weeks in the Tower broken her spirit?

There was a fraction of a pause. "She did. She knew there was no point in contesting it. Her proctor made no protest."

As the hours ticked past, Jane was filled with increasing dread at the prospect of what was to happen in the morning. She was torn between feeling desperately sad for the innocent Elizabeth, who was to lose her mother to a horrible death, and relief that Henry was free of Anne at last, and would come to their marriage unencumbered by the complications caused by his first two marriages. Her internal conflict must have been obvious, for when Henry left her, he cupped her face in his hands. "Be strong," he said. "I will be here in the morning."

Sunshine streamed through the windows as Jane knelt in the chapel, unable to endure the tense and hushed atmosphere in the house. It was too beautiful a morning for a bloody execution.

She prayed harder than she had ever done—for Anne, first and foremost, but also for Henry and for herself, that God would not turn His face from them both in wrath at this day's act.

It was at nine o'clock that she heard the thunderous sound of a distant cannon, followed by a dreadful silence interrupted only by the merry sound of birdsong. Feeling faint and dizzy, she gripped the altar rail for support. It was done. Now she must live with the guilt. She doubted it would ever leave her.

Part Four

From

Hell into

Heaven

Chapter 25

1536

Mother was suddenly behind her, genuflecting. She hastened to Jane and put her arms around her. "She is at rest now," she soothed. "You must put this behind you. Cease your prayers. There is much to be done."

Jane crossed herself, rose and curtseyed to the crucifix on the altar. With a heavy heart and a spinning head, she followed her mother out of the chapel and upstairs to her bedchamber, where the tailor and his assistants were laying out the new gowns on her bed for inspection. They were gorgeous, spread out in all their glory, in an array of colors—a beautiful sage green, a glistening gold, a rich black, a figured crimson damask, a plush scarlet velvet and a gleaming white satin. But Jane could only think of the body that had been butchered and the blood that had been spilt that morning, blood that must still be warm. It felt so wrong to be admiring clothes only minutes after Anne had died.

"You must choose one for your wedding dress," Mother said briskly. "Any of these will be perfect, but I think white, for purity? Unless you think gold would be more appropriate for a queen?"

Jane swallowed. "I will wear the white," she said. "And the green for my betrothal."

At ten o'clock, Henry arrived. He was wearing black, and looked pale, as if he had not slept. "The Queen died boldly," he said, as they all hastened to greet him and make reverence. "Jesu take her to His mercy." He crossed himself.

"Was it quick?" Jane asked.

"Cromwell said it was over before you could say a Paternoster," he told her. "She would have known nothing about it."

"Thanks be to God!"

She was utterly relieved to see him. It was a comfort to be close to him.

"Cromwell and most of my Privy Council were there," he related. "They said she spoke well of me from the scaffold, and commanded her maids to be always faithful to me—and to her whom, with happier fortune, they looked to have as their queen and mistress."

So Anne had guessed that he would marry her, Jane. And she had been gracious about it at the last, and about the husband she had betrayed.

"I left many in my Privy Chamber exulting," Henry went on, sitting down in the tall chair by the empty hearth. "Francis Bryan told me that in the streets of London, the people were making great demonstrations of joy after the gun was fired. And soon they will have more cause to celebrate. This morning I informed the Privy Council that we are to wed. You may imagine how happy they were to hear it. There is now no obstacle to an alliance with the Emperor, and that will be a boost to England's trade."

"Your Grace's subjects have much cause to rejoice," Sir John observed.

Henry smiled at him. "Even though your daughter is little known, Cromwell tells me that her friends have been assiduous in proclaiming her virtue and her kindness." Jane felt herself blushing. She hoped that the people had also been told of her love for the popular Princess Mary, whom many believed had been much wronged. That must surely stand in her favor. And a queen who cleaved to the old faith would be welcomed not only by Spain, but also by France and the rest of Christendom.

Henry remained at Chelsea all that day. He did not mention Anne again, and Jane was glad of that. Anne's shadow was looming over them darkly enough as it was.

That evening, as they supped together, he spoke of their wedding. "Everything will be ready in a week or so. Cranmer will officiate. Your family will, of course, be present. Then we will have a few quiet days to ourselves before you are proclaimed queen, which I mean to have done at Whitsuntide." He took her hand and kissed it. "I cannot wait to hold you again," he said. "But first, we must be betrothed. I am going directly to Hampton Court tonight. I will send a barge for you early tomorrow morning. Be ready to depart at six, before too many people are about. I want to keep our betrothal a secret for now."

On parting, he kissed her lovingly. "Good night, sweetheart. I shall think the time long before I see you tomorrow."

The morning was cool and misty as Jane and her family boarded the unmarked barge. Edward, Nan, Thomas, Dorothy and Dorothy's new husband, Clement Smith, had arrived late the night before, elated and unperturbed about the fate of the Queen, and today they were all wearing their best attire. Jane was dressed in the green gown, with her hair loose, as became a maiden. Everyone was barely awake, and there was little conversation in the cabin as the boat was rowed upriver to Hampton Court. The events of yesterday seemed unreal today, the horror mercifully a little distant.

After this morning, she would be bound to Henry eternally. It was what she had long desired, and yet she could not help feeling apprehensive and on edge. Mother was watching her. She smiled nervously. Father, sitting next to Jane, patted her hand. "All will be well," he murmured. He looked gray and drawn.

Soon the mighty red-brick palace came into view, and the barge pulled in by the landing stage. From here, a covered gallery led to the King's privy lodgings. Yeomen of the Guard stood on watch, and an usher was waiting to escort them to Henry's presence. They passed along the gallery where he and Jane had often met during their courtship, and Jane noticed that Anne's portrait had been taken down.

Henry received them in a closet hung with blue damask. Archbishop Cranmer was waiting with him, looking a little strained. Of course, he had been the creature of the Boleyns, and, like them, hot for Church reform. How must he feel, joining the King to one who loved the old faith, and who was now in a position of great influence? Yet he gave no hint of hostility; a smile of welcome lit up his lugubrious features.

Jane took her place next to Henry, and his hand folded over hers. The ceremony lasted only a few minutes, the contract was signed, and then Henry was sealing their betrothal with a kiss. Her family crowded around congratulating her. That seemed strange, as it was usually the custom to congratulate the lucky gentleman. But it seemed there was no doubt as to whom was the luckier on this occasion. The King was doing her an honor in taking her as his wife.

Mother blushed furiously as Henry kissed her, while Father and Harry looked on proudly. Edward and Thomas were slapping each other on the back, for once. They were now set on their course for advancement, and both aiming to scale dizzying heights.

It had been arranged that Jane and her family would return to Chelsea immediately after the betrothal, and that Henry would remain at Hampton Court. He looked wistful at the prospect of parting from her, and walked with them all the way to the landing stage. When they arrived, he waved the others on to the barge so that he could have a few private words with her.

"Tomorrow is Ascension Day," he said, "and I will be wearing white mourning out of respect for the late Queen. It is just a gesture, so if you hear of it, pay no mind. And I'm sending Elizabeth to Hatfield, where her lady governess will look after her. Anne saw her so rarely that I doubt Elizabeth will miss her. It is Lady Bryan she cleaves to."

He paused. "Today I have to arrange for the settlement of the Constable of the Tower's account for money spent on Anne. I also have to redeem the jewels and clothing she wore yesterday." Jane winced. It made it all too real. "Normally, all the Queen's jewels are handed down, but I think I am right in assuming that you would not want these particular pieces."

"No, I would not," she told him.

"Then I shall send them to the Jewel House for safekeeping."

"Why do you have to redeem them?" she asked.

"It is customary for the attire of a condemned criminal to be distributed to the Tower officials as perquisites," Henry said. "The sumptuary laws prevent their wives from wearing Anne's rich attire, so they would prefer their value in coin."

Jane shuddered inwardly at the thought of Anne's clothing. It would surely be encrusted with her blood, and beyond recovery. Besides, who would want to wear it? "What will happen to her clothes?" she whispered.

"They will be burned," he said shortly. "I've had the rest sent to the Royal Wardrobe. They'll take off the jewels and reuse them."

Just then, Jane noticed the vaulted ceiling of the gallery. There, untouched, were Anne's initials, entwined with Henry's, obviously overlooked in the hurry to erase all memory of her.

"You should go," Henry said, "much as I hate to part with you. Take this." He pressed into her hand a heart-shaped brooch adorned with the jeweled motto "My heart is yours." "Until next week," he said, bending down and kissing her before she had a chance to thank him. "I will find your absence unbearable, I know it."

She clung to him, not caring who saw them. "Until next week!" she murmured, smiling through her tears.

She kept busy, to stop herself brooding about Anne. Her brothers had all gone back to court, and Father was looking up old soldiering friends in London, so Mother had leisure to help her with her trousseau. They wrote to Lizzie in Yorkshire, to inform her in the strictest secrecy of Jane's coming wedding. Lizzie was too far away to be able to travel to London in time for it, but there was a gown to be made up for Dorothy, who was to be a maid-of-honor. Mother thought the remaining bolt of crimson damask would do very well.

"What does a royal bride wear on her head?" Jane asked.

"A chaplet of flowers, much as any other bride, I should think," Mother replied. "You put the crown on after you're married!"

Jane smiled, and went into the garden to select the flowers she would pluck at the last minute to make her chaplet. She picked some now, for the hall table, and went into the still room to find a vase and arrange them.

As she was standing at the table, absorbed in her task, she heard voices coming from beyond the open door that led to the kitchens. Her own name was spoken. She realized that the servants were muttering about Anne's fall.

"You know, long before her death, there was some arrangement." It was the royal chef himself speaking; she recognized his French accent. "It will not pacify the world when it is known what has passed, and is passing, between the King and Mistress Seymour. It is strange that, having suffered such ignominy, he has shown himself more glad than ever since the arrest."

"And we all know why!" someone said, as Jane's heart began to thud in her chest.

"I've never heard of a queen being thus handled!" another exclaimed.

"But everybody is rejoicing at her execution," a young man protested.

"Mark me, there are some who murmur at the mode of procedure against her and the others, and people speak variously of the King." The chef was clearly enjoying himself. "Think about it! They said she danced with her lovers, but it is no new thing for the King's gentlemen to dance with the ladies in the Queen's chamber. Nor can any proof of adultery be drawn from the fact that the Queen's brother took her by the hand and led her into the dance among the other ladies. And you have this charming custom in England whereby ladies married and unmarried, even the most coy, kiss not only a brother, but anyone else they greet, even in public. They made much of her writing to inform her brother that she was enceinte, but I hear it is the custom with young women to write to their near relatives when they become pregnant, in order to receive their congratulations. From such arguments as these, no suspicion of adultery could reasonably be inferred. There must have been some other reason that moved the King."

Jane was trembling. Was this the kind of evidence on which Anne had been condemned? Had they no stronger proofs? If so, they had built up a house of cards against her, and innocent blood had been shed. All along she had felt that there was something amiss somewhere. She tried to calm herself, remembering that four others beside Rochford had been accused with Anne, and what she herself had seen with her own eyes . . . and that Anne was no innocent. Even if she had not poisoned Katherine, she had hounded her to her death, and had probably tried to poison Bishop Fisher; and she would have had the Princess executed. No, Anne had deserved death!

"It could have been the desire for an heir that led the King to proceed against her," a rough voice said; it belonged to the gardener, who had shown himself very friendly to Jane. "And his desire for a new marriage."

"I think he got rid of her for fear that the Emperor, the Pope and the Catholic princes of Europe would band together against him," someone else opined.

"Very likely," the chef agreed. "But remember, just as she enjoyed herself with others, or so we are told, he, while the Queen was being beheaded, was enjoying himself with another woman."

This was intolerable! Jane stepped into the kitchen. She had rarely felt so angry. "Hold your tongue!" she cried, as they all jumped and gaped at her in dismay. "You lie! You know nothing of what you speak, and no honest person would believe it! Some might construe it as treason." She glared at them, one by one, wishing she could tell them that she was now betrothed to the King; but very soon they would hear her proclaimed queen, and then they would be sorry!

Henry wrote with news. Cromwell's man Thomas Heneage had filled Norris's office of Groom of the Stool, and Bryan was now chief Gentleman of the Privy Chamber in Norris's place. For him, preferment had come speedily. Jane was pleased. Bryan had long been her friend and one of her staunchest supporters, and had worked indefatigably to make her queen. She would probably never know how far he had undermined Anne's position.

She frowned when she read Henry's next paragraph: "It will be impossible to keep news of our betrothal a secret for long. There is much talk here that by midsummer, there will be a new coronation." Well, the gossips would not have long to wait. She was glad that Henry had mentioned her coronation. So far, he had said nothing about it. She rather dreaded it, knowing she would find it an ordeal, but it was her due.

She felt she ought to try once more to heal the rift between Henry and his daughter. She wrote back to him, choosing her words carefully: "I have been thinking about the Lady Mary's Grace, who must be relieved to know that the cause of her unhappiness is no more. If you could now receive her back into your fatherly embrace, I know that it would be a comfort for her, who loves you greatly."

Henry was touchy when it came to the subject of his elder daughter, but he surely could not object to that? He would know that it proceeded from kindness. A reconciliation was the first step; hopefully that would lead in time to Mary's restoration to the succession.

She was bitterly dismayed to receive an unequivocal response: "Darling, you mean well, but Mary refuses to acknowledge my laws and statutes, and if she continues in her obstinacy, I will proceed against her. I will not be satisfied until she acknowledges that her mother's marriage was incestuous and unlawful, and recognizes me as Supreme Head of the Church." Jane must realize, he added, that if Mary persisted in her assertion that she was the King's true daughter, she would remain a threat to their children. The way must be made clear for their undisputed succession.

Reading this, Jane wept for Mary. Henry was asking the girl to go against all her deeply held convictions, and betray everything her mother had suffered and fought for; in fact, he was asking the impossible. This was not the Henry she knew. It was not the action of a loving father. Could he not find it in his heart to let bygones be bygones? She had expected better of him. She herself believed that Mary was legitimate, and wanted her restored to the succession; she accepted that Mary would take precedence over any daughters she bore the King; but even Mary would acknowledge that Jane's son must succeed. Why must Henry be so unkind and unreasonable?

There was another reason why his letter had upset her. She, and all her friends and supporters, especially Chapuys and the Exeters, had believed that once Anne was removed, Mary would be restored and Henry might return to the Roman fold. But in a few lines, he had made it plain that there would be no going back. They had built their castles in the air, and all for nothing. The tasks she had set herself would be all the harder now.

What would Henry do if Mary kept defying him? Would he use coercion or force, or worse? Mary was now twenty, but Jane remembered her as a young girl plagued by the emotional and physical consequences of the conflict between her parents. Mary had not enjoyed good health during her years of exile, and her life had been despaired of more than once. Was it fair to put intolerable pressure on one who was known to be weak and sickly, and still grieving for her mother?

Mary should know that she could count on Jane to do everything in her power to help her. Jane knew she had a great ally in Chapuys, who had championed the Princess's rights for years. Bryan had said that even Cromwell was secretly sympathetic toward Mary; he might also use his considerable influence on her behalf.

She replied to Henry, asking him only to use kindness with Mary, for then he might be more likely to obtain what he desired. He an-

swered in a slightly testy tone that he had sent Norfolk and a deputation of the Privy Council to see Mary and demand her submission
in regard to her mother's marriage and the royal supremacy. He was
hoping that his daughter would come to her senses. Jane prayed
that she would. It would make her own task so much the easier.

It was now more than a week since Anne had died. Jane had struggled to put it out of her mind as she busied herself with preparations
for her wedding, which afforded a welcome distraction, and Mother
would not allow her leisure to brood. Jane had worried that the
strain she had been under would affect the babe, but she felt well,
with no hint of the kind of sickness Anne had suffered. Now Henry
had sent for her, and tomorrow she was to leave this house for good
and go to York Place, where they were to be married two days hence.
It had come upon her so quickly, and she had felt uneasy about marrying him so soon after Anne's death, but she understood the need
for haste. She hoped that his subjects would too.

She and Mother spent their last day at Chelsea making sure that
everything was packed and ready for the morrow. Her wedding
gown was folded away in a chest of its own. Father fell asleep in his
chair after dinner, and Jane caught Mother looking at him with a
worried frown on her face. She knew that both of them had put on a
cheerful front for her benefit, and that something was very wrong,
for Father had eaten little during the time they had been with her,
and was looking grayer than ever. But he had made it plain that he
did not want to discuss his health, and that he was determined to go
on as normal. Yet it taxed him, she could see, and it troubled her
deeply. She could not imagine a world without his solid presence.

The Lord Chamberlain himself conducted Jane and her parents from
the landing stage where they had disembarked, and through the
spacious gardens. Ahead lay the vast, sprawling palace of York Place,

said to be the largest in Europe. Henry had lavished a fortune on converting Wolsey's former town house into the most sumptuous of royal residences, with walls painted with checkers and black-and-white decorative patterns. Jane had visited York Place before, of course, but now it was as if she were seeing it anew.

The crenellated gatehouse ahead of them straddled the highway that passed right through the palace complex. Its checkered brickwork, oriel window, Tudor badges and terra-cotta roundels of Roman emperors bespoke the very latest in architectural style. Further down the road, toward Westminster, there was another gatehouse, in the classical style. She caught her breath as they passed into the great hall and then entered the King's lodgings, where Henry was waiting to receive them. The ceiling of the long gallery was painted in the most vivid, intricate manner, and was unmistakably by Master Holbein. It was beautiful.

From now on, her life would be lived in surroundings of similar splendor. Mother was speechless for once, her mouth gaping in an astonished O.

All the principal rooms in Henry's lodgings had high bay windows overlooking the Thames, and ceilings marvelously wrought in stone and gold leaf. The windows blazed with heraldic glass, and on one wall there was a great mural of Henry's coronation. Jane noticed that Queen Katherine's figure had been painted over.

The first thing she saw on entering the privy chamber was an alabaster fountain. Only later did she notice the wainscots of carved wood, painted with a thousand beautiful figures, for now Henry was coming toward her. She sank into a deep curtsey.

He raised her, and embraced and kissed her. "Welcome, Jane!" he said in a voice filled with emotion. "Welcome, darling!"

He insisted on escorting her to the Queen's apartments himself, and bade her parents come too. He was ebullient with excitement.

Taking Jane by the hand, he led them through a little door in his privy chamber to a secret gallery. Its windows overlooked the privy gardens, which were a masterpiece of formal design. At the other end of the gallery, the door opened onto the Queen's privy chamber, which was almost as lavishly adorned as the King's.

Jane hesitated. This place was familiar, and redolent of Anne. She could almost smell her perfume. This was where Anne had held court, had entertained, among the throng that had flocked around her, those unfortunate gentlemen who had died on her account.

Henry was smiling at Jane, looking at her expectantly. He had given her paradise, and wanted her to be brimming with happiness.

"I am so deeply honored," she said, making herself smile, when all she wanted to do was be away from here.

"I am so glad you like your lodging," Henry beamed. "I spent a King's ransom on these rooms."

He opened another door. Jane looked at Mother. There was no help to be had there. Mother was utterly overawed.

Jane followed Henry into the bedchamber. It was as she remembered. There was the great French bed hung with curtains of cloth of gold, and the magnificent carved overmantel. No woman could have had a finer place to sleep, but Jane could only think that this room had been Anne's, that it had witnessed her most intimate moments, as well as her fears and her despair. Henry had slept with her here.

She had not the courage to ask him if there was another lodging—any lodging—she might occupy. She knew it would be the same at all the royal palaces. These were the Queen's lodgings. The Queen must occupy them. Henry had beautified them all for Anne.

He was now leading her into another chamber, in which there was a long dining table with a great chair upholstered in velvet at the head.

"Your dining hall!" he announced. Her gaze took in the array of gold and silver plate on the oak buffet, the portrait of a younger Henry on the wall above the massive stone fireplace.

"In truth, I am overwhelmed," she told him. "Your goodness to me is boundless!"

Henry smiled and squeezed her hand. "Come," he commanded.

When they returned to her privy chamber, she was astonished to find a host of ladies and servants waiting for them. As one, they all made the deepest reverence.

"Jane, I have not quite finished drawing up your household," Henry explained, "but these good people will serve you until all your officers are appointed, and then we'll have everyone sworn in together. I am increasing the number to two hundred." He smiled ruefully. "I would add that word of our betrothal has somehow been leaked, and there has been a great rush for places." He leaned in closer. "You should tell them to rise."

Jane hurriedly collected herself. She had been thinking that from now on, she would not need to lift a finger to do anything for herself; always there would be someone to do it for her. She remembered wondering how she, a mere knight's daughter, would ever find the courage to exert her authority over so great a personage as Lady Exeter. Now she stood before a household of Lady Exeters.

She swallowed. "Please rise," she said, in a voice that sounded hoarse. When they did so, she was relieved to see Margaret Douglas, Margery Horsman, Anne Parr and Mary Zouche, all familiar faces. Margery was smiling at her. Mary Norris was with them, but she was not smiling.

She would be mourning her father. Jane hoped that Mary did not blame her for his death.

"My good niece Margaret is to be your chief lady-of-honor," Henry said, as Margaret stepped forward and curtseyed. Timidly, Jane extended her hand to be kissed, as she had seen Queen Anne do. She was glad she had donned her sumptuous black velvet gown.

"I am glad to be serving you, Mistress Jane," Margaret declared, in her lilting Scots accent.

"I hope you will be my friend," Jane said. God knew, she had need of them!

"Your other ladies-in-waiting are Lady Monteagle, Lady Rutland and Lady Sussex," Henry said, as the three ladies came forward. "I intend to appoint three others." Jane would rather have not had

Lady Rutland, who had been hostile to her when they both served Queen Anne, but that lady was now smiling as she rose from her obeisance. How the wind did change!

"I thought perhaps you might like your sister-in-law, Lady Seymour, as one of your ladies," Henry murmured, with a wry grimace.

"I would rather not," she whispered, shrinking from the exhausting prospect of the domineering Nan Stanhope shadowing her waking hours, with her dogmatic opinions, her critical eye and her jealousy. "May I call on her as an extra lady-in-waiting when I need one?"

Henry grinned. "Very sensible! The woman terrifies me."

The chief officers of the Queen's household had come forward. Most of them, Henry explained, had transferred from the service of the late Queen. "But if you wish to replace any with those who are more congenial to you, I would not object," he told her.

Now the maids-of-honor, the chamberers, the ushers and the grooms were presented. Jane was a little dismayed to see pretty Joan Ashley, who had been Henry's mistress not two years ago, though that, she knew, was well and truly over. There was Bess Holland, Norfolk's mistress, and the cause of his estrangement from his Duchess. Bess was a cheery soul, and both Jane and Henry liked her.

It felt strange to have Margery Horsman, Mary Norris, Anne Parr and Mary Zouche curtseying before her. It brought home to Jane the distance that must now be between them. She knew—and regretted—that it was not fitting for a queen to make confidantes of her maids. Anne had done it, but Katherine only when her household had dwindled to the point where there was no one else; and Jane was resolved to emulate Katherine and distance herself from Anne's style of queenship. So, painful as it would be, she must now set herself apart from her maids and make friends with the great ladies who were to attend her. She could not see Lady Rutland being a congenial companion, but she had high hopes of Lady Monteagle, who had been born Mary Brandon and was the daughter of the King's great friend the Duke of Suffolk.

Mary was twenty-six and very beautiful; she had hated Anne Boleyn, so was likely to be sympathetic to Jane. Henry was deeply fond of her.

Henry addressed her household. "Serve your mistress well, and be loyal to her, and discreet in all your doings. Do not speak of her marriage until it is proclaimed. Now, be about your tasks, and make all ready for her." As the household dispersed, leaving Jane and her parents alone with Henry, he turned to her. "I will leave you to settle yourself, darling, and we shall dine together later."

He kissed her hand and left by the door to the secret gallery. As Mother shooed the maids toward the bedchamber, Father sank down gratefully on a bench.

"Well, daughter, you have done us proud!" he said. "To think that tomorrow you will be our queen!"

"I can't quite believe it," Jane replied. "It seems like a dream." And a nightmare at times, for still she could not get the horror of Anne's end out of her mind, or the guilt she felt, rightly or wrongly. And now there would be reminders of Anne at every turn.

Leaving him to rest, she joined Mother, who was instructing the maids to take the greatest care when lifting Jane's wedding gown out of its chest.

"And it must be ironed and laid out on a flat surface ready for tomorrow," she commanded. "Young lady, those fingernails are not fit to touch it. Go and clean them!" Anne Parr hastened away, shamefaced. Margery threw a secret smile at Jane. Jane pretended she had not seen it.

"Margery, could you unpack my chaplet of flowers and put it in water?" she asked.

"Of course, Madam." Margery bobbed and did as she was bid.

"Oh, what gorgeous shoes!" Anne Parr exclaimed as she returned, seeing the crimson velvet slippers embroidered in gold that Jane would wear on the morrow. "May I try them on?" It was the kind of thing Jane would have agreed to in her former life, when they had all taken an interest in each other's attire, but she knew she must nip such familiarity in the bud.

"They are the Queen's shoes, Anne," she said, "and it would not be fitting for her maid to try them on."

They all stared at her, and she wished the ground would swallow her up. It had sounded so stiff and mean, and not at all as she had intended, but she bit off the urge to apologize. As their mistress, she owed them no explanation. Yet she could leaven her severity. "You may all carry my train tomorrow," she told the maids, and smiled. They looked at her uncertainly.

"But Madam, I think that is my privilege, and the other ladies'," Eleanor Rutland said.

Jane stood her ground. She must establish her authority. She did not like the implication that she was unaware of court etiquette. "My Lady Rutland, it is traditional for maids to attend a bride. When I am crowned, you ladies may carry my train."

Eleanor bristled. "The Lady Margaret is unmarried."

"Yes, but she is royal, and I intend that she shall be at the head of those who bear my train."

Eleanor's eyes flashed, but Margaret came to Jane's rescue. "It will be my pleasure!" she declared.

Jane walked away and went into the privy chamber to sit with her father. She was uneasy, and worried that already she had alienated most of those who would be living in close proximity to her. It was not a good start.

Chapter 26

1536

The white satin gown fell in stiff folds to the floor. The long train was heavy, and the bodice tight, but Jane knew she had never looked better, with her long hair cascading down her back and her head crowned by the beautiful chaplet of flowers. Around her neck she wore Henry's cross. Mother had wept when she saw her dressed for her wedding, and even Father had looked as if he might shed a tear.

They were all there, crammed into the Queen's closet—her three brothers, proud as peacocks in their bright silks, Dorothy looking very pretty in her new crimson gown, Nan resplendent in green damask, Bryan and Carew both wearing an air of jubilation, and her ladies and maids decked out in their finery. Jane was aware of them all looking on as she and Henry knelt before Archbishop Cranmer and the wedding ceremony began; but when the time came to make her vows, she had eyes only for Henry, who held her gaze as he spoke the words that would make her his. Then the Archbishop pronounced them man and wife—and she was Jane, by the grace of God, Queen of England!

Henry, looking magnificent in white cloth of silver, with an enormous ruby glinting on his chest, turned to her. "My lady and Queen!" he exulted, and kissed her heartily on the lips. When they turned around, everyone knelt in reverence. It came as a shock to see her parents with their heads bent to her, and she hastened to raise them. Then everyone was crowding around, congratulating them, and Mother was weeping tears of joy, and Father looked ready to burst with pride.

In a joyous mood, Henry led Jane to his presence chamber, and there she was enthroned next to him in the Queen's seat under the canopy of estate, as their guests and favored courtiers came to pay their respects.

She felt quite dizzy at being the focus of such attention and honor, and prayed that she was playing her part well. She knew that the eye of every great lady would be upon her, and could imagine them thinking, There she goes, the little upstart!

The King stood up. "Be it known by one and all that I have today dowered Queen Jane with a hundred manors in four counties, with forests and hunting chases, and the palaces of Baynard's Castle and Havering-atte-Bower." As everyone clapped, a page stepped forward and gave the King an elaborate inlaid box. Henry sat down and turned to Jane. "This is yours, Madam. It contains the documents relating to your dower. The income from these properties will amply support your estate as queen. There is no need to trouble yourself: your officers will administer your lands and income."

"In all matters, I will do as your Grace directs," she said.

"You do not need to ask me for money for your little pleasures," he told her, looking at her tenderly. "The keeper of your privy purse will supply any money you need."

"Thank you," she answered. She knew he would deny her nothing. Her estate must reflect his own magnificence. She also knew him to have a generous heart when it came to giving.

After dinner, which was served in his privy chamber, Henry disappeared briefly and came back with something wrapped in cloth of gold. "I have a wedding gift for you," he said. She gasped when she saw an exquisite gold cup engraved with the initials H and the Latin I for Jane entwined in true lovers' knots, four antique medallion heads, and the Queen's arms supported by dolphins and cherubs and surmounted by a crown. Her new motto was delicately graven around the stem.

"Henry, it's beautiful!" she breathed.

"I thought you would like it, darling," he said, kissing her. "Holbein designed it."

They supped alone together that evening. Jane ate well, aware of Henry gazing at her intently across the table. Afterward, he escorted her back along the connecting gallery to her apartments, so that she could be made ready for bed. Taking her hand, he kissed her gently on the lips and left her to the ministrations of her women. They were respectfully subdued as they undressed her. She suspected that they must have guessed by now that she was with child, but they gave no sign of it as they put on her nightgown and cap, which were edged with gold and silver embroidery, and brushed her hair until it shone.

"Is there anything else your Grace needs?" Margery asked.

Jane smiled at her. "No thank you. I will get into bed now. Pray tell the King I am ready."

They left her alone as she climbed into the elegant French bed and sank into the feather mattress, thankful that Henry had rejected the idea of a public bedding ceremony out of hand. "I've never had one, and I don't intend to start now!" he had declared, looking prim. "What happens between us in our bed is private, and will stay so!"

The door opened, and he appeared, clad in a red-and-gold brocaded night robe and a matching nightcap.

"Darling!" he said, and put down his candle. Climbing in beside her, he held her close, and she could feel his need for her. How she wanted him!

"We must think of the babe," he said. She did not gainsay him, for much hung upon this pregnancy, but it was disappointing to be spending her wedding night being chaste. She was grateful when he guided her hand down to his member and began caressing her breasts. At least they could share some intimacies while they waited for the child to be born.

Jane sat up and pulled on her night rail. She must be decent before she summoned her ladies.

Henry watched her appreciatively as she returned from the privy in the corner.

"This morning is your uprising as a new wife," he said.

She smiled at him. "I know. From today, I must bind up my hair and cover it with a hood. It must be for your eyes only."

"Indeed!" he grinned. "But as queen, you are allowed the privilege of leaving your hair loose on ceremonial occasions when you wear your crown."

"Where is my crown?" she asked, kneeling beside him on the bed.

"In the Jewel House at the Tower," he told her. "I will have it sent for, if you wish to see it." She wondered if it had been made for Anne. She would have preferred to wear Katherine's crown, but did not like to ask.

"When shall I be crowned?" she asked.

"As soon as I can arrange it, darling," Henry said, his eyes gleaming. "But first, let me kiss you again."

Henry had planned a hunting expedition for the afternoon. That morning, the ladies dressed Jane in a new scarlet riding habit. She sensed that they were a little wary of her, but they responded readily enough to her conversation.

"I do rejoice to see your Grace as queen," Margaret Douglas told her warmly.

"I rejoice to have your ladyship as my chief lady-of-honor." Jane smiled. She was aware of Margery Horsman looking a touch downcast. She felt badly about having ended their close friendship, and about the clumsy way she had gone about it—but what else could she have done? She was the Queen now, and for better or worse, things had to change.

In the morning, Jane rested on her bed, but found that she could not sleep. Rising, she went into her closet to fetch a book from the chest containing her personal belongings, and heard Lady Rutland's voice in the room beyond.

"It does seem strange that within one and the same month that saw Queen Anne flourishing, accused, condemned and executed, another has been assumed into her place."

Jane froze.

"I don't think it strange." That was Lady Monteagle. "The King needs an heir; that is why he has remarried so soon. And Queen Anne made a cuckold of him. The crimes she was found guilty of have no parallel in Christendom."

"Yes, but did she commit them?"

"Of course she did. Her fate was the judgment of the Almighty."

"I do wonder! And now we have this proud and haughty upstart in her place."

Jane could listen no more. "Lady Rutland, have you duties to attend to?" she asked, stepping through the door. She smiled at Lady Monteagle. Eleanor Rutland reddened, muttered an apology and hastened away.

"I fear I have made an enemy, Mary," Jane said.

"Your Grace heard what she said?"

"Yes. I know she was a friend of Queen Anne."

"Yes, and she fears your Grace dislikes her on account of that." This came as a surprise.

"I would be her friend, if she were not hostile to me."

"Then, Madam, I pray you show her some sign of favor, and I think all will be well."

"I am grateful for such kind advice," Jane told her, liking Mary Brandon more by the minute. "Tell me, do people really think me proud and haughty? Are the maids-of-honor upset at my not being familiar with them as I used to?"

Mary flushed. "A little, Madam."

"Will you tell them, please, that you think I am sorry for it, but that I have said I am minded to be a queen as Katherine was. I think they will understand."

"I will do that," Mary promised.

After dinner, on her way to the courtyard where Henry was assembling his hunting party, Jane could have kicked herself. She was not half the woman Katherine had been, so how could she aspire to take her place? Instead, she should be endeavoring not to appear proud and haughty. Lady Rutland's words had stung.

Henry stared at Jane. "You are not riding in your condition?" he muttered, taking care that none of the company should hear him.

She had not thought of that. "I have seen many pregnant ladies ride, and none took any hurt. And I am feeling so well. Please let me ride with you. People will talk if they see me in a litter."

He did not look happy. "Very well. But I'll have my groom bring you the gentlest palfrey, and you must not go faster than a trot."

They rode out as far as Tottenham, eight miles north of London, where they looked around the ancient parish church and dined at the nearby Lordship House, which had reputedly been owned by Robert the Bruce, King of Scots. Now it belonged to their hosts, the Compton family. Henry's close friend Sir William Compton had died of the sweating sickness eight years before, and he still held the family in affection.

Inevitably, the talk at table touched on Anne's fall. Sir Peter Compton observed, "In destroying her, God revealed His will. The news of her judgment was music to my ears."

Henry nodded. He did not seem at all averse to discussing his late wife on the day after his wedding. "She has earned the greatest infamy," he observed. Jane saw that he appreciated others' expressions of sympathy and solidarity.

"In charity, I pray that God will have mercy on her soul and pardon all her offenses," Jane said.

Sir John Russell, a man high in the King's counsels, looked impressed. "Your Grace has found as gentle a lady as ever I knew, and as fair a queen as any in Christendom."

Henry took Jane's hand. "I do assure you, my lord, I have come out of Hell into Heaven for the gentleness in her, and the cursedness and unhappiness in the other."

"We all rejoice that your Grace is so well matched with so gracious a woman." Sir Peter smiled. Jane's cheeks were burning, but it was heartening to be the object of such approval.

"Did your Grace hear back from Peterborough?" Sir John inquired. Henry frowned. "I did. Apparently, the report spoke truth."

"What report, Sir?" Jane asked.

"On the day before Queen Anne was beheaded, the tapers that stood about the Lady Katherine's tomb kindled of themselves, and after Matins, they quenched of themselves. I sent thirty men to Peterborough to find out the truth, and they could discover no trickery. Mary had witnessed it. No one could explain it. And the ignorant folk who saw it are now saying it is a sign that God approves of my punishing the woman who supplanted my true wife. They have been warned not to spread such sedition. Katherine was never my true wife, and nor was Anne. You, Jane, are my only true Queen." He raised her hand and kissed it.

She did wonder about the candles. She preferred to think of their rekindling as a sign that Katherine smiled upon her marriage.

Henry came to her bedchamber that night, and they lay closely entwined for some time, talking and kissing and holding each other. When he had fallen asleep, his head on her shoulder, she lay there wakeful. Moonlight was streaming through the open casement and the damask curtains were stirring gently in the breeze. Her mind teemed with thoughts of the future. She envisaged herself, full in years, as the matriarch of the Tudor dynasty, with Henry, a magnificent elder statesman, at her side, and a brood of great strong sons encircling them. There would be daughters too, of course, for the King to marry off to secure the friendship of foreign princes. And Mary would be there, and Elizabeth—well married, both of them, and loved by all.

At first, she dismissed the dark shadow on the wall as a trick of the light. It was some moments before she realized that there was nothing to account for it. It looked like a woman with a halo around her head—or a French hood! It was a woman in a French hood, she was sure of it. Suddenly, terror gripped her. It was Anne, come back to haunt her—Anne, who would take the greatest of pleasure in spoiling her happiness. Anne, her enemy in life, and now in death.

She wanted to huddle under the counterpane, but she could not draw her eyes away. Was there vindictiveness in Purgatory? Or was Anne already in Hell, doomed to walk the earth for all eternity, and torment those who had destroyed her? Had she appeared thus to Cromwell? Did she haunt his dreams?

She was dreaming, she must be. She blinked, and the shadow was gone, yet she was not aware of having woken. There were things that could not be explained by rational deduction; she had sometimes seen or felt them. She lay there trembling violently, frightened to rouse Henry or call out, lest she summon up the apparition again. Her maids would come running. They would think she was mad! They would gossip, and speculate why she thought herself haunted. They would guess at the burden of guilt she bore.

It must have been a dream, she told herself. All the same, she got up and lit a candle, banishing the darkness. It was a long time before she slept. In the morning, she felt sure it had indeed been a dream. And then the cramps began, and when she arose, she saw blood on the sheets. She knew at once what was happening, and her teeth began chattering.

She shook Henry awake, tears streaming down her cheeks.

"What is it?" he cried, sitting bolt upright. Then he saw the blood.

He was very kind. There was not a word of reproach, even though he had cause, after she had insisted on riding yesterday. He soothed her, summoned her women and bade her rest. Then he waited in the outer chamber.

The cramps worsened. It was sheer agony, so a midwife was hurriedly summoned. Presently Jane felt something pass from her. Mary Monteagle clapped a hand to her mouth, staring in distress at what the midwife had in her hand. Jane caught a glimpse of a tiny infant, no bigger than her own palm, before it was concealed in a cloth and whisked away.

The pains eased then, but the sense of loss and failure was great. As she lay there weeping, Henry came in, still in his night robe, and sat by her side, holding her hand.

"Sleep now," he said. "The midwife tells me there is no reason why we should not have another child, and soon."

"I am more sorry than I can say," she sobbed.

"It was God's will," he sighed. She looked up at him and saw tears in his eyes. He was suffering too.

"Oh, my darling," she said. "I would not have had this happen for the world."

"I know that," he answered, squeezing her hand. "Now rest."

When he had gone, a suspicion began germinating in her mind. If the shadow had not been a dream, was it her child that Anne had come for? And if it had only been a trick of the light, could it be that God was punishing her for her part in Anne's fall? If so, would He ever permit her to bear Henry a son?

She was soon up and about, and telling herself sternly not to dwell on irrational fears. She was still bleeding intermittently when they returned to York Place, but she felt well, if deeply saddened, for she could not forget the tiny creature that she had nurtured for that short time, and mourned it deeply. But she put on a brave face for Henry, telling herself that there would be other children. She was only twenty-eight, after all.

She received a letter from Eliza Darrell, asking for a place in her household. She had fond memories of Eliza, who had served with her under Queen Katherine. Eliza explained that since Katherine's death, she had fallen into penury. She had hoped to enter the Lady Mary's service, but since she saw no hope of Mary ever being taken back into favor, she had presumed to petition the Queen. Jane told Henry about her request.

"Would you like to have her, sweetheart?" He was being so kind to her, for all that she had let him down badly.

"Very much," she told him.

"Then you must send for her."

When Henry arrived that evening, he was attended by a page carrying an iron-bound casket of chased gold.

"Set it on the table," he commanded, and opened the casket. It was a treasure chest of jewels, winking and glittering in the candlelight. "These are yours now," he said, with a flourish of his hand.

"Mine?" Jane was awestruck.

"Yes, darling. These are the Queen's jewels, handed down from consort to consort. Some of these pieces are very old." He drew out a heavy gold collar. "This was my mother's. And this dates from the thirteenth century." He lifted up an enameled brooch. "It belonged to Eleanor of Castile, who was dearly loved by King Edward I. Now another beloved queen will own her brooch."

He handed it to Jane. She was staring at the wealth of jewelry before her.

"Take them out! Look at them. They're yours," Henry enjoined.

She recognized pieces that Queen Katherine had worn before her jewels were cruelly wrested from her by Anne. Here were the long ropes of pearls that had graced her bodice. The jewel that Jane liked best was Katherine's brooch with its black diamond pendants and the initials IHS, representing Christ's name in Greek.

"It will be an honor to wear these," she whispered. "You are too good to me, Henry."

"It is your due," he told her.

She wore the brooch the next morning when she stood before her assembled household. Henry was not present, and she was doing her best to bear her royal honors with dignity.

She tried not to let her voice falter. "I have called you here this morning to say that I expect high moral standards among you all. You will observe the proper protocols and etiquette at all times, and show yourselves devout and virtuous. Ladies, you must attire yourselves sumptuously—as I see you already do—but please dress modestly." She paused to clear her throat. "Your trains must be three yards long, and each of your girdles set with two hundred pearls." There was a suppressed gasp, which she tried to ignore. If they wanted to serve her, they must look the part. "You are to wear gable hoods and no other. French hoods are banned, for they are immodest." There was a murmur of protest, quickly stifled, but again Jane ignored it. Anne had favored the French hood, therefore she wanted it banned at her court.

Her ladies were attired exactly as she had ordered when, three days after her marriage, they followed her to the landing stage at York Place, where they boarded the Queen's barge, on which her arms had been painted over Anne's, and followed the King's to Greenwich. That evening, Jane sat in solitary splendor under the canopy of estate in her presence chamber, wearing a gorgeous gown of creamy damask and a pearl-edged gable hood with frontlets of goldsmiths' work. She was to dine in public as queen for the first time, a prospect that filled her slightly with dread. She remembered watching Queen Katherine at table and thinking that she could not endure to be the object of such scrutiny. Yet she was learning that she had inner reserves of strength she had not dreamed of.

Her servants placed a table before her on the dais, and set it with a cloth of the finest white linen, which was laid with vessels of gold and silver-gilt, with a great gold salt in the shape of a ship. Dinner was served to her with much ceremony, as the courtiers looked on. She took deep breaths and resolved to make Henry proud of her.

Two days later, on Whitsunday, the King finally emerged from seclusion to preside once more over the court. He wore a triumphant expression when the trumpets sounded in the great hall at Greenwich and the royal heralds proclaimed Jane queen as a great throng of lords, ladies, bishops, Privy councillors, courtiers and the great officers of state looked on. Throughout the realm, the same proclamation was being made, in towns and in villages. Garbed in cloth of gold, Jane bowed to acknowledge the loud acclamations, then followed Henry in procession to Mass, with a long train of ladies walking behind her. She thought she would never get used to people bowing as she passed, but it gratified her nonetheless. Who could not take pleasure in being the object of such deference?

At the altar, she made her offering as queen, and afterward dined again in her presence chamber, with her officers and household in attendance, ready for the long ceremony of swearing-in that was to take place that afternoon.

Henry had not attended the ceremony of oath-taking; he had been in Council. When he joined her in her privy chamber for supper, he was tense and brusque. She began to wonder if she had offended him in some way, but soon the reason for his anger became clear.

"The Privy councillors who visited Mary at Hunsdon reported back to me today," he growled. "Norfolk had ordered her, in my name, to acknowledge her mother's marriage to be incestuous and unlawful. She refused out of hand. He reduced her to tears, but still she remained obstinate." Jane could detect no flicker of sympathy in him. All that mattered, it seemed, was that his will must be obeyed. Other people's consciences were of no account, and anyone who opposed him, be they never so close, must be punished. In that moment, she felt hatred for him, for the first time, and it upset her. As for Norfolk, he was despicable. He had presided over his niece Anne's trial and passed sentence, and thereby retained his post of Lord Treasurer; and clearly he hoped to retain favor with the King by bullying Mary.

"Whatever Mary has done, she is of your blood, and the Duke should not have spoken to her so harshly."

"Hmm." She suspected that Henry was unhappy about it, but would he admit it? "I think it is time to intimate to Norfolk that it might be politic for him to retire to his house at Kenninghall," he said.

"As ever, you have made a wise decision," Jane told him. Norfolk was one of the most powerful men at court, and she feared that he might one day champion the cause of his great-niece, Elizabeth, to further his own ambitions. "And Mary? What will happen to her?" she asked.

Henry bristled. "She will be brought to heel!"

He did not stay with her that night, and she cried herself to sleep.

In the morning, as Jane sat in her chamber trying to establish a happier rapport with her ladies, Master Cromwell was announced. He bowed low before her as she extended her hand to be kissed.

"Your Grace, might we speak alone?" he asked.

Jane smiled at her women, who curtseyed and withdrew.

Cromwell's expression hardened. "Madam, I need your help. It is essential that the Lady Mary be restored to favor. Until your Grace has a son, which we all pray for daily, the King has no certain heir. His daughters are both bastards now, and his only son is baseborn. As things stand, the Lady Mary is our best hope for the future. But she has continually defied his Grace over this matter of her mother's marriage, and this morning he has expressed his resolve to have her arraigned for treason."

"No!" Jane cried. "She is his daughter!"

"Under the law, Madam, she is also guilty of treason. She has written to me, begging me to intercede for her with the King, which I am happy to do, but first we have to rescue her from her folly."

"I will plead with his Grace," Jane said at once.

"I was hoping you would say that, Madam." Cromwell smiled.
"Surely he cannot refuse so gracious a bride."

Jane was relieved to receive a summons to Henry's presence chamber. When she was announced, she was surprised to see ranks of
courtiers assembled there, standing aside to let her pass. She curtseyed low to Henry and joined him on the dais. He looked at her
contritely.

"I am sorry I did not visit you last night, darling," he murmured,
taking her hand and kissing it. "I was vexed with Mary, and I got
one of my headaches." He had them increasingly often, sometimes
with blind spots and strange flashes of light, and they all but incapacitated him.

"I trust you are better now," she replied. It had been painful to
discover that there was a side of him that she could hate, but her
anger with him was now overlaid by her concern.

"Much better for seeing my Queen." He nodded to a man standing nearby. It was the Garter King of Arms, who was holding a
scroll. "And now, Jane, you shall see how I reward your family's
loyalty. Summon Sir Edward Seymour!"

Jane felt a thrill as Edward advanced toward the throne and knelt
before the King, and the Garter King of Arms read out a patent of
nobility creating him Viscount Beauchamp of Hache, the property
of their ancestors in the county of Somerset. Then Henry's voice
rang out, appointing him chancellor of North Wales, governor of
Jersey and Lord Chamberlain to the King, and confirming a grant of
numerous manors in Wiltshire.

Edward's normally stern face was lit up with triumph and pride.
This was what he had dreamed of, and worked tirelessly for. But
Jane knew that, for all his abilities, he owed his ennoblement largely
to her becoming queen, and was glad that she had helped to bring
him to this pinnacle. She saw her parents looking on joyfully, and
Nan, who would be insufferably proud after this, and Thomas, puce
with envy, and the eyes of the courtiers, some jealous, some calculat-

ing, some smiling. Edward stayed kneeling as the King placed the mantle of estate around his shoulders and the coronet on his head. He made his oath of homage and stood up a peer of the realm, the most influential Gentleman of the Privy Chamber.

Harry was summoned next, and made steward and receiver of the Queen's manors in three counties. "He will administer them well for you," Henry said. She understood why Harry had received no higher office. For all his kind nature and steady application, he lacked the ability, the ambition and the will to rise further.

She had expected Thomas and her father to be called next, but apparently the investiture was at an end, and Edward's relations and friends were crowding around him, offering congratulations. Chapuys, Bryan and Carew were among them. Cromwell stood a little way off, looking on benevolently. Jane rose and descended from the dais to embrace her brother and add her own felicitations.

When she and Henry were alone in her candlelit bedchamber that night, she thanked him for his munificence to her family.

"It is no more than they deserve," he said, turning in the bed to face her. "I expect you are wondering why I did not honor Thomas. Well, Jane, the truth is that he is a young hothead and not yet ready for high office. If he settles down and conducts himself well, he may win preferment in the future."

"You have the measure of him." Jane smiled. "But there is one, Henry, for whom I would humbly solicit some small token of your esteem, and that is my father."

Henry was silent for a moment. "You must have noticed, darling, that he is a sick man and unfit for any office."

"I know. I am worried about him. He doesn't seem to be getting any better. My mother is aware of it, but she puts on a brave face."

Henry reached out and drew her to him. "Would you like me to ask my physicians to examine him?"

"It is most kind of you, but he will not admit he is ill. We do not mention it."

"Then I do not see what you can do," Henry murmured. She wept then, and he held her tightly against his broad chest, and then desire flared in him, and although she was still bleeding a little, she let him kiss away her tears and make love to her.

Afterward, as they lay close together, she gathered her courage. This was her moment. "Henry, do you intend to proceed against the Lady Mary?"

She felt him grow tense. "I do, Jane."

"I beg of you not to do this," she urged. "I beg of you!"

He drew away from her. "Jane, you must be out of your senses. She has committed treason, against all reason and her duty to me. She is the most unnatural daughter in the world!"

She said nothing. She lay there, trying to quell her thumping heart.

Now was not the time to pursue the matter.

"Do not meddle in this, sweetheart," Henry said. "I do not want to quarrel with you. God knows, I had enough of that with Anne!"

"I am sorry if I spoke out of turn," she said. "I was hoping that the Lady Mary could return to court and keep me company."

"You know I cannot allow that until she has acknowledged her mother's marriage to have been incestuous and unlawful."

"It is a hard thing for her to do, Henry." Even so, why did Mary not give Henry what he wanted, for expediency's sake, and then ask for absolution?

Henry reached across the bed and took her hand. "It was your tender heart speaking, I know. But Jane, I intend to instruct my judges to proceed, according to law."

"What will people say of you if you do that? What of the Emperor and the new alliance?"

"What I do with my own daughter is my affair!" he snarled, his anger erupting. "And you, Madam, would do well not to meddle in matters that do not concern you."

It was as if she had been slapped. Desperately, she tried not to cry.

"This is a fine way to end a special day," Henry said, breathing heavily.

"It is," she agreed. She would not apologize.

In the night, he took her again with no word of love, but with increased mastery, as if to show her where the power lay in their marriage. Afterward, she did weep, silently, into her pillow. But in the morning, he was his old loving self again, and with renewed hope in her heart, she told herself that, given time and careful handling, she would win him round.

Edward came to see her. They sat in her closet, for privacy.

"Cromwell is cajoling and bullying Mary to submit to the King's will," he told her.

"I know." She related what Cromwell had said.

"Chapuys fears that Cromwell is working against your hopes of her being restored to the succession."

"He shares those hopes, I assure you."

"There will be no reconciliation with Rome."

"I know," she said sadly. "The removal of Anne has not changed the King's opinions at all. And while that grieves me, I think you would not be sorry if England remained in schism?"

"I would not, personally, but we need the Imperial alliance. It's good for trade, and the Emperor supports you as queen. It is an advantage to have powerful friends abroad. No, Jane, I am for reform, you know that; and I am also for us, the Seymours. Norfolk has left court under a cloud. With him gone, our star will be even more in the ascendant. We don't need Cromwell!"

"We do, Edward. We need him to save the Princess from herself."

Chapter 27

1536

Cromwell came to see her late that night. He looked tired, and wasted no time in getting to the point. "Your Grace will be comforted to know that the King's justices are reluctant to proceed against the Lady Mary. They have suggested to his Grace that instead of being tried for treason, she be made to sign a paper of submission, recognizing him as head of the Church and her mother's marriage as incestuous and unlawful. It is the best solution, and I have persuaded the King to agree. It was not easy." He took out his kerchief and began mopping his brow. "His Grace was very angry. He told me that my birth made me unfit to meddle with the affairs of kings." He smiled self-deprecatingly. "He also called me a villain and a knave, knocked me about the head, and thrust me from the Privy Chamber. Already, Madam, I am regretting lending the Lady Mary my support. I fear I have laid myself open to accusations of misprision of treason."

Jane shook her head in sympathy. "I am sure the King will not go that far. He knows that you have his interests at heart—and he likes you."

"I trust to that, Madam. One must deal with such trials with humor and patience. It is a small price to pay for a happy outcome."

"Then you will not abandon Mary?" she asked anxiously.

He shook his head. "No, Madam. But I have today sent her the list of articles she is to sign, with a politic letter, written with a view to making her comply. If you read it, you would think the worst of me, and I would not incur the odium of such a gracious lady." He sketched a courtly little bow. "That is why I have come to explain myself."

"What have you written?" she wanted to know, intrigued.

He hesitated for a moment. "I deplored her unfilial stand against the King her father. I said I was as much ashamed of what I have said to her as a friend as afraid of what I have done for her. I told her that, with her folly, she will undo herself and all who have wished her well. I said—forgive me, Madam—that I think her the most obstinate and obdurate woman that ever was, and that I will only venture to intercede for her with the King if she signs the articles. I warned her I could not vouchsafe her any hope of escaping her father's wrath, and would never think otherwise of her than as the most ungrateful daughter to her dear and benign father." He paused. "You understand why I had to write thus. Not only must she be made to see the error of her ways, but the King will see the letter. I cannot be seen to be her friend."

"Of course. I pray she will take heed. Thank you for coming to tell me this, Master Cromwell. I cannot say how much I appreciate your masterly efforts."

Cromwell bowed. "I am always happy to be of service, Madam."

At dinner the next day, Henry was in a foul temper. He came in limping and flung a piece of paper on the table. "Read that!" he commanded.

It was a letter from Mary.

> I congratulate your Grace on the comfortable tidings of
> your marriage and beg leave to wait upon Queen Jane, or

do her Grace such service as it shall please her to command
me, which my heart shall be as ready and obedient to ful-
fill as the most humble servant that she has. I trust, by
your Grace's mercy, to come soon into your presence,
which shall be the greatest comfort I can have in this
world, having a great hope in your Grace's natural pity. I
pray that God will send your Grace shortly a prince, at
which no creature living would more rejoice than I.

"She expresses all the right sentiments," Jane observed. "I cannot
doubt that she is sincere, and that she is longing to be forgiven by
you."

Henry snorted.

"What will you say to her?" she asked.

"I do not intend to reply," he said. "I feel no natural pity for her,
and I will not receive her again unless she puts her signature to the
articles that have been sent her."

Jane was silent. They had reached an impasse. Henry was determined to be obeyed. But, much as she craved his love, Mary was
stubborn. She believed she would be risking her immortal soul by
betraying her mother's memory, and that was entirely understandable. Yet could she not see that she was on a headlong course to di-
saster?

"I do hope that she will sign," she replied.

"She had best do so, if she has any sense," Henry growled. "I have
Chapuys badgering me night and day, bleating about the alliance
and what the Emperor will say if she defies me and I punish her for
it. I told him I will not have anyone interfering in what passes between me and my daughter, or undermining my laws. I recognize
no superior, and I will not have anyone imagine that I can be led by
force or fear."

"I am sure that the Emperor must realize that, Henry. He has not
made any threats, has he?"

"No. But I lived under the threat of war on Katherine's account.
I do not intend to have my daughter put me in the same case."

_____

After dinner, Henry suggested a walk in the privy garden. His anger had burned itself out, and Jane suspected he was regretting venting it on her. As they wandered along the gravel path between the rose bushes, he took her hand.

"You must forgive me, Jane. I am a rough man when I don't mean to be, especially with you, darling."

"I understand that you were upset about Mary," she said, noticing again that he was limping. In bed, she had seen the old wound on his leg and not liked the look of it. "Are you in pain?"

"Yes," he admitted. "My leg has been playing up lately. My physicians say it has become infected. I was going to play tennis this morning, but I was too lame. I'm sorry, it was that too which put me in a bad humor."

"Do the physicians say how long it will take to heal?"

"Not long. They have put on a poultice and bound it up. At least I can walk."

They sat in the shade of a mulberry tree, Jane with her embroidery and Henry with his book, a theological tome on transubstantiation.

"I have always loved theology," he told her. "There's nothing better than a good debate. And now I am the spiritual father of my people, and ought to be conversant with doctrine."

"I have heard that you know more than most doctors about Scripture," Jane said.

"That may be so!" He looked pleased. "I could trounce several I could name in an argument!" His arm curled around her and she turned her face to his. They kissed, and then he resumed reading his book. They sat there in companionable silence.

The next day, Jane summoned her head gardener, Master Chapman, and asked him to escort her and her mother around her privy garden. It was laid out in the shape of a knot, with low box hedges in

an intricate design around a fountain at the center, and colored rail-
ings in the Tudor colors of green and white marking the boundary.
Jane's panther emblem perched snarling on its hind legs atop a pole
at the entrance.

"I would like more flower beds," she told the gardener, "and some
fragrant herbs. Maybe you could lay these out on the other side of
the outer path."

He looked at her with interest. "That would be a new idea,
Madam."

"It's just that I love the scent of flowers."

"You should see her garden at home," Mother told him.

"I made it myself," Jane said. Chapman looked impressed, and
she sensed in him a kindred spirit. "I should like to work in this
garden too, from time to time, if I would not be trespassing on your
territory."

He seemed surprised. "Whatever your Grace pleases."

She was aware of Mother curtseying low. The King was approaching, not limping as badly as he had been. In his arms he carried a
little white poodle wearing a velvet collar.

"For you," he said, beaming at Jane.

"Oh, it's adorable!" she cried, as he placed it in her embrace. The
little thing nuzzled her hand as she petted it. "Your Grace spoils
me."

"It is my pleasure," he declared.

She put the dog on the path and immediately it ran over to the
hedge and lifted its leg. They all laughed.

"What will you call him?" Henry asked.

Jane thought for a while. "I rather like Noble, because he looks
it."

"Noble he is, then," Henry said. "A most fitting name."

Noble was sleeping on a cushion by the silk fire-screen in the empty
hearth when Henry arrived for supper that evening. He bent down
and fondled the dog's silky ears before joining Jane at table. "I have

another gift for you," he said, and placed in her hands a magnificent ruby pendant in a setting of gold acanthus leaves. "Master Holbein designed it," he told her. "I had it made specially for you."

"It's stunning," she said, gazing at it in wonder. "How can I ever thank you for all the gifts and blessings you shower upon me? Truly, this is exquisite. Master Holbein is a most versatile artist."

"There is nothing to which he cannot turn his hand," Henry said. "Let me put it on for you." He rose, draped Jane's veil over her hood so that it lay in the fashionable whelk-shell manner, and did up the clasp of the pendant. His hand snaked down to where her breast rose plumply from her bodice, and briefly caressed it. A warm feeling crept through her. They would be lovers tonight, she knew. Perhaps, God willing, she would conceive another child.

"I want Holbein to paint you," Henry said, resuming his seat. "A coronation portrait. I've started to make plans for your crowning. It is customary for kings and queens to lodge in the Tower before they are crowned, but the Queen's lodgings there have been stripped of their contents." They were both silent for a space, with the specter of Anne between them. Those rooms had been emptied after she left them for the last time. "I'm having an inventory of the furniture you will need drawn up," Henry said.

Jane felt a tremor. She did not want to stay in those lodgings. Anne's misery and terror would be imprinted on the walls. "You will be there with me?" she asked.

Henry understood her reluctance, she was sure of it. "You may sleep in my chamber, in the King's lodgings," he told her. Then abruptly he changed the subject. "Parliament meets next month. Its chief business will be to settle the succession on our children."

"I am praying daily that God will send us a son," Jane said, thinking of that lost little one with a pang.

"He will," Henry assured her. "He smiles on this marriage, I feel certain."

"I do hope so," she murmured.

———

The next day was one of glorious sunshine, and Henry woke early. "Fine weather for hawking!" he declared, eager to be up and ready for sport.

"I will ride out with you, if it pleases you," Jane said. The prospect of a day in the saddle was enticing. She could almost feel the wind in her hair.

"No, darling," Henry said. "It is too soon after your miscarriage."

She subsided back on the pillow in dismay, foreseeing that she might never get on a horse again. Henry bent over and kissed her. "Why not go for a trip along the river?" he suggested. "Or take some food into the park with your ladies?"

That brought back the uncomfortable memory of the last time she had been in Greenwich Park, and what she had seen there.

"I might go on the river," she said.

"Then I wish you a good day," he said, eager to be gone. "I will send your women in to you."

"I think I will have a bath," she declared, but he had gone.

When the door closed behind him, Noble scrambled onto her bed, and she lay there cuddling him while her bath was prepared. Bored, she jumped up and opened the window, letting the morning breeze stream in with the sun's rays. Below, in the garden, Lady Rutland was sitting on a bench with Bess Holland. Their voices drifted upward.

"And do you know what I heard the King say, before he left this morning?" Eleanor said. "I was giving instruction to two of the new chambers and he saw us and said this was the second time he had met them, and that he was sorry that he had not seen them before he was married. He said it in jest, of course, but I did wonder."

Jane swallowed. It would have been in jest, surely. It was the kind of thing Henry would say.

"You know the old adage, though," Bess replied. "Marry in haste—"

"And it was in haste!" Eleanor interrupted. "People are saying that the King caused his wife and the others to be executed only for his pleasure, and that he was made sure to the Queen's Grace six months before."

"Don't listen to them," said a voice in Jane's ear. It was Mother, come up behind her to say her bath was ready.

"And I was trying to make friends with Lady Rutland," Jane said bitterly.

"I wouldn't waste time on her," Mother retorted.

"But it's sedition."

"Report her to the King then, child, or deal with her yourself."

That decided Jane. "Will you ask someone to send her up to me?"

"With pleasure," Mother declared.

The bath could wait. Jane put her night robe on and sat down in the high-backed chair by the hearth. Mother seated herself firmly on the smaller chair on the other side. "Countess or not, I'll see she shows you proper respect," she stated.

"You sent for me, your Grace?" Lady Rutland sank into a curtsey.

"Yes." Jane was deliberately cool. "Could you explain to me why you spread unseemly gossip and sedition against the King and me?"

Lady Rutland colored. "I do not understand what you mean, Madam."

"I heard your conversation with Bess Holland just now. I do not appreciate such vile insinuations, and I doubt that the King would. I have tried to be your friend, but I see I have troubled myself for nothing."

The Countess looked afraid. "I am sorry, your Grace. It was but idle gossip."

"People have been locked up for less. And it was all lies."

Mother nodded severely.

Eleanor Rutland fell to her knees. "Please do not dismiss me, Madam. It would bring great shame on my husband."

Jane sighed. Her anger was abating, and she did not want an unpleasant atmosphere in her household. "I do not intend to dismiss you, my lady. God knows I have few enough with whom I can be friends. The Lady Margaret and Lady Monteagle are congenial company. Why not let us all be merry together, and loyal? Do you think you can manage that?"

Eleanor seized her hands and kissed them. "Oh, Madam, I will try. I have listened to too much gossip, and I am truly sorry for it. I too am of the old faith. I rejoiced when you became queen, really I did, but when you made it clear there was to be a distance between you and those who serve you, unlike with Queen Anne, I heeded those who were put out by it. They called you haughty and arrogant."

"The very idea!" Mother snorted. "She is the Queen now. What did they expect?"

"I know," Jane said, loosening Eleanor's hands. "I regret that distance, but it exists, and Queen Katherine observed it without attracting any criticism. But I was not born royal, as she was, and I fear that the late Queen's lax ways did me no favors. Now, let us put this behind us. My bath is waiting."

Eleanor rose and curtseyed low. "Thank you, Madam," she said fervently, and left.

"You won't have any more trouble with that one," Mother said. "And I'm relieved, because I have to tell you that Father and I are returning to Wulfhall. He is not well, as you know."

Jane faced her. "I do. Try to get him to see a doctor, Mother. I am worried about him, and so is the King. He has offered the services of his own physician."

"Bless him. I am worried too," Mother admitted. "I am hoping that, with a rest in the country, and lots of healthy air, your father will amend."

It was an emotional parting, for Jane was convinced that she would not see Father again, and from the worried expressions on her brothers' faces, they feared that too. Together they stood on the King's landing stage and watched as the barge sailed out of sight up the Thames. When it had gone, Jane dabbed at her eyes and walked blindly into the covered gallery.

Chapuys had not yet been formally presented to Jane, for he had been ill with a fever, which struck her as rather sad, having happened at a time when some of the things he had worked for were coming to pass. But now he was better, and she was to receive him. She dressed carefully in a new red damask gown with the outline of a crown cleverly woven into the bodice, and cloth-of-gold sleeves.

After mass on Sunday, the day before she was to make her state entry into London, Henry himself brought the ambassador to the Queen's apartments and formally presented him to her. Chapuys bowed low and kissed her hand.

"I congratulate your Grace on your marriage, and wish you prosperity," he said, regarding her kindly with those warm, sensitive eyes. "I have no doubt that, although the device of the lady who preceded you on the throne was 'The Most Happy,' you yourself will bear the reality." She smiled at his courtly turn of phrase. "I am sure," he told her, "that the Emperor will be rejoicing as much as the King himself does at finding so virtuous and amiable a wife, the more so since your brother was once in his Imperial Majesty's service."

Jane was impressed that Chapuys knew about that, but Edward must have told him, for it was fourteen years since he had been deputed, with Father, to attend the Emperor when he visited England.

Chapuys was still congratulating her. "It is almost incredible to see the joy and pleasure that Englishmen are displaying at your Grace's marriage, especially as they believe that you are continually trying to persuade the King to restore the Princess to his favor."

"As indeed I am, my lord ambassador," she replied, looking around nervously to see if Henry was listening. But he had moved away and was talking and laughing with Margaret Douglas and Mary Monteagle.

"It is not your least happiness," Chapuys was saying, "that without the labor of giving birth, you have gained such a daughter as the Princess, from whom you will receive more joy and consolation than from any child you could have yourself." That was rather extravagant, she thought, and then it came to her, in an instant of clarity, that Chapuys—who had never been known to display an interest in any woman—cherished feelings for Mary. Nothing else, not duty or loyalty, could explain his utter devotion to her. "I beg your Grace to favor her interests and deserve that honorable name, the Peacemaker."

"I will do that," she assured him, "and I will labor especially to earn that name." There was a long pause. She was nervous, at a loss as to what to say, and her mind had gone blank, but there was Henry, suddenly at her side, come to her rescue.

"You must forgive her Grace," he said. "You are the first ambassador she has received, and she is not yet used to such receptions. I feel sure that she will do her utmost to obtain the title of Peacemaker, as besides being naturally of a kind and amiable disposition, and much inclined to peace, I believe she would strive to prevent my taking part in a foreign war, if only out of the fear of being separated from me." Jane smiled at him gratefully. She realized he must have heard at least part of the conversation about Mary, and was relieved that he had not been angered by it.

Chapuys gave a little bow in her direction. "I see that your Grace has chosen a wife of virtue and intelligence, who bears her royal honors with dignity. I congratulate your Grace on this new felicity, and rejoice at the removal of all the obstacles to the long-desired alliance between England and Spain. I assure your Grace that you can rely on the firm friendship of the Emperor. Truly, God has shown special care for you. Many great and good men, even emperors and kings, have suffered from the arts of wicked women, and it is greatly to your credit that you detected and punished conspiracy before it came to light. Would you not agree, Madam?"

Jane smiled as Henry thanked Chapuys, but she deemed it wise to say nothing.

"I see that her Grace adds discretion to her other virtues," the ambassador observed.

Jane clung to Henry as he entered her, moving her body in rhythm with his. Their lovemaking was prolonged and tender, but there was always a point where he seemed to lose all awareness of her and it ended in a rush. But he was affectionate afterward, and tonight, when he was spent, he subsided next to her and grasped her hand.

"Jane, I do love you. It's like coming into harbor after long days of tempest." He raised himself on one elbow. "Did you know that on the day after Anne died, King François offered me the hand of his daughter, Madame Madeleine? I said that, at sixteen, she was too young for me, and besides, I've had too much experience of French bringing-up with Anne, and would never, ever have taken a French bride."

For a moment, Jane was too busy rejoicing that he had passed over a French princess for her to comprehend what else he was telling her.

"What do you mean, French bringing-up?"

His face flushed in the dawn light. "Well, her light ways with men, for a start—and other things that I forbear to tell you." He was prudish when it came to talking about intimate matters.

She sat up, her hair tangled about her bare shoulders. "Now you do have me intrigued!"

"It is not fit for a lady's ears." His lips pursed primly.

"Are you telling me that you knew something was amiss all along?"

He sighed. "Jane, I had my suspicions from the first time I bedded her. She had vaunted her virginity, but she knew practices no virgin should know."

"Practices?" Jane could not imagine what he was talking about.

"Strange ways to please a man—except they did not please me! I realized she had lied to me, that the virtue she had so long trumpeted had been mere pretense. And she had learned those things in France."

Jane was little wiser. "I've heard that the French court is a byword for licentiousness."

"There's no doubt of that," Henry agreed, swinging his legs over the side of the bed and pulling on his nightshirt. She noticed that the bad place on his shin was less inflamed. "François keeps a *maîtresse-en-titre,* who rules over his court just like a queen." He grinned. "Fear not, that is one French custom I shall disdain to adopt!"

"I should hope so!" Jane laughed. Yet still she wondered what he had meant about Anne's "practices." They could not have been very nice, whatever they had been.

Jane's stomach was fluttering with nerves at the prospect of appearing in public on the morrow. When she arrived for a private dinner hosted by Edward in his apartment, she feared she would not be able to eat at all. But a goblet of good Bordeaux wine steadied her, and she was distracted from her anxiety by the arrival of Master Cromwell in company with Chapuys, friends despite their political and religious differences.

Nan was the only other woman at table, and she played her part to perfection as hostess, effortlessly directing the servants, steering the conversation and sometimes expressing her own, rather strident views.

"The Princess Mary has to see sense!" she declared.

"I am doing my best!" Cromwell said. "Messire Chapuys and I were discussing this earlier."

Chapuys turned to Edward. "We agree that it would do great good, not only to the Queen your sister and all your kin, but also to the realm and all Christendom, if the Princess were restored to her rights; and I beg that you will use your good offices in those interests."

"Indeed I will," Edward said, his manner a trifle stiff. He was diffident about Mary; he wanted to see a Seymour king on the throne.

Cromwell leaned forward, lowering his voice. "You may not all be aware of just how hard I have worked for the marriage of the Queen and the restoration of the Princess. You, Eustache, will recall the displeasure and anger the King showed me on Easter Tuesday. Well, it was for fear of that displeasure that I thought up and plotted the affair of the late Queen, in which I took a great deal of trouble."

Jane froze. Thought up? Plotted? "But you had evidence laid before you, did you not, Master Cromwell?" Her voice was hoarse.

"Indeed, I did, Madam, and I acted upon it." He smiled at her. She feared he was dissembling. Which had come first—the proofs, or his plotting? And what had he meant when he said he had thought up the affair? She dared not ask, for she did not want to know the answer. She had not forgotten the fatuous questions that had been put to her by the Council. She had thought then that they had been trying to construct a case and had very little to go on.

Chapuys was watching her. "I think Master Cromwell meant that he had already seen the evidence, and decided it was time to act on it." Cromwell nodded sagely.

That contradicted Cromwell's boastfulness, but she did not like to say so. Henry had been angry with him. That had been the day when Chapuys had acknowledged Anne as queen, and they had all thought that her star was again in the ascendant. Anne had meant to destroy Cromwell. The obvious conclusion was that Cromwell had gone home and plotted her destruction. The proofs—such as they were—had been obtained afterward. And he had not done it to make Jane queen, or for Mary's benefit. He had done it to save his own skin.

She toyed with her food, feeling nauseous. The others had seemed to see nothing amiss in what Cromwell had said. The talk had returned to Mary. Pleading an early start on the morrow, Jane departed as soon as courtesy permitted, knowing that she could no longer comfort herself with assurances that Anne had been guilty as charged. What if she had not been guilty at all?

Chapter 28

1536

London was en fête, and crowds were lining the riverbanks, eager to see their new Queen make her state entry into the City. Seated beside Henry in the royal barge, gowned in cloth of gold and dripping with jewels, Jane forced herself to smile as they sailed from Greenwich to Westminster, escorted by a colorful procession of smaller boats, all gaily decked out for the occasion. Behind followed a great barge carrying the King's bodyguard in their scarlet-and-gold uniforms.

As the royal procession passed along the river, the people cheered, and warships and shore guns sounded salutes. At Radcliffe Wharf, by Limehouse, they halted at the quayside so that the King and Queen could watch a pageant mounted by Chapuys in their honor to demonstrate his master's approval of their marriage. Resplendent in purple satin, he was waiting for them in a pavilion embroidered with the Imperial arms, and when the pageant was done, he signaled to two small boats, one carrying trumpeters, the other a consort of shawms and sackbuts, and bade them leave their moorings and provide a musical escort for the royal barge as it resumed its stately progress toward Westminster. The French ambassador, standing on the riverbank nearby, looked on jealously.

Jane could hardly bring herself to watch as the Tower loomed ahead, stark and sinister, despite its walls being festooned with banners and streamers. As the procession paused to take the salute from the four hundred guns lined up along Tower Wharf, all she could think of was that those same guns had announced Anne Boleyn's death three weeks earlier. Anne was still there, within those walls, her body decomposing beneath the pavement of the Tower chapel. Thomas had told Jane, with ghoulish relish, that there had been no provision for a coffin, so her bloody corpse and head had been buried in an arrow chest, with little ceremony.

Jane glanced at Henry, who was standing beside her in the middle of the boat, taking the salute, but if he was troubled by morbid thoughts, he gave no sign of it. Jane swallowed. If she did not pull herself together, she would go mad with anxiety and guilt. The grim fate of Anne was best forgotten; it had not been her doing. But then the nagging voice of conscience reminded Jane that, by willingly poisoning his mind on her friends' advice, she had helped to convince Henry that he should rid himself of Anne. And when she had told him of her ill-fated pregnancy, she had probably sealed Anne's fate. But she had never intended her harm.

Her eyes ranged over the citizens of London, who were crowded all along the banks, shouting their loud approval of their new Queen. They had no moral qualms; nor did Henry. Ah, but did any of them know that Anne's fall had been thought up and plotted by Cromwell?

Stop it! she admonished herself, as she smiled and waved to the people. It was irrational that she herself should feel guilty on account of what Cromwell had done. Had she not kept silent about what she had seen at Mireflore? All she had worked for had been an annulment, not Anne's destruction. And she had believed there was good evidence, until others had expressed doubts—and by then it had been too late. Since then she had searched her soul to discover why she felt so guilty. She had confessed and been absolved. Her

chaplain had dismissed her doubts. What was she tormenting herself for?

At Westminster, she and Henry alighted from the barge and
walked hand in hand in procession to Westminster Abbey, where
they heard High Mass. As the Host was elevated, Jane bowed her
head and, for the first time that day, felt a sense of exultation. It
brought home to her why she had resolved to become queen, and of
the good she hoped to achieve. She remembered Father James, long
ago, speaking of Cicero and the concept of the highest good. Which
was better: a heretic posing as queen, undermining true religion
and plotting against the rightful Queen and her child; or a virtuous
queen committed to restoring true religion and the rights of the
lawful heir? There was no contest as to where the highest good lay.

There was to be no procession through the streets of London.
Henry had said that must wait until her coronation. She was relieved, because today's ceremonies had been overwhelming enough,
and she was grateful to reach the sanctuary of her apartments in
York Place.

"You did so well, darling!" Henry complimented her, as they sat
down to supper that evening. "The people loved you! And when you
gladden them with a prince, they will love you all the more."

"I pray that happy day will come soon," she answered. It would
be three weeks before she could hope that she had conceived this
month.

Henry smiled at her. "It will not be for the want of trying!"

He broke his manchet loaf and dipped it into his pottage. "Darling, both Katherine and Anne were crowned within weeks of becoming queen, but you may have to wait. My treasury is so depleted
that I cannot afford the expense of another coronation at present. I
hope soon to have some of the wealth of the monasteries diverted to
my coffers, and then I can give you the coronation you deserve."

"I am content to wait," she told him.

"It will not be for long. I am planning it for late October, and
having a new barge built for you like nothing ever seen before in

England. It will be fashioned like the bucentaure, the ceremonial barge the Doge uses when he weds Venice to the sea."

"That would be wonderful!" She smiled, wondering how much it was going to cost, and hoping that it would not be paid for with wealth stolen from the Church.

He served her with some choice morsels of chicken in a sauce of verjuice. "You will sail in your new barge from Greenwich to the Tower, then make a triumphant progress through London, with the usual pageantry, and so proceed to Westminster, to be crowned in the abbey on the following day."

She had seen her crown; Henry had kept his word and had it brought to her. As she had hoped, it was the one worn by Queen Katherine, an open coronal of gold set with sapphires, rubies and pearls, and of a great weight. It was be a crown she would happy to bear; it would make her feel a queen indeed. She was painfully aware that she had none of the majesty of Katherine nor the confidence of Anne.

Jane stood in the gallery above the Westminster Gate at Whitehall, waving goodbye to Henry as he rode in procession to open Parliament. Behind her stood her ladies. Lady Rutland was going out of her way to be friendly, Lady Monteagle was always as charming as her sweet face, and Margaret Douglas seemed nowadays to be nurturing some delicious secret. Jane made a mental note to speak to Margaret—but first she would find out what Henry felt about Thomas Howard's courtship.

Edward had attended the state opening of Parliament. She had watched him ride to the Palace of Westminster, resplendent in his viscount's robes, and was pleased when he came to her lodgings shortly before dinner to tell her what had passed.

"When the Lord Chancellor made his opening speech to both

Houses, I was surprised to hear him speak at length about Queen Anne's crimes," he said, shrugging off his mantle. "He put it rather delicately, almost lamenting that, having been so disappointed in his first two marriages, the King had been obliged, for the welfare of his realm, to enter upon a third, and said it was a personal sacrifice not required of any ordinary man."

"Really?" Jane felt diminished by that. "I don't think sacrifice played any part in it!"

"I'm sure it didn't, but presumably the King felt the need to justify his hasty remarriage before Parliament and the people. He cannot be seen to have acted out of personal desire, which is why the Lord Chancellor asked what man in middle life would not be deterred by the crimes of the late Queen from marrying a third time. And yet, he said, our most excellent Prince, not for any carnal reasons, but at the humble entreaty of his nobility, had again condescended to contract matrimony, and had taken to himself this time a wife of apt years, excellent beauty, and pureness of flesh and blood, whose age and fine form give promise of issue."

Jane felt her cheeks burning. "He made me sound like a brood mare!"

Edward shook his head. "It was the right thing to say. The succession must be assured, and everyone in that chamber appreciated that. There was great applause, and the Lord Chancellor, on behalf of the Lords and Commons, thanked the King for his selflessness and the care he had shown for his subjects. He called you a right noble, virtuous and excellent lady."

She was still warm with embarrassment when Henry arrived, in high good humor, and she had to dissemble her discomfiture and smile as he told her how Parliament had rejoiced at their marriage.

In the afternoon, she watched from the oriel window in the King's Gate as Henry jousted at a tournament held in her honor—the first since that fateful one on May Day. Then it had been Anne in the place of honor—and the next day she had been a prisoner in the Tower. Had she had any inkling of what was to come? Or of how devastatingly the wheel of fortune could turn?

Jane realized that her ladies were clapping. The King had won. "Bravo!" Margery cried, almost jumping up and down in excitement. Jane smiled at her, and into that smile she put all the regret she could muster that they could not be friends as before. To her great relief, Margery smiled back. Belatedly Jane joined in the applause.

She had not wanted Henry to joust. She had asked if his leg would permit it, and he had insisted that it was much better, and even if it was not, he would not let it stop him. But what would happen, she had wondered, if he took a fall, as he had in January, and was killed? He had no certain heir. There would be civil war, without a doubt. She thanked God now for his victory, and his delivery from danger. One day soon, he would have to accept the fact that, at nearly forty-five, he was no longer a young man, and too old for jousting.

When Henry joined her in the gallery, she and her ladies congratulated him, much to his gratification. Then he led her to his chamber and gave her a paper granting her a property called Paris Garden, which lay on the Surrey shore of the Thames.

"As ever, you are so good to me," she said, and kissed him.

"Mary has written to me," he informed her, and she was surprised that his mood was still benign. "It seems she has received good advice from Chapuys and the Emperor, and has finally seen sense. She begs me to pardon her offenses, and says she will never be happy until I have forgiven her. She wants to prostrate herself humbly before my feet to repent of her faults, and prays that Almighty God will preserve us both, and shortly send us a prince, which she declares shall be gladder tidings to her than she can ever express."

"This is the happiest news you could have given me!" Jane exclaimed, feeling as if a great weight had been lifted from her shoulders. "I knew she would do the right thing in the end." Of course, it had not been the right thing as far as Mary was concerned, but she would soon see the benefits.

Henry did not appear to share her joy. He seemed thoughtful. "Is she sincere?" he asked. "I expressed my doubts to Cromwell this morning, and he assured me she is. But I wonder."

"I am sure that her submission was the result of much heart-searching," Jane said, "and that Master Cromwell is right." Was Henry now demanding sovereignty over his subjects' inner thoughts? What mattered was that Mary had begged pardon for defying him. He had bullied and threatened her, and she had capitulated. What more did he expect? Again, she felt that disconcerting dislike for him.

"I want her to sign a declaration that her mother's marriage was incestuous and unlawful, and that she recognizes me as Supreme Head of the Church," he said. "Nothing less will persuade me that she loves me."

Despairing of him, Jane imagined how Mary must feel, bereft of her mother, hounded by her father, alone and frightened. She must sign. They were only words on a paper, after all. God would know that she did so under duress.

"She has signed it!" Henry cried, bursting into Jane's chamber without any ceremony and thrusting the document into her hands. She saw Mary's signature by each article, written, as she declared, freely, frankly and for the discharge of her duty toward God, the King and his laws. By a few strokes of the pen, she had repudiated everything she held sacred.

"I am very glad," she said at length, then read the covering letter in which, in groveling terms, Mary begged Henry's forgiveness for having so extremely offended him that her heavy and fearful heart dared not presume to call him father.

She looked up. "I hope this satisfies your doubts. Surely there is now no bar to your reconciliation."

"It is most gratifying," Henry said. "She should have come to her senses long since. I should not have been made to wait for her to obey me. I am not only her father, but her King!" He spoke in an injured tone.

"But you will forgive her?"

"Presently. First, I am sending Sir Thomas Wriothesley of my Council to Hunsdon, to obtain a fuller declaration of her faults in writing. If she complies, he will ask her to name those ladies she would like appointed to her service, should I decide to increase her household pending her return to favor."

This was taking it too far! He was so suspicious! "But what more can she say, other than that she is sorry and repents of her offenses?"

"She can account for her faults."

And so she did. Wriothesley reported to Henry and Jane that Mary had been pathetically grateful for his assistance. And Cromwell showed them her long letter acknowledging her faults and thanking him for his kindness in furthering her cause with the King. Henry read it, looking pleased. "She has shown herself a dutiful daughter at last," he said. "I am happy to extend my paternal love to her once more."

Jane did not know how she kept her silence. Love was not conditional upon people behaving as you wanted them to. Love was something you felt, instinctively, naturally and often unbidden. She could not doubt that Henry loved his daughter; but he loved his kingly authority more, and she herself was now under no delusions that it would take precedence over his love for her too, should she defy him in any way.

Yet he had been unhappy about the rift, she was sure of it, and his unhappiness had made him cruel. She was beginning to understand why he acted as he did. Always there would be this dichotomy between the King and the man. He feared anything that smacked of disloyalty or treason, so much so that he could think the worst even of those who were closest to him. It explained why it had been easy for him to believe the charges against Anne.

As soon as she could, Jane sent for Chapuys. When he arrived, she sent her women into the inner chamber. "You know that the Princess has made a full declaration of her faults," she began.

"Madam, she has never done a better day's work. I assure you, I have relieved her of every doubt of conscience. The Pope will himself grant her absolution."

"We and our friends have good cause to rejoice at her submission," she told him. "We have worked for months toward a reconciliation, and I am now looking forward to receiving the Princess at court. She will be a friend and companion to me."

"You may be assured of that, for she bears the greatest love and goodwill to your Grace. Many here at court welcome the prospect of her return to favor, and the common people will rejoice when they hear of it, for they have always loved her."

"It is the first step toward what we both hope to achieve," she told him. "And I am comforted to know that you have salved her conscience. It was a dreadfully difficult thing for her to do. But already her circumstances are improving. The King has sent his officers to Hunsdon to see that she has everything she needs, and they are to tell her that it will not be long before he brings me to visit her. I cannot tell you how glad I am."

"I rejoice to hear it!" Chapuys declared, sounding quite emotional. "I never thought to see this day. The good Queen will be celebrating in Heaven."

On the feast of Corpus Christi, attired in a low-cut gown of cloth of gold, Jane mounted her richly caparisoned horse and rode beside the King the short distance from York Place to Westminster Abbey, with the lords preceding them and her ladies following on horseback. In the cool of the church, the bishops and clergy preceded the nobles and the King up the nave, and Jane followed, with Margaret Douglas bearing her train.

As High Mass was celebrated, she knelt in reverence, aware that, with the coming of autumn, she would be enthroned in this great abbey, and Archbishop Cranmer would place that glittering crown on her head.

The royal barge was filled with minstrels playing for the King and Queen as they made their journey from Greenwich to York Place. The balmy summer days had brought no new hope of a child, but they had seen many jousts and triumphs, all in Jane's honor, and pageants on the river, and now it was back to Whitehall for St. Peter's Night, which was always marked by a parade of the Marching Watch of the City of London.

In the afternoon, they watched from the privy garden at York Place as a water battle was staged on boats bouncing on the Thames, cheering as loudly as everyone else as the mariners fired guns and tried to board the other vessels. But in the shouting and confusion, one man toppled into the river with a splash, and two others were shot by mistake. As the crowds gasped, Henry raised an arm. "Stop!" he roared. "Cease your fighting!"

Two of the sailors had dived into the water after their fellow, but when they surfaced, he was not with them. Meanwhile, one boat had taken the wounded away, making its way toward St. Thomas's Hospital in Southwark. Jane felt sick, and close to tears.

"I will not stop your sport," Henry was shouting, "but you must continue with wooden swords and stuff your guns with wool and leather."

The mariners obeyed, and battle was resumed, but in a more subdued fashion. Jane was glad when it was over and she and Henry were able to proceed to the gatehouse to watch yet another tournament in honor of their marriage.

That evening, they stood in a window in the Mercers' Hall in Cheapside, looking out on the torchlit procession of the scarlet-clad Marching Watch, who appeared very proud and brave in their liveries. Afterward, Henry and Jane attended a reception hosted by the Lord Mayor, and then their barge took them back to Greenwich. It was dark when they approached the palace, and torches had been lit all along the quayside. Lights shone too from various windows, and

from one, smaller than the rest, very high up. It took a moment or
two for Jane to realize that it was not shining from the palace at all,
but further away, from Mireflore, the tower on top of the hill.

A chill raced through her. What business had anyone to be there
at night? Maybe someone was using the tower as a secret trysting
place. But why would they leave a light shining?

It troubled her, that light. Irrationally, she could not help connecting it to what she had seen at Mireflore in April. And then,
lying awake long after Henry had taken her and fallen asleep, she
began to wonder if the tower was haunted.

In the morning, she was able to shrug off her fears, especially
when Mary Monteagle told her that Margaret Douglas would come
late to attend her, having overslept after a late night. It occurred to
her that Margaret might have been meeting Thomas Howard at
Mireflore. Well, she would satisfy her curiosity.

"Ladies, we are going for a walk in the park," she said. "We can
explore that old tower."

Mary Norris paled. "But it's haunted, Madam!"

Jane felt a tremor. "Haunted?"

"Yes. Lights have been seen, and noises heard."

"It's true, Madam," Joan Ashley said. "Margery has seen the
lights."

"When?" Jane asked, more sharply than she intended.

"About two weeks ago," Margery replied. "There was a light
moving from window to window, as if someone was walking about
with a candle."

At that moment, Margaret walked in. "Your Grace, I am sorry to
be so tardy," she apologized.

"I hear you were late to bed last night," Jane said.

Margaret's cheeks flamed almost as brightly as her hair. She hesitated. "Yes, Madam," she admitted.

"You weren't in the old tower, by any chance?"

"No, I wouldn't go there," she said. "It's a bad place. They say
sgàiles walk there. It's what we Scots call the shadows of the dead."

"That's nonsense," Jane said, with more confidence than she felt.

"We shall go and lay these so-called ghosts to rest." Margaret looked at her dubiously.

They followed her with marked reluctance as, armed with the key, she led them out to the park, Noble racing ahead, delighted to be out for a run. There was little of the usual chatter and laughter that attended such expeditions. As they ascended the hill and approached the tower, she caught their mood and was filled with increasing foreboding.

The door creaked as she pushed it open. There were the stark, gloomy paintings and the cobwebs, just as before.

Anne Parr squeaked and fled.

"Forgive me, Madam, but I cannot enter here," Margaret declared, and hurried after Anne. The other women huddled by the door. Even Noble would not come when he was called, but stood barking from what he evidently considered to be a safe distance.

"I am surprised you educated ladies pay heed to the tales you have heard," Jane admonished them. "They are stories to frighten children." But she herself was resisting the urge to run. "Will no one accompany me upstairs?"

They looked at one another. No one volunteered.

"Very well," she said, "I shall go by myself. There is nothing to fear up there."

She ran up the spiral steps, wishing she had not come on this foolhardy escapade, yet knowing she must not lose face before her inferiors. She reminded herself that it was broad daylight, and that ghosts favored the dark!

In the first-floor chamber, the dust lay more thickly now. She could see no footprints. No one had been there in weeks.

Holding her skirts high so as not to dirty them, she continued to the upper chamber, and was suddenly enveloped in such a shroud of misery and yearning that it took her breath away. The sadness and longing were like a physical presence, suffocating her, cutting her off from all happiness and all hope. It was like being in a long, dark tunnel with no end to it.

With a cry, she flung herself back down the stairs. On the spiral below the first floor she had to stop to catch her breath and compose herself. The wave of misery had vanished as soon as she had left the upper chamber, but the memory of it was vivid, and she was shaken to her core.

This had not happened to her when she had visited that room on the day Anne and Norris had been there. The despair she had felt was theirs; she was as sure of that as she was of her own existence, and was now able to guess what had really happened here on that April day. The love that had been between those two had been hopeless; she understood that now, and doubted very much that they had succumbed to their longing for each other. She thanked God and all the saints that she had not given voice to her suspicions.

Strangely comforted, she joined her ladies, who looked mightily relieved to see her. Noble fawned around her skirts.

"Are you all right, Madam?" Margery asked.

"I almost fell down the stairs," she said, "but I am all right."

The celebrations continued. Had ever honeymoon been so prolonged? They watched a firework display; early in July, they attended the magnificent celebrations for the triple wedding of the Earl of Westmorland's son and two daughters, with Henry riding in procession from Whitehall in disguise as the Sultan of Turkey—although everyone knew who it was—and Jane basking in the people's acclaim. She was relieved when he said he was not taking part in the jousts. His leg was playing up, and he made little of it, but she could sense his frustration.

All this time, Parliament was in session. One evening, Henry invited Master Cromwell to join them for supper, and spoke of the new Act of Succession that was to be passed on the morrow.

"As things stand, Jane, Elizabeth is legally my heir, under the Act of Succession passed after I married Anne. But a bastard cannot inherit the crown. And so this new Act will ratify the annulments of my pretended marriages with the Lady Katherine and the Lady Anne, and vest the succession in our children."

Cromwell smiled, spearing a piece of beef on his knife. Jane shrank from him these days; it felt as if she were eating supper with a snake.

She wondered if he sensed her suspicions of him. "Madam," he said, "Parliament understands the great and intolerable perils that the King has suffered as a result of two unlawful marriages. It recognizes the ardent love and fervent affection he feels for his realm and his people, which impelled him to venture upon wedlock a third time. Everyone is agreed that your marriage is so pure and sincere, without doubt or impediment, that your issue, when it shall please Almighty God to send it, can never lawfully be deprived of the right to the succession."

Everything depended on her bearing a son. She could almost feel her womb cramping inside her. Pray God she would conceive this month!

"And what happens if, God forfend, his Grace and I have no issue together?" she asked.

Henry stared at her in dismay. "We will!"

"In that case," Cromwell said, "Parliament has granted his Grace the power to appoint any person he chooses to be his successor, including the issue of any other lawful marriage."

She trembled at that. Already they were providing for what would happen in the event of her death, and while her rational self told her that was sensible, the part of her that remained acutely sensitive over Anne's fate was sounding all kinds of alarms. What if she failed to bear a son? Would they do to her as they had done to Katherine and—God forbid!—Anne?

"The Lady Margaret Douglas is my only true heir at present," Henry said. "I cannot consider her half-brother, the King of Scots, for he is an alien and as such is barred from succeeding here—and I certainly don't want England becoming a satellite of Scotland. But I pray God you will be fruitful, darling. I do not want to name anyone as my heir for now. Any person so named might take great heart and courage, and fall into disobedience and rebellion."

"I am sure that God will smile upon our marriage," Jane said, thrusting down all her fears.

Jane was eager to ensure that Mary would have all the fine attire she needed when she returned to court. To this end, she sent Edward to Hunsdon to obtain a list of the Princess's requirements. He rode off, richly garbed, as became the fine lord he now was, and weighed down with his new honors.

"You should take her a gift," Jane had said.

"What do you suggest?" he had asked. "A jewel? A prayer book? She is very religious." He made a face. Mary's long adherence to Rome irked him almost as much as it angered the King.

"Maybe a fine horse?" Jane had suggested.

"A capital idea!" Edward pronounced. "I'll send my man to Smithfield to buy one."

"And please tell the Princess from me that the King's gracious clemency and merciful pity have now overcome his anger. He is again her loving father, and longs to see her."

"I will tell her," Edward had said.

"She has written again to him, promising she will never vary from her submission, and praying that God will send us children."

"It is what we all pray for," Edward said piously, looking at her speculatively. "You are not . . . ?" He had been devastated when she told him she had lost a child.

"Not yet. And Nan? You have hopes too, the more so now you have a title and estates to pass on."

He had looked momentarily downcast. "Not yet."

"Then I will pray that God will bless you too."

After Edward had departed for Hunsdon, Henry let it be known that he would shortly be reconciled to Mary, whereupon his courtiers immediately began racing off there to ingratiate themselves with her.

Edward, when he returned, was furious. "They were clamoring to see her, the bloody vultures. I had to send them away. Mary is ill. The strain of making her submission has been too much for her."

Henry, when he heard, was deeply concerned. Being Henry, it never occurred to him that he had been the prime cause of Mary's sufferings; it was all her own fault. Nevertheless, he was sufficiently worried to defer her official reception at court until she was better.

"We will visit her ourselves," he told Jane, and so it came about that, on a sunny July morning, she found herself riding the few miles eastward to Hackney, both she and Henry dressed in plain attire so as not to attract attention.

"I had my officers summon Mary in the night and bring her in secrecy to the King's Manor," Henry had explained. She was waiting for them there, very nervous and looking like a shadow of her former self. She had been sixteen when Jane had last seen her, when Mary had been allowed to visit Queen Katherine at Eltham for a brief spell. Four years ago now. Even then she had been plagued with numerous ailments, made worse by the rift between her parents, yet she had been a pretty, diminutive girl, with beautiful red hair and the freshness of youth. Now, as Henry raised her from her deep obeisance, she looked ill and haunted, and she was much too thin.

"My most dear and well-beloved daughter!" Henry breathed, clasping her to him. Jane saw that he had tears in his eyes, and guessed that he too was shocked at Mary's appearance.

He was gentle with her, kindly and affectionate.

"I have brought your good mother, Queen Jane, to meet you," he said, and Mary went to kneel, but Jane would not let her, taking her hands and embracing her instead.

"You cannot know how good a friend you have in the Queen," Henry said.

Mary ventured a smile. "I know I am much beholden to your Grace," she told Jane.

Henry led them into the great chamber and bade Mary be seated between him and Jane. He regarded her with that intense blue gaze, his face filled with emotion. "I deeply regret having kept you so long away from me," he said, and at that Mary's composure broke and tears streamed down her face.

"Oh, my dearest father, how I have missed you," she wept.

Henry was choked. "I will not let it happen again," he promised. "We must forget the past and look to the future. There is nothing I would not do for you, my child, now that we are in perfect accord again."

Jane took from her purse a little velvet bag and pressed it into Mary's hands. "And I would be your Grace's friend." She smiled.

"There is nothing I would like better, Madam. You were always kind." Mary's eyes were dewy with gratitude. When she opened the bag, she could not speak. There in her palm lay the most beautiful diamond.

"In token of our new friendship," Jane told her.

"And this is from me," Henry said, handing Mary a tasseled purse. "It is a thousand crowns for your little pleasures. From now on, you need have no anxiety about money, for you shall have as much as you wish."

The afternoon passed pleasantly after that, as Mary and Henry began to relax in each other's company, and Jane cherished good hopes of the future. Mary expressed delight in the horse that Edward had given her, and Jane assured her that she had many friends at court. After Vespers, when they made ready to leave, promising to see Mary again soon, the Princess's haunted look had gone, and she was in much happier spirits. "I promise you, you shall be well treated from now on," Henry called down from the saddle. "When you are restored to health, you must come back to court. You will enjoy more freedom than you ever had, and I will see to it that you are served with solemnity and honor, as the second lady in the land after Queen Jane. You will want for nothing!"

He blew her a kiss, and then they were riding away through the gatehouse and heading for the London road.

"No father could have shown himself more loving," Jane said.

"No stepmother could have been more welcoming!" he countered. "I am glad that Mary and I are perfect friends again."

"And so was she, I could tell. She is overjoyed to be back in favor." It was, Jane reflected, the happiest outcome that she, and even Chapuys, could have wished for. Mary now wanted for nothing but the name of Princess of Wales, and that was really of no consequence, for she would have everything else more abundantly than before.

True to his word, Henry began to send her gifts of money, while Jane, working down Edward's list, sent costly court gowns. Master Cromwell gave another fine horse and, at the King's instigation, began overseeing the reinstatement of Mary's household.

"Read this, Jane," Henry said at breakfast some days after their visit, and handed her a letter. It was from Mary, thanking him for the perfect reconciliation between them. Jane was touched to see that Mary had again expressed the hope that her dearest mother the Queen would shortly bear him children.

She went to bed in a happy mood. It was six days since her flowers had been due, and she was nursing a secret hope that she might be with child. All was well between Henry and Mary, and she believed there was a good chance that her hopes in that direction might come to fruition too. If she had a son, Henry would surely be more amenable to restoring Mary to the succession.

Chapter 29

1536

She did not see Henry the next morning, for he was in Council. Neither did she see Margaret Douglas.

"She should be in attendance, Madam," Eleanor Rutland said, looking irritated.

"I'll wager she's dallying with Thomas Howard!" Mary Monteagle grinned.

Jane could have kicked herself. She had meant to speak to Henry about that, and find out what he felt about the courtship, but it had slipped her mind. She suspected that he would not regard Norfolk's younger, landless brother as a suitable husband for his niece. He would want some advantage for himself from her marriage. She feared that Margaret was living in a paradise of fools.

Margaret had still not appeared when Henry arrived for supper that evening. His every look and gesture proclaimed him a man who had been much wronged, and who was righteous in his anger and his sorrow.

Sitting down heavily in his chair, he waved the servants away and regarded Jane darkly.

"What is the matter?" she asked, fearing that she had upset him in some way.

"Would you believe me if I told you that my niece, Margaret, has presumed secretly to precontract herself to Lord Thomas Howard?"

"She has not?" Jane was aghast. It was hard to credit that Margaret had been so foolish.

"Norfolk wrote to me," Henry growled. "His daughter had told him. She had abetted them in their misconduct, and confessed all, lest she be found out. And of course, in view of what has recently befallen his traitorous niece, the late Queen, he is already fearful for his own neck, and thought to win my favor by disclosing this treason."

"Treason?" The word struck Jane like an icy chill.

"What else could it be?" Henry flared. "No princess of my blood should be given or taken in marriage without my consent. Lord Thomas's presumption is outrageous, and I am bitterly disappointed in the Lady Margaret, having cherished such a high opinion of her and her virtue." He banged the table with his fist. "How dare she defy my laws and promise herself without my permission? Her marriage is in my gift!" While he was in this furious humor, Jane feared to say anything lest she too incur his displeasure. Yet she had to speak out for Margaret. She had seen the lovers together, many times, in Anne Boleyn's chamber. She was convinced that they had intended no treason, although they had been unbelievably foolish. "I do not understand," she said. "How can this be treason?"

His eyes narrowed. "It is strongly suspected that, in precontracting himself to my naughty niece, Lord Thomas aspired to the crown, and I am convinced that he falsely and traitorously imagined that if I died without heirs of my body, he would ascend to the throne by reason of his marriage. Margaret is popular, and he had reason to trust that the people of England would want her for their Queen. But in so plotting, Jane, he was guilty of maliciously subverting the new Act of Succession—and impugning the succession is treason!" He was simmering with rage.

Put like that, it all sounded pretty damning for the couple. But it struck Jane that the whole case against them had been founded on belief and supposition.

"Have they been questioned?" she asked.

"They have. It's clear that Lord Thomas was seduced by the Devil into disregarding the duty of allegiance that he owes to me, as his most dread sovereign lord! He has contemptuously and traitorously conducted himself, and suborned Margaret by crafty, fair and flattering words."

Jane found that hard to believe. Margaret had been as enamored of Thomas as he had been of her; he had had no need to suborn her. Jane herself had read their poems to each other, and been moved by the love expressed in them. And Thomas was a mild-mannered man with a poet's soul; she could not imagine him scheming for the throne and using Margaret to that end.

"What will happen to them?" She could barely bring herself to utter the words.

"They have this day been imprisoned separately in the Tower," Henry told her, his lips pursed.

Fear spread its tentacles. Not the Tower! It was less than two months since Anne had been executed there. Surely Henry would not condemn his own niece to the same fate?

"Parliament is adding a clause to the Act of Succession," he said. "From now on, it will be treason for any man to espouse, marry or deflower a woman of royal blood. Both shall suffer death."

Jane had to act. Margaret had not a treacherous bone in her body. She clutched at his sleeve. "You will not go so far, surely? She is your own niece, your flesh and blood!"

He sighed. His anger was burning itself out now. "No, Jane, I will not. I think she was deceived. Certainly she was foolish, and she should have known that her marriage was mine to make. A spell in the Tower will teach her a lesson. Fear not, she is being held there in some comfort, in the Queen's lodgings."

Jane shuddered. What comfort could there be in being immured in a gilded prison knowing that its last occupant had left it only for her death not long since? It would be a hard lesson for Margaret.

"And Lord Thomas?" She must not appear to be too sympathetic.

Henry frowned. "Parliament will deal with him as he deserves. And now let us change the subject, for I can feel one of my headaches coming on. Have some herrings." He passed her the dish. "Tomorrow I will be knighting Cromwell and raising him to the peerage as Baron Cromwell of Wimbledon."

She was in no doubt that Cromwell was being rewarded for his zeal in uncovering the treason of Queen Anne. But did Henry know or suspect that Cromwell had gone further in that than just gathering proofs and drawing up a case? "He has served you well," she said.

"Indeed he has. And I am appointing him Vicar General. Parliament has enacted that all monasteries with an income of less than two hundred pounds a year be dissolved. He will oversee that."

She found it hard to hide her distress.

Henry was watching her. "Jane, these houses are redundant or corrupt. There is no need to look so unhappy."

She thought of all the poor religious who had dedicated their lives to God, and who must now leave their abbeys and priories, places they had perhaps come to love. Some would be in great grief.

"Sir, I beg of you, be charitable to the monks and nuns who are turned out!" she cried, falling to her knees before him.

"Get up," he said gently. "I have told you, they will be able to move to the larger monasteries, and if they prefer to return to the world, they can claim a pension. No one will suffer. You must think of the benefits." He helped himself to more chicken. "The revenues from those houses, and the sale of their property, will double the Crown's income. This can only strengthen the throne."

Yes, but it will undermine the Church! She held her tongue. She did not want to make him angry again.

Cromwell craved an audience. She bade him be seated, and he eased his heavy bulk onto a turned stool, perching there uncomfortably. Since that dinner of Edward's, she had been wary of him, and she believed he sensed it, for he seemed to be doing his best to ingratiate himself with her.

"The Lady Mary has written to me," he said. "She has expressed
her gratitude for my advice, and promises to continue to follow it in
all things concerning her duty to the King. She was pleased to say
that she takes me as one of her chief friends after the King and your
Grace. Madam, I have had made for her a ring inset with portraits
of the King, yourself and her Highness. The King has graciously
offered to take it when he next visits her."

"We are to see her at Richmond later this month," Jane said. "I
am sure she will be delighted with your kind gift."

At that the courtesies dried up. He had made his point, and reminded her of their former alliance, but she knew they could never
be allies again. Still, he could prove useful.

"This matter of the Lady Margaret," she said. "It troubles me."

"Madam," Cromwell said, "I assure you that I am doing all I can
on the lady's behalf. But I cannot be certain of the outcome. She and
Lord Thomas have committed a grievous offense. Parliament is to
debate it next week, and the King is pressing for the extreme penalty."

"But he promised me he would spare her!" Jane cried.

Cromwell leaned forward. "And that is indeed his intention. But
first she is to be taught a lesson, that you do not with impunity
usurp the prerogative of kings."

"Then she is to be kept in suspense?" The prospect was horrifying.

"We both have prevailed upon the King to be merciful in the
past," Cromwell said, again speaking as if they were allies. "But I
think we must not press him too far this time."

"And Lord Thomas?"

"Alas, Madam. The King is not inclined to show mercy."

The Lady Margaret and Lord Thomas had been attainted for treason,
and now languished under sentence of death. Henry gave Jane the

news as he stumped into her chamber, scattering her women with a wave of his hand. He was in a morose mood.

"The matter was so plain that the Lords and Commons did not hesitate," he recounted. "But as it is clear that criminal intercourse did not take place, and you have interceded for her, I will spare Margaret."

Jane found herself trembling. "Has she been informed?"

Henry's eyes glittered. "Not yet."

She sank to her knees by his chair. "Henry, I beg of you, put her out of her misery. Think what it must be like to face the horrifying prospect of dying at just twenty years old. She will believe that it really will happen; after all, the Queen of England has just been beheaded. And for all she knows, she might be burned at the stake. Oh, Henry, the anguish of mind she must be suffering is unimaginable."

He had heard her out with a frown on his face. "Think you I do not imagine what it is like to face execution?" he asked. "She should have considered this when she precontracted herself."

"But Henry, what she did was not then an offense."

"It was offensive to me!" he snapped. "You and Cromwell seem to forget that the actions of those two not only deprived me of a valuable political asset, but also threatened my very life!"

She seized his hand and wrung it. "I know them, Henry. I cannot believe that Lord Thomas had designs on the throne."

"He is a Howard!" Henry barked. "They all have designs on the throne in one way or another. Locusts, the lot of them! Darling, you are a sweet innocent with a kind heart." He squeezed her hand. "To please you, and Cromwell, I will spare both their lives. But they must remain in the Tower for the present. I trust that satisfies you."

It was enough, for now. Fervently she kissed his hand in gratitude. "You are the kindest, most gracious sovereign that ever lived," she told him. He liked that, she could see, although he still seemed preoccupied and downcast.

"You couldn't really have thought I would execute my own niece?" he murmured, nuzzling her throat. "I love her too dearly, even though she has behaved herself so lightly, to my great dishonor. And she is my only heir." Suddenly, to her utter amazement, he was weeping.

"Henry, whatever is wrong?" she cried, folding her arms around his broad shoulders. Was he still grieving for their lost child?

"Oh, God, Jane, I can hardly bring myself to speak of it. I have just come from the doctors. My son is gravely ill."

Jane had seen the Duke of Richmond in the court only two days before. She had noticed that the youth had been coughing and had a livid flush to his cheeks. But he had been laughing with his crony, Norfolk's son, the volatile Earl of Surrey, and she had not been at all concerned. She did not much like Richmond, an arrogant young man with a ruthless streak, but he was the apple of the King's eye.

Henry was weeping profusely against her breast. "A humor has fallen into his chest. There is no hope, they say. My boy, my precious boy! Oh, Jane, why does God punish me so? I am frustrated at every turn when I try to provide for the succession. I was going to name Richmond my heir and successor, and have him proclaimed by Parliament, though of course he would have ranked after any children we may have. But now there is no one to succeed me apart from that naughty girl in the Tower. You do see, do you not, why I am so grieved at her offense?"

"Oh, darling, I do see, and I am so very sorry about Richmond. Is there nothing the doctors can do?"

Henry mopped his eyes with a large white kerchief. "Nothing! He is in God's hands now."

That night, the shadow appeared again. Henry was snoring, having cried himself to sleep, and Jane was lying wakeful, cradling him in her arms. Suddenly it was there, stark and black, silhouetted against the wainscot.

She shrank back into the warmth of Henry's body, shutting her eyes against the presence. Quaking, she wondered if the shadow was a harbinger of evil, and what its appearance tonight might presage.

She made herself open her eyes. It was gone, and again she thought perhaps she had dreamed or imagined it. Possibly it was a trick of the light after all.

But when the Duke of Richmond died four days later, she wondered.

Henry was devastated. "It was that cursed Anne and her brother—they poisoned him!" he burst out, as they stood looking down on the still white corpse, dressed in its ducal robes. "I knew it all along, what they intended!"

"But Henry," Jane soothed, "they have been dead for two months. Surely no poison could be that slow to work?" There was no reasoning with him.

"What they gave him fatally undermined his health," he insisted. "The doctors think he had been ailing for some weeks before he became really ill. No, Jane, this was the work of their malice!"

She thought of the shadow. Had Anne come to claim Richmond? If so, she could not have thought of a more deadly way to repay Henry for signing her death warrant. It stood to reason that she could not rest. She had scores to settle. Anne had every cause to haunt the woman who had supplanted her. It was easy to believe that she was having her revenge.

Richmond's death was kept secret.

"I dare not raise fears over the succession," Henry explained mournfully. He had aged this past week. At night, when he came to her bed, it was for comfort, not desire. There were new lines of grief etched into his face, and more gray in his red hair; Jane was already aware that he was overeating and putting on weight. His leg pained him from time to time, so he could not always enjoy the sporting pursuits he loved, nor get the exercise he needed.

Norfolk, as Richmond's father-in-law, had been commanded by Henry to have the late Duke's body wrapped in lead and conveyed in a farm wagon to Thetford Priory in Norfolk for a private burial.

Immediately, Henry regretted it. Norfolk was summoned, and Jane was astonished to see the King erupt in fury.

"Why did you not bury my son with the honors due to him?" he shouted. "I'll have you in the Tower for this!"

"I was but obeying your Grace's own orders," Norfolk replied, in his choleric way. "And when I deserve to be in the Tower, Tottenham shall turn French!"

Henry glared at him. "You will build him a proper tomb, in the church at Framlingham, so that he can lie in suitable state!"

Norfolk bowed, full of chagrin. "Your Grace may rest assured that it will be done. May I ask what is to happen to my daughter now that she is widowed?"

"Find her another husband!" Henry snapped, still angry. "The marriage wasn't consummated, so she is still a maid."

"But your Grace, she is your daughter-in-law."

"And your daughter! Take her home with you, and don't show your face here again. I have not forgotten the treason of your villainous niece and nephew!"

Norfolk scuttled away, plainly mortified. Jane felt a pang for the young Duchess of Richmond. She had not liked her, for Mary Howard had been a friend of Anne Boleyn, and hostile, but to be widowed so young, and consigned to the protection of that martinet of a father of hers, was a bleak fate. God send that Norfolk found her a husband before too long.

As Jane and Henry rode side by side along the leafy lanes of Kent, she reflected that it was to have been Anne accompanying him on this trip to Dover to inspect England's defenses. She recalled the night when it had been canceled. No one had guessed then that Anne was about to be arrested.

She felt so depressed about the burden of guilt she bore that the magnificent cathedrals of Rochester and Canterbury passed her by in a haze of towers, spires and stained glass. When they arrived at Dover Castle, she could take no pleasure in seeing her phoenix badge in the jewel-colored windows newly installed by the King's master glazier. But that night, she and Henry were lovers again, and after that her mood gradually lifted. The King roused himself from his grief, and there was a hint of a holiday spirit.

From London, Cromwell kept Henry informed of all the news, with messengers racing to and fro.

"Elizabeth is outgrowing her clothes," the King remarked, looking up from the latest letter. They were standing on the battlements of the Great Tower at Dover, high on the magnificent cliffs, with the English Channel spread out before them.

Jane was standing away from the parapet, holding on to her hood, for the wind was strong here, whipping her veil about her face. "She must be growing fast," she said. The thought of Anne Boleyn's motherless child was even more unsettling than thinking of Anne herself.

"Cromwell is attending to it. Apparently Elizabeth's governor is allowing her to dine and sup every day at the board of estate, and Lady Bryan does not approve. But I commanded it. Bastard she may be, but she is still my daughter."

"I'm told she is a very intelligent child."

"Too intelligent by far!" Henry observed. "On the day after her mother died, she was asking her governor why it was that she was now being called the Lady Elizabeth instead of Lady Princess. And she not yet three!"

Jane's heart bled for the little girl. "And what did he answer?"

"He instructed Lady Bryan, on my orders, to tell Elizabeth that her mother has gone to Heaven. She is too young to be burdened with the details. She will find out soon enough, poor child. Anne should have thought of that."

Jane could not imagine how Elizabeth would feel when she learned of her mother's fate.

"Fortunately Mary has conceived a special affection for Elizabeth," Henry was saying. "It seems that forcing her to serve Elizabeth was a sound idea after all, for who could not but love such a goodly, gentle child?" That sisterly love had flourished against all the odds seemed incredible. "Mary's health has improved sufficiently for her to go to Hatfield this week. She writes that her sister is in good health and that I will have cause to rejoice in her in time to come. She sent us both her best wishes for our health, and called you her good mother."

That was heartening, and it was heartening too to see that Henry's affection for his younger daughter had been in no way undermined by Anne Boleyn's fall.

Henry was looking down on the massive ramparts of the castle, his brow furrowed. "I've had to order that Elizabeth must keep to her chamber and not come abroad. There is much gossip and speculation that she is not my child, and that Norris was her father. I do not want it reaching her ears, or talk of what happened to her mother. So it is best she remains in her apartments, with supervised time in her privy garden."

"That is very wise," Jane observed.

He nodded. "And I've ensured that her household is staffed by older and sober persons. There were too many young people around her."

"You think they were light of morals?"

A pause; a heartbeat. "I am remembering the young people who laughed and flirted with Anne in her privy chamber. Look what that led to! Elizabeth is her mother's daughter as well as mine. Already she's a little coquette. It must be schooled out of her, which is why I want mature servants attending her. She must be constrained to virtue."

Jane felt yet more sorrow for Elizabeth. She would always bear the stigma of being Anne Boleyn's child.

When Jane's flowers appeared in August, Henry sighed and looked downcast.

"At least you can join me for the hunt," he said.

They spent most of that month out in the fresh air, chasing across the broad meadows and sun-dappled woodland of the Thames valley, enjoying good sport. On a single day, they brought down twenty stags. It should have restored Henry's good spirits, but he was still mourning Richmond, despondent at his hopes of an heir being dashed, and still vexed with Margaret Douglas. One night, he flung himself into Jane's chair and regarded her with eyes full of self-pity.

"What is wrong?" she asked, hastening to embrace him.

"Oh, Jane!" he groaned. "I am weary of the burdens I bear. I feel myself growing old. I doubt now that we shall have any children."

"Nonsense!" Fear made her sharp. "You're in the vigor of your age, as I well know! Try to be cheerful. Take a little wine—and come to bed." It was the most daring thing she had ever said to him, for no virtuous wife initiated lovemaking, and he commanded her as her king as well as her husband, but it worked marvels. Soon they were rolling on top of the counterpane, fumbling with laces and garters, and coming together in a breathtaking climax. And afterward, Henry lay there with a broad smile on his face at last.

Later that month they visited Mary at Hunsdon, and Jane was delighted to see her stepdaughter looking a healthier color, although she was still thin and confessed to being plagued by headaches. As they talked, a small red head and curious eyes came peeking around a pillar.

"There you are!" came Lady Bryan's voice, and then she saw who was present and dropped a hurried curtsey.

"Come here, you little minx!" Henry cried, and Elizabeth ran to him, to be scooped up in his arms. "Say hello to Queen Jane, your new stepmother."

Jane marveled how Elizabeth had grown since she had last seen her. The plump contours of infancy had all but disappeared, and now she was a sturdy little girl. Henry kissed her heartily and told her how pretty she was, while Mary looked on tenderly, if somewhat wistfully. Mary was still nervous in Henry's presence, and probably a touch resentful, if the truth be known, for Elizabeth was too young ever to have offended him, and it was obvious that his love for her was uncomplicated. Certainly the child knew well how to work her wiles on him. Stroking his beard, and planting little kisses on his cheek, she regarded Jane speculatively, then put out an imperious hand to be kissed. They all laughed.

"No, sweeting, it is you who must kiss the Queen's hand, as you should know," Henry reproved. Jane gave Elizabeth her hand and received a rather haughty peck, then, impulsively—for she must be worthy of the name of stepmother, and make up in some small way to Elizabeth for what she had lost—she reached out her arms and took the child; she was heavy and not at all sure that she wanted to be held by her stepmother, but when Jane smiled and spoke gently to her, telling her that they were going to be firm friends, she relented a little, and soon she was telling Jane that she knew all her alphabet and her numbers up to twenty. Then she was clamoring to be put down, and climbing on Henry's knee as he sat talking to Mary. He did not object to being interrupted, and was very affectionate to her. It came to Jane forcibly that they looked like an ordinary happy family: father, mother and two daughters. Who, watching them, could have guessed at the tragedies and dramas that lay behind this touching tableau? She realized that she herself was in no small way responsible for restoring harmony, and that made her feel infinitely better. Good had come out of bad, and that was something to thank God for.

She made a point of sitting close to Mary and asking whether she had all she needed. Mary seemed pathetically grateful.

"It is good to have your Grace as a friend," she said. "I cannot say how much I appreciate all you have done for me."

"I longed for years to help you," Jane told her, taking her hand. "I was glad to be able to do so."

"My health is wonderfully improved," Mary said.

"Then you will soon be ready to come to court," Henry said. "We will have a public reunion for all the world to see."

Mary looked a little daunted at the prospect.

"And Elizabeth must visit court too," Jane said, trying to extricate Noble from Elizabeth's none-too-gentle clutches. "Would you like that, Elizabeth?"

"Yes," Elizabeth said, letting go of the little dog and twirling around in a fair imitation of an almain, a dance greatly favored at court.

"She is her mother's daughter," Mary murmured, as Henry got up and showed Elizabeth how to do the steps properly. "Your Grace should keep an eye on her. I cannot help but love her, for she is so endearing, and yet I fear she is no blood kin to me."

Jane stared at her. "I beg your pardon?"

"She is Mark Smeaton's child," Mary muttered low. "Can't you see the likeness?"

"Not at all." Mary must be disabused of this silly idea at once. "You only have to look at her to see who her father is—and he himself, who has most cause, has never expressed a single doubt!"

Mary looked unconvinced, but then Henry came back, carrying a squealing Elizabeth under his arm, and there was no chance to say anything more. When Mary bade them farewell, she embraced Jane warmly, so clearly she had not taken offense at their disagreement.

Seeing Henry with his daughters, and how loving a father he could be, had brought home to Jane his desperate need for a son. She could not bear to think of the child she had lost, and how she had failed him. It seemed cruel that she, the child of such fecund parents, had not immediately proved fruitful.

She was worrying too about her father's health. He wrote rarely these days, which seemed ominous in itself. Mother's infrequent letters were always relentlessly cheerful, yet Jane feared that the truth was being kept from her. Edward had said that Father was no better, and even the normally flippant Thomas was concerned.

As they rode away from Hunsdon, Jane began to feel overburdened. There were things she could not discuss with Henry, who was dealing with his own demons, and there was no one else in whom to confide. Margaret Douglas was in prison. Eleanor Rutland had been making an effort to be amiable, and Mary Monteagle was friendly enough, but Jane did not know either of them well, which was probably her own fault because, being constantly aware of the need to be on her dignity, she had not encouraged the intimacies of normal friendships. And easy camaraderie with her maids was now forever barred to her.

Henry leaned over from his saddle. "You're quiet this evening, darling. Are you well?"

"I am just tired," she prevaricated.

"We'll soon be at Waltham," he said. "The harbingers have gone ahead. Supper will be ready for us."

She made herself smile at him.

"Why, darling, how happens it you are no merrier?" Henry asked, coming into her chamber the next morning to find her staring into space while her women bent over their embroidery. "Leave us," he ordered them.

"I'm lonely," Jane said, when they had gone. "I feel all over the place."

Henry's eyes brightened. "Could you be with child?"

She wondered. She had felt overemotional lately, but had put it down to worry and guilt, and shadows in the dark. "Not that I know of," she said. "But now it has pleased you to make me your wife, there are none but my inferiors with whom to make merry, your Grace excepted—unless it would please you that we might now enjoy the company of the Lady Mary at court. Surely she is well enough now."

"We will have her here, darling, if she will make you merry," Henry promised. He stood up, walked over to the window and stood there looking out, with his back to her. "God knows, we need some cheer. My councillors now speak as if there is no hope of an heir. It's very depressing. But I hope, darling, that we will prove them wrong." He turned and attempted a smile.

"We have only been married for three months!" she reminded him.

"Of course. I am being an old pessimist. Come, let us walk in the gardens. It's a beautiful day." He held out his hand.

Chapter 30

1536

September was unseasonably hot. Jane sat fanning herself in the shade of an oak tree in Greenwich Park with Noble stretched out and panting on the ground beside her. Her flowers were a week late. It was what she had been longing for.

A week later, she told Henry. "I think I am with child."

His face was transformed. "Darling! Thank God, thank God! You cannot know how I have prayed for this. I had almost given up hope." He folded her in his arms, carefully, as if she were made of Venetian glass. "This is wonderful, wonderful news. Now, you must look after yourself. No more riding!"

His spirits revived joyfully as he began to make plans for the Prince's household and the tournaments there would be to mark his birth. He was even discussing suitable marriage alliances for his son.

"And you must be crowned, Jane, as soon as it can be arranged. I promise you, I will perform wonders." Immediately he instructed his councillors to put everything in place, and set carpenters to work preparing Westminster Hall for the coronation banquet. No expense was to be spared. Thanks to the work of Cromwell and the King's commissioners, the royal coffers were now filled with wealth plundered from the monasteries. With that prim, disapproving look, Henry had read out to Jane some of the reports of the visitations. "I had never realized the scale of the corruption!" he growled. "Lechery, sodomy, over-luxurious living! Shrines exposed as fakes! I read these things again and again. I tell you, Jane, I am scandalized that the word of God was not being observed as it should have been in these houses." His lips pursed in self-righteous indignation. "I was right to close them down! By God, I will purge my Church of all superstition and popery!"

She did not want to believe the things he had told her, and indeed she could not believe them. They were all too timely, these shocking revelations. Maybe there had been some sinful things going on in the monasteries—but how much of it had been fabricated by the King's commissioners?

She said nothing. A lot of this money was being spent on her. It felt like the wages of sin.

And then, suddenly, everything came to a halt.

Plague! Jane heard her ladies uttering the word in panic, and her heart almost stopped. Dreadful memories of the sweating sickness surfaced; it had been eight years ago, but still they were vivid, and she thought immediately of Margery and Anthony, snatched away in the flower of youth. All that death, all that suffering . . . Nothing must threaten the precious burden she carried.

And now here was Henry, crashing through the door, his face white with fear. "Darling, there is plague in London. In this hot weather, the contagion will spread like fire. We are removing to Windsor for safety. We must take no chances."

Not for years had there been such a hasty packing-up of household stuffs and furnishings, as courtiers raced about gathering their belongings and fetching their horses. The stables were mobbed. Henry was bawling orders, hurrying everyone up and growing furious in his impatience. Jane was glad she was not suffering from nausea as some ladies did. She felt well, physically, if a little tired. Yet she was troubled in her mind, and terrified of the plague. Desperately she needed this child to live. She could not get to Windsor fast enough.

At last they were on the road. She lay in her litter, a kerchief tied around her mouth and nose to protect against infection, as Henry had ordered. It was hot, and the roads were dusty and rutted. She thought of what it must be like in the stifling, stinking city, where people were dying and the plague pits were being filled as fast as men could dig them. And the physicians could do nothing. People would be huddling indoors behind locked doors, sunk in fear, melancholy and grief, all mirth departed.

The relief was overwhelming when the great round tower of Windsor came into view, and she saw the massive castle, dominating the landscape for miles around. She was glad to lie down in her lodgings, feeling rather lost in the vast bed with its gold-and-silver canopy and silken hangings. It had been made for his mother, Henry told her, when he came to her that night, in a much calmer mood.

"Your coronation must be postponed, sweetheart," he told her. "I've set it for the Sunday before All Hallows' Day."

"Hopefully the plague will be gone by then," she said.

"I do pray so! Now, darling, get some rest."

She shut her eyes tightly, not daring to open them in case *she* was there. And when, finally, she slept, plague stalked her dreams.

Chapuys asked to see her, and they walked along the North Terrace, admiring the spectacular view of the countryside for miles around, with the spires of Eton College rising in the near distance.

"Something is troubling your Excellency," Jane said.

"It is indeed, Madam." Chapuys's kindly eyes were pained. "This closure of the monasteries is not only wicked, but disastrous for the people of England. There are hordes of monks and nuns being turned out into the world with only small pensions to live on. And they, who have succored the sick and the poor, are now dependent on their parishes or charitable persons. And whereas in the past the monks and nuns looked after vagrants, they themselves are now in many cases reduced to begging."

This was not the picture Henry had painted. Had he just fed her platitudes, or had he not foreseen the consequences of his actions? Or was Chapuys exaggerating because, like her, he was opposed to the Dissolution with every fiber of his being?

"The parish officers will find it hard," he said. "People say they are stretched as it is, supporting the poor." Jane remembered seeing long queues of the destitute in Bedwyn Magna, waiting for alms.

"Already it appears that in some places they cannot cope," Chapuys informed her. "Your Grace, something must be done. The people are angry and resentful. They are protesting against these impositions, and against the loss of their abbeys and the banning of ancient religious traditions. Holy shrines are being desecrated! It is now forbidden to seek miracles, so the sick and the dying are deprived of all hope." He was shaking his head in despair, the good, earnest man.

"The King says that the monasteries are in decline." She felt she had to make some show of loyalty to Henry. She did not wish to be drawn into discussions about religion or politics.

"Your Grace, if that is so, then why are the people so appalled to see them destroyed? They are not fools. They know why this is being done. I have witnessed their horror as they watch the King's men breaking up sacred images of the Madonna and saints, and smashing their axes through beautiful stained-glass windows. They see the treasures, the rich vestments and altar plate, the very stones and the lead from the roofs being carted away to enrich the King; and there is much murmuring against those who are buying up the lands and converting the abbeys into fine houses. The people see it as sacrilege! And on top of all that, they are taxed heavily to support Church reforms they do not want and have to succor the displaced monks and nuns! Madam, I flee to you in the hope that you can beg the King to see the error of his ways and put a stop to it all."

"Messire Chapuys, I have tried several times, and failed. The King knows my views."

"Warn him, Madam! Warn him of what might happen if he persists in this iniquitous folly. The people are outraged, and they are grieved. They will tolerate only so much. I say this for the King's own good."

"I know you do," she said, pausing. "Believe me, I will try to make him listen. I promise. These are matters too weighty for me to discuss with you. For now, I must go and change, for I am to sit for Master Holbein. Farewell." She left him with a sinking heart.

Her ladies dressed her in a gorgeous gown of scarlet velvet, with a kirtle of damask and oversleeves embroidered in gold thread. The heavy pearl-and-ruby necklace matched the jeweled biliment on the neckline of the gown, and the great pendant ouche had been designed by Master Holbein himself. On her head they placed a gem-encrusted hood, with the veil folded over it in the fashionable whelk-shell style.

Henry had decreed that Holbein should paint portraits of them both to mark Jane's pregnancy. Her hands were to be folded over her stomach, as if cradling the child that lay within. By the time the portrait was finished, she would—God willing—have quickened, and all would understand the significance of the painting.

Holbein had just been appointed King's Painter. He had a studio in York Place, but had escaped from London with the rest of the court.

"He is an exceptional artist, and worthy of my patronage," Henry had said, "and Cromwell finds him very useful, for while he is working away on his portraits, he hears all kinds of things."

Jane had seen Holbein's portrait of Henry, and been taken aback by its astonishing power and presence, highlighted in real gold leaf. She had been looking forward to seeing how he painted her. But during the sitting she was fretting about what Chapuys had said, and when she was shown the preliminary sketch, she saw that Holbein had captured her mood, for she looked tense and preoccupied, her lips unflatteringly pinched.

She looked like a woman who was frightened of broaching a contentious subject with her husband.

Henry had just arrived in Jane's chamber for supper, and was washing his hands, when Cromwell's secretary appeared.

"A report from Lord Cromwell, your Grace," he said, bowing, and waited patiently while the basin was removed and a hand towel presented to the King.

Henry took the scroll. "Thank you, Ralph. You may leave us." He sat down at the table. Jane watched his expression tauten as he read the report.

"The plague has now spread beyond the City to Westminster," he said. "It has struck down several in the Abbey itself. Darling, I think we should put off your coronation for a season."

"It is best to be safe," she said. "We must think of the child."

"Indeed! I would not risk your life, or his, for the world."

"We are still safe here?"

Henry patted her shoulder. "If we were not, I would have moved on long since."

On the last night of September, the specter manifested itself again. Cowering in fear, Jane asked herself what it could portend this time. Would the plague get them all? Or would she lose this child too? She was consumed by anxiety.

Within days, she had the answer.

The news came by fast messenger from London. There had been a riot in Louth, in faraway Lincolnshire.

Stamping up and down Jane's chamber, his staccato tones betraying his rage, Henry gave her the bare facts. "It was in protest against my religious reforms. In those parts, and especially in the north, the old ideas are much entrenched. But, Jane, this was no ordinary riot. It was well organized by men of substance—traitors, all of them!"

It was what Chapuys had predicted. She wished she had spoken to Henry of the ambassador's concerns, but she had been too faint-hearted, too preoccupied with her fears. And anyway, what could Henry have done? He would have had no time to take action. More to the point, would he have listened to her, or dismissed her fears and been angry at her interfering?

"I've called an emergency meeting of the Council, and they will be waiting for me now," Henry told her. "Fear not, darling. I will deal with these knaves as they deserve!"

But as the days passed, and the October leaves turned red and gold, it became clear that the trouble was escalating. This was a revolt. A rebel army was gathering, and men were swarming to join it. News came that the men of Norfolk had swelled the insurgents' ranks; then they heard that the rising had spread to Yorkshire.

"The rebels have occupied York!" Henry thundered, beside himself with rage. Jane thought she could detect fear also in him. This was a serious rebellion. She trembled for them both, for the child beneath her girdle, and for her sister Lizzie too. Lizzie was living with young Henry and her infant daughter, Margery, in a house in York, struggling to survive on her widow's funds. Jane had sent her money, and worried about her, and Lizzie's last letter had given her cause to hope that matters were improving, for it seemed that her sister was being courted by Sir Arthur Darcy, the younger son of Lord Darcy, a northern peer. But now she was terrified lest Lizzie was in danger, for the rebels might not look kindly upon the Queen's sister.

"Were many killed or injured?" she asked, dreading the answer.

"No," Henry said. "It seems these northerners are all of one mind. A supposedly respectable burgher of York called Robert Aske has set himself up as the rebels' leader. They have been joined by the men of Hull, led by a wretch called Robert Constable. Even Lord Darcy has declared for the insurgents, and surrendered Pontefract

Castle to them, against his allegiance to his King! He always was a troublemaker. By God, when I get my hands on him, he shall pay for this with his head!"

At his mention of the name Darcy, Jane stiffened. She could not have her sister implicated in this lord's treason.

"Henry, I must tell you. Sir Arthur Darcy is a suitor for the hand of my sister, Lady Ughtred."

Henry's eyes narrowed. "Then write to her now. Tell her to have nothing more to do with him."

Everyone at court knew that the situation was serious. There was a hushed atmosphere of fear and feverish conjecture, and all entertainments were canceled. Henry spent long hours with his councillors, making plans to deal with the rebels. And when word spread that an army of forty thousand was marching south, panic broke out.

"Calm yourself, Madam!" Henry commanded, after Jane had run in terror through the castle to find him, and had burst in on him as he sat in his closet in conference with Cromwell, who had risen to his feet on seeing her.

"But people are saying that a rebel army is marching on us!"

"It is true," Henry said, looking as if he bore the weight of the world on his shoulders. "They are calling it the Pilgrimage of Grace. It is supposed to be a peaceful protest against my reforms."

"Nonetheless, it seems these traitors are prepared to back up their demands by armed force," Cromwell said. "They carry banners showing the Five Wounds of Christ, and call their rebellion a crusade. They want the King to heal the breach with Rome and restore the monasteries and the old ways." His tone betrayed his contempt.

Jane sank down on a bench, her heart racing. Why, oh, why didn't Henry give his people what they wanted? Then they would go home and there would be no more trouble. They would all be safe. Couldn't he see that his policies were wrongheaded and sacrilegious, and that the rebels had good cause for their protest? For all her fear, she herself could only applaud them for it.

"Madam, this rebellion is the most serious threat to the King's authority we have faced," Cromwell said, regarding her severely. She thought he must know where her sympathies lay. She wanted to tell him that her chief loyalty, despite everything, was to her lord and husband.

"I am leading an army north against the rebels," Henry told her.

"No!" she cried, springing up. "You might be killed!"

"Darling, it will strike fear into these traitors to see their King at the head of a great army, come to mete out justice." She could see the light of battle in his eyes, his elation at the prospect of a great victory. How all peoples would hold him in esteem and fear for stamping out the revolt!

"Please don't leave me!" she begged. "I am so frightened."

Henry seized her hands. "Think you Master Cromwell will not be zealous in ensuring your safety? I will be leaving many stout men to guard you. There is nothing to fear."

"But what if you are killed or taken prisoner?"

Henry's face darkened. "You must not entertain such doubts, for I assure you I do not. And darling, I need you here, to be regent in my absence."

She was astonished. She had not realized he had such trust in her. "But how will I know what to do?" she faltered.

"Archbishop Cranmer and my Privy Council will act as your advisers," Henry said. "You should have more confidence in your own wisdom and ability, Jane. And chiefly you will be a figurehead, presiding over the court in my absence."

She pulled herself together. She must show him that she was worthy of such an honor. She had often heard Queen Katherine recalling how she had acted as regent when Henry had been fighting in France, and how the Scots had invaded. Katherine had been active in dealing with that threat, and England had won a great victory. She must profit by Katherine's example.

"I am greatly honored that you should trust your kingdom to me," she said. "I will not fail you."

She knew there was no gainsaying Henry. Cromwell had poured

some wine to calm her, and she sat there sipping it as Henry planned his campaign and barked out orders, with Cromwell scribbling furiously. The tiltyard at Greenwich was to be converted into a workshop, so that the royal armorers could repair his old armor, which was being got out of storage at an inn in Southwark.

Jane was barely listening. All she could think of was that Henry was going miles from her to face danger.

He was not going. She could not hide her relief.

Huffing with annoyance and disappointment, he sat down dejectedly in the window embrasure in her chamber. "The fact is that I cannot raise sufficient forces in the little time I have. So I am sending Norfolk and Suffolk north with those men I have mustered, and ordered them to use conciliatory measures before resorting to force. Scoundrel he may be, but Norfolk's a fine general, and Suffolk is stoutly loyal. A rabble of peasants with scythes and billhooks will be no match for those two. I am confident that they will crush the rebels."

"It rejoices me so much to hear that you are not going north," Jane said, reaching out for his hand.

"I wanted to lead my men in person," he scowled, "and teach those rebels a lesson. I will not have my laws subverted and mocked!"

She was returning to her apartments when a man stepped out of the shadows.

"Messire Chapuys!" she gasped. "You gave me a fright!"

"I am sorry, your Grace," he said, bowing, "but this Pilgrimage of Grace is most worrying. It could cost the King his throne, you realize."

Yes, that had occurred to her, in the darkest hours of the night. "He is taking strong measures to deal with it," she said.

"I am aware of that. But Madam, the whole dangerous situation could be defused if only he would listen to reason. Has your Grace spoken to him, as you promised?"

"Not yet," she admitted, forbearing to say that Henry had been so angry lately that she had feared to do so.

"Then I beg of you, speak now! Do it tomorrow, when everyone is listening."

Tomorrow she would be enthroned beside Henry beneath the canopy of estate in his presence chamber. The whole court would be assembled to hear him declare how he meant to deal with the rebels.

Dared she do it? She trembled at the very idea.

Chapuys had noted her hesitation. "I will be there, Madam, and many who wish you well and would see the monasteries restored."

He was surely exaggerating. She was aware of the stampede of courtiers clamoring to buy monastic estates and property. Yet there must be some, like herself, who secretly deplored the Dissolution. And she was really their last hope—unless the rebels prevailed.

"I will do it," she said resolutely. Chapuys smiled.

She sat there, decked out in her finery, looking down on the sea of bared heads, and listening as Henry spoke from the throne, outlining the actions to be taken in his name by Norfolk and Suffolk. Her heart was thumping so loudly she was sure he could hear it, and her hands were clammy with sweat. In a moment, he would finish, and then she must make her plea. If she did not do it now, the moment would be lost.

They were applauding him, their cheers resounding around the ornate chamber. He sat there acknowledging them, hands firmly grasping the arms of his chair, determination in his face. She saw Chapuys watching her, smiling encouragement.

Now. As she stood up, a hush descended. Henry looked at her in surprise, then his brow furrowed as she fell on her knees before him. Not a whisper could be heard. As she took a deep breath, she could sense people leaning forward to hear what she had to say.

"Sir," she said. "Sir . . ." The words would not come out. She cleared her throat. "Sir, I beg you, for the sake of peace and of those of your loving subjects who regret the passing of the old ways, please think kindly upon the monasteries. I urge you to restore those you have closed. It is wrong for subjects to rebel against their Prince, but perhaps God has permitted this rebellion as a punishment for the ruin of so many churches."

She broke off, realizing that Henry was shaking with fury. "You forget yourself, Madam!" he snarled. "This has nothing to do with you. I might remind you that the last Queen died in consequence of meddling too much in state affairs. Go and attend to other things!" He pointed to the great doors.

She had gone too far. Mortified, her face flaming, and her heart juddering as if it were breaking, she rose unsteadily to her feet and curtseyed. Then she hastened through the throng, the ranks of courtiers parting for her, staring, smiling, murmuring behind their hands. Her ladies hastened after her, and she slowed her pace in an attempt to retrieve her dignity.

She had forfeited his love, she knew it. Back in her lodgings, she threw herself on her bed and wept. So much for Henry's trust in her wisdom! He had put her down as he might swat a fly. That he could speak to the mother of his child so! She should have learned her lesson before, that his kingly authority meant more to him than anything, or anyone. It was Anne who had made him like this, and now he would no longer allow any woman to have it in her power to rule him. Well, never again would she interfere in politics. She would make that clear to Chapuys and everyone else. She would keep her head down, nurse her broken heart in silence, be adoring, respectful and submissive, and attend to domestic affairs. It was the only way to retain Henry's favor.

Eleanor Rutland tapped on her door. "Your Grace, the Prioress of Clementhorpe is here to beg your aid in saving her convent."

Jane dabbed at her eyes. "Tell her I can do nothing," she called.

———

She was surprised to see Henry that night. She had gone to bed feeling fragile, with his words ringing in her ears, and was trying ineffectively to sleep. Then Mary Monteagle was at her bedside. "The King is here, Madam."

Mary vanished as Henry entered. He was wearing his velvet night robe and cap, and a very mournful expression. He came and sat on the bed.

"I am sorry for my anger today, Jane, but you should not have interfered in a political matter that does not concern you."

She was about to explain her motives when she realized that she had best hold her tongue. He had apologized; she must show herself contrite. "I am truly sorry to have so offended you," she said, feeling the tears welling up. "I thought I had forfeited your love, which means more to me than anything on this earth."

"Darling, that could never be!" he said, grasping her hand. "I know you spoke out of sincere conviction, even if it was misguided, but I cannot have my Queen questioning my policies. St. Paul says a wife should keep silence and learn from her husband."

"As I intend always to do," she told him.

"Then we are friends again." He smiled, shrugging off his robe and climbing into bed. "And to cheer you further, I have sent for Mary."

"Nothing after our reconciliation tonight could give me more pleasure!" she declared, feeling infinitely relieved. It had been anger and embarrassment, nothing more, that had made him speak brutally to her, and it had been an error of judgment to make her plea in public. There had been no need for heartbreak. Now his hand was on her stomach.

"I hope the little one quickens soon," he whispered.

Chapter 31

1536

As the dukes rode north, news of Mary's imminent arrival at court spread, and crowds gathered at the gates of Windsor, where apartments were being prepared for her. When Henry summoned her old governess, Lady Salisbury, back to court, the people cheered her, and Jane made a point of inviting this venerable old lady to drink wine with her and tell her about the old days. She had been in awe of the Countess back then, for the former Margaret Pole had royal Plantagenet blood, and was a peer in her own right; but now she was glad of her very congenial and spirited company. Together they ensured that all was in place for Mary's coming.

It had turned cold at last and the plague was mercifully abating. Jane stood with Henry by the roaring fire in the presence chamber, waiting to receive Mary, their courtiers crammed into the vast apartment, all agog to see the King formally receive his daughter back into favor. Mary appeared in the doorway, dressed in the rich clothes he had provided; behind her was the train of gorgeously attired ladies he had appointed. She curtseyed twice, at the door and once in the middle of the chamber, and then fell to her knees before the King.

"Sir," she said nervously, "I do crave your fatherly blessing."

"And I do readily give it, my well-beloved daughter," Henry replied, taking her hands, raising her and kissing her with evident affection.

Jane also embraced and kissed her, noting that Mary looked drained, and that she was trembling. "You are most welcome here!" she said.

Henry turned to the Privy councillors standing nearby. "Some of you were desirous that I should put this jewel to death!"

Jane cringed at his tactlessness. Mary should not be hearing this! "That would have been a great pity, to have lost your chief jewel in England," she said quickly.

Henry smiled. "No, no!" he replied, and patted her belly in full view of everyone. "Edward!" He could not contain himself. "Edward!"

She felt herself blushing. She had not quickened yet, so he ought not to have revealed their secret. And they had not even discussed a name! She was aware of people staring at her, and the hubbub of murmuring.

Just then, her attention was caught by Mary, who was swaying on her feet, her face deathly pale. Before Jane could reach out to steady her, the Princess had collapsed in a faint. Uproar broke out. A worried Henry was on his knees, begging his daughter to come to her senses and patting her cheeks. "Send for the physicians!" he cried.

"And for a cool damp cloth and some wine!" Jane called. Mary opened her eyes and stared around, bewildered.

"Be of good cheer, daughter," Henry said. "All is well, and nothing now will go against you." Jane gently mopped Mary's forehead with the cloth, and soon the color came back into her cheeks. Henry raised her to her feet, took her by the hand and walked up and down with her until she was herself again. Then he commanded her ladies to take her back to her lodgings.

After resting, Mary joined Henry and Jane for a private supper. She did not eat much, and seemed tense.

"Mary, there is no cause now to fear," Henry reassured her. "She who did you so much harm and prevented me from seeing you for so long has paid the penalty."

Mary looked at him uncertainly. He had conveniently forgotten how he had hounded her into submission after Anne's death.

"To please you, I want you to have these," he said, and handed over a small gold chest that had been sitting beside his plate. Mary opened it. "These were my mother's personal jewels," she said in wonder. She held up a thick strand of pearls. Then she frowned. "But this cross—this was *hers.*" She said the word with such venom that Jane was startled.

"So it is fitting that you should have it," Henry said. "Compensation for what that woman made you suffer. I am giving half her jewels to you, and half to Elizabeth."

"Thank you, Sir," Mary said. "I am overjoyed to have my mother's, but you will forgive me if I do not wear these."

"We understand," Jane said, before Henry could speak.

"Sell them, if you wish," Henry added. "But you will need a goodly collection of jewels since, at your stepmother's request, I am assigning you lodgings at Hampton Court and Greenwich and my other great houses."

Jane extended a hand to Mary. "And we will be friends. You shall have precedence over all other ladies, being first after myself."

Mary smiled back. There were tears in her eyes.

As the days passed, Henry grew tense waiting for news from the north. "The dukes should be there by now," he said. "I would I knew what was happening."

Jane was worrying about her sister. Lizzie had not replied to her letter; maybe she had not even received it. And if Mother and Father, down at Wulfhall, were aware of the threat from the Pilgrimage of Grace, they would be fretting too—and for Jane's safety. For if the worst happened, and Henry was overthrown, what would happen to her?

To divert herself from her fears, she asked Henry if Elizabeth might be brought to court, and he agreed. Elizabeth would be safer in Windsor than north of London at Hatfield or Ashridge. The child arrived accompanied by Lady Bryan and a new gentlewoman, Kate Champernowne, whose beautiful sister Joan had served alongside Jane in Queen Katherine's household. Kate was round-faced and snub-nosed, nowhere near as lovely as Joan, but she was kindly and exceptionally well educated—and good with Elizabeth.

They were to dine with Henry's daughters today. Jane took Mary by the hand, walking alongside her as an equal. At the door to the presence chamber, Mary stood back to let Jane go first.

Jane shook her head. "No," she said, "we will go in together."

Mary waited behind Jane's chair as they all stood for the fanfare announcing the arrival of the King, and remained standing until he was seated. Basins were brought so that Henry and Jane could wash their hands, and Mary performed the duty of presenting napkins, so that they could dry them. Then she seated herself at the high table, a little lower down than Jane. Elizabeth, placed at a table set at right angles to the dais, demonstrated perfect manners, but showed off from time to time, with Henry looking on indulgently.

Most of the time, Elizabeth remained in her apartments, where Jane sometimes visited her and played with her, as did Mary and Lady Salisbury, whom Mary regarded almost as a second mother. It was wonderful to see Mary rejoicing at the reversal in her fortunes, delighting in the fine clothes that had replaced her old, worn gowns, and the money she now had to lavish on her charities and reward those who had done her kindnesses. At last she was living as a young royal lady of twenty should, hunting, gambling, dancing, playing music and laughing at the antics of Janie, her new woman fool.

Henry enjoyed Janie's jests too. One evening she had him nearly crying with mirth.

"God, that woman's jokes are priceless!" He chuckled.

"What do you get when you cross an owl and a rooster?" Janie asked, reveling in her sovereign's admiration.

"Tell us!" he commanded.

"A cock that stays up all night long!" She grinned archly. That set them all giggling again, but Mary looked puzzled.

"I don't think she understands it," Jane murmured. "She seems to be innocent of men. She knows no foul or unclean speech."

"I don't believe it," Henry replied. When Janie the Fool had finished, and the servants were making ready for the masque that was to follow, he beckoned Francis Bryan over. Bryan was dressed up as Theseus, bracing himself to slay the Minotaur. He looked even more like a satyr. "Francis, the Queen says my daughter is an innocent, but I cannot credit it," Henry said. "Dance with her. Test her virtue for me. Use a word that might make her blush."

"Sir, that is unkind!" Jane reproved gently.

"It will do her no harm," Henry said. "Don't be too rude, Francis."

Bryan grinned and went away to take his place, ready for the masque. When the dancing began, Jane watched him bow to Mary and lead her out to the floor. Mary was smiling and gracious. She did not look offended by anything he said.

Soon afterward, Bryan returned to the King. "I don't believe it," he muttered. "I asked the Lady Mary if she would like to see my yard, as it was very impressive. She said, with perfect guilelessness, that she had not known that any courtier lodgings had yards, and that she would like to see it but it would be more proper if she brought her ladies with her. I don't know how I stopped myself from laughing."

"Francis, you are a villain!" Jane exclaimed.

"By God, she is innocent!" Henry declared.

She was not only innocent, but damaged. The torments occasioned by the Great Matter, the loss of her beloved mother and her forced submission had taken their toll. Jane knew that all Mary longed for, more even than being restored to the succession, was a husband and children; yet Henry had so far failed to arrange a marriage for her. Jane was of the opinion that all these factors accounted for Mary's various vague but debilitating illnesses and her women's problems, about which she could not speak without blushing furiously. She even blushed when Jane asked if she would like her to press the King to find her a suitable match.

"I am a bastard, Madam!" she cried, with tears in her eyes. "No prince will want me, and there is little likelihood that my father will allow me to marry a commoner. I must face the fact that while he lives, I will only be the Lady Mary, the unhappiest lady in Christendom." And nothing Jane said could comfort her.

She spoke to Henry about it.

"I will think on the matter," he said. "But let's wait until after young Edward is born. Then I will feel happier about Mary marrying, because her husband could not have designs on my throne."

Jane was feeling well, if a little tired, so she was appalled, at dinner one day early in November, to feel a stickiness between her legs.

"If you will excuse me, I feel a little faint," she told Henry.

He was all concern. "Go and lie down, darling. Ladies, look to the Queen!"

It was as she had feared. The babe was bleeding away from her. Mary Monteagle, who was attending her at the close stool, brought cloths and comforted her as she sat there, weeping inconsolably.

The bleeding got heavier, and the horribly familiar cramping pains began. By afternoon, Jane was lying on her bed, reconciling herself to the fact that her hopes had once again been dashed, and to having to break the news to Henry, which she had insisted on doing herself. Already he had been sent for.

"Darling, I am sorry to hear that you are unwell," he said, hurrying through the door. Then he saw her face, which must be blotched from crying. "No!" he groaned, and for a moment she thought he would weep too.

"It is God's will," she said gently, tears welling again. "I am so deeply sorry."

"What do I have to do to placate God?" Henry cried, balling his fists. "This marriage is pure, without any impediments! Why does He withhold sons from me?"

If a mere human could presume to know why God was angry with Henry, Jane thought she did. And if He was displeased with her too, it was not hard to see why. What more could she do to expiate her guilt? She had tried to save the monasteries; she had played a mother's part to Mary and Elizabeth; she was devout at her prayers. She did no one ill. Did not all this count against her part in bringing Anne down?

"We must pray, and we must try again," she said, with more conviction than she felt.

"How many times have I heard that?" He sighed.

"I am so sorry, Henry. I took the greatest care."

"I know." He patted her hand, sighing. "Often it seems to me there is no reason for these things."

She was up and about the next day, suffering only the dullest of aches and a trickle of bleeding. To take her mind off her loss, she kept herself busy. Hearing that an aging gardener who had kept the Queen's garden at Greenwich beautiful had fallen on hard times, she sent to Cromwell, asking him to provide financial assistance. "You could not do a better deed for the increase of your eternal reward in the world to come," she wrote. She commanded her park keeper at Hampton Court to send a gift of venison to the gentlemen of the King's Chapel Royal, who had pleased her with their singing. She ordered a survey to be made of her lands and property, and was happy when her officers reported that they found all her tenants and farmers as glad of her as hearts could be, and that they were speaking of the year that had seen her marriage to the King as a year of peace in England.

They were flattering her. For two months now, the rebellion had flourished, the pilgrims having been joined by more and more supporters from the northern parts. Thankfully, most lords had rallied to the Crown, and the south was not infected by the treachery of the rebels.

"You know what this betokens!" Henry said cheerfully, looking out of a gallery window at the frosted gardens below. "My reforms and the Dissolution find favor with the majority of my subjects. But it's December now, and the time for fighting is past. My councillors have urged me to deal gently with these rebels, so I intend to play for time. A little dissembling is called for." He gave Jane a knowing smile.

"What do you mean?" she inquired.

"I've sent a comfortable message to Master Aske, telling him I will meet his demands, and promising that Norfolk will ratify the agreement. I've said that I will ride north later. I've promised a royal pardon to all the rebels, and I've told them that you will be crowned in York Minster, and that a Parliament will be held at York."

Jane was staggered. "And what of the monasteries and your reforms?"

"I've given them what they want."

"Henry, do you mean you will stop the Dissolution?"

"Jane!" He looked down on her, almost with pity. "You are a sweet innocent! No, darling, I do not mean any of it. The law is the law. But there are more ways than one to catch a snake. I've invited Master Aske to spend Christmas at court, on condition that he disbands his army."

Jane trembled for Aske, who by all accounts was a sincere man standing up for principles she shared. Did he suspect that he might be walking into a trap? But Henry was beaming munificently.

"We'll show him some royal hospitality, eh? Win him round!"

When they left Windsor for York Place, now renamed Whitehall and designated by law the principal residence of the King and the official seat of government, Mary went home to Hunsdon, where, at her invitation, Elizabeth was soon to visit her.

At Whitehall, they found Master Holbein hard at work on a huge mural that Henry had commissioned for his privy chamber. It was to depict the Tudor dynasty, and the sketches showed the founders, Henry's parents, King Henry VII and Queen Elizabeth, in the background, with Henry and Jane in front. For her sitting, Jane had

worn a gown of figured cloth of gold with a long court train, six
rows of pearls slung across her bodice, and the Tau Cross. Noble had
been there, and had settled down to sleep on her train, whereupon
the normally taciturn Master Holbein, with a grin, had insisted on
including him in the picture.

His portrait of her was finished now, and it was very fine, but she
thought it made her look prim and wary, and was dismayed when
people said it was a good likeness. Henry liked it, though; it was
hanging in the closet he used as a study.

Jane was conferring with Master Hayes, the King's goldsmith,
about a New Year's gift for Henry when Nan Stanhope—or Lady
Beauchamp, as everyone, even her intimates, must now call her—
came to her chamber looking most put out. Master Hayes quickly
concluded his business and bowed himself out. As soon as he had
gone, Nan erupted. "The Earl of Surrey has gone too far this time!
Just because his father is back in favor, he thinks he can do as he
pleases. And because the King likes him, he gets away with it."

"What has he done?" Jane asked.

"Got rather forward and passionate—even though he knows his
advances are unwelcome to me. He's doing it to rile Edward. He'd
never deign to notice me otherwise, as he hates the Seymours. He
thinks we're lowborn upstarts. Edward is furious."

"Do you want me to speak to Surrey?" Jane asked.

"Would you? Edward warned him off, but he took no notice. He
keeps waylaying me and making indecent suggestions."

"We can't have that! It's outrageous. Go back to Edward. I'll
summon Surrey now."

She called one of her ushers. "Please inform the Earl of Surrey that
the Queen wants to see him at once."

Surrey arrived, a tall nineteen-year-old youth, exuding arrogance
and volatility. He was well traveled, learned, famed for his poetry,
and French in his tastes and manners, like his cousin Anne Boleyn.
Yet neither this, nor his wild pranks and profligacy, had cost him

the King's esteem. Jane suspected that in some ways, Henry saw Surrey almost as a son, for the Earl had been much beloved by the late Duke of Richmond, and there was no doubt that he had a talent for jousting and more than his fair share of erudite talent. Indeed, Surrey carried himself as if he were a prince of the blood!

He executed a most flamboyant bow, but she kept him standing. Just as she was about to open her mouth to reprimand him, Henry was announced.

"Why, my lord of Surrey, what brings you here?" he asked, clapping the young man on the back.

"That is what I am waiting to find out, your Grace," Surrey said, smirking at Jane. "The Queen summoned me. It sounded most urgent."

"As indeed it is," Jane said. "Sir, the Earl has been forcing his attentions on Lady Beauchamp, despite both she and Lord Beauchamp making it clear that they are unwelcome. My brother is very angry, and Lady Beauchamp has complained to me."

Henry regarded Surrey ruefully. "Alas, foolish proud boy, what were you thinking of? If the lady says no, she means no."

"Sir, in my experience, no often means yes, or maybe," Surrey protested. "I did not think she would disdain to have an earl at her service."

"By God, man, her husband will be up in arms!" Henry exploded. "You will not approach her again."

"No, your Grace," Surrey muttered, glaring at Jane.

When he had gone, Henry shook his head. "That boy has a talent for making enemies! One day he'll go too far."

Nan was gratified to hear that the King himself had warned off Surrey, but soon afterward she was waxing indignant again, for her rejected swain had renounced her, in the most unflattering terms, in a poem that he had taken care to circulate at court, and now everyone was laughing at her.

Henry was annoyed, but it was too late. The damage had been done. "One day I will repay Surrey for this," Edward swore through gritted teeth. "I will have my revenge!"

Margaret Douglas and Lord Thomas Howard still languished in the Tower. Jane had repeatedly begged Henry to release them, but he remained adamant that they had not yet suffered sufficient punish-ment for their offense. The world must be warned that usurping the King's privilege was a serious crime.

"But how long will you keep them in prison?" she asked, as they sat late after supper, drinking wine in the firelight.

"At my pleasure!" Henry retorted, and she knew by that not to press further.

"Of course. But I am still short of a lady-in-waiting."

"I know," he replied, refilling his goblet, "and I have given it some thought. You might consider Lady Rochford. She was in seri-ous financial difficulties after Lord Rochford's execution, and ap-pealed to Lord Cromwell for help. When I heard, I made Lord Wiltshire increase her allowance. He wasn't best pleased, for he hates her, and he told me he did it for my pleasure alone."

"But he is her father-in-law."

"Yes, and she testified to his son's incest with his daughter." Hen-ry's mouth set in a grim line.

"She never liked Queen Anne."

"She had good reason! And she loves the Lady Mary. She under-stands the ways of courts, and I feel that she deserves some recogni-tion for the part she played in uncovering those vile treasons."

"Then I am happy to welcome her into my household."

Lady Rochford arrived from Kent a week before Christmas, wrapped in furs against the bitter weather. She showed herself grate-ful for her appointment and set about making herself useful, dis-playing a proper deference to the Queen. But there was something about her catlike face, with its pointed chin, pouting mouth and discontented expression, that Jane found repellent. When her women were sitting together, exchanging the latest gossip and tell-ing each other risqué tales, Lady Rochford took a gleeful interest in the lewd details, which Jane found unbecoming. Of course, Lady

Rochford deserved sympathy for what she had suffered, but Jane could not help thinking that Lord Rochford, bad man though he had been, had had reason to stray. If she could have found cause, she would have dismissed Lady Rochford without hesitation; but for now she had to live with her prickly, unsettling presence.

Mary joined them at Whitehall, with Elizabeth; she had specially asked for her half-sister to be invited. The plan was that they would travel with Henry and Jane to Greenwich, where they were to keep Christmas. But the winter was severe and the roads were iced up and treacherous. In London, the Thames had frozen over. Three days before the festival, they wrapped themselves warmly in furs and mounted their horses, with Elizabeth in her father's arms, and rode along the river from Westminster to the City, the child shrieking in delight. Jane was nervous lest her palfrey slip on the ice, but it was exhilarating being out in that vast expanse between the two shores, with the cold wind whipping at her cheeks and crowds lining the banks to see them pass.

"Merry Christmas!" Henry called again and again from his saddle, with Elizabeth lisping the words in imitation and waving to the people. The City of London was gaily decorated in their honor with tapestries and cloth of gold hanging from the windows, and holly wreaths on many doors. At every street corner, priests in rich copes stood waiting to bless the royal party, and hundreds had braved the bitter chill to watch the procession, cheering loudly. Jane was touched to hear so many people calling her name and Mary's, as they rode side by side to St. Paul's Cathedral for the service that would mark the beginning of the Yuletide celebrations.

When it was over, they emerged to a thunderous ovation, remounted and spurred their horses back across the frozen river, cantering toward the Surrey shore, with Mary and the rest of their retinue following, much to the delight of the crowds. Soon they were approaching Greenwich Palace, where Jane was to preside for the first time over the twelve days of Christmas festivities. But she was relaxing into her role as queen now, gaining confidence daily and no longer so nervous about what people thought of her. She had learned to remember that she was the Queen, and that everyone owed her reverence, whatever they thought of her.

Master Aske was waiting for them at Greenwich. Henry granted him an audience that first evening, with Jane present.

"Be you welcome, my good Aske," he said, as the man fell to his knees, clearly overawed to be in the presence of his sovereign. Aske bowed most courteously to Jane, and when she extended her hand to be kissed, he smiled up at her. "I believe we are third cousins, your Grace, through the Cliffords." He spoke with a broad Yorkshire accent, and was plainly dressed, but in good black cloth, as became a lawyer and a godly man.

"Then welcome, cousin," she smiled.

Henry inclined his head graciously. "It is my wish that here, before my Council, you ask what you desire and I will grant it."

Aske looked troubled. "Sir, your Majesty allows yourself to be governed by a tyrant named Cromwell. Everyone knows that, if it had not been for him, the seven thousand poor monks and priests I have in my company would not be ruined wanderers as they are now."

Henry nodded. "Lord Cromwell has a lot to answer for." Jane was amazed to hear him say so. Was Cromwell to be sacrificed to appease the rebels?

"Tell me, what do you wish for?" Henry asked. "I fear that I have not been made properly aware of what is happening in my kingdom."

Aske clearly had his answer ready. "Sir, we ask for the monasteries to be restored. We want to see heretical bishops and evil advisers punished, certain commissioners prosecuted, and the repeal of all laws that are against God's word. We also ask that Parliament sit in York to debate these matters."

Jane listened to all this with mounting perturbation. Any moment now, Henry would explode in fury. Those who dared to question his laws were on very dangerous ground indeed, as she had bitter cause to know. She held her breath.

"All these requests I will grant," Henry said. "There will be redress for those who have been wronged, and you shall have safe passage home after Christmas. For now, in token of my good faith, I should like to give you a present to mark the season." What good faith? Jane wondered. This was another of those occasions when she found herself disliking her husband.

Aske's eyes widened as Henry presented him with a jacket of crimson silk. "I cannot thank your Majesty enough," he said. "I know you are a good man, and sincere. I will send the order for my people to disband, and tell them that we have the King himself on our side."

"I will be true to my word," Henry said.

Jane forced herself to keep smiling, but she watched Aske depart with a sinking feeling in her stomach, knowing that this honest man, this devout man, would soon find that he had been betrayed.

On St. Stephen's Day, an usher bade her attend the King in his closet. Soft-slippered in her velvet finery, ready for the day's feasting, she made her way there at once, and found him standing at the window overlooking the Thames, which was framed with wall paintings depicting the life of St. John the Baptist.

His face was grave, his voice tender. "Darling, sit down. I have bad news. Your father is departed to God. He died at Wulfhall five days ago."

Dead. Her father, dear to her despite all the scandal he had caused. But that was long in the past now, and all she could think of was that he was gone from her forever. She wept helplessly against Henry's jeweled doublet, as the first awful spasms of grief shook her. And then, when she thought of Mother, and how bereft she must feel, she cried anew.

Henry called for her brothers. She could tell from their faces that they already knew. They begged leave to depart, Edward because he must take possession of the estates that had come to him as heir, and arrange the funeral; Thomas in hope of wresting anything from Edward that he could; and Harry to comfort and succor their mother. Henry granted it willingly.

"I ought to go too," Jane said. "I would be with my mother."

"No," Edward said. "You are the Queen now. Mother has enough to cope with without having to stand on ceremony."

"But I would come as a private person," she protested.

"Wait until the new year and the better weather," Henry counseled. "After the funeral, your mother will be in need of comfort. And you are needed here at court."

"Of course," Jane said, pulling herself together. "Where is the funeral to be?"

"At Bedwyn Magna church," Edward told her. "He wanted to be laid to rest in Easton Priory, but that has been dissolved because it was ruinous. Thanks to his Grace's kindness, I have just bought the land and the buildings." Jane could not speak. Her tears were welling afresh at the knowledge that, thanks to this wretched Dissolution, her father could not be buried in the place he had chosen.

She dabbed her eyes. "If you will forgive me, Sir, I will not join you for the festivities today. I would pray for my father's soul. And you, my brothers, may God speed you on your journey. Give my dearest love and sympathy to Mother."

There was no court mourning. Sir John had never been a prominent figure, and few were aware of his passing. After a day spent in sorrowful seclusion, Jane put on a brave face and played her part, trying to suppress her grief. The revelry around her made a mockery of it, and she felt guilty for joining in. But Henry said it would take her mind off her loss, and besides, she was the Queen, not just a bereaved daughter. So she could not even pay her father the tribute of wearing black.

Chapter 32

1537

When the new year of 1537 had been rung in, Master Aske went home, convinced that his sovereign was on his side, and Edward and Thomas returned to court, leaving Harry at Wulfhall to run the estate. Mother was bearing up bravely, they told Jane, and the funeral had been well attended. Edward had given instructions for a fine monument to be raised in Father's memory. Evidently the scandal Sir John had caused had been buried with him.

Henry gave Thomas a command in the navy, saying it would suit him well and channel his abilities in the right direction, and Bryan was willing to keep Thomas's position open while he was away. Thomas was jubilant. Nothing could have appealed to him more than the prospect of adventure on the high seas, and he went about the court swaggering like a bantam cock, boasting to any who would listen of his promotion. Monasteries were still being dissolved, taxes remained heavy, and nothing more was said of Parliament being held in York, or of Jane being crowned there. Before long, Master Aske would realize that nothing had changed and that

Henry had no intention of honoring his promises, and the rebels would know that they had been duped.

In February, Jane was not surprised to hear that they had regrouped. "No more fair words!" Henry thundered. "Norfolk is to ride north again, and this time I'm sending a great army with him to teach those traitors a lesson they will not forget. They will learn the hard way that they must not presume to question the will of their King!"

He had come to supper seething, and not just on account of the rebels.

"You may have heard of my cousin, Reginald Pole." He spat out the name as if it were poison. "Lady Salisbury's son. Last year, he wrote a vicious, offensive and treasonous treatise against me—after all I had done to advance him! That's why he's in exile in Italy. Today, I received two reports from Rome. That scoundrel of a pope has rewarded him with a cardinal's hat! And he has appointed Reginald to plot an offensive against me while I am occupied with this rebellion! Apparently all the princes of Christendom are being encouraged to unite in opposition to me! And that my own kinsman should consent to it! It's treason of the worst kind!" His eyes were glittering with hatred. "I have summoned Reginald back to England, on the pretext that I want him to explain certain difficulties in the treatise; but I know he will not come."

"He must know what awaits him," Jane said.

"Yes, but his family are here," Henry said. She caught her breath. He raised an eyebrow. "They are of the old blood royal. Lady Salisbury thinks she is grander than I am, as her father was brother to King Edward IV and the usurper Richard III. He was a traitor too! By God, Jane, the whole family is tainted with treason. I'm convinced that the true object of this new offensive is to depose me and set up Lady Salisbury or one of her sons on the throne. Reginald's out of my reach, but they aren't, and by all that's holy, I will make them suffer!"

She had rarely seen him so incensed, yet she detected the fear behind his anger. He was wary of his Plantagenet relations, the

Poles and the Exeters. Always, at the back of his mind, there lay the suspicion that they would plot to win back the throne; and there was resentment too, for he was in no doubt that they thought themselves more royal than he was, and that the Tudors were an upstart dynasty with a weak claim to the Crown.

"Cromwell is writing to Lady Salisbury to inform her of her son's treason," Henry told her. "We shall see what she says." He pushed his plate away and threw down his napkin. "I'm sorry, Jane, but I can't eat tonight."

Three nights later, he was still in a grim mood. "Lady Salisbury has written to me. She expressed horror at what Reginald has done, and said that he is no son of hers. But Cromwell has warned me that, out of fear, she and her sons might unite with the Exeters against me. From now on, they will be under surveillance." He smiled at Jane grimly. He would kill them all in the end, she feared. He would never be comfortable while they lived.

"I've had word from the north," he told her, loading his plate with food. At least his appetite had returned, even if he was still acting like an angry bear. "Martial law has been imposed there, and Norfolk and Suffolk are dealing with the rebels as they deserve." She could imagine what that meant. "Wiltshire has gone to help. He makes no secret of his desire to win back my favor."

Of course, the man who had condemned his own son and daughter to death would not hesitate to crave the favor of the King who had signed their death warrants. It seemed that Wiltshire was ready to do anything to preserve his position at court. All he had lost had been the office of Lord Privy Seal, which Cromwell now enjoyed. Jane wondered how Wiltshire managed to sleep at night. But his ambition was notorious, and so was the fact that he always acted in his own interests.

Jane had planned to visit Wulfhall in February, but Henry did not want her traveling abroad without him at such an uncertain time, and part of her felt relieved to hear it. She was feeling unaccountably tired, and put it down to her grief for her father. She wrote to Mother, explaining the situation, and Mother wrote back with her blessing, saying she was in health and that Harry was managing well in Edward's absence. Jane was to recover her strength before she contemplated making the journey.

Jane sent another letter to Lizzie, but there was no reply. Her anxiety deepened. Pray God her sister was safe!

Norfolk crushed the rebellion and hanged as many traitors as he could lay his hands upon. The north was a forest of gallows trees. But in London, the bells were ringing out, and in churches thanks were being rendered. Nevertheless, Henry was stern in his triumph. "Over two hundred have been executed. Their bodies will be left to rot on their gibbets, as a warning to any who dare contemplate rebellion in future."

"What of Lord Darcy?" Jane asked.

"He has been taken, and is being brought south to the Tower. Aske and Constable have gone into hiding, but they will be rooted out, never fear!"

Cromwell, standing by, looked as pleased as a fat tomcat who had caught a mouse. "This victory has strengthened the throne. His Grace is now more powerful than ever, and he will be more respected than before throughout Christendom."

"I rejoice to hear it," Jane said. "But I fear for my sister, Lady Ughtred."

Cromwell smiled. "You will be pleased to know that I have word of her, Madam. She is in York, well and safe, although I gather young Darcy is still a suitor for her hand." Henry grunted, frowning.

"Then she cannot have received my letters conveying the King's wishes," Jane said.

"Your Grace must not worry. Sir Arthur Darcy was not involved in the rebellion."

"I am most relieved to hear it." She turned to Henry. "And now, Sir, I can rejoice fully in your great victory!"

There might be another reason for rejoicing too, but she was not certain yet. It was too soon.

Henry came to her bed that night and took her with renewed vigor. "I feel a new man," he said afterward, cradling her in his arms. "You know, darling, if I have learned one thing from the late rebellion, it is that I have perhaps gone too far in my reforms. Last year I had Convocation and Parliament set forth ten articles of doctrine for my Church. I felt they offered a middle way between traditional religion and the more radical beliefs of the reformers. But now I know I should have leaned more toward the traditional, to discourage any other would-be rebels."

It was what the rebels had asked for! Jane held her breath.

Henry wound a strand of her hair around his finger. "I've asked Cranmer to write a book outlining the doctrines of the Church of England. It's to be called *The Institution of a Christian Man,* and it will signal a return to more traditional tenets of faith."

This was good news. "The reformers will be unhappy," she said.

"They will have to be. We've just seen where reform has led us. My reforms must be of the right kind, what the Church needs."

She took a breath. "And the monasteries?"

"Are hotbeds of popery and vice! No, Jane, that law stands."

The middle of March brought the first warm day of the year, and with the coming of spring, Jane knew with glorious certainty that her hopes were realized. "I am with child again," she told Henry, when he came to bed intent on making love to her.

Instantly, he drew back. "You are sure?"

"I have missed two courses. There can be no doubt. I have been feeling tired and my breasts are tender, but I am very happy."

He embraced her gently. "Sweetheart, I have prayed for this!

Maybe Heaven is smiling on me after all. A son to crown my victory—it would be like one given by God." His kiss was full of joy. "We must take the greatest care of you this time."

She thought of all the things that could go wrong. She might miscarry again, or bear a dead baby, as Anne had done. She had never forgotten how Anne had suffered. And then there was the pain of childbirth to endure. Or the child might be a girl. Suddenly she was filled with fear.

"What is it, darling?" Henry murmured, still holding her closely.

"It is just that I worry that we will be disappointed yet again."

"You must not worry. Just rest and keep calm. When you are past your dangerous times, we will tell everyone the glad news. And then you shall be crowned!"

Norfolk and Suffolk returned to court in a blaze of glory, to be warmly received by their King. Norfolk was back in high favor, and the battle lines were being drawn between the Howards and the Seymours, the old guard against the new. Edward's anger at Surrey still festered, and Surrey went out of his way to provoke him. Naturally, Norfolk took his son's part.

"I blame Surrey!" Edward said, sitting next to Jane in her privy garden. "He's a troublemaker. He can't stand the fact that we Seymours now occupy a higher eminence than he does. He's so jealous."

"And will have more cause soon," she replied. "I am with child."

"Jane! That's marvelous news!" Edward's smile was radiant. "When?"

"October, I think."

"A Seymour king on the throne—think of it! Surrey and his friends will be green with envy. No Howard can compete with that. I can't wait to see his face when he hears the news."

"You must be patient. It will not be announced for a little while." And nothing was certain in this business of getting heirs.

"I will tell no one then. I trust you are well?"

"Perfectly. The King's doctors assure me that all is progressing as it should." Dr. Butts and Dr. Chambers had asked her a lot of questions, then departed nodding their heads sagely.

"Good. I will pray for a happy outcome. My own prayers have been answered too. Nan is also with child, and it is due around the same time as yours. You can support each other!"

Jane congratulated him warmly, with genuine pleasure. But if he thought she was about to indulge in expectant-mother confidences and cozy little chats with Nan, he was mistaken. They would be wrangling over every last aspect of the whole process of childbearing and rearing. Nan would always have to be right, and Jane did not think she could face it.

Edward, however, was preoccupied with something of graver import. "Jane, this rivalry with Surrey. It's not just about Nan. I am for reform, while the Howards are stout Catholics and see themselves as champions of the old ways. And they want supremacy at court. They won't attain it, of course, but that won't stop them trying. Be on your guard."

"They cannot complain about me. I am for the old faith too."

"You're a Seymour, sister. That's bad enough."

The warm weather continued, but Henry could not enjoy it. The trouble with his leg had flared up again, and now the other leg was affected too. He was limping around with bandages under his hose, feeling very sorry for himself.

"I intended to go north next month, to overawe those subjects who dared to rebel against me," he told Jane as they sat watching Surrey slaughtering Sir Thomas Wyatt at tennis, "but to be frank with you, with this humor in my legs, my physicians have advised me not to go far in the heat of the year."

"I do feel for you," she murmured. "Are they very painful?"

"Very," he admitted.

They did not improve. The next day, he was confined to his bedchamber. Jane sat with him, looking on anxiously as his physicians tried remedy after remedy, and administered poultices he had devised himself. He bore it all ill-temperedly, barking at them when the treatment hurt.

"Why not try a herbal bath?" she suggested. "I have heard they can be most efficacious." He took her advice, but to no avail. His incapacity, and the pain, depressed him and made him irascible. As King, he could not be seen to be losing his grasp on affairs, and she knew what it was for him, who had led such an active life, to be incapacitated. Moreover, he was a fastidious man, and found his condition distasteful and humiliating. In despair, she summoned his fool, Will Somers, knowing that if anyone could rouse Henry's spirits, he could. Somers was a kindly soul, an unobtrusive and constant presence in his master's life, and he alone was allowed to speak plainly to him. Sometimes she thought he was the only true friend Henry had. Everyone else wanted something from the King. Somers was not like that.

"Well, Hal, what a state you're in," he said cheerfully when he arrived, wearing his old brown gown and twirling his stick with the bells attached—the staff of his office. "Old lady been beating you up, has she? Or was it the dastardly French?" Jane had to smile.

"Go away," Henry growled.

"But I like it here!" Will retorted, hunkering down by the fireside and warming his hands. "Come on, Hal! What can't be mended must be borne bravely. And the Queen's here, looking ever so pretty. Won't you give her a smile? She has a lot to put up with while you're stuck in here. All those clamoring courtiers—and that long-faced brother of hers. Not much company when you're used to that fine fellow what sits on the throne. What's his name? People are forgetting . . ."

"All right, all right," Henry conceded. "You've made your point, Fool. But it's miserable being stuck in here, as you put it, with two bad legs, when the sun is shining outside."

"Could be worse, Hal. Could be three bad legs—or four."

Jane let them get on with it, suppressing a smile. Hopefully Will would work his usual magic on Henry. But he was having to work especially hard at it today.

The next day, she was sitting sewing in Henry's chamber when an usher announced the arrival of a French merchant.

"Oh, no," Henry moaned. "Not now. But I did agree to see him and I suppose I must do so."

"You can buy me a gown!" Will cried. Henry gave him a none-too-gentle cuff, and he leapt away and huddled behind a chair.

The merchant approached, bowing obsequiously, and laid out his wares for the King to see. Henry cast baleful eyes over the latest velvet bonnets, lace trimmings, biliments, embroidered gloves and other exquisite luxuries from Paris.

"I'm too old to wear such things," he muttered.

"But these are beautiful," Jane said, trying on a pair of the gloves.

"Very well, set them aside." He peered at the other items. "Hmm. That rich collar is well made. I'll have it. And that hat. I'll have the furs too, and a bolt of that linen."

The merchant bowed, and added them to the pile. "I have something special that your Majesty will like." He placed a burnished silver mirror, adorned with cupids, before Henry.

"That also," Henry said. Jane suspected that he was beginning to feel better. He never could resist the chance to adorn himself in fine clothing, and loved to see all the men at court rushing to copy each new thing he wore.

Within three days he was up and about again, his bad mood banished.

"I trust you are feeling well, darling," he said to Jane, when she came to see how he was.

"Never better," she told him.

"Good! Because we are going on a pilgrimage to Canterbury, to the shrine of St. Thomas."

She was astonished to hear it. "But surely it is now forbidden to worship at shrines?"

"Not any more. And we have need of the intercessions of the holy blissful martyr."

"It does my heart good to hear that," she breathed. "But I shouldn't be riding."

"You can travel by litter, resting on cushions. It will do us both good to go on progress."

They had passed through Rochester and Sittingbourne, and were now entering Canterbury. Jane waved from her litter at the citizens lining the streets to see them, and soon she and Henry were entering the massive cathedral and kneeling together in front of the gold-plated, bejeweled shrine, one of the most famous in Christendom. Head bent, Jane beseeched St. Thomas to intercede for her, that this child might live. She knew with absolute certainty that Henry was offering up the same prayer.

From Canterbury, they rode to Dover, where the King inspected the new pier, after which they made their leisurely way back. The progress ended when they arrived at Hampton Court. Jane admired the remodeled Chapel Royal, with its crystal windows and beautiful fan-vaulted blue-and-gold ceiling, with its drop pendants, piping putti and the King's motto, "Dieu et mon Droit," blazoned on the arches. She noticed that a stained-glass window depicting St. Anne, the patron saint of her predecessor, had been removed. As usual, the pew for the King and Queen was in a gallery above the main body of the chapel, looking down on the black-checkered floor; and their arms had been set in stone plaques on either side of the door. It was all quite magnificent; Jane had never seen anything like it.

"And timely too." Henry smiled. "Our son will be christened here."

The crowning glory of Hampton Court, however, was the King's new hall, a huge chamber with an impressive hammer-beam roof, a tiled floor and a fine minstrels' gallery above an oak screen. The walls were hung with Henry's pride and joy, a set of exquisite tapestries depicting the story of Abraham, which had cost him a fortune.

The Queen's lodgings had been remodeled for Anne, but she had never used them, as they had been unfinished at her death. Jane did not like Anne's taste, so Henry had ordered that these apartments be refurbished in the antique style, with linenfold paneling and gilded and mirrored ceilings. A private gallery connected her bedchamber to the King's, and a staircase led down to her newly laid-out privy garden, which she regarded with much pleasure. There would be a balcony from which she and her ladies could watch the hunting in the park. However, the workmen were still not finished—in fact, Hampton Court resembled a vast building site, and Jane found herself accommodated in the faded splendor of Queen Katherine's old second-floor rooms overlooking the Inner Court. Jane's bedchamber contained a rich bed surmounted by a wooden roundel painted with her arms, and draped with hangings she had embroidered herself through the long winter months, in anticipation of the works here being finished. But she knew now that that would not be before her child was born.

Jane took Nan to see her new lodgings. But Nan, picking her way, skirts lifted, over timbers and buckets of paint, had to spoil it all. Looking around her, she gave Jane a knowing smile. "Very impressive. But don't you think it's splendid to the point of vulgarity?" The little green-eyed demon leered out from her eyes.

"I think it's the most beautiful apartment," Jane said.

"Well, after Wulfhall, it must seem so," Nan retorted, still smiling.

"Wulfhall is a lovely old house," Jane countered, becoming irate. She knew she would brood on Nan's unkind remarks later.

"Yes, but it's not exactly a palace, is it?"

"No, it isn't meant to be, and according to what you've just said, you don't like palaces either. Too vulgar." She smiled back. Before Nan could answer, she went on, "Now, I should be grateful if you would leave me to rest a while."

And Nan could not gainsay her, for she was the Queen. Pink-cheeked, she made an exaggerated curtsey and left.

Late in March, Jane received the Master of the Hospital of St. Katherine-by-the-Tower.

"Your Grace," he said, kneeling. "St. Katherine's was founded in the twelfth century by Queen Matilda of Boulogne, the wife of King Stephen, and it has served as both church and hospice under the traditional patronage of the queens of England. We ask that you continue this noble tradition."

"Willingly,"—she smiled, nodding to him to rise—"and I take great pleasure in remitting all annual dues." Out of the corner of her eye, she could see Lord Cromwell waiting.

"Your Grace!" cried the Master, pink with gratitude. "That is most kind."

She gave him her hand to kiss, and he withdrew, doffing his bonnet again. Cromwell took his place.

"Madam, I have had a letter from Lady Ughtred in York," he told her, beaming.

"That is marvelous news! Is she well?"

"She is indeed, Madam. I wrote to her, at the King's behest, offering to help her if she was ever in need, and she has replied, asking me to persuade his Grace to grant her one of the redundant abbeys." Was his smile a little smug? How embarrassing, that her own sister was looking to profit from the Dissolution. "Apparently she hopes to turn farmer."

"She needs to improve her circumstances, my lord."

Cromwell cleared his throat. The smug smile had vanished. "There is another way she might do that. I have a son, Gregory, a promising young man, if I say so myself, and well set up in property. Your brother, Lord Beauchamp, has indicated that a match between him and Lady Ughtred might find favor with you."

Was there no end to the man's ambition? Now he wanted to ally himself by marriage to the King. Yet given how he had plotted to bring down Anne Boleyn, that tie of kinship might be Jane's best protection should she too fail to give the King a son. And Cromwell was a powerful friend to have. Moreover, it would be wonderful to have Lizzie near at hand, and the nephew and niece she had never seen. Little Margery could be a playmate for her own child . . .

"Indeed it does, my lord," she answered, "but the last I heard, my sister was encouraging the advances of Sir Arthur Darcy."

Cromwell looked pained. "A most unsuitable match, given that his father is in the Tower as a traitor, and can look soon to lose his head. And I am credibly informed that Sir Arthur is a lukewarm suitor at best."

Was there nowhere the man's tangled web of spies did not reach?

"I will write to my sister," Jane promised, "and if she is willing, and the King pleases, the marriage shall have my blessing."

The next day, Henry took her on a trip along the river to Whitehall to see Holbein's mural, which was now finished. When they entered the privy chamber, Jane involuntarily took a step back, for the effect of the vast painting was overwhelming. The four regal figures stood in a splendid antique setting with a classical roundel, grotesque pillars and friezes, trompe l'oeil decoration, and shell-shaped niches, but it was Henry's dominating presence that drew the eye. He looked so majestic and powerful, feet firmly apart, hands on hips, gazing out with steely authority, that she felt overawed. Truly this was a masterpiece, and Henry was delighted, praising Master Holbein and clapping him on the back. The artist took it all with his usual quiet deference.

"That's how I want to appear to my subjects," Henry said. "Not just as their King, but as head of the Church."

"Everyone will want a copy," Jane said.

"That is to be encouraged. It shows loyalty and approval of my reforms."

Chapter 33

1537

By the time the April blossom flowered, she had missed three courses, and there was a slight swell to her belly. Her pregnancy seemed well established, and Henry conveyed the happy news to the Privy Council at Whitehall. Then the Lord Chancellor stood in the great hall, as Henry and Jane looked on from the dais, and announced to the assembled court: "We do trust in God that the Queen's Grace is now pregnant and will bring forth many fair children, to the consolation and comfort of the King's Majesty, and of his whole realm." There was thunderous applause, caps were tossed up into the air, and everyone came pressing forward to express their congratulations. Henry was jubilant as he received the good wishes, the epitome of a powerful, virile king, while Jane sat there blushing and nodding her head in acknowledgment.

Heralds were sent speeding forth to all parts of the realm to proclaim the news.

"Everywhere there are celebrations," Edward exulted, coming to see Jane a few days later.

"The King is a new man," she told him. "He is so much better, in body and in heart."

"And all because you are with child, my clever sister!"

The good tidings soon crossed the sea. From Calais, Lady Lisle, wife of the Governor, who was cousin to the King, sent two tiny silk nightgowns with caps she had herself embroidered in gold, miniature versions of the nightwear Jane had made fashionable among her ladies, along with the request that one of her two daughters be considered for the Queen's service. "God send that your Grace be safely delivered of a prince," she wrote, "to the joy of all faithful subjects."

Henry fussed around Jane, making sure that she did not exert herself, that she got plenty of fresh air, and that the choicest delicacies were served to her. To please her, he appointed Edward a Privy councillor and granted him extensive lands; and when Thomas returned from his first voyage overseas, he made him a Gentleman of the Privy Chamber. Harry was summoned back to court and knighted, and brought with him a long list of instructions from Mother as to what Jane must and must not do while she was carrying her child. He had promised to return to Wulfhall in time for the harvest. God willing, Jane thought, there would be a better harvest not long afterward. She was counting down the months until October, when the babe was due.

She was feeling less tired now, and very well, but she was hungry all the time, and had a craving for quails, which were unfortunately in short supply. Henry went to considerable trouble to have some shipped over from Calais, commanding Lord Lisle that if none were to be found there, a search must be made in Flanders. Whatever the cost, Jane must have her quails! And Lord Lisle did not fail her. In the last week of May, a large crate of the birds arrived, and she and Henry tucked into a dozen at dinner, and a further dozen at supper.

"I don't think I could look at another quail for a long time," Henry said, wiping away the meat juices with his napkin.

"I could!" Jane told him. "They were delicious. I do hope that Lord Lisle can send some more."

"He will," Henry said. "His wife wants to see her daughter in your household!"

"I might have to agree to it, at this rate!" Jane replied, laughing.

Early in June, thanks to the warm weather, Jane was alarmed to hear that plague had infested London for the second year running, with as deadly consequences as before. Not a moment too soon, Henry immediately ordered the court's removal to the safety of Windsor.

"Have the horses spurred on, please!" Jane cried from behind her linen mask and the leather curtains of her litter. "I just want to get there. I can't bear the thought of anything happening to this baby."

Henry, riding beside her, spoke firmly. "Be calm, sweetheart. Panicking will not do you or the child any good. And we cannot go faster. I would not have you jolted about too much."

But she would not be quieted. She was horribly afraid of the plague, especially when she heard that in London it was killing a hundred victims every week.

Secluded at Windsor, she bargained daily with God, observing every feast day in the Church's calendar and fasting to absolve herself of the burden of guilt she carried, begging that He should spare her and her child from the pestilence. In the end, Henry and everyone else became very concerned about her, and he grew stern with her and forbade her to be so rigorous in her devotions.

"Certainly you must not fast!" he commanded. "It is bad for the child. Now take comfort, for I have forbidden anyone from the city to approach the court. And I am postponing your coronation once more, not only on account of the plague, but because I think it unwise to put you through the strain of a long ceremony just now. But I promise you, darling, you will be crowned after our son is born."

Her spirits were lifted by a letter from Lizzie, who was eager to accept Cromwell's proposal. Arthur Darcy had accepted the situation with unflattering equanimity. "He said he would have been glad to have married me, but was sure that some southern lord would make me forget the north," Lizzie wrote scathingly. She was winding up her affairs in York, and making preparations for the journey to London.

Jane was sad to read that little Margery was to be left behind. "She is not strong enough to make the journey," Lizzie had explained, "and although I am loath to part with her, the nuns of Wilberfoss Priory are willing to take her in, with such keep as I can provide from the sale of my goods. It is a small house, with only eleven sisters, yet they are all saints, and she will be well cared for there. And when, God willing, she is stronger, I will send for her to come to me."

Jane could have wept for her sister, and she worried that Wilberfoss would be closed down, but an opportunity like this marriage did not come every day, and it would ensure that Lizzie, Henry and Margery lived in comfort and security for the rest of their days.

Jane was more than four months pregnant when the child first stirred within her, a little fluttering like a butterfly's wings. She was sitting with Henry in the great park, watching her maids playing catch with a ball.

"Oh!" she exclaimed, as the fluttering came again. "Henry, feel!" She grabbed his hand and placed it on her belly, across which her kirtle was now stretched tight.

"The child?" he asked, in wonder.

"Yes, wait! There!"

"By God, it is! You have quickened!" He was ecstatic. "We will have it announced at once!"

When the announcement was made, she was in her apartments, where she had her women loosen the laces on her stomacher, exposing the mound of her belly for all the world to see. Thus attired, she processed through the court to dine with the King in his presence chamber, and as she passed, the courtiers made reverence to her, as the mother of the heir. On the table there was a dish of quails, sent this time by the Lady Mary.

On Trinity Sunday, Londoners braved the plague for a special Mass of thanksgiving in St. Paul's Cathedral, and the Te Deum was sung in churches throughout the realm. This news of her quickening was joyful to the people, who fully appreciated the King's need for an heir, and were thankful that the bloody specter of a disputed succession had receded. They lit bonfires and celebrated in the streets.

At court there was more cause for rejoicing, for at noon Margery Horsman married Sir Michael Lister, Keeper of the King's Jewels. The King and Queen attended, but left after the ceremony on Henry's insistence.

"You must keep taking the greatest care of yourself, darling," he said, himself escorting Jane to her bedchamber so that she could rest for the afternoon. In fact, on his orders, she spent the summer resting, undertaking no public engagements. She enjoyed her enforced leisure, and the peace of her quiet daily routine. It being improper for a doctor to attend the Queen—or any woman—in childbed, the King's physicians had given place to a midwife, very clean and highly recommended, who was already installed in the palace. Jane found it comforting to know that, in churches throughout the land, prayers were being offered up for her safe delivery.

Henry was in excellent spirits; she had never seen him merrier. He hunted daily in Windsor Great Park, and the game he killed was served to Jane alongside her favorite quails, with which Lord and Lady Lisle kept her well supplied. One evening, as she was enjoying a second helping of them, Henry laid down his knife and reached across to her.

"I know you think I was wrong to order the closure of the smaller monasteries," he said, "but I assure you, I do not mean to wipe out the religious houses entirely. And to please you, and show God that I am still a true son of the Church, I am reestablishing Stixwold Priory in Lincolnshire, for the salvation of your soul and mine."

He never ceased to astonish her. He was a man of so many contradictions. And that he should do this for her moved her profoundly. Maybe this was the turning of the tide, and she would win through in the end.

"I cannot tell you how much that pleases me," she told him, taking his hand and raising it to her lips. "God will reward you for it, I am sure. And I venture to ask that you will grant me another favor. I heard that Bisham Priory has just been surrendered to your Grace, and that saddened me, because its church contains many noble tombs. The earls of Salisbury and Warwick lie there. Would you consider restoring that house too, for my sake?"

Henry looked uncomfortable. It was no secret that his father had kept the last earl of Warwick a prisoner in the Tower from childhood, for no reason other than the fact that the boy's Plantagenet blood made him a threat to the Tudor dynasty; and he only left it for the scaffold, an innocent by all accounts. Queen Katherine had sometimes spoken of him; she had said that her marriage to Prince Arthur had been made in blood, for her father had made it plain that it would not go ahead until Warwick was removed.

"I will do more than that," Henry said. "I will re-establish Bisham as an abbey."

"Posterity will thank you," she told him, "as fervently as I do."

But that night she dreamed, and in her dream she saw a great abbey in ruins. It was Bisham, she knew, although she had never seen it. She awoke suddenly, troubled. Had it been a portent? Henry lay beside her, snoring evenly, and she would not wake him. She was glad of him in her bed. He had not made love to her since finding out that she was with child, but he came for company, he had told her. It had heartened her to hear, from the Duchess of Norfolk, that he had not slept with Katherine or Anne while they were pregnant— and then Lady Rochford had spoiled it by recalling how he had found solace for his enforced abstinence elsewhere. Yet Jane did not think he had been unfaithful to her. She was sure she would have guessed—and that Lady Rochford would have taken the greatest pleasure in telling her!

The next morning, as she took her breakfast, she could hear that lady's voice coming from the bedchamber. She could not make out all the words, but she heard Lady Rochford mention someone who had been hanged in chains. She exchanged glances with Mary Monteagle, who was in attendance. Mary looked uncomfortable.

"Who has been hanged in chains?" Jane asked.

"Madam, it was the rebel, Master Constable," Mary faltered. "They caught him, and Master Aske. We thought it best not to upset you." Evidently Henry had thought so too, since he had said nothing of this.

"What do you mean, hanged in chains?"

"The Duke of Suffolk, my father, told me that he was chained and suspended in a gibbet over the gate of Hull, where he was left to die."

Jane shuddered. How long had it taken him to die? "And Master Aske?"

"A traitor's death," Mary whispered. Horrified, Jane grieved for that honest good man, butchered for his beliefs. She could not bear to think of his sufferings.

"What of Lord Darcy?"

"Madam, he was beheaded on Tower Hill last month. His head is even now on London Bridge."

She said nothing to Henry. To him, these men had been rebels and traitors, and he had dealt with them as the law demanded. She had not known Constable, or Darcy. But Aske, God rest him, had been acting on principle—a principle she shared. She could only pray that his hopes would come to fruition now that Henry had restored two of the dissolved houses. What would he not do for her if she bore him a son?

As the balmy days passed, she was overcome by a pleasant euphoria, as if she and the child were cocooned in a safe little world of their own. She no longer feared the plague, which seemed to be abating a little and had crept nowhere near Windsor.

Her peace was interrupted only by that hothead Surrey. Edward's anger and resentment, together with Surrey's hatred and disdain, had escalated into a bitter feud. Jane was shocked when Edward arrived in her chamber one afternoon, his face all bruised and bleeding, his rare temper aroused. She was glad that Henry was there.

"Surrey punched me in the face," Edward told them, as she sent her maids for water and a cloth.

"By God, he shall hear about this!" Henry flared. "I will not have fighting within the verge of my court, and for those who draw blood, the penalty is the loss of their right hand."

"Sir, the Duke his father would never forgive it!" Jane cried.

"The Duke cannot gainsay it! It is the law," Henry countered. "Tell me, Lord Beauchamp, did you provoke this attack?"

Edward flushed. "Sir, I suggested that my lord of Surrey was sympathetic to Aske and his rebels."

Jane shook her head furiously at Edward.

Henry frowned. "And is he?"

"I thought so, Sir. I expected him to refute it."

"Hmm. I will confer with Cromwell."

When Henry had gone, Jane turned to Edward. "If Surrey loses his hand, the Howards will be out for revenge. I pray the King shows mercy. There is enough enmity as it is."

Edward shrugged, dabbing his head. "I care not. It's what he deserves."

Presently, Henry returned. "I have discussed the matter with Cromwell, and we feel there is no evidence that my lord of Surrey is disloyal, so I am inclined to be lenient. He shall be imprisoned here at Windsor for two weeks, in which time I hope he will have learned the folly of his action."

"I thank your Grace," Edward said, brightening. But Jane remained pensive, nursing fears that this day's quarrel had sowed the seeds of a bitter harvest.

Jane summoned Margery Horsman, who, as Lady Lister, had been promoted to be a lady-in-waiting. For all their mutual goodwill, there was still a certain tension between Jane and Margery, and Jane still regretted the loss of their easy friendship. She was more confident now, more established in her role as queen, especially now that she was carrying the heir to England, and was sorry that she had felt the need to hold herself so aloof early on. She hoped that, now that Margery had been advanced in rank and position, they could be friends again.

She smiled at Margery. "Do sit down. I would like you to write a letter for me, to Lady Lisle. I need a new maid-of-honor to replace you. Lady Lisle has been assiduous in sending me quails, and she keeps asking if I can take one of her daughters. I owe her a favor, so I would like you to extend an invitation to her daughters to present themselves at court. I wish to see them both before choosing the one I want to serve me."

"Very wise, Madam." Margery smiled. "But what will happen to the one who is not chosen?"

"The Duchess of Suffolk will take her. It is agreed. Tell Lady Lisle that her daughters must bring two changes of clothes, one of satin, the other of damask. I will provide wages and food, but she must see that the young lady I choose is properly kitted out, and impress upon her that she must be sober, wise and discreet, obedient above all things, and willing to be governed and ruled by my Lady Rutland and my Lady Sussex. She must serve God and be virtuous, for I hold that those things are more worthy of regard than any other."

She hesitated, shifting heavily in her cushioned chair. Her belly was now very large and she had unlaced her gowns to their fullest extent, wondering if her pregnancy was further advanced than she had reckoned. "I am always wary of young girls coming to the court. It is full of pride, envy, scorn and derision, and there are too many temptations. You might like to warn Lady Lisle of this, but do stress that my household is not like the previous Queen's." She paused, toying with her pearls. "Do you remember how unhappy I was serving her? You were a good friend to me." She looked hopefully at Margery as she said this, and to her relief, Margery smiled.

"Your Grace was a good friend to me too," she said.

"And would be again. I was wrong to put a distance between us, but I was so conscious of my new dignity, so terrified lest people should look down on me, a country girl raised up to wear a crown, and so unsuited to it in many ways."

"I think I understood that, Madam, even as I sorrowed over the loss of your friendship. Nothing would please me more than to be honored with it again."

Jane held out her hand, took Margery's and squeezed it. "Thank you, dear friend."

The Lady Mary arrived at court. "As an unmarried lady, I can't be a gossip at your Grace's confinement, but I can be one of the first to welcome my new brother," she said, as Jane embraced her. Then, late in July, Lizzie made the long journey south from York. It was good to see this sister who was so much younger and had been through so much in her nineteen years, and to meet her boisterous young son, who had nevertheless had manners drilled into him. Lizzie had a becoming maturity about her these days; she was missing her daughter dreadfully, but Cromwell hastened to assure her that his agent in Yorkshire had just informed him the child was in good health.

Cromwell was now a Knight of the Garter, the highest order of chivalry to which an Englishman could aspire. He was clearly delighted with his future daughter-in-law, and at pains to do her honor and make her welcome. He had made his house at Mortlake ready for her and Gregory, and early in August, Jane traveled there by barge to attend their wedding. Gregory seemed a pleasant young man, and she was confident that the couple would be happy.

Lizzie thought so too. "It is good to have a husband near to my own age," she told Jane when they made their farewells. "Anthony, good man that he was, was forty years my elder. And the thing that comforts me most in the world is that Lord Cromwell is contented with me, and says he will be my good lord and father."

"He has every reason to be pleased with you," Jane said. She kissed Lizzie farewell and made her way between the avenue of torches to her barge.

At the end of August, her ladies reported that wagers were being laid in the court as to the sex of her baby and the date of its birth.

"The doctors are all saying it will be a boy," Jane said, "as do the soothsayers and astrologers the King has consulted." It disturbed her every time Henry told her he had seen a fortune teller or had his horoscope cast, for it brought home to her just how much was riding on the outcome of her pregnancy, and how high his hopes were. "I pray Jesus, if it be his will, to send us a prince!" she breathed.

Edward was away at Elvetham, supervising the building works and enjoying some good sport with his hounds and hawks while he was about it. When September came in, he wrote to Jane, sending commendations to her and the King, and adding the fervent prayer that God would soon send him a nephew. So much was hanging on her bearing a boy. But there was nothing she could do save wait and pray. It would not be long now.

Chapter 34

1537

Early in September, they returned to Hampton Court, where the child was to be born. Henry was tense with anticipation, fussing over Jane like a mother hen, and fearful lest she do anything to imperil the child, which was now very active, as if eager to be born.

Jane thought she might be a month or less away from her time when, in the middle of September, she formally took to her chamber. She found the ceremony that marked the occasion daunting. Accompanied by her ladies, the officers of her household and a great company of courtiers, she attended Mass to pray for her safe delivery, then processed into the great hall, where she seated herself on her chair of estate and was offered spiced wine. As she sipped it, her chamberlain, in a very loud voice, asked everyone to pray that God would send her a good hour.

She stood up then, handed the goblet to Eliza Darrell and formally bade farewell to the courtiers. Then the Lady Mary and the Duchess of Suffolk led her to her bedchamber, her ladies and gentlewomen following, and took their leave of her. As the damask curtain was drawn across the doorway, the world outside was shut off.

She gazed around her bedchamber in astonishment, blinking in
the dim light. She had known that she must go into seclusion for
her confinement, and that no man save the King and her chaplain
might see her, but she had not realized that while she had been in
the chapel and the hall, the room had been transformed. New tapestries adorned the walls, the ceiling and even the windows. Only
one window had been left uncovered, and although it was full day,
the candles had been lit. It was also very warm in the room, for it
was hot outside, and the first thing she did was ask them to open the
window and let in some fresh air.

New carpets had been laid on the floor, and next to her rich bed,
where she would spend her lying-in period, there was a pallet bed,
on which she would be delivered. Over its counterpane of scarlet
furred with ermine and bordered with blue velvet, a sheet of fine
lawn had been laid, and a mantle of crimson velvet and ermine, for
her to wear after giving birth. An altar had been set up nearby, and
holy relics set upon it, so that Jane could hear Mass and pray for the
protection of God and His Holy Mother during her travail. Her
court cupboard was laden with gold plate for the service of her
meals. The midwife stood ready, a spotless white apron over her
dark dress.

Her male officers had been temporarily stood down. For the duration of her confinement, her ladies would serve in their place, as
butlers, carvers and cupbearers. Every necessity would be brought
to the chamber door.

It all felt somewhat stifling and oppressive, and she was glad of
her married ladies, and her sister Lizzie, who, as gossips, would sit
and make merry with her, and cheer her through her travail. She had
written to ask Mother to come, but Mother was recovering from a
summer ague, and was not up to making the long journey from
Wiltshire. Jane would have given anything to have her there, for
Mother had borne ten children, and was very experienced. Her presence would have been a great comfort. For as the weeks had passed
inexorably, the euphoria that had distanced Jane from her fears

seemed to sustain her less and less. She knew that childbirth was a hazardous event, and that she or her baby—or, God forfend, both— might die. Many women did, having suffered who knew what horrors, and others—she had heard it whispered—had been left damaged. She clung to the knowledge that her midwife was highly experienced and expert at her craft—and a very amiable and capable woman. She made Jane take herbal baths to relax her, and taught her how to breathe so that she could ward off the worst of the pains of labor.

"It is best to give birth in a sitting or squatting position," she told her, "because if you lie down, you are pushing the babe upward, rather than down, and it is harder work."

"Is it very painful?" Jane asked, dreading it.

"Every mother has a different experience, Madam, but yes, it can be. But it isn't a frightening pain, and it is all worth it in the end, for when you hold your son in your arms, you will forget it." Jane fervently hoped so.

She was sitting up, resting in her chair, and wishing that she could go out into the garden, when Margery brought Lady Lisle's daughters to see her, newly arrived from Calais. Interviewing them both, Jane immediately took to the elder, Anne Bassett, a pretty young creature, fair of face and hair, and well mannered.

Asking them to wait outside, she turned to Margery. "I like Anne best. What do you think?"

"She has good qualities, Madam. She has been educated in France and is highly accomplished. But her attire is not up to standard."

"I agree. That French hood will have to go, and I'd be grateful if a gown of crimson damask and a gable hood could be found for her to wear in my presence until she has proper attire of her own. What was her mother thinking of?"

Margery set about finding what was necessary, as Jane recalled Anne Bassett and welcomed her to her household. "But," she told the delighted young lady, "you must obtain two new gable hoods and two good gowns of black velvet and black satin. Lift your skirt a little. No, that linen shift is too coarse. You need fine lawn. In the meantime, suitable clothing will be lent to you." Her eye alighted on Anne's girdle. "How many pearls does that have?"

"A hundred and twenty, I think, Madam," replied the maid, looking increasingly perplexed.

Jane sighed. "Not enough, I fear. Write to your mother and ask for another girdle. And tell her that if you do not appear at court in the proper clothes, you will not be allowed to attend the christening."

"Yes, Madam."

Seeing Anne Bassett's bewildered face, Jane pulled herself up. She was doing it again, compensating for her knightly birth by emphasizing the magnificence of her estate as queen. She reminded herself that she had every right to do so, on account of the precious burden she carried—and yet she must not lose sight of her humanity. She smiled at Anne. "I hope you will be very happy at court," she said.

As Jane heaved her swollen body over in bed that night, she thought she caught a glimpse of the shadow out of the corner of her eye. When she made herself look again, there was nothing to see, but the notion that it had been there struck terror into her. It was the last thing she wanted to see at this time. But if it was Anne—and by now she had convinced herself that it was—she would have good cause to manifest herself, for Anne would be jealous of Jane bearing a son. She would not want Jane to accomplish what she had failed to do. Jane trembled for the safety of her baby. She wished she had the comforting presence of Henry beside her in the bed. But that was not allowed during her confinement.

There was cause to fear, for with the hot weather, the plague had returned, and London was suffering horrors. Henry came, limping, to see her, to assure her that they were safe at Hampton Court. "Darling, there is no need to be afraid. As before, I've ordered that no one from the city is to approach the court, and I've warned Cranmer not to leave Lambeth Palace until the pestilence has died down."

His assurances did not dispel Jane's anxiety. She was full of fears. Had it been the shadow she had seen? And if so, had its appearance presaged something awful?

Henry was watching her with concern. He raised a heavily beringed hand and caressed her cheek. "Stop worrying, sweetheart. No harm shall come to you."

She put on a brave smile. "Is your leg hurting you?"

He sighed. "A little. Norfolk wants me to ride north. He says my presence there will quell any last vestiges of rebellion."

"You will not leave me?" she cried, filled with foreboding.

"No, Jane. Both legs are inflamed, and my physicians advise me not to go far in the heat of the year. And I would not go anyway, because of your being close to your time, for which I give most humble thanks to Almighty God. But you must stop fretting. It will upset the child."

"I will try, Henry," she promised. "You always give me wise advice."

"I am pleased to see you so loving and conformable that you are ready in all things to content yourself with what I think expedient," he said, "especially considering that, being a woman, you take to heart every unpleasant report or rumor that foolish persons blow abroad."

She bowed her head. She knew she must be strong for the child.

"As soon as my legs stop playing up, I am going on my usual hunting progress," he told her. "Never fear, I have agreed with my Council that I should not ride far from you. I will stay within sixty miles from here at the furthest, especially as you think you might be further gone than you thought at the quickening. Believe me, I never forget what depends upon the prospering of our hopes, both for our own quiet, and for the welfare of my realm."

She was a little reassured by that, although sixty miles did seem a long way, but she was dismayed when, two days later, he told her that because of the plague, he wanted to minimize the risk of infection by reducing the number of people staying at Hampton Court.

"So I am removing with my household to Esher, and there I will await the happy news."

"I will miss you," she told him, trying not to cry.

"It is not far," he said. "I can be here in an hour if I am needed." He went on happily to describe the Garter stall he was having prepared at Windsor for the Prince, but she was hardly listening. All she could think of was that he was going from her and that of all the people she wanted with her at this time, he was the one she needed the most.

"Not long to wait now, your Grace," the midwife said, pulling down Jane's smock. "You may look daily for a prince."

But the Prince did not now seem in any hurry. Mary, having promised to attend the christening of the child of one of her tenants, hastened to Hunsdon at the end of the first week in October, fully expecting to miss the happy event, but when she returned, Jane was still up and about.

Two days later, in the afternoon, she felt a slight cramp, as if her flowers had come, and then another. There was a gush of water from her womb.

"Your Grace should go to bed," the midwife said. "Your travail has begun, but as this is a first baby, it may take some time."

The King was informed, and word came from Esher that he had sent heralds to London with the news. Soon, God willing, the bells would be ringing out to announce glad tidings to the people.

The pains were now coming regularly, and Jane found that the only way to ease them was to walk up and down. As they grew sharper, and closer together, it was better to lean forward with her hands pressed on the table. Before long, she did not know what to do with herself, the pangs were so strong, and they continued that way all night.

And then everything slowed down, and she was glad of the respite, although worried about what it portended. The midwife assured her that it was not unusual. "The pains will pick up again later," she said. Jane spent the day resting on her bed and chatting with her ladies. They made music for her, and laid out the exquisite tiny layette that had been prepared for the infant. Two cradles stood ready, the great gilded state cradle bearing the arms of England, in which the Prince would be shown off to visitors, and the smaller one in which he would sleep. That afternoon they told her that, in London, the bells were still ringing and Masses were being offered up for her in every parish church, with congregations spilling out into the street. A solemn procession had made its way from St. Paul's Cathedral to Westminster Abbey, with the clergy in their ceremonial copes and the Lord Mayor and aldermen leading the merchant guilds and livery companies of the City; all had prayed for her safe delivery.

At five o'clock, the pains began again, and they grew more severe as the evening wore on. As each wave took her, she cried out for relief. Eleanor Rutland and Mary Monteagle tied a birth girdle around her, a long scroll of parchment on which was written a prayer of supplication to St. Margaret of Antioch.

"Her intercessions are especially helpful for women in childbirth," Mary said. But St. Margaret was evidently busy elsewhere, for Jane felt no lessening of the torment.

"Open all the doors and cupboards," Lizzie urged. "It opens up the womb."

But that had no effect either. Jane was now in such distress that the midwife hurriedly made up an infusion of poppy seeds, tansy, parsley, mint, cress, willow leaves and birthwort, which brought on a blessed drowsiness, so that she slept through the worst of the onslaughts.

At midnight, however, she awoke to unimaginable agony and

began screaming. In her drugged state, she had forgotten why the
pains were coming, and knew only that if she screamed loudly and
long enough, someone would have to make them stop.

As the drug wore off, she became aware of the women crowded
around the bed, and their anxious murmurs. Again she screamed, so
that they would take notice.

"You must push, Madam!" the midwife urged. "Push now! The
babe is ready to be born, but without your help, he cannot be."

She pushed, feebly at first, for she was overcome with exhaustion,
but then the midwife bade her press her chin down on her chest, and
that helped. Miraculously, she found that when she pushed, the pain
was less, and so she made one great tremendous effort, and strove
with all her might.

"They don't call it travail for nothing!" The midwife smiled.
"Well done, Madam, nearly there." The women were crying out
encouragement. "The head is crowned!" the midwife pronounced.
"One more push, Madam—now!"

Jane pushed, and suddenly the child was being wrenched from
her, and she felt as if her body were being torn in two. Then the
pains ceased. It was over. She lay there, drained, and heard her child
cry.

"Blessed be God, a prince!" the midwife shouted.

They laid the child in her arms. He was wailing lustily, a fine
child with a heart-shaped face and a pink, healthy color; he had
Henry's blue eyes and her own fair hair and pointed chin. She had
triumphed. She had borne England an heir, and as she gazed down
in wonder at her son, she was consumed with the most powerful
love she had ever felt in her life.

Suddenly, there was much bustle, for all that it was darkest night
outside. Lady Rochford hastened to the door and spoke to whoever
was on duty outside. "Send messengers to Esher at once to wake
the King and inform him that the Queen has been happily delivered
of a prince." Lying there contentedly, with her child in her arms, as

her attendants cleaned her and made all tidy, Jane envisaged the messengers galloping the few miles to Esher, bearing the joyful news. How she wished she could see Henry's face when they delivered it.

He was there within the hour, followed by Mary, and by then Jane had been lifted into her great bed, and the Prince was lying beside her, swaddled and wrapped in a robe of velvet and ermine, with a little gold bonnet tied on his head, and looking very tiny in his great state cradle. "Let me welcome my son!" Henry cried, as he burst into the room.

Bending over the cradle, he swept the baby up in his arms, tears of joy pouring down his face.

"He's gorgeous!" Mary cried, weeping too as she leaned in to admire the babe.

Henry turned to Jane. "Darling, how can I ever thank you? You have given me the most precious jewel in all the world—a healthy boy. Twenty-seven years I have waited for this moment! At last England has its heir, and my dynasty is assured. We need no longer fear the kingdom being rent by civil war."

He was bursting with pride, beside himself with elation.

"He shall be called Edward," he said, gazing down adoringly at the child. "Edward, because he was born on the eve of St. Edward the Confessor, our royal saint. Edward, Duke of Cornwall and Prince of Wales." Jane was pleased that it was her brother's name too. He would be so proud when he heard. And Edward was a good old English name. It suited the child.

"God bless you, my precious boy." Henry laid his son gently in the cradle, as Mary and the other women looked on, misty-eyed; then he bent over the bed and kissed Jane with profound tenderness. "A thousand thanks to you, my darling, for bringing me such joy." She smiled up at him, tired but happy. He turned to her ladies. "Send for Cromwell!" he commanded. "I would speak with him now. Darling, I will be back presently. This cannot wait."

Mary sat down next to Jane and took her hand. "I am so pleased for you," she said.

"Even though this child takes precedence over you in the succession?" Jane asked.

"Even so!" Mary declared, peering dewy-eyed into the cradle. "Perhaps now that he has a son, my father will feel happier about arranging a marriage for me."

"I will press him on that, never fear." Jane had known that once she bore a prince, she would be in a position of great influence, for Henry would be eager to please the mother of his son. It was marvelous now to be enjoying that power.

When he returned after conferring with Cromwell, he was still jubilant. "I've had heralds dispatched to every part of my kingdom to proclaim the Prince's birth. At eight o'clock, the Te Deum will be sung in St. Paul's Cathedral and in every parish church in London. But for now, darling, you must have a well-earned rest, and I will try to sleep too, although I doubt I will. I must just look once more upon my son, to assure myself that he is real!" As he gazed into the cradle at the slumbering infant, Jane stretched out her hand and took his.

"Stay with me," she asked. Her ladies looked startled, Mary blushed, and the midwife was clearly outraged, but Jane did not care. "I just want you here, close to me, on this night of all nights," she told him. He looked searchingly at her for a space, and nodded. "Leave us," he said. "I will call if the child wakes."

The women curtseyed and departed, and he took off his bonnet, gown, doublet, breeches and shoes, and lay down beside Jane in his slops, shirt and hose, folding his arms carefully about her. She relaxed against him, loving this new bond of love and blood that bound them, the blessing of parenthood. It was hard to believe that her ordeal was over and that their son lay in the cradle snuffling gently in his sleep. The midwife had been right. You did forget the pain—and it was all worth it, a thousand times over.

She felt vindicated, as if a great weight had been lifted from her. In granting her the blessing of a son, God had made it manifestly clear that He smiled upon her. She resolved to put the past behind her. Anne could not trouble her now.

They were woken at eight by the glad sound of church bells ringing out the momentous tidings. Jane's first thought was for the child, and she leaned over and looked into the cradle. He was sleeping peacefully.

"He cried in the night," Henry murmured. "The wet nurse came and fed him. A wholesome woman with great paps! He will do well with her. He's a fine boy, and takes suck lustily."

Jane picked up her son and cradled him, crooning soft words. His milky blue eyes blinked up at her. What could he see? she wondered. Did he know her already for his mother?

Henry caressed the tiny hand. "They'll be ringing the bells all day in the City, and all over England. My subjects have much to celebrate. And I must be up and about, to receive everyone's congratulations."

Jane regarded him wistfully. "It's at times like these that I wish we could just be a private family and enjoy our son. Thank you for this night. It meant so much to have you to myself for that precious short time before all the world clamors for us."

He kissed her, long and lovingly. "A part of me has always wanted to be a private man, and I think that's why I understand my subjects, and why they say I have the common touch. I know how you feel. But we are not private persons, Jane, and in that cradle lies the next king of England."

"I know that very well," she said, a touch sadly, "but he's still my little boy."

He smiled at her and rose from the bed. "You are looking well and rested this morning."

"I am feeling well," she told him.

"Well, you must do as the midwife commands!" he instructed. "I will be back later to see you and Edward."

"I look forward to it," she said with feeling.

In the evening, he came to take supper with her, and a table was set up by her bed.

"I'm so hungry!" she told him, resting back against her pillows as Margery fed her with a spoon from a bowl of broth. "This is invalid fare. I could eat an ox!"

Henry wagged a finger. "You must do as you are told!"

Munching happily, he was full of what had been happening. "They're still reveling in London! We have all hungered for a prince so long that there is as much rejoicing as at the birth of John the Baptist! They've hung banners and garlands from all the windows and doors, and lit bonfires in the streets; the waits are playing in Cheapside, the bishops have provided a feast for the people, and everyone's making great cheer, especially since the Steelyard merchants very generously provided hogsheads of free wine and beer for the people. Can you hear the guns at the Tower?"

She listened, and heard a faint, distant boom.

"I ordered a two-thousand-gun salute, in honor of the Prince's birth."

"It is wonderful to hear of such celebrations!" Jane said.

"Aye, darling, and I have asked the Lord Mayor to ride through the streets and thank the people on my behalf for their demonstrations of love and loyalty, and pray them to render praise to God for our Prince."

"Is Edward pleased?" she asked, regretting that her brothers could not visit her.

"He is delighted. He said it was the most joyful news that has come to England these many years."

"He awaits his own child," she said. "Nan must be near her time."

"God send they are as blessed as we are," Henry said.

London's bells ceased their clangor at ten o'clock that evening. Jane was aware of the sudden silence. She was feeling so well that the midwife had allowed her to sit up in bed, and she was taking the opportunity to write letters announcing the birth of her son. It was the Queen's privilege, and she was very proud to be doing it, but the first letter she wrote had been to Mother. The next was to Thomas, whose ship was patrolling the English Channel. Now she was writing to Cromwell. She thought she had composed this one rather well. It sounded suitably regal: "We have been delivered and brought to bed of a prince conceived in most lawful matrimony between my lord the King's Majesty and us. It is our command that you convey the news to the Privy Council. Jane the Queen." She was still hungry. She called for her maids. "Please send down to the privy kitchen and see if they have anything better than that tasteless broth," she instructed.

"What do you fancy, Madam?" they asked.

"Some fish in a sauce, if they have it. Or meat will do."

They brought her roast lamb in a Malmsey wine sauce. It tasted delicious. She ate it as she read some of the letters of congratulation that were pouring into the palace. Henry had told her that his secretaries were working round the clock to announce the royal birth to foreign princes and other dignitaries.

And then Lizzie came hurrying into the bedchamber, her eyes shining. "Edward is outside! Nan has borne a son, and he is also to be called Edward, after his father and in honor of the Prince, for that he was born on the same day!"

"That's marvelous news! He must be so proud!"

As Nan would be, of course. And there was every good reason why their child should be called Edward, but the uncharitable little devil in Jane's head whispered that, in choosing the name, Nan was proclaiming to the world that her son too would have an important place in it. Already Jane could feel the rivalry flowering.

"He wants you to be godmother," Lizzie said.

"I shall be glad to accept," she declared, thrusting aside her unkind thoughts. All in all, it had been an auspicious day for the Seymours.

Late the next morning, she indulged herself as she felt she deserved, sitting up and enjoying some spiced roast capon for dinner, as young Edward slept soundly in his cradle by her bed. And then Henry arrived, and the claims of the outside world could be denied no longer.

She knew he had long been busy giving orders for the establishment of the Prince's household. So many officers and servants to wait upon so tiny a child! There were four hundred of them!

"All is ready for the Prince," he said.

She had known that she must be parted from her son, so that he could be cared for by his lady mistress and his wet nurses and nursemaids in the splendid apartments that had been prepared for him near the tennis court. There was a pretty garden outside, where he could take the air, and Henry told her that the princely lodging, which had been decorated during her confinement, was of the greatest splendor. She wished she could see it for herself. Her child would have the best; in that, she could rely on Henry. Oh, but her heart sank to see Lady Bryan come forward to take the baby, Lady Bryan, who had been lady mistress in turn to the King's daughters, and had given such good and sensible service. With her was the head nurse, a motherly lady called Sybil Penn. "Come, my lord Prince," Lady Bryan said. "We must say goodbye to our lady mother." She lifted Edward and gave him to Jane, who took him in her arms, drinking in every pore of him and kissing him as if she would devour him. It was such a wrench to give him up to Lady Bryan, and to see that lady carry him off. She felt as if her heart were breaking.

She looked down at her empty arms and fought off tears.

"He will be brought to you daily," Henry said, "as often as you command it. And when you are up, you can visit him. His nursery is only a short step from here."

She managed a smile. "I intend to be a devoted mother."

He nodded approvingly. "In the meantime, you must regain your strength."

She winced. They had bound her breasts to dry up the milk, and she felt sore. The women had been recalling how Queen Anne had insisted on suckling Elizabeth, but the King had forbidden it. Well, he would have no need to quarrel with Jane. She felt no desire to feed Edward. He was thriving on his nurse's milk, and that was as it should be. It was well known that a woman could not conceive while she was feeding an infant, and a queen's duty was to bear children. Nevertheless, she fervently hoped that she would not have to undergo the pains of travail again just yet. Yet if she did, the midwife had told her that it would be easier next time.

As she lifted herself into a more comfortable position, she noticed that Henry was looking pensive.

"Is something wrong?" she asked.

"There is still plague in London," he told her. "I cannot afford to take any chances with our son's health. I've ordered that every room, hall and courtyard in his apartments be swept daily and washed down with soap. Everything that comes into contact with him must be scrupulously clean."

She approved of his fastidiousness. It was one of the things she liked about him, along with his practical approach. He saw a problem and he dealt with it. It was very reassuring. The anxiety that had sprung in her on hearing him speak of the plague receded.

"The christening will take place on Monday night," he said. "Because of the plague, I've commanded that the number of guests attending be greatly restricted. But all will be done with the proper pomp and ceremony. I have been giving some thought to choosing the godparents. I trust you will be content with Archbishop Cranmer, the Lady Mary, and the dukes of Norfolk and Suffolk?"

Cranmer, given the chance, would infect her son with Protestant heresies, if her suspicions of him were correct. At the very least, he would lead young Edward down the reformist path, away from the traditions she herself believed in. Norfolk would play his part, if only because he wanted to stay in favor, but no Howard could ever love a king with Seymour blood. Suffolk, though, was loyal to the King, come what may, and there was no doubt that Mary would love and protect her new brother.

"I am content." She smiled. She would not spoil the perfect harmony between them by opposing any of his choices.

Henry might have restricted numbers, but there were still four hundred people present at the Prince's christening. Late on Monday evening, shortly before midnight, Jane heard them all gathering in the Inner Court below her apartments. She could see through her window the flickering light of many torches illuminating the darkness, as she lay on her ornate bed, on a counterpane of crimson damask lined with cloth of gold. Wearing a crimson mantle edged with ermine, and her hair loose over her shoulders, she received the congratulations of the godparents and the most high-ranking guests. Beside her sat the King in a richly upholstered chair, bursting with pride in his son, who was being much admired.

Lady Exeter lifted the Prince out of his state cradle, and as she held him aloft, Henry himself placed a velvet mantle with a long train about his son's shoulders. Three days old now, Edward was wide awake and behaving very well, as if aware of the solemnity of the occasion. Lying on a cushion, he was carried away by Lady Exeter, with the Duke of Norfolk supporting his head, the Duke of Suffolk his feet and the Earl of Arundel carrying his train. Beyond the door stood four Gentlemen of the Privy Chamber, who were to hold a canopy of cloth of gold above the Prince as he went in procession to his christening in the Chapel Royal. Behind walked the nurse, Sybil Penn, and the midwife, carrying herself very proudly.

As the company departed, their footsteps fading into the distance, Jane lay savoring her moment of triumph, and Henry called for wine. They sat there together, holding hands, listening to the sounds of the procession forming below them. It would be led, Henry explained, by knights, ushers, squires and household officers, followed by bishops, abbots, the clergy of the Chapel Royal, the entire Privy Council, all the foreign ambassadors and many lords. Even the Earl of Wiltshire had been invited, although it must be bitter gall to a man of his ambition to see Jane succeeding where his own daughter had failed. But Henry bore him no grudge; he had even allowed him to keep his place on the Council.

The four-year-old Lady Elizabeth was present too. Henry had decreed that she should take part in the christening, for he wanted all the world to see that both his daughters were happy to give precedence to their brother. It had been arranged that Jane's brother Edward should carry Elizabeth in the procession, and that she should present the chrisom, the richly embroidered white robe in which the Prince would be clothed at his baptism. The Lady Mary would follow, attended by many ladies. And Thomas would be there, having seen off four French ships and made it to court in time for the ceremony.

"The lords and ladies will be a goodly sight to behold," Jane said, wishing she could be present as Archbishop Cranmer baptized the Prince in the silver-gilt font that had been set up on a dais draped with cloth of gold, which Henry had described to her. He had thought of everything. A closet formed of tapestries had been constructed in the chapel, and in it were set a basin of perfumed water and a charcoal brazier, so that the Prince should not catch cold when he was undressed. When the ceremonies were over, the Te Deum would be sung yet again. Trumpets sounded in the distance. Henry smiled at her. The company was returning. Presently, they heard the Garter King of Arms cry, "God, of His almighty and infinite grace, give and grant good life and long to the right high, right excellent and noble Prince Edward, most dear and entirely beloved son to our most dread and gracious lord, King Henry VIII!"

And then the Prince was borne in state back into the Queen's bedchamber, with Mary following, holding Elizabeth's hand, and the guests of honor crowding in behind them.

Lady Exeter laid young Edward in his mother's arms, and Jane gave him her blessing. Then Henry took him, weeping for joy, and blessed him in the name of God, the Virgin Mary and St. George. The tiny Prince was becoming a little fretful, so he was carried back to his nursery, and refreshments were served: hippocras and wafers for the nobility, bread and wine for everyone else. Henry ordered that alms be distributed among the poor who had gathered at the palace gates. It was nearly morning before the last guests kissed the hands of the King and Queen and departed.

"There'll be much celebrating this day, with bonfires and toasts," Henry said.

"And great joy made, and thanksgiving to Almighty God, who sent us so noble a prince to succeed to the crown of this realm," Jane replied. "I doubt I shall sleep!"

Henry kissed her good night. "You were perfect, darling. Every inch the Queen. I am so proud of you," he told her, and left her to rest.

Jane lay there feeling happy and secure. She still could not quite believe that she had borne the heir, who now slept safely in his nursery. Soon she would be churched and out in the world again, enjoying her new status as the Prince's mother. She imagined herself teaching her son to read, as—Henry had told her—his mother had taught him, and taking an interest in his marriage, as was a queen's duty. Her dream of herself and Henry growing old, surrounded by their children, did not now seem so fanciful. And now that he had his cherished boy, Henry would become the benevolent ruler he had been before Anne had made him frustrated and cruel. Jane had always seen the good in him, even as she had deplored his ruthlessness. And Edward's arrival signaled a new golden age; the courtiers knew it, and the people of England, out there celebrating through the night, felt it too. She fell asleep, dreaming happily.

Chapter 35

1537

At Jane's command, Lady Bryan brought Edward to see her the following morning, and her heart filled to see that he was contented and replete with milk, and that his swaddling bands were spotlessly clean. He was adorable, her little boy, and as she held him in her arms, she felt such a tug of exultant love that it brought tears to her eyes.

"His little Grace is such a good child, Madam," Lady Bryan reported. "He takes his feed and goes to sleep without a fuss. Of course, we have a little cry now and then, but he is easily soothed when his cradle is rocked. And he takes such an interest in everything! Already he is a very forward child."

Jane smiled. "I know that I can rely on you to care for him well, Lady Bryan. Tell me, who has replaced you as the Lady Elizabeth's lady mistress?"

"Lady Troy, Madam, although I think that Kate Chapernowne had her eye on advancement. But Lady Troy is sound."

"I am glad to hear it, as I am glad that you are looking after Edward." When Edward had been borne away, she rested until dinner time, when they brought her the salmon she had asked for, in a rich wine sauce with onions and verjuice. An hour or so later, she wished she hadn't eaten so fully of it, for she began to get griping pains in her belly, and soon she was rushing again and again to the close stool, heedless of the midwife's orders that she stay in bed. Her chamberers came running to help her, but she was so ashamed of the mess and the stink that she called for them to go away, and herself cleaned up the muck, and her body, where she had befouled it.

When, finally, the onslaughts abated, she crawled back into bed, feeling ill, weak and drained. Her heart was pounding alarmingly, and there was an unpleasant tingling, especially in her hands and feet. Her women looked concerned, and summoned the midwife. Lizzie sponged Jane's brow and Margery chafed her hands.

"Now, Madam, I told you not to get up!" the midwife reproved her. "This is what comes of taking foolish risks." She was enjoying her brief reign, especially ordering the Queen of England about. "Now your Grace must stay there, and if the laxness comes again, call me."

Jane nodded meekly. "I am so thirsty," she croaked.

"Bring some wine," the midwife commanded, "and some milk to line the Queen's stomach." The maids did as they were bid, and Jane eagerly gulped down both drinks, but her thirst persisted.

By suppertime, though, she was feeling much better, and called for some eggs in moonshine, an old childhood favorite that Mother had made by cracking the eggs into a syrup of rose water and sugar. Henry, come to see how she was feeling, regarded them with distaste.

"They are tasty, Henry. Try a spoonful."

He made a face. "I think you should have kept to the broth," he said. "And now, sweetheart, for your health's sake, you must get some rest. I've seen young Edward, and he is thriving."

He doused the candles himself, and left her to settle down, and she slept. But in the night, she woke, feeling very sick, and had to hurry, groping through the dark, to the close stool, where she vomited up a revolting mess of eggs and the marchpane biscuits she had eaten after supper. And then her bowels turned to water again, and she had to call for help, for all that it humiliated her to have her women see her reduced to the lowest state of humanity. After the first violent attack, there were several more, seizing her with relentless frequency. It was all the women could do to keep her clean, and the midwife was clearly frightened by the responsibility she bore.

"Send for the King!" she cried.

"No!" Jane protested. "I do not want him to see me like this. And it's four in the morning; he'll be asleep."

But they defied her, and presently she heard Henry's voice in the outer chamber, inquiring about her in anxious tones.

"Sir, she does not want you to go in." That was Lady Rochford. "Very understandable," she heard Henry say. "I will wait here for my physicians." He was squeamish about anything like this, and he had a horror of illness, so she was surprised he was staying at all. But then the griping pains took her again, and she forgot all about him.

By six o'clock, when dawn was breaking, there was nothing left to vomit up or let loose, but she felt utterly exhausted and ill. The doctors looked down on her as she lay prone in her bed, and their faces were grave. They had examined her urine, had her horoscope cast, bled her to balance the humors in her body, and given her orris root and blackberry juice to drink. They had also sent for the Bishop of Carlisle, her confessor. There was no cause for alarm, they reassured her; it was just to offer her spiritual comfort. She watched dull-eyed as the chamberers did their best to freshen the air for the Bishop's arrival.

A learned former schoolmaster of Eton, much praised for his erudition and eloquence, Bishop Aldrich had always been a congenial spiritual director. Giving her a heartening smile, he prayed by her bed and administered the sacrament of unction for the sick, anointing her with holy oil while offering up a supplication for her recovery.

"Am I going to die?" she asked him. "Everyone seems so worried."

"If I thought that, I would have given you extreme unction," he

told her. "Naturally we are all concerned for you, as clearly you have
suffered much."

"Where is the King?"

"Still in the outer chamber, in his night robe."

"Please ask him to go back to bed. I will sleep now, and hopefully
I will feel better for it. But before you go, Father, could you ask my
maids to bring me something to drink. This raging thirst will not
go away."

"Your Grace should drink boiled and strained water," he advised.
"I have found it very efficacious for maladies of the stomach."

"Very well, please ask them for some. Thank you."

But the midwife decreed that she had never heard the like! "Everyone knows water is bad for you. I'll send for some ale." It was
duly fetched, and Jane managed a few sips before falling into a deep
slumber.

She slept all morning, and when she woke in the afternoon, to a
room that had been aired and sweetened with bowls of dried herbs
and flowers, she felt much better, apart from a dry mouth and the
tingling. She drank some more of the ale, and it did her good.

Henry was sent for, and was at her side within minutes. "Thank
God you are improved!" he cried, kissing her heartily on the forehead. "I was so worried, and so was everyone else. Word got around
that you were ill, and people were crowding into the galleries and
courtyards. We had to put out a bulletin to explain what was happening."

She realized what a lucky deliverance she had had. "My confessor
led me to believe it was not as serious as I feared. I thought I was
dying."

She saw that Henry had tears in his eyes. "So did I!" He grasped
her hand. "But you are better now, truly?"

"Truly! See, I am sitting up in bed. The sickness has gone. I feel
much restored."

"Then I will go to the chapel and render thanks to God for sparing you. You are so precious to me, Jane. The thought of losing you . . ." He wiped away a tear. "But now that you are well, we can continue with the celebrations in honor of the Prince's birth. And— this will come as a great health to you—tomorrow, I am having Edward proclaimed Prince of Wales. Your brother Edward will be made Earl of Hertford, and Thomas is to be knighted. I'm planning to send him on a diplomatic mission, to see how he conducts himself. Does that please you?"

"How could it not?" she cried. "They must be so proud. Henry, you are so good to me and mine." It thrilled her to think that, thanks to her—and, of course, in part to Edward's own abilities— the power and prosperity of her family were now assured.

Two days later, on the Friday, Edward was a week old, and England was still celebrating. Jane was feeling much better now, and Henry had taken to dining with her again.

"I have a favor to beg," she said.

"Hmm?" He deftly carved her two choice slices of beef.

"I crave that you will pardon the Lady Margaret Douglas. Now that you have an heir, she is displaced from the succession and can no longer cause mischief."

Henry nodded. "She shall be pardoned and released."

"Both she and I are indebted to you." She laid her hand on his. "And Lord Thomas?"

"I hear he is very sick. If he amends, I will set him at liberty."

"I am saddened to hear that he is ill. I will pray for him."

"It's more than the fool deserves," Henry grunted. "And if I do let him out, he had better not try to see Margaret or write any more silly poems to her."

"What of their precontract?"

"Dissolved. I have a mind to marry her to an Italian prince, to forge bonds with the Medici of Florence. They're very rich. And Margaret will love Italy. By the way, now that you are better, I'm planning to return to Esher tomorrow to make the most of what's left of the hunting season. But I will be back for your churching, which the midwife tells me will be early next month, if all goes well."

"I will miss you," she told him, "but it is dull for you here. Go and enjoy the chase. I will be all right."

That evening, when she got up to use the close stool, which was now permitted, she found that the small exertion made her feel unusually breathless. Lying in bed, the shortness of breath persisted, and around ten o'clock, she felt a pain in her chest, and then another. It frightened her, and the more anxious she became, the worse the pain grew.

Immediately, the King was informed, and he came hastening back, all concern, to Jane's bedside, his doctors at his heels. By then, Jane's heartbeat was racing, and the pain was stabbing her every time she took a breath. She was in terror that she would suffocate.

Dr. Chamber did his best to calm her. "Your Grace is fretting over a trifle. If you calm down, you will feel better. Relax and breathe deeply." She lay flat, heartened by his words, trying not to feel scared. But even as her muscles unclenched, the pain and the shortness of breath were still there, and her heart was still pounding away. She saw Dr. Butts look anxiously at Dr. Chamber. What was wrong with her?

"It's easier if I sit up," she told them, and they helped her to rise in the bed, plumping her pillows and easing her down gently onto them.

"Do not worry, Madam," Dr. Chamber said. "All will be well." Then he and Dr. Butts disappeared with Henry into the outer room. Jane watched them go with fear in her heart.

Henry came back, smiling, but she could sense his tension. "They think it's an ague of sorts, and nothing serious."

"But I have no fever," she panted. "And it's getting worse!"

He frowned. "The fever may come out presently. And being so afraid can only make things worse. Try to sleep, darling."

She caught his wrist. "Stay with me!" she pleaded.

He nodded. "Of course. I will not leave you until you are amended."

She did manage to sleep, but when she woke, there was still a dull ache in her chest and that awful shortness of breath. Breathing shallowly helped, but not much.

Henry could not hide his anxiety. He summoned his doctors back, and they examined Jane again, and conferred with him, looking perplexed. They don't know what is wrong, she realized. Henry went into the outer chamber, but the door did not fully close behind him, and she heard him say, "Order all the London clergy, with the Mayor and aldermen and all the guilds, to make a solemn procession through London to St. Paul's, to make intercession for the preservation of the welfare of the Prince and the health of the Queen."

At least he had mentioned Edward first, which suggested that he was not overly worried about her. But as Saturday passed, her symptoms worsened, and by Sunday night, she could not lie flat without the sensation that she was suffocating.

"I must sit up!" she gasped, and they brought more pillows. The pain was a constant torment. Henry was distraught, her women were at a loss to know what to do to ease her suffering, and the physicians seemed to be able to do little beyond shaking their heads.

Henry lay next to her all that night, keeping his distance, for she could not tolerate his leaning against her, and holding her hand. While he slept, she struggled to breathe, lying there wakeful in the cool draft from the window, which she had insisted on keeping open. Moonlight shone through it, illuminating a shadow on the wall. No! Not now! And then, for the first time, she could see clearly those unmistakable features: the narrow face, the pointed chin, the dark eyes flashing with menace, glaring at her malevolently. Now she could not doubt who it was who had visited her in the dark reaches of the night, or of what her appearance heralded. I am going to die, she thought desperately.

Night thoughts, she said firmly to herself in the morning, but by now she was grasping at straws. Breathing was so difficult that she had to lean forward, with her arms braced on either side. She was unable to get comfortable, moving restlessly this way and that, and horribly anxious.

"Open the window!" she gasped.

"It is open, Madam," Mary Monteagle replied, unable to hide her concern.

"I must have air!" Jane whispered. "I am so cold."

"She is not making any sense." That was Henry, fear evident in his voice. He had stayed with her throughout, his hunting plans abandoned.

"Her ankles are swollen," the midwife observed.

"Dear God!" he cried. "Can't somebody do something? Summon the doctors again!"

"Air, please!" Jane begged, and Margery grabbed some sheets of music that Henry had left by his lute on the table, and began fanning her with them.

The doctors came, and made a great bustle about her. After an hour or so, she felt her struggle for breath easing slightly, and the pains seemed a little less severe. "There is every hope of recovery," Dr. Chamber pronounced when she whispered the good news. Jane saw the look of utter relief on Henry's face, and the glint of a tear on his cheek. He left her for a moment to confer with the physicians, and came back beaming.

"God willing, you will be better soon!" he said, taking her hands. "If so, I will go to Esher as planned, but if not, I could not find it in my heart to leave you until I know you are beyond danger."

She stared at him. "I have been in danger?"

He nodded. "The doctors say so. But, thanked be God, you are somewhat amended, and Chamber and Butts tell me that if you remain stable through the night, they are in good hope that you will be past all danger."

She was breathless again at dusk, and could not face food, so Henry had hurried off to sup alone, promising to be back soon to wish her good night. He had been gone an hour when the pain returned with a vengeance and she could not get her breath.

"She's turning blue!" the midwife cried. "Call the doctors, quickly, and the King!"

She pulled Jane forward by the arms. "Breathe, in and out, in and out!" she commanded. Jane struggled for breath. Her limbs felt dreadfully cold, and she saw that her hands were gray.

"Help me!" she panted. "Can't breathe."

The door was flung open and Henry crashed into the bedchamber. "Mother of God!" he cried when he saw her. "Jane! Jane!" The doctors came running in his wake.

She could strive no more. Her lungs were giving up. She wanted to stay with Henry, she so wanted to stay, but she had no breath anymore, and no strength to fight for it. And she was cold, so cold. But there was one thing she must do. She must see her little boy, her precious one, one last time, and give him her blessing, a blessing that would have to last for all of his life.

She sank back on the pillows, feeling as if she were fading into nothingness. "Edward," she whispered. But then her breath failed her and she could speak no more.

"Should I fetch the Prince?" It was the Lady Mary's voice. She had come, God bless her, in her stepmother's hour of need.

"No, Madam, we dare not take the risk," Dr. Chamber said.

"There is no risk!" Henry countered. "I am here, and I would not be if there was any fear of infection. Bring the child." His voice came out in a sob.

"I will fetch him." Was that Cromwell? Was even he here? It was like being in a dream, with faces and voices merging into a blur.

"Hurry! There is no time."

"No!" That was Henry, crying out in anguish.

She opened her eyes, knowing she must try to say goodbye. There was so much she wanted to say to Henry, that should be said. But she was beyond words, and she must conserve the little breath she had for Edward.

She heard the bell in Base Court chime twice. The shadow was there on the wall, beckoning to her. She raised a hand weakly and pointed to it, shrinking in fear. If this was what awaited her in eternity, she was surely bound for Hell.

"What is she doing?" Henry asked.

"She is delirious, I think," Mary said.

She was aware of the Bishop of Carlisle kneeling beside her, giving her the Last Sacrament, anointing her with sacred oil and forgiving her sins. Inwardly she prayed that God would watch over Edward and Henry when she was no more, and absolve her of any guilt, hoping that the remorse she had suffered in this life, and her sincere repentance, would count in her favor when she came before Him for judgment. When she looked again, the shadow had gone. Had she dreamed it? Was she going to Heaven after all? And would Anthony and Margery and Father be there waiting for her? How she wished Mother was here with her.

Henry was clutching her hand, his head bent over it, weeping inconsolably. She heard Cromwell speak. "They are crowding into the Chapel Royal. If prayer can save her Grace . . ." She did not hear the rest of what he said.

"Never was lady more popular with every man, rich or poor," Mary said.

"Sir, I have sent for the Duke of Norfolk to come and help take charge while your Grace is occupied here," Cromwell said. His voice fell to a murmur and she heard it break. She had not dreamed he was so fond of her.

"God, I would I could do something for her!" Henry cried, his voice close beside her. "All my power is for nothing. My most precious jewel is slipping away, and I am helpless. Oh, darling, do not leave me!" He collapsed, sobbing, his arm stretching out toward her.

She was dimly aware of the child being laid beside her. She could hear him snuffling, feel his warmth against her icy skin. Gasping for breath, she tried to raise her hand in blessing, but she had not the strength, so she blessed him in her heart, her darling son, her little future king. She had given him life, and he gave her hope of redemption, and for the future. And as her life ebbed away, it was his heart-shaped face, innocent and beautiful like no other, that she took with her into the light.

Author's Note

Jane Seymour's career spanned three of the most tumultuous years in England's history. She was at the center of the turbulent and dramatic events that marked the Reformation, a witness to the fall of Anne Boleyn, and an adherent of traditional religion at a time when seismic changes were taking place in the English Church. Had she left behind letters giving insights into her views on these events, we would know much more about the role she played in them—but she didn't, and therefore she remains an enigma.

Historians endlessly debate whether or not Jane was the demure and virtuous willing instrument of an ambitious family and an ardent and powerful king; or whether she was as ambitious as her relations and played a proactive part in bringing down the Queen she served. It is impossible, given the paucity of the evidence, to reach a conclusion. And yet a novelist approaching Jane Seymour must opt for one view or the other. For me, this posed a challenge, which set me poring once more over the historical evidence on which this book is closely based, looking for clues as to how to portray her.

What do we know about Jane Seymour, apart from the bare facts of her story? We know that, at the outset of the Dissolution, she pleaded for the monasteries to be restored. This places her firmly in the traditionalist camp, as does the fact that she had served Katherine of Aragon for some years, and probably stayed with her for a time after Katherine had been banished from court.

Jane was perhaps overshadowed, or even dominated, by her ambitious brothers. And yet while she was for the old faith, the eldest, Edward, the future Lord Protector of England, was a reformist, so obviously Jane had a mind of her own.

In keeping with her reactionary views, and perhaps out of personal devotion, she took up the cause of Katherine of Aragon's daughter, the Lady Mary (whom Jane, in the novel, always speaks of as the rightful Princess, despite her having been bastardized), and pleaded with Henry VIII to restore her to his affections and bring her to court.

The fact that Jane asked this not only for Mary's sake, but because she was lonely and needed a friend of similar status strongly suggests that when she became queen, she felt the need to pull rank and distance herself from those she called her inferiors. I don't see this as snobbery, but as the action of a knight's daughter who felt at a disadvantage, perhaps wanting in dignity and confidence, beside the great ladies of the court, and who felt the need to emphasize her exalted rank.

One senses a certain gaucheness in her, inferred from her nervousness when officially receiving the Imperial ambassador Chapuys. She left barely a letter. We might detect an understandable triumph in the one she wrote, in formal terms, announcing her son's birth, which suggests that by then she had gained in confidence. Her recorded utterances are few, but they suggest a humane and sympathetic personality. Her daring plea to Henry to save the monasteries speaks volumes for her moral courage, for this plea was made at a time when the Pilgrimage of Grace was on the march, and effectively she was siding in her opinion with the rebels who were opposing the King's reforms and demanding that the Dissolution be halted. On this evidence, we see Jane as a thinking, caring woman who was not afraid to speak out on principle.

Yet there are many who see her in a more sinister light. Some would agree with Jane's Victorian biographer, Agnes Strickland, who thought her conduct "shameless," asserting that her willingness to entertain Henry VIII's courtship "was the commencement of the severe calamities that befell her mistress," and thundered: "Scripture points out as an especial odium the circumstances of a handmaid taking the place of her mistress . . . a sickening sensation of horror must pervade every right-feeling mind, when the proceedings of the discreet Jane Seymour are considered. She received the addresses of her mistress's husband . . . she passively beheld the mortal anguish of Anne Boleyn . . . she saw a series of murderous accusations got up against the queen, which finally brought her to the scaffold." Strickland conveniently forgot that Anne, only a decade earlier, had begun scheming to supplant *her* royal mistress, and had later tried to compass that lady's death. Moreover, her criticism was born of her religious and moral convictions, while that of Jane's modern detractors is more likely to arise from their partisanship of Anne Boleyn.

But the only evidence for Jane's involvement in Anne's fall is her agreeing to denigrate Anne in Henry's ears. That isn't the same as conniving in the plot to annihilate her. Anne's arrest on May 2, 1536, came as a surprise, or shock, to most people; prior to that, the assumption was that if Henry got rid of her, it would be by annulment. Aside from Thomas Cromwell, who later attested that he had "thought up and plotted the affair of the Queen" after April 18, 1536, the coalition that formed against Anne early in 1536 can have had little idea of where their ambitions would lead. Nothing we know about Jane Seymour suggests that she tried to compass Anne's death, as Strickland alleged.

Many of Katherine of Aragon's contemporaries—indeed, most of Christendom—held the view that her marriage to Henry VIII was valid, a view that an objective study of the relevant canon law supports. Jane clearly adhered to this opinion, and she must have regarded Anne Boleyn as no more than the "other woman" who had usurped Katherine's place and been the cause of her troubles. She cannot have regarded Anne as Henry VIII's lawful wife, and that view doubtless underpinned her encouragement of the King's advances. As she did not recognize his marriage to Anne, this would not have seemed like adultery to her. In fact, as in the novel, she probably saw Anne as the author of many of the ills that were blighting the kingdom—the mistreatment of the rightful Queen and her daughter, reform that looked like heresy, and the shedding of the blood of good men.

What did she expect—that the King would marry her? Probably not for some time, although her family may have hoped to profit by the affair. Both she and they must have been aware that Anne Boleyn in her day had been a mere maid-of-honor when the King had determined to marry her. But Jane had seen Henry pass from mistress to mistress, so maybe she meant to make the most of his interest while she could, and in this her relations, particularly her ambitious brothers, may have put pressure on her. Or maybe, as is entirely possible, she loved him. Anne knew about the affair, and was resentful. We hear (in the memoirs of Jane Dormer) that there were "scratchings and by-blows" between the Queen and her maid. It was a mistress's privilege physically to chastise those who served her. I do not believe it was Jane who was doing the scratching and slapping.

The situation changed in the early months of 1536, when that unlikely coalition of court conservatives and radicals united to bring Anne Boleyn down. Jane was asked to keep reminding the King of Anne's failings whenever she could, and it seems she complied. Again, she would have seen this as an opportunity to rid Henry—and England—of a pernicious influence, though she could not have envisaged any worse consequence than an annulment.

Maybe Jane found the charges believable, or was willing to. (The storyline involving Mireflore is pure fiction, and carries on the thread begun in my previous novel, *Anne Boleyn, A King's Obsession*.) But why was she so anxious to be informed of the verdict at Anne's trial? Was it because she was longing to be queen? Or was it because she was suffering from guilt and dreaded to hear that she would be queen, literally, over Anne's dead body?

We do not know the answers to these questions. We do know that

Henry VIII expected obedience and conformity from Jane after they were married, and was protective toward her, being aware of her inexperience. She did not involve herself in politics, and Chapuys noted that she would not be drawn into a discussion about them. It is highly unlikely, therefore, that she was embroiled in the dramatic events of late April and May 1536, although she may have been privy to some of what was going on. Did she feel to some extent that she was responsible, because she had helped to poison Henry's mind against Anne and encouraged his courtship? This theory underpins my portrayal of her.

And did she preserve her virtue before marriage? Henry had begun courting her by October 1535, and their affair gathered momentum until February 1536, when Jane returned a purse of gold he had sent her, asking him to save it until such time as she made a good marriage.

After that, in March, Henry installed her brother and his wife in apartments at Greenwich, where he could come by a secret gallery and visit her with her relatives as chaperones. Suddenly, five months after their relationship had begun, her virtue was to be protected.

The previous year, Henry had considered ending his marriage to Anne, but had been deterred by advice that it would be an admission that he had been wrong to put away Katherine and would be expected to take her back. But now Katherine was dead and Anne had just miscarried of a son, and there could be no awkward consequences of an annulment. Yet Henry dithered. Ridding himself of Anne would still have looked like an admission that he had been wrong to marry her. It was not until late April, when shocking evidence was laid before him, that he was resolved to be free of her. And there was the seemingly virtuous Jane waiting in the wings. We know that he had broached the subject of marriage before Anne's arrest on May 2. I suspect it was probably after he had read the evidence against Anne.

And yet there was perhaps another reason why he decided to marry Jane. What exactly had passed between them prior to February? Certainly Jane had given Anne cause to be jealous. On June 26,

1536, one John Hill was accused of slandering Henry, saying he was
"made sure unto the Queen's Grace about half a year before"—
meaning that, around December or January, he had either asked her
to marry him, or—more likely—made her his mistress. As a historian, I would discount this statement as mere calumny, but there is
another report that strangely corroborates it. In June, Dr. Ortiz, the
Imperial ambassador in Rome, stated that the new Queen Jane was
"five or six months gone with child." It was probably unreliable,
garbled gossip, not to be made too much of, and yet it is not beyond
the bounds of possibility that Henry and Jane had been lovers in the
winter of 1535–6, up until February (when she or her family saw
that Anne was vulnerable to the machinations of her enemies, and
that a vacancy might soon be created), or that she was pregnant
when he married her.

That would explain the haste with which Anne Boleyn was
brought to her death. In 1929, in an otherwise quaintly romanti-
cized biography of Henry VIII, Francis Hackett posed several perti-
nent questions:

> Why the months of delay in leaving Anne, the hesi-
> tation, and then the violent haste? Why the marriage
> with a nobody? Why, at last, a precipitate marriage
> without any bargaining for a bride with the French
> or with the Emperor? Why execution rather than
> divorce? Anne's death would have become doubly
> necessary if Jane were quick with child. All that
> Henry needed to urge him into a decision was to
> know that Jane Seymour could become a mother.
> His mania was to secure a male heir. Their precipi-
> tate marriage [took place] within ten days, without
> any decent preparation, without a word to the pub-
> lic, without anything more ceremonious on Henry's
> part. Hence Jane's quiet first months, Henry's ad-
> mission in a few months [August] that he could not
> be a father, and hence the long interval from the date

of marriage before Edward was [conceived]. Hence
the urgent, the peremptory, reason, for Anne Boleyn's
elision.

Anne's speedy fall could also be explained by Cromwell needing
to move quickly to preempt the King taking pity on her and showing leniency, but there was no need for Henry to be betrothed to
Jane on the morning after the execution, or for him to marry her ten
days later—unless Jane was pregnant. Already, when she had
pleaded for Mary, he had reminded her of the children they would
have together. All Mary's letters written in June express the hope
that the Queen will bear a son or be fruitful. Of course, both Henry
and Mary could have been voicing general hopes for the future. And
if Jane was expecting, she must have lost the child before it quickened (a not unusual occurrence), or the King would have announced
her pregnancy. This is the reasoning behind what I realize may prove
to be a controversial aspect of this novel. As a historian, I would not
claim that Jane probably was pregnant when she married, only that
the possibility should be borne in mind.

There may have been another doomed pregnancy. Among the papers of the Duke of Rutland at Belvoir Castle, there is an account,
published by the London printer Thomas Colwell, of the Lady Mary
being received back at court in 1536. This is the report that mentions Mary fainting and Henry patting Jane, who was "great with
child," on the stomach, saying, "Edward, Edward!" The phrase
"great with child" did not then necessarily mean that Jane had a
swollen stomach, only that she was expecting a baby. We find the
term used to describe women in early pregnancy.

Colwell flourished as a printer from 1560 until his death in 1576.
The account he published places this event at Windsor on December 17, 1536, but we know that Mary had returned to court in October while on December 17 the court was held at Whitehall. There
are other flaws in the narrative—it states that "commandment was
made that she should be called Lady Princess, and the other Lady
Elizabeth," which is incorrect—but the detailed description of the

meeting itself is convincing, and may actually relate to Mary's visit to the court at Windsor in October 1536, and be based on eyewitness testimony or a contemporary source lost to us. It is inconceivable that some form of ceremony would not have marked Mary's return to court.

Yet, while accepting subsequent evidence in this document, most historians ignore or discount this account, probably because of its flaws—not unusual in a narrative written between twenty-three and forty years after the event it describes—and because Jane could not then have been expecting the future Edward VI, even in December 1536. But what if she had been pregnant with another child in October 1536? It is highly unlikely that she would have been expecting a baby conceived in February, or there would be other references to her advancing condition—as in 1537, when she certainly was pregnant—such as an announcement to the Privy Council, public rejoicing and prayers offered up, especially as the child would have been due in November. And in August, Henry had said he did not think he would have children by Jane. Yet there remains the possibility that there was a second pregnancy, a child conceived in August and lost in October or November. It is perfectly possible for a woman to have two miscarriages and a successful conception in quick succession; in fact, the likelihood of a successful pregnancy is greater if conception takes place within six months of a miscarriage. I know this theory too will be controversial, and while as a historian I would be cautious about committing to it, this is fiction, and I could not resist posing the question, What if . . . ?

I have refrained from developing a storyline based on notorious claims that Jane suffered a Caesarean delivery. Rumors to that effect were current in London at the time, but in 1585, a Catholic writer, Nicholas Sander, hostile to Henry VIII, wrote that when Jane "was in severe labor in a difficult childbirth, all her limbs [were] stretched for the purpose of making a passage for the child, or (as others stated) having the womb cut before she was dead, so that the child ready to be born might be taken out. The travail of the Queen being very difficult, the King was asked which of the two lives was to be spared. He answered, the boy's, because he could easily provide himself with other wives." A Caesarean operation is then said to have been performed, but there is no evidence for one being carried out on a living mother before 1610, and if it had been, the result would have been a speedy and agonizing death.

Not until the twentieth century could this procedure be safely carried out. Yet the story gained wide currency, and persisted. In his chronicle of 1643, Sir Richard Baker claimed that Jane "was fain to be ripped," and in an old ballad, "The Death of Queen Jane," which survives in various versions, perhaps the earliest dating from 1612 (although a ballad called "The Lamentation of Queen Jane" was licensed in 1560), Jane is in labor for six days and more, and begs that her side be cut open so that her baby can be saved, and Henry reluctantly concedes.

There is another reason why I did not build on this myth. Traditionally, it has been assumed that Jane died from puerperal fever, yet there is no mention of fever in the sources. And when I studied them, and looked at the chronology, it looked as if she actually suffered two distinct illnesses.

She was in labor from the afternoon of October 8, 1537, until her son was born at 2 a.m. on the twelfth. On the evening of the twelfth she was signing letters announcing the birth, and late at night on the fifteenth, she was sitting up in bed, hosting the guests who had attended the christening. Thus there were probably no complications to her labor, and the birth was normal. I myself was in labor for a similar time with my first child, and Jane's experience in the novel mirrors mine (except I had pethidine, not a Tudor herbal infusion!).

Not until the afternoon of October 16, four days after Edward was born, did Jane become unwell. Her condition was described by her chaplain, the Bishop of Carlisle and her physicians in a bulletin stating that she had suffered "an natural lax, by reason whereof she began to lighten [become more cheerful] and (as it appeared) to mend, and so continued till toward night. All this night she hath been very sick." The word "sick" meant ill in a general sense, not necessarily that she was vomiting.

Some historians have understood the word "lax" to mean post-partum bleeding (from which several theories have evolved), but from *c.* 1400, the word (which is sometimes given as "laske") meant "loose bowels"; the word "laxative" derives from it.

Jane recovered the next day, Wednesday, and there are no further reports of her being unwell again until the evening of Friday, October 19. Her condition worsened over the weekend, and on Monday night she was in "great danger." On Tuesday evening, the King was summoned to her bedside, as it was clear that she was dying. She passed away at two o'clock the next morning, October 24. After her death, her illness was attributed to "the fault of them that were about her, and suffered her to take great cold, and to eat things which the fantasy in her sickness called for." The bulletin and this report are the only evidence relating to her illnesses.

The first suggests she had food poisoning, which was unpleasant, but cleared up quickly. The reference to her eating unsuitable foods might be corroborative. The mention of Jane being cold in the second report has been the basis of claims that she died from puerperal fever, but that condition was recognized then and would surely have been described as such; the coldness was more likely to have had an entirely different significance.

I showed the historical evidence to Suzanne Schuld, a registered nurse of more than thirty years' experience focusing on critical care and emergency medicine; she in turn showed it to her colleagues Melissa Rockefeller, MD; Karen Maury, MD; and Michele Sequerra, MD. I also showed the evidence to Sylvia Howard, a midwife with decades of experience. I am enormously grateful to these five medical experts for their groundbreaking theories and opinions, which shed new light on why, and how, Jane Seymour died, and which inform the final pages of this novel. Any mistakes in my interpretation of the information they gave me are mine alone. It is summarized as follows.

As I suspected, there were almost certainly two distinct illnesses, and the first was probably food poisoning—my original theory. In regard to the second illness, as there was no report of fever, puerperal sepsis or endometritis (which have similar symptoms) seem unlikely. On the evidence we have, death was probably due to a combination of dehydration and embolism, leading ultimately to heart failure.

Possibly Jane had a thrombosis in a leg or in her pelvic circulation, and pieces broke off and migrated to the right side of her heart and lungs. Rushing to the close stool while suffering from food poisoning, or getting up to enable her servants to clean or change her bed, might have dislodged a piece of clot.

Embolisms do not always lead to instant death, and not all are fatal. Jane could easily have had one or more small ones that would have put a strain on her heart and respiratory muscles and worn out her ability to breathe, especially if she had less oxygen-carrying capacity due to anemia. Contemporaries remarked upon her "whitely pale" skin, which may indicate that she was anemic.

If Jane was anemic, and dehydrated after suffering food poisoning, her heart would have been under tremendous strain. The addition of an embolism may have been more than it could endure. Her heart was relatively young so it would have taken longer to wear out, hence the duration of her last illness.

Combined, anemia, possible postpartum blood loss after a long labor, dehydration from diarrhea and extended bed rest or inactivity could have caused an embolism, and probably more than one—not enough to trigger instant death, but enough to put Jane gradually into cardiorespiratory failure, shock and death. Her symptoms at the end, especially being cold, suggest she was cyanotic, or turning blue in her extremities.

Suzanne Schuld, who has seen this condition many times, very kindly described to me the stages of Jane's last illness, and explained the medical terminology of the doctors' theories for me, for which I am hugely grateful.

Aside from the theories I have outlined above, this book is substantially underpinned by historical sources. The earlier sections have been heavily fictionalized because we have only a skeletal framework of evidence for Jane's early years. Parts of the text are based on passages from an earlier, unpublished novel I wrote about Jane Seymour, which I had entitled *A Certain Young Lady*.

The family ancestry, as outlined by Sir John Seymour in the novel, is now known to have been somewhat less colorful. Although the Seymours claimed descent from one of William the Conqueror's Norman knights, supposedly surnamed St. Maur after Saint-Maur-sur-Loire, his birthplace in Touraine, their first certain ancestor was William de St. Maur, who held manors in Monmouthshire in 1240. Jane's branch of the family was established in Wiltshire by the end of the fourteenth century.

There is no evidence that the real Jane wanted to be a nun, but given her courageous pleas for the restoration of the monasteries, she must have had a strong devotion to them, or to particular religious houses, and it is credible that she might at some time have contemplated taking the veil. We do not know why it took so long to find her a potential husband, or why her younger sisters were married first, but that could be explained by her wish to become a religious. There is no evidence that Sir Francis Bryan was ever a suitor to Jane, although he was certainly a very good friend to her, and not always out of self-interest, so far as can be determined.

That there was some kind of scandal in the Seymour family several years before Jane attracted Henry VIII's attention seems likely. By 1519, Edward Seymour had married Catherine, daughter and coheiress of Sir Edward Fillol. She bore two sons, John in 1519(?) and Edward in 1527(?), then seems to have retired to a convent. Her father, in his will of 1527 (which Edward later contested), stated that "for many diverse causes and considerations," neither Catherine "nor her heirs of her body, nor Sir Edward Seymour her husband in any wise" were to inherit "any part or parcel" of his lands, and he left her £40 "as long as she shall live virtuously and abide in some house of religion of women." He died in July that year.

Possibly a scandal then came to light, which resulted in Catherine being cast out of the Seymour family. Left destitute, she was probably driven to enter a nunnery (although there is no evidence that it was Amesbury, which I chose because of its proximity to Wulfhall), so that she could thereby claim her inheritance. She had died by early 1535, whereupon Edward immediately married the formidable Anne Stanhope, a lady whose pride would become notorious.

But did Catherine have an affair with her father-in-law, Sir John Seymour? A marginal note in a seventeenth-century edition of Vincent's Baronage in the College of Arms states that Edward had repudiated Catherine *"quia pater ejus post nuptias eam congovit"*—"because she was known by his father after the nuptials." The only other evidence, written by Peter Heylin in 1674, claimed that a magician had conjured a "magical perspective" for Edward, enabling him "to behold a gentleman of his acquaintance in a more familiar posture with his wife than was agreeable to the honor of either party. To which diabolical illusion he is said to have given so much credit, that he did not only estrange himself from her society at his coming home, but furnished his next wife with an excellent opportunity for pressing him to the disinheriting of his former children." It seems that Edward did have suspicions about the paternity of his sons by Catherine, for he disinherited them both, at his wife Anne Stanhope's instigation, in 1540.

If an incestuous liaison was involved, there was all the more reason for secrecy and the affair being hushed up, but we should remember that Sir William Fillol disinherited Edward as well as Catherine, for reasons that are not clear. Possibly—as I have chosen to show in the novel—he disapproved of Edward's treatment of his wife, which had perhaps driven the unhappy girl, unforgivably, into his father's arms.

I have given the name Wulfhall in its older form, which derives from the Saxon Ulfela (Ulf's Hall, after the thane who owned it) that appears in the Domesday Book in 1086.

That Chapuys had feelings for Mary was suggested to me by his biographer Lauren Mackay.

There are supernatural threads in the novel. Jane's aversion to Beddington Park is based on my own reaction to the house (now a special school called Carew Manor) when I drove there one evening to point it out to a historian friend, and we both felt so spooked that I hurriedly reversed, wanting to get away (although I fully accept that my overactive imagination was probably responsible). At Beddington, Jane dreams of a face in the church tower—possibly Sir Walter Raleigh, whose head is buried there. She is also haunted by the shadow of Anne Boleyn. But is it real, or a projection of her own guilty conscience? In the park at Hatfield, she is afforded a glimpse of the future, for in 1558, Queen Elizabeth I received the news of her accession while seated under the same tree. Jane's dream of a ruined abbey is prescient, for Bisham Abbey was dissolved in 1538, less than a year after her death.

A note on titles: Jane always thinks of Katherine of Aragon, and for preference refers to her, as the true Queen. She calls Anne Boleyn queen only when she is constrained to. Those who support Katherine also covertly refer to her as Queen, and to Mary as the Princess, even after both have been deprived of their titles. The Imperial ambassador, Chapuys, would never refer to Anne Boleyn as queen; he wrote of her as "the Lady" or "the Concubine." In the novel, those who are plotting against Anne follow his lead and refer to her as "the Lady."

I owe a great debt of gratitude to the wonderful team at Ballantine whose creative dynamism and support has immeasurably enhanced this book: Executive Editor Susanna Porter, Associate Editor Emily Hartley, Associate Publisher Kim Hovey, cover designer Victoria Allen and publicist Melanie DeNardo.

Huge thanks to all my readers for buying my books; to the history lovers who engage with me on Facebook; to the bloggers who have so generously reviewed and promoted my books; to those who feature my work and articles in historical publications; and to all the event organizers who have invited me to give talks and presentations. I am deeply touched by your interest and support.

I am grateful to my historian friends for listening to my theories and giving me their invaluable insights: special thanks to Tracy Borman, Siobhan Clarke, Sarah Gristwood, Elizabeth Norton, Linda Porter, Nicola Tallis, Christopher Warwick and Josephine Ross.

Lastly, as ever, boundless thanks to Julian Alexander, for being such a brilliant and supportive literary agent over the past thirty years; to my family, for celebrating successes with me, and for putting up with me when the pressure gets tough; to my lovely children, John and Kate; and to Rankin, who is my North Star and gives my life direction and meaning.

Jane Seymour

THE HAUNTED QUEEN

Alison Weir

A READER'S GUIDE

THE UNHAPPIEST LADY IN CHRISTENDOM

In this short story that Alison Weir has written as a special addition to our paperback edition, Mary Tudor, Henry VIII's daughter with Katherine of Aragon, recalls what happened in the aftermath of Jane Seymour's death and looks forward to the coming of Henry's fourth wife.

Oh, what lamentations were made for the death of my dear stepmother! Even at a distance of twenty years, I can still feel the reverberations from her loss. Yet no one took it more heavily than the King my father. I don't remember ever seeing him so affected by anything. As soon as the Queen had breathed her last, he stumbled from the room, tears streaming down his face, and withdrew to his apartments, refusing to see anyone.

My father could not bear anything to do with death and soon departed from Hampton Court, leaving instructions that the funeral was to be done with the greatest magnificence. I was chosen as chief mourner—I, for whom Queen Jane had done more than for anyone. She could never have filled the shoes of my sainted mother—no one could—but she had done her very best to restore me to my rightful place in my father's affections, and for that I shall always be grateful.

We ladies who had loved her took turns to keep watch over her body. After the wax chandlers had done their work, and we had put on the mourning habits that had hurriedly been made for us, she was laid on a bier covered with a rich pall of cloth of gold and dressed in a robe of gold tissue and some of her jewels, with the

Queen's crown on her head. Her fair hair lay loose like a cape of pale gold, her face was painted in an attempt to give a semblance of life, and there was a strong smell of herbs and spices in the bedchamber.

We followed in procession as the bier was reverently carried to the presence chamber, where her body would lie in state for a week. The officers of the Royal Wardrobe gave us white kerchiefs for our heads and shoulders, to signify that our good mistress had died in childbed. As Masses were sung night and day for her soul, we kept vigil, lamenting and weeping, while I tried to ignore a raging toothache.

I had plenty of leisure to mourn my loss and think back on the blows life had dealt me. My childhood had been so happy. The only one of six children to survive, I was cosseted and loved by my parents, both of whom I adored, and brought up to be courteous, decorous, learned and merry—merry, that is, until my father was led astray by Anne Boleyn. How I hated her, the source of all my mother's woes, and mine. Through those dreadful years, I could barely bring myself to utter her name, and never, ever would I acknowledge her as queen. How could I, when my mother was my father's true, lawful wife? But Father had been seized with a temporary madness, so in thrall was he to his enchantress, and so my mother and I endured humiliation upon humiliation.

Throughout four long, terrible years of exile from court, Mother and I were kept cruelly apart, and I was often ill. Declared a bastard, to my shame and horror, I was made to wait upon my half sister, the baby Elizabeth, although I would never call her princess, which riled Anne Boleyn still further. In spite of all, I came to love Elizabeth, since I was never likely to have babes of my own to cherish. For what prince would want me, disinherited and demeaned as I was?

When my mother became gravely ill, I was desperate to see her. When she died, it was as if the sun had fallen out of the sky and I was adrift in a black void of grief. And then Anne Boleyn's wickedness was revealed, by a great stroke of providence and the perspicacity of Thomas Cromwell—how she had betrayed my father with a string of lovers and plotted to kill him. She paid for it with her head.

It was as if my mother had been vindicated, although there was no reversing of my bastardy. Instead, Elizabeth and I were now bastards together, and I did my best to take the place of the mother she had lost, even though I could not—and still cannot—believe that she is truly my sister. She has the look of Mark Smeaton, the lowly musician who confessed to adultery with that whore Boleyn.

Anne did repent of her cruelty to me at the last. She went on her knees to my friend, Lady Kingston, wife of the Constable of the Tower, and begged my forgiveness by proxy. But how can you forgive the person who ruined your life and robbed you of your future?

Praying by the Queen's bier, I could not stop thinking of my poor baby brother, who was now motherless. As soon as it was my turn for respite, I would hasten to his nursery to see that he was thriving, and watch him as he lay in his cradle swaddled up snuggly and making little snuffling noises as he slept. All I could think of was how tragic it was that he would never know his mother.

One night, as I emerged from my vigil, swaying with weariness, I saw someone waiting for me. It was Lord Cromwell, who had turned out to be an unlikely friend in my great troubles. I had never trusted him, but last year, when the King my father demanded that I sign that dreadful declaration acknowledging that his marriage to my beloved mother had been incestuous and unlawful, and I had shrunk, horrified, from doing so, Lord Cromwell had given me wise counsel and tried to protect me from my father's wrath. It had been a hard lesson in pragmatism, and I cannot bear even now to recall that I did sign, in the end—and I doubt I will ever forgive myself. But I can see that my father wanted to ensure an undisputed succession for his children by Queen Jane.

Cromwell looked anxious. He lowered his voice. "Madam, I am

worried about the King. I hear that he is keeping himself too close and secret," he confided. "He has taken his loss very hard."

I felt tears welling again. "We all miss the Queen terribly. It is a great tragedy."

"Almighty God has taken to Himself a most blessed and virtuous lady," said Archbishop Cranmer, joining us. "But consider what He has given to us, to the comfort of us all—our most noble Prince, to whom God hath ordained your Highness to be a mother as well as a sister."

I did not want Cranmer's comfort. How could I? It was he who broke my mother's marriage, and for that alone I could never like or approve of him. (And, in the end, I punished him as he deserved, the great heretic.)

I turned back to Lord Cromwell. "Maybe it is best to leave the King's Grace in peace for now."

He regarded me sadly. "And maybe we should not. Some of his councillors think he should be urged to marry again for the sake of his realm. He has his son at last, after waiting all these long years, but the Prince is but an infant and might at any time succumb to some childish ailment."

I was shocked. "But the Queen is not yet buried! For decency's sake, my lord, let it alone for now."

"Some feel that the matter is pressing, my lady."

We left it there, and I took myself off to bed, shaking my head. But a few days later, Cromwell was waiting again as I emerged from the presence chamber to seek a clove for my toothache.

"I have word from Windsor," he said. "The King is now taking his loss reasonably. The councillors have laid their concerns before him. He is, of course, little disposed to marry again, but has framed his mind to be impartial to whatever they think best, for the tender zeal he bears toward his subjects."

"I pray he will not be maneuvered into a fourth marriage too soon," I said.

"Has your Grace ever known his Majesty to do anything he does not want to do?" Cromwell asked with a wry smile.

"Of your charity, pray for the soul of the Queen!" Lancaster Herald cried, as the court assembled in silence to pay its respects. After a long week, we were relieved when the obsequies began, for not all the spices in the world could mask the stink from the body, and we were glad to see it coffined and moved to a catafalque set up in the Chapel Royal, where we were to keep vigil beside it for a further seven days.

There was a great public outpouring of grief. Crowds gathered as my stepmother's coffin was carried with great solemnity to Windsor, where my father had decreed that she should be buried. And there she was laid to rest, with all the pomp and majesty that could be. She had been our Queen for just seventeen months, but the people had taken her to their hearts, just as they had my sainted mother. She had given England a prince, which my poor mother had been unable to do, and for that we were all profoundly grateful, since it warded off the prospect of civil war. And I was grateful for many other things, especially for her vain attempt to halt the wicked closure of the monasteries. My father was very abrupt with her. Even so, he loved her truly—more truly than he ever loved that witch Boleyn.

After the funeral, Father came out of seclusion, but the joy had gone out of him and he had put on an alarming amount of weight, for grief and the sores on his legs prevented him from taking his usual exercise. He sat alone, brooding and wearing deepest black. It was as if a pall lay over the court.

"I must marry again." He sighed. "I have but one son, and I must ensure the succession by siring others."

We were at supper in his chamber. He had sent for me to join him, saying that he needed company to lighten his spirits. Lord Cromwell had been invited, too, and looked up eagerly when Father raised the matter of his marriage.

"There are great advantages to be gained by a foreign alliance, sir," he said.

"And for others," Father said. "The King of England must be the most eligible catch in Christendom."

I smiled, but I was wondering if, with three dead wives and two divorces behind him, the princesses of Europe would agree.

"Indeed, Sir. There should be many ladies who would be delighted to be honored by your hand, but the problem is that, just now, there are very few suitable brides available. Some are of the Protestant persuasion, and others not politically desirable."

Father waved a dismissive hand. "I'll rely on your judgment, Thomas."

That November, I went home to Hunsdon, hoping that a quiet and peaceful life in the country would help to heal my sorrow. I took Elizabeth with me, since Lady Bryan, who had been my lady governess and Elizabeth's in turn, had been transferred to the Prince's household. I think Elizabeth felt the loss of Lady Bryan far more painfully than that of her mother, for Lady Bryan had cared for her daily. Yet she was a resilient child, sharp-witted and self-contained. I did my best to fend off awkward questions about Anne Boleyn, wishing to spare her the brutal truth. Even if she was not my blood sister, I loved her as one.

I heard that my father was looking for a bride in France to counterbalance the vast power of the Emperor. It hurt me to hear that he did not want another Spanish bride like my mother. Being her daughter, and half-Spanish, I have always hated the French. But King Francis had marriageable daughters, and it was said that there were other beautiful ladies of high rank available in France.

My father liked to keep his intentions hidden, and it was in character that, even as he considered a French marriage, his ambassadors abroad were told to report on other likely brides. Rumors were rife, even at Hunsdon, and soon I was delighted to hear that the King was now bent on marrying the young Duchess of Milan, niece to the Emperor.

Messire Chapuys, the Imperial ambassador at court, wrote regularly, keeping me informed of what was happening at court. God rest him, he was one of my truest and most devoted friends—and I suspect he wished he could have been more to me. I loved him dearly, but there could never have been anything between us—and yet, when I tried to imagine the husband I might one day have, he had many of the qualities of Messire Chapuys, and even looked like him a little.

Chapuys wrote that the Duchess of Milan was sixteen years old, very tall and of excellent beauty. My father was entranced by reports of her loveliness. No doubt he saw her youth as an advantage, anticipating that her character could the more easily be molded to suit him.

But then, mercurial as ever, he changed his mind. Chapuys informed me that he was now seeking a big wife, since he himself was big in person. I inferred from this that he had put on more weight, which concerned me.

The big wife he had in mind was a French noblewoman called Marie de Guise. She was mature and sensible and—more important—had borne her late husband two sons. But, after receiving advance warning of my father's imminent proposal, she hastily married her other suitor, the King of Scots.

Father shrugged off his disappointment and sent his painter, Master Holbein, to Brussels to paint the portrait of the Duchess of Milan. With thoughts of marriage in mind, he discarded his mourning garments. When I went to court at Easter, I was dismayed to find him looking older than his years and suffering from constant pain from a sore on his leg. He was forced to submit to the barber surgeons and have it lanced, which relieved the pain but did not cure him. It galled him to have the sporting activities he loved curtailed: no longer could he ride in the lists, but was obliged to sit and watch younger, fitter men doing what he had once done better. Increasing immobility was making him fat, and his red-gold hair was thinning. Yet he still dressed sumptuously, setting a new fashion for short full-cut gowns with built-up shoulders and bulky sleeves. Soon every man at court was wearing one.

Pain and advancing infirmity made Father's temper highly unpredictable. I was not the only one to suffer the fearful lash of his tongue, and poor Cromwell got bawled at every week. You could hear the King shouting, calling him a knave and other, worse names I would blush to repeat. Sometimes he even pounded him soundly on the head. I once saw Cromwell emerge from the privy chamber with rumpled hair, shaking with fright, but smiling bravely. In certain moods, my father could be dangerous.

He was in such a mood when he heard that my mother's old chaplain, Father Forrest, was still speaking out in her favor from his prison. Immediately, he gave orders that the old man be taken to Smithfield and there roasted in chains over a fire. Father Forrest was a dear, kind soul, very upright and devout, and he had loved my mother devotedly, so I was devastated to hear of his unimaginable sufferings. Sometimes I thought my father was the most cruel man in all the world.

Summer came, and with it the King's spirits seemed to revive. He ordered that my little brother be brought to Hampton Court, so that all his children could be together. Attended by his vast retinue, Edward arrived, gorgeously dressed in cloth of gold and cradled in the arms of Lady Bryan. He was eight months old and thriving, with a solemn heart-shaped face, blue eyes and a pointed chin that gave him an elfin look. I never wearied of looking at him. I would sit watching him take suck from his wet nurse, Mother Jack, and took pleasure in seeing my father proudly carrying him around in his arms, showing him off to the courtiers, and holding him up at a window, so that the crowds below could see their future King.

Edward had a loving nature—before the Protestant heretics got at him—and always came joyfully to me in those days. When I asked my minstrels to play for him, he leaped in my arms, as if he would dance. Truly, I felt no resentment toward this child who now took precedence over me. I had never wanted to be queen of England. All I wished for was a husband and children, and a peaceful existence.

That summer, France and Spain signed a truce that left England dangerously isolated. Since my father had broken with the Pope and declared himself Supreme Head of the Church of England, he had been vulnerable to the hostility of Catholic princes. Yet still he hoped to marry the Duchess of Milan. I was at court when her portrait arrived, a magnificent full-length masterpiece that showed a demure young woman with an enigmatic smile and bold eyes. Father was captivated and immediately dispatched an embassy to Brussels with a proposal of marriage. Back came the young Duchess's pert answer. If she had two heads, she said, one should be at his Grace's service!

Father spluttered and swore at her impudence. Never would he take a bride who had shown such disrespect toward him!

"His Grace is now inclined to heed my advice and seek a bride among the Protestant princes of Germany," Cromwell told me, as we strolled together in a garden filled with the scent of late roses. "I think he would be willing to set aside his religious scruples if it meant making an alliance that could tip the balance of power in Europe in England's favor once more."

"But—a Protestant queen?" Those German princes were permanent thorns in the Emperor's side—and threats to the unity of Christendom.

"The princesses I have in mind have been brought up by their mother as strict Catholics," Cromwell replied, smiling. "It is their brother who has turned Lutheran. I speak of the children of the Duke of Kleve, who has an enlightened approach to religion. Duke

John has two unmarried daughters, Anna and Amalia. He has hastened to offer the hand of Anna, the elder, to the King, being sensible of the fact that it would be a brilliant match for her."

"I trust she is no giddy sixteen-year-old like the Duchess of Milan," I said, unhappy at the prospect of seeing my father married to the princess of a small German duchy. Heavens, I had no idea of where it even was!

"She is twenty-three," Cromwell supplied.

"It will seem strange having a stepmother only a year my senior."

Cromwell picked a rose and handed it to me, an unusually chivalrous gesture in a man who was normally so hard-headed. "We shall see. These negotiations take time—and I fear that the King's Highness is lukewarm in the matter."

I took Elizabeth back to Hunsdon. Lady Bryan wrote regularly and reported that the Prince was growing fast. He had stood alone and grown four teeth before his first birthday, and when I read that, I grieved afresh for Queen Jane, knowing how much joy and pride she would have taken in her son.

I was deeply concerned for my beloved old governess, Lady Salisbury. She was of the old Plantagenet royal blood and had been a dear friend of my mother. The two of them had once hoped that I might marry Lady Salisbury's son Reginald, which still seems to me to have been an excellent idea. Yet my father would have none of it. He distrusted his Plantagenet kinsfolk, fearing they would plot to seize his throne. He would not see that, by marrying me into the old royal House—which had been displaced when my grandsire, King Henry VII, had won the throne at the Battle of Bosworth—he would have united the two royal lines. So Reginald had entered the Church, and was now a cardinal, while I was still only the Lady Mary, the unhappiest lady in Christendom.

I had adored Lady Salisbury. When, as my father's sole heir, I was sent to Ludlow Castle to learn how to be the Princess of Wales, Lady Salisbury came with me, easing the separation from my mother and ensuring that I was kept happy, healthy and well-diverted with my lessons. Against all the odds, those two years at Ludlow were happy ones.

At eleven years old, I returned to court to find Anne Boleyn flaunting herself. Lady Salisbury did not like or approve of her, and so Anne made my father dismiss her. In her place was a Boleyn aunt, who was instructed to beat me. She did her best for me though, concealing her sympathy under a rough tongue, and protected me from the worst of her niece's vindictiveness. How I missed Lady Salisbury in those bleak years when I was deprived of my mother's company. And how overjoyed I was when, with the advent of the good Queen Jane, my old governess was welcomed back to court. It was heartening to hear the people cheering when she arrived and to be folded in those loving arms again.

But now the taint of treason had infected the Pole family, and my beloved Lady Salisbury was in peril. Two years earlier, from the safety of Italy, Cardinal Pole had written a tract damning my father's marriage to Anne Boleyn, and in such insulting terms that it was a good thing he was out of reach in Rome. Had my father been able to arrest him, he would surely have lost his head, for Father was no respecter of cardinals, as the execution of the venerable Cardinal Fisher had shown. Fisher, like Sir Thomas More, had been among the few who had upheld my mother's marriage. That was why they had to die.

My father was never one to forgive and forget. Obsessively suspicious of his Plantagenet kinsfolk, he convinced himself that the Poles were a pack of traitors. I was shocked to hear that Reginald's younger brother Geoffrey had been imprisoned in the Tower for aiding him. I was even more appalled when the older brother, Lord Montagu, and his cousin, the Marquess of Exeter, were executed for having plotted to assassinate the King. It was hard to believe that the Marquess, a kindly man of principle who had supported my mother, could have been guilty of such a horrible crime. I would not believe it.

I could not bear to think of how my dear Lady Salisbury was bearing the loss of her sons—one dead, one in prison and one in exile. Her grief must have been terrible, for they were everything to her. I prayed for them all, and for their families, who remained prisoners in the Tower, with no hope of release. It seemed that Father was determined to eliminate or neutralize every remaining member of the House of Plantagenet.

That Christmas of 1538, I helped Elizabeth to make a cambric shirt to send as a New Year gift for Edward. We kept the Yuletide season as merrily as we could at Hunsdon.

In the new year, I received the most unwelcome news. The Duke of Kleve had proposed a double alliance. My father should marry his daughter, and I should marry his son, the abominable Protestant William. Dear God, I prayed, deliver me from such a fate!

It was my father who saved me from my unwanted suitor. He realized that the marriage would render any he himself might make with Anna or Amalia incestuous, and my father would not risk that. His first two marriages had been annulled on the grounds that they were incestuous—though of course my mother's wasn't, not at all. But my father never would admit that he had been wrong.

Soon afterward came the most awful news from Rome—the thing I had been dreading for some years now. Aghast at the executions of Montagu and Exeter, the Pope had excommunicated my father.

I prayed for him as I had never prayed before. What must it feel like to be cut off from God and Christian fellowship and the sacraments of the Church? How dreadful to know that your soul is in mortal peril! But, of course, my father was adamant that the sentence of the Bishop of Rome—as he liked to call the Pope—had no force in England. It would make no difference. Yet it was soon clear that France and the Empire were now more hostile than ever toward him. Daily, the prospect of an alliance with Kleve grew more attractive.

As the March winds shrilled around Hunsdon, there came another letter from Chapuys. Lady Salisbury's house had been searched by the King's officers. They had found a banner embroidered with the royal arms of England, a banner made for a sovereign. It looked damningly as if my dear old governess had been plotting to seize the crown.

"It's ludicrous!" I cried to my dear lady-in-waiting, Susan Clarencieux. "Lady Salisbury is sixty-six, far too old to be plotting rebellion! There is not a disloyal bone in her body." Yet she had been sent to the Tower all the same. I wept when I read how rigorous her imprisonment was, how she was being kept in a cold cell without adequate food or clothing. I despaired of my father. Where was his humanity? Clearly he wanted her out of the way like the rest of her kinsfolk. That was made plain in May, when Parliament passed an Act of Attainder against her, depriving her of her life, title, estates and goods.

"No!" I wailed, when the news came. "Not dear Lady Salisbury!"

I waited, tremulous, for news. I heard that Father had seized all her property, but there was, thankfully, no word of his ordering her execution. As the weeks went by, I began to relax, anticipating that he would leave her to languish in prison, or even release her. I prayed that day would come soon.

The coldness between England and the two allies, France and the Empire, grew, to my distress. Like my mother, I had always wished to see England and the Empire bound in eternal friendship. But when the Emperor and King Francis signed a new treaty, my father finally resolved to press ahead with the Kleve marriage. He sent envoys to Germany, followed by Master Holbein with instructions to paint the likenesses of the princesses Anna and Amalia, so that Father could decide which pleased him the most.

Chapuys wrote that my father already fancied himself in love with the lady. He had even said he would take the Lady Anna without a dowry if her portrait pleased him. And please him it did.

I own that portrait today. It's a little miniature in a carved ivory frame, which opens to reveal Anna smiling demurely. It's a good likeness—to a point. And the whole world knows that, when my father saw it, he made up his mind at once that he wanted to marry Anna.

I had mixed feelings. I wanted to see him happy and contented again, as he had been with Queen Jane. And yet I feared that the Protestant cause would be greatly advanced if Anna of Kleve became Queen. Brought up a Catholic she might have been, but her brother now ruled Kleve and might yet have infected her with his heresies. God forbid, she could turn out to be another Anne Boleyn, which was what the reformers were all hoping for.

I was staying at Hertford Castle in October, when word reached me that the marriage treaty was signed. We heard that the ambassadors from Kleve had been royally entertained by the King. Chapuys reported that great preparations had been set in train for the reception of the Princess Anna. No doubt I would soon be summoned to court to meet my new stepmother. Fervently I prayed that she would be as kind and well-disposed to me as was Queen Jane.

My father was planning a Christmas wedding at Greenwich, to be followed by twelve days of festivities and Anna's coronation on Candlemas Day. I was gratified to hear that he was in exuberant spirits, and that his leg was troubling him less. He sounded impatient to meet his bride!

We all waited expectantly. It had been two years since the death of Queen Jane. Now England was ready for its new Queen. Setting aside my reservations, I resolved to welcome her warmly and make a friend of her, if I could. She would have need of it, I was sure.

QUESTIONS AND TOPICS FOR DISCUSSION

1. When you began reading this novel, did you have any preconceptions about Jane Seymour's character? If so, did the novel change those perceptions in any way? Did you like Jane as a character?

2. What was your impression of the Seymour family? How did the dynamics within the family change during the course of the novel? Was it a happy family? How well did its members cope with scandal?

3. Did the young Jane really understand what becoming a nun would entail? What made her change her mind?

4. What did you make of Jane's relations with Sir Francis Bryan? What motivates his interest in her?

5. Jane's compassion for her sister-in-law impels her to acts of kindness. Do they also show wisdom and emotional intelligence?

6. Why did Jane come to love Henry VIII? What was her attraction for him? Did he truly love her? In what ways was she a contrast to Anne Boleyn?

7. How does Jane see Anne Boleyn? Was her conduct as shameless as her Victorian biographer, Agnes Strickland, claimed? Or did

she have strong moral grounds for encouraging Henry VIII's courtship?

8. Do you think that Jane deserved to feel guilty about Anne Boleyn's fate? Why is the novel subtitled "The Haunted Queen"?

9. In what ways did Jane show moral courage?

10. Is it likely that Jane had one or more aborted pregnancies before she bore the future Edward VI?

11. Was Jane a good queen? In which ways was she at a disadvantage? Do you think she overcame these challenges?

12. Did you find the author's new theory about the cause of Jane's death convincing?

ABOUT THE AUTHOR

ALISON WEIR is the *New York Times* bestselling author of the novels *Anne Boleyn, A King's Obsession; Katherine of Aragon, The True Queen; The Marriage Game; A Dangerous Inheritance; Captive Queen; The Lady Elizabeth;* and *Innocent Traitor* and numerous historical biographies, including *Queens of the Conquest, The Lost Tudor Princess, Elizabeth of York, Mary Boleyn, The Lady in the Tower, Mistress of the Monarchy, Henry VIII, Eleanor of Aquitaine, The Life of Elizabeth I,* and *The Six Wives of Henry VIII.* She lives in Surrey, England, with her husband.

alisonweir.org.uk
alisonweirtours.com
Twitter: @AlisonWeirBooks

ABOUT THE TYPE

This book was set in Garamond, a typeface originally designed by the Parisian type cutter Claude Garamond (c. 1500–61). This version of Garamond was modeled on a 1592 specimen sheet from the Egenolff-Berner foundry, which was produced from types assumed to have been brought to Frankfurt by the punch cutter Jacques Sabon (c. 1520–80).

Claude Garamond's distinguished romans and italics first appeared in *Opera Ciceronis* in 1543–44. The Garamond types are clear, open, and elegant.

Chat.
Comment.
Connect.

Visit our online book club community at
Facebook.com/RHReadersCircle

Chat
Meet fellow book lovers and discuss what you're reading.

Comment
Post reviews of books, ask—and answer—thought-provoking
questions, or give and receive book club ideas.

Connect
Find an author on tour, visit our author blog, or invite one of
our 150 available authors to chat with your group on the phone.

Explore
Also visit our site for discussion questions, excerpts, author
interviews, videos, free books, news on the latest releases,
and more.

Books are better with buddies.
Facebook.com/RHReadersCircle

RANDOM HOUSE